A TRILOGY OF DESIRES SEBASTIAN & LOLA PARTS I-III

STEELE INTERNATIONAL, INC. A BILLIONAIRES ROMANCE SERIES BOOKS 1, 2, 6

CHARMAINE LOUISE SHELTON

A Trilogy of Desires Sebastian & Lola Parts I-III
Copyright © 2020 by Charmaine Louise Shelton

All rights reserved. No part of this book may be reproduced or transmitted in any form or by any means, electronic or mechanical, including but not limited to photocopying, recording, or by any information storage and retrieval system without written permission from the author.

ISBN: 978-1-7363429–6-1 (Paperback)
ISBN: 978-1-7363429-4-7 (eBook)
Published by CharmaineLouise New York, Inc.
Sexy Fantasies Fulfill Your Desires Publications

A Trilogy of Desires Sebastian & Lola Parts I-III is a work of fiction. Names, characters, businesses, places, events, and incidents are either the product of the author's imagination or used in a fictitious manner. Any resemblance to actual persons, living or dead, or actual events is purely coincidental.

CONTENTS

HEIGHTEN MY DESIRES
SEBASTIAN & LOLA PART II

DEEPEN MY DESIRES SEBASTIAN & LOLA PART III

FREE BOOK

Get the start of the STEELE International, Inc. A Billionaires Romance Series with *Discover My Desires Sebastian & Lola Prequel* FREE!

Click Cover Below or visit **bit.ly/CLBooksNewsletter** to subscribe to my newsletter for latest news and launches, books from my author friends, and sizzling reads in book promotions. Plus, start reading the steamy billionaire romance *Series Prequel* of Sebastian Steele and Lola Lewis.

Their stories. Their discovery of unknown desires…

Discover my
DESIRES
SEBASTIAN & LOLA PREQUEL
Charmaine Louise Shelton

Discover my
DESIRES

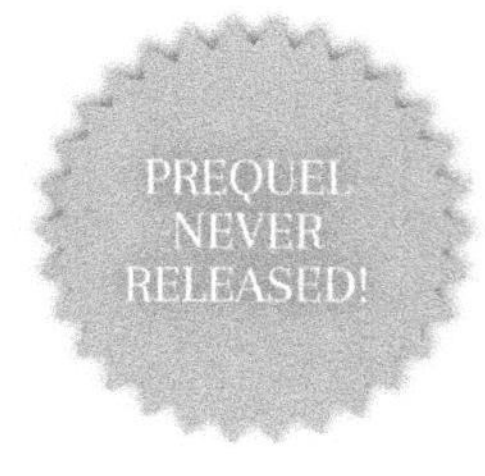
FREE BOOK!
PREQUEL
NEVER
RELEASED!
EXCLUSIVE FOR SUBSCRIBERS!

ALSO BY CHARMAINE LOUISE SHELTON

STEELE INTERNATIONAL, INC.

A BILLIONAIRES ROMANCE SERIES

Discover My Desires Sebastian & Lola Prequel

(Available Exclusively to Subscribers)

Fulfill My Desires Sebastian & Lola Part I

Heighten My Desires Sebastian & Lola Part II

Ignite My Desires Roger & Leonie Part I

Stoke My Desires Roger & Leonie Part II

Justify My Desires Roger & Leonie Part III

Deepen My Desires Sebastian & Lola Part III

Capture My Desires Malcolm & Starr Part I

Embrace My Desires Malcolm & Starr Part II

Cherish My Desires Malcolm & Starr Part III

A Trilogy of Desires Sebastian & Lola Parts I-III

A Trilogy of Desires Roger & Leonie Parts I-III

A Trilogy of Desires Malcolm & Starr Parts I-III

Series Extras

Series Playlist

STEELE INTERNATIONAL, INC. - JACKSON CORPORATION
A BILLIONAIRES ROMANCE SERIES CROSSOVER

Tempt My Desires Lachlan & Haley Part I

Tease My Desires Lachlan & Haley Part II

Grant My Desires Lachlan & Haley Part III

Intrigue My Desires Harris & Kat Part I

Decode My Desires Harris & Kat Part II

Honor My Desires Harris & Kat Patt III

A Trilogy of Desires Lachlan & Haley Parts I-III

A Trilogy of Desires Harris & Kat Parts I-III

Series Extras

Series Playlist

ABOUT STEELE INTERNATIONAL, INC. A BILLIONAIRES ROMANCE SERIES

Welcome to the titillating world of the multibillion-dollar global company and the love affairs of the family that controls it.

STEELE International, Inc. is a series of interconnecting Billionaire romance. Follow the Steele family as they fly around the world chasing the women they love and their happily ever afters. Get ready for glitz, glamour, and steamy romance books. What's better than that? The Jet-set Life-style has never been hotter...

The Desires Series is not for the tea set; it's for the top-shelf vodka straight up in a pretty crystal glass coterie!

Don't miss any of the sizzling romance books in the STEELE International, Inc. A Billionaires Romance Series:

Discover My Desires Sebastian & Lola Prequel

STEELE
INTERNATIONAL, INC.
A BILLIONAIRES
ROMANCE SERIES

Fulfill my DESIRES

SEBASTIAN & LOLA PART I

Charmaine Louise Shelton

Fulfill My Desires Sebastian & Lola Part I
Copyright © 2020 by Charmaine Louise Shelton

All rights reserved. No part of this book may be reproduced or transmitted in any form or by any means, electronic or mechanical, including but not limited to photocopying, recording, or by any information storage and retrieval system without written permission from the author.

ISBN: 978-1-7352917-1-0 (Paperback)
ISBN: 978-1-7352917-0-3 (eBook)
Published by CharmaineLouise New York, Inc.
Sexy Fantasies Fulfill Your Desires Publications

Fulfill My Desires Sebastian & Lola Part I is a work of fiction. Names, characters, businesses, places, events, and incidents are either the product of the author's imagination or used in a fictitious manner. Any resemblance to actual persons, living or dead, or actual events is purely coincidental.

I dedicate my first contemporary romance novel to all who like me have Sexy Fantasies floating in their heads.

Fulfill Your Desires.

xoxo
Charmaine Louise

ABOUT FULFILL MY DESIRES
SEBASTIAN & LOLA PART I

Lola Lewis is feisty, business driven, and focused on her luxury lingerie company—she has no time for relationships. Battles her desire for punishment at LEVELS New York... Wait, what?

Sebastian Steele is heir apparent to his family's luxury real estate empire; a playboy who's never with the same woman twice—a string of steamy encounters at LEVELS. Until his latest hookup, who just happens to be the owner of the company he's meeting with the next morning...

Can they overcome the taboo: never mix business with pleasure?

Travel with Sebastian and Lola from New York City to Monte Carlo to St. Barth's as their love affair sparks in this soul mate romance story.

Sebastian and Lola's love story is a standalone trilogy in the series. Get a glimpse of their dynamism in other books.

Anthem: "Erotica" Madonna
https://www.youtube.com/watch?v=WyhdvRWEWRw

Playlist:
https://www.youtube.com/playlist?list=
PLXwYvn0e218Bfsk5rVIJamWHOMjuDvWCv

Visit CharmaineLouiseBooks.com

SEBASTIAN

"Good evening, Mr. Steele," one of the two stunning greeters purrs as I step into the lobby for LEVELS New York.

This is the flagship location of the global, luxury, members-only BDSM/dance clubs in Manhattan's Meatpacking District. They chose the historic location as a play on the area's name. Put a club where men pack their meat into willing women and willing men allow women to pack them with their toys. The theme for the lobby is minimal and industrial. The fixtures and furniture that appear well worn are high-end, modern replicas used to add authenticity without the grime of old pieces. The two sides have coordinating greeter stations that allow access to the separate Dine & Dance levels and the BDSM levels. The other greeter turns her head in my direction and briefly smiles at me before she returns her attention to a couple entering the BDSM side.

My cousin Lucien Jackson cooked up the idea and roped my younger brother Malcolm into it. Lucien literally cooked it up since he thought of it as he finished his hospitality and culinary training at Le Cordon Bleu in Paris.

Who the hell goes through that prestigious training to come up with a titty bar? Well, five years later his idea proves it's bigger than that and has a high profit margin with more locations in Paris and London. That's all that concerns me: will it add to STEELE International's bottom line? Yes, well, it's a go. No, then no go.

LEVELS is one of many business partnerships that STEELE has with Jackson Corporation. World-renown for their award-winning eateries, choice cigars, and distinguished liquors and wines, their products pair well within STEELE's casinos, hotels, resorts, and residential and retail properties.

On the personal side, my mother is best friends with the Jackson Matriarch. They spent most of their adult lives together forming a closer bond than they have with their blood siblings and relatives. Not sharing DNA doesn't keep our families from being a close-knit group.

"Good evening," I respond as I make my way to the D&D elevator.

Once inside, I place my keycard against the panel to select the third floor for the Level 4 Restaurant. I'm a Global All-Access member. I can choose from any of the seven levels: 7th Sky Lounge that offers a stunning, 360-degree view of Manhattan and across the Hudson River to New Jersey's shoreline, a bar, restaurant by day dance club by night, a coverable pool that's open during the warmer months, and a glass-retractable roof; 6th and 5th multilevel dance club with two bars and a lounge for food and drinks; 4th Level 4 Restaurant and bar open for breakfast, lunch, and dinner; 3rd has twelve private suites for members to continue their pleasure apart from the BDSM levels; 2nd

Peepshow for BDSM with seating alcoves, primary stage, mini-stages, performance rooms, and a bar that serves non-alcoholic mocktails; below ground the Cellar a BDSM dungeon with mocktails bar. The Dine/Dance members only have access to the party levels—Sky Lounge, Dance Club, and Level 4 Restaurant.

Tonight, I need to eat and fuck hard in that order. I'm bound to find a female at the restaurant or bar who's willing to be my pet for the evening. One night only, maybe two if she's not clingy or a gold digger, but two fucks is my maximum. I'm not looking for a relationship and damn sure not marriage, just enough time to satisfy my Dom needs and my physical release for the moment. A short-term encounter to balance out my business-focused life.

As president of the Retail Properties Division of STEELE, I bust my ass fourteen hours a day to make it super profitable and to prove that I deserve my future role as CEO of the entire luxury real estate development and management company when my father retires next year. It's not just my last name getting me into the head position. I'm damn capable since I've worked my way up the ranks to learn our multigenerational, multibillion-dollar business combined with my Harvard undergrad and MBA degrees.

My father, Morgan, trusts me to carry the legacy into the future and my younger brothers and sister respect me and accept my leadership. Each sibling works at STEELE: Malcolm president of the Entertainment Properties Division; Roger, president of the Residential Properties Division; Harris and Haley, fraternal twins, co-founders of the subsidiary STEELE Technology and Cyber Security. At 35, I take my role as the eldest seriously, so I don't have time for nor care to get involved in a relationship. Thanks to Lucien and Malcolm, LEVELS provides exactly what I need.

As I step off of the elevator, I take in my surroundings. The bar is bustling as usual with the crème de la crème of society. They hobnob with top-shelf drinks. Seating ranges from the leather and black metal stools at the long, reclaimed-wood-covered bar to the dozen high-top tables styled to match. The bar along the right wall features a floor-to-ceiling mirrored wall of shelves of only the best spirits and wines—most are from the Jackson labels. The bartenders serve signature cocktails. Tables on the left complete the layout of the open-plan room. A path between the two areas leads to the LEVEL 4 Restaurant's maître d' station. There, the patrons eat delicious meals prepared by chefs trained by Lucien. My destination awaits.

As I stride towards the maître d', my gaze alights on several recognizable faces enjoying nightcaps at the bar area's high-top tables. Tonight, the U.S. Attorney for the Southern District of New York, the former governor of California, and a high-powered female CFO of a Wall Street investment bank are present. The club caters to the most wealthy and influential in society. They prefer the relative safety that one can expect from the ironclad nondisclosure agreement that LEVELS requires every member and their guests to sign.

I smile and nod in greeting—every Steele is instantly recognizable—but keep it moving as I'm not here tonight for small talk. As I approach the hostess at the dining area's maître d' podium, I also notice several pairs of lust-filled eyes including those of a few men track my movement as I walk past them. Sadly for the men, I'm strictly a female to a male individual. As I approach the station, the maître d' on duty tonight looks up with an alluring smile on her pretty face.

"Good evening, Mr. Steele," says Susan, as her name tag

denotes. She angles her chin down to allow her to peek up at me from beneath her long eyelashes without direct eye contact.

"Your usual table, Sir?"

I don't miss her emphasis on Sir as a sub innuendo. Susan is one of many LEVELS employees who want to have my marks on them and my dick in every one of their holes. Disappointingly for the staff though, I don't mix business with pleasure. That can only end in a messy situation and unnecessarily complicate matters—doesn't fit with my trajectory.

"Good evening, Susan. That's good, thank you," I reply.

Susan's full lips curl up into a dazzling smile as she visibly preens. Her reaction as though I petted her head for a job well done after I fucked her throat and she didn't spill a single drop of my copious amount of cum. Susan seductively sways her hips, long legs stressed by stilettos and her form-fitted, black mini dress molded to her curvy body. She leads me to my table in the center of the room with an unobstructed view of the large dining area and of the bar. A spot from which I can easily observe all the patrons to cherry-pick my companion for tonight. However, the sight before me has me second-guessing my no business/pleasure rule. Susan deliberately bends over the table to straighten the napkin, giving me a visual of her cuffed to my pommel horse and a cane in my hand. Damn if my cock didn't just twitch from looking at her plump bottom and grip-worthy hips. Fortunately, I hadn't unbuttoned my suit jacket, or my piqued dick would be on full display.

I give the heads, on my neck and at my groin, firm, shakes to clear the vision. Then, without making eye contact, I thank Susan, take my seat, and pick up the menu discouraging further attention.

With an audible sigh, Susan bids me, "Enjoy your dinner, Mr. Steele," and walks away. Then on second thought she turns and offers, "Should you need anything at all, please let me know."

Keeping my gaze on the menu, I nod, and Susan dejectedly walks away with less sway to her hips, albeit still an eye-catching vision. Sorry, sweetheart.

If I'm not entertaining business associates or attending social gatherings like charity functions, I frequently dine at Level 4. I prefer that then eating takeout at home or hiring a personal chef to cook for only one person. Both are extravagances that I can afford, but why waste resources with my mutable schedule that changes as often as I change boxers.

Dinner out at whatever time is convenient in a city with thousands of excellent restaurants suits my lifestyle. Level 4 is one of them with a menu that offers the expected fare typical of Continental cuisine of pastas, meat, and steaks with favorable sauces. Lucien complements the usual dishes with appealing specials that change daily to keep the choices fresh and habitual guests like me from getting bored.

The client care is impeccable. So, I don't flinch when the server quietly appears at my side and places a napkin-covered basket with an assortment of warm, fresh-baked breads on the table. I glance up to see a youthful man who is model-perfect and well-groomed with a clean-shaven jaw, slicked-back ebony hair, and intelligent brown eyes. His all-black uniform of a long-sleeved shirt, pants, butcher apron, and shiny Oxford shoes is spotless—the de rigueur fashion for LEVELS employees.

"Welcome to Level 4, sir. My name is Andrew and I'll be your server this evening. May I take your drink order?"

"Thank you, Andrew. I'll have a bottle of Pellegrino," I respond with a pleasant smile.

"Very good, sir. We have some lovely specials tonight. May I share them with you?"

Since I plan to play tonight, I select a light meal comprising the tossed salad to start and the grilled langoustines with white wine sauce entrée. A clear head is best for my evening plan of play.

As Andrew heads to the kitchen to submit my order, my gaze wanders around the room admiring the decor. Just as with the lobby and the bar, Lucien and Malcolm stayed true to the original use of the warehouse. Clean lines and antique pieces for the decor: floor-to-ceiling mullion windows allow natural light to filter through to the room during the day, now dimly lit for dinner; light fixtures hang from the ceiling where the dark metal duct work and copper pipes are visible; exposed brick walls; the floor poured concrete; the well-heeled patrons sit on antique leather chairs at wooden tables. The guys really did a hell of a job with their enterprise. Few can pull off and maintain a high-end, respectable establishment, especially one that's a combo BDSM/dance club with a restaurant.

Perfectly situated for visibility by those at the bar and within the dining room, sit two lovely beauties laughing and tossing their long, glossy hair over their shoulders. Their eyes roam the vicinity hoping to connect with potential partners. The duo is more focused on attracting company for the evening, then on eating the salads that they absent-mindedly move around on their plates.

The blonde spots me watching them, and a grin appears on her face lighting up her baby blues. As she nods her head to show her friend she's spotted a potential hookup, her little pink tongue pokes out to dampen her glossy, lush lips.

I wonder if her pussy is as shiny and wet as that mouth.

Her friend shifts slightly in her seat to adjust her position casually. As she runs her red-manicured hand through her sable-colored, shoulder-length hair, she spies me. The green darkens with lust when I wink at her. With a smirk, I turn my attention to Andrew as he places my salad in front of me. Now that I have the attention of both women, I nod and eat. I know they're interested, so no need to rush my meal. They'll be a double order of tonight's dessert special.

I spend the next thirty-five minutes purposely ignoring them. I only allow my gaze to shift occasionally in their direction, never direct eye contact. That dominant behavior —and who I am—will keep them intrigued. As they cross and uncross their legs, the movement affords me a better view higher up their toned thighs. Green Eyes has on a clingy, silk wrap dress that showcases her ample cleavage, the red color complementing her bronze skin. The blue of Luscious' eyes, enhanced by the cobalt color of her strapless, stretch-jersey dress, make them as prominent as her pebbled nipples. Delightful.

First item on tonight's agenda is complete—dinner eaten, now it's time to fuck.

They automatically place the bill on my membership account, so no need to waste time signing the check. I stand and take my time to button my suit jacket, drawing the attention of my pets. Once our eyes lock, I walk past their table to head to one of the high-tops at the bar.

Susan gives me a wistful stare and bids me, "Good night, Mr. Steele. We look forward to seeing you again soon."

"It was a pleasure as always, Susan. Good night," I offer her in consolation.

Moments after I settle at the closest available table, I feel one hand caress my back and another hand lands on my forearm.

I glance to my left and am greeted with a sultry, "Hello." Green eyes glitter in the candlelight like vivid emeralds.

A squeeze to my forearm draws my attention to my right to see freshly glossed lips beaming, "Hello. There aren't any other tables available, would you mind it if my friend and I share with you?"

"Would your friend and you mind sharing me for a fuck?"

Without missing a beat, Green Eyes responds breathlessly, "Absolutely."

SEBASTIAN

Not one to waste a second on a prime opportunity whether business or pleasure, I turn on my heel and lead them through the bar. Again, I smile and nod at more members. This time among them is the CEO of a high-end, privately owned retailer whose stores serve as the anchor in several of STEELE's malls. He's with a breathtaking model who's not his wife, whom I've seen on his arm at functions we've attended in the past. Well, to each his own as long as it's consenting adults. Just another reminder of why I'm not in a relationship. Right now I'm loyal to STEELE spending the vast majority of my time on our company leaving no room to split my loyalty with a woman. In no way am I a cheater.

Before reaching the elevator, a petite figure suddenly steps in front of me causing me to stop in my tracks. I glance down and recognize the pretty face of a fling from two weeks ago, but can't recall her name.

"Baz, I've been trying to reach you!"

With a frown, her arched eyebrows scrunch and her full

lips pout. "Taylor insists that he gives you my messages, but I haven't heard a peep from you!"

Suddenly, I'm flanked by Green Eyes and Glossy Lips who possessively link their arms through mine while imposingly towering over my petite fling.

She takes a step back. Her brown eyes shoot venomous daggers at them. Then she turns her glare to me, tilting her head back to look me directly in the eye.

"Well, now I see what's kept you busy, Sebastian," she accuses.

Her lips no longer turned up in a coy smile. Rather turned down scornfully.

With the realization I need to diffuse this situation posthaste and not allow it to derail my evening plans, I gently detach my pets. Then, I offer my petite agitator an ingenuous look, taking her lightly by the elbow to move us away from their ears.

"I did not intend to ignore you nor to cause you any hurt," I tell her in a sincere, but no-room-for-debate tone. "We had a lovely evening together, but as I explained to you in advance, it was a onetime situation for us to achieve mutual satisfaction. Nothing beyond that night."

I cock an eyebrow at her and smirk, "I believe that I was a man of my word."

She blushes prettily from the exposed café au lait skin of her bosom to her curly hairline. Then, she looks up at me from beneath her eyelashes.

Demurely she replies, "Yes, you most certainly are a man of many… words."

Her lust-filled gaze travels from my eyes to my broad chest before it rests on my crotch. She smiles coyly when she notices the large bulge straining against the zipper of my custom-tailored trousers.

She flicks her little pink tongue across her lips. With a sultry smile, she returns her simmering gaze to my face.

"It appears that you require some help. Would you like me to ease your need? I know how much you enjoyed me on my knees."

I sense tonight's pets impatiently shifting behind me and needing to wrap this conversation up now.

"Sweetheart…"

"Kimberly. My name is Kimberly, Baz."

"Kimberly," I sigh, "as tempting as your offer may be, I set my plans for the night. Please excuse me. Good night."

The once hopeful expression on her face drops. Her almost forgotten pride replaces hope as she pivots in her strappy sandals with her head held high to make her way to the bar.

Damn. I'll have a word with Taylor as the head of membership to let him know not to accept any messages for me. Particularly since he never told me about Kimberly's efforts to communicate with me. I'll also have the concierge send flowers and a pleasant note to her home in the morning. I find pleasure in many women who willingly let me fuck them, but I'm not a cad. No one deserves to feel hurt, even unintentionally.

After shooting quick texts to Taylor and to the concierge, I turn to my pets who as expected did not move from where I left them.

"Pardon me ladies," I say when I rejoin them, "you have my undivided attention for the rest of the night. Shall we?"

We reach the elevator as the doors open to more members coming for dinner at Level 4 or to have cocktails at the bar.

The three of us are alone on the ride down to Level 3, where my personal suite is always ready for me. In the reflective doors, I spy the women appraising me and eyeing each other, relishing the catch they know I am.

I stand at least seven inches taller than them at six feet four inches. My thick, black hair styled slicked back highlights my gray eyes and sharp cheekbones. It's late, so my five o'clock shadow covers my firm jaw. The cut of my bespoke Saville Row double-breasted vest suit emphasizes my fit physique.

They notice my Patek Phillipe as I adjust the cuffs of my custom shirt. Turning in my A. Testoni Oxfords, I ask their names—can't keep referring to them as Green Eyes and Glossy Lips.

"I'm Emma," says the blonde in a low, sultry voice, "and this is Natalie."

Emma is the leader in this duo.

The elevator doors ping as they open. The foyer sparsely decorated and dimly lit sets the mood for carnality. The hypnotic thrumming of sensuous music piped in through hidden speakers add to the intensity and expectation of the sexual activities that happen behind the twelve closed doors. On this level, they carpet the floor to mask the sounds of footsteps.

Politely gesturing them out of the elevator ahead of me, I say, "Nice to meet you, Emma and Natalie. I am Sebastian."

They smile and move aside to allow me to lead them down the quiet, dimly lit hallway to my corner suite. At the door, I place my palm on the plaque to disengage the lock. No need to dig for keys, Lucien and Malcolm thought of every convenience, and Harris and Haley implemented the best technology for security.

Once again, I wave Emma and Natalie ahead of me. Their eyes dance in delight once they see how my decked-out suite compares to others. As members, they would have access to the private suites, but none are as elaborate as mine. One of many investor perks.

I look at the suite through their eyes: set in the middle of the room is an impressive, handmade to my specifications mahogany wood, king-size bed with four thick carved posters and a brass lattice canopy with rings strategically attached; the mattress covered in matching deep-blue silk sheets, velvet duvet, and velvet accent pillows, a deep red cashmere blanket draped over the foot; from the mahogany coffered ceiling, along with the Swarovski crystal chandelier and recessed lights, hang various hooks; the walls and ceiling panels covered in blue silk damask; the floor carpeted in almost black-blue, silk on silk; a large, double-door armoire has drawers filled with anal plugs, clamps, cords, cuffs, vibrators, and a plethora of other toys; a St. Andrew's Cross and pommel horse take prime spots on the wall opposite the armoire; below windows treated to not allow visibility from the outside sits a chaise with brass rings; on either side of the entry door hang an assortment of canes, crops, feathers, paddles, and whips; one door next to the armoire leads to the all white, Carrara marble bathroom that has a walk-in shower big enough to hold four, an extra-large claw-foot tub, double vanities, and a separate water closet for the bidet and toilet; the other door is my dressing room filled with suits, casual wear, and footwear.

The opulently decorated suite perfectly reflects my tastes for elegance and experience as a BDSM Dom. The other suites are just as resplendent in their sumptuous decor. They vary based on their individual color schemes and BDSM fixtures.

Returning my gaze to Emma and Natalie, I notice them staring toward the St. Andrew's Cross and pommel horse.

They shift from foot to foot as though just the mere sight of those items has their cores dripping honey.

"Emma, Natalie, we need to discuss a few things."

Their heads swivel to me, their eyes bright with lust.

"First, you are lovely and beautiful," I start and they visibly preen pushing their ample bosoms out and swishing their curvy hips. "I want to be clear that tonight will be all about your pleasure, but will only be for this one night. I do not commit to relationships of any kind. This is purely fucking. Do you understand?"

I let that statement settle in their minds. Particularly after the Kimberly encounter, I want to be extra clear in my intentions.

Emma glances at Natalie to gauge her response. Then through some unspoken agreement, Emma turns to me and they nod simultaneously.

"Words please, ladies."

Again in unison, they affirm, "Yes, Sir."

"Second, I know that you are members and have signed the nondisclosure agreement and consent form, but I want to further emphasize that what we do is confidential and consensual." I pause again and wait for their verbal assent.

"Last, tell me your experience level with BDSM such as your hard limits and safewords."

At that, the passion reignites in their eyes and their faces flush with excitement. They all but bounce on the balls of their feet as they gush over their preferences.

Emma's lush tits almost spill over the top of her strapless dress. The dark pink of her areoles is as visible as the taut tips of her nipples.

Natalie runs her fingers up and down the opening of her wrap dress practically pulling it off revealing the bountiful curve of her under boob.

Now that the details are complete, I can get some relief for my aching cock that at this point has the imprint from the zipper teeth of my trousers.

"Natalie, come here," I command.

Immediately, Natalie sashays her way to stand in front of me.

"Ah ah… crawl to me on your hands and knees with that plump ass high and your head low."

The flush of her face and chest increases as she gracefully drops to her knees and lowers to her hands, keeping her ass high as I commanded. Her eyes don't rise from the floor as she makes her way to me.

"Obedient girl," I cajole—a natural sub.

I turn my attention to Emma, issuing the command for her to remove her dress in a slow striptease.

With a coy smirk, she faces away from me, raises her arms overhead, and begins a well-practiced shimmy of her body. Her round ass and curvy hips move to their own beat in a sensuous display of enticement.

My balls grow heavy.

Pressure on the top of my right shoe draws my attention away from the blonde vixen and to the top of Natalie's glossy, sable-haired head. Her lips press to the top of my left shoe, and my dick twitches. Yup, a natural sub.

I squat before Natalie and lift her chin with the tip of my index finger to bring her eyes in line with mine.

"Oh, Pet, so far you are a delightful little girl. Make me proud and give my cock some attention."

As I rise to my full height, my fingertip guides her to her knees.

"Unwrap that pretty dress, I want to see your tits bounce as I fuck your face," I smirk down at her.

With a blink, Natalie unties the bow of her dress. Like a

present at Christmas, her tits bounce free. My mouth salivates at the lush beauty of her ample, natural breasts and taut nipples that beg to be suckled and clamped.

As the dress falls to the floor, Natalie reaches for the fly of my trousers. A whimper falls from her lips when my massive length at last springs free from the constraint of my pants. Her enormous eyes fly to mine and she swallows thickly.

"Yes, Pet. You will take all of me everywhere before the night is over, starting with your mouth… Now!" I growl at her as she visibly shivers at the thought of my colossal dick in each of her holes.

An indistinct murmur from across the room distracts me from watching Natalie's full lips part to take my length into her mouth.

Emma, not wanting to be out of our play, has her dress off. Her long legs for days ending in stilettos on display. She strokes her fingers over her bare mound, her eyes locked on Natalie who's deep throating me with gusto.

"Come," I command, trying to keep my voice from shaking with the intense jolts zinging through me.

Instantly, Emma drops to her hands and knees with her ass high to emulate Natalie's crawl. As she reaches Natalie's rear, I raise my hand to signal Emma to stop.

My cock has now reached the back of Natalie's throat. She's humming in delight while cradling my balls in one of her little hands, making the tingle start at the base of my spine. Shit, at this rate, I'll blow my load before we even get started.

I withdraw my dick from Natalie's hot, wet mouth with a pop, as I gently push between her shoulder blades to return her to all fours. I turn to Emma with a smirk, "Eat Natalie like you want me to eat you, Pet."

The gleam in Emma's eyes sparkles as she eyes her friend's plump ass and glistening pussy dripping wet from sucking me off. Unconsciously, Emma licks her lips in anticipation.

I step back to remove my clothes and watch as Emma grips Natalie's hips and plants her face between Natalie's butt cheeks, a moan spilling from her lips.

The sight and sounds of Natalie mewling and trembling in ecstasy has my hand reaching to stroke my thick cock and smearing the pre-cum across the tip with my thumb. I walk to the armoire to get a strip of condoms, clamps, red silk cords, and an enormous dildo. Then, place the treats on the tray table next to the bed. I call to my pets to join me.

Natalie gives a sharp cry and jumps as Emma must have nipped her clit. Damn, that one needs to learn that I'm the Alpha here.

"Pets, here, now," I command.

Emma reluctantly stops her ministrations on Natalie's pussy and they crawl over to kneel at my feet beside the bed. Emma's lips and chin are shiny from her friend's juices while Natalie has a dazed look on her reddened, damp face.

"On the bed, Emma, on your back, arms and legs spread. Natalie, stand above Emma, feet on either side of her hips, arms overhead."

I attach the red, suede-lined cuffs to Emma's wrists and ankles, ensuring that the fit is snug, yet comfortable. I suckle on her left nipple as she moans, then place the clamp on the tight bud. I repeat the process on her right nipple, smirking at her discomfort.

Once I have Emma situated, I turn my attention to Natalie. I stand behind her to tie her arms with the cords above her head to one of the brass rings on the lattice canopy. Then, tug on the cords to make sure that her arms have room and not stretched too tight. I give her ass two resounding slaps that makes her lift to her toes and squeal. Her flesh jiggles at the impact and immediately turns bright pink.

I have to taste her pussy; the scent is potent from Emma's feasting.

On my knees behind her, I raise her right leg, holding under her thigh. Then, I spread her pussy lips with the fingers on my other hand, revealing her engorged clit and slippery core. A deep inhale of her tantalizing aroma makes my dick jump. I eat her with relish, her moans and cries spurring me on.

The sight is too much for Emma and she twists beneath us as she whimpers her dissatisfaction at being ignored. I reach down and spank her pussy three times. The sound of my fingers hitting the wetness of her labia is loud in the room. Oh, Pet, you will wait your turn patiently or get reprimanded.

I feel Natalie's inner walls quiver as her orgasm nears. I pull away to growl, "Do not cum until I tell you or I will punish you."

Her eyes squeeze shut as she tries to push the orgasm away despite my unending onslaught. I lave, lick, and lap at her core, drinking her ambrosia. Her hips move and I grip her tighter to keep her in place. Then using her pussy juices for lube, I press my thumb against her back hole, applying enough pressure to pass the tight ring of muscle. Natalie nearly jumps in the air and wails in anguish from keeping her orgasm at bay.

Another few licks and a few thumb thrusts and I pull back enough to command, "Cum for me, Pet. Cum now!"

Natalie lets go, screaming my name as a gush of her honey pours down my throat. I don't relent. Instead continue to nip and to suck her pussy, drawing three more orgasms from her until she's limp, dangling heavily on the cords.

I stand and kiss her deeply, letting her taste her sweetness on my tongue as I hold her close to my chest and release the knots. As her breathing returns to normal, I lower her to the bed to lie beside Emma who's red faced and moaning pitifully.

"Your turn, Pet," I remark to her.

I position my cock at her mouth and my lips at her weeping pussy. We'll get some mutual satisfaction before I fuck them both.

Emma's fiery mouth closes around my thick dick in pure bliss. The suction of her cheeks is intense and draws my balls up tight. The moans she makes as I fuck her face and eat her pussy reverberate up and down my spine. My hips buck and I begin to piston, timing my movements to my tongue fucking her pussy. Emma lets off a keening moan and I feel tremors from her pussy on my tongue. I pull out and give her wet pussy lips three quick spanks as a reminder not to cum until I allow her release.

A whimper escapes from her mouth around my dick. I return to my ministrations, adding the dildo to increase her sense of fullness. I continue to eat her and edge her for at least ten more minutes—she'll blow when I blow.

Soon, I can't hold back my load and I work her even harder with the dildo in her pussy and my mouth on her clit. I reach between us and remove the clamps, knowing the return of the blood to the sensitive areas will set her off. She wails and I feel her pussy clench down hard on the dildo, I tell her, "Cum, Pet, cum now!"

Her sweat-glistening body stiffens, her back arches off of

the bed, and a resounding scream of my name wrenches from her lips, as she convulses in unending waves of ecstasy.

My cock falls from her mouth and my seed spills on her face, neck, and breasts as I roar my release. A release so strong that my toes curl and I see a white flash in front of my eyes. The pleasure makes me collapse to Emma's side opposite Natalie. I catch my breath, then uncuff Emma, tenderly rubbing her wrists and ankles. Her face is now serene with her eyes closed as a languid smile plays on her swollen lips.

Damn, that was good.

The intense pleasure of multiple climaxes forced from them wore my pets out, so I go to the bathroom to get warm, wet washcloths to clean them gently. When I return to the room, Natalie is kneeling on the bed with her hands clasped behind her head. Her large breasts jutting towards me, her knees spread wide revealing her distended clit, and her eyes downcast in a classic sub position. My dick twitches to life at the sight.

"I'd like to satisfy you, Sir," Natalie purrs.

"Oh, would you, now," I ask as I gently clean a still passed out Emma, but who breathes steadily.

"Yes, Sir, if I may," Natalie replies.

I place the washcloth on the tray table by the bed, pick up the strip of condoms, and turn to Natalie, my cock standing proud.

"Well, Pet, I see we will use these after all."

LOLA

Rupaul's 1993 hit song blares from the surround-sound speakers of the photography studio. My best friend and muse Leonie Beaulieu—*The Lion* as she's known in the modeling world because her name means brave as a lion and her long, mahogany hair looks like a mane —strikes alluring poses in a piece from the new collections for my eponymous luxury lingerie company Lola's Coterie.

These collections are extra special since I designed them specifically as exclusives for my New York City and Las Vegas boutiques. No, they're not open yet, but my goal is to have them open by my thirtieth birthday that's four months away. Ambitious, yes, but I never back down from my goals nor from a challenge.

* * *

"LOLA, sweetie, come give your father and me a kiss good night," my mom yells down the hall from the front door to our apartment.

While my parents go to dinner with their friends from out of town, I'm staying at my childhood apartment on Manhattan's Upper Eastside for the weekend. I need to take a break from my studies at FIT, the prestigious Fashion Institute of Technology in Chelsea.

I fell in love with lingerie when I saw Elizabeth Taylor wearing a silk lace-trimmed slip in the classic movie Butterfield 8. The bombshell leaning against the wall in nothing but her slip and high-heel shoes sipping liquor from a crystal glass. Her image remained forever etched into my thirteen-year-old brain. From that day onward, I knew that I wanted to give women an air of sultriness in sexy lingerie.

The specialized high school that I attended allows students to graduate at seventeen. So, I applied and attained acceptance to FIT, the internationally recognized hotbed for talented designers, this past fall. I love my studies in design and business and take extra courses so I can finish in three years instead of four—hence the need for a break.

So instead of hitting the books—as I have each weekend over these last two semesters—my mom and I spent the day planning my eighteenth birthday party that's in two months. As their only child, my parents dote on me and I adore them. We are close since it's just the three of us—no extended family—and mean everything to each other.

Now, my parents head out. They offered to stay in and order Thai my favorite food, but I told them to go have fun. Especially since they had plans with their friends before I came home unexpectedly.

"Have fun and tell Mr. and Mrs. Shaw hi for me," I say as I kiss and hug my parents.

The landline ringtone for the apartment intercom wakes me and I almost roll off of the sofa where I fell asleep binge-watching

GOT. I sit up to reach for the handset to answer it, as I wonder the time.

"Hello," I clear my voice.

"Ms. Lewis, the police are here to see you," responds the doorman.

My heart palpitates, and I glance around for the clock on the television. It's 12:15 a.m. I jump and drop the handset as the front doorbell chimes.

The two uniform police officers appear grim when I open the door. Tears fill my eyes and my vision blurs.

"May we come in, Ms. Lewis?"

With a nod, my throat too tight to respond vocally, I step back and they enter the foyer.

"We're sorry to inform you, your parents died in a car accident..."

* * *

"SHANTAY, SHANTAY, SHANTY," shouts Leonie singing her personal anthem as she twirls for the camera, her infectious laugh brings me out of my reverie. My eyes glisten with unshed tears and my face is flush with emotion.

I change my focus to peer around the room, taking in the sight of my success: the studio bustles with activity; the famous fashion photographer known for his glamorous shots of women who appear sexy and not slutty even in the skimpiest of lingerie like the cream, lace teddy and matching barely there thong that Leonie prances in; his assistants moving back and forth swapping lenses and adjusting the lighting; the makeup artist who has a wait list of six months touches up Leonie's full lips; meanwhile, the hair stylist that *Vogue* named the *Best of the Decade* adjusts Leonie's bed-head updo, their assistants eagerly standing to the side holding brushes and pins; my assistant Blair Thomas animatedly talking on her mobile while typing on her tablet; a table of food and beverages overseen by the caterer.

Lola's Coterie is in dedication to my parents. I envision each success as a kiss and a hug from them; each setback I hear my father whispering his favorite saying in my ear, "Lola, are you a wolf or super wolf? Because there are no sheep in this family." As I harness the super wolf that they raised me to be, it pushes me to work harder to turn each setback around. At their funeral, I promised them I would never forget how much they loved and believed in me and that I would make them proud. In my heart, I know that they're pleased with all that I've accomplished in such a scant time—graduated FIT at twenty; completed an apprenticeship here in Paris at twenty-four; opened my first boutique on the Champs-Élysées at twenty-five; the second location on London's Bond Street at twenty-eight; expansion back home in New York City and another in Las Vegas in a few months…

"*Chérie*, stop thinking so hard!"

A glance to my left shows Leonie strutting in my direction, her wavy hair now loosely flowing down her back, a predatory stare sets her amber eyes glittering. Long, toned legs make quick work of the distance between us. I raise my hazel eyes to glance up at her standing at six feet, four inches in her five-inch mules reminds me of the difference between our body types. My petite, five-foot-five-inch, curvy body so opposite to her tall, voluptuous frame.

The Parisian-born, feline beauty is the perfect spokesmodel for Lola's Coterie. Her sensuous, statuesque figure reminds me of the bombshells of yesteryear and the '90s supermodels, full bust, small waist, shapely. Her golden, caramel skin that looks great with any color or material reflects her biracial heritage—her mother is Tunisian and her father is French.

And, yes, everything looks good on her. Rupaul would be proud.

"Lola, you didn't hear a word that we said to you," Leonie accuses tossing her head and pursing her lips.

"Sorry, what did you say," I ask abashed for being caught not paying attention to this important photoshoot.

Leonie flutters her eyes and blows out a lengthy breath in mock annoyance, then laughs, "Yes, you are as they say, busted!"

Looping her arm through mine, Leonie walks us to the racks of lingerie to select the next pieces.

"Seriously, are you okay," Leonie asks with concern on her face.

I turn to her with a bright smile and respond, "Definitely. I was thinking about how far Lola's Coterie has come since we met six years ago."

Leonie's amber eyes glow as she laughs, "Oh, *Chérie*, you've done so well!"

With an exaggerated roll of her eyes, she continues, "I remember Luc insisting that I meet a new lingerie designer and I thought, *mon Dieu*, really?"

At twenty-five, Leonie was at the height of her career with well-established designers and cosmetics companies pleading with her agents to book her for shows and exclusive contracts. So, an up-and-coming designer like myself was far from her radar. Luckily, my guardian angel and mentor, Luc Montaigne, knew her and insisted that she meet with me.

"Ah, persistent Luc… very handsome and sexy. How

could I say, no? But really, I knew that if he said you were worth it, you must be special."

As we reach the racks, Leonie stops to hug me before she continues, "*C'était fait accompli*!"

Yes, it was a done deal.

Leonie and I hit it off right from that first meeting. Two years apart, only children, driven, and confident, we complement each other well. Leonie's fun-loving personality balances my serious demeanor and my feistiness balances her easy-going behavior, particularly when men try to paw all over her when we're dancing at clubs. Yes, this native New Yorker will rail on someone in a minute, even in fluent French. We're sisters in every aspect except DNA.

"*Ooh la la c'est magnifique*!"

The beige, satin-trimmed, embroidered tulle chemise with matching bra and thong is extraordinary with the gold thread of the lace covering only the soft cups and along the hem leaving the center sheer tulle. The front of the panties matches the lace and has bands of satin along the hips connecting in the rear for the thong. A matching bra is available, worn with the panties not under the chemise. The delicate set is my favorite in the collection for the New York boutique.

"I absolutely must model this next. It's divine," Leonie croons as she carries it to the dressing room.

Soon, Leonie emerges looking like a goddess. Her hair is curled in ringlets cascading around her face and down her back, the shiny mahogany shines beneath the lights. Her makeup is soft with a touch of nude gloss on her lips. The cups of the chemise barely contain her breasts, a hint of the dark nipples peek through. Her toned torso framed by the sheer core of the chemise, while the dainty embroidered hem grazes the tops of her thighs. A slight glimmer of gold body makeup adds sparkle to her caramel skin. As she pads over to the set, Leonie is the epitome of feline feminine grace.

"Gorgeous, darling, absolutely marvelous," gushes Henri as his cameras click in rapid succession taking frame after frame of Leonie as she turns to the left, then turns to the right.

I glance up to heaven and smile.

* * *

Luc Montaigne

"Bon soir, Monsieur Montaigne," greets the maître d' at Arpège. *"Comment ça va ce soir?"*

"Bon soir. C'est bien, je vous remercie," I reply with a smile I'm fine this evening.

The three Michelin star restaurant is buzzing with the sounds of patrons chatting while they dine on the award-winning food.

This is Lola's favorite restaurant in Paris. I first brought her for dinner almost five years ago to celebrate the opening of her flagship boutique on the Champs-Élysées. A year later we returned for the anniversary of our initial meeting.

I have to smile to myself when I think back on her literally falling at my feet one evening as I was leaving Banque Montaigne's headquarters. The parcels in her arms flew in the air and landed on the sidewalk when she tripped over a trail of fabric from a bolt of lace. Fortunately, I caught her before she too landed on the asphalt. The curses in English and in French that rushed from her mouth were explicit enough to redden even a sailor's face.

After she regained her footing, the words worsened when Lola realized that she broke the heel on her shoe. I heard her mumble the expletives under her breath as we collected her packages and bolts of material.

"Mademoiselle, let me help you. You can sit inside to situate your shoe," I said, hands full of packages as I showed with a tilt of my chin the front doors of my bank's headquarters.

Mesmerizing, hazel eyes gave me the once over. With a nod the petite beauty, apparently I didn't seem threatening, allowed me to guide her into the lobby.

"Monsieur Montaigne!" Called one of the security staff, "*Laissez-moi vous aider.*"

I handed the packages to him and to the other guard before I took her by the elbow and led her to one of the lobby sofas. The scent of her alluring perfume stirred my once-lifeless loins.

"*Merc*i, Monsieur Montaigne," she said, holding out her hand.

"You're very welcome, mademoiselle," I responded, surprised that she caught my name. As I took her small hand in my large one, she surprised me once again with a firm shake.

"Once I fix my shoe, I'll be on my way."

"My dear, your shoe is beyond fixing," I laughed and she joined in holding the two pieces of her shoe in both hands.

The sound of her laughter was like a breath of fresh air that I hadn't experienced in over a year. Before allowing my mind to drift as it so easily did in those days, I asked her where she planned to go with such an assemblage of goods.

"I'm an apprentice for a lace maker and was returning to his atelier with supplies," she responded, her eyes shining with exuberance.

It was then that I noticed how much younger than me Lola was, at least eighteen, maybe twenty years.

"I see, your dedication is admirable to carry so much so late in the evening."

"Yes, well, his work inspires me… Anyhow, I must go, thank you, again."

She stood and made to lift her packages.

My gut told me to not let her go so quickly. Her apprenticeship, dedication, even her tempestuous little mouth, noticeably a lush and kissable one, intrigued me. My reaction shocked me, but not enough to stop myself from offering to give her a ride.

"My car and driver are out front, please allow me to take you to the atelier. Your shoe and those packages are not a pleasant combination."

I paused and held my breath for her reaction.

Again, she appraised me, then nodded. With a perfectly arched eyebrow raised she responded, "Well, I know who you are. I'll text Monsieur Thibault to let him know that you're bringing me to his studio now."

"Sorry I'm late!"

With a blink, I look up and see Lola leaning down to double kiss my cheeks in greeting. I didn't notice the time pass as I reminisced.

Her pretty, heart-shaped face flushed from rushing to the restaurant is even more appealing. Her wavy, black hair flowing down her back is in stark contrast to the cream silk blouse tucked into a black leather pencil skirt. I laugh to myself when I notice that she's wearing shoes similar to the ones she had on that long-ago evening, this time paired with black fishnets.

Still a temptress for this older, yet fit, man.

"Oh, *petite chérie,* no need to apologize. No doubt Leonie took longer than expected," I joke. Leonie is the utmost professional who never displays a diva attitude.

"Of course," Lola winks, going along with my jest. "She's infatuated with the new collections and coerced me into giving her most of the samples!"

The server arrives to take our order and Lola requests her favorite dishes.

Once we're alone, I sit back. With a stern tone I ask, "And if Leonie has all the samples, how do you presume to present them to the president of STEELE International's Retail Properties Division the day after tomorrow?"

Lola nearly chokes on her sip of wine as her gaze flies to mine, eyebrows hitting her hairline.

"What?" She sputters, delicately wiping her lips with the linen napkin.

"Mmhmmm," I respond, pulling on the cuffs of my custom-tailored dress shirt.

"What do you mean… What are you saying, Luc, tell me!" Lola demands, mouth agape.

A minor part of my mind wonders what my thick length would feel like filling her inviting mouth—six years and I still barely restrain myself. As usual, dispersing the thought with a quick shake of my head, I smile at my unsuspecting little protégée. Despite occasional tangents, I make every effort to maintain the father-figure role with Lola serving as her benefactor to guide her in her business endeavors.

"A business associate of mine has a partnership for his stores with STEELE. He told me word was out that they're looking to make up for a poor deal and need to move fast with one that will offset the loss."

Intrigued, Lola leans forward and my eyes briefly drift to the gap in her blouse created by the movement.

"So, what does that mean?" She insists, eyebrows scrunched.

"It means, *petite chérie*, that now is an excellent time to negotiate boutiques in New York and Las Vegas where STEELE has several properties. Rents on Fifth Avenue, on Prince Street, and in their premier Vegas shopping mall are not inexpensive. Lola's Coterie can benefit from long-term leases set now when STEELE is not in the best position to play hardball," I finish with a relish.

"Oh, Luc"—Lola jumps from her chair and pulls me into her warm embrace—"you are *incroyable*!"

Again seated, Lola is all business, the smart, feisty woman I met six years ago resurfaces.

"When do we leave?" Her hazel eyes twinkle with glee.

LOLA

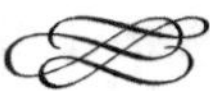

Luc Montaigne

What else is new? I ask myself as I sit on my G650 waiting on the tarmac at Le Bourget Airport for Lola and Leonie—Double L Trouble I nicknamed them.

Not only did Lola reinvigorate my desire to live a year after I tragically lost my wife and unborn son and only heir. But my relationship with Leonie developed from mere acquaintances introduced at one or another society gala to another young woman whom I've taken under my wing.

Both have blossomed into confident, business-savvy women determined to achieve their goals. Lola's set on her luxury lingerie company going global. Leonie starting a new career in upscale residential interior design. Developed over the years from her appreciation of staying in remarkable properties as a highly sought-after supermodel who travels the world.

The vibration from my mobile alerts me to an incoming text.

We're 10 minutes away! :)

It wasn't foresight that made me ask my pilot team to schedule the flight plan for five and not four this afternoon.

Ça va

"Monsieur Montaigne, Ms. Lewis just sent a text that she and Ms. Beaulieu are ten minutes away," Blair informs me.

I glance up and smile, "*Merci*, Blair."

Lola's assistant is the daughter of a friend who three years ago mentioned that the attractive brunette was interested in fashion and not their family's manufacturing business. Lola was trying to handle all aspects of her company despite my advice to focus on the creative design side and let an assistant handle the day-to-day tasks. After a one-month trial period, Blair proved herself to be efficient, dependable, and clever when balancing the activities that didn't need Lola's constant or immediate attention.

"You're welcome, Monsieur Montaigne," Blair replies, a blush forming on her cheeks.

What I find amusing is how flustered she gets around me. Leonie lasciviously teases that Blair wouldn't mind handling personal calls for *Le Renard Argenté*.

Silver Fox, I chuckle to myself. Yes, my black hair now has some gray sprinkled in it and I do workout regularly and eat healthily, so the nickname is appropriate for an attractive, fifty-year-old man. Obviously, Blair agrees.

"I have the latest copy of the *Financial Times* if you would like to read it. There's an interesting article on the banking industry and additional security measures to protect clients' personal information," Blair says to engage me in conversation to extend our interaction.

Not wanting to hurt her feelings since I read the advance copy yesterday afternoon, I tell her that would be interesting.

With a flash of her bright smile at me, she turns on her heels to retrieve the newspaper.

"*Pardonnez-moi,* Monsieur Montaigne, Monsieur Richard confirms we are ready to depart when the rest of your guests arrive."

"*Merci,* Daphne," I respond to my head flight attendant.

"Here's the article," Blair says as she bustles past Daphne giving her a face and sitting beside me holding the newspaper in my direction.

"We're here!"

"Arrivé, arrivé!"

A chorus from the private jet's door brings our attention to Lola entering the plane, followed by Leonie.

I stand and make my way to them, thankful that the spacious cabin has the headroom to accommodate my six-foot-four-inch frame.

"*Bonjour, Chères,*" I greet L&L with double kisses and hugs.

"*Bonjour, Renard Argenté,*" winks Leonie peering over my shoulder at Blair and Daphne.

"*Bonjour,* Luc," Lola adds, "so sorry! The traffic was ghastly!"

"I can imagine… That's why I left earlier," I tease her with a quirk of my eyebrow.

Turning to Daphne, I ask her to inform the pilots we're ready to depart.

Daphne scurries past me with a side-long stare before she hurries to the cockpit to deliver my message to the crew. Leonie and Lola titter in amusement while they seat themselves—Lola across from me and Leonie stretches out in the adjacent four-seat cluster.

"Ms. Lewis," Blair clears her throat, "do you need anything at the moment?"

Lola shifts in her seat to address Blair. "I'm fine, thank you. You can get settled now," Lola nods her head to the rear of the jet where the other assistants and two members of my staff sit buckled into their seats.

With a nod to Lola and a coquettish glance at me, Blair heads down the aisle. Her plump *derriere* encased in a form-fitting dress and lifted by the high heels that adorn her feet. The sight makes my cock twitch. Discreetly adjusting my bulge, I stride to my seat and buckle up just as the twin Rolls-Royce engines roar to life.

* * *

Lola

The level of luxury that Luc's multibillionaire status affords him always astounds me, even after experiencing it vicariously for over six years. The finer things in life were not new to me since my mother was a high-powered medical attorney and my father was one of the world's top cardiologists. But millions and billions are very different, rich and über-wealthy have two different meanings and degrees in access. The rich fly first class or perhaps charter; the wealthy own private jets like Luc's G650. The best money can buy and customized to suit his every whim. With a base price that starts at sixty-five million dollars, you should be able to have whatever you want. The atmosphere at eight thousand feet tires you out? Poor baby.... Gulfstream structures its gold-standard of private aviation to simulate the pressure of three thousand or four thousand feet, so you're well rested and comfy when you arrive at Teterboro. A tidbit I picked up from the pilots when they proudly gave me a tour. Eye roll sure, but it damn sure beats commercial and rental.

That fateful night I fell into Luc's arms changed the course of my life.

"Oh, hell... Dammit... Motherfucker!"

"Merde!"

I knew I should have taken a taxi instead of walking with all of this stuff.

"Oof, putain!"

"Mademoiselle, let me help you. You can sit inside to situate your shoe."

I peer up at my savior to see the hottest, older man, ever. Dark blue eyes ringed with black thick lashes; short, jet black hair the kind that you want to run your fingers through; an aristocratic nose; cleft chin to run your tongue over. The face of a god loomed close to mine as he held my arms to prevent a spectacular fall.

His stunning visage rendered me speechless, so I could only nod in response.

As he led me to an impressive old-world bank, I noticed the cut of his immaculate, custom three-piece suit. My designer eye caught the perfect stitching and the alignment of the stripes, not an easy feat. His sturdy arms easily carried my parcels while I carried the offending bolt of lace that almost caused my demise.

Immediately upon entering the plush lobby, security rushes to take the offending items out of his arms. Okay, so this guy was the owner of this bank, hhhmmm. Actually, I later learned, not only the owner, but the CEO & Chairman of the Board of his family's multigenerational, multibazzillion banking empire.

Once inside, I quickly situate myself. I need to get going or Monsieur Thibault will have to stay later than expected.

"Merci, Monsieur Montaigne," I say as I shake his enormous hand firmly. You can always tell the character of a person by their handshake, my father's voice pops into my head.

"Once I fix my shoe, I'll be on my way."

Monsieur Montaigne looks at me as if I have two heads—how could I blame him after our comical encounter—and offers to give me a ride. I sense that he is trustworthy, but to be safe, I send a text to Monsieur T. to let him know that I'm getting a ride to his atelier.

THAT WAS, as they say, the start of a beautiful friendship. Luc became my advisor, benefactor, and confidante. As we became more acquainted, my original attraction to him developed into a mentee to a mentor, or my guardian angel as I tell him. He can never replace my father, but he fills in as a father figure over the years.

The banker in Luc added the role of financial manager. His wise investments turned my inheritance into a multi-million-dollar cache. So, yes, I can afford luxuries, but I still revel in Luc's wonderful fortune.

"Let's go over your presentation."

Aside from being my mentor, Luc is the Vice Chair of Lola's Coterie and a major investor. My company's success is as ingrained in him as it is in me.

"The presentation must not leave room for questions and predispose any concerns so that by the end of it we can focus on the negotiations," Luc continues.

We spend the next couple of hours making revisions and rehearsing until it's memorized and flows naturally.

"That pretty much sums it up and the numbers are tight," Luc beams at me.

The pride that he shows makes my heart swell. He's tough and demands the best, not allowing me to slide or to cut corners. Luc's keen business sense combined with my creativity and vision have led to the successful growth of Lola's Coterie in only five years.

The expansion to New York City and Las Vegas is not out of reach. I'll definitely make my goal of the two boutique openings by my thirtieth birthday. I'm super excited. STEELE International, Inc. here we come.

I glance to my left and notice that Leonie has her head buried in one of her schoolbooks. I'm so proud that's she successfully made it to her last year at the Paris American Academy for her bachelor's degree in interior design. She's so nervous about her ultimate project where she must design an entire house. I'm sure that she'll find someone who will let her redo their home.

"Hey, Bookworm," I call to her, "ready for some dinner?"

Leonie peers at me over the top of her reading glasses. Her amber eyes glint in the light; her wavy mane pulled atop her head in a messy bun with a pen holding it in place; her ample bosom peeking from the slightly unzipped jacket of her velour tracksuit. Even dressed casually with books and binders piled around her, Leonie effortlessly looks like a sex kitten, a little nerdy kitty.

Leonie smirks, "Bookworm, huh, okay *Ms. Are My Numbers Right?*"

I laugh and stand to stretch my arms overhead, rolling my shoulders to get the kinks out after sitting for so long.

"I'm not the only nerd," I retort as I head to the bar to get a bottle of water.

"Do you guys want anything?" I ask.

"Let Daphne or Stephanie get that for you," Luc admonishes me with a frown.

When I do mundane tasks that a member of the staff should handle for me, Luc twinges. Raised in the French nobility, he's the last *duc* in his aristocratic family's line. I tease him relentlessly and call him a snob. He always gives me that arrogant Gallic shrug: sticks out his lush lower lip; raises his thick eyebrows and broad shoulders simultaneously; followed by a patronizing, "*Bof.*"

I roll my eyes and purposely lob a bottle to him he catches effortlessly. As I return to my seat, I hand one to Leonie who promptly uncaps it, curls her lips into a smirk, and drinks straight from the bottle.

"*Pardonnez-moi, Monsieur,* I didn't mean to offend you," I jest.

With a gleam in his beautiful, blue eyes, Luc also uncaps his water and drinks from the bottle.

"How are your studies, Leonie? It must please you that this is your last year," asks Luc. He's just as concerned with Leonie's success as he is with mine.

"*Tres bien*!" Leonie declares with an ecstatic grin. "I just have to find a house for my last project. It's a hands-on redo from consultation to plans to placing the last flower in the vase."

She playfully bites her fingernails and trembles nervously.

"Let me ask around. I'm sure we can persuade someone to proffer their home," Luc nods sagely.

After eating a delicious six-course meal served on the finest Bernardaud china and vintage wine in Lalique crystal glasses, we drift into separate areas of the jet. Luc moves to the bedroom after Leonie and I decline the use of it. Instead, Leonie reclines her chair into a bed to sleep and I remain upright, my nerves not allowing me to rest for the rest of the flight.

An hour or so later, five o'clock in the evening New York time, we land at Meridian Teterboro the deluxe FBO at the private jet airport. We don't linger as the ten of us hop onto one of Luc's Sikorsky S-92 Executive luxury helicopters. Designated to take us the seven miles from New Jersey to Manhattan's West 30th Street Heliport in less than fifteen minutes. Yup, the billionaire level is fierce. A thirty-minute drive in excellent traffic conditions is an inconvenience for someone like Luc.

Somehow, Blair finagles a seat next to him and periodically brushes her thigh against his. I laugh to myself when I notice him shift in his seat. I guess her touches are getting to Luc. Leonie nudges me and winks, then both of us burst into giggles, drawing Luc's attention our way, his face reddening in embarrassment. Blair looks uncomfortable, too, and turns her gaze to the scenery outside of the window, a flush creeping up from her chest to her hairline.

Soon we disembark and stride to the awaiting vehicles. Two Mercedes-Benz Sprinters for the larger luggage and trunks for the collections. Two Escalades with drivers for the staff. Luc's Black Badge Rolls-Royce Cullinan for the three of us—the most gorgeous SUV ever crafted. His New York driver greets us as he holds the door open.

"Let's have breakfast at the Astor Court at 7:30 tomorrow morning. That will leave us plenty of time to review the presentation once more and to arrive at The STEELE Tower for the ten o'clock meeting," Luc tells Leonie and me.

I frown, "I'm so nervous. I probably won't eat anything, but I'll have some tea and possibly toast."

"Oh, *Chérie,*" Leonie croons. "You'll be *formidable*!"

Ever my cheerleader, I smile at Leonie and nod my thanks.

"Bon," Luc injects. "Get some rest and don't worry. You're ready."

He drops Leonie and me off at the St. Regis New York

where we'll stay in the Presidential Suite. Luc continues to his palatial Fifth Avenue penthouse overlooking Central Park.

A smartly dressed doorman opens the door as the Cullinan pulls up to the hotel's entrance on Fifty-fifth Street around the corner from Fifth Avenue.

"Good evening, welcome to the St. Regis New York."

"Thank you."

"Merci."

"Enjoy your stay," he enthuses.

Two bellmen swiftly appear to take our carry-ons and to usher Leonie and me up the red-carpeted stairs. Another doorman greets us with a flourish, "Good evening ladies, welcome to the St. Regis New York."

"Thank you."

"Merci."

Luc's driver called ahead to inform the concierge of our imminent arrival, so he greets us at the entrance and takes us directly to our suite. Suite is an understatement for what's more like a grand apartment. It features a large foyer that leads to the formal dining room, living room, exquisite wood-paneled library, three bedrooms, four bathrooms, powder room, and a complete kitchen. The floor-to-ceiling windows open onto large balconies with spectacular views of Central Park, Fifth Avenue, and Fifty-fifth Street. A personal butler is on call to oversee our every need. With a five-figure per night rate, it has every luxury imaginable for a home away from home.

I spend most of my time in Paris, so I don't have a residence in the city. I sold my childhood apartment years ago. If, or rather when I lease my New York and Las Vegas boutiques, I'll purchase an apartment here to have a base in the United States. I'll split my time between here and Paris.

"... will you require any further help this evening, *mademoiselles*?"

I catch the tail end of the concierge's comments, so I wait for Leonie to answer him and the butler.

"We're fine for now, *merci*," she responds.

"Very well. We'll take our leave," they bow slightly and exit the suite.

Leonie twirls and flops onto a silk-covered, pillow back sofa, placing her long legs up on the armrest with a sigh.

"It's only after six. What should we do?"

I anxiously wring my hands and flop onto the twin sofa opposite her.

"I can't sleep and besides, we need to adjust to New York time to avoid jet lag," I answer hesitantly.

"Okaaay, so what should we do?" Leonie persists.

I sit up, face Leonie, and with a neutral face tell her, "Let's go to LEVELS New York."

Her eyebrows almost fly off of her face as she raises them in surprise and straightens on the sofa.

"LEVELS... really? Didn't Simon want to take you to the Paris location, but you chickened out?" She asks shocked, her amber eyes wide.

I think back to last year when I had my third date with Simon Blanchet—the second man with whom I'd had sex—during which he spanked me. The punishment gave me the most intense feelings ever. Sure, it was only my second time having sex in my entire life, but the feelings were incomparable. After Simon fell asleep, I slipped out of his apartment. Embarrassment flooded me that I—an independent woman who owns a company—would reach such intense satisfaction from being spanked by an Alpha male. No way!

To avoid thinking about it, I redoubled my efforts on the

success of Lola's Coterie and I haven't been in a relationship since that night.

Part of the reason I want to go is it's in New York. Plus, I won't risk bumping into Simon, especially since I refused all of his calls and texts. The other reason is that I need to get my nerves in check and the release that I felt after Simon's spanking was mind-blowing.

"Yes, but now we're in New York and not in Paris. Plus, you'll be with me. Let's go," I declare, standing and heading to one of the three bedrooms to get ready before I wimp out.

Leonie lets out a wolfish whistle and prances to one of the other bedrooms.

LOLA

For three hours, we soak in the oversize bathtubs to loosen our travel-weary muscles, wash and style our hair, then artfully apply makeup to our faces. Our heels click on the hotel lobby's marble floors. Leonie and I strut arm-in-arm from the elevators to the front doors. We pass well-dressed guests on their way to dinner or to one of the city's happening night spots. Several do a double take when they recognize *The Lion* with her glossy, mahogany hair flowing behind her like a mane. The supermodel whose stunning visage graces magazine covers on the newsstands and on the billboards in Times Square impresses even the most jaded New Yorker. With her signature predatory smile on her face, amber eyes twinkling, Leonie prances past the gawkers and nods at the doorman as he smiles sheepishly at her. We glide down the stairs and sweep into the chauffeured Bentley Bentayga that I hired for our seven-day stay.

"Good evening, Ms. Lewis and Ms. Beaulieu," the driver greets us as we settle into the plush leather seats. "My name is Stan, and it is a pleasure to be your driver while you are in

New York. Your requested beverages are in the center console."

"Good evening, Stan. Please take us to LEVELS New York in the Meatpacking District, thank you," I reply confidently.

As the quintessential professional, Stan's face remains neutral even though I'm sure that he knows LEVELS is a hedonistic establishment and responds, "Yes, Ms. Lewis, right away."

While Leonie's mobile commands her attention, I gaze out of the window, ever amazed by the constant activity on the city's streets. Tourists gaping at the store windows of the pricey retailers; vendors with pretzel carts on the corners; natives bustling past everyone else as they hurriedly make their way to their destinations.

I open the window and close my eyes to take in a whiff of my former home. The various smells fill my nostrils, reminding me of the marvelous times. As a child, ice skating with my dad at Rockefeller Center. Lunch with my teenage friends at Serendipity's. Going to the boutiques on Madison Avenue with my mom to shop for my high school graduation dress and shoes.

Although the pain is still fresh, I truly miss the place of my childhood. A boutique here will be the impetus for me to return, especially since I'll be so busy that I won't have time to dwell on my anguish. The boutique will provide fresh experiences and better memories, reestablishing my presence here.

A squeal from Leonie breaks my reverie.

"Gio invited me to Monaco for the Grand Prix next month!"

She does a shimmy in her seat and taps her toes on the SUV's floorboard. Her exuberance makes me laugh.

"I thought you were over *Mr. Thinks He's God's Gift to Women*," I taunt her.

Giovanni Mattei is a wealthy nobleman from an aristocratic family dating back to the Middle Ages and her on-again-off-again paramour.

"Bof," Leonie scoffs. "He's angling to get off of my shit list. Two weeks ago, he sent that oil painting from his Paris gallery that I had my eye on. I promptly returned it. Last week it was a beautiful pair of yellow diamond earrings with a note. 'They remind me of your eyes right after you cum screaming on my cock'... Returned to sender!"

I'll give it to him, Giovanni—that handsome devil—definitely has the confidence of a man used to getting whatever he wants in life. He doesn't give a damn about how others view his arrogance.

"Then, why are you going on and on about the Grand Prix," I ask with my eyebrow raised.

With that infamous Gallic shrug—Leonie is as bad as Luc—she responds, "I always have fun! It's the best time in Monte Carlo. You know that you enjoy it as much as I do. The thrill of the tight turns. The roar of the engines. The glamorous crowd losing themselves cheering on their favorite team..."

"Oh, like you're not one of the glamorous crowd," I tease her.

"*Mais oui*!" She retorts. "It's just such a thrill to watch. Heart pounding!"

"Or is Giovanni 'a thrill to watch. Heart pounding!'" I laugh.

The Bentayga stops in front of a renovated warehouse in a prime spot of the Meatpacking District that offers unobstructed views of the Hudson River and of the New Jersey coastline. The building is six stories and has a brick facade with oversized windows treated to block outsiders from seeing through the panes of glass since the interior is not visible.

Two men in custom-tailored black suits stand outside. A queue that extends around the corner of people in expensive attire patiently await admittance to the club. Not surprising given LEVELS is for the überwealthy and influential, too refined to behave boorishly. The hopeful patrons are not rambunctious as one would ordinarily see waiting outside a Manhattan nightclub.

One doorman opens the Bentley's door while Stan opens the other.

"Welcome to LEVELS New York, ladies. May I have your names?"

When Leonie and I emerge, he pulls out a mobile device from the breast pocket of his jacket.

"Lola Lewis and Leonie Beaulieu," I respond.

After a quick perusal of the screen, he ushers us through the front doors to the lobby.

"Taylor is waiting for you at the greeter station to your right. Enjoy your evening."

While still in Paris this morning, I spoke with Taylor as the head of membership and purchased two seven-day, all access passes for Leonie and for me. I knew if I waited until I arrived that I may have chickened out, again. Plus, the cost wasn't a trifle to waste.

"Good evening, Ms. Lewis, Ms. Beaulieu. I'm Taylor Hunt. Welcome to LEVELS New York," he greets us as we approach. "Please allow me to give you a tour. Would you like to check your coats?"

Leonie and I decline since we have on outfits more suitable for a lover's tryst than for a tour of the entire club.

Taylor then introduces us to Chester the greeter for the

BDSM levels—just like the doorman, the two men are very attractive and impeccably dressed. Next, Taylor leads us to the other greeter for, as he explains, the Dine/Dance levels. He guides Leonie and me onto the elevator that quickly whisks us to the Sky Lounge on the 7th Level. As I suspected the view is spectacular. A few boats bobbing on the river and lights from properties on the New Jersey coast shining in the night sky. From there, we go down to the Dance Club on levels 6 and 5. The deejay is pumping some booty-shaking songs. Partiers are definitely shaking their things on the dance floors. The bartenders are busy serving drinks. Taylor explains that this is where the queue out front hopes to gain entry. He notes that it's an excellent way to vet more members and keep things fresh for existing ones. As we head to the elevator, he says that the restaurant also allows outsiders on certain days for the same reason. The Level 4 Restaurant and bar are in contrast to the club with soft jazz music playing and well-heeled patrons dining on delicious-smelling food and sipping tasty cocktails. The D&D side is on my list as a place that I would frequent regularly.

We return to the main level and take the BDSM elevator to Level 3 to view the twelve private suites. As we exit the elevator, a devastatingly handsome man towers over us. My vision locks on his magnetic gray eyes and a thrill rushes through me as if a jolt of electricity shocked me. I suck in a breath and my step falters.

Leonie reaches for me, but his powerful hands catch me by the forearms and hold me in place.

His eyes darken to a slate gray and he inhales sharply as if he experienced the unexpected jolt, too.

"Pardon us, sir," Taylor says to the sizable man and reaches for my elbow.

The man gives him a glare with what I must have imagined was a low, feral snarl.

I regain my composure and extricate myself from the man's tight grip.

"Excuse me," I assert and move around him only for his imposing form to block my path. A bit of a dance ensues as I sidestep him and he blocks my path, again. His intoxicating musky scent, a mix of bergamot, patchouli, and vanilla wafts into my nose and beckons to me, making my pussy clench.

Leonie senses my frustration and takes me by the arm to elbow our way past him, muttering, *"Âne."*

He definitely is an ass. But, I can't help but to peek over my shoulder at him as he speaks animatedly with Taylor, the man's eyes darting between Taylor and me. Resigned to ignore him, I turn away to take in the dimly lit foyer. I note the minimal style of the decor and the silence only broken by the soft hum of sensuous music. The alluring atmosphere prepares you for the carnal activities just inside the doors of the suites that line the hallway.

"I apologize, Ms. Lewis, Ms. Beaulieu. Please right this way," Taylor approaches and gestures down the hallways. I peer beyond him to find that the gray-eyed stranger left the floor. My disappointment is palpable.

After the brief encounter, I find it hard to concentrate on Taylor's commentary as he shows us some suites that are unoccupied. My mind is back with the handsome stranger.

Did he really snarl possessively? He couldn't have. The thought he could have makes my nipples tighten and my pussy throb—what a caveman.

Leonie takes my arm once again since I failed to notice her and Taylor walking to exit the suite.

"Are you all right?" Leonie inquires with a frown. "He was such a brute. Did he really snarl?"

I snort and cover my mouth, laughing. I didn't imagine a thing!

"Now, we'll go to Peepshow on the 2nd level. It's the perfect spot to give in to your voyeurism..."

Once again, my mind drifts this time to a scene with Captain Caveman...

"MINE!"

Comes his snarl as he roughly yanks me from the arms of my would-be playmate for the evening. I nearly topple over in my mules as the gray-eyed stranger pulls me close, my back to his hard chest. I tense as his enormous cock hardens and lengthens against my plump bottom. He ignites a flame deep in my core, my juices immediately pour from my seam and trickle down my thighs.

I peek up and over my shoulder at him. His upper lip curls, his nostrils flare, his eyes the color of molten platinum shoot poisonous darts at the Dom who was preparing me for a scene.

My unknown cockblocker wants to take me as his very own.

As I decide whether I want this to happen, the Dom puts his hands up and beats a hasty retreat—even he couldn't best this caveman.

Suddenly, I'm hoisted onto the stranger's shoulder as though I weigh nothing. He swiftly strides to one of the darker areas of the dungeon. I kick my legs and pummel his back—my small fists ineffectively hit a wall of steel and earns me three swift smacks on my rear. A zing shoots through my core, pumping more of my juices between my thighs.

Curses pour from my mouth as he sits on a red velvet sofa in the alcove and drapes me over his hard, muscular thighs. My belly presses against his thick dick that promptly pulses when our bodies collide.

He makes quick work of lifting my chemise and snatching my thong down my thighs. The skimpy material keeps my legs bound above my knees. My bare ass and pussy exposed to his view. He gently runs his hands over my lush curves—quite a contrast to his previous brutish behavior. I shiver under his delicate touch, his rough hands caress my supple skin...

"Owweee," I yell as the first smack of his palm against my soft tush shocks me from the gentle lull. I reach back to shield myself with my hands, only to have him grab both of my wrists in one gigantic hand and hold them against my lower back. His other hand never misses a beat and continues to spank me—left, right, left, crease of my ass and thigh, right, left. I dance on his lap.

"You are mine. No one else will ever touch you again."

He growls as he punctuates each word with a hard spank, drawing heat and pumping blood to the surface of my bare, jiggling ass.

A sudden shift in his movements brings two of his thick fingers to my seam—I'm sopping wet for him.

"Is this all for me?"

His voice deepens with lust as he slides his fingers in and out of my pussy, fucking me, the wet sounds loud in my ears. As if I were a puppet on a string, I widen my legs to allow him more access to my slippery core, but don't respond.

My lack of a verbal answer results in another volley of spanks —left, right, left, crease of my ass and thigh, right, left.

"Yes!" I scream as I squirm on his lap attempting to get out of his reach and to close my legs.

"Open!" He commands, and my thighs instantly part again, my traitorous body taking over from my brain.

"So, sweet."

The sound of the caveman licking his fingers clean of my essence makes me gush even more than before.

A dark chuckle falls from his mouth. He bends to press his lips against my ear to whisper, "You like being mine and receiving the sting of my palm on your luscious ass, don't you, Pet? How would you like to have my colossal dick in your little ass?"

I whimper and tremble, aching to have his thick cock in all three of my holes. I can't deny that I want this beast to take me harshly in every single one of my holes, bent over and fucked by him like a feral animal...

"HONESTLY, ENOUGH ALREADY!" Leonie chastises me for bumping into her from behind, my mind in my oh so vivid erotic fantasy.

"You're all gaga for that guy," she continues.

We stopped at a greeter station in front of the doors to Peepshow. Taylor is holding bracelets and explaining the differences in the colors: partnered subs wear collars given to them by their Dom; partnered Doms wear gold bracelets; available subs wear red; unattached Doms wear white; voyeurs wear black.

Without looking Leonie in the eye, I select a red bracelet. If I want to get spanked to ease my nerves for my meeting in the morning, then I have to show my availability, I assure myself.

Leonie, being the best friend that she is to me, doesn't make a comment and selects a black one. I see, *The Lion* on the hunt.

We remove our Burberry trench coats, hand them to the greeter Jane, and accept the tickets from her.

I had to wear my favorite set from the new collections. The beige, satin-trimmed, embroidered tulle chemise and thong made specifically for me. My size D breasts would never fit the sample. To adjust the piece for my petite frame, I shortened the length to just skim the tops of my thighs.

Gold, strappy sandals adorn my feet, adding five inches to my five-foot-five-inch frame. My black hair cascades down my back in soft waves, brushing the curve of my plump bottom. I feel extra sexy and ready to do a scene with a capable caveman—I mean Dom.

Leonie chose the new black lace, strapless jumpsuit that ties above her bosom paired with marabou mules and her hair in a high ponytail.

The statuesque beauty and my curvy, petite self turn heads as Taylor walks us through the room. We pass seating alcoves filled with members in various stages of sex. A main stage and several smaller platforms showcase demonstrations in bondage and edging. We continue through performance rooms with viewing windows where members watch others live their fantasies. A bar that Taylor points out only serves non-alcoholic mocktails to keep everyone's minds clear.

The atmosphere is all about bacchanalia with the melodic thrum of sensual music and the moans and groans of men and women as the backdrop to intense sexual play. The air is heavy with the scent of perfume, cologne, and sex. I swear that above all, I can detect the caveman's cologne. A faint trail of his scent tickling my nose, adding to my already overstimulated body.

Finished with the tour of this level, we walk down a flight of stairs to a set of heavy wooden double doors with two large, iron circular pulls. A riveting pair oversee the entrance. A man dressed only in a minuscule, black leather jock strap, his enormous bulge slightly covered. A woman in a black latex butt-cheek-baring tube dress, both have black leather collars around their throats.

Taylor explains that this is the Cellar, LEVELS' BDSM dungeon.

I feel a twinge of excitement and my face heats from just thinking about what's behind those imposing doors.

As the couple opens the deceptively light doors, the sights and the sounds that surround us are incredible. The Peepshow is tame compared to the Cellar.

My eyes scan the expansive, grand hall, austere in design. A multi-beamed high ceiling; cobblestone floors; brick walls; lighting that resembles flickering torches in brackets on the walls and in metal stands scattered around the room; an assortment of what looks like Medieval torture devices placed in clusters. My gaze bounces from one area to another. An older man cuffed to one of the several St. Andrew's Crosses, his head thrown back in pure ecstasy. His engorged dick eagerly sucked by a younger man on his knees. A woman in a swing, her thighs glistening with her pussy juices and stretched wide to accommodate the large man standing between them aligning her core to his massive cock. Several men and women attached to hooks hanging from the ceiling in varied positions being whipped by Doms and Dommes with canes, floggers, and paddles extending from their hands. Still others lead naked subs by leashes while they crawl on their hands and knees to one of the partitioned rooms for a bit of privacy. Here and there voyeurs stand watching, mesmerized by the decadent, sexual activities.

The sight has my throbbing pussy so wet that I can feel my juices coating my inner thighs. The aroma of my arousal rising to fill my nose and to join with all the other scents. I shift subconsciously on my feet. Then I look around once more. My gaze reaches the bar on my right where my sight settles on hungry, lust-filled, gray eyes. Once again they magnetize me pulling my soul into the orbit of their black moons.

SEBASTIAN

Fuck... me.

My rock hard dick weeps pre-cum against the tightened confines of my trousers just at the sight of my Petite Seductress. Standing at the entranced to the Cellar in that see-through getup flaunting her every lush curve, her big, pillowy tits on full display makes me drool. I picture myself suckling her firm nipples as she bounces up and down on my thick, rigid length.

I'm even more riveted by her now than I was when she fell into my arms at the elevator on the private suites' floor upstairs. Her alluring floral scent enveloping me, sharpening my senses. I cannot believe that I couldn't control myself and snarled at Taylor like a possessive jerk. I was already on edge since my mind was on that bad, stupid ass deal that I fucked up and need to fix like yesterday. But as soon as my hands gripped her forearms, even through the barrier of her trench coat, my mind got a jump that reset it. I felt a jolt shoot down my spine to the tip of my cock, making it stand at full attention to salute the hazel-eyed beauty. My heavy balls demand that I blow my load deep in her pussy, coating her womb with my virile life force.

Damn.

When she and her companion a beautiful supermodel who I easily recognized stepped away, I quickly pulled Taylor aside. I grilled him about my Petite Seductress. Against the privacy rules of LEVELS New York. Yes. But when do I ever let such inconsequential encumbrances impede what I want? Never.

And I want her.

The one piece of information that I could not coerce him into divulging to me was her name. Taylor insisted that detail went too far beyond the privacy boundary, even for me. Since it was the number one rule that members and guests exchange names consensually to keep the integrity of the club intact and everyone secure. Well, that minor detail definitely won't stop me. I determined that she has a week-long All Access trial membership, she's single, and that she's not lovers with the supermodel.

Then, I told him to end their tour in the Cellar instead of at Peepshow, as is his routine. There, I could gauge her reaction to full-on BDSM. If she was hesitant, then I would have to pass no matter how much I'm attracted to her because vanilla lovemaking is not my style. I fuck and dominate, period.

Now, I sit riveted as I watch my Petite Seductress' reaction as she takes in the lascivious sights and sounds of the Cellar. Her eyes round in awe and not in fear. A heated flush on her face from her excitement. She shifts from foot to foot, discreetly rubbing her thighs together to ease the pressure building from her watching the members play. Her unconscious behavior confirms that she is perfect as my next hookup. Yet I wonder if she's new to the BDSM lifestyle and if she's open to being a sub.

My gaze travels to her slight wrist when she wipes her damp brow. I notice that she wears the red bracelet... Hmmm. So, my Petite Seductress may be virgin to the scene, but she's ready for indoctrination.

I squint and imagine introducing her to the pleasure in the pain, trusting me to take control of her body, to bring her the ultimate sexual satisfaction.

I will make her body my personal playground.

Her feverish gaze once again skips around the room, this time locking with mine as I sit at the bar drinking in the sight of her.

My Petite Seductress' eyes widen even more and she flushes deeper, embarrassed by my witnessing of her sexual arousal by the mere sight of others in promiscuous acts.

A predatory grin slowly spreads across my face. My eyes glint like steel in the torchlight as I rise from my perch on the barstool and stride over to capture my prey.

LOLA

Oh my God, no.

He's headed towards me. The lusty gleam in his eyes rivets me in place. I'm captured by the raw power that emanates in waves off of this striking man. I can only watch wide-eyed like a rabbit as the wolf approaches me through the crowd. He does not waver for a second. His predatory eyes solely focused on me.

For the second time tonight, my knees wobble and threaten to buckle beneath me.

Where is that strong, independent woman when I need her? I ask my inner *I Am Woman Hear Me Roar*. She's lost out to my body that's inwardly doing a series of jubilant cart-wheels, eagerly awaiting his eminent arrival.

"Le monde est fou!" Leonie exclaims shaking her head, her swishing ponytail hitting me on the cheek breaking the caveman's magnetic pull on my body.

That's putting it lightly. The Cellar is a crazy world. I peer around once again, a shiver racing down my spine.

And I love it.

"Do you want to remain on this level or return to Peepshow? Taylor says they set a demonstration with a popular Domme and her male sub to start in fifteen minutes. I'd love to watch!"

I glance up into Leonie's amber eyes, glowing with ardor. She's just as galvanized by LEVELS as I, its potent draw entices one to step out of their comfort zone and to relish in their sexual fantasies.

I intend to partake.

"Actually—"

"Excuse me."

A quiver instantly shoots through my body, sparked by the deep rumble of my caveman's voice. It ignites my very soul like jet fuel thrown onto a campfire. The slow burn becoming a blazing inferno, scorching everything all around it.

Leonie and I simultaneously pivot on our heels to stare at him, his commanding tone brokering no denial to his call.

"I see that you're wearing the red bracelet."

He gestures to my wrist and I lift it as if he's moving my puppet strings, again. Yes I am, I think dazedly, once more pulled into his spell.

"What do you want?" Leonie demands, hands on her hips.

Our roles have reversed where she's the feisty one who's keeping overly amorous suitors away from me.

With a slow blink, my caveman turns his gaze to Leonie and cocks his eyebrow.

"I appreciate your protectiveness of your friend, but I mean her no harm. I assure you of that fact."

Taylor moves closer to the gray-eyed stranger and smiles reassuringly at Leonie and me.

"*Mademoiselles,* allow me to introduce you to—"

"Baz, and you are?" Interrupts the stranger.

"I'm—"

I quickly cut Leonie off and purposefully glance at her and at Taylor, "It is too soon. So, we'd rather not reveal our names."

"I understand and respect your wishes. Since you chose the red bracelet, I gather that you are interested in being with a Dom?"

I glance away, nervous now that the opportunity for a spanking presents itself. Am I interested? Am I ready? I hesitate. Then, I remember my anonymity and can let go of my inhibitions. I can allow this Dom to dominate me, to release the tension that's inside of me before my meeting tomorrow.

"Yes, I am. I take it you're an experienced Dom?" I question him with a tilt to my head and a raised brow.

"I am a Dom with fifteen years of experience and partnered with many subs. Would you like to see my dossier?"

That's why I sense that LEVELS New York is a safe club. They vet every member and guest and maintain a file on them with periodic background checks and references. The security and privacy measures are unparalleled.

I turn to Taylor who smiles and nods, offering to get my potential paramour's file from the membership office.

I glance at Leonie and she can barely contain her glee. That was a quick change in her stance. I'm not the only one impressed by this Dom.

Finally, I return my gaze to the Dom, scanning his face for veracity. Deep in my soul, I know that he is the one to take me to the next level of my desire to be a sub. If only for this one night.

He holds out his gigantic hand—cocky isn't he—and I place my small one in his. His predatory smile returns and I tremble, my pussy clenches as I expect what the night will bring for me.

We make our way through the members in the Cellar and back through the double doors, two other sentinels comparably attired pull rings from this side. Careful to climb the stairs without stumbling in my sky-high sandals, I tighten my grip on Baz's hand. He looks down at me and smiles reassuringly. This man is beyond gorgeous as his gray eyes sparkle with mischief. I can only imagine what I'm about to experience with him.

We speak no words as we cross the floor at Peepshow and take the elevator upstairs to the private suites. As I stand slightly behind him, I observe him in the elevator doors' reflective surface. He's at least six inches taller than me even in my five-inch heels, so he's well over six feet; his face is a work of art with smoky gray eyes, chiseled jaw, and sexy stubble; his black hair is as thick as his eyelashes and I imagine tugging on it as I climax from him gorging on my pussy juices; his wide powerful shoulders taper to a narrow waist and slim hips, ending in muscular thighs and calves; his enormous feet make me wonder at the size of his cock. The ding of the door opening at our floor brings my eyes back up, only to find that he's smirking at me with a knowing expression in his captivating eyes. Damn, busted.

Baz still holding my hand, leads me down the hallway to the suite on the end. Then he places his hand on the plate to unlock the door before ushering me inside. As I hear the lock engage in acknowledgement of my commitment to this encounter, he breaks the silence.

"Tell me about your experience with BDSM and being a sub."

Baz's questions come as I stand in the middle of what must be his domain alone. I take in the strong, masculine ambience of the decor and the collection of various implements and equipment around the room. My eyes settle on what looks like a pommel horse that's typically used in gymnastics. However, I can sense by the brass rings strategically attached to it that the piece of equipment has a unique use in BDSM. The thought of being cuffed to it, my bare ass exposed to Baz, makes me shift on my feet as my core oozes with need for him.

I turn to Baz. I notice how confident he is standing there in his dress shirt, the top buttons undone and his custom-tailored trousers falling just right on his narrow hips; he laid the jacket and the tie over the wooden valet next to the suite's door.

"I've never been in the lifestyle and I'm not a sub," I pause and gaze directly in his eyes to gauge his reaction. His face remains neutral, not giving away his thoughts.

Not sensing judgement, I continue, "My last lover is a Dom, and he persuaded me to allow him to spank me one night. I... I enjoyed it." I lift my chin defensively and prepare myself for any negative word that he may say in response.

Instead, a low growl emanates from his lips. I blink in surprise at his possessive behavior, but before I can comment, he nods and motions for me to continue, as though he never emitted a sound. Perhaps, I misheard, I think to myself. Then I face the wall lined with whips, canes, and paddles. Slowly, I bring my gaze back to Baz.

"I want to experience that release again. I'm not a sub nor interested in a relationship. I'm a busy woman who doesn't need a Dom nor a man in my life permanently. But, for tonight, I seek the pleasure that I experienced from being spanked."

I stop and ask, "Are you able to give that to me?" There's nothing more for me to say, it's his turn.

He pauses for a moment and runs his thumb over his lower lip, thinking, assessing me and my remarks.

I hold my breath, hoping that he will agree—my body wants him to be the one. Yeah, my roar is definitely on hiatus.

"I can give that to you. However, I want to fuck you, rough and long. Can you give that to me... along with your trust?"

"Yes."

His gray eyes darken nearly to black, and he licks his full lips.

"You need a safeword that you will use only if you want the play to stop completely."

For a moment, I consider what it should be and decide on the word panther. Baz with his jet black hair, gray eyes, and feline grace reminds me of a sleek and powerful panther. He's definitely one to admire, but not one to cross —my limit ends with him.

"Panther," I say out loud.

Again, a neutral, unreadable face.

"Since you're new to BDSM, we will not jump into the more advanced play. But, I will demand your submission and push your limits, so use your safeword only if you absolutely want all play stop. The point is to explore your sexuality."

I nod my agreement.

"Words, Pet."

He says sharply. His authoritative tone and his use of the word pet makes my pussy juices flow once more and I shift restlessly. I'm ready to get started.

"Yes, Sir," I respond.

His eyes widen and his nostrils flare as if he's turned on

by my use of the word sir. Or perhaps, he can smell my arousal because I surely can smell the sweet nectar.

"Crawl to me on your hands and knees, ass high, head low."

I flinch, surprised by his demand.

"If you hesitate, I will punish you. That is your only warning."

As much as it thrills me to imagine him punishing me for my transgressions, I don't know what his form of punishment entails, so I comply.

As I crawl to him, my first response is mortification: who does he think he is to demand that I crawl to him? Then, my feelings shift as my body takes over from my mind: my breathing quickens, my nipples tighten to points, my pussy leaks and contracts. Innately, I hold my position and keep my eyes lowered to the floor when I reach where he stands.

"Such a dutiful girl, Little Pet."

He rubs my head as he praises me and I arch into him, a mewl falling from my lips surprising me.

The tug on my scalp as his fingers twine in my hair pulls my head back, my gaze meeting his as he lifts me to my knees.

"Since the moment you fell into my arms, you have had me hard enough to cut a diamond. Now, you will take every one of my ten inches in your pretty, little mouth. All the way to the back of your throat and suck me off without spilling one single drop."

A gasp escapes from my slacked-jaw mouth. Did he go all the way there with me?

"That is five extra spanks."

I blink and whimper, more in delight at being spanked longer than in trepidation.

As if sensing my desire, Baz chuckles darkly, "You would like that wouldn't you?"

My nod turns into a cry as Baz yanks my hair. "Words, Pet," he admonishes me.

"Yes, Sir, I'd like that very much," I whimper.

"We shall see. Now, take out my hard dick and show me how much you like pleasuring your Dom."

Without the slightest hesitation, I reach up to unbuckle his belt, unzip his pants to lower them past his hips. Directly in my face is the biggest bulge that I have ever seen—grant it, I've only had two lovers, but neither is this huge. His bulging cock tents the black silk of his boxer briefs. I hook my fingers into the waistband and tug them over his dick and down his muscular thighs. It clarifies my wonderment at his shoe size in relation to his cock. Baz is massive.

I swallow and peek up at him through my eyelashes to see an arrogant smirk on his handsome face. The urge to wipe the smugness from him causes me to grasp his cock in one hand and his balls in the other. I heft their weight and stroke them before I lean forward and lick the drop of pre-cum off of the tip with my tongue. I hum around his girth in satisfaction when he groans as I take him to the back of my throat. Sucking dick is my favorite for the power that it gives me over the man. I've made an art out of it.

I glance up again and smile, satisfied that Baz has his head thrown back and his mouth is hanging open, more groans slipping out.

I turn my attention back to his dick and really go at it. Drawing him in deep with my lips pressed all the way down his shaft to press against his manscaped crotch. I pull back to swirl the tip of my tongue around his bulbous head. Then follow up with a long lick along the vein on the underside of his girth to his heavy balls. To add to the sensation, I suck his full sac into my mouth and stroke it with my tongue. Minutes later, Baz's legs quiver as I hold the backs of his thighs, his six-pack abs tighten, and his cock grows larger, throbbing under my ministrations.

Baz tightens his grip in my hair and locks my head in place as he fucks my throat. His eyes are wild and his lip curls, a guttural snarl ripping from his mouth as an abundant amount of his cum spews down my throat. I remember not to spill a drop, so I seal my lips around his girth and swallow repeatedly.

"Fuck me," Baz groans as his dick—still large even when flaccid—slips from my mouth with a pop and he sinks to his knees staring at me in amazement.

"Damn, where did you learn to suck cock like that? Actually, never mind."

Somewhat piqued, I say defensively, "I've only had two lovers in my entire life, so don't act like I'm some promiscuous tart!"

I stand abruptly, but before I can get to the door, I'm pulled back against his hard chest.

"Please forgive me. I did not mean to offend you."

Baz turns me in his arms, but I keep my eyes on his chest. With the tip of his index finger, he lifts my chin to bring my gaze to his regretful eyes.

"I just don't want to think of you with someone else…"

His words trail off and he looks surprised that he said them as if shocked by the admission. He pulls back and lets go of me, running his hand through his hair.

"Are you using your safeword?"

With his abrupt change in topic, I'm perplexed and pause too long.

"If not, that is ten extra spanks."

With a shiver, I say, "No, Sir, I am not using my safeword."

"Splendid girl, Little Pet. Come."

I drop to my hands and knees and crawl after him. He stops at the pommel horse and I suck in a breath.

"Stand and undress for me."

I rise with a tremble coursing through me. My fantasy comes to life.

Slowly, I reach under my chemise and shimmy my thong down my legs, kicking it to the side once it reaches the floor. I bring my hands to my neck and trace the edges of the embroidered cups before pinching my nipples through the material with a low moan.

Baz grunts and strokes his hardening cock as he removes the rest of his clothes.

I smile coyly and trail my hands down the sheer panel covering my middle to grasp the hem. Slowly, I lift it up and over my head, my full breasts bounce free. The sudden feel of Baz's hot, wet mouth on my left nipple makes my knees quake and I bite my lower lip to hold back a groan. The powerful pulls as he suckles zing my core. His hands heft the weight of my heavy breasts as he moves from one nipple to the other, lavishing them with equal attention. My head falls back as I cry out in ecstasy—it's been too long since I knew a lover's touch.

I hastily push that thought aside, this isn't about love, it's about release.

His hand skims down my belly and cups my bare mound. His fiery breath tickles my skin as he teases my pussy lips, "All this wetness just for me?"

"Yes, Sir," I moan and grind my mound into his large palm.

"Ow! Oh, ow!"

Five quick spanks to my pussy has me rising onto the balls of my feet and trying to move away from Baz. But his arm tightens around my waist, pinning me in place.

"You did not think I would forget your extra spanks, did you, Little Pet?"

His sneer followed by a pinch to my tender nipple makes me jump—and my pussy contract.

"Lean over the pommel horse. It is time for your spanking," he demands.

My body is ablaze, the inferno is still smoking hot.

I happily drape myself over the horse, my strappy heels lengthening my legs, allowing my toes to skim the floor. My body thrums in anticipation. A slight nag dances at the edges of my mind, questioning my decision to do a scene as a sub with a Dom just to get over my nerves. Is that a plausible excuse? Or do I want to be a sub and not the independent businesswoman? Is it possible to be both?

The sense of Baz's rough hands sliding along the inside of my soft thighs as he lowers himself to the ankle restraints brings me back to the suite. Soft kisses trail after his fingers, lulling me into a stupor. He expertly attaches the cuffs and checks that they're not too tight. A sharp crack of his palm to my left butt cheek dispels the haze and I cry out. Baz glides his hands down my arms and closes the cuffs securely around my wrists, again he checks the fit.

"What is your safeword, Pet?"

"Panther, Sir," I whisper as my muscles tighten to prepare for the blow.

Instead, Baz strokes his palm over my shoulders and down my back.

"Relax, Little Pet. I promise that I will not hurt you more than you can comfortably take. Remember to test your boundaries. The pleasure will follow the pain. Free yourself to receive it," he croons in my ear, his lips brushing the shell.

His palm reaches the curve of my ass and I try to settle, but I'm still tense.

"Thirty plus the five extra. I want you to count them for me."

"Yes, Sir," I whisper.

"Louder, Pet."

I raise my voice and declare, "Yes, Sir!"

The first strike hits my right butt cheek, left, the crease of my ass and thigh, right, left. I dance on his pommel horse, oddly almost like my fantasy, and count each one out loud.

At fifteen, Baz pauses and slides his thick middle finger along my dripping seam, collecting my juices.

"You want this spanking, Pet. Your little pink pussy swollen and dripping for me."

Another finger joins the first, and he finger fucks me, driving his long fingers into my slippery core. His fingers leave me and I'm bereft. The sound of his groan and tongue licking his fingers clean make me blush.

"So sweet, just as I knew you'd be."

"Oh. Oh. Oh!" I wail as Baz spanks my pussy five times.

The sting morphs into pleasure and my pussy clenches around his fingers as they slide back into me.

"Fuck!"

I can feel my orgasm rising to the surface and I buck against Baz's hand.

Left, right, left, crease of my ass and thigh, right, left.

"You do not cum until I give you permission. And be still! Control your body."

As the spanking continues, they get harder and the intensity mounts. I can barely concentrate to count and beg

Baz to let me cum. Finally, after what seems like a century, I hear those sweet words.

"Cum for me, Little Pet!" Baz commands as he thrusts his engorged cock deep inside of my dripping sheath. I scream as I clench his dick and shudder as I cum.

Baz grips my hips hard enough to leave fingerprints that will match his palm prints on my ass. He grunts as his hips piston like a jackhammer into my pussy. The sounds of my wetness are loud in his suite.

"Uh. Uh. Uh. Uh," I cry out as Baz increases his pace and pounds into me, pushing me to the brink once more.

"Cum, again!" He shouts.

I babble that I can't take anymore, but Baz is not hearing it. He demands that I cum again as he spanks my stinging butt cheeks.

His dick grows even bigger and throbs as it scours my sheath.

"Cum!"

I grip his dick with all the strength that I have left and scream my release as wave after orgasmic wave hits me. It's so good that I sob and shake my head from side to side, overwhelmed with emotions.

As Baz slams into me one last time and roars his release, at last my mind lets go to float. My mind is free of tension and worry about my meeting in the morning. With a long drawn-out wail from my fifth electrifying orgasm, I give in to the sweet surrender of subspace.

Eventually, I return to myself, aware of my surroundings: Baz is holding me tightly on his lap, sitting against the headboard of the giant bed. My head is against his bare chest and I can hear the beating of his heart.

"How are you?" He asks softly.

The rumble of his voice goes through his chest to my ear.

"Incredible. Sore. Thirsty," I respond with a shy smile, my throat scratchy from my screams.

Baz holds a glass of water to my lips and I gratefully drink all of it.

As the haze lifts more, I realize that we're both still naked. The navy silk sheets caress my bare skin.

"I need to go," I make to get off of his lap, but Baz tightens his grip on my waist.

"That was intense and long. You should stay and get some rest. No one will disturb us. This is my private suite."

The offer is tempting, but I can't allow feelings to develop and I know that I'm vulnerable right now. Plus, it must be late and I need to return to the St. Regis. Breakfast is early and I want a clear head for the meeting.

So, with a heavy heart, I decline Baz's offer and climb off of his lap. The delicious touch of his hands sliding along my flanks, then my hips as I move away tempts me to stay. But, no.

"Would you like to meet tomorrow night?"

I stare at him over my shoulder, surprised that he would ask since we agreed that this would be for only one night, no commitments. I'm further surprised when I answer yes.

* * *

LEONIE DECIDED that she would watch the BDSM demonstration and Taylor offered to keep her company. Not just because he wanted to make sure we enjoyed ourselves, rather *The Lion* completely captivated *him*. She knew my reason for coming to LEVELS. Now that she saw I was in the capable hands of an experienced Dom, Leonie was happy to see me let go.

Stan drove back for me after he took Leonie to the hotel earlier. So, as I ride alone in the Bentayga, I lean my head against the plush headrest. My indescribable scene with my wild, possessive Caveman replays behind my closed eyes.

Tomorrow promises a monumental day and an incredible night.

SEBASTIAN

"Get your head in the game, Steele, and out of your ass!"

The glorious vision of her glistening, pink pussy and tight, puckered hole gets soundly knocked out of my brain. My personal trainer and former MMA champion Borya *The War Defender* Alexeyev delivers a roundhouse kick to my left flank.

Damn… that shit hurts likes a motherfucker.

"First, you're ten minutes late—"

Whack!

"Looking all bleary-eyed—"

Bam Bam!

"Now, I'm beating your weak ass like a *kiska*—"

Before Borya's next series of blows can hit me, I quickly crouch low and use my leg to sweep him off of his feet. The giant Russian lands on his ass with an oomph.

"What were you saying, asshole?" I sneer as I do my best Mohammad Ali float like a butterfly sting like a bee moves, cracking my neck side to side.

"Da, mal'chik!"

Alexeyev punches his fists together as he effortlessly backflips to land on his feet.

"*Da,* that's more like it, Steele. Be here or go jerk off. No room on this mat for *zhopas* with the smell of *kiska* on their breath! Meow. Meow."

Sufficiently chastised and pissed that I'm letting some hookup fuck with my head, I refocus.

I fake a charge at Borya, then at the last second turn and back kick him, the momentum throwing him off balance and causing him to stumble forward. I follow the kick with a few, well-placed punches then taunt him as I float backwards, fists in the air, "I am the greatest!"

It's later than my usual start time of 5:15 a.m. I couldn't sleep after I arrived well past midnight at my duplex penthouse on the fifty-fifth and fifty-fourth floors of The STEELE Tower. SI's remarkable gray-tinted glass skyscraper for our headquarters and commercial, retail, and residential properties on Fifth Avenue and Fifty-seventh Street in the heart of Billionaires' Row.

My mind replayed the scene with my Petite Seductress repeatedly, keeping my dick amped up and begging for access deep inside of her tight, wet pussy. From our initial contact with my hands gripping her forearms. To my dick pummeling her pussy, my balls slapping against her clit. To my palms sliding along her small waist and lush thighs as she rose from my bed. I can't shake the need to have her. It's disturbing since I've never gotten caught up in a tryst before. She's got me all scattered.

Shit, I have to get my mind on straight for my meeting later this morning with a lingerie company based in Paris interested in expanding into the United States. This retail expansion deal must make up for the fiasco. The blight on my record that shall go unnamed and locked away, never seen nor heard from again. No matter what, I can't let that situation or any other disrupt my rise to CEO and Chair next year.

The session with Borya goes on for another hour. The Russian is always ready to hand me my *zhopa*. Workouts with him are brutal and challenge me to bring my A game. I'm forced to focus or get my ass kicked, literally.

"You ended better than you started, Steele. Still weak, but better. Whatever's turning your mind into mush must be worth it. Since you dared to step onto the mat half cocked with me!" Borya says. A deep, rumbling sound that's his version of a laugh. The grimace on his face the closest to a smile that his lips can create.

"Okay, okay, see you tomorrow," I respond and wonder if my Petite Seductress is worth it. Why do I care if she is or if she isn't?

* * *

ASIDE FROM A FULL gym on the first floor of my penthouse duplex, another of the many benefits of living at The STEELE Tower is I can ride the family's private elevator. It links our residences on the fiftieth through fifty-seventh floors to our headquarters on the nineteenth through twenty-ninth floors. The commute to my office is less than five minutes, so despite being late to my workout session, I arrive at my office as usual at seven.

I exit the elevator on the twenty-ninth floor for the executive level where my father, Malcolm, Roger, and I have offices. Our finance and legal departments along with various conference rooms occupy the remaining space. The

STEELE divisions have designated floors below along with Harris and Haley's STEELE Technology and Cyber Security.

As always, power surges through me as soon as I enter any of the STEELE global offices. Pride swells in appreciation for my forebears. They laid the groundwork for the following generations to grow SI into a multibillion-dollar, luxury real estate development and management corporation. Each subsequent generation adding to the business' success. As the head of this generation, it is my duty to continue that upward trajectory set by those before me.

Through the gray-tinted, floor-to-ceiling windows, the city stretches out before me with unobstructed views. Central Park to the north, the Hudson River to the west, the East River opposite, and the rest of Manhattan to the south from Midtown to Battery Park. On a beautiful, cloudless day like this morning, the panoramas are riveting.

The decor—as sleek as the exterior—features platinum silk wall treatments, ebony wood floors, dove gray and white leather furniture, crystal light fixtures, Lucite tables, steel accents, and original artwork. The reception area has a spacious desk. Three attractive receptionists with headsets in their ears and custom-tailored light gray dress suits and skin-tone heels that serve as uniforms sit behind it.

The majesty of our power awes all who enter SI's offices.

"Good morning, Mr. Steele!" The trio chorus pleasantly.

"Good morning, Sue, Angela, Katrina," I respond with a nod and a smile.

On my way to my corner suite of offices, I pass Roger's offices and notice that he's in town early. He's based in our Paris branch, but spends about twenty percent of his time here.

"Hey, when did you get in?" I ask him as I stroll up to his desk.

Roger lifts his head and hits me with that intense stare. His gray eyes are just like mine, our family trait.

"Late last night. The investors canceled our meeting because of an ill associate, so I flew out earlier than planned."

He replies as he rises from his chair and comes around the desk to give me a bro hug and slap on the back.

I settle into the chair opposite his desk while he leans against it, crossing his long legs clad in custom-tailored trousers at the ankles, hands resting on the edge.

He catches me up on the happenings with two of the new builds that he's managing in Positano and Monte Carlo. I fill him in on the meeting with Lola's Coterie that I'm having with my team in a few hours. As the middle child, Roger—*The Responsible* as his childhood nickname implies—seeks to balance everyone and acts as mediator, so I invite him to sit in on the meeting. It's always useful to have his perspective.

My mobile buzzes, interrupting our conversation. I retrieve it from my pants pocket and realize the time is 8:20 already. Tina Nickles, one of my two assistants, texted to ask if I were running late. I type a quick response that I'm in Roger's offices and will be there in ten minutes. Between Tina and Melody Lawson, they keep a tight rein on my schedule because they know how valuable my time is and that I dislike wasting it.

I return to my conversation with Roger for a few more minutes, then head to my offices. The workout session and bonding with my younger brother has me back in the game.

* * *

Lola

Oh boy, is my ass sore.

I reposition myself on the seat of Luc's Cullinan, the buttery soft leather not easing the pain from Baz's punishing blows to my bottom. A galvanizing reminder of our incredible play last night.

Even after I soaked in my bathroom's tub at the St. Regis, the blend of essential oils and Epsom salt did not fully ease the tenderness.

Now, I sit here enduring the soreness of my ass. My disappointment at the dull ache in my well-used pussy crying out for Baz's thick, long, tasty dick to fill it. I dreamt of him taking me repeatedly in the Cellar. I awoke this morning at six o'clock not by my alarm. But by a powerful orgasm that ripped through my pussy causing it to clench so tightly that it thrust me upright, crying out at the climax. I shiver just at the memory.

"Is everything all right?" Luc asks me, concern etched on his handsome face.

I feel my cheeks heat of embarrassment as though Luc can read my lewd thoughts.

Out of the corner of my eye, I spot that Leonie grins like the Cheshire Cat and gives me a knowing look with her eyebrow arched.

"I'm fine, just excited to get the meeting started," I respond to Luc, completely ignoring Leonie.

"How are your nerves? Did you satisfy them last night?" Leonie ribs me, suppressing a chuckle.

My face flushes deeper and I reach into my handbag, pretending to retrieve my mobile to avoid looking into Luc's eyes.

"Pretty satisfied, the long soak in the tub did me good," I nod my head in affirmation.

"I'm sure that it was long..." Leonie quips.

Fortunately at that moment, we pull up to The STEELE Tower which is a scant distance from our hotel. Once we're on the sidewalk, I do the decidedly non-New-Yorker move and crane my head back. I look up at the imposing glass building that appears to reach endlessly into the sky—it's magnificent.

We stride into the gray glass and steel lobby that has a three-story atrium with several high-end retail stores. The other stores are just as exclusive and make up the rest of the seven-story, luxury mall, the only one of its kind on New York City's posh Fifth Avenue. I'm determined to make Lola's Coterie New York its newest addition.

Security confirms our appointment with STEELE's president of Retail Properties and escorts us to the elevator for the executive floors on twenty-nine. We're quiet as the elevator speeds nonstop to the floor. The doors open to an opulent reception area with stunning 360-degree views of Manhattan. Once again, I'm suitably impressed by the strength and power that STEELE International exudes.

One of the three receptionists who's not busy on the telephone or speaking with another visitor welcomes us. Then, she informs us that the models are in one of the conference rooms. Our assistants, the glam squad, and the select pieces from the New York and Las Vegas collections are there, too. The receptionist calls for one of the security guards to escort Leonie to the room so she can join the others to prepare for the mini fashion show. Melody, an assistant for Mr. Steele, arrives to take Luc and me to another conference room where the meeting will occur.

"Would you care for some coffee, tea, or bottled water? Pastries and fruit are also available," Melody offers to us.

"Coffee black, *merci*," responds Luc with a charming

smile that makes his deep blue eyes glitter like sapphires to which Melody blushes. In an attempt to hide it, she hurries to the breakfront for the beverage.

I head to the sleek, black, wooden table to check the presentations that Blair must have placed at one end. As if on the same wavelength, Blair appears in the doorway and smiles brightly at Luc, then at me.

"Good morning, Monsieur Montaigne!" She chirps.

"Bonjour, Blair."

Not having the patience to deal with Blair flirting with *Le Renard Argenté* before my meeting, I interrupt her before she can say another word.

"Blair, please help me with these," I say pointing at the various remotes that control the conference room's audio-visual system.

Melody assists us and soon we have my laptop connected and working properly. Her mobile chirps and she excuses herself to collect Mr. Steele and his team.

Once the door shuts, I turn to Luc and bite my lower lip as a touch of nerves threatens to rise.

Luc pulls me into his comforting embrace and I wrap my arms around his waist, drawing positive energy from him.

Suddenly, the doors open and we quickly pull apart to face our potential partners.

* * *

Sebastian

What the ever-loving fuck is she doing here? Better yet, who the fuck is that old guy rubbing himself all over my Petite Seductress!

I damn near blow a gasket. The woman who's invaded every fucking cell of my body in less than twenty-four hours has the arms of another man wrapped around her. A man who's abso-fucking-lutely comfortable holding her so damn close. What… The… Fuck.

"—the founder and CEO of Lola's Coterie. Luc Montaigne, CEO of Banque Montaigne and vice chair of Lola's Coterie. Ms. Lewis, Mr. Montaigne, this is Sebastian Steele, the president of Retail Properties."

No one but my traitorous seductress notes that I faltered mid-stride when I entered the room. So Walter Smith, the director of development, continues with the introductions. I missed her first name, but assume it's Lola since the name of the company is the founder's name.

Lola's hazel eyes widen even more than they had last night in the Cellar and she flushes deeply. Obviously, she's as dumbfounded as I. Unconsciously, her hand moves to cover her round ass that I know is still sore and covered in my palm prints.

This is surreal. And fuck me if my dick didn't grow hard.

A lull in the room draws my attention from the little vixen to my team who watch me with curiosity in their eyes. Roger is staring between Lola and me with that damnable intense gaze of his that never misses a thing. He would catch the tension between Lola and me.

I quickly recover and continue to stride over to Lola and Luc, thankful that my suit jacket prevents anyone from seeing the big bulge in my pants. I give them each a firm handshake—well, I may have squeezed Luc's hand more than necessary. He babbles on about Delcour who made the introduction for this meeting and I let Montaigne know that I'm not impressed by him. The little vixen pipes up about starting the meeting and I check out her luscious hips sway in that tight skirt as she walks to the head of the table. Oh, so the sub wants control.

As I lower myself into the seat opposite Lola, pinning her with a penetrating Dom stare, I remind myself of my earlier pledge. No matter what, I can't let this situation or any other disrupt my rise to CEO and Chair next year. Game on.

LOLA

How is this even possible? What in the hell did I do to deserve this karma? I ask myself in utter disbelief that Baz is Sebastian Steele, the president of STEELE International, Inc.'s Retail Properties Division. The man who I'm supposed to dazzle with my company's stellar growth and expansion plans. The same man who spanked my ass, saw my pussy, and fucked me raw.

Holy shit…

His expression and the falter in his stride, show that he can't believe this either. What are the chances that we would encounter one another at a BDSM club; share an intense scene and have crazy sex; later come face-to-face at a business meeting the next morning? Incredible.

The thought reminds me of my sore butt. I didn't even realize that I touched my ass until the arrogant smirk on his face appeared. Baz, I mean Sebastian… didn't miss the subtle movement.

I bite my lower lip in consternation as I wearily eye him strutting towards me.

The feel of his palm touching mine in a firm handshake causes a zing of electricity to shoot up my arm straight to my core. Against my will, my pussy obediently clenches for its Dom. The expression in his eyes turns feral at the contact before returning to neutral. Once again, like a puppet on a string, I shake his hand.

As if sensing my discomfort, Luc steps forward and holds his hand out to Sebastian.

"Good morning, Monsieur Steele, it's a pleasure to meet you. Pierre Delcour speaks highly of you and STEELE International."

"Yes, Monsieur Delcour is an honorable man, Monsieur Montaigne," Sebastian responds with a hint of a growl in his tone. "Let's determine if you are, too."

I glance to Luc as his face slightly grimaces, then I notice how tightly Sebastian is gripping Luc's hand. Sebastian's unprovoked aggression snaps me out of my stupor—this isn't the Cellar and I'm not a sub. Who the hell does he think he is behaving this way? I didn't come this far to let some caveman frazzle me.

"Mr. Steele, Luc and I appreciate you and your team meeting with us on such brief notice. Shall we get started?"

Without waiting for Sebastian's response, I strut to the head of the table and signal to Blair to close the doors. I begin the presentation once everyone settles in their seats. Sebastian sits opposite me, his gray eyes unreadable, his face set in a neutral expression. No sign of what happened last night impacting him today, hmmm. Unlike me so, I take a deep breath to re-center my thoughts and proceed as Luc and I practiced. My gaze travels to each person seated around the table to encourage their engagement during my thirty-minute pitch. After I finish, Luc's assistant opens the door to start the mini fashion show. As each model enters, I explain the relevancy of the piece for the specific boutique location and the craftsmanship that is the hallmark of my designs. Leonie, as my muse, begins and ends the show with her trademark predatory gait and mesmerizing aura.

At that point, Luc takes over for the financial portion of the presentation. I sit in awe of him and his innate ability to charm and to win over people so easily. The confidence that Luc exudes makes everyone around the table sit up straighter after being wowed by my story and by the models. After he's completed the details on the growth rate and expansion numbers, we answer the team's questions without a hitch.

Two hours later, the meeting ends with Sebastian rising from the table and announcing they will get back to us in a few days, before he abruptly leaves the room. Throughout the entire presentation, he sat there stoically and mum. I couldn't gauge his reaction, even when the scantily clad models with Leonie in the lead pranced around the conference room. That man confounds me!

Luc waits until Sebastian's team and his brother Roger exit the room before turning to me with a raised eyebrow.

"Je ne tolère pas l'impolitesse," he scoffs, the corner of his upper lip curled in disgust.

I can't stand rudeness either I nod my head in agreement with him and gather my laptop and portfolio. Blair and Luc's assistant handle the rest of the items in silence.

"Well, Mr. Steele may have been a cold fish, but we impressed his team and engaged them. I'm pleased with the presentation and I know that we did our best. Like my father used to say, 'Nothing beats a failure, but a try.' Thank you everyone," I smile.

Despite my mind racing, trying to figure out my next

move and holding back my disappointment. I expected more than a cold brush-off.

Does he think less of me since I played a sub for him last night and now he can't perceive me as a serious businesswoman? Would he have had more respect for me if I hadn't given him head like a professional? Should I have pulled him aside and cleared things up? Why the fuck did I go to that damn sex club?

"Did you notice his brother Roger's face when Leonie entered the room?" Luc asks.

I shake my head no. My focus was on the meeting and trying to get a read on Sebastian to notice his brother—the president of Residential or something—and Leonie. Besides, it's unusual if a man doesn't drool when he sees her.

Melody reappears as we finish gathering our belongings and walks us towards the elevator. As we pass a set of offices, Sebastian is leaning against his desk laughing with some red head standing in front of him. His gaze briefly meets mine without acknowledgment of me before he looks back at her when she places her hand on his chest. He laughs even more at something she says in his ear.

My vision goes red, and my brain explodes.

SEBASTIAN

Look at the vixen teetering over here in those fuck-me shoes, her hazel eyes trained on me, her heart-shaped face red in anger. I want to bite those tightly pressed lips. The spitfire has my eager dick expanding.

Poor Tina didn't stand a chance as Lola sidestepped her way around my assistant as she fruitlessly attempted to block Lola from barging into my office.

"Who the hell do you think you are, asshole?" Lola demands, hands on hips and feet planted wide on the floor. Her fight stance beats Borya's by aces.

"Please excuse the interruption, Chloe. We'll continue our meeting momentarily," I tell her. I never take my eyes from Lola. Who looks as though she's about to throw Chloe out of my office by her long, red hair if she doesn't leave fast enough.

"I'm so sorry, Mr. Steele!" a flustered Tina starts, "Ms. Lewis, please come with me."

The scathing look that Lola gives Tina makes me shudder just as much as Tina trembles in fear.

"It's all right, Tina," I assure her. "I'll handle Ms. Lewis."

"Handle... Handle? I'll give you something to handle, you jerk!" Lola screeches as Chloe and Tina scurry out of the office giving Lola a wide berth. They're followed by Melody, who had appeared at the door openmouthed and wide-eyed. As she leaves, she slowly shuts the door watching me for a sign to call security. I shake my head and gesture for her to go.

I peer beyond Lola to see more shocked expressions on the faces of Luc, Leonie, Roger, and the team from the meeting. Still others stare from their spaces. The situation prompts me to walk around my desk. Where I press the buttons to darken the glass walls of my office and remotely lock the door. This provides much-needed privacy for our unexpected encounter. As loudly as Lola is speaking, I'm glad that my office is soundproof, too. As she continues her rant, she stands in front of me poking my chest with her long, red fingernail in emphasis.

"Don't you dare think less of me because of what happened last night! I'm a successful businesswoman who deserves respect! I will not allow you to discount my achievements and blow off my expansion plans! Sitting in that room all high and mighty, as though you had more important things—"

I swipe the surface of my desk clean. The items hit the floor with a crash. I deftly grab the wrist of her jabbing hand, spin her around, and put her hands on her lower back. I press her against the top of my desk with my torso.

"Are you forgetting who's the Dom and who's the sub here?" I growl into her ear, satisfied when she trembles beneath me and expels a heavy breath. I push my hips into her plump ass, my thick cock wedged against her crack.

"Well, let me remind you, Ms. Lewis," I tell her gruffly and stand.

The snap of my large palm spanking both cheeks of her ass slides Lola across the surface. I remove my tie and secure both of her wrists against her lower back. I wrap the fingers of my left hand around the back of her neck to hold her in place. My right hand delivers a quick succession of smacks that have Lola dancing up on her toes. She squirms to dodge the startling blows.

"Don't you dare!" She splutters attempting to rise from the position. "I did not give you permission to spank me and you are not my Dom and I am not your sub!"

My hand stops midair as I realize with a start that I want to be her Dom and I want her to be my sub. I want my Petite Seductress for more than one night. My body craves her, I need to have more of her. I conclude that I have two choices. Ignore my inner caveman who wants to claim her and walk away with just that one glorious night. Or give in to the feral beast and fuck her out of my head while she's here this week.

In the brief span of time for my thoughts to form, she takes advantage of the break in the spanking to rise and face me. The breathtaking blow from her head butting my chest brings my focus back to Lola. She's stunning with her eyes bright and her cheeks flushed in anger and thinly veiled passion.

She's wrong in her conclusion that I think less of her because we had a Dom/sub scene and intense sex. No. Lola is a brilliant, determined woman who accomplished a huge and rapid success despite the tragic loss of her parents. I learned those details from the synopsis that my development team assembled on her company and on her personal life. The expansion plan is spot-on and would be a positive addition to the profitable roster of STEELE retail partners. It wasn't a delay tactic nor a dismissal when I told them that my team would be in touch. The details that Lola presented today need an in-depth review by my team, finance, and legal. More than likely, they will have revisions and recommendations that will require a follow-up meeting. That's all a part of the negotiations, but there's no doubt that we'll move forward with the deal. It promises to make up for my recent mishap. Especially if we expand into Los Angeles and Miami in the United States and Abu Dhabi and Dubai in the United Arab Emirates. Those epicenters for the wealthy who appreciate fine craftsmanship and sexy lingerie. I shake my head and snort at her false assumption.

"Oh, so now you're laughing at me? It's not enough to make a fool out of me, but to add insult to—"

I silence her newest tirade with a knee-jellifying, ground-shaking kiss that renders her speechless. Lola's taste is addictive and I seal my decision with our lips crushed together—I haven't had enough of her and I damn sure need more than one night.

Gently, I pull back and watch Lola's beautiful, hazel eyes flutter open to gaze into mine. In that moment, I see and sense her need to have love and to give in to someone whom she can trust. It may have to do with the loss of her parents at such a young age and not having any siblings or other relatives to comfort her. Or the loneliness of chasing her business success. I can relate with the loneliness, but ignore it. No wonder Montaigne latched onto her—old, scheming bastard. An overwhelming instinct of protectiveness for Lola takes over me. I brush her soft cheek with the pad of my thumb and cup her face, holding our stare.

"Lola, you are mistaken. What you shared with me last night was a gift that I cherish. You put your trust in me and I value and respect you for it."

As she attempts to interrupt me, I put my thumb to her kiss-swollen lips and continue.

"You decided that you wanted to do a scene with me during which you wanted a spanking. The sex was as much for your satisfaction as it was for mine—I pushed you to your limit for orgasms before I allowed myself release. You learn that a sub holds all the power, not the Dom."

I remove my thumb from her lips to allow her to speak.

"Then, why were you so aggressive when you saw me and closed off during the meeting? You walked out without even a glance my way," Lola laments, her beautiful face set in a scowl of frustration.

I pause and reflect on my behavior and the reasons for it. The realization that I'm jealous of her relationship with Montaigne and that jealousy being the impetus for my actions makes me uneasy. I don't want to develop feelings for Lola for many reasons: I don't mix business with pleasure; I'm not interested in a relationship; I have a business to grow. The one exception is to fuck her despite our pending business deal. That she isn't interested in a relationship either, as she stated last night. Then proved when she left even though I offered for her to stay validates the exception for my next offer.

"As per the norm, my team vetted your company prior to our meeting, so we knew what to expect. The specifics you presented today require an in-depth review. More than likely, a follow-up meeting will be necessary to discuss revisions and recommendations. All necessary before we move forward with the deal."

I allow her time to cogitate.

With a nod of acceptance, she tries to slip out of my embrace. But I hold her tighter and she looks up at me questioningly.

"I have an offer for you," I start and my Petite Seductress lifts her elegant brow further.

"Really… do tell," she smirks.

"Let's set the deal aside and leave it to our teams to hash things out until we need to make the ultimate decision. I propose that you and I spend our time more pleasantly," I respond, then pause again to judge her reaction.

"What do you have in mind?" She purrs with a tilt to her head, eyeing me through her long, dark lashes.

"That for the week you're here, I teach you the beauty of a Dom/sub relationship and you get thorough use of your LEVELS New York guest membership."

Her hazel eyes darken to black as desire runs through her body. The telltale scent of her arousal from the spanking a moment ago grows stronger when she shifts from foot to foot. She rubs her thighs together to soothe the ache that's built in her core.

It intrigues my Pet.

* * *

I CAN'T BELIEVE I'm anxiously sitting at the Cellar's bar hoping that Lola will meet me here. I'll think about it, she told me. Really… Even while her nipples peaked against the silk of her blouse and her body quivered at the thought. What the fuck?

Now, who's playing hard to get. Except I'm the one who's hard. So hard that my pent-up dick is about to punch a sizable hole in my trousers and blind me with the force of my balls unleashing. I've been on edge since ten o'clock this morning, eleven hours now—not to mention since she left me in bed last night. Shit, Lola even refused to let me walk her to her car, not wanting anyone to see us together as I recall. Annoyed that she didn't want people to know that we spent time together. Further annoyed that I'm annoyed.

Lola is fifteen minutes late. If she doesn't show up in three minutes, I will split in two the sexy Milk Chocolate Bunny. She's been eye fucking me this whole time. Even after I showed her the gold bracelet and reminded her it matches me with a sub for the night.

My mind is on a nonstop Lola Loop: thinking of her soft coos as I finger fucked her; remembering how good her tight cunt seemed wrapped around my swollen dick; and most of all, the sweet taste of her juices. Tonight I have to feast on her honeypot.

The sweet thing walks towards me and I give her an encouraging look since at this point Lola's missed the deadline. Moments before the tasty delight reaches me, Lola saunters into the Cellar. She looks beyond fuckable in a chestnut brown colored, leather bustier that pushes her succulent tits to her throat, a skimpy silk thong, and a pair of thigh-high leather boots.

Damn, my dick jumps and weeps as I groan out loud.

Just as we make eye contact, Lola gets stopped by that bastard Patrick Rockett, another Dom and the CEO of STEELE's biggest competitor Rockett Construction before she reaches me. That motherfucker is a pain in my ass. He's already fucked me over with that poor ass deal, sliding in and lowballing the contract. Now, he's after my Petite Seductress. I don't think so, asshole.

"Hi, looks like your sub didn't show up. Her loss is my gain—" starts the Milk Chocolate Bunny.

"Excuse me, she's here," I respond, rising from the

barstool without taking my eyes off of Rockett. He's damn near drooling on Lola when she laughs at some inane thing he's said in her ear.

As the bunny follows my trail of sight, she adds, "Well, she's hooked up with Pat—"

"No," I bark at her, my blood boiling at the thought of Rockett taking what's mine, again. Then, a sense of contrition hits me when she steps back in surprise at my sharp tone. "I apologize. Excuse me," I quickly add, then stalk over to Lola and Rockett.

"—I already told you I'm meeting someone—" Lola is telling him.

"Rockett, the lady is with me," I cut in and position myself between him and Lola, forcing Rockett to back up. I've got an inch on him even if he outweighs me by about 20 pounds of muscle still fit from his rugby days. I'm swifter and a trained fighter.

"Damn, mate, no need to get in my face," he responds with a sneer.

"Wanna be sure you're clear," I retort and glare at him until he backs down mumbling about me being a sore ass over the deal. I ignore him. My Pet is here now, even though in the back of my mind a niggle reminds me I'm a wimp for allowing more feelings where there should be none.

I shake it off and face my Petite Seductress, who's even more bewitching up close. She's added some eye makeup that enhances the flecks of gold in her hazel orbs. If I'm not careful, I could get lost in their depths especially as Lola stares at me like I'm her protector.

"Are you all right?" I ask, noticing a bit of unexpected, but pleasant warmth at the thought.

"Yes, he just wouldn't take no for an answer," She sighs in frustration. "Colossal jerk."

"Yeah, he is a colossal jerk. Come, we'll use one of the private areas… No need for an audience," I tell Lola. I make a mental note to tell Taylor to remind Rockett of LEVELS' rules of engagement.

I put my hand on Lola's waist, my fingers brushing against her soft skin exposed between the bustier and the thong. I guide her to one of the Cellar's alcoves separated from the main hall by heavy blood-red velvet curtains held by metal links suspended from the ceiling. Within each alcove a multitude of BDSM toys and equipment offer various levels of pleasure and pain. I choose an alcove with my favorite piece—the St. Andrew's Cross.

"Oh, of course, we don't want that woman to have more of a reason to eye fuck you," Lola mocks with a tilt to her head and her lips pursed.

I smack her bottom twice and nearly cum as it jiggles and my palm print blooms red on her still sensitive skin. As I pull her back to my front, I growl in her ear, "Are you sassing me, Pet?"

"Well, Sir"—she emphasizes the sir cheekily—"I'm merely pointing out the obvious."

I bend my knees and grind my hard cock into her ass while I press the flat of my hand against her mound, locking her ass to my pelvis.

"I'll tell you what is obvious. I will show you another use for your cocky mouth. Then you are getting this plump ass paddled. After which I will keep you on the edge until you beg me to cum on my dick."

I warn the vixen, the sound of her soft mewls zinging my balls.

Enough time wasted. I stand to my full height—Lola teeters on those sky-high boots—return my hand to her waist and walk us to the alcove. Time to start our evening.

LOLA

Holy shit! My pussy creams not only from the wild vision that Baz depicts. But from his massive cock grinding into my ass and his gigantic hand cupping my mound. His long fingers stroking my engorged clit through my thin, silk thong. I tremble and a mewl escapes my parted lips on a lengthy sigh. Damn, I can't wait to have Baz fill me and take me roughly.

I agreed to his offer to introduce me to the Dom/sub world so I can get my fill of him in more ways than one and to satisfy my curiosity. The spanking Simon gave me opened my body to pleasure and release that I never knew existed. The key with Baz is to remember that this is only for the week and that I don't have the time for a relationship —my relationship status is Lola's Coterie. I can't allow Baz's training to impact our business deal negatively. Fortunately, he seems just as keen as I am to keep things purely sexual. I must stay focused and not develop any feelings for him. Easier said than done, especially when Baz has my body buzzing just from his words and from his touch. My inner cheerleader urges me to stay in the moment and to have fun, business completed for the day.

"So, what do you have in mind, Sir?" I ask. He guides me to a secluded corner of the Cellar where an alcove with ominous red velvet curtains held open by gold cords beckon us to enter.

"I told you, your mouth needs filling and your ass needs punishment," he retorts looking down at me with a smirk. His gray eyes filled with lust, shining like liquid platinum. Damn, is he the most vampish man I've ever met?

Without further interruptions, we reach the private alcove and Baz loosens the curtains from their cords. As they flow closed, he turns and his eyes gleam at me in the dim space lit by a pair of torches in metal stands. I peel my eyes from his lust-filled gaze and take in my surroundings.

A standing wooden cross that has cuffs on the four corners—similar to the one Baz has in his corner suite upstairs—dominates the area; a leather bench is along the stone wall; an antique wooden chest sits beside the bench; my eyes widen and I gasp when I recognize different whips, crops, and… a few paddles. Some paddles are smooth wood, while others have holes or studs on their surfaces. The sizes vary from as large as a cricket bat to as small as an oven mitt. Instinctively, I cover my bottom with my hands and glance at Baz who's studying me with an intense stare. Oh dear, why did I mouth off.

"Come here, Pet," Baz chides.

I gulp and keep eye contact with him as I walk in his direction. I pray that my shaky knees won't give out and I collapse into an undignified heap at his feet.

"Ah… Ah… Ah," Baz intones with a wag of his long finger and a shake of his gorgeous head.

With a tilt to my head, I pause in the middle of my stride

and ponder what I'm doing wrong. Then, it hits me… I'm a sub for all intents and purposes now, and subs don't walk and keep their eyes level with their Dom. As gracefully as possible in my tall boots, I drop to my hands and knees. I attempt to recapture the moment from last night when I crawled to Baz. I keep my ass high and my head low. Once I reach him, I sit back on my haunches and await his next command. Am I a bitch in heat or a successful businesswoman, I question myself. Again, my inner cheerleader tells me to leave it at the door and to fulfill my desires.

"Good, girl, Little Pet," Baz croons with a smile on his handsome face. I notice that he's shaved the five o'clock shadow that he had earlier today and last night. This guy's face is a work of art. His sculpted cheekbones, strong jawline, and nose that he must have broken at some point and it healed slightly crooked gives him a more edgy and less pretty boy appearance. His full lips are so kissable that I lick my own and bite my lower one to hold back the moan that's threatening to burst forth. I quiver in anticipation.

"You were so sassy a minute ago and I warned you what was in store for your flippant mouth," Baz reminds me with a smirk. "Time for your first lesson, a sub does not talk back to their Dom nor do they flirt with other Doms—"

"I wasn't flirting with that guy!" I protest. "He was—"

"Lesson number two, a sub does not interrupt their Dom and never yells at them," Baz chastises me. "For those grievances, you will receive five extra strikes of my paddle. But first, it's time for you to fill this hole with every inch of my length."

As Baz traces my lips with his fingertip, my mouth waters from the memory of how good he tasted, like saltwater taffy from the Jersey Shore, sweet and salty. I lick my lips in anticipation and reach up to open his fly.

"I apologize, Sir, please allow me to make up for my naughty behavior," I purr with a voice so thick with lust that I barely recognize it as my own.

Baz grunts his approval. I slowly unzip his trousers exposing his black silk boxer briefs stretched to capacity by his dick so hard and ready to be free it's pulsating behind the material. I happily uncage the Beast and push Baz's pants and briefs down his muscular thighs. A drop of pre-cum greets me once his massive cock springs free, nearly taking my eye out. Mmm mmm.

Without hesitation, I set to work, cupping his heavy sac as I flick the droplet onto my tongue, savoring his salty-sweet taste and musky scent with a groan. I swirl my tongue around his swollen tip and massage his balls before I wrap my other hand around the base of his girth. In tandem, humming, I move my mouth lower on his head as one hand strokes his dick and the other squeezes his balls. Baz grunts in appreciation. A quick upward glance and I see he's watching me with heavy-lidded eyes black with lust, mouth parted in absolute bliss. His look encourages me to take him deeper into my mouth until his bulbous tip hits the back of my throat. He groans in response, his fingers fisting my hair holding my head at the perfect angle for him to fuck my face.

"Damn, Pet, your mouth feels so good. I've been hard all day for you. Fuck!"

His hips jerking forward, fucking my mouth in earnest follows Baz's exclamation. I meet his cries with my moans reverberating around his cock, driving him further into oblivion before he cries out.

"Fuck, Pet, I'm going to cum so hard. Fuck! This is how you use your mouth with a Dom. No... more... sassing... me!" He punctuates each word with a forceful thrust.

Tears form in my eyes. I have to concentrate to keep my breathing at pace with his thrusts since Baz is holding my head so tightly that my scalp stings and I groan in pain.

"Yes, Pet! That's it! Take it… Take every fucking one of my ten inches. Fuuuuuuuck!"

With that, Baz's dick expands in size and pulsates with rope after rope of his cum shooting down my throat. He locks my lips to his crotch and jerks his hips to get every drop out and into my mouth. I swallow profuse amounts of his seed—delicious…

As Baz's length lessens, he pulls his dick from my mouth. I suck on it until it comes away with a pop, a trail of my spit connecting my lips to his tip. I smirk and lick my lips, satisfied that I had a powerful hold over such an Alpha male that his knees shook and he threw his head back completely undone. Now, I understand what Baz means by the sub has all the power. My inner cheerleader does a series of cartwheels in jubilation.

As Baz tucks himself back into his pants, he stares at me with a dazed look. Then shakes his head as if trying to rid his mind of some unwanted thought. I sit back on my haunches and daintily wipe my mouth with my fingers. Then wantonly lick the cum that's there into my mouth. His eyes darken further.

"Now that I used your mouth suitably, it is time for your spanking."

Baz holds his hand out to help me from the floor—used, ha, I love sucking his dick—and leads me to the cross.

"This is the St. Andrew's Cross," Baz starts as he positions me with my front to the cross and my back to him.

"We place subs on the cross for various reasons. Tonight, it's holding you in place while I administer your punishment, naughty, little girl," he continues as he buckles red, suede-lined leather cuffs to my wrists and ankles.

"Tell me why you're being punished, Pet," Baz quizzes me.

"You're punishing me because I was sassy when I commented that other woman would have another reason to eye fuck you if we stayed in the main hall for our training session," I answer snarkily.

"Ow," I yelp when Baz smacks my bottom unexpectedly.

"Another lesson. How do you address me and in what type of tone?" He barks.

I know right away that my tone wasn't submissive. But I take a moment to realize that I didn't end my response with Sir, so I add it to the sentence and answer contritely. After a placated grunt, I hear Baz walk away from me. My mind runs wild as I think of which paddle he'll choose for my punishment. Will it be the small one that has holes in it, the large one with indentations, or the medium one that's plain? All too soon, Baz is back and the hardness of one paddle against my skin makes me explode with desire as he rubs it along my thighs and buttocks.

"You are new to BDSM, Little Pet. So I will not take you to the extremes with one of the more advanced paddles. Tonight, I will use a classic one made of wood and only six inches in length and 5 inches wide. I will administer ten strikes for the punishment and five more for your insolence. I want you to stay still and count for me. Absorb the pain and take your mind off of it by focusing on the numbers. Do you understand?"

Baz asks as if I have a choice. Actually I do as he reminded me this afternoon, that the whole situation is my decision and he will respect my desires.

"Yes, Sir, I understand," I respond, anxious about the

pain level. Yet giddy to reach subspace knowing that I can trust Baz.

"What is your safeword, Little Pet?" Baz asks me, while ripping the silk thong off and rubbing the paddle against my bare skin.

"Panther, Sir," I moan as my juices flow down my legs.

"Good, girl."

Whack. Whack. Whack. Whack. Whack. Whack. Whack.

I try my best to stay still and to count as Baz unleashes blow after blow on my bottom. The impact of them sending shock waves through my body, radiating from my ass to my hands and feet. I lean into the St. Andrew's Cross, thankful that it is sturdy and won't let me crumble to the floor. Once we reach the seventh blow, I'm not sure how much more I can take. As if sensing my distress, Baz pauses.

"You are doing well. Are you still with me, Little Pet? Or do you want to safeword? Then we stop right now."

The pause gives me time to re-collect myself and I shake my head no.

"Words, Pet," Baz admonishes my non-verbal response.

"No, Sir, I don't want to stop," I vocally answer, my juices slipping to a puddle below the cross. It hurts, but the pain is morphing into pleasure, the release that I crave. "Please don't stop, Sir!"

The last few hits send me into a place where I can just let go and not worry about business, being lonely, my parents, fighting my desires—I'm free.

* * *

I WAKE to strong fingers smoothing a cool gel onto my heated buttocks and thighs. I lie face down with my head resting on my hands on the leather bench. A low hiss issues from my parted lips when Baz's fingers touch a sore spot on my left cheek. I open my eyes and push against the bench to sit up, but a firm press between my shoulder blades prevents me from rising far from the soft leather.

"Lie down. I am almost done massaging the salve into your skin. It will not hurt much longer," Baz commands and assures me at the same time. "This is aftercare when a Dom tends to their sub once the scene is over. How do you feel otherwise?"

I don't want to keep my Dom waiting too long for my answer. So, a quick head-to-toe scan of my body reveals that other than my bruised rear, I'm pretty relaxed. Albeit fuzzy in the brain.

"Good—" I wince when Baz touches the crease where my thigh meets my ass. "Except for a few painful areas on my rear, Sir."

"Mmm mmm," Baz responds in a low rumble that makes my pussy clench and weep all over again. "Enjoy this moment of relaxation now because your punishment continues shortly."

I whimper and adjust my position on the bench. Three rapid smacks to my pussy makes me yowl and squirm.

"Enough!" Baz demands. "Time is up. Follow me."

Gingerly, I sit up on the bench, certain not to put too much pressure on my punished rear. As I drop to my knees, I realize that the salve has lessened the sting from the paddle. With an appreciative sigh, I crawl behind Baz until he stops at the St. Andrew's Cross.

"Not again!" I wail, kneeling up to stand. "It's too soon and my—"

Baz cuts my words off when he wraps his fingers around my throat and leans in so close that our noses touch.

"You will not tell your Dom what is best for your punishment, nor will you raise your voice to me!"

As he keeps his grip firm on my neck, Baz continues in a dangerous whisper, "Understood, Pet?"

At the sensation of his fingers applying pressure to impede my breath and the fury glowing in his gray eyes, my traitorous body quivers with pleasure. Despite my brain, yelling at me to tell Baz to fuck the hell off.

I nod.

"I will have your words, Pet!" Baz thunders at me.

"Ye... Yesss, Sir," I stutter.

Still holding my throat, Baz stands. I clumsily rise to my feet. A sense of shame at disappointing my Dom washes over me. The burn of tears behind my eyes.

"You will learn, and quickly, what is correct and what is wrong. Or, you will not sit on your plump bottom for the rest of this week."

Both of us suck in a breath—me at the thought of the pain and the pleasure of his promise. While Baz looks taken aback by the reminder of this being for a week—at least my inner cheerleader hopes that's the reason.

As he regains his composure, Baz continues, "Stand with your back to the cross, Pet."

Immediately, I obey his command and get into position, careful not to let my butt cheeks come into contact with the hard wood. I keep my gaze at his chest while I await Baz's next form of punishment. Without delay, he cuffs my wrists and as he lowers himself to a squat; he trails the tips of his fingers along my inner thighs and calves. Once my ankles are secure, Baz buries his nose in my folds and inhales deeply.

"Oh, Pet, your arousal smells divine," he croons, then with a lick to my pussy lips, he groans. "So sweet, just like honey. Tell me your pussy is my personal honeypot, Pet. All mine!"

Baz's deep, passionate growl sends shivers up and down my spine, a gasp falling from my lips when his tongue flicks my swollen clit. A not so gentle nip to it makes me jump and bump my butt against the cross.

"Nooo," I wail as the pain radiates through me.

I open my eyes when Baz suddenly stops his ministrations to my core and stands before me, a frown on his face.

"No? No, your pussy is not mine? Then, who does it belong to?" He snarls, eyes blazing.

I gasp and quickly respond, "To you, Sir. To you! I hit my butt on the wood and it hurt. That's why I cried out no!" I insist to compel him to return to devouring my pussy.

With a nod, Baz turns and walks to the wooden chest. I crane my neck to see what he's removing from it, but can't get an unimpeded view from this angle. When he returns, he's holding a red silk scarf and his trouser pockets are full.

"Edging is orgasm control where at the peak of arousal the Dom refuses to grant the sub release, preventing one from going over the edge to climax. I will keep you at a top level of arousal for an extended period. If you cum without my permission, I will punish you. Do you understand?" Baz gazes intently at me.

The thought of not being able to cum coupled with knowing that Baz is so good, that I'm scared I won't be able to hold on to my orgasm. I look away from his captivating gray eyes to think without his influence. The sounds of others in throes of passion fill my ears and makes me want more. Decision made, I look back at him.

"Yes, Sir," I respond, my curiosity overtaking my nerves.

"I will deprive you of three of your senses."

He holds up the blindfold and presents ear plugs from one of his pockets.

"I bound your hands so you cannot touch. Your sight and sound are next. I want you to only feel what I am doing to you with no distractions. It will be intense, so use your safe-word if you want me to stop completely. Remember to push beyond your limits as much as you are comfortable."

"Yes, Sir," I reply with an affirmative nod for double surety.

With my confirmation, Baz places the earplugs in and pauses with the scarf in front of my eyes. I smile shyly at him and he places the soft material around my head and ties it securely.

His lips crush mine. I gasp at the sudden kiss and he pushes his tongue past my open lips. Our tongues duel and mate as he dominates my mouth. The sensation of his thick fingers sliding along my pussy lips as he nips the lips on my face draws a moan from me. His tongue and two of his fingers act in tandem as he repeatedly plunders my mouth and my pussy. When he adds a third thick finger, I'm amazed that my juices gush in a torrent and the stirrings of an orgasm surface. I bite back a scream as I attempt to rein in my climax. My pussy walls clench around Baz's fingers and I pant into his open mouth. Suddenly, three smacks hit my pussy and my orgasm retreats from the shocking pain. I whimper and toss my head from side to side in irritation.

Warm wetness engulfs my left nipple. I arch my back into the ecstasy of Baz's mouth suckling my breast, the suction intense, bordering on painful.

"Aaahhh," I moan when he fondles my right breast, testing its weight in his palm before pinching my nipple between his fingers. A sharp bite to my left nipple makes me shudder and cry out. Baz's mouth immediately moves to my right nipple and suckles relentlessly until another sharp bite on that nipple makes me squeal. Kisses to each nipple followed by kisses and nips trailing down my belly to my mound dulls the pain in my nipples.

Baz's tantalizing tongue plays my pussy like a fine instrument and makes me sing mezzo-soprano in absolute pleasure. He pulls my engorged clit into his mouth and nips it before a sharp bite closes around it and I wail in agony that morphs into pleasure. Baz returns to his concerto and I return to the brink, yet again. This time, I hold on longer than before. Deep breaths help me maintain a bit of control over my orgasm. Baz adds his fingers to my pussy, stroking them in and out. My juices coat them more with each thrust and my orgasm builds with their plundering.

Suddenly, he slides his hands above my core into virgin territory—my asshole. I jerk and attempt to lift off of the cross once again inflaming my butt when it strikes the wood. I'm pinned into place against the cross by Baz's other hand on my hip. All the while, he continues his path to my forbidden hole and his tongue laves my clit, scooping out my honey. I clench my fists and my pussy walls with a shout when he slides one finger to the knuckle inside of my ass. I pull against the cuffs and jerk from his hand on my hip as his finger goes deeper, and the pain increases. The muscles of my hole resist Baz's dark trespass. Once he fully seats his finger deep within me, I pant and try to breathe deeply—until he thrusts his finger and adds the second one, stretching my puckered hole. As quickly as the pain hit, it changes into pleasure and I moan and beg.

"Baz, ppp… please let me cum," I wail. "I can't hold on anymore!" I cry as he speeds up his finger and his tongue. It's pleasurable torture and I can't hold it anymore.

Just as the orgasm under the surface rises, Baz stands,

removes his finger from my ass, and tugs on my nipples and clit. The pain is excruciating and I scream as blood rushes back to the sensitive areas. What. The. Fuck. Was. That.

Before I can even speculate on the possible causes, Baz's mouth surrounds one of my tender nipples. Then the bulbous head of his hard cock is at my pussy entrance pressing between my folds with a demanding urgency. I wail and try to match his pistoning strokes, thankful that I'm so wet that his massive dick glides unimpeded through my core.

"Uh. Uh. Uh. Uh."

Faced with Baz's unrelenting onslaught, I can only give into my orgasm as it breaks the surface and crashes through me. My body convulses and I scream through wave after wave of my unbound release. I've never cum so hard in my life and revel in the unending pleasure until it becomes too much and I beg Baz to stop.

"Please, Baz, no more… I can't take another orgasm," I wail as tears fall from my eyes.

Baz ignores my pleas as he continues to pump into me like a machine, still hard, his pelvis crushing mine, his heavy balls slapping my pussy lips. I tighten up again as another set of orgasms rips through me and I cry out.

"Oh! Oh! Oh! Oh!"

Just before my last orgasm crests, I clench as tight as my ravished pussy can on Baz's cock. I'm rewarded with his dick expanding and jetting his seed into the condom. Another round of orgasms triggered as my pussy milks his cock for every drop.

Breathless and spent, my head hangs and I pass out.

SEBASTIAN

This stunning beauty in my arms is really getting under my skin. It's not just the earth-shattering sex. But the combination of how Lola's body responds to me as a sub and how she still fights me with the spunk of her independent-woman mind. I've never experienced a woman who challenges me and I want to stay buried deep inside of her. Hell, if I'm perfectly honest with myself, Lola is the first woman I want to go bare with. I have the urge to mark her with my scent and to coat her womb repeatedly with copious amounts of my seed. I won't stop until her womb grows my baby. Lola is the one who could bear my heir as the leader of the next generation of the STEELE Dynasty. I know this is a dangerous territory that I'm diving into, but I can't ignore these sensations. Screw that, fucking her this week will push these crazy thoughts out of my head —I'm just caught up in this climatic moment.

A small sigh draws my attention to my Petite Seductress who's now staring at me with eyes full of ardor as she savors the afterglow of subspace. I stroke her cheek with my thumb and smile when she stretches like a cat, her luscious tits lifting to my face. I can't resist drawing one of her succulent nipples into my mouth and she mews, tangling her fingers in my hair to hold me close to her bosom. Damn, my dick jumps and I want to take her again and again. I shake off the thought since she's had two rough nights and hasn't been sexually active in a while. Instead, I satisfy my craving by toying with her breasts. Neither of us is ready to stop.

"Oh, Baz," she purrs. "You feel so good, baby… Please don't stop… Fuck!"

In the back of my mind, I know that I should correct her for calling me by my nickname instead of by sir. But I don't want to—it sounds right, just as right as her calling me baby.

Nope—I'm screwed big time.

My fingers slowly ghost over her belly and cup her mons —Mine! Before I slide them along her puffy pussy lips swollen from the pounding that I gave her. Yet they're still wet and getting more moist as her arousal increases. Tenderly, I slide one of my fingers into her core, slowly rubbing her G-spot. I increase the rhythm and use my thumb to stroke her distended clit until Lola breaks beautifully for me.

"Mmmmmm… Ooo… Baz… Right there… Oo… Oo… Oo… Aaaaaahhhh… Yes!"

Lola's writhing and her wanton wail force cum to ooze down my turgid shaft and coat my balls that ache to fill her with my displaced seed. I lift her languid form. Then crush her to my chest burying my face in her soft hair inhaling the aroma of her floral perfume mixed with our scent of carnal sex. Our synchronized heartbeats pulse rapidly from our desire and reverberate through my mind, body, and soul leaving an indelible mark. I'm silenced while I process our connection.

After a few minutes, Lola wraps her slim arms around my neck and cuddles into my chest. Sweet sounds of her contentment slip past her lips as she adjusts her position.

"That was amazing, Sir," she coos. "Thank you so much."

With a kiss to my neck, Lola rises, but I hold her firmly in place on my lap—no repeat of last night with her skipping out so quickly. It hits me she's returned to the more formal sir, than Baz or baby of moments ago. Before I can question whether or not I'm disappointed in the change, I issue a command.

"Be still, Little Pet," I tell Lola. "Your aftercare is not over. Your body needs to reacclimate from our play. How do you feel?"

With an audible sigh—there's her independent woman breaking past my sub—Lola lifts her head to look me in the eyes. Gone is the ardor of subspace.

"Very good, Sir. Relaxed and clearheaded," she responds, then looks over her shoulder towards the drawn curtains, her wish to leave obvious in her agita.

Just as well since I need to stay in control and not allow impulsive behavior to lead me astray.

"Excellent, Pet," I tell Lola. "However, I sense that you are impatient to leave. Did I not treat you well…"

A flush of embarrassment colors Lola's face and she stammers a quick response.

"Oh, you treated me very well, Sir! I didn't mean to imply otherwise. It's just that…"

Lola's blush darkens and spreads to her chest, her hands twisting in her lap.

"What is it, Little Pet?" I ask her. "Subs should always be truthful. They hide nothing from their Doms."

As she peers up at me from beneath her lashes, Lola murmurs that she's embarrassed that others in the Cellar heard her passionate cries and will think she's a loose woman. I stroke her hair to gentle her and smile when she fully lifts her gaze to mine. The worry that's in the depths of Lola's eyes is real—she's truly concerned that others will think less of her. When in reality, everyone at LEVELS is here for the hedonistic atmosphere where they are free to explore their desires safely.

"No need to worry, Little Pet," I say as I continue stroking her long, wavy raven-colored hair. "Members and guests are in the same position as you—no pun intended—so we do not judge one another. LEVELS is a welcoming environment. Does that make you feel more comfortable?"

With a nod and a coy smile, Lola responds with an affirmative hum, slipping her arms around my waist and nuzzling her lips against my hard pecs.

We continue to sit quietly, absorbed in our separate thoughts. The sounds of the Cellar activities no longer white noise in the background: a woman's piercing scream followed by her plaintive moans; a man's guttural shouts of release; the slap of leather meeting skin; the soft sobs of desperation floating to us just beyond the curtains. No, Lola need not concern herself with shocked faces upon our departure from this private alcove when we leave our little bubble.

My mind drifts to my calendar to decide what time is best to meet Lola tomorrow night. She has so much more to learn and I'm eager to test her pain levels since she responded so nicely to the nipple and clit clamps. The set that I used tonight were entry level. The weighted clamps will bring Lola closer to her limits. Just as I'm envisioning how lovely Lola will look tied to my bed upstairs spread-eagle with her juices glistening on her pink pussy and her tight puckered hole on display before me, it shatters when I remember that I have a charity gala to attend. STEELE International is the patron sponsor, so I can't decline the invitation. I sigh in annoyance.

"Are you all right, Sir?" Lola asks as she pulls her torso away from my chest—I miss the warmth of her embrace.

"I have a charity gala tomorrow night that I must attend since STEELE is the patron, so we cannot play tomorrow. Unfortunately, your lessons will have to skip a day, Little Pet," I respond, stroking her back to get some skin-to-skin contact with her.

"Oh," Lola pouts, her full bottom lip poking out. I can't resist the temptation to bite it before I soothe the sting with a deep kiss that has Lola going from a squeal to a sigh of bliss.

An interesting idea pops into my head as I kiss her sweet lips. I can invite Lola as my guest, an opportunity for her to engage with New York's elite before her boutique opens. Yeah, I'll just keep telling myself it's for business and not because I can't go a day without seeing her curvy ass.

"You should come with me as my guest so you can mingle with the attendees influential in the city and beyond," I start, gaining belief that it's only for business. "They will be good to know since you're opening Lola's Coterie here." I add as further encouragement.

Lola looks hesitant and studies my face for a moment, trying to decide whether I'm asking as a date or truly as business. I struggle to maintain a neutral expression—I want her to say yes. Decision made, Lola nods and with an equally neutral face responds that it's a smart business move. We discuss details. I offer to buy her a dress and accessories since it's a formal event, and she didn't travel with a gown. To which, Lola bristles and frowns before telling me she can take care of her clothes. I refrain from spanking her for her attitude because again she intrigues me, switching from sub to sass like a pendulum. We discuss the logistics and put on our clothes to leave the club.

As we walk through the Cellar and out to our awaiting cars, I possessively keep my hand on Lola's lower back. I guide her past members, some of whom follow us with their gazes. My eyes land on Rockett who's also eyeing us. I smirk at him—there's no denying that it was me making Lola scream in pleasure.

LOLA

Another day my ass and pussy are sore—that damn Sebastian Steele whose hand and cock are like steel.

I attempt to sit comfortably on the buttery soft desk chair. My temporary workplace is in one of the guest offices at Luc's Banque Montaigne United States headquarters in Midtown on Park Avenue. The navy blue, ribbed-knit, midi dress I chose has enough stretch in the material to prevent any chafing and hugs my curves for a little vavavavoom action. Paired with stilettos and my hair in a high ponytail add height to my petite figure. From the appreciative looks that I garnered as I left the St. Regis, followed Luc through his building, and to the office, confirm that men approve my outfit of choice. I feel good, even if achy.

"—halt production and set the date back or use the lace from the last collection?"

My body is in the office. But my mind is back in the Cellar, reliving the nirvana that I found twice upon waking in Baz's arms after he forced multiple orgasms from my quivering pussy. Pure rapture. The elated smile playing on my lips dips when I notice Blair staring questioningly at me.

"Excuse me a moment," I tell her as I gingerly rise from the chair and walk to the en suite bathroom. First, I have to clear my head. Then get back to work. I dab my eyes with a damp washcloth—thank goodness for waterproof makeup—and the back of my neck, hot from the lustful thoughts. I gently massage my ass to ease some dull pain before I return to the chair.

"What were you telling me, Blair?" I ask once I'm perched on the seat.

Blair smiles and repeats the situation to me. The artisan being upset with the quality of the lace. How Blair tried calling the atelier, but Pierre—Monsieur Thibault's son who runs the business side for him—was not available. Lola's Coterie is my top priority, not reminiscing about earth-shattering sex. So, I roll my shoulders back and forth a few times to ease the tension, then get to work.

* * *

JUST BEFORE NOON, I hear the sexy baritone of Luc's voice as he speaks to Blair in his native French. If he were anyone but my mentor, I would swoon as often as Blair does whenever he's near. *Le Renard Argenté*. I laugh to myself, then glance up when Luc saunters into the office and lowers his tall frame into a chair opposite my desk.

"And how are you, *petite chérie*?" Luc asks me, his dark blue eyes twinkling with mirth from his conversation with Blair.

"Well, I'm fine, *Renard Argenté*," I tease him with a smirk. "How are you is the better question?" I continue, raising my eyebrow and glancing towards the office door at Blair's desk for emphasis before returning my gaze to him.

Luc clears his throat, tugging at the Full Windsor Knot of his tie as he shifts in the seat.

"Comfortable?" I ask sweetly, bringing my hands up to rest my chin on top of them, awaiting his response.

"Indeed, I am."

Ever the aristocratic gentleman to not discuss another's private life, Luc parries my question with one of his own.

"Leonie tells me you've been attending lessons these past two nights. Something about improving your learning curve?"

Now, it's my turn to squirm and I bump my rear against the base of the armrest and yelp.

"Are you truly all right, *petite*—" Luc starts.

But thankfully, my mobile buzzes with a text from Leonie informing me she's in the Bentayga outside of Luc's building.

"Oh, that's Leonie. I have to meet her to pick out an outfit for tonight's gala. The one I told you Sebastian invited me to mingle with influential people," I hurriedly tell Luc as I grab my handbag and practically run out of the office. I don't wait for his response—I feel like a naughty teenager about to get reprimanded by her father—and rush past Blair to head to the elevators.

* * *

"*Oui, fermez la bouche, Leonie!*" I exclaim when I slide into the back of the Bentley SUV without so much as a bonjour to my big mouth best friend. "Why did you insinuate anything to Luc about my lessons?" I stress the word lessons with air quotes and an exaggerated eye roll.

Leonie's melodic laughter rings out in the luxury SUV while Stan attempts to maintain a professionally neutral expression. My accomplice who drives me to LEVELS New York for my trysts with Sebastian is a two-faced Janus. I glare at Stan through the rearview mirror and watch as his neck reddens at the collar of his suit jacket, his eyes refusing to meet mine in the mirror. I slam my back against the seat and fold my arms under my breasts with a huff. Then suck in a sharp breath when I hit my bum on the seatbelt buckle. Leonie doubles over, laughing even harder than before. As she wipes tears from her eyes, she turns to me and giggles.

"*Je suis désolé, Chérie!*" Leonie swears with her hand over her heart.

"Yeah, well, you are sorry and you better keep your mouth shut," I grumble as I rub my rear.

Since we have had little time to talk, Leonie fills me in on her activities over the past two days: her rounds at New York's most prestigious design houses; a visit to the New York office of her modeling agency; an interview at *Vogue*; prep work for the PSA commercial she's shooting tomorrow that encourages adolescent girls to follow their dreams.

Just as the SUV stops on Fifth Avenue and Fifty-seventh Street, Leonie briefly mentions Roger Steele. She became unsettled when he stared at her so intensely during the fashion show at our meeting. With no time to delve deeper, we lose the comment as we slide out of the Bentley.

It's good to catch up with Leonie. But my spirits really lift when we step onto the hallowed ground of Bergdorf Goodman—the venerated retail mecca of class, elegance, and sophistication for women, men, children, and home. It's situated directly across from The STEELE Tower. The thought of Baz adds to my upliftment. I'm surprised, but I can admit that Baz makes me happy. With a smile playing on my lips, Leonie and I begin the hunt for a showstopper gown that will turn heads and make my re-entry into Manhattan's elite spectacular.

"Oh, *Chérie*," Leonie coos as we eat a late lunch at BG Restaurant on the seventh floor of Bergdorf's overlooking Central Park. "You will make Sebastian turn back into that crazy, possessive caveman when he sees you in your dress!"

I bite my lower lip to hold back a moan as I think of Sir spanking me for wearing the hourglass-enhancing, iridescent orange and gold sequin gown. It definitely checks off my boxes for an ultra glamorous scene-stealer with its long sleeves, dramatic padded shoulders, and pooling train. The exquisite gown will definitely make me stand out on the red carpet.

"I know," I cry gleefully as I clap my hands together and dance in my chair, unable to contain my excitement—damn my sore ass.

* * *

IT'S JUST 6:30 p.m. So Baz isn't late, but still I wait anxiously for him to arrive at the Presidential Suite that Leonie and I share at the St. Regis New York. An hour ago, the glam squad completed my styling, stressing the gold flecks in my hazel eyes to complement the tonal colors of my gown; my hair blown stick straight floats down my back to the curve of my ass like an arrow for Sir's strong palm. I recheck the contents of my new sleek-shaped and innovative-designed evening clutch made from gold satin and 18-karat gold-plated aluminum. When at last the butler announces Baz's arrival, I pivot in my Aquazurra gold, mirrored-leather sandals with slender, foot-framing straps to face him.

Baz's wolfish gray eyes lift from staring at my round ass before I turned around to slide seductively over my body. His gaze travels from the top of my head to the hem of my gown. His eyes brighten with unmistakable lust when his gaze slows at my hips. Baz's nostrils flare as though he's inhaling my essence. Then licks his full lips as though he tastes my unencumbered arousal on his tongue. Scandalously, I went sans lingerie. Baz slides his palm over the front of his bespoke tuxedo jacket, smoothing his hand against the noticeable bulge forming in his perfectly tailored trousers.

I've definitely brought out Captain Caveman—again.

SEBASTIAN

Damn, my Petite Seductress went all out tonight. That dress makes her look like a golden, shimmering mermaid basking in the setting sun. Like a siren, she calls me to my death—the end of my playboy days is neigh if my dick has any say in the matter. Absentmindedly, I rub my growing cock that, with a mind of its own, lengthened when my eyes took in the glorious sight of Lola's ass encased in her hip-hugging dress. When she turned, I almost let loose with a wolf whistle and growled my approval—my dick stood up at attention, silently weeping a salute to my bewitching goddess.

"Good evening, Mr. Steele," she purrs with sinful lips curled up in a smirk, fully aware of my body's response to her exquisite beauty. "You look delicious in your tuxedo."

"Tha—" I begin, but have to clear my throat since my voice was too thick to be coherent with my cock remembering those lips wrapped snuggly around its girth.

I try again, "Thank you, Ms. Lewis. You are a divine sight. Shall we?"

I walk towards her with my elbow bent in suggestion that we depart. My Petite Seductress smiles at me from under her eyelashes—her hazel eyes dazzle me—and hooks her arm through mine. With a nod, I return her smile and we exit the suite.

As we sit in the back of my chauffeured Mercedes-Maybach S 650 Sedan the proximity to Lola drives me mad. Her perfume teases my nose. Her thigh brushes against mine as she re-crosses her legs. If I'm not mistaken, I swear that I can detect a hint of her arousal as she sits beside me. I want to pull her across my lap and spank her for wearing such an alluring dress. It hugs her ample curves than trails behind her, guiding my eyes up to her ass. She captivates me.

Unfortunately, I extended this invitation as a business opportunity, not as a date. Even more annoying, I'm sure the same people, the men specifically, that I wanted Lola to mingle with will ogle her. Their fantasies about gripping her hips as they pound into her tantalizing pussy makes my head explode.

"Fuck!" I growl.

"What's the matter?" A bewildered Lola asks me.

It's only then that I realize I spoke aloud. Damn, I'm definitely losing it.

"Nothing, babe," I respond, shaking my head and caressing her cheek with my thumb to soothe her.

Lola stares at me wide-eyed and again I realize that I spoke out loud what should have remained in my head or not even in my head. I called Lola babe. I quickly shift in my seat and press the intercom to ask my driver Michael how far we are from the venue. I refuse to make eye contact with Lola even though I feel her staring at me, waiting for me to address the term of endearment. Not happening.

"We're behind a queue of cars waiting for the valets, Mr. Steele. It should only be a few minutes," Michael informs me.

The annual gala raises funds for the nonprofit children's hospital that's one of the few organizations outside of STEELE Foundation's roster that I support. My mother Shelley runs our family's foundation that builds and manages attractive, affordable housing for urban, lower-income families. The name is a play on the house foundation, being strong and supportive like steel.

The children's hospital is a favorite of mine since I volunteered there as a teenager and witnessed firsthand the importance of quality healthcare for all children. Our mother insisted that we did more than as she called it "lounge around the pool working on our tans" during the summer. I'm thankful that she was so determined to have us experience life beyond that of typical offspring of the über-wealthy.

The Maybach pulls up to the front of STEELE42, one of our award-winning entertainment venues. It specializes in weddings, parties, and galas for society's best both in the United States and abroad. A buzz surrounds the area with paparazzi and news crews angling for the best shots and interviews on the red carpet. The energy is high and reaches into the sedan, drawing us out as a valet opens Lola's door and Michael opens mine.

Lights flash and the photographers yell my name to turn my head in their direction. As I reach Lola, I can't help but smile at her radiance—she looks spectacular with the light-bulbs flashing off of her iridescent gown. I will have the best-dressed woman on my arm tonight. Lola smiles as her hand wraps around my forearm and like a pro saunters along the red carpet. When the paps call for her to pose, as a good sub should, she looks to me for approval, then poses like the best supermodel. My dick aches for her.

Once we arrive inside, we stop and chat with other attendees. I introduce Lola to key guests and mention her lingerie boutique. The women love it. Some of whom are already familiar with it and have pieces from Lola's Coterie. Their excitement to meet the creator palpable. The men as expected nonchalantly check Lola out and I struggle not to deck someone.

"Oh, Sebastian, this is a beautiful venue. Are all the STEELE properties as refined?" Lola asks, looking up at the vaulted ceiling where the constellations twinkle in the dim lighting. I want to lave her throat and suck on it until I leave my bright red mark as a warning to others to back the fuck off.

"Yes, they are," I reply instead. "This is one of my favorites. It was a bank and when we refurbished it, we strove to keep the integrity of the space. We kept the original ceiling, columns, teller windows on the sides, the vault, and more original details."

"It's impressive," she murmurs.

We spend the evening mingling during the cocktail hour, chatting with potential shoppers. We place bids on a few interesting items from the silent auction. Then, eating a fantastic dinner—Lucien's catering division handles the food and drink.

"Excuse me," Lola says to me and the other guests at our table.

"Where are you going?" I have to pause as I realize how needy I sound.

"I just need to freshen up. Don't worry, I'll be right back," Lola says as she rises and I follow suit to pull out her chair.

I watch my Petite Seductress glide past tables with eyes

that follow her movements and growl. Suddenly, a red satin gown blocks my view. I glance up for the source, I see Kimberly, the LEVELS New York member that I fucked a few weeks ago.

"Baz, it is you," Kimberly purrs as she sits in the still warm seat that Lola just vacated. "What a lovely surprise!"

"Hello, Kimberly, how are you?" I try for polite since I don't want to upset her again.

"Better now that I'm with you," she responds rubbing my thigh way too close to my crotch. As she inches her fingertips higher, Kimberly leans towards me to whisper in my ear.

"How about we skip this stuffy gathering and head to Peepshow for better entertainment?" She says before licking the shell of my ear with the tip of her tongue.

Kimberly mistakes the shudder of revulsion that runs through me at the thought of being intimate with her or anyone besides Lola and places her palm on my crotch. Just as my hand grabs her wrist I hear a cry of pain from Kimberly.

"Pardon me, I forgot my clutch."

Unbeknownst to Kimberly and me, Lola returned to the table. Judging by how Kimberly cradles her foot, Lola must have stepped on it with her pointy heel when she took her bag off of the table. With a balls-shrinking stare directed at me, Lola storms away and straight into Rockett. Fuck me.

"Whoa, there, lass," Rockett tells Lola as he grips her forearms to keep her from tumbling backwards from bumping into his hard body.

"Oh, excuse me," Lola responds as she presses her palms against his chest.

"Well, let's take this tango to the dance floor!" Rockett

laughs and throwing a glare at me over her shoulder, Lola lets him lead her away.

Lola

I cannot believe that Sebastian would flirt with that woman and let her grope his junk as soon as I left the table. I saw her eye fucking him from across the room. He's like a fucking magnet for women. Well, two can play that game, I grouse to myself as Patrick expertly spins me on the dance floor. He's actually handsome in his tuxedo and his big, muscular body is impressive. Not to mention his sexy Scottish accent. How Jamie Fraser!

As I chance a peek in the table's direction where Sebastian and I are sitting, I see him scowling, his gray eyes black with anger as his eyes lock with mine. With a smile, I return my attention to Patrick and try to ignore the pang in my chest.

Sebastian

That… fucking… Rockett.

He always shows up at the worse fucking times. He thinks he's hot shit, twirling my girl around and holding her close under the pretense of dancing. If he grinds his dick in her, I'll kick his ass right here, right now.

Not to mention Kimberly—cockblocker once again. Her babble continues on some mundane topic. Who the fuck knows or cares? When all I can see is red as I watch Lola in the arms of another man, my enemy to boot. Without even acknowledging Kimberly, I stalk over to the laughing pair.

"Lola, a word," I tell her as I clasp her elbow and pivot to walk off of the dance floor. A tug back makes me turn around to see Lola's hazel eyes blazing and her face contorted in rage. With a snarl, she yanks her elbow free.

"Take your hand off of me—" Lola starts, and I flash back to my office, the scene of her previous tirade.

Quick to defuse the situation, I grab her by the waist and crush my lips to hers, not giving a damn who sees, or that this is a business engagement.

I feel Lola melt into me and with a sigh open her mouth to give my probing tongue entry. As we continue our unplanned, passionate kiss, Rockett, Kimberly, the gala, and the world fade to nothing—all we know is the other. At that moment, I decide I'm all in with Lola, my Petite Seductress.

LOLA

The week ends where we started—in the conference room at The STEELE Tower with the same cast of characters as our first meeting. This time, Dom Pérignon Rosé Vintage 2005—somehow Baz knows my favorite champagne—flows as we sign the contracts for Lola's Coterie and STEELE International, Inc.'s multiyear, multimillion-dollar partnership. My expansion into the United States is in place with New York City and Las Vegas in four months. Amazingly Los Angeles, Miami, Abu Dhabi, and Dubai within the year, too. I'm so thrilled that I dance around the table with Leonie while Luc and Sebastian laugh and Roger stares—Leonie is right, he's intense.

Not only is my company on track, but I've had an unbelievable time with Baz. We spend every night at LEVELS New York furthering my Dom/sub lessons and pushing past my limits—who knew I was such a hedonist. Sometimes, I still hesitate when Baz commands me since my mind wants to have a say in the matter. Or I'll flat-out refuse, mainly because I'm yearning for the pleasure of his punishment. But, I'm learning to let go and just feel as Baz demands.

I glance across the room at him and shiver when his pupils dilate and his gray eyes turn black with desire for me. I'm wearing a pink sapphire suit with a pencil skirt and a waist-length jacket, a matching lace bralette, nude high heels, and flesh-tone silk stockings. I purposefully wore the fitted outfit to tease him right within the walls of his empire. I'm the sub and I hold all the power, that lesson I've definitely mastered.

"I'm so excited for you, *Chérie,*" Leonie squeals and hugs me close. "Your dreams are coming true!"

"I know!" I exclaim. "It's so awesome! We have so much to do! I can't wait to get started." I continue and hug her back.

"*Oui, petite chérie,* but no need to think of it all at this very moment," Luc interrupts as he joins us and pulls me in for a warm embrace. "*Jouissance du présent!* Let's have dinner tonight at Per Se, your favorite New York restaurant, to celebrate."

My heart drops when I realize that I have to decline since I already have plans with Baz. I feel even worse since I have spent no time with Leonie and Luc the entire week. I only see Leonie in the suite and Luc at the office in passing. Only brief pleasantries—every non-work moment is with Baz.

"Lola and I already have plans for this evening," Sebastian cuts into the conversation, staring challengingly at Luc while placing a possessive hand on my lower back.

They contentiously eye each other like two Alpha lions fighting to claim the last lioness in the Serengeti. My insides tingle knowing that Baz wants me so much that he'll square off with my beloved Luc. My instinct tells me that Luc is only tolerating Sebastian for my sake. Their initial introduction did not sit well with Luc at all. He may be a tad jealous of the personal time that I'm spending with Sebastian.

"What are you doing that you can't have dinner with me, again?" Luc asks after I tell him I have plans for the evening.

"I'm meeting with Sebastian. You know that I told you he's introducing me to people who are worth connecting with—"

Luc cuts off my response.

"Bof! He isn't the only one who knows people to introduce you to, you know that, Lola. I think you're getting too involved with him, especially since we haven't completed the deal yet. Do you think that's a wise decision?"

Somehow, Luc twists it around and makes me guilty for not putting Lola's Coterie ahead of my personal life. I'm sure that he knows I'm not spending time with Sebastian for business. But Luc is too much of a gentleman to call me out on my half-truths.

"Okay, let's have dinner tonight. Just give me a moment to tell Sebastian that I can't make it," I give in to Luc. I owe him so much and I wouldn't be here pitching a deal if not for his contact.

It pissed off Sebastian rightfully so that as he said I chose Luc over him. Damn these men in my life...

As I watch the two of them puff up, I wonder if Sebastian is in my life. Or am I just a conquest for him—the playboy as my obsessive Google searches revealed. What I know for sure is over this week, he's made me admit to myself I am lonely and I want a good, strong man in my life. If it's Sebastian I can't say for sure, but my inner cheerleader is gleefully doing jumping splits and waving her pompoms in the air.

"How about you, Luc, Leonie, Roger, Blair, and I celebrate the deal over dinner and afterwards the two of us can continue with our plans?" I hopefully suggest to Sebastian as a compromise.

Sebastian rolls his eyes and Luc grunts. I take the reactions as their agreement since they didn't say no nor did they duke it out. So, I grab two fresh glasses of Dom from the sideboard and continue my merry dance around the conference room with Leonie. I will not let their overabundant testosterone ruin my joy.

AGAIN, hoping to keep the men in my life appeased and not ripping each other's throats out, I organize the rides to Per Se. Sebastian and Roger riding in Baz's S 650. Luc and Blair in his Cullinan. Leonie and me in my Bentayga. We plan to meet at the restaurant at eight o'clock. Leonie and I arrive last—both of us took extra care with our looks and attire. I wonder at the reason for Leonie's primping, but then notice the appreciative eye that Roger gives to her as we walk towards the bar where the others gathered. My eyes scan the group for Baz, but don't see him.

"Where's Sebastian?" I ask, hating that I sound whiny.

Roger shifts uncomfortably as he stands next to the barstool he vacated for Leonie to sit and looks over my shoulder. I follow his gaze and see Sebastian off to the side in an animated conversation with a gorgeous blonde woman who has her hand on his chest. A slight cough from Roger draws my attention away from the good-looking couple. Luc just raises his eyebrow and folds his arms across his chest. Blair standing next to him looks at me worriedly.

"Le playboy occupé à une autre tâche à ce moment," Leonie spits out while she glares at Sebastian.

"Come, we will sit. I reserved the private East Room for our *fête*. Tonight, we celebrate your success, *petite chérie*. Nothing else matters, *non*?" Luc says and places his hand on my lower back to guide me to the maître d'.

I allow Luc to take control of the embarrassing situation while I attempt to restrain the tears that burn behind my eyes. I refuse to let them fall. Fuck Sebastian.

I sit between Luc and Leonie—my support for so long. Then peruse the menu to occupy my hands and to take my mind off of the pang in my chest. It doesn't matter anyway since this is the last night of our agreed upon D/s lessons; I remind myself. I just hate that I've allowed Sebastian past the wall I built to keep my heart safe from pain the night of my parents' death.

"Oh, the oysters and pearls are on the tasting menu tonight. Your favorite!" Leonie says, nudging me and smiling. "I can't wait to savor the flavors of the hand-cut tagliatelle. *C'est magnifique*!!" She closes her amber eyes and kisses her fingertips for emphasis.

The server is collecting our drink orders when Sebastian finally enters the room, his eyes search the table until his gaze lands on mine. I glance away, still hurt that he would so blatantly flirt with another woman in front of everyone and knowing that I was arriving soon. This answers my questions. I was just a conquest for the Dom playboy.

Sebastian sits in the chair opposite mine at the circular table and continues to stare at me, trying to get my attention. I dutifully ignore him and turn to stare out of the window at the stunning views of the Manhattan skyline and Central Park clear across Columbus Circle to Fifth Avenue. The other side of the East Room is a glass panel that overlooks the restaurant's main dining room. But prior to our arrival, Luc had the staff close the silk drapes for privacy.

The festivities proceed first, with Leonie and Luc offering toasts—Sebastian's toast is irrelevant and I choose not to listen. Then they present the savory dishes for the nine-course meal. Just before they serve the cheese dish, I excuse myself to go to the ladies' room and whisper to Leonie that I'm fine to go alone.

As I'm reapplying my lipstick, the door to the bathroom's antechamber opens and Sebastian walks in, locking it behind him. With a determined expression on his handsome face, he strides over to me. I attempt to duck around him, but he cages me in between his arms with my butt against the counter below the mirror.

"Get out of my way!" I seethe through my clenched teeth as I push into his hard chest. A futile effort to move his solid body that towers over me.

"No! You've ignored me all night—" Sebastian starts.

"Well, that's just rich, isn't it… I ignored you all night?" I snarl and try to knee him in his philandering balls. Unfortunately, he deftly blocks my blow and smashes his pelvis into mine. His thick shaft presses up and against my mons, eliciting a strangled moan from my pursed lips as his tip hits my clit.

"Fuck you, Sebastian!"

"Yeah, Pet, that is exactly what you will do… fuck… me."

He thrusts his hard cock against my mound with each word. Then flips me to face the opposite direction. Sebastian yanks the bottom of my dress over my head, bends me across the counter, rips off my thong, and kicks my legs apart.

"You… ignore… me… all… night… because… you… are… pissed… that… I… am… speaking… to… another… woman…"

Sebastian lands hard smacks to my ass between each

word that he utters out of his mouth. He continues to berate me for not giving him a chance to explain. I dance on my toes and squirm to avoid the punishing slaps to no avail. My ass is on fire and I can't hold back a wail when his fingers spank my dripping pussy.

"Enough, Sebastian," I cry.

"No, it is not enough!" He growls in my ear as I hear him unzip his trousers before he slams his gigantic cock past my wet, swollen folds to enter my core.

He's so deep that his bulbous tip hits my cervix. Like a madman, Sebastian pistons his hips, jamming my pelvis into the counter until I grasp the edge as a counterbalance. The sounds of our grunts and my juices sluicing fill the air along with the scent of our feral sex.

I can't help my body's response to Baz's brutal assault: a sheen of sweat and goosebumps break out across my skin; my heart races; my pussy walls suck him in to take every inch deeper with each thrust. I mewl when his long, middle finger swipes my seam collecting the dew dripping down my spread thighs. I moan in pleasure until I yelp when Baz presses that same finger against my puckered hole. Ignoring my pleas, he pushes past the rings of muscle until he encases his finger completely in my ass. His colossal cock in my pussy and his thick finger in my bottom hole leaves little room in my core.

"So tight, Pet," Sebastian hisses in my ear as he flattens my body to the counter with his heavy torso. "Tonight, I will take your last hole."

The words rumble through me as his dick swells and pulses before one last deep thrust that lifts me clear off the ground. His roar of release sends a zing to my core, stimulating my walls to milk every drop of his seed. For a moment, we collapse onto the counter and pant.

Sebastian slowly stands and as he withdraws from my sheath, his cum oozes out and drips to the floor—my pussy clenches to re-collect the spillage.

"Shit!" Sebastian exclaims.

I hastily rise and adjust my rumpled dress.

"What? You suffer remorse for forcing yourself on me, asshole?" I retort, still pugnacious despite my body thrumming with delight.

"I didn't wear a condom, and I came bare inside of you." Sebastian responds sheepishly, looking at me with wide eyes. "I've always worn a condom… I don't know what came over me… I—" He mumbles more to himself than to me.

He walks into the bathroom and returns with a damp linen cloth that he hands to me. I stare at it, then at him before snatching the cloth to clean myself.

"I'm on birth control. No need to get your panties in a bunch. I'm the one that should worry since you're a manwhore who can't keep it in his pants!" I chastise him with a glare, wiping our combined juices leaking from my pussy and from between my thighs. "I've only had two lovers and can guarantee that I don't have any sexually transmitted anything. Who knows about you," I add pointedly.

When Sebastian doesn't respond, I glance up to see him gazing at me with an unreadable expression on his face. He's so damn sexy, hair mussed, flushed skin, darkened gray eyes. I shake my head and sigh—if only.

"Whatever," I say as I toss the soiled cloth in the bin and limp towards the door—damn, did he ravage me. Sebastian's hand whips out and he stops me mid-step.

"I'm clean… I get tested regularly. It's just that I've never been bare in my life and my behavior shocked me. I apologize, Lola. Do you forgive me?"

The sorrowful expression on Baz's face takes me aback

and I can't stop my hand from cradling his face. He closes his eyes, takes a deep breath, and nuzzles his cheek into my palm. I study his face and can sense that he's truly unsettled. If my instinct is correct, it's because he's falling for me and it shocks him. We stay that way until Baz opens his eyes and gazes down at me.

"I know it's your celebration party, but can we go now? I want to be alone with you."

His gray eyes nervously slide across my face, trying to judge my reaction.

I could let him hang out there, but I have the urge to be alone with him, too. Is it too fast? Am I getting too involved with Sebastian? Will he hurt me? If I were a fortuneteller, maybe I could answer my questions, but I'm not. So, I won't repair the crack in the wall around my heart just yet. I want to see where this—whatever this is—takes us.

"Yes, Baz," I give in.

SEBASTIAN

I've seriously lost my shit, but I don't mind. It felt damn good to fill Lola's womb with my seed. Perhaps it was my subconscious that made me follow her to the bathroom and take her so thoroughly and bareback. Because that's what I really want—Lola's belly big with my baby. Lola as the mother of my child would lock her to me forever. No, that's not so bad, I muse—the caveman in me beats on his chest in triumph at the conquest of his mate. I'm glad that I didn't let that jerk Luc stop me from following Lola.

However, I regret hurting her feelings by getting caught up with Bridget Heimonen, the Finnish model that I played with at Peepshow last week. I didn't fuck her, just toyed with her a bit and that's why she accosted me demanding more as soon as I walked into the restaurant—what luck. Definitely a stunner, but not my type. Hell, no one's my type anymore.

Only Lola has got to me, the real me inside, beyond my playboy exterior. I thought in a week I could fight the instant, soul-stirring attraction. Just fuck her out of my system under the guise of training her to be a sub and to enjoy the pleasures of a Dom/sub relationship. Never have I desired a woman more. She challenges me at every turn. Her body makes her an adept pupil—despite her protests—easily responding to stimuli of all kinds. But her intellect and emotional fortitude combined with her innate submissiveness make Lola superior to all those who came before her, including Bridget. Not a day goes by that I don't think about Lola and want more from her.

"Why are we stopping here?" My Petite Seductress asks as she peeks out of the sedan's window, tilting her head back to get a glimpse of The STEELE Tower's upper floors.

I didn't tell her we were going to my penthouse and not to LEVELS New York. I wanted to get her out of Per Se without a scene or any delay. So I just let her assume that we were going to the club. My intentions for bringing Lola to my home is to see how we interact in my personal space. We need time together beyond public places like the office, the club, social gatherings, or restaurants. If this can be more, then I have to be sure that we can be together intimately. Not only sexually.

It's also a place no woman besides my female family members have been. I only have sex at LEVELS or a hotel. This is special.

* * *

THE DOORMAN OPENS Lola's door before I'm forced to admit the truth. I hop out and take her hand as she stands in bewilderment. Swiftly walking through the grand doors for the residence side of the Tower, I nod as the concierges greet me. Distracted by the opulence of the lobby, Lola scurries along beside me, turning her head in every direction. I don't slow my pace until we reach my family's private elevator and gently tug her through the open doors. As they close, I place my hand on the plate to select the main level of my duplex on the fifty-fifth floor.

"Sebastian, where are we going? This looks like residences and not your headquarters," Lola demands, trying to pull her hand loose from my firm clasp, garnering my immediate attention. I refuse to let her hand go.

"I said that I want to be alone with you, Lola."

I respond not answering her question instead mentally urging the high-speed elevator to hurry before Lola's quarrelsome nature breaks through disrupting my plan.

"Thanks for the non-answer," she retorts with a raised eyebrow and pursed lips.

In response, I grab her wrists to pull her arms over her head and push her into the corner of the elevator with my much larger body. A small oomph pops out of Lola and I bend down to bite her luscious lip into my mouth. I groan at the contact and rock my hips rhythmically into her pelvis. The all-encompassing kiss leaves her breathless and pliable in my arms. I need Lola in a blissful state to prepare her for my next offer.

We kiss—her flavorful taste a mixture of the rich foods and fruity wine that she had at dinner tantalizing me. The doors ping open to the foyer at the entrance of my penthouse duplex high above the rooftops of Manhattan. I bite Lola's lip as I slowly pull away from her delectable, curvy body and pin her with my lust-filled gaze once her eyes open—she's soft and loose, perfect. I grasp her hand in mine again and place my palm on the plate next to the door to trigger the lock. Then gesture for Lola to enter ahead of me knowing that the 360-degree, unencumbered view from the expanse of wall-to-wall, floor-to-ceiling windows will astonish her. She won't have time to question me further.

As if on cue, Lola sucks in her breath at the sight and teeters over in her fuck-me heels to the wall of windows that faces south. The famous skyline is breathtaking in its magnitude with the infinite lights contrasted against the ink-black night sky. Even I'm impressed whenever I take time to stare out.

However, I'm more intrigued by my Petite Seductress' ass in her dress as it swishes from side to side. My dick lengthens at the memory of the pounding that I gave her in the lounge. I follow her and stand flush against her body as she places her small hands on the glass as if she could touch the lights beyond. I bend down and nuzzle my nose against her neck, breathing in her seductive perfume and the maddening smell of our sex. I grind against her, pushing her body into the glass and placing my big hands on top of hers, holding her in place.

The vixen ignores my advances and peppers me with questions about the view, the decor, the fucking construction—shit, I just want her. So in response, I unzip her dress and slide it down her body. My fingers skim along her soft skin, sending shivers across her body and goosebumps to rise. Then unclasp her sheer, nude-colored lace bra. Two of my fingers push into her exposed core, not surprised to find her sopping wet—her thong still in my pocket.

"Is all of this for me, my Little Pet?" I demand as I slip my fingers in and out of her channel, delighted that she's still so tight even after repeatedly taking the girth of my ten inches.

"Yes, Sir," she mewls, arching her back and pressing her mound into my hand, seeking even the slightest bit of relief.

"Who do you belong to?" I demand, pinching her sensitive gem between my thumb and forefinger with one hand and alternating pinching her hard nipples with the other.

"Aah... You, Sir... Only you," she moans greedily grinding her mound against my palm.

I swat her pussy quickly three times.

"Whose is it?" I demand.

"Ooohhh... You, Sir... Only you!"

I slip my fingers wet with her arousal to her virgin ass and apply pressure to the puckered hole with the tips. Her gasp makes my cock twitch and my balls fill with my seed.

"What did I tell you earlier, Little Pet?"

"Th— That you will take my last hole, Siiir?" She pants, wiggling her hips to extricate my probing digits from her snug hole.

"Correct. Tonight, I fully claim you. Undress me, Little Pet," I command.

With no hesitation, Lola faces me and quickly removes my jacket, tie, and shirt, trailing her fingertips along my chiseled chest, six-pack abs, and the v-cuts of my Adonis belt. She drops to her knees gracefully, unbuckles my leather belt, opens my trousers, and pulls them down with my boxer briefs. My heavy cock falls free, nearly striking her in the face. With a moan, she takes me into her mouth and twirls her tongue around my tip, massaging my balls.

"Oh no, Pet," I reprimand her. "Did I tell you to suck me?"

As she pulls back with a disappointed sigh, Lola lifts her hazel eyes darkened by her desire and shakes her head.

"Words, Pet," I remind her.

"No, Sir, I just want to give you pleasure since I know how much you like my wet, warm mouth on your delicious cock. Am I wrong?" The minx asks with a sly smirk.

I respond by lifting her to her feet and putting her across

my bent knee, foot braced against the window, spanking her ass in rapid succession. She will not sass me tonight. Her lustful cries drive me crazy and I can't wait any longer to make her dark hole mine. I pick her up and effortlessly carry her to the sofa, positioning her on her knees facing away from me with her hands braced on the back. She looks at me over her shoulder, her long hair partially covering her face, her eyes wide with trepidation and desire. I rub down her spine to her reddened globes to gentle her before I kneel behind her and lave her sweet pussy with my flattened tongue. As though I were starving, I eat her like she's a plate at Per Se. I lick her seam, suck and bite her pussy lips, then nibble on her clit before I plunge my tongue into her core. Orgasm after orgasm drawn from her until she collapses against the sofa, sweat glistening on her damp skin.

I rise to my full height to rub my dick along her pussy lips, covering it with her juices—a natural lubricant—before I press my tip to her puckered hole. Lola stiffens and I swat her ass to get her out of her head. I lean into her body as I press against her hole, putting only the tip of my cock inside of her ass. I grip her hips when she pulls away and lean over to growl into her ear.

"Be still, Little Pet. Open up and let me in. I need to feel your tight, virgin ass wrapped around my big dick. Your last hole is mine!" I growl as I fully seat my member deep inside of Lola's ass, not stopping at the resistance.

"Oh... Fuck... Baz... Ooohh..." Lola cries as I move in and out of her ass, the snug fit gripping my dick and suctioning it back in.

Fuck, she feels so good. I won't be able to hold out much longer. So I play with her clit, tweaking and pinching it until she thrusts back against me, pummeling her ass. Her passionate cries have me on the edge.

"Come undone for me, Lola! Give it to me. Give me everything!"

I roar as I feel that tingle start at the base of my spine and shoot to my expanding cock. I unleash my full load deep in Lola's well-used ass. Just as I come, she screams her release shaking and swearing as her body responds to mine giving me what I commanded.

* * *

"WHO IS SHE, SEBASTIAN?"

Damn, leave it to my Lola to not forget about my earlier unintentional indiscretion with Bridget. I know better than to lie to her, so I tell her the truth.

I pull her onto my lap also knowing that I need to keep my hands on her to prevent Lola from spiraling out of control before I can finish.

"Her name is Bridget Heimonen, a Finnish model that I played with at Peepshow," I start and Lola squirms to get out of my grasp.

I hold her in place, then continue, "Despite what you may believe, I don't fuck every woman I see and I didn't fuck her. What you saw was Bridget attempting to persuade me to have sex with her. I was telling her I'm not interested and I'm involved with someone. So, you were angry with me and ignored me for no reason."

I finish with smacks to her butt cheeks.

"Then, why did you take so long to get to the room?" She questions with a frown, still doubting me.

"Melody forwarded a business call to my mobile I had to take. I wasn't with Bridget. I had stepped out to the vestibule to speak freely."

I give her a moment to absorb what I said and unconsciously hold my breath, hoping that she'll believe me and won't get angry again.

"Oh," she says, still thinking too much and not letting go.

"Listen, Lola, I've never been in a relationship before and I'm sure that I'll get things wrong like tonight proved, but I'm trying. I get that we haven't known each other for long. Our initial plan was for me to teach you about D/s. But to me, it feels like more and I'd like to explore it. I can't make any promises. But I'd like to see where things take us."

I hold up my hand to stop her from interrupting me and continue.

"I know how important your company and its success is to you. So, you have my word that I won't let this interfere nor harm the business partnership that Lola's Coterie has with STEELE International. We can even include an addendum to the contract if that will ease your mind."

I stop to give her a chance to respond.

Lola is quiet for so long. I pull back to get a better view of her face. She's staring out the window with a pensive and sad expression on her lovely face—my heart drops.

With a sigh, she turns her gaze to me. I brace myself for a no, made worse by me opening myself up to a woman for the first time in my thirty-five years.

"Baz, I'm scared, too. I shut myself off from love since my parents died thirteen years ago. The only people that I've allowed to get close to my heart are Luc and Leonie."

I struggle to maintain a neutral face when she mentions Luc being in her heart—a place that I now realize I wish to be.

"This past week with you has been amazing..."

I tune Lola out when I realize that she's trying to let me down nicely. I just nod when I think I should, but I don't hear a word she's saying to me. The distance in her eyes tells me enough. It's not until she smacks my chest I tune back in.

"You weren't even listening to me!" She yells.

Feeling stupid for getting caught not paying attention and wallowing in self-pity, I can only shake my head in acknowledgment with a glum expression.

"Oh, I get it. You thought I was rejecting you so you tuned me out, huh?" Lola asks with an eye roll.

Again, I go with the truth. "Yes," I admit.

She shakes her head and mumbles something about unbelievable and how she opened her heart to a big baby.

I grasp her face and demand that she repeats herself.

"I agree with you, loser! I want to see where this goes, too!" My Petite Seductress exclaims, her eyes glowing.

"Oh, well… Damn… Okay… Let's do this!" I laugh and wrestle her beneath me as she squeals in delight. For once, my brain and my dick are in agreement.

* * *

I STRETCH in my king-size bed as I awaken at my usual 5 a.m. The warmth of a soft body presses against my side and a small hand rests on my hard dick. With a start, I sit up and glance down to see Lola squinting up at me in with a startled expression on her sleepy face.

Shit, I forgot.

Smiling at her, I lean down. This morning, I learn the benefits of being in a relationship as Lola and I make good use of my hard dick and her warm, soft body.

. . .

As we finish eating a hearty breakfast that Lola made for us—the benefits keep rolling in—I take a deep breath and dive off the deep end.

"Now that we completed the expansion deal, you must be in the city more. What are you going to do about your living arrangements?"

Lola pauses, sipping her green tea and eyes me over the brim of her cup. I maintain a nonchalant air and take the last bite of my omelet before turning in the kitchen banquette to face her. Like a pro negotiator, Lola just as nonchalantly completes her sip and carefully places her cup back on the saucer before she speaks.

"I will meet with the realtor that Luc recommended finding an apartment."

That damn Luc, again. I barely hold back a growl. But I know that I can't push her too much on him or she'll balk.

"Sounds good. What will you do until you find a place? We have meetings scheduled over the next few weeks that will require your presence," I say, blowing on my coffee and taking a sip from the mug.

"The suite is still available for a few more days, so I'll stay there," Lola hedges aware of where I'm going with this line of questioning.

"Yeah, I can see where that could be appealing. The St. Regis is near to STEELE and you're already settled. Too bad you must move to another hotel once the next guest's arrival date comes."

"True. Or, I can just stay at Luc's Fifth Avenue penthouse until I find a suitable place of my own. If not, he's already told me I can just live there when—"

I cut her off with a growl, yank her from the banquette, and swipe the surface clear with my forearm before depositing her on top, wedging myself between her thighs.

"No… You will check out of the hotel today and move in here with me! You will not stay with any other man. I don't give a damn if he's old enough to be your father as you so told me the other night. You are mine and I will take care of you!"

I dictate, all cool negotiator behavior thrown right off one of the balconies of the fifty-fifth floor.

The vixen laughs at me so hard that she snorts and falls back onto the tabletop clutching her stomach. Tears pop out of her eyes, squeezed shut in her glee. Yeah, she got me to lose my cool, again. This woman will be the death of me. I know. With only one of my t-shirts on, her natural D-cup tits shake and the hem rides up past her waxed mound. My dick comes to attention and I lean over her to whisper in her ear.

"Laugh all you want now. But soon, you will cry and beg me to let you cum. But, I will not, Naughty Pet."

Instantly, Lola stops laughing and looks at me with her head slanted to the side trying to assess the situation. I hold a straight face until she hiccups, a laugh caught in her throat from the whiplash change in my mood.

Yes, Pet, the Dom is never far. Now, it's my turn to laugh as the vixen shivers in anticipation and her nipples harden.

SEBASTIAN

A few hours after I punish my Pet to her satisfaction, we take a much-deserved soak in my en suite bathroom's sunken tub. Afterwards Lola and I leave my duplex to drive over to the St. Regis New York. We'll gather her things and check her out of the hotel.

The elevator doors open at the fifty-second floor and I smile in anticipation of seeing my younger brother leaving his penthouse. My jaw drops when Leonie and Roger fall through the doors too engrossed in a passionate kiss with their arms wrapped around the other, to notice that they're not alone.

Lola and I exchange shocked looks—me because he's *Roger The Responsible* and not prone to one-night stands nor to overt public displays of affection. As he hikes Leonie's long, shapely leg around his hip, thrusting at her pussy I cough.

"Good morning!" Lola singsongs delightedly, her eyes twinkling in merriment.

Roger nearly drops Leonie in his haste to find the source

of the unexpected greeting. She in turn squawks flailing her arms out to find purchase on the wall. Equally surprised, it's Roger's turn to pick his jaw up from the floor at seeing me with a woman coming from my apartment. I'm able to suppress my laugh until Lola bursts out laughing. Leonie joins in, her amber eyes dance in delight. She and Lola giggle and converse in French about how funny the whole situation is and how they can't believe they're so busted. Meanwhile, I peer over their heads at Roger who's trying his best to remain stoic while studying the floor indicator to avoid my eyes.

"So, what's up, man? Good night?" I rib him.

A flush creeps up his neck from beneath his shirt collar as he ignores me.

Pressing on, I add, "I take it the dessert was more than satisfying? A bit of sweet passion fruit filled with lots of seeds? *Succulente, n'est pas?*"

At that, Lola and Leonie's laughter increases, filling the elevator with their unrestrained guffaws and snorts. Fortunately for Roger, the doors open and he grabs a still laughing Leonie by the hand to drag her out of the elevator. I put my arm around Lola and follow them through the lobby to the sidewalk where our cars and drivers await.

"Seriously, where are you headed?" I ask, looking from Roger to Leonie. "Lola and I plan to get her things from the hotel and bring them back here."

Leonie bugs her eyes out at Lola and starts speaking rapidly to her in French, gesturing animatedly with her hands. With a glance at me, Lola pulls Leonie to the side, murmuring a response. Leonie's eyes filled with concern dart to mine, then back to Lola before speaking rapidly, again. I hear Luc's name mentioned with not going to be happy and too fast. As the Dom in me is about to charge over and relieve my sub of Leonie's haranguing, Roger finally speaks.

"Better question, what's up with you? I've never seen you bring a woman to your home before and definitely never move them in if that's what you meant by bringing Lola's things back here."

I run my hands through my hair and turn to glance back at Lola, whose attempts to calm Leonie are proving difficult. For a moment, I consider whether we are rushing by moving in together after only a week. But my heart seizes when I think of her in Luc's penthouse or anywhere besides with me. Fuck it. I follow my instincts in business and have been successful. So with matters of the heart, I'll do the same.

With true confidence, I respond, "You're right, I've never had a woman over to visit nor lived with one. But Lola is not just anyone. She's the one who I want to build a relationship with. Not just fuck for the night—"

"Whoa, brother, The One?" Roger's eyebrows shoot to his hairline and he looks stunned.

I'm as stunned when he repeats my words back to me. I tip my head to the side and consider my statement. Is Lola The One? Or was that a mistake? I shrug and shake my head as Lola puts her arm around my waist and leans into my side. I peer down at her and my heart skips a beat when I take in her gorgeous face smiling at me so full of trust and security. I smile back, slip my arm around her shoulders, and kiss the tip of her nose before turning back to Roger to respond.

"Yes."

Roger gives me his intense stare for almost a full minute before he nods.

"I'm taking Leonie back to the hotel for her to pack

while I do some work at the office before we fly back to Paris this afternoon. I'm giving her a lift since Lola and Luc are staying for the meetings."

I eye Roger. But let it go as he let what I told him go—for now at least.

"Superb idea. We'll see you soon," I clap him on the shoulder and nod at my driver Edgar to open the Maybach's door. Lola and I slip inside and settle in for the quick ride to the St. Regis.

"Everything okay with you and Leonie?" I ask, hoping that her best friend hasn't dissuaded her from moving in with me since she's quietly looking out of the sedan's window.

Lola turns to face me and nods her head, "We're good. She's worried, that's all."

I study her face and ask for confirmation to allay my fear, "Are you worried?"

Lola's eyes brighten and her face lights up as she takes my hand and squeezes it before answering, "Not even for a minute!"

I tug her onto my lap and nuzzle my nose against her slim neck. Holding her close, I inhale her sweet, natural aroma under the scent of my body wash. She giggles as my warm breath tickles her skin and tangles her fingers in my hair, holding me close to her before tugging to pull my lips to hers. We share a soul-stirring kiss that solidifies our new relationship.

We arrive at the hotel and stride to the elevators, barely noticing the other guests bustling in the lobby. I put my arms around Lola's waist to hold her back against my front as the elevator fills. The proximity combined with her wiggling her plump globes on my once flaccid dick turns it into a battering ram. I nip her neck with my teeth to still her before I throw her against the wall and fuck the shit out of her—damn the other guests. This woman drives me wild.

Once the elevator clears, I take control and flip us to press her against the wall bending my knees to push my pelvis up and into her ass. Lola moans as she wantonly thrusts back against me, urging me on. My hand slips under her dress and cups her mons, pushing two fingers roughly inside of her tight channel, her ever-ready cream easing the way for my probing digits.

"Ooh, baby… Fuck!" Lola groans, widening her legs to give me more access when I repeatedly stroke the textured area of her sensitive G-spot.

I grind my thick staff into her bountiful bottom. As I inch her dress up to her hips with my other hand and add a third finger. Lola turns into a screaming banshee as she comes, shaking and panting, gripping my fingers with her pussy walls.

"Who do you belong to, Little Pet?" I demand my fingers continuing to thrust in and out of her spasming, dripping pussy.

"Uh… Uh… Uh… Uh," is all that Lola can say as another orgasm rips through her core, her trembling body leaning heavily on mine.

I pinch her nipple with my other hand and she squeals.

"Who do you belong to, Pet?" I repeat.

"Ooohhh… You, Sir… Only you!" Lola pants.

She comes undone, gripping my fingers as she cums for the third time as the ping sounds announcing that we've reached the Presidential Suite's floor.

I gently withdraw my fingers from her pussy rippling with aftershocks and pat Lola's mound while softly kissing her neck, the skin damp with sweat. A groan falls from my mouth as her dress slides back down, covering her lush curves. I extend my other arm to prevent the elevator doors from closing while I lap her sweet honey from my fingers and hand. When Lola turns, her eyes shine with satiety as she bites her fleshy, lower lip. I pat her ass when she passes me to exit the elevator, a smirk on my face knowing that I gave her such pleasure capable of making her swoon.

"Everything good?" Comes the deep rumble of Roger's voice edged with laughter.

I snatch my fingers from my mouth and whip around. My brother and Leonie emerge from the other elevator having witnessed me sucking my digits and patting Lola's ass. Now, it's our turn to experience embarrassment. The four of us laugh and Leonie links arms with Lola sashaying to the suite's double doors. Roger gives me a shove and follows them. I trail behind, enjoying the last remnants of Lola's delicious essence.

* * *

"YOU HAVE MORE clothes than I do! Are you sure this is for two?"

Lola calls out from my bedroom's oversized dressing room and walk-in closets—equivalent to two New York studio apartments combined. She's adding her clothes, shoes, and handbags to the custom racks, drawers, and shelves.

"Whatever. Am I supposed to walk around nak—" I start.

But the words get stuck in my throat. Before me is a dick hardening sight. Lola bent at the waist—a red lace thong disappearing between her mouthwatering ass cheeks uncovered from my T-shirt she's wearing—placing shoes on the lower shelf. My bollocks go crazy.

Lola glances over her shoulder at me with a puzzled

expression in her eyes since I stopped mid-word. She laughs when she sees my mouth hanging open and my eyes fixed on her enticing bottom. She shimmies her hips and the T-shirt slips further to reveal her voluminous breasts bouncing free. With a low growl, I loosen the string on my sweatpants to free my dick, too. I advance, lining my rapidly hardening shaft with her seam and impaling her instantly. Both of us groan in mutual satisfaction as we join as one in absolute carnal rapture.

Since I entered Lola with no preparation—yes, she definitely drives me mad—I spank her ass to give her pussy time to grow accustomed to my girth and length. I move at a slow, rhythmic pace. Lola's juices coat my cock as her arousal catches up to mine. The feeling of being bare inside of Lola is indescribable. My cock feels every surface of her pussy walls, including the texture of her G-spot that I brush my tip against each time I re-enter her channel. The increased movement of her ass hitting back against my groin pushes my dick deeper within her drenched folds, my tip touching her womb.

Again, my inner caveman surfaces and grunts as I mount Lola and increase my pace plundering faster and harder wanting to plant my seed deep into her fertile womb. I adjust my grip, placing one hand on the top of her shoulder to hold Lola in place. The other hand I place under her opposite thigh to lift it, changing the angle to go even deeper. The sounds of our mating reverberate around the room.

I feel Lola's walls tremble, milking up and down my shaft as I squeeze her clit with the fingers under her thigh. She tosses her head back and wails my name as she convulses with her orgasm. I lift her off of the floor to drive up into her pulsating pussy. Mad in my desire to fuck her raw, I chase the orgasm brewing at the base of my spine.

"Fuck yes, baby... Take it... Take all of it... YES!" I shout my voice gruff with desire.

My movements become disjointed as I feel Lola cum for the fourth time and my dick swells deep within her sopping wet pussy. I shift to face the wall and brace Lola against it as I ram into her again and again until I can't hold back any longer. I grip her hips tightly and possessively bite the sensitive area where Lola's shoulder meets her neck as my orgasm rips through my body. My cock jerks deep inside of her, erupting with seed that coats her womb. I can't stop thrusting like a feral animal claiming its mate until every drop of my jizz spews from my tip.

My knees weaken and I lower us to the floor, pulling a boneless Lola into my lap. My spent dick falls from her pussy that's dripping with our combined essence. I stare at the puddle forming beneath our entwined legs, transfixed by our coupling. Lola sighs and lays her head against my chest where my heart beats helter-skelter.

If the last twenty-four hours are any proof of how we'll interact in my private space, then we'll be more than fine.

LOLA

The past week has been a blur of meetings at STEELE's New York headquarters where Baz arranged for Blair and me to use one of the office suites on the executive floor. Close, but not distractingly so as he stated. Apartment hunting with the realtor Baz insisted that I use. He didn't want me working with Luc's recommendation. Then there's the passionate sex every evening after which we soak in the large, sunken tub in his en suite bathroom. It's a ritual we instilled from our first night together. A girl could get used to this life. Demanding work and just as rigorous sex. Both satisfying.

Speak of the devils. Right on time for our next meeting, Baz and Luc stride into my office with Blair close behind them, eyes firmly fixed on Luc like a lovesick puppy. It makes me wonder if they're spending time together outside of business hours. If they are good for them since it'll be a distraction from Luc questioning my move into Baz's duplex. I roll my eyes thinking about his overly dramatic reaction when I told him I wouldn't need to stay at his penthouse. Oh, well, I'm a big girl, I shrug to myself. Both men briefly greet me as they continue to debate some topic on their way to the conference table next to the wall of windows. I take a deep breath. Here we go.

"Hello, gentlemen. What rousing topic are you discussing?" I ask as I join them at the table, eyeing one and then the other with my brow raised questioningly.

"He thinks—"

"You should—"

They start at the same time.

"What I was say—"

"Anyway, the best—"

My shrill whistle rings through the space ending all conversation and they stare at me stupefied. I remove my fingers from my mouth and put my hands on my hips.

"Enough, already," I admonish them. "I have a lingerie business to run, not an MMA match to referee. Again, what are you talking about?"

Luc looks chastened, and Sebastian clamps down on his lips, champing at the bit to speak. So, I turn to Luc and gesture for him to speak.

"Pardon, Lola," Luc begins sincerely. "I am concerned that the..."

We finish that meeting and a few others with Sebastian's team before we break for lunch delivered by Mangia that Blair and Tina arranged in one of the conference rooms. I rise and stretch my arms overhead to ease some tension from the compression of my spine caused by sitting for hours. When I open my eyes, I see Sebastian glaring at Luc and Luc staring at me. Oh, boy.

"Well, those went well," I state, as I walk to my desk while discreetly adjusting the neckline of my navy silk wrap dress. "I have an appointment with the realtor after lunch, so I won't be back until tomorrow."

"Lunch is ready," Blair announces from the door.

Luc's eyes leave mine and glance over at Blair who smiles at him tentatively.

"*Tres bien,*" Luc responds with a nod as he stands and buttons his suit jacket. "Shall we?" He asks, gesturing to the door with a sweep of his right hand.

"Actually, I need a word with Lola. We'll join everyone shortly," Sebastian answers in a domineering tone, keeping his steady gaze on me.

Luc hesitates, protectively looking between Sebastian and me. Then nods again as if surmising that I'm safe before he follows Blair out of the office who also hesitates to assess the situation. I give Blair a confident smile to ease her mind and she turns to follow Luc. Sebastian goes to the door and locks it, then comes to my desk to press the button to darken the glass walls. Double oh, boy.

Sebastian leans his rear against my desk and crosses his arms over his massive chest and his long, muscular legs at the ankle, his eyes never leave mine. I shiver from the dominant stare like a rabbit caught in the predatory sight of a gray-eyed wolf on the hunt. My nipples bead and my pussy drips in response. He's so close that I can detect his sexy cologne that I now know is Creed Aventus. The iconic name derived from ventus—the wind—illustrating the Aventus man as destined to live a driven life, ever galloping with the wind at his back toward success. How apropos. I'm in the office, where I'm an independent, successful businesswoman and not in our bedroom or at LEVELS New York. I refuse to submit to him. I won't be the first to give in and speak and I won't turn away from his eyes.

Sensing I'm not about to back down, Sebastian ends the

standoff. Judging by the flare of his nostrils, he can scent my arousal just as much as I can feel it.

"So, you do not think Luc wants you?" Sebastian questions with a tilt to his head and that blasted unwavering stare.

I steel my shoulders to draw on my resolve to not submit before I respond.

"Luc is like a father to me and—" I answer, but Sebastian abruptly raises his hand to stop me.

"What father acts like a jealous lover when his daughter moves in with the man that she is seeing?" He questions.

I try to respond, but Sebastian is on a roll and continues as though I didn't even open my mouth to speak.

"What father marks his territory by pissing around his daughter? Most importantly and worse… What father ogles his daughter's tits as they strain against her dress???"

Sebastian's voice rises with every word until he's hissing the esses in dress and he's towering over me.

I swallow, but hold his gaze thinking he's not so far off, but I can't let him get even more upset. So, I try to diffuse the situation with a deflection.

"Oh, Baz, don't you see how Luc and Blair act when they're together?" I rush on before he can interrupt. "She's mad for him. It's been for some time. He's spending a lot of non-business hours with her going to dinner and to the ballet."

I slide my palms up Sebastian's biceps to clasp my fingers behind his neck, leaning my body into his until he drops his arms to his sides. I brush my breasts against his hard chest and gaze warmly into his eyes as they darken with lust.

"Blair just asked me this morning if I mind her leaving early today to go with Luc to an event in Greenwich,

Connecticut. I figured you could skip out early, too, so we can go to Peepshow at LEVELS since we haven't been in over a week. What do you think, Sir?" I purr in his ear as I lick then nip the outer shell.

His body jerks in response, and he wraps his arms around me as he growls in my ear.

"I know what you are doing, Naughty Pet. You cannot manipulate me by pressing your bountiful breasts and sultry pussy against me."

I yowl when he bites and tugs on my ear with his teeth and try to pull back only for him to crush me to his unyielding body.

"We will go to Peepshow, and we will perform a punishment demonstration for your bewitching behavior, Naughty Pet."

My pussy clenches and I whimper as he quickly spanks my right butt cheek, left, crease of my ass and thigh, right, left. I dance on my tiptoes and whine against his neck.

As he halts, Sebastian stands and I sway in his arms. Disappointment courses through my body that he ended his reprimand. My pussy continues to pulsate to the beat of his spanks, aching for his massive cock to fill it completely.

"A sample of what will occur tonight. Now, let us eat lunch."

* * *

THE VIEW across the East River is spectacular where I stand on the terrace of the Sutton Place penthouse I have to make mine. It reminds me of the one I had from my family's apartment further north of Fifty-seventh Street. I smile at Robin Sanchez-Waghorn, the realtor that Baz recommended to me. She's very knowledgeable and has shown me six apartments that are exactly what I'm looking for in my new home. But this sunny, spacious penthouse in a magnificent, Rosario Candela designed building is by far my favorite.

"I'll pay full price and want to close in a week," I tell Robin with a smile excited that I've found the perfect home.

"Fantastic!" Robin exclaims. "This is the most distinguished Sutton Place building. I'm confident that the board will approve your application as you'll be an impressive addition to the residents. Would you like to take another walkthrough before we leave?"

I slowly spin in a circle to take another glimpse, then head back to Baz's penthouse to get ready for our date tonight. I pause at the thought I consider going to Peepshow to serve as a punishment demonstration as a date, but nothing Baz and I have done is conventional. So, with a shrug to myself, I follow Robin through the penthouse and out of my soon-to-be front door.

TONIGHT, I want to be brazen. I chose a lingerie set from my new Las Vegas collection: the bra creates a flesh-tone barely there illusion with its sheer stretch-tulle cups; it's framed with delicate eyelash-trimmed lace and has black crossover straps and binding that highlight my curvy shape; I also made the briefs of sheer stretch-tulle outlined with contrasting black binding; added detail of panels trimmed along the waistband with more eyelash lace to highlight the deep cutout front and back. The overall appearance is my naked body crisscrossed by black lace and straps as a play on being tied up.

I hear a sharp intake of breath behind me as I stand in front of the full-length mirror in the dressing room. Startled, I peek over my shoulder to see Baz standing in the doorway staring at me with his mouth agape. My outfit struck him speechless—mission accomplished.

"Oh, hi," I say nonchalantly as I adjust my boob in the tiny cup watching his reflection in the mirror. "I'm almost ready," I add as I slip my feet into the nude-colored five-inch mules.

I sense his presence close behind me. My gaze returns to his reflection where he stands holding a wide, black leather choker with a silver ring attached to it. Baz lifts it in front of me and puts it around my neck. I dab it lightly with my finger, just realizing its purpose.

"From now on when we go to LEVELS, you will wear this collar. It shows that you are a sub who is the partner of a Dom and not available to anyone else." He tells me, gazing into my eyes. The closure locks in place and he reaches into his pants pocket to remove a delicate silver chain that he clips to the collar's ring.

My eyes follow the length of the chain as it dangles between my overflowing cleavage. It trails down my stomach to end in a leather loop Baz holds in his right hand. Now, my mouth hangs open as I peer back up at Baz who has an unreadable expression on his face.

"I... I..." I stutter not able to form a coherent sentence as alarm bells go off in my head sounded by my independent-woman self. I clear my throat to try again, "You expect me to wear a collar with a chain on it like I'm a dog on a leash?" I end on a shout, my face reddened in anger and embarrassment. What was I thinking getting involved in this Dom/sub shit? I ask myself angrily.

Sebastian raises his eyebrow and cocks his head before he braces my hands against the mirror and issues a barrage of spanks on my exposed ass as he responds.

"When will you learn to not question your Dom, disobedient girl? How many times do I have to remind you who's the submissive and who's the Dominant? You asked to learn the ways of D/s. Yet you question my putting a collar on you in a haughty tone. For that you will receive ten more lashes during our demonstration."

I'm forced to watch myself get spanked. To stand witness to the flashes of emotions that flit across my face as Sebastian continues his tirade as he watches my reactions in the mirror. From my initial anger to shock to pain to acquiescence, at which point he stops since after that blistering punishment, I'm submissive.

He stands and dabs my tearstain face with his handkerchief, "You must trust me if this will work. It does not mean the collar degrades you. It signifies that you are mine just as this gold bracelet that I wear signifies that I am yours."

My eyes quickly jump to his at the mention of mine and open wide at yours. Sebastian's eyes widen with mine when he realizes how I interpreted what he said to me. He hesitates a moment as if deciding whether to clarify his statement or leave it to hang between us like the chain between my breasts. Does it mean more than what's on the surface?

He leaves it alone when he tells me to freshen up so we can leave. Then strides out of the dressing room. Leaving me to wonder.

NOW THAT THE spanking Baz gave me in the dressing room has my head back in sub mode, I can just let go and feel. But that doesn't stop the nerves from happening. They flutter below the surface as Sir leads me by the delicate chain attached to the collar around my neck through the crowd at Peepshow. His destination, one of the mini stages that serve as spur-of-the-moment demonstration areas for members to show off their BDSM skills to those that gather to watch. Thankfully, he didn't book the primary stage—my heart would have definitely jumped out of my chest. The only reason that I gave in so easily to the mini stage is tonight's Masquerade Night. A time where everyone wears masks and can really enjoy the freedom of anonymity as they amp up their hedonistic deeds.

To keep my mind off of what's about to occur, I focus on Baz as he walks in front of me. He looks even more commanding and sexy than usual. Tonight's attire an all black outfit: heavy, leather boots; leather pants that fit oh so right front and back on his firm ass and massive bulge; an untucked, loose-fitted, long-sleeve shirt with laces instead of buttons; topped off with bed-head tousled hair and slight stubble on his gorgeous face. Yum.

All too soon, we step up onto a mini stage that I realize is in the middle of the crowded room. It has a vamp red leather spanking bench and various implements. Leave it to Baz to want to be the center of attention. Great. I give myself a mental pep talk and square my shoulders as I peer around at the people who have already turned in our direction in anticipation of a show. Again, I'm thankful for the gold mask with a black feather plume. Baz turns me to face him—his face half covered with a simple black mask like Zorro—and bends to place his lips to my ear.

"Now, Little Pet, I want you to relax and trust me. I will not embarrass you nor allow anyone else to make you feel poorly about your choice. Remember this is your decision and we will stop if you use your safeword. Do you understand?"

"Yes, Sir," I muster up in a strong, confident tone even

though my stomach just flipped and I'm glad that I skipped dinner.

Sir addresses the group to inform them we will exhibit a punishment due me for putting another man ahead of him. He announces twenty lashes plus ten extra because of my flippant response to the collar with a flogger. I'm not sure if fear or arousal or even a combination reddens my face. But I shiver and my pussy clenches, eager for what Sir is about to do to me.

I slip out of my mules. Sir makes quick work of placing me on my belly across the bench with my wrists and ankles in matching vamp red suede cuffs. He adjusts the legs of the bench and my thighs open wide. If not for the scrap of material my barely there briefs offer as coverage, everyone would have an unobstructed view of my pussy and puckered bottom hole. Fortunately, the black material of the crotch hides the wet stain made by my sopping pussy. It doesn't go amiss by Sir I learn when he runs his fingers across the silk and slips two of his thick digits inside of my channel. I moan piteously when he removes them after three languid thrusts and steps away from me.

I tremble as rampant thoughts run through my mind. Then stop instantly when I feel the leather fringes of the flogger drag along the sole of my right foot, along my calf, up my thigh, across my right cheek. The hit to my left butt cheek resonates with a thwack before the fringes continue along the path of my left leg. I bleat out one. I fist my hands and try to stay still. A lesson I learned over the weeks that I must do or I risk receiving additional spanks. Sometimes that's a pleasurable thing. But tonight, I'm not so keen to stay on the stage for longer than necessary.

Sir continues his ministrations with the flogger and adds my pussy into the mix causing me to yelp instead of bleat.

By the twentieth lashing, I'm fighting to stay still. Not to avoid the leather fringes on my hot, sore globes and thighs, rather to get relief for my core that's vibrating from trying to hold back my orgasm. Another sub lesson in control taught to me oh so well by Sir. At somewhere around twenty-three, I can't keep up with the count and become incoherent, even drunk-like. I reach subspace where pain morphs into pleasure. I can let go by putting my trust in Baz to take care of me. Since I can't utter my safeword, I can only rely on him to stop if he senses that I'm in distress. I float blissfully.

A second of pressure at my channel entrance follows a full-on thrust as Baz enters me with his massive cock. The force so strong that I shift along the bench, my wrists and ankles sliding in the cuffs saved from abrasion by the soft suede linings. From a distance I hear grunts and cries of lust as Baz chases his release while my body responds with wave after wave of orgasms. The erotic energy that surrounds us causes the group watching to join in seeking their own pleasure. A bacchanal-like atmosphere reaches a frenzied peak and we come as one with Baz's dominant roar heard above all.

I LANGUIDLY WAKE to warm water dripping on my breasts and the sound of humming. I peek around and realize that we're no longer on a mini stage in the middle of Peepshow. Rather, we're in the oversize bathtub of Baz's suite upstairs surrounded by fragrant bubbles instead of lust-driven revelers. With a contented sigh, I lean back against Baz and let him tend to me as my eyes drift close, again.

SEBASTIAN

Three weeks in and I'm not disappointed or ready to call it quits with Lola. In fact, I'm settling into our routine with some minor adjustments to my usual schedule. That includes changing the time for my training sessions with Borya to 11:00 a.m. since I'd rather roll around with Lola in our bed satisfying my morning wood than sparring with the giant Russian. Especially now as I block his deadly kicks with my forearms.

"Da, mal'chik!" He says with a satisfied grunt since I survived his latest onslaught. "Your focus is back and you seem much more relaxed, less uptight, *da?* Is the time better? Or are you getting some *sladkaya kiska?*" He taunts, hoping to piss me off and I'll lose concentration as we start round five on the mat.

"Otvali, Alexeyev!" I growl as I go at him with a series of strategically placed punches and kicks that send him reeling backwards. No one disrespects my girl.

After the grueling hour and a brisk shower, I call Lola in her office. It's on the opposite end of the executive floor where I situated her into a suite of rooms initially as her temporary headquarters. However, I'm sure that I can persuade her to make it permanent.

"Hey, babe, do you have a minute to talk shop?" I ask her.

I laugh to myself about one of our scenes. Lola pretends she's a newly hired shop girl in one of her boutiques. While I'm a buyer who forces her to model the lingerie for me before I ravage her delectable, curvy body.

"Sure, what's up?" She asks, although she sounds distracted.

Lola's tone of voice gives me pause. So I ask her what's wrong. She tells me that the Sutton Place penthouse she bid on didn't pass inspection and that they can't sell it. This happens after they couldn't close within seven days as was part of her original offer. Instead, the sellers requested thirty days. I didn't mind the delay since I look forward to coming home to her every night. She sounds so disappointed, her voice thick like she's on the verge of tears. Good thing I can cheer her up.

"I'm sorry to hear that, darling. Robin will find an even better penthouse for you, don't worry. Okay? Besides, you get to stay with me longer. You know you'll miss waking up with my tongue deep in your sweet, little pussy, licking your cream for my breakfast."

We talk some more and then I spring the excellent news on her.

"Remember how we wanted Lola's Coterie in the west wing of the Vegas mall closer to the entrance from the casino? Well… As it turns out, we had to end the lease for one of the anchor stores early because of the owner's impending divorce and can offer it to you—"

I have to pull the headset from my ear as Lola's shrieks of joy threaten to deafen me. I put our call on speaker and sit back in my chair as I hear her yelling the wonderful news to Blair. Then silence. As I'm checking the connection to figure out what happened, I look up to see Lola running at top speed despite the high heels across the floor towards my office. With a laugh, I get up and open the door for her just as she jumps into my arms, wraps her legs around my waist, and smothers me with kisses. My dick hardens and lengthens from her warm core pressed against me. I carry her inside and kick the door shut before striding to my desk to darken the glass walls for some much-needed privacy.

Yeah… not… disappointed… at… all.

THE VIEW of the world-famous Las Vegas Strip sparkles like rare and exceptionally beautiful, fancy color diamonds as my G650 private jet flies into McCarran International Airport. I never tire of seeing the bright lights flashing in the middle of the bleak desert. I squeeze Lola's hand as we touch down and kiss her soft, fragrant cheek. Her spirits are much higher now that we've checked off the Mile High Club for her in the bedroom at the back of the jet.

"The view is phenomenal, Baz!" She exclaims leaning closer to the window, her excitement like that of a child staring into the windows at FAO Schwarz during the holidays. "I love Vegas! The shows, the shopping, the atmosphere! I can't wait to see the space!"

As soon as the pilot gives the all clear, we gather our things and walk to the cabin's exterior door. I can't wait to start the surprise that I have in store for Lola. I hate to see her sad. Although secretly, I'm glad that the penthouse fell through. Perhaps it's a sign that she's meant to stay with me indefinitely.

I have my Vegas driver Dario take us along the entire

Strip so that Lola can oh and ah. Then we double back to the driveway for one of the two STEELE five-diamond resort and casino properties in the middle of the action. We'll stay in my penthouse that's on one of the top six floors. The penthouses act as a bridge to connect the two properties with the mall between them from the ground level to the third floor.

The valet opens the door of my Black Badge Rolls-Royce Cullinan for Lola while Dario opens my door. I stride around the back to reach Lola and take her hand in mine. We walk through the ornate, but tasteful main lobby towards the private reception foyer for the twelve Bridge Penthouses designed to attract high rollers and the über-wealthy clientele. Various staff members greet me by name. A few of the woman give Lola the once over. They can't compete with my girl's beauty, so I don't even bother to acknowledge their lust-filled stares. The center of my attention is practically skipping beside me. She's so happy about the retail space for Lola's Coterie. At least she's able to get her first choice in the boutique if not in her penthouse.

We pause at the etched-glass, double-doors for the doorman to allow us entry to the separate foyer. Beyond are three reception and two concierge desks, four sitting areas, and a bank of three private elevators, each accesses two of the Bridge Penthouses in this tower. Lola looks up at the two intimidating security guards who flank the entrance, then at me. I shrug like it comes with the territory and she smiles, her hazel eyes more dazzling than the lights on the Strip. So, entranced by Lola, I barely hear the greeting from one of the two concierges as we pass their desks on our way to the elevators.

"Good evening, Mr. Steele!"

I reluctantly pull my gaze from Lola and look towards

the voice to see the female concierge walking towards me with an envelope on the properties' signature stationery.

"I have a message for you, Sir." She tells me in a seductive tone and emphasis on the Sir.

"Thank you," I respond, taking the envelope. She brushes her fingers against mine and smiles flirtatiously.

I have to hold back from rolling my eyes and I feel Lola stiffen next to me. "That will be all, Margaret," I finish brusquely, noting her name so I can tell Malcolm to have human resources correct her behavior or replace her. STEELE has a reputation to uphold. We will not tolerate staff wooing us, nor our guests. This is not a brothel, nor are our employees anything but professional and respectable.

We get on the elevator, and I quickly send a text to Malcolm. As my fingers fly across the screen, I hear Lola huff. I glance up to see that she has her back to me and is staring at the floor indicator with an annoyed expression on her pretty face. I finish my text before I slip my arms around Lola's waist to pull her back to my front and nuzzle the side of her neck. I take a deep inhale of her sultry perfume and close my eyes when my cock grows against her round bottom—damn, this woman drives me wild. Sadly, we don't have time to christen my suite, so I only hold her until the doors ping open.

"Come on, babe, we have to get ready for dinner," I tell her as I take her hand and lead her into the entryway. I know it's bad when Lola doesn't react to the breathtaking views of the Strip and the desert beyond.

"Hey," I start as I lift her chin to bring her eyes to mine. "I just sent Malcolm a text to report that concierge's inappropriate behavior."

Lola twists her mouth to the side and raises her perfectly sculpted eyebrow with another huff. So, I continue.

"Despite what you may think, I have not nor will I ever have sex of any sort with an employee. As a rule, I do not mix business with pleasure."

To that, she jerks back and widens her eyes at me—damn. I take her hands in mine and bend my knees to bring our eyes on the same level.

"Lola, let me be very clear, you and I are not in that category. You made me break my rule… Only you have ever made me want to set it aside. Understand?"

Lola pins me with a stare, then exhales and nods her head in acceptance.

"Words, Little Pet. I will have your words," I correct her.

"Okay… Okay!" She replies all sass with an eye roll. When she spins on her heels to head towards the wall of windows, I give her ass a sufficient swat. I enjoy watching it jiggle under her pants as she yelps in surprise.

After a quick tour, we go into my bedroom to get ready. Lola emerges from the dressing room in a black sexy as fuck cutout, fringed stretch-cotton and mesh, sleeveless maxi dress. The plunging neckline enhances her ample D-cups. I want to yank on the wispy fringe and delicate ties that criss-cross the open back to feast on her mouthwatering, curvy body. Her luscious globes in matching black briefs peek out from under the sheer skirt. It falls to a billowy, ruffled, asymmetric hem where her legs are on display in high strappy heels. I let out a low wolf whistle in appreciation.

"You like?" Lola asks coyly as she spins and the dress lifts and falls around her beautifully.

"More than like," I start as I put my hands under the vee of the neckline to knead her more-than-a-handful breasts. "I love it," I finish as I pinch her pebbled nipple between my fingers and nip her neck.

The vibration of my mobile in my trousers pocket

bumping against my thick dick reminds me we don't have time for carousing. Instead, I step back from my Petite Seductress to answer the call from Malcolm.

"Yeah... Great, thanks for taking care of that for me."

I end the call quickly and take Lola by the hand to leave the penthouse before we sidetrack my surprise plans.

Lola glides through the Bridge Penthouses foyer with her head held high. Purposefully ignoring a much-subdued Margaret who stands behind the concierge desk and doesn't even dare to look in our direction. I chuckle to myself and kiss Lola's hand to prove that she's it for me. She turns her head and beams a beatific smile at me, and my heart soars.

I lead her through the bustling main lobby and action-packed casino to the high-end mall. My excitement builds with each step in anticipation of her elated response to my spectacular surprise. She never questions where we're going or why we're headed away from the restaurants. She trusts me to take care of her—the Dom in me is pleased.

When we arrive in front of the large retail space recently vacated by the former anchor tenant, I punch in the code for the door lock. As I step back, I gesture for Lola to enter ahead of me. The interior is black since the lights are off and they covered the windows and doors with paper to block the inside from passersby's view. So she sidesteps to the left to let me guide the way and claps her hands in delight.

"Is this it? Is this the space for Lola's Coterie?" She asks bouncing on the balls of her feet, holding her beaded clutch to her chest.

"Maybe," I tease her with a Cheshire Cat grin.

"Don't tease me."—THWACK—"My heart can't take it." She says as she hits me on the chest with her clutch.

"Okay... Okay. Wait there while I turn on the lights," I tell her and walk into the darkness.

I get a few feet when the lights flash on and loud screams of surprise echo throughout the vast space. Lola screeches and jumps back as Leonie, Roger, Luc, Blair, Tina, Walter, Malcolm, Lydie Jackson, and the servers wave, clap, and stomp their feet. I join in and swoop Lola up in the air, then carry her over to the table set for dinner. As I put her down, she fists my hair and brings my face to hers for a passionate kiss. It almost makes me want to kick everyone out so I can have my way with her. Reluctantly, I let her go when Leonie grabs her arm to pull Lola in for a hug.

"*Félicitations*!" Leonie exclaims, beaming with her amber eyes aglow.

Luc comes over next and kisses her cheeks before pulling Lola into an embrace. "*C'est une excellente nouvelle pour* Lola's Coterie, *petite chérie*!" He extols, hugging my Lola, again. *Le bâtard*.

"Let me introduce you to my brother Malcolm and Lydie," I interrupt hurriedly taking her from Luc's embrace.

"Lola, this is my brother Malcolm, and this is Lydie Jackson an old family friend and the overall vice president of Jackson Corporation," I introduce Lola when we reach them.

"Not so old and not only a friend!" Lydie laughs as she hits me playfully on the chest leaning into me as she shakes Lola's hand. "So, you're Lola." Lydie adds giving Lola the once over in the direct way Lydie has with people.

"Yes, I am. Can't say that you're familiar," Lola says haughtily before turning her back to Lydie and shaking Malcolm's hand.

I'm just about to smack my younger brother in the back of his head for daring to let his eyes dip to Lola's breasts, when Lydie takes my arm. She announces that she needs to speak with me. As she turns us away, I see an emotion that's a combination of irritation and disappointment flit across Lola's face. Then she pastes on a pleasant smile and nods at us without meeting my eyes.

As Lydie drones on about some joint business idea that she and her brother Lucien want to present to STEELE, I can't take my eyes off of Lola. She's laughing with Luc and Malcolm, both of whom she has enthralled. She's so beautiful, charming, and smart that she's a magnet for men like Luc, Rockett, Malcolm—but Lola is mine. So, I tell Lydie to set the date in a couple of months when she and Lucien have more details. Lydie mumbles something about not seeing me as much recently and now has to wait two months for a meeting. But I barely listen as I make my way back to my Petite Seductress.

"—I'd love to go dancing! What a marvelous way to continue the celebration!" Lola gushes to Malcolm as she squeezes his hands between hers. "Let me tell Leonie. She'll love it, too."

Lola goes to pass without acknowledging my presence, so I grab her by the waist and pull her close to press my lips to her ear.

"I have plans for us after dinner," I growl and nip her delicate lobe.

Her only response is to flick at her ear like I'm a pesky gnat as she pushes me in the chest to move pass, again not meeting my eyes. I let her go to avoid a scene and watch as she hurries to Leonie and they wiggle their hips mimicking dance moves. Out of my periphery, Luc approaches me and I brace myself for dealing with his shit.

"This is an excellent space for the boutique. We will do well so near to the high traffic of people entering and exiting the casino," Luc says as he holds his hand out for a shake.

I can't let this man get under my skin with his reference to we as Lola and him. So I shake his hand and hold a civil conversation with him until the servers announce that dinner is ready.

The night is less of the original idea that I had of us laughing and celebrating the boutique. Correction, Lola is thoroughly enjoying herself first throughout the meal, engaging with everyone but me. Now in one of the resort's nightclubs, dancing with Leonie. The two of them attracting the attention of every man in the damn universe. I notice that Roger looks as glum as I feel. I haven't spoken with him about his deal with Leonie, but I can tell he has feelings for her.

Fuck it. I will not sit here sipping glass after glass of the Jackson Special Blend Scotch, moping for the rest of the night. Nor do I want to take Lydie up on her many requests to dance despite her pouting. So, I slap Roger on the shoulder and we stalk over to our dancing queens.

I stake my claim by coming up behind Lola. Entwining our fingers and raising our joined hands above her head to wrap them around the back of my neck, I dip my knees to grind my pelvis into her ass. I make sure she feels how much I miss her attention. At first she stiffens, but then loosens up when she realizes that it's me and not one of the lame dudes salivating around them. We dance like we have sex—hot, heavy, sweaty, long.

A few hours later, we stumble off of the penthouse elevator kissing while wrapped in each other's arms. I bend down and toss her over my shoulder in a fireman's carry. She squeals and slaps her palms against my back.

"Let me down, Captain Caveman!" A tipsy Lola yells, laughing and snorting. "You're a beast! Grrrr!"

I smack her ass a few times as I stride over to the wall of windows, then stand her facing the exterior where the sun is just beginning to rise. I lace my fingers with hers and press our palms to the glass, bending down to rest my chin on her shoulder. At first she squirms, but then settles as we quietly watch the natural blazing colors of the sky outshine the artificial lights of the Strip.

Our bodies speak to one another without words, stoking the fire of our burgeoning relationship. Lola turns to me, cupping my face in her hands as she stares longingly into my eyes. I tilt my head to nuzzle my cheek into her palm, then shift to place a gentle kiss on it. With a sigh, Lola leans into me and wraps her arms around my neck. I scoop her up into my arms and carry her to the bedroom where I revere her body until neither of us can stay awake any longer.

LOLA

"*Non,* I don't want to talk about it!"

Leonie exclaims slicing her hand through the air to cut off my questions regarding Roger and her and why she's sexting with Giovanni Mattei.

Only three weeks ago Leonie and Roger were dancing it up at the nightclub in Vegas. Now as we sit eating pastries and sipping tea in Angelina Paris, the legendary 1903 tearoom near *le Jardin des Tuileries,* Leonie is going at it with Giovanni. I'm surprised that my best friend isn't sharing with me whatever happened between Roger and her.

"Are you not telling me because Roger is Baz's brother and you think I'll say something to him he'll tell Roger?" I guess putting my hand over the screen of her mobile and pushing it to the tabletop.

Leonie dramatically blows out a pfft of air and rolls her eyes, tossing her long mane of wavy, mahogany hair over her shoulder. She sits back and regards me silently, her amber eyes drilling into my hazel ones. I mimic her position, prepared to wear her out until I get answers. I miss her and want the time that I'm here for the week to catch up. Hence, the afternoon tea with her and why I'm not at the office taking care of some business that I can't handle via teleconference or video conference from New York.

"No, that's not it. I know you wouldn't tell anything to Sebastian," Leonie twirls a section of her silky hair around her finger while she stares into the distance. "I just don't know what to make of him. I thought it could have been *un coup de foudre*. You know, a stroke of lightning or love at first sight..."

She trails off and looks away sadly, twirling and untwirling the same lock of her hair. I realize that she's serious and the bolt of lightning must have hit at the initial expansion meeting when I noticed them staring at each other strangely.

"Well, what happened? You were definitely close in the elevator at their residences in The STEELE Tower and Vegas..." I prod her to keep talking about what happened next.

"Yes, but he's so serious and uptight. If I didn't study when I said that I would, he would chastise me for not being focused... I'm not a child!" She slaps her hand on the table and the dishes clatter, but fortunately don't break.

I can tell she's really distraught and get up from my chair to hug her, offering words of understanding and comfort. It's rare that Leonie gets upset and I hate it when she does. After a moment, she pulls herself together and gives me a squeeze before shooing me back towards my seat.

"Anyway, I'm going to the Grand Prix—"

I cut her off by waving my hand in the air, "I'm going with you! I will not let you get caught up with *God's Gift*, especially when you're feeling down and are vulnerable. No rebound sex!"

I hold up my hand to stop her from interrupting me, "No! It's next week and I'm here anyway, so I'll just leave when the race is over. We'll be a part of the glamorous crowd." I add using air quotes reminding her of what she told me a couple of months ago.

"*Fantastique!*" Leonie exclaims clapping and jumping up to hug me.

Of course, the surrounding guys gawk at *The Lion*.

It does not thrill Sebastian at all that I've extended my stay in Europe to include a few days in Monte Carlo for the Grand Prix. He growled his disappointment and attempted to command me with his Dom-mind control back to New York. My best friend needs me and that's final.

Sebastian lost it when he wanted to scene over the mobile video view and I told him I couldn't because I was getting ready for dinner with Luc. He ended our call abruptly saying that he had a meeting that he had to get to and he'll talk to me later. The man is maddening, grrr!

* * *

THE SUITE that Baz arranged for me at the STEELE Monte Carlo is palatial with a beautiful view of the sparkling azure water of the Mediterranean Sea. But the many vases filled with gorgeous, delicious scented flowers are all that matter to me. Each card has an original message from Baz from the sentimental—I miss you; The bed's too big without you—to the raunchy—My dick will fall off; I can't taste your pussy on my lips anymore. I take pictures of them and send them to Baz via text.

I add a message of my own—a photo of me naked, lying on a chaise on the terrace overlooking the Med. The sun is glistening on my skin, shiny from the suntan oil I slathered all over my body. I'm caught in the throes of ecstasy. My long, wavy black hair fans around my head as it's thrown back with my mouth open in an O. I cup my large, heavy breasts and pinch my nipples into tight buds while I widen my thighs to put my slick pussy on full view. Before I can sit back up, my mobile is ringing with a call from Baz.

"What the hell, Lola!" He shouts when I answer. "Who the fuck took that picture!"

He's so loud that I have to hold the mobile away from my ear. I can still hear him yelling without being on speaker. Once his tirade is over and it's quiet except for his heavy breathing, I respond.

"Why hello, darling. The flowers are gorgeous, tha—"

"Don't give me that shit, Lola! Answer me!" He shouts, cutting me off as he lets loose a string of curses that would give a sailor lessons.

Oh dear, he's really pissed and I need to calm him down pronto.

"Baz, I took the picture," I start.

But he interrupts me demanding to know how I got the angle, what's or rather who's around me, can they see me, on and on. Oh boy, my Caveman is definitely losing his shit.

"No one is around me. I put my mobile on the ledge and used the timer. And no, I wasn't naked when I set up the shot. I had on a robe. Only for your eyes, baby, only you," I purr into the phone.

Now, Baz's breathing is heavy for other reasons. We continue the call with a scene where I'm on a deserted island and he washes ashore naked, the survivor of a shipwreck...

* * *

"THIS IS THE LIFE," I sigh contentedly as I sip a refreshing Sea Breeze cocktail in a tall, frosty glass.

"Oui, Chérie. Nous sommes très heureux d'être ici, sur Plage du Larvotto," a radiant Leonie agrees sipping her champagne.

I think how happy I am that I came with Leonie to Monte Carlo. Yesterday and today have been amazing, especially since Giovanni is busy with his pre-race activities.

At the moment, we have on bright colored, skimpy, string bikinis with the tops on since the paparazzi are always near for the Grand Prix festivities happening around the clock. God help me if Baz sees a topless photo of me online.

Leonie and I took a break today to relax on the beach with some of our friends here for the race or who live near. It's one of the few sandy spots on the Monaco coast. Sure we could have spent time at pools at the hotel or at their luxurious villas. Instead, we want to feel the sand between our toes and splash in the warm waves of the Med.

Tonight we're going to a party on a royal's yacht with more of the glitterati. Then, the race is tomorrow and the after parties begin. It's a whirlwind of fun in the sun with my best friend. So worth it.

SEBASTIAN

I stand here with steam coming out of my ears. I still haven't stopped fuming since I saw those photos all over the internet, social media… fucking space. Lola prancing around town in a pair of short booty shorts. Wearing some tiny ass bikini that didn't do much to cover her big tits. Gamboling in the surf on the shoulders of some motherfucker. A tight ass dress that hugged her curvy body on a yacht. I nearly had a stroke.

I barely kept my sanity enough to tell one of my assistants to arrange my flight plan ASAP. Then, in the air, more photos surface of Lola at the race, this time in a simple, halter dress. It's not what she's wearing, rather what she's doing—being swung around by some asshole after the race in the pit because their team won. Yeah, I was okay with her hanging with her best friend, but not okay with all the attention she attracts. Damn!

Little does she know that I'm at the Grand Prix after party being held at one of Roger's new specs. It's a hillside villa used as the venue to showcase the property and to encourage buyers. When she called me earlier, I pretended that I was in a meeting and couldn't talk. Actually, I was over the Atlantic Ocean mentally pushing my G650 to go faster. When I landed, I went to Roger's personal villa so Lola wouldn't know that I was in Monte Carlo ready to pounce on her.

"Hello, sexy."

I glance down to see a buxom redhead in a designer dress stroking my biceps and running her tongue over her pink, glossy lips. I know that she's not one of the high-end call girls that spend their time in locations where the rich and famous congregate. The invitation list is for a certain caliber of attendee and the security is airtight. So as not to offend a potential owner, I flash her a charming smile and ask her to excuse me. I pull my mobile from my pants pocket to answer a pretend call. She nods and reluctantly releases my arm. Gracing her with an award-winning smile, I stride away and don't look back.

Loud cheers erupt from the lower terrace and the deejay stops the music to announce the winning team. I weave through the guests as I rush over to the wall, fully expecting to see Lola with them as she told me she was going to the post-race party. Yup, there she is laughing with Leonie who's in the arms of the driver whose tongue is down her throat. I search around, but don't see Roger, who probably won't be happy to see Leonie with some other guy. I know I'm pissed with Lola.

"Mattei! Mattei! Mattei!" The crowd chants. He grins, keeping his arm around Leonie as they pose for the cameras. Lola is opposite them with her arm looped through the same ass from earlier. Fuck… that.

As if by kismet, Lola's gaze sweeps around the villa and lands on the terrace where I stand glowering down at her.

She does a double take when she recognizes me. I merely stare at her and can sense even from this distance her astonishment at seeing me here. I refuse to move—the Dom in me is on overdrive. She whispers something in Leonie's ear, who promptly lifts her shocked gaze to me on the terrace, before hurriedly making her way through the crowd.

Just as she nears another woman stands in front of me and puts her hand on my chest, babbling in French something or the other about the race. Lola pauses for only a moment before stepping to us and forcibly putting herself between me and the woman while telling her in French to back off. The woman startles. Then rapidly disappears into the crowd, the scent of her perfume wafting behind her. My eyes never left Lola's face. I wait for her to make the first move.

"Baz! What are you doing here? Why didn't you tell me you were coming when we spoke earlier? I've missed you so much!" She exclaims, reaching her arms around my neck to pull my face to hers for a hungry kiss.

Once in her arms, my angry mind can't deny my aching soul's need for her. So I lift Lola into an embrace, kissing her like she's the air that I need to breathe. Suddenly, all is right in my world. No longer agitated or feeling that something is absent from my life. In this moment, I realize Lola is a vital part of me I can't be without. Even for little more than a week.

"Oh, Baz. I'm so glad that you're here," Lola sighs as I lower her to the ground, sliding her body against mine, relishing the feel of her so close to me at last.

I take in the sight of her in a long-sleeve, antique gold metallic wrap, mini dress and sandals. I want to unwrap her curvy, little body and drive my hard cock deep inside each of her three holes to remind her she belongs to me and me only.

"I missed you too, babe," I tell her sincerely, stroking my thumb on her soft cheek flushed a pretty pink from her excitement. "You look beautiful."

Lola giggles and twirls making the hem of her dress rise showing the tops of her shapely thighs. I have an urge to sit Lola on the wall and have my way with her despite the other people around us. Sure that she wouldn't agree, I settle for another embrace, resting my chin on the top of her head.

That's when I catch sight of Roger staring from a distance at Leonie with that guy Mattei. Roger's facial expression is indecipherable to a stranger. However, I'm his brother so I can tell by the stiffness around his mouth that he's struggling to keep a straight face and his emotions under control.

The couple he was speaking with is oblivious as his eyes dart from them to Leonie who's the center of attention sipping champagne amongst the jubilant racers. When the peals of her laughter rise above the music and other voices, Roger visibly vibrates with white heat. I can't just witness my younger brother's turmoil and not try to fix it.

"What's up with Leonie?" I ask Lola pointedly.

Lola shifts uncomfortably before asking, "What do you mean?"

I cock my head and give her my Dom stare to compel her to tell me what's going on. When she ignores my look, I pivot and walk towards the stairs to ask Leonie for myself.

"Sebastian! What are you doing?" Lola shrieks as she attempts to catch up to me in her fuck-me heels, careful not to misstep. "Don't you dare say anything to Leonie! It's Roger you need to speak to not—"

Lola halts and I turn to see her standing wide-eyed with

her hand over her mouth. Aha! I knew there was something going on.

"What do you mean it's Roger I need to speak to?" I frown, stalking back towards her.

"I promised Leonie that I wouldn't say anything and I'm not. If you want answers, then speak to Roger," she replies with a lift to her chin and hazel eyes blazing in pure pertinacity.

Lola's loyalty is admirable, if not annoying. I nod and make a note to ask Roger tomorrow. I will not ruin Lola's and my evening after we've been apart for a long nine and a half days.

"Sebastian, what are you doing here!"

I turn to see an anxious Leonie looking around the bustling terrace, more than likely seeking Roger. I can tell the moment that she sees him when Leonie's cat-like eyes flash wide with hurt, then narrow to angry slits. Meanwhile, he's whispering in the ear of another stunningly beautiful, well-known supermodel.

Leonie continues to glare at the couple until Roger raises his head as though sensing her presence and pins her with his signature intense stare. They continue to glower at each other until Mattei glides up behind Leonie and slips his arms around her waist, burying his face in her neck, lustily whispering in Italian. The scornful eye that Roger throws at Leonie is strong enough to make me flinch. In response, she lifts her chin defiantly and takes Mattei by the hand, only stopping briefly to ask Lola if she minds if Leonie leaves. With a wistful smile, Lola shakes her head, then pins Roger with a scathing glare.

"Nice to see you, Leonie," I tell her more determined than ever to find out what's happening between her and my younger brother. On the surface it appears as though he's at fault given Leonie's reactions.

"*Bon soir*, Sebastian," she replies attempting to keep her smile in place. "Take care of my girl. She's missed you," Leonie tells me softly.

Before they walk away, I give Mattei the once over to let him know that he better not fuck with her. My investigator will do a full background check. I'll prevent anything that has the potential to impact Lola negatively, including some hotshot hurting her best friend.

Then, I turn to face Roger. He pretends the conversation with the model captivates him. Yet, the set of his shoulders belie his genuine emotions—he's agitated. Yeah, there's more to this story. I'll get it out of somebody, just not tonight. The only significant mystery I'm solving is how quickly I can get Lola out of here and back to the hotel.

"Babe, let's leave too so you can show me how you set up that scandalous photo," I growl against the shell of Lola's ear.

At first she's rigid, still thinking about Leonie and Roger. When I discreetly slip my hand inside her dress to cup her mound artfully playing her clit, she loosens right up and moans her agreement. I bring my finger to her mouth for her to suck it clean while I nibble on her lobe and grind my erection into her back.

"Mmm mmm," Lola hums, sucking my digit and sending a zing to my throbbing cock.

"Let's go… Right… Now," I grab Lola's hand and part the crowd, suppressing the urge to bulldoze through them. Lola's laughter at my eagerness fills my ears.

We get into Roger's convertible Aston Martin Vanquish and zip to the hotel. If I were racing in the Grand Prix, I would beat Mattei by miles. When we arrive, I toss the keys to the valet. I take Lola by the waist to keep her steady on those sky-high heels as we rush through the lobby to the elevators. I walk as though I have blinders on to avoid interacting with the staff—no delays, no opportunities for flirtatious concierges.

Unfortunately, we share the elevator with two other couples. So I can't get my hands on Lola until we arrive at the top floor that only has four suites the size of four-bedroom apartments. The hotel only reserves this floor for royalty and the über-wealthy. Lola barely gets to swipe the keypad before I'm untying the bow on her dress. The alluring floral scent of her perfume increases my desire for her as I bury my face in the side of her neck for a whiff.

"Baz, I want to taste you on my tongue. Feel you stretch my throat," Lola says in a low and sultry voice.

She gracefully lowers to her knees in front of me, unbuckling my belt and unzipping my pants. My achingly hard cock is finally free from the tightened confines of my trousers and right where it has wanted to be all this time.

"Hmmm… So big… So thick. Ooh, are you crying for me, baby?" She asks, putting the tip of her little pink tongue on the bead of pre-cum dripping from my dick. "Yummm!" Lola hums around my pulsating dick sending vibrations shooting through me, her full lips wrapped around my girth and her hooded, hazel eyes staring up at me.

The sight of my enormous cock filling her small mouth makes me growl and I grip her silky hair tightly in my fists to guide her movements.

She works my shaft like her favorite lollipop. Down, suck, up, swirl, suck. Her salacious eyes stay on mine. I've never had a woman experience as much pleasure from giving me head as Lola. Her body quivers with excitement as she takes me to the back of her throat, then down until I can see the outline of my cock in her neck. She reaches into her open dress and strokes her clit making my dick jump and her gag. I cup her big, pillowy tits and knead them before I sharply pinch her pert nipples, eliciting a strangled groan from her mouth.

She continues with her pattern—down, suck, up, swirl, suck. On her next down stroke, I pull her hair to get her attention and hold her steady with her lips pressed to my groin until she gags. Then, I fuck her fast, pumping my hips and fisting her hair until her eyes water. She ineffectively pushes against my thighs, taut with the power I'm using to fuck Lola's throat.

When I can't hold back any longer, I thrust deep one last time and throw my head back roaring my release as my seed pours down her throat. Lola swallows every single drop. The universe explodes behind my closed eyelids. I can't hear any sound except for the thrumming of my blood rushing in my ears. Then I pant as I slowly return to Earth. I gaze down at Lola, who's still beautiful despite the trails of mascara, smudged lipstick, and messy hair. Her pride in bringing me to my knees clear in the satisfied smirk on her face.

"So good baby," I praise Lola, rubbing my thumb over her lips swollen from my unrestrained fucking of her face.

I lift my girl up into my arms and carry her through the suite to the moonlit terrace, the warm breeze drifting over from the Med. I want to make her come undone for me on the same chaise she posed on for that photo she sent two days ago.

SEBASTIAN

My meeting lasted longer than expected, so I rush into the penthouse. Instead of going upstairs to change, I detour to the kitchen to apologize to Lola for keeping her waiting for me. She left work early to go grocery shopping, then to cook dinner for us—her specialty Bouillabaisse in homage to our time spent on the Mediterranean coast two weeks ago. I kiss her where she's sitting at the breakfast bar sipping a glass of white wine, my favorite Jackson Scotch sits in a Waterford crystal snifter beside her. My mobile chimes an incoming text, so I lean my hip against the bar to respond and chuckle when I read Lydie's message.

"What's so funny?" Lola asks, peering at me over the rim of her glass.

"Huh?" I respond distracted by returning the text and laugh some more.

Lola nudges me and repeats her question. To which I answer nothing, then place my mobile on the counter. I give her a quick kiss on the forehead and head to the bedroom to put on a pair of sweats and a long-sleeve T-shirt. When I return to the kitchen, Lola looks pissed.

"What's the matter?" I ask, curious what changed her mood so abruptly.

She just glares at me, her nostrils flaring from her heavy breathing for a full minute before she responds.

"What the fuck, Sebastian? You told me in Vegas that Lydie is just an old family friend even though she was flirting with you and rubbing all over you all damn night!"

That's when I notice that Lola is holding my mobile in her hand, shaking it at me accusatorially. I make the mistake of getting defensive.

"Why are you going through my mobile, Lola!" I stalk over to her and reach to take the device from her.

Incensed, she takes a deep breath and rips me an extra one, then throws my mobile at me which I easily catch. Her eyes are like sharp daggers, her face is bright red, and she's breathing heavily, again. I know that I should back down, but I don't appreciate her invading my privacy. Lydie is only a friend and I should repeat that fact but I won't on principle.

"I wasn't going through your mobile, you pompous ass! It was unlocked, and I saw a name that started with an ell and thought it was Leonie! I'm not the girlfriend who snoops!" She snarls at me, even more pissed than before.

Without thinking of the consequences, I let my temper get the better of me.

"Who said you're my girlfriend, huh?" I retort.

Instantly, Lola recoils as though I slapped her in the face and she blanches, then blinks rapidly before spinning on her heels and rushing from the kitchen. I throw my head back and shout in frustration. I refuse to run after her and wait a few minutes hoping that she'll calm down and I won't have to deal with this shit. It's been an interminable day and I'm not in the mood to coddle her when she's in the wrong. Despite a niggling in my mind telling me to apologize and make this right.

After I finish my drink, I go out into the hallway and call her name. When I don't get an answer, I check every room and don't see her. I dial her mobile number and it just rings until her voicemail picks up. Next, I call the concierge to ask if he saw her leave. He confirms that Lola left the building fifteen minutes ago.

Fuck!

Lola

I cannot believe that Sebastian spoke to me that way and accused me of invading his privacy. Most of all, I'm beyond hurt he said I wasn't his girlfriend after three solid months together. In fact, the dinner tonight was for our anniversary —I just hadn't told him that was the reason I cooked. I knew it was too good to be true.

The crosswalk light turns red and I bring my attention to my surroundings. When I walked as quickly as I could without running through the lobby, I didn't pay attention to the direction I took. I just had to put as much distance between me and him. The pain was so intense that I got an instant headache. I rub my temples, then I see that I'm still on Fifth Avenue, only a few blocks south of Luc's penthouse. My subconscious taking me where I'll find comfort, I wonder.

Fortunately, I had the sense of mind to snatch my handbag when I left our—I mean—Sebastian's duplex. So, I take my mobile out and notice several missed calls and text messages from him. Too bad.

Instead of calling him back, I send a brief text to Luc to let him know that I will spend the night at his place. He'll see it in the morning when he wakes given that it's after one in the morning Paris time. The doormen know me, so I have no trouble getting in his building and use the code to call for the private elevator. Once inside, I take a shower and crash in one of the guest rooms.

Sebastian

I can't sleep. I pace and drink Scotch all night until the sun rises. My voicemails and text messages to Lola range from angry to conciliatory to blaming her to begging her to come home. I'm worried sick.

The shrill ring of a telephone startles me as I must have fallen asleep. I jump up at the sound and realize that I'm on the couch in my home office and the landline is ringing. I rub my hand over my bleary eyes and cradle my pounding head in my hands. Damn, I'm hungover. I don't make it to the telephone and wonder why they didn't call my mobile. Not seeing it anywhere, I get up and head to the desk to call the number.

A crunch under my foot and a sharp pain causes me to look down. I see shattered pieces of my mobile on the floor. Fuck! I must have thrown it, and that's why they're calling the telephone. Cursing, I fall into my desk chair and pick a piece of glass out of the sole of my foot. The house intercom rings and I answer it with the hand not staunching the flow of blood from my foot.

"What!" I growl.

"Mr. Steele, sir, I apologize for disturbing you, but your office called asking me to ring you. Your assistants have been trying to reach you. But didn't get an answer and they're concerned," the concierge quickly tells me.

"Shit. What time is it?" I ask, wondering why I don't have a clock in here.

"It's eleven-thirty, Mr. Steele," he replies.

"Fuuuck!" I yell. Then add a thanks before hanging up to call Tina.

"Sebastian Steele's office, Tina speaking."

I give Tina some instructions: cancel my appointments for the day; deliver a new mobile to me at home immediately; let my cleaner know there's broken glass in my home office that needs removal. I'm taking the day off and do not disturb me. Once I finish my call with Tina, I wrap my t-shirt around my foot and drag my sorry ass to my bathroom to get my shit together.

* * *

It took me four excruciating days to find Lola. Now, I stand here on a private beach watching her sit at the shoreline as she stares out at the Caribbean Sea. Those days taught me I should have listened to her and put my ego to the side. The accusations I made of her and not admitting that I was wrong as soon as she clarified she wasn't snooping didn't help the situation. Our first fight and it's all my fault—dummy.

Lola's movement to stand draws me back to the present. Hungrily, I watch her rise wearing a black string bikini bottom and a white cropped tank top. Sand clings to her luscious butt and her long hair blows in the breeze, covering her eyes so she doesn't see me standing a few yards away from her. She tosses her hair over her shoulder and looks up. She pauses in the middle of her step and shields her eyes with her hand since the sun is obscuring my features. So she doesn't get frightened, I walk towards her and call her name praying that she will forgive me and come home. I can tell it will not be easy when I notice she squares her shoulders, folds her arms under her braless breasts and quickens her pace, ignoring me. I refuse to give up.

"Lola, I'm sorry, I shouldn't have said those terrible things, and you didn't deserve that cruel treatment, especially not by me." I raise my voice to tell her as I walk closer to her.

She only hesitates for a moment, then shakes her head. When she nears me, Lola gives me a wide berth to reach the villa's seawall gate. I follow her. But she turns and puts her hand up to stop me.

"I can't right now," Lola says before opening the gate.

"Please, Lola. Please let's talk. I was wrong. Won't you listen to me? Please?" I urge, knowing that if she closes that gate I'll beg her to give me a chance.

Lola pauses again with her back to me. This time she raises her hand to wipe at her face. Fuck… She's crying. I'm such a miserable asshole.

Without thinking twice, I rush over and pull Lola to my chest, wrapping my body around hers. I refuse to let go when she squirms to loosen her arms I have pinned to her sides. I bury my face in her hair and clutch her even tighter.

"Baby, please forgive me. I fucked up and I want to make it right. Please let me make it up to you. Please," I beg huskily in her ear, dragging my lips down to her neck and nuzzling her sensitive spot. "I don't want us to be apart. It's hurting both of us, please."

Her body trembles with her emotions. I turn her around to face me, bending my knees so we're eye level, holding her by the shoulders.

"I warned you at the beginning that I've never been in a relationship and would undoubtedly fuck up," I pause staring intently into her hazel eyes red from her tears. "And I did... superbly. I apologize. What can I do to earn your forgiveness?" I ask sincerely.

One tear falls from her eye as she stares into my soul, weighing the veracity of my words. I can read the emotions rolling across her tearstained face. I can tell that Lola is fighting an internal struggle. So I lean in slowly, giving her the opportunity to pull away. Then I brush my lips along the tracks from her tears, tasting the salt, placing my lips softly against hers.

She whimpers and I press my tongue past her lips and against her teeth, demanding that she open for me. When she denies me entrance, I bite her plump, lower lip and push my tongue between them as they part with her moan.

A deep passionate growl rumbles through me. I sweep her mouth with my probing tongue to capture her taste again and to conquer her resistance. I end the searing kiss by nipping, licking, and sucking down her throat as she offers it to me, acknowledging my dominance. Then lower my head to latch onto the tightened buds of her nipples through the cotton of her tank top. Suckling strongly, pulling hard enough to draw pants and gasps from her slack mouth.

Immediately, Lola's response to my demands is to arch her back. She twists the fingers of one of her hands in my hair at the back of my head to anchor my mouth to her breasts. The other hand grips my shoulder to anchor her to me.

As I keep one arm around her waist, I place the fingers of my other hand inside of her bikini bottom and dive into her sopping wet channel. I need to stretch her tight pussy to prepare her for me to reclaim her. I swat her wet pussy lips a few times to punish her for leaving me. My palm smacks her engorged clit, and she mewls in pain and pleasure, grinding her mound into my hand.

I can't wait any longer as the crude sounds of my hand spanking Lola's soaking pussy combined with her thrashing drives me mad. I lift her up, slamming her back into the seawall while I unzip my jeans. I drive my aching, weeping cock to the hilt deep inside of her in one unyielding thrust.

Lola cries out in pain and ecstasy at my brutal invasion of her tight pussy. She wraps her legs around me, digging her heels into my ass to push me deeper. We both groan, feeling every one of my ten inches graze her G-spot and stroke inner walls. Lola meets each of my frantic thrusts with one of her own, her body bowing to ease my way inside of her. Suddenly, the dam breaks. Lola screams curses at me for hurting her so badly, for not trusting her like I tell her to trust me, and for being a big asshole. I can't help but to agree with her.

The rhythmic sound of skin on skin mixed with the squelching of her soaking pussy drive me into a frenzy. I grab under her thigh and lift her calf to my shoulder, changing the angle to drive up deeper into her. Each thrust sending my tip to graze her cervix. Each time that I withdraw, her greedy pussy grips my cock, refusing to let me go. She feels so good, so tight and wet, that I lose control and pound into her pussy with guttural grunts.

Once again, I lower my head and suckle and bite her pebbled nipples until she squeals and her pussy clamps down on my thickening cock. Lola cries out in wild abandon with her eyes squeezed shut, tossing her head side-to-side, babbling in the throes of ecstasy as she cums over and over and over. Now that she's peaked, I ram into her like a feral beast chasing my orgasm. I don't stop until I feel my dick pulsate and shoot rope after rope after rope of my essence deep into her core. Unable to remain standing, I sag to the sand with Lola limp in my lap.

"How did you find me?" Lola asks as we soak in the outdoor sunken tub, the air fragrant from the fresh, tropical flowers in the surrounding garden.

"I tried asking Leonie and Luc, but they refused to tell me," I answer annoyed, still pissed with them. "So, I had my investigator do the search." I hedge, not wanting to divulge the methods he used, including hacking her mobile and laptop.

"Hhhmmm... I see," Lola says, more than likely envisioning the lengths to which I went to get the information.

I run my sudsy hands over her full breasts and cup their weight in my large hands as I knead them to distract her from this line of questioning.

"What is Lydie to you, Sebast—"

I cut her off, but she raises her hand and turns in the tub to face me, putting herself out of my reach.

"Don't... Tell me the truth. We both know that I saw her text where she calls you Sebbie, reminds you she'll be in town soon, and to be ready for her with no distractions. What does she plan to do with you? Am I a distraction, Sebastian?"

Lola is trying hard to keep a straight face. But I can see the hurt in her eyes and hear the tears in her voice. I go to comfort her. Once more she stops me. I sigh and lean back against the tub lifting my face to the sky wishing that I could erase the whole encounter. But, I remind myself to listen to her and to set my ego aside.

"Lydie is a childhood friend… Period. She calls me Sebbie because she couldn't pronounce Sebastian when she was little. It's not a term of endearment. At… all." I stop to gauge Lola's reaction. Then, continue since she nods in understanding. "In Vegas at your celebration dinner, she told me about a business idea that she and her brother Lucien want to present to STEELE. So, I told her to book the meeting when they had it fleshed out. Our families are close because our mothers were best friends before they married and had us. So we do lots of partnerships as I explained to you a few weeks ago. The meeting is in two weeks."

I won't allow her to stay out of my arms a second longer. Instead, I move to her and lift her onto my lap, sloshing water out of the tub and onto the stones.

"You are not a distraction in any way. You know what you are?" I ask her, cupping her small face in my hand.

She shakes her head, and I raise my eyebrow.

"No, Sir," she whispers.

I smile at her correction to use her words and not a shake of her head.

"You are my girlfriend, Lola Lewis. And I am your boyfriend. Exclusive… Period," I tell her unconsciously, holding my breath in hopes she doesn't disagree.

Her silence makes me nervous as she looks pensively out at the Caribbean, but I hold out on saying more. I leave it to her to respond. After a while, she slowly returns her gaze to mine.

"I understand that you're new to relationships and I haven't had but two. So, yes, we'll both make mistakes. And I too apologize for yelling instead of asking you about the text. I just felt that the way she behaved in Vegas insinuating that she's more than only a family friend. The flirtatious tone of her text combined with you laughing while reading her messages. Then your harsh defensive reaction... It just appeared she was more to you and I was less."

Lola ends quietly with a little shrug and her eyes downcast, glistening with unshed tears.

Her raw pain hits me in the chest like a sledgehammer and I flinch. It's visceral. I lift Lola's face to meet my gaze and kiss her deeply. Desperate to put all of my unspoken emotions into it, to prove to her how much she means to me—more than I can express with mere words.

Lola senses the depth of my feelings for her. She wraps one of her arms around my neck, burrowing into my body. With her other hand, she guides my hardening shaft into her warm sheath to meld us into one.

LOLA

The words I love you bang behind my teeth, demanding I speak them out loud. But I swallow those three words back, afraid to open myself to hurt more. Rather, I connect with him in the only way that a woman and a man can. I cover his body with mine and put him inside of me like a key in a lock. I clamp down on him, holding his member in place. Then lower myself until he's fully seated in my core.

Slowly, I circle my hips and rock back and forth as his girth stretches me. I plant my feet on the bottom of the tub to give me better leverage. Lifting myself up and down, I ride Baz as my passion builds and increases my pace. I grip his strong shoulders never taking my loving gaze from his eyes black with ardency matching my fervor.

He must sense that at this moment I need to control our carnal union—not his dominance. Baz places his firm hands on my flanks keeping me balanced as I use my body to pound onto his, impaling my tight pussy on his massive dick unceasingly.

As my passion peaks, my inner walls quiver signaling my impending orgasm. Suddenly, Baz's fingers pinch my clit. I spiral out of control, screaming his name as my muscles ripple with wave after wave of contractions from the rapid, pleasurable release of my orgasm.

While I'm still amid my mind-blowing release, Baz effortlessly lifts me off of his lap—it's his turn. He flips me around onto my hands and knees, tightly grips my hips, and slams his engorged cock inside of my still spasming sheath. A possessive, feral growl rips past his clenched teeth.

Baz bucks and pumps into me, his fingers digging into my slippery flesh so firmly that he's bound to leave marks. His guttural groans make my inner walls grip his length as he drives deeper and deeper within me. Baz continues to jackhammer into my hole until his enormous dick expands impossibly further before he lodges himself in my core and roars his release. My name a prayer falling from his lips.

The sound is so loud that it resonates all around us and makes my body shiver in response to his triumphant outcry. I collapse into the water as he drops his heaving chest onto my back and cradles my head in his arm—we're completely spent by our erotic exertion.

* * *

My body thrums from two days of nonstop coupling as we lie on the exclusive beach for STEELE St. Barth's. Baz risked my ire, but refused to stay at Luc's private villa after we recovered from the tub. Once again, Baz insisted that I belong to him and that only he will see to my needs, including shelter. He also told me I could forget moving out of our penthouse when I admitted I stayed that first night at Luc's penthouse. Baz's possessive Captain Caveman really turns me on and I can't deny him anything when he's all testosterone.

Despite Lola's Coterie New York and Las Vegas boutique openings in a month, I don't regret taking a break after working long hours every day to meet the deadlines. It's worth it to relax here with Baz.

"Hey, the sun is scorching. I'm going in for a dip. Do you want to join me?" He asks putting his aviators on the bed of the cabana.

"Not right now, I can barely walk... Remember?" I smirk.

Baz busses his lips against my stomach above my string bikini bottoms and I giggle, ruffling my fingers through his thick, black hair. He lifts his gray eyes to mine and trails his tongue along the edge of bikini. I massage his scalp and stare back at him. He buries his face on my mound and inhales deeply of my instant arousal. A sharp nip makes me yelp and jump away from his mouth.

"Are you denying me, Pet?" Baz croons as he kisses the painful spot.

My nipples pucker and I suck in a breath when his finger slips beneath the material and slides inside of my pussy. I clench on his digit and close my eyes, raising my hips from the bed.

Baz adds another thick finger and thrusts both of them in and out as my walls vibrate. He continues his assault until I clench on his fingers mere seconds from my climax. I arch my back, welcoming the pleasure barreling towards me.

Abruptly, Baz removes his fingers and towers over me sucking the digits into his mouth watching me intently with hooded eyes. I drop onto the bed with a frustrated growl, then rise onto my elbows to see him walking away from me to the surf. Damn, he's built like a god. His powerful body's well-defined muscles are magnificent beneath his olive-toned skin deepened by the few days in the sun. I lie back closing my eyes reliving the divine pleasure that Baz's body gives to mine.

Flirtatious peals of laughter and the sounds of splashing wake me from my daydream. I rise back up onto my elbows to find the source of the interruption. Some topless trollops are splashing Baz and giggling like hyenas when he rises from the water, the sun glistening on his wet skin, looking like Adonis Rising from the Waves. He pushes his hair back out of his eyes, then says something to the two women that I can't hear from this distance. But his gestures are obvious as he points in my direction and nods his head. They just laugh and move closer to him without ceasing their childish deluge.

To hell with that nonsense! With a menacing growl, I leap off of the cabana's bed and stalk over to the giggling groupies. I'm on fire by the time I get to them. So, I let them have a piece of my mind—the uncensored version. I call them every name that I can think of except for the one their mothers gave to them.

Meanwhile, I can tell that Baz is attempting to hold in his laughter by keeping his Dom face in place and his arms folded across his sculpted chest. I almost forget what I'm snarling at the two hussies when he flexes and makes his pecs and biceps bulge.

I swivel my glare back to the bimbos, scared and not sure how to handle a petite firecracker seconds from exploding. So, they turn on their heels and scamper away, their fake asses implanted on the tops of their thighs. I watch them with smoke curling from my flared nostrils. No longer will I idly stand by and allow anyone to take my man!

SEBASTIAN

It's been just over two weeks since Lola and I returned from what felt like a honeymoon or at least the start of a new chapter in our relationship. She really put it in perspective when she told me to envision Luc as Lydie and me as her. Just imagining reading a text from Luc to Lola that I interpreted as flirtatious makes my blood boil. So, I get an idea of her reality. We've moved on and promised each other that we would talk things out, not yell or accuse. All is good in our world. I muse as I wait for Lola in my office so we can go to dinner at Le Bernardin with my roommate from Harvard and his newlywed wife.

My thoughts as I stare at the Manhattan skyline standing behind the desk in my office.

"Sebbie!"

I'm surprised to hear Lydie calling out to me since she and Lucien are not due in until tomorrow afternoon for our meeting. Turning to face her, I realize Lucien is here, too. Lydie is a tall, gorgeous woman with waist-length dark brown hair that flows down her back and intelligent green eyes—the signature Jackson family trait. She's only six inches shorter than me in high heels. Her long, shapely legs easily close the distance between the door and my desk. Lydie wraps her arms around my neck and kisses my cheek, the edge of her lips close to the corner of mine.

Just at that moment, Lola walks into my office and starts when she sees Lydie in my arms, her hazel eyes darkening. I quickly step away, removing my hands from Lydie's back and attempt to convey with my eyes that nothing bad is happening. To Lola's credit, she visibly shakes off her triggered ire and replaces her frown with a smile.

Lucien who caught my reaction and followed my gaze quickly surmises the situation and defuses it by extending his hand to Lola with a charming smile.

"Hello, I'm Lucien Jackson and this is Lydie my sister. We're close friends of Sebastian and his family," he adds to dispel any thoughts of romantic involvement between Lydie and me.

Obviously, Lola appreciates Lucien's gesture and her tepid smile warms tenfold, making her hazel eyes glow.

"Nice to meet you, Lucien. Sebastian speaks highly of you"—she responds shaking his hand—"Lydie and I met."

She looks beyond Lucien to Lydie, who still stands beside me.

"How lovely to see you, again, Lydie," she continues as she saunters over to me and lifts her lips for a kiss I eagerly provide slipping my arms around her.

"You're early. Isn't your meeting tomorrow afternoon?" She sweetly asks Lydie as Lola turns in my arms to lean her back against my front, blocking Lydie from me. My dick jumps at Lola staking her claim on me.

"Well—" Lydie scowls, folding her arms across her full breasts, but Lucien cuts in to respond to Lola.

"Yes, I flew in from Paris earlier than expected. So, we thought it would be nice to have dinner tonight. Are you free?"

Lola tilts her head back to look at me over her shoulder since she knows we already have plans and she'll defer to me to answer Lucien's question. My dick lengthens at her submissive behavior outside of sex and play.

"We have dinner plans already with my roommate from Harvard—" I start.

"Oh, do you mean Scott or Alan?" Lydie interjects.

I have to restrain myself to keep from rolling my eyes at her attempt to show her familiarity with my life to one-up Lola. I can tell that she picked up on Lydie's ploy when Lola's shoulders stiffen.

I pointedly ignore Lydie's question and continue my sentence, "and his newlywed wife at Le Bernardin in thirty minutes. So we must pass. However, we're all on for the opening of Lola's Coterie New York tomorrow night, including Malcolm."

Lola relaxes against me again and I inwardly sign in relief.

For the second time, Lucien prevents Lydie from speaking by bidding us good night and taking her by the arm to escort her out of my office. He turns and winks at Lola and me as he shuts the door.

* * *

THE NEXT MORNING, I wake as usual before Lola. Since our connection in St. Barth's, I take time to watch her sleep so peacefully before I fill my mouth with her sweet juices, then ravage her waking body. As I lie on my side resting my head on my forearm, I reach out gently to swipe a lock of raven hair blocking her face so I can see. Lola is so beautiful.

I'm glad that we didn't derail after the encounter with Lydie—I owe Lucien one. Lola and I had a fantastic time with Scott and Lauren. It was the first time that Lola met a close friend of mine. Not because I didn't want her to meet anyone, rather we've been busy and I don't have many friends outside of my family including the Jacksons.

It was also interesting to observe Scott fall head over heels in love with Lauren and marry her so quickly. Scott, who like me was a self-professed bachelor and dedicated to his family's business. I remember teasing him about it being a shotgun wedding. With a far-off look in his eyes, he told me he can't wait to settle down and to one day have children with Lauren. Then, he looked back at me and told me when the right woman comes along, the one who's worth it, she'll change my mind like Lauren changed his. I thought he was nuts and declared that wouldn't be me.

Now, I run my fingertip along Lola's silky cheek, and she murmurs my name. Even in her sleep she responds to my touch. She satisfies my Dom plus she's smart, funny, gorgeous, and not a gold digger. I brush my thumb over her full lower lip and she opens her mouth with a sigh. Is Lola beginning to make me rethink my life? Perhaps Scott isn't so crazy.

As if sensing my thoughts and growing desire for her, Lola opens her eyes and stares at me, then pulls my face to hers and kisses me passionately. All thoughts, questions, answers, fade away. I roll on top of her soft yielding body and settle myself between her welcoming thighs. My inner caveman grasps her butt in my hands to hold her steady as I plow my cock to the very end of her wet sheath, possessing her fully.

"Mine!" I growl into her ear as she mewls.

* * *

LYDIE AND LUCIEN want STEELE International to partner with Jackson Corporation's new members-only, high-end, jet-set hot spots. The concept is a combination of beach bar, restaurant, and dance club with the first location at our hotel and marina in Monte Carlo followed by our St. Barth's resort. They want to roll the spots out at key STEELE properties worldwide over the course of five years.

The name as expected is typical Lucien—Jackson Hole a play on a watering hole for drinking liquor and accessible body areas. Their brands of liquors and cigars would be the exclusives and Lucien would create the menus and signature cocktails. The three areas would be the bar, the restaurant, and the beachfront that offers cabanas, beds, and chaise lounges. Sexy hosts, bartenders, and servers plus dancers and live bands and deejays would round out the staff and entertainment. Basically, Jackson Hole would be LEVELS on the beach minus the BDSM.

I think back to Lola and me on the STEELE Resorts' beaches in Monte Carlo and St. Barth's and can visualize the attraction and the benefit. However, the main and the only relevant requirement: will Jackson Hole at STEELE add to our bottom line?

We continue talks for a few hours with our teams weighing in, making recommendations, switching properties, expectations, and so forth. It's easy to make a speedy decision since our companies have partnered on so many successful endeavors over the years. The rehashed idea satisfies all parties.

"That ran smoothly," Lydie pushes her chair back from the conference room table and stretches her long legs.

I can't help but admire their sinuous lines as her skirt rises to reveal her bare thighs. Still, she's not Lola and I've never felt a sexual attraction to Lydie. I'm her confidante and close friend since we're the eldest of our siblings. She's working to take over the helm at Jackson Corporation from her father just as I am with STEELE from mine.

Over the years, she's turned to me for advice, especially since she craves approval from her father Connor. Lydie will do anything to prove she's as good as a son to lead. The son in question is Lachlan, my best friend and the second oldest of the Jackson clan. He's two years younger than me and one year younger than Lydie. Lachlan being the eldest son—Lucien is the third child and Laurent is the fourth—is the President of Liquor and their father's preferred heir. But Lachlan is a reluctant heir apparent because he loves his older sister more than he wants to please Connor. He refuses to hurt Lydie, knowing how much she wants to run their company.

For now, Uncle Connor is holding out on making an ultimate decision since he's not retiring for at least two years. He's also hoping in that time, Lydie will marry and turn to her family life and Lachlan can step up to the helm.

"Yes, I'm thrilled with the outcome and eager to get in touch with the Los Angeles-based architecture firm Hawkins, Brown, Dennis LLP that specializes in high-end bars, restaurants, and clubs. A business acquaintance worked with them recently. She recommends them and says that one of their associate architects is extra creative and forward thinking—"

As Lucien goes on excitedly about the plans, my mobile vibrates with a text. I pull it from my trousers pocket and discover it's a message from Lola. I smile to myself and open it immediately.

Hi! Melody said your meeting is over. Hope it went well ;)

I text her back: *Hi, babe. We're all set, thanks. Just wrapping up.*

Okay. I'm looking forward to the opening tonight! TTYL

"Earth to Sebastian..." Lydie says tapping her Montbanc, gold, fountain pen on the table to get my attention.

"Yeah, just a second," I tell an impatient Lydie while I shoot a quick response that I can't wait to see which dress I'll rip off of her later.

"This girl has you—" Lydie starts.

But Tina interrupts as she comes into the conference room to tell me I have an urgent call from one of my project managers that needs my immediate attention. I tell Lydie and Lucien that I'll catch them later at Lola's opening as I leave the conference room.

LOLA

I've been so busy since Sebastian and I returned from St. Barth's. It's been a whirlwind of activities to prepare for Lola's Coterie New York's opening: print and television interviews with various fashion, beauty, and business editors and correspondents; model selections and alterations for the fashion show; fix last minute glitches; complete the staff; confirm the attendee list; so on and so on.

Not to mention the Las Vegas boutique's opening two weeks later and all that entails—just in another city. I've flown out a few days to take care of some details and even hired a second assistant Billie Chandler who's based in Vegas to handle that office. Sebastian's director of their West Coast retail properties recommended her to me.

Billie is a Southern belle originally from Savannah, Georgia. But the contractors and anyone else who's tried to take advantage of the petite, brown-skinned beauty have learned beneath her sweet accent and big green eyes is a feisty woman. She's like me—can charm the best of them, but can turn into a spitfire when necessary. Billie is an absolute godsend, I smile to myself.

When I'm in Vegas, I stay at Baz's suite. However, I'm keeping New York as my base. Not just because I made myself the promise to buy a place here if the company's expansion deal went through, but also because I enjoy being with him. It's been so good recently. I'm afraid to jinx it or scared something will happen. I try to shake the fear that haunts the edges of my mind and tell myself to just live and not worry about unexpectedly losing what I love. Do I love Sebastian? I definitely feel deeply for him and almost told him those three words when we were in the bathtub in St. Barth's. Once these two boutique openings happen, I think I may tell him anyway and just let whatever happens unfold.

I woke this morning to Baz touching my face and looking at me tenderly, then taking me forcefully with his punishing and possessive ravishing of my body. My nerves have been on edge all this time, so it helped to reassure my feelings for him and to calm my agita.

It was the first time that we had sex in a few days because I've come home late, exhausted from my busy schedule. Baz has been patient especially for a man who's used to fucking for hours each day. But he gets why I'm driven and determined to make my company a success—another reason that I'm falling for him. I'm still on track for my expansion plan by my thirtieth birthday that's right after the Vegas opening. I haven't even planned what I will do, yet. I've been all over the place.

The morning flew by and it's already time for lunch. Blair called for delivery of salads—I don't want to be a bloated balloon in my sexy, revealing dress tonight. I send a text to Baz to check in on his meeting with Lucien and Lydie. Ugh!

Baz tells me she's only a childhood friend and they're not romantically interested in each other, only confidantes. But somehow, I perceive Lydie wants more. Until me, she may have only held back because Sebastian hadn't made a move and has been a serial playboy who fucks different women without commitments. I think she was just biding her time until he was over that phase, but now he's seriously involved with me and it's bothering her. I can handle Lydie secretly lusting after Sebastian. But if he betrays me, our relationship ends. I put those disturbing thoughts aside and send him a quick text.

Hi! Melody said your meeting is over. Hope it went well ;)

He texts back: *Hi, babe. We're all set, thanks. Just wrapping up.*

Okay. I'm looking forward to the opening tonight! TTYL

There's a longer pause than before, so I scroll through my email. My mobile dings with a new text from Baz.

I can't wait to see which dress I'll rip off of you later...

I giggle, but don't respond because I just received an email from Billie that I need to handle and Luc walked into my office. Work now, party later.

"Hi, is everything okay?" I ask Luc who has a frown on his face.

It's good to see him since we usually spend time together regularly when I was in Paris full time. I'm thankful that he's been here for the past few days helping me to tie up loose ends and just being the rock that I've depended on for so long. Now that I think about it, I've spent more time with him than I have with Baz over this week. A reversal from the first time we were in New York. Despite the frown, Luc is as dashingly handsome as ever in his bespoke three-piece charcoal gray suit, white dress shirt, cobalt blue tie, and black Oxfords.

"Oui, tout est bien," he says waving his hand with a half smile that doesn't reach his stunning, dark blue eyes enhanced by the color of his tie.

I don't believe him for a minute, but I don't press him for the truth. As if on cue, Blair comes in with the food delivery bags, but pauses when she sees Luc. Then her eyes fly to mine with a worried expression. She stands there frozen in place with the bags dangling from her hands as though she's not sure how to proceed.

I glance between the two of them and surmise that something is amiss with the pair, confirmed when Luc avoids my gaze. To break the tension and to act normal, I ask Blair to set up the conference table by the windows with lunch. I talk to Luc about Billie's email that shares some of her concerns about the Las Vegas boutique. Luc looks relieved and grateful for the subtle distraction.

"Tell me, what's happening?" He asks as he leans forward, elbows on his knees, eager to move beyond the tension in the office.

We discuss the details over lunch. Luc has the best advice and puts my mind at ease. It's decided that we won't delay the boutique's opening and instead I will stay in Vegas afterwards to settle the issues and to monitor the outcome. I call Billie to fill her in so she can take care of the next steps. She's on her way to the airport for tonight's opening, but can handle it before her flight takes off. That crisis averted, we move on to other business for the next couple of hours.

A SHARP WOLF whistle pierces the air as I stand in front of the dressing room's center island putting my earrings on. I peer over my shoulder to see Baz standing in the door looking every inch the powerful Alpha billionaire in his custom black tuxedo and patent leather dress shoes. He's leaning against the doorframe with his hands in his pockets, smirking at me. Sexy devil!

"My… My… My… look what we have here…" he says as he stalks towards me with a glint in his predatory, gray eyes.

I shiver in anticipation as his eyes rake my body from head to toe. I can tell he sees my nipples pucker against the pewter chain mail, floor-length, vee-neck, backless gown that clings to my body. The sheer detailing under my bust and zigzagging along the sides add to its sexy appeal. The glam squad worked their magic with my hair split down the middle and brushing against the sides of my breasts and sultry makeup. I slowly turn in a circle with my hand on my hip to give him the complete view. The five-inch metallic sandals give my ass a lift and elongate my legs. I'm proud of the dress since it's my novel idea to debut an evening gown collection based on lingerie soon.

"Hot damn, Little Pet. Who are you trying to impress tonight?" He croons as he steps into my personal space.

With a coy shrug, I respond, "My Dom, Sir."

Baz hisses in a breath and bites his lower lip as if trying to control himself. With a shake of his head, he refocuses and pulls a red box from the breast pocket of his jacket. The click of the closure reveals an extraordinary pair of giant diamond drop earrings that glitter in the light. My mouth falls open and instinctively, I reach out to gingerly touch them.

"For you, Little Pet. Allow me," Baz says as he hands the box to me and removes the diamond studs that I had just put on, then replaces them with his gift.

I turn to stare in the mirror on the island and grin broadly at the sight of the exquisite diamonds dangling from my ears—they're so big. I glance at his reflection and beam.

"Thank you, Sir"—I turn to slip my arms around his neck and press my body into him—"They're incredible."

THE RED CARPET is bustling with photographers, television crews, and international glitterati. My heart pounds in my chest as I step out of the Maybach and take Baz's hand. Feeling my nerves, he squeezes my hand and puts it into the crook of his elbow, pressing it close to his side as he bends down and softly kisses me. The paparazzi go wild and scream our names. I seem like a movie star!

We make our way down the carpet, posing for pictures and chatting with reporters. Leonie and Giovanni are just ahead of us. When Leonie hears them calling my name, she turns and makes her way back down the carpet towards Baz and me. Giovanni holds her hand possessively.

"*Chérie,* this is your night!" She gushes.

The supermodel looks fantastic in a sexy outfit: a white, silk satin, elbow-length shirt that only reaches above her navel with the top buttons open to show off her cleavage; a low-slung miniskirt made of Swarovski crystals with a slit up to the belt buckle at her waist; clear strappy sandals with double buckles above her ankles. Her long legs and flat tummy are amazing. Her smile is as dazzling as the crystals. Leonie tosses her back-length hair and twinkles her amber eyes as she hugs me close. The paparazzi reach a frenzied peak and thousands of flashbulbs pop.

Luc appears in a classic tuxedo cut perfectly to emphasize his height and muscular frame. He, too, hugs me and congratulates me on my success—ours I correct him with a smile. I swear that there are tears in his eyes, but he blinks and the moment passes. All of us pose for the cameras before we walk through the doors of Lola's Coterie New York.

The boutique is breathtaking and resembles my other locations, but with a nod to New York with the Manhattan skyline featured in the hand-painted wallpaper instead of Parisian street vignettes. It's the largest of my boutiques with three floors and includes a section for custom design requests. It was Baz's idea to make this location different and do the same for the others. Not cookie-cutter replicas, each distinct. I've already commissioned redesigns for the London space to continue the concept.

The night is like a dream. The boutique impresses everyone. A few hours later, the party winds down. I slip away to have a moment to myself as my emotions hit. I find a spot near a corner that's slightly obscured by an étagère and watch the scene in front of me with a wistful smile.

"Oh, no, that's nothing. Our families expect Sebbie and I will marry. He's just sowing his wild oats as they say—"

"Well, he seems pretty involved with the designer—"

"No, Sebbie is just getting her out of his system before we settle down next..."

The voices trail off as they pass, not realizing that I'm standing here. I recognize Lydie's voice, but not the other woman. I'm stunned. My stomach knots and bile rises in my throat. With a slight cry, I rush to the staff area clutching my arms to my chest.

Somehow, I'm able to regain my composure. More like I hear my father's words in my mind, "Lola, are you a wolf or a super wolf? Because there are no sheep in this family." I make my way back to the main salon. Even the sight of Lydie's hand on Sebastian's forearm doesn't make me lose my shit. I also remember that we promised to talk things through, so I'll wait until I speak with him. However, I can't bring myself to go over to Sebastian. Instead, I walk over to the temporary bar, finish a glass of champagne, and take another as I turn to decide where to stand.

As I scan the clusters of people who remain, I catch Sebastian's eye. He smiles and bids me over. But I shake my head and sip the bubbly. He frowns and walks over, Lydie's eyes follow him like a hawk tracking its prey. I have to take a deep breath to hold on to my calm.

"I was looking for you," Sebastian says as he puts his hands on my hips and draws me in for a kiss.

I avert my face and ask softly, "Were you?"

Sebastian leans back and squints his eyes, trying to gauge my mood. It's a struggle, but I keep a neutral face. He can tell something is off. So, he pulls his mobile from his trousers pocket, sends a text, then takes the flute from my hand and places it on the bar.

"Let's go," he commands and grabs my hand striding through the crowd ignoring people attempting to engage us in conversation. Once we get outside, he doesn't hesitate at the calls of the remaining paparazzi and puts me in the sedan. He doesn't say a word until we're in the penthouse.

"What's wrong?" He asks.

I open my mouth, then close it.

Sebastian flares his nostrils and pins me with his Dom stare.

I inhale a deep breath and square my shoulders, "Are you sowing your wild oats with me before you marry Lydie?" The words rush from my mouth and my stomach churns just hearing them.

Sebastian visibly flinches and takes a step back, frowning as he runs his hands through his hair.

"What the fuck are you talking about?" He asks, barely containing his fury.

I cross my arms over my breasts and plant my feet, bracing myself for a fight. "Do not curse at me!" I retort. "That's what I overheard your 'family friend' telling some woman twenty-five minutes ago!"

"Whaaat???" Sebastian yells and stops pacing to stare at me, his mouth set in a line.

I throw my hands up and repeat myself, then add that he told me she's just a confidante in air quotes. My snarky response sends Sebastian in a tizzy and he stalks towards me. I back up until I bump into the wall. I raise my hands and push on his chest as he pins me in place with his enormous body.

"And you believe her?" He seethes in my ear.

Fuck if my body doesn't react to his dominance and my pussy throbs and gushes.

"I'm asking you aren't I?" I boldly quip, glaring up at him with my eyebrows lifted.

"Are you asking me or are you accusing me, Lola?" He continues in a low rumble glaring right back at me.

"I'm asking you, dammit!" I yell and hit his hard chest with my small fists, trying to hold my angry tears back and ignore his massive bulge poking my stomach.

Sebastian searches my eyes for what seems like an eternity. Then his features relax and he lifts my hands above my head placing his palms against mine twining our fingers pressing the backs of my arms against the wall. I whimper and squirm to move away. He's too much, too big, and I can't think with him so close and so dominant.

"No, I am not sowing my wild oats with you nor am I marrying Lydie. I do not understand why she said those lies.

But, I will find out," he ends ominously, breathing it in my ear as he brushes his lips and nips along my jawline.

My body shudders and I arch my back, baring my neck to him in submission. Fuck! It's a love-hate situation that makes me so angry with myself. I love the way I feel with Baz, but I hate that I submit so easily to him. It messes with my mind. The question if it's worth it falls aside. Baz bends his knees and rocks his erection against my mound as he whispers words of desire and need along my skin, amping up my arousal. I moan and pull against his powerful hands, aching to touch him and hold him buried within me, soothing the pain in my heart.

"I'm yours, Lola… Only you… I promise," he croons.

Baz takes off his bow tie to knot it securely around my wrists, pressing my arms back against the wall. When he's done, I maintain the position like a good sub.

The telltale sound of his zipper reaches my ears as Baz frees his cock and I shudder, my nipples hardening. He lifts my gown up to my waist and pulls my thigh around his flank as he thrusts his throbbing cock deep inside of my dripping pussy.

"So good, baby… Fuck," Baz's voice is rough with male desire as he rocks his hips pushing his bulbous head further inside as my channel adjusts to his size. "So tight and wet. All for me, Lola? Are you mine?" He groans when he's fully seated within my welcoming depths and my inner walls tighten around his girth.

I hiss in a breath as he nudges my cervix. Fuck, he's so long and thick. I sense every inch and texture of his gigantic dick as it stretches my channel. I lift my other leg around his waist and dig my heels into his sculpted ass.

"Move, dammit… Fuck me!" I yell, pushing my arms

against the wall and arching my back, my heavy breasts rising to his face.

I hear Baz growl and he widens his stance as he pummels me with his colossal cock, slamming my back against the wall with each painful thrust.

"Are you mine, Lola?"

He demands an answer I'm hesitant to give. Although my body already said yes when my juices gushed more to coat his dick easing its passage in and out of me.

"Harder!" I yell, writhing wantonly.

"Are you mine, Lola!"

Baz shouts as he rises onto his toes and uses his thigh muscles to pin me in place while he pulls my dress off of me. Then cages me in with his hands against the wall under my shoulders.

The sub is bare, and the Dom fully clothed, only his dick exposed for the brief moments when he pulls back before driving deeper back inside.

I lower my arms around his neck and hold on, trembling as he forces orgasm after orgasm from me, my body drenched in sweat.

"Are… you… mine… Lola!" He punctuates each word with a savage thrust that repeatedly bangs me back into the wall.

Baz won't stop until I answer, he's like a machine using his power and strength to tear down my defenses. I sense another round of orgasms threaten to undo me and I clamp down on his punishing cock to force his release so I can avoid the answer.

Baz howls in response. He lets my pussy have it as he pistons in and out before he withdraws completely, pushes me to kneel before him with my hands clasped behind my head, and jerks his shaft as he unleashes a torrent of his hot cum at my open mouth eager to have his seed. It's so much that it rushes down my neck, covers my breasts, and drips to my thighs. I watch enthralled as he coats my body, then reaches down and rubs his seed into my skin, marking me as his. The smell of our sex permeates the air.

"You are mine, Lola, whether or not you want to admit it," he says, his voice hoarse from his yelling.

I bow my head.

SEBASTIAN

"Oh, look!" Lydie exclaims nodding her head in the direction beyond where I sit at our table at Eleven Madison Park.

We're meeting for dinner so I can ask her about the comments she made at the boutique opening two weeks ago. Since Lydie has been out of the country on business, we couldn't meet in person. Other than texting with her to set the date, I've avoided all contact. The timing is good because Lola's not here since she and Luc left for Las Vegas three days ago. Unfortunately, I couldn't rearrange meetings, so I'll fly out in the morning—the opening is tomorrow night.

I turn in my chair to glance over my shoulder. A man in his mid-thirties across the restaurant on one knee proposing to the stunned woman at his table. I continue to watch in fascination as the woman covers her mouth and tears fall from her eyes. Even at this distance, I can see the enormous diamond nestled in a blue jeweler's box sparkle as the stone catches the lights.

As I watch the scene unfold before me, a vision of Lola

and me in a similar situation pops into my head. I wonder how Lola would react. Would surprise overwhelm her? Or have a nonplussed attitude? Would she clap her hands and dance like she does when she's excited? Hell, how would I feel… Am I even ready to get married now or…

A light touch on my hand displaces the daydream. I turn back around to Lydie who has now curled her fingers around mine, smiling softly at me. I stare at her and wonder at what she said about us expected to marry. Has she always felt that way? She's never mentioned it to me, nor has my family. Could I marry Lydie and be happy? Was she even serious when she said it? Or just saying it to avoid an arranged date like the ones her father forces on her for a potential business merger between powerful families?

As I study more closely the way her green eyes shine and how she's leaning towards me while rubbing her thumb across my palm confirms she's definitely not pretending. She's in love with me. Fuck!

How the hell did I miss it all this time? Or is it only recently since I started dating Lola? Now that I think about it, Lydie has complained about not seeing me as much as during my pre-Lola days. Even then, Lydie and I only saw each other every few weeks because I was busting my ass trying to salvage that wreck of a deal I lost to Rockett.

Sure, Lydie and I have been close from birth. Since we are only a year apart and being that the Jacksons are an extended family of ours, we've spent much of our lives together. Yet, it never occurred to me to view her romantically—at all. Lydie has teased me relentlessly about being a playboy, but never hinted at wanting me for herself. I just assumed that she just wanted me to be careful or to slow down. Now, I doubt it. This is some crazy shit.

Lydie has always been a grounded woman. She's not an

airy ingenue. She's driven like me and focused on proving herself as the most able of the Jackson children to run their company when their father retires in two years. So, I'm, perplexed by this 180-degree turn in her behavior.

"How romantic!" Lydie enthuses squeezing my hand and smiling. "We should send them a bottle of champagne! I'll be so excit—"

I yank my hand from hers and abruptly cut her off.

"What are you going on about, Lydie?" I demand, scowling at her.

"Wh… What do you mean, Sebbie?" She asks clutching her hand to her breasts as though I stabbed her with a knife from my place setting.

"Why did you tell some woman that our families expect you and me to marry and that I'm just sowing my wild oats with Lola? What the fuck is that about?" I ask, my voice rising as I nearly lose control.

Lydie shifts uncomfortably in her chair and looks around to check if anyone overheard what I said to her. She looks down and adjusts the napkin in her lap, stalling for time before she faces me.

"What makes you think I said those things?" She asks in a gloomy voice.

"Lola overheard you and asked me about it," I retort, not giving a damn who hears me. I'm pissed.

At the mention of Lola's name, Lydie drops the coy manner and her green eyes pierce me as her face contorts in anger. She leans over the table to whisper-yell at me.

"How dare that gold digger whine to you about me! She's just another one of your bed warmers! You can't be serious about her? We're the more likely pair, Sebastian…"

As she continues her rant, I sit back stunned speechless staring at someone I do not recognize. I would have never imagined this venomous harpy in front of me as Lydie. I can only give her the excuse of snapping under the pressure that she puts on herself to please her father. Perhaps she feels that I could be the business merger Connor seeks.

I take time to get my thoughts in order and allow her to finish. After a few minutes, she stops, red-faced, chest heaving, and nostrils flared. Her eyes flit across my face to judge my reaction. I keep a neutral expression and regain control.

"Lydie, I apologize if at any point in the years we have known each other, I gave you the impression that we could be more than friends"—I raise my hand when she opens her mouth to speak—"Our families are close and you and I have shared more than I have with other women. But that does not equate to a romantic relationship, nor a potential one. I will forgive your comments about Lola and will not discuss them with her as it is best that the three of us remain cordial for our families' relationship."

I lean forward for emphasis, "However, do not for one minute believe that you can continue to slander Lola's name. Nor insinuate that you and I have a rapport beyond friendship. Do you understand, Lydie?"

The Dom in me takes control.

She sits back in her chair and studies my face. I can see the emotions play across hers as she decides what to do next. I hope that she understands and we can move forward without a blight on our friendship, but I mean what I said.

Once again, Lydie looks down at her lap and adjusts the napkin before she brings her gaze to mine. Her face set in an expression that I've seen her use in board rooms—cool and detached. Good, she's settled down.

"Sebastian, I did not realize how serious you are with her. I must admit the thought occurred to me you and I would make a brilliant team as we are so alike and close. But

I can admit that I was wrong and understand you. Accept my apology," she replies humbly, but still an Alpha female.

"I accept your apology and appreciate your understanding," I respond with a nod.

She places her napkin on the table and rises as she tells me she has an early meeting and needs to get home. I stride around the table and help her from the chair. With a dismissive wave of her hand, she refuses my offer to walk her to her car and leaves the restaurant poised and dignified.

I watch her walk away and wonder if this will negatively impact our families and our business partnerships. But the Lydie I know is gracious. She would never cause a disruption. I can only hope that Lydie is in control, again.

* * *

"Hi, babe, I just landed. Where are you?" I ask Lola as I settle in the back of my Cullinan at eight o'clock the next morning. I'm eager to see her and flew out at six New York time.

"Baz… Hi…" Lola responds distractedly.

I can hear a male's voice whispering in the background. What… the… fuck!

"Who are you with, Lola?" I demand sitting up and gesturing to Dario to drive faster.

"What?" Lola's voice rises and I can hear a door shut.

"Who… are… you… with?" I seethe envisioning her lush body damp and sated from fucking some asshole in Vegas for a business convention. Fuck, it better not be Luc!

"Listen, Sebastian, I don't have time for your Captain Caveman shit right now! I'm in the middle of a crisis!" She screams.

Fuck, there I go, again…

"Sorry, darling. I didn't mean to accuse you of anything.

It's early morning, and I just heard a man's voice in the background. Forgive me?" I ask in a conciliatory tone.

A beat passes, then Lola tells me to meet her at the boutique because there was a water leak that caused damage. I tell Dario where to drive and immediately make calls. The first to my younger brother Malcolm, who's already at STEELE Las Vegas. Heads will roll if they don't get shit fixed before Noon. My girl will not worry about a thing, just enjoy her boutique opening as planned.

I merely nod at staff who greet me as I rush through the lobby and casino to reach the mall entrance where Lola's Coterie Las Vegas sits. There are curtains in the windows and on the door to prevent passersby from seeing inside until the opening party. A security guard dressed in the STEELE Las Vegas uniform stands beside the door. When he sees me, he immediately opens the door and I stride in, scanning the group of workers and people for Lola.

"Sebastian!" I hear her cry out.

Lola is running towards me, her face red and swollen with tears. I hold her close when she throws herself into my arms and buries her wet face in my chest. I rub her back and kiss the top of her head, inhaling her intoxicating perfume. I can't help my dick from reacting to her curvy body, but ignore it so I can focus on the situation.

There's water tricking down from the HVAC unit on the second floor. The contractor told me it was worse before and that they expect to have it repaired in an hour. The actual damage is to the lingerie, furniture, and flooring. Malcolm called his associates at film studios and I called house staging designers I work with regularly for their inventory that Lola could use until she replaces the original pieces. Jets are on standby to bring lingerie from her Paris, London, and New York boutiques. I relay this information to Lola and she looks at me like her hero. My dick jumps and she smiles coyly at me when she feels it bump against her belly.

"So, it'll be fine, darling," I murmur as I brush my lips across hers. Damn, I miss her and she smells so good.

"Lola, Mr. Steele… Excuse me."

We turn to the voice and Billie stands there holding her hand over her mobile needing to speak with Lola.

"I will talk to Malcolm and the workers. Don't worry," I tell Lola as I kiss her forehead. "Nice to see you, Billie," I smile at the pretty assistant who nods, flashing a charming smile.

"Sebastian."

I turn to my right and see Luc walking towards me. I realize that it probably was him whispering in the background. I know that I trust Lola, I just don't trust him despite Lola saying he's her mentor and may be involved with Blair. I take a deep breath to stave off my irritation.

"Luc," I nod and firmly shake his extended hand.

"I'll update you on the situation…"

ONCE AGAIN, Lola takes my breath away. This time in a sleeveless, deep-vee neckline, silver, intricately patterned mini dress with garnets sewn onto the delicate sheer material. Silver metal sandals add five inches to her height. Her raven hair is up in a messy bun and her makeup is a dewy natural except for the smoky garnet eyeshadow. She looks like a classy showgirl from Moulin Rouge. This time, I gift her with rare, red diamond earrings and matching bangles, two on each arm. Lola teared up when I put the set on her and thanked me with a kiss full of promises. She never asks for anything and it makes me want to give her the world. Gold digger, my ass.

I never leave her side as she mesmerizes everyone around her. Lola glows with pride and confidence, graciously accepting the well wishes and congratulatory remarks from the guests. When she and Leonie pose for photos, the flashes are blinding. Leonie looks just as ravishing in a floor-skimming, sheer gown embellished with tiny crystals that molds to her voluptuous body, only a flesh-tone thong beneath it. I'm still no closer to finding out what happened between her and Roger—everyone is mum. Mattei can't seem to stay away from her. I investigated his background and nothing stands out as dangerous. He's a billionaire from a prominent noble family. So, I'll just monitor things. I smile as Lola saunters over to me and wraps her arms around my waist, holding me close. I whisper how I will make her strip for me later and her face flushes as her laughter rings out.

* * *

"OKAY, brother, give it to me straight," Malcolm says to me as we eat breakfast at one of the resort's restaurants the next morning.

I kept Lola up all night as promised, now she's passed out in our suite upstairs. So, I'm catching up with him. It's been a while since we spoke in depth about anything besides business. Undoubtedly, he wants to pry into my private life.

"What?" I ask nonchalantly, sipping my coffee.

"Don't hedge with me, Baz. What's up with you and Lola? You've gotten close fairly quickly..." he responds, cocking his head to the side.

They're not used to me being with a woman longer than

a few hours. I've been too busy to spend time with everyone like normal. Only Roger has seen me with Lola. So, I know that my family has loads of questions. When we get back to New York, I'll invite everyone over for dinner and formally introduce them to her. I'm sure that Lola will like to get to know my family, especially since she doesn't have a lot of friends who live there permanently. Her fashion crowd travels all over the world. A regular set of people may help her acclimate and not think so much about her parents. She and Haley are less than a year apart and besides my mother the only women. Perhaps they'll get along well.

"Yes, we have and I'm thrilled. I never thought I would be in a long-term relationship at this point in my career. But Lola… Lola just does it for me."

I can't explain it any more than that and Malcolm understands.

"When we get back, we'll have everyone over and introduce her formally. Is that all right with you, Dad?" I tease him.

"Whatever, fucker." Malcolm eyes me, then nods to himself. "Mr. Playboy is pussy whipped!" He guffaws loudly and the patrons turn to stare, including the two women who have been giving us the come-hither expression that we've chosen to ignore.

"Your time will come, bro, don't think for a minute it won't happen to you," I laugh along with him.

"I THOUGHT I TOLD YOU?" Lola responds.

"No, you didn't tell me you were staying for a week after the opening," I grouse. "I hoped that we could spend a few days in Cabo San Lucas to relax."

Lola stops rifling through the files on the living room coffee table to peek up at me.

"Oh, I'm so sorry, baby," she says as she opens her arms for me. "I must have completely forgotten with all that was going on. Forgive me?"

I grudgingly go to her, and she pulls me in for a kiss. I try to convey my need to be with her alone on the beach, but she doesn't get the message.

Pulling away, Lola turns back to the files mumbling that she promises to make it up to me when she gets back. I almost reply with a snide comment when the elevator dings and Luc steps out. Great.

LOLA

Baz left two days ago after staying with me for two extra days. I had to make up for bolloxing his plans to surprise me with a trip to Cabo San Lucas. So, I surprised him with a day at the spa where I played the masseuse and gave him a very, very happy ending. We had a delicious dinner at the resort's three Michelin star Italian restaurant with Leonie, Giovanni, Luc, Blair, Billie, and Malcolm—who flirted shamelessly with Billie. It appears as though things are back on with Luc and Blair. They spent the evening whispering to each other. Everyone has the hots for my beautiful, smart, and sassy assistants. I hope that I don't lose them soon; I laugh to myself. Baz and I spent the second day at my office on the third floor of the boutique, each doing our work. Afterwards we had an early dinner. Then retired to the suite where I worshipped my Adonis for the rest of the night and early morning before he had to go to the airport. I miss him already.

That's why I'm hustling through my work to leave a day earlier than scheduled. Luc had to return to Paris for a board meeting yesterday. But thankfully he already put in his time helping me with some heavy lifting. I had Blair stay so she can pitch in with Billie to get through some issues I don't have to address personally. So far, we've gotten through most of the pressing matters and I'm on target to fly out on a redeye flight.

Baz arranged for Blair and me to use one of the STEELE corporate jets. I already asked them to adjust the flight plan, but to keep it secret so I can surprise Baz. I can't wait to see his expression. I'm sure that he'll be super excited. I without a doubt will be, I think gleefully.

* * *

"THANK YOU, Stan. I know it's late or rather early morning!" I smile as I hop into the back of my Bentayga.

Just as I hoped, I finished my work and some additional interviews Malcolm arranged for me at the last minute with some prominent Vegas magazines and news shows. He's nice and told me that everyone is looking forward to meeting me. I smile, not sure what he means, so I'll ask Baz after I jump his bones.

I'm literally bouncing on the seat as we make our way from the West 30th Street Heliport to The STEELE Tower. I look out of the window thinking about all that I've accomplished in these past four months. I remember the first day when Stan picked us up from the same place. Then, I shiver when I remember how I felt when Baz grabbed my arms to keep me from falling when I bumped into him at LEVELS New York. What did Leonie call it? *Un coup de foudre.* Indeed, love at first sight, I sigh.

The penthouse is quiet as I walk in on the bedrooms level, but my skin tingles as if in warning. As I put my bags down, I look around trying to pinpoint what's bothering me. A sound from the direction of the guest suites makes me head in that direction. My sneakers are silent on the tile floors.

As I get closer to the partially open door of the first guest suite, I head into the outer lounge to reach the bedroom. I hear a woman sobbing softly and a male murmuring. My heart skips a beat and my stomach flips. Who is in there? I don't remember Sebastian mentioning a couple staying with us. I brace myself as I walk closer to the door and peak inside.

"—your happiness is a top priority for me and I will do anything to make it happen."

Sebastian is shirtless, only wearing sweatpants sitting on the rumpled bed stroking Lydie's face, wiping tears from her eyes as she gazes at him lovingly. Her mussed hair from his fingers running through it. She's in one of his t-shirts.

I have to cover my mouth with both hands to keep the gasp from escaping my lips. Tears form in my eyes, and I back away from the door. Without looking where I'm going, I bump into a table and a low squeak pops out of my mouth. My hands move behind me to catch my balance. Not wanting them to spot me, I quickly slip out of the lounge and into another guest suite. I press my ear to the door to listen for either of them coming to check on the sound.

"I see nothing. We must have misheard a noise… Let's get back to the bedroom."

My heart shatters as I listen to Sebastian. Before I physically break down, I crack the door open to check if I can make it back to the elevator undetected. Sure enough, I witness them returning together to the guest suite. Sebastian has his hand on Lydie's waist holding her tightly and she's leaning heavily into him. Once they're inside, I run to the foyer, grab my bags, and leave.

Once again, I find myself walking from Sebastian's duplex to Luc's penthouse in the middle of the night. This time, I'm not going back.

* * *

Sebastian & Lola's Story Continues: *Heighten My Desires*

STEELE
INTERNATIONAL, INC.
A BILLIONAIRES
ROMANCE SERIES

Heighten my DESIRES

SEBASTIAN & LOLA PART II

Charmaine Louise Shelton

Heighten My Desires Sebastian & Lola Part II
Copyright © 2020 by Charmaine Louise Shelton

All rights reserved. No part of this book may be reproduced or transmitted in any form or by any means, electronic or mechanical, including but not limited to photocopying, recording, or by any information storage and retrieval system without written permission from the author.

ISBN: 978-1-7352917-3-4 (Paperback)
ISBN: 978-1-7352917-2-7 (eBook)
Published by CharmaineLouise New York, Inc.
Sexy Fantasies Fulfill Your Desires Publications

Heighten My Desires Sebastian & Lola Part II is a work of fiction. Names, characters, businesses, places, events, and incidents are either the product of the author's imagination or used in a fictitious manner. Any resemblance to actual persons, living or dead, or actual events is purely coincidental.

I dedicate this novel to all the independent single ladies who find pleasure in the arms of powerful, possessive men.

Fulfill Your Desires.

xoxo
Charmaine Louise

ABOUT HEIGHTEN MY DESIRES SEBASTIAN & LOLA PART II

Sebastian proved a playboy billionaire never changes, or did he? Lola gave up on love and her desire for dominance thanks to his love for another. But what you see is not what you always get…

Will their love bond them, or will outside forces keep them apart forever?

Travel with this highly explosive match around the globe as they chase each other and their business dreams. New York City, Los Angeles, Paris, London, Dubai, Abu Dhabi await in this scintillating romantic suspense Sexy Fantasy.

Sebastian and Lola's love story is a standalone trilogy in the series. Get a glimpse of their dynamism in other books.

Anthem: "BedTime Story" Madonna
https://www.youtube.com/watch?v=CSaFgAwnRSc

Playlist:
https://www.youtube.com/playlist?list=
PLXwYvn0e218BG3nYwPgZE6voUwr2QbU1F

Visit CharmaineLouiseBooks.com

LOLA

"Oh... Oh... Oh... Fuck... Yeesss... Sssir!"

The sounds coming from my mouth reverberate around the Cellar as my Master rains an onslaught of ruthless blows to my bare ass and thighs. I lie naked, face down, cuffed to the red leather spanking bench atop the main stage in the middle of the room. My poor bottom and puckered hole are on full display for all the members—the crème de la crème of society—at LEVELS New York to witness. His chosen punishment for me since I had the absolute audacity to scene with another Dom. Yes, it was revenge for my Master denying me pleasure when I wanted it and needed it the most. Do I regret it? Absolutely not, I affirm as I relish the pleasure in the pain.

"Tell me, Naughty Girl. Why did you choose to disobey me and scene with another Dom although you belong to me only and I expressly told you your climax will wait until you earned it?"

He demands in a clear voice that resonates throughout the Cellar for everyone to hear my greedy sins.

Thankful for the break in my spanking, I try to draw out the much-needed reprieve. With a voice hoarse from my cries, I tearfully reply to my Master.

"Ppp… Please—Hiccup—Please… Sir, I do not know what came over me—"

WHAP… WHAP… WHAP

I yowl from the punishing blows. Then attempt to twist my bruised bottom from his hard hand. The pain more intense since I'm mortified by the already large crowd gathered and growing quickly upon hearing my pitiful cries.

"Wrong answer, Naughty Girl. Let us try it again, shall we?"

He continues with a snarl, "Tell me, Naughty Girl. Why did you disobey me and scene with that Dom despite being told that you will have to wait until you earned your climax?"

WHAP… WHAP… WHAP… WHAP

I take a moment to clear my throat enough to squeak out my response, now chastened by his reprimand.

"Sssir... I was a naughty girl… And I was desperate for relief after you took me to the edge for over two hours this morning… I couldn't concentrate at work… Sssoo… I sought a Dom who would scene with me just until I reached my release nothing further… And… And… I did not expect you would ever find out…"

I end on a pitiful whisper, praying that my Master doesn't punish me further for admitting the full truth. I purposefully came to LEVELS tonight seeking my unsanctioned pleasure behind his back.

WHAP… WHAP… WHAP… WHAP… WHAP

"Is this where you sought your pleasure with a Dom behind my back, Naughty Girl? On this soaking wet pussy that is dripping your juices down your thighs in a puddle on the floor?"

I cringe and scream as my Master repeatedly spanks my swollen, throbbing pussy with his unforgiving fingers. My arousal almost peaks and I pant to catch my breath so I can answer him.

"Yeesss… Ssir!"

I keep my answer brief as my Master has taught me and because I hope to assuage him quickly so that this embarrassing punishment will end.

"Well, Naughty Girl, I can tell by the sweet smell of your arousal and by your engorged clit that you are enjoying this spanking. Which leads me to believe that you need another form of correction to ensure that you understand your mistakes and will avoid such erroneous behavior."

With that, my Master squats behind me to remove the red, suede-lined cuffs that anchor my ankles to the spanking bench. I watch him from over my shoulder admiring his devilishly handsome face scowling, his eyebrows scrunched above his piercing gray eyes that lift to meet mine. I nearly swoon at the sight of him and feel my pussy clench in need of his ten-inch, thick member.

"Do you like what you see, Naughty Girl?"

He asks as he gently ghosts his fingertips along my calf, up my thigh, and up to my—

"Ooowwweeee!" I screech when his large palm slaps my sore butt cheek. Fuck, that was unexpected. Smiling faces tell lies is the truth.

My Master chuckles darkly as he strides to the front of the spanking bench where his bulging cock strains against his trousers on a level with my hooded eyes. I lick my glossy lips and seductively look up at him through my eyelashes.

"Ah, ah, ah Naughty Girl, I know how much you enjoy

sucking me off, but no pleasure for you tonight. You will only have my ten inches in your tight little ass," he admonishes me. "Come."

My heart sinks.

He finishes unbuckling the cuffs at my wrists and helps me from the bench. Then takes my small hand in his large one as he leads me to the wicked St. Andrew's Cross. A cane leans against the well-worn wood, polished from so many uses by Doms and their subs. Tonight, it's my turn. I shudder at the thought, not sure if it's in fear or desire.

Without words, my Master cuffs me once again, this time spread-eagle to the cross, my back to the awe-struck audience. I close my eyes when I realize more members have gathered on the other side. High-profile faces peer at me with rapt attention. They can fully see my naked body, my heavy, D-cup breasts with pebbled nipples, and swollen pussy lips fully exposed. My face is as red as I imagine my burning ass must be.

"Now, Naughty Girl, you will count out loud the ten lashes of the cane. If you miscount, we will start from the beginning. Do you understand?" He asks loudly, playing to the infatuated crowd who oh and ah in response.

I take a deep breath and open my eyes to look at him before I reply in a resigned sigh, "Yes, Sir, as you wish."

The whistling sound of the cane zipping through the air is my only warning. At first impact, I feel no pain. Then the sensation hits me like a shot and I scream out the first stroke.

"Ooowwww… One…"

My Master unrelentingly canes my ass and thighs, already reddened and marked with his large palm prints from the spanking that he gave me only moments before. I wantonly writhe against the St. Andrew's Cross, counting each of the savage hits until I can no longer think coherently and the sounds of the Cellar fade away.

My last image before I enter subspace is that of my climax galloping towards me. It's so intense I won't be able to rein it in. My only prayer is that my Master doesn't stop my punishment and allows me to cum. If he brings me back from the edge, that would be pure torture. Fortunately, all thought ends as the welcoming darkness of floating freely consumes me.

"No… other… Dom… is… to… ever… touch… you… Pet!"

I wake to my Master growling in my ear as he savagely emphasizes each word with a harsh thrust of his massive dick in my tight ass. Just the sound of his voice sends me spiraling towards another climax. His authoritative power makes my pussy walls clench down hard on nothing in my empty channel and takes my breath away. I pant and push back meeting every thrust with one of my own—my sore, bruised ass slapping against his groin sending shock waves through my body. Damn, he feels so, so good! This is what I needed, I resolve, secretly pleased with my punishment.

Now, as the muscles of my pussy and ass tighten from my impending orgasm, I keen and ball up my hands. My fists pound the cross I'm now braced against with my feet on the floor, my Master having removed the four cuffs. He holds me with one arm hooked around my waist and the other hand clasping my throat to keep me in a submissive position. I feel his cock swell and he speeds up his movements. My Master becomes frantic, chasing his orgasm before he throws his head back and bellows my name with his release. His dick spews copious amounts of cum, some sliding down to coat my pussy and thighs. With a final upward thrust that lifts me onto the tips of my toes, he pumps the last of his jizz deep inside of me. I scream his name as I cum with him.

"Sebaaasstiaan!"

The sound of my hoarse voice screaming aloud rips me from my dream. I bolt upright in the bed sweating, breathing heavily, wildly looking around for the LEVELS members, the Cellar, and my Dom… Sebastian.

I flop back down against the pillows, noticing that the sheets are in disarray tangled around my body. Not the arms of my former lover holding me in his warm embrace as I hoped. The realization sinks in my brain past the haze of my sexy fantasy that I'm not in New York at all. Rather, I'm at the resort in Fiji for the eight-day fitness retreat as my birthday gift to myself.

A much-deserved getaway after the last four months of expanding my luxury lingerie company, Lola's Coterie to New York City and Las Vegas. Plus the short-lived, sizzling relationship that I had with Sebastian Steele, the Alpha billionaire whose company STEELE International, Inc. owns the retail spaces that my new boutiques are in. The third and fourth after my flagship in Paris and second location in London.

I made a vow to myself I won't go into my birthday dependent on any man. So I chose to end things with Sebastian upon returning home from Vegas early to find him with Lydie Jackson in the penthouse duplex that we shared on the fifty-fifth and fifty-fourth floors. Conveniently in The STEELE Tower above my boutique. The Tower is a modern, gray-tinted glass fifty-seven story mixed-use skyscraper on Fifty-Seventh Street and Fifth Avenue on Billionaires' Row in New York City.

Better to be alone than with someone who tells me one

thing but does another. For the third and final time, I will not allow Sebastian Steele to dupe me into believing Lydie is only an old family friend and confidante. Especially when I saw them with my own eyes on the bed in one of the guest suites at the penthouse. Sebastian in only sweatpants, soothing Lydie who was in one of his T-shirts with mussed hair, smiling lovingly at him. No, my thirtieth birthday marks a whole new decade for me and the continuation of my plan to expand Lola's Coterie globally. That's my sole focus once again.

I roll over with a groan and leave the stifling confines of the empty bed. I rip the damp, silk, babydoll nightie off of my hot, drenched body that's still reeling from a sleep-induced orgasm. Then head to the en suite bathroom of my cliffside villa on the private Fijian Laucala Island to shower before my first session begins. The retreat's host is Starr Knight, the owner of the Beverly Hills-based fitness studio and wellness center Starr Light Fitness & Wellness. I pray that she can help me get my head back in the game with her mediation, yoga, Pilates, and whatever else she recommends for an aching heart. I'll need the works, I reflect with a resigned sigh.

LOLA

Last night was wild. I cannot believe that I dreamed of Sebastian. Ugh!

I should have known it wasn't real. I've never and would never ever call him Master and definitely would never choose punishment butt-ass naked in front of anyone. Well, maybe with a mask on like I did that time he flogged me on a mini-demonstration stage in the Cellar during Masquerade Night at LEVELS New York.

Seriously, I wonder if my subconscious wants me to be so submissive. Or is my Independent Woman stepping up again to remind me not to be in a D/s relationship. For her, that includes the sub-during-sex-only version like I had with Sebastian. After four months of that experience—granted it was fantastic and I miss it/him—I'm still torn between letting go and just feeling as he always told me. Even more so since Sebastian has betrayed my trust. That precondition is the foundation for any D/s intimacy. I can finally admit that I love him, but I have to love myself more. I really need—

"Lola... Hello there... Lola?"

The gentle voice seeps through my introspection and shifts my focus from the painful inner turmoil to the present.

Damn. Here I sit on my yoga mat in the middle of mediation class meant to clear my thoughts. Yet my mind is running in a million directions—and some circles—thinking about that man. Get it together, Lola!

I open my eyes to see the angelic face of Starr, her deep brown eyes filled with concern as she peers at me. She's a beautiful woman in her late twenties or early thirties. Her chestnut-colored skin dewy in the humidity. Her long, curly, dark brown hair pulled up in a topknot. Starr has a sexy body to die for—five feet, six inches, fit, yet still curvy. I smile and laugh softly, embarrassed that I didn't really meditate as that was the purpose of this session. Starr's dimples highlight her sculpted cheekbones when she returns my smile.

"Come on, girl, the session ended. Do you want to tell me all about it over breakfast?" Starr asks as she gives me a hand up from my mat. "Everyone has a story to tell. I could see by how much you were frowning while moving your lips as you talked to yourself with shut eyes. Your mind definitely has something to work out. Yoga simply won't do!"

With a loud snort of laughter at just how on point she is with her assessment, I agree and accept her invitation. Starr loops her arm through mine as we head out of the thatched-roof, wooden pavilion overlooking the sparkling, cyan-colored South Pacific Ocean. The hues of which range from the darkest to the lightest blues and greens so varied in depth, like the emotions swirling through me.

"Okay, start from the top. No judgement and totally confidential!"

Starr says enthusiastically as she laughs and crosses her heart once we sit at a table on the veranda of the beachfront restaurant at the luxury private island.

I let my hazel gaze travel out across the vast, jewel-toned ocean. I take a contemplative moment to gather my thoughts in a coherent description of the last four months. Then I turn back to face an attentive Starr. From the moment that I met her at the welcome dinner last night, I innately knew that she'd be a caring and trustworthy person who would keep confidences. It's a combination of her hippie vibe, openness, and bubbly personality that makes me relax and fill her in on the details, not leaving one chapter out of my story.

Instantly, the soul-crushing weight of despair from the unexpected loss of another loved one lifts off of my chest by the end of my tale. Just as importantly, I'm relieved to see that Starr is true to her word and doesn't judge my chosen submissive behavior. Nor does she think me crazy to miss a man who cheated on me the entire time that we were together.

"Yeah, I guessed right, didn't I? You have some story! Whew!" Starr laughs as she jokingly fans herself from the all-encompassing heat of the intense relationship that Sebastian and I shared.

"Pretty much," I reply, joining in her infectious laughter.

It seems like such a relief to talk about it out loud to someone else—not talking to myself like Starr spied during class. I haven't even told my best friend and closest confidante Leonie *The Lion* Beaulieu, the world-renowned supermodel who's not only my BFF, but the muse for Lola's Coterie.

The stunning Parisian-born, feline beauty's name means brave as a lion. Her long, mahogany hair looks like a mane, prompting the accolade. She's the perfect spokesmodel for my lingerie company since her sensuous, statuesque figure reminds me of the bombshells of yesteryear and the '90s supermodels—full bust, small waist, shapely body. Her golden, caramel skin that looks great with any color or material reflects her biracial heritage—her mother is Tunisian and her father is French.

In fact, I haven't seen Leonie since the Las Vegas store opening nearly two weeks ago. I've been dodging her questions regarding Sebastian and our breakup because I needed time to digest it all and wasn't ready to talk about it. Now I can.

"Well, I'm glad that you joined the fitness retreat. Set on an idyllic tropical island with only yourself to focus on gives you the chance to gather yourself and to explore your fresh path," Starr says sincerely.

Holding both of my hands in hers and gazing in my eyes, she continues to drop more sage advice.

"Don't let anyone make you feel any kind of way about your past choices nor the future ones that you make. It is your life to live as you see fit. Your mistakes or successes sculpt you into who you really are destined to be. A yogic piece of advice is to be equally thankful for what you perceive to be good and for what you perceive as bad. It all happens for a reason. Either way, you don't let it disturb your inner peace. Strive for tranquility no matter the outer circumstances."

I nod with tears glistening in my eyes at her kind and impactful words. I needed to hear them and they make me realize that everything will work out fine. We sit in silence for a while, watching the waves lap lazily onto the sandy shore and allow the sounds of nature to soothe our souls.

Once the tears wash away my sadness, I turn to Starr and offer her an appreciative smile.

"Enough about me!" I start. "Tell me about you. A friend of mine who's a wellness editor told me she loves taking your classes when she's in LA. It bummed her out when she couldn't come to your first international retreat. I'm glad that I could take her spot. Lucky me!"

Starr claps her hands in delight, her chocolate brown eyes twinkling as she leans forward, eager to share her tale.

"I've always loved being active and caring for my body in a natural and healthy way. Of course I learned it having hippie parents and growing up in LA! My mother's name is Sun Knight and my dad's name is Peace Knight for goodness' sake!" She laughs and throws her hands up, shrugging her shoulders resignedly.

"No way! Are those their actual names?" I ask, giggling.

Starr shakes her head and laughs, "Absolutely not! Belinda and Jordan Knight. They met at a festival and the rest is history as they say. Anyway, I wanted to combine my love of wellness with helping others. So I completed my fitness certifications and studied at Stanford for undegrad with a BA in economics, then stayed to get my MBA. I opened my center six years ago at 25. It was my initial goal. Now, I want to expand into international fitness retreats at luxury resorts and add a second center location in the Caribbean. This retreat is a test run."

As Starr shares more of her story, I find the parallels of our lives another good sign: only children; 31 and 30; smart; independent, founders of thriving businesses with plans for growth. I definitely found a kindred spirit in Starry Knight as I nicknamed her since her eyes twinkle like stars in a clear night sky. We promise to stay in touch after the retreat ends. Especially since my LA boutique is opening in about eight months and I plan to spend a lot of time there in the coming weeks.

I also pay it forward, as Pierre Delcour did when he told Luc Montaigne about the opportunity to meet with STEELE for my expansion plan. They were looking to make up for a terrible deal and needed to move fast with one that would offset the loss. Luc along with being the billionaire CEO of Banque Montaigne and the Vice Chair of Lola's Coterie is my advisor, benefactor, and father-figure. Despite what overly possessive Sebastian believes. Monsieur Delcour's thoughtful act led to my multiyear, multimillion-dollar partnership.

I promise Starr I'll tell Malcolm Steele who's one of Sebastian's four younger siblings and the president of their Entertainment Properties Division about her fitness center expanding into luxury resorts. We finish up our lengthy tête-à-tête, trading stories about the men in our lives. Then head to the next session where Starr will teach the attendees how to strengthen our cores with Pilates.

After a delicious dinner of native fish prepared with savory Fijian flavors, I retreat from the retreat. I stretch out in the sunken tub on my villa's veranda to soak my sore muscles from the exercises Starr and her instructors put me and the group through. For the first time in months, the aches are not from the rigors of having sex with Sebastian for hours.

It feels fantastic to lean back against the porcelain and let the fragrant essential oils amplified by the warmth of the water lull me into a peaceful state of bliss. The sounds of the ocean waves lapping against the rocky cliff are hypnotic. Finally, I let my mind drift into a meditative trance.

* * *

By the end of the soul-cleansing, mind-centering retreat, I'm back on track. I've stuck with my original plan to stay in New York as my base and will visit my Paris flagship and London boutique every few weeks or as needed. Once the LA construction starts, I'll go to the West Coast as often as necessary—the retail space is still undecided at this point.

The most important decision is that I will not let the situation with Sebastian change my mind about returning to my childhood home. I left it once before when I graduated from the Fashion Institute of Technology and moved to Paris. Since my parents died in a tragic car crash, New York was no longer home for me. My goal with the initial expansion was to buy an apartment in New York to split my time between there and the other cities. I will not allow the Sebastian fiasco to deter me.

Therefore, I took time before leaving to make some very necessary arrangements to prepare for my return. The realtor, Robin Sanchez-Waghorn—who helped me to find the Sutton Place penthouse of my dreams that unfortunately fell through—has arranged a rental apartment. Hopefully, I'll stay for only two months until she can help me find a permanent place. Blair Thomas, my New York assistant, has already moved our offices from The STEELE Tower's executive floor to the third floor of our New York boutique. After we signed the deal, Sebastian had arranged for me to be close, but not distractingly so as he stated. Thankfully, Blair also moved my things out of Sebastian's penthouse and into the rental, leaving the keys with the building's concierge. Now, I'm all set for my new decade of Independent Woman.

RAWR!

SEBASTIAN

Two Weeks Prior

Damn, I miss Lola. These past few weeks leading up to the openings of her New York and Las Vegas boutiques have been hectic for her. Suddenly having to stay an extra week in Vegas to wrap up some issues added to her schedule. I understand and respect her determination to grow her company. Hell, I'm no different with my focus on replacing my father as the CEO of STEELE International next year. But I still miss my Petite Seductress.

Who would have thought the self-proclaimed playboy would end up in an instant, living-together relationship with a woman whom he can see spending the rest of his life?

I preferred one night only. Perhaps two if the woman wasn't clingy or a gold digger. But only two fucks, enough time to satisfy my Dom needs and physical release for the moment. Only a short-term encounter to balance out my business-focused life. If someone would have told me that four months ago, I would have told them they have the wrong guy. No. Way. No. How. Not. This. Guy.

Well… I'm lying in bed missing my baby and wanting to wrap myself around her curvy, sexy as fuck body. My dick is hard thinking about Lola. Rolling over, I let out an agonized groan when I see the time is only 11:30 p.m. and I've been in our big, empty bed for only half an hour. Fuck! I need to take a long, cold shower and jerk off my aching, weeping cock before it explodes from the pressure of being engorged. Maybe I should call Lola for some FaceTime sex. That would—

The ringing of the penthouse intercom interrupts my pathetic pity party. Who the hell would visit me at this hour, I wonder. I tick off in my head where my family could be other than in their penthouses on the fiftieth through fifty-seventh floors above and below mine. My parents are on holiday at their Italian Rivera villa in Positano; Malcolm is at STEELE St. Barth's to review logistics for the second Jackson Hole at STEELE Resorts beach club project; Roger isn't in the city, rather at his flat in Paris where he spends around eighty percent of his time; the twins Harris and Haley are downstairs in their respective penthouses. Besides, to reach me all they'd have to do is take our private elevator and not go through the lobby. So, I pray that it's merely a late-night visitor and not some unwanted news.

"Steele," I answer as I slip into a pair of sweatpants so as not to greet them naked.

"Mr. Steele, this is Blake the concierge. I apologize for the late call, but there's a woman here demanding access to your penthouse."

In the background, I hear a woman yelling, sounding belligerent towards a security staff member before the concierge moves away from the disruptive scene. He continues in a lowered voice.

"Excuse me, Mr. Steele. The woman appears highly

intoxicated and her behavior is erratic. Would you like us to call the police or escort her off of the property?"

I have to think who the hell it could be since Lola is in Vegas and The Tower's residential and commercial staff know her. Suddenly, I hear the woman screech her name. Fuck me, it's Lydie Jackson.

My mind goes into overdrive. Despite assuring me she understood we could never have an intimate rapport and Lola is my girlfriend, Lydie's gone on an obvious bender. Drunk off her ass if the commotion is any sign of her state.

We're only family friends and I'm her confidante. Damn, her younger brother Lachlan is my best friend. Now Lydie is in the lobby at this late hour to speak with me. Knowing I can't let her carry on nor do I trust her to go home and stay if my driver took her, I have to let her come up. I'll put her in a guest suite and deal with her in the morning once she's sobered up. Thank God Lola isn't home, or she'd have my balls and I'd have two emotional women on my hands. Damn.

"Thank you, Blake. I will handle the situation. Please escort Ms. Jackson to the family's private elevator and enter the code for my first floor," I tell him.

"Yes, sir, right away. Good night, Mr. Steele," Blake responds.

I take the stairs down and turn on the lights for that floor and start the coffee machine in the kitchen. The voice-controlled virtual assistant that Haley designed—the little techie nerd—handles the tasks. Then, I head to the front door to await the screaming banshee.

As soon as the elevator doors open onto the foyer outside of my duplex, I can smell the liquor rolling off of Lydie in waves. She's in a complete state of dishevelment. Her mussed hair tangled with knots as though she had been running her fingers through it or pulling it out. Makeup smeared around her eyes gives her the look of a raccoon. Black streaks of mascara from crying coupled with her puffy and red face attest to her despair. What appears to be an entire bottle of Scotch stains her light green dress. I notice the broken high heel of her shoe as she limps unevenly, staggering towards me.

"Sssebbieee."

She sing-songs, her arms reaching out to me as she stumbles across the tile floor. I cannot believe this is the polished, well-kept, in control woman who is the overall vice president of Jackson Corporation and who garners the utmost respect from hard-as-nails titans. Lydie is a total mess.

I'm shocked speechless and surprised as she jumps and wraps her legs around my torso. I have no choice but to catch her and hold her under her ass as I stagger backwards from the unexpected collision.

"Arrre youu feeeelinggg meee up, Sssebbieee?" Lydie cackles before leaning down to bring her lips to mine as she humps her pussy against my stomach.

I nearly drop her on her ass—feeling her up. Fuck no!

Without answering her, I put her back on her feet. As she slides to the ground, I grip her elbow. I really don't need this shit, but I have a responsibility to take care of her in this inebriated state. I lead her to the kitchen and settle her at the banquette—she'd fall on her face if I put her on the stool at the breakfast bar. After, I walk to the coffee machine to reverse the drunkenness with two cups of strong espresso or more. On my way back to her, I grab some crackers from the pantry. All the while, I ignore her singing at the top of her voice about her love for me à la Beyoncé.

Yeah, I think to myself, Lydie is crazy right now and Lola

would definitely lose her shit. With a sigh, I unwind Lydie's fingers from my wrist as I set the cups and the box of crackers on the table in front of her. I have to get her to consume this stuff and get sober really quickly.

"Lydie"—I start, suddenly pulling away as she grapples with the drawstring of my sweats—"You need to drink this and here, have a cracker. Cut it out right now!"

"BUT I LOOOVE YOUUUU, SSSEBBIEEE!" She wails loud enough to hurt my ears.

This situation has to get under control now. So, I switch to Dom and not a friend.

"Listen, Lydie, right now you will drink this espresso, both cups and if necessary more, and eat some crackers. After you finish, we are going upstairs to get you cleaned up and in bed—"

"Ooohhh, Sssebbieee, let's go to bed, right now!" Lydie makes a grab for my hand, but I move away in time.

I press the espresso cup to her lips and command her to drink. After what has to be an eternity, but the kitchen clock only shows half past midnight, Lydie is functional and we go upstairs. I leave her in a suite and rush to my bedroom to get a T-shirt for her to wear. Fortunately, she's in the shower when I return, so I leave the t-shirt on the bed and wait in the separate lounge. Shortly, Lydie appears looking chastened, but teary, and I motion for her to sit on the sofa while I stay in the chair opposite. With a nod of her head, she humbly agrees. We have to clear this shit up once and for all.

"Lydie—" I start, but she lifts her palm up to interrupt me.

"Sebastian, I have to apologize for my behavior. I… I had a rough day with my dad. You know the usual, proving myself to him and dodging merger marriage demands. I… I needed to take the edge off, but had too much to drink instead."

She looks down at her hands she's wringing in her lap. With a deep breath, she continues, "I'll rest until the morning and go home. That is, if you don't mind."

I will not force the issue since she looks remorseful, and it's late. So I stand and walk with her to the bedroom. Once she's settled against the pillows, I sit beside her on the rumpled bed. I stroke her face to wipe the tears from her eyes—I can't stand to see a woman cry or show such hurt, especially Lydie. I feel bad because I wonder if I led her on over the years since we've been close. I have to reassure her and let her know that I care and understand about her deal with getting her father's approval despite her happiness. It's important to me she knows that and I will support her in any way other than as the business-merger marriage that her father is insisting of her.

"Lydie, again, I want to be clear I apologize if I ever led you to believe that we could be more than friends. We cannot. Lola and I are a couple. Understand those two things. However, your happiness is a top priority for me and I will do anything to make it happen—"

A noise from outside of the room stops me and I walk over to the door, not sure whether I misheard. I hear Lydie scamper out of the bed and follow me into the hall since I see nothing in the lounge. Funny, it smells like Lola's perfume. I sniff deeper and shake my head, realizing that I miss her so much that I'm imagining her here now. I turn back to Lydie who I didn't realize was directly behind me and I bump into her. I reach out to steady her by holding her waist as I lead her to the bedroom.

"I see nothing. We must have misheard a noise… Let's get back to the bedroom."

Still a bit unbalanced, Lydie leans heavily into my side and I guide her back to bed where she slips in and I turn off the light.

As I walk back to my bedroom in the opposite wing, I swear I can still smell Lola's alluring perfume in the hallway. My ache for her increases tenfold, as though her perfume is a trigger for my arousal. Fortunately, she'll be home the day after tomorrow. So I'll get my fix of her body and the light she brings into my life that changed me from a playboy to a one-woman, or rather one-Lola man.

* * *

WHO WOULD HAVE GUESSED two weeks later after returning from Las Vegas, Lola would move out of our penthouse into a rental way across town somewhere and move her office from the suite on the executive floor of STEELE's headquarters to the third floor of her New York boutique?

Fuck, not me.

Well, she did and I can't even believe this shit. I should have known something was up when I called her the day after Lydie left my duplex and Lola didn't answer my calls or my text messages. It got to where I contacted Luc—I was desperate—and he told me he and Lola were in back-to-back meetings all day. Even though that niggled at the back of my mind since Lola always texted me back, I let it go. The day turned to night. Still no response. I told my flight crew to set a plan to fly out there so I could see for myself what the hell was going on. I stepped into the lobby to get into the car for the airport and stopped in my tracks. Lola sent a text she was busy all day and going to bed. I found it odd that she texted and not called. On top of that, her text was bland with none of her usual smiley faces or xoxo. Now, I know.

She broke up with me out of the blue. Un-fucking-believable!

There I was pining away for Lola like a wuss and she dumps me with no hint of an issue. After the Vegas opening, I surprised her with a trip to Cabo San Lucas. A treat to unwind by the beach, drink Honey Bees, and get lost in each other with no distractions for a week. Unfortunately, she told me she had to stay in Vegas to wrap up some loose ends and that she was sorry she forgot to tell me.

So being the understanding boyfriend, I stayed two extra days to offer her my support. Yeah, she made up for botching my plans by treating me to a spa day with a mind-blowing happy ending. Lola played my masseuse, and I was her client with a stiff dick in need of her special rubbing.

After those two days, I fly home. Three days of missing my girl later, Lola texted me: she needs time on her own since she's been with me immediately upon arriving in New York; she feels she's losing herself jumping into a relationship with me so quickly; we should take a break and not be exclusive.

Not. Be. Exclusive. What the fuck does that mean?

Now, I'm sitting in Aquavit waiting for Lola to get here. She has to explain what changed her mind in three days from her kissing me and telling me she'll hurry home as soon as she can to bye-bye sucker.

At first I didn't know her location: Vegas or New York or on the moon. I finally persuaded her to tell me, and when she said that she'd been here for two days, I lost it.

We argued. She hung. I called back. I left voicemails. I sent text messages. Finally, she responded that we could meet today. But she refused to come to the penthouse, nor did she want to meet for dinner. Instead, it's lunch and now she's late.

It reminds me of our first night together at LEVELS. When we knew who we were as opposed to our initial first-time meeting as strangers doing a D/s scene together the night before her meeting with me for Lola's Coterie. I sat at the bar in the Cellar waiting as anxiously for her arrival, hoping that she showed up as I am now. And there she is, walking in the restaurant. Finally.

Lola is gorgeous and I feel my chest constrict when I think of us being apart after being together almost every day for four months. I was getting settled into our routine and WHAM. I watch as she makes her way to me. I can't take my eyes off of her. I want to pull her into my arms and never let her go. With a sigh, I stand when she's closer to the table to greet her.

"Hi," I start, surprised at the hitch in my usually dominant voice. "How are you?" I ask as I bend down to kiss her lips, aching to connect with her skin to skin.

She turns her head slightly so that my lips brush her cheek, then responds, "I'm good. How are you?"

So it's like that.

"I will not lie and say that I'm good—"

"Are you calling me a liar?" Lola demands, scowling up at me as she stops sitting in the chair I pulled out for her.

"Whoa, babe"—I raise my hands palms forward in defense—"I would never call you a liar. I am not good. I miss you and want to make things right between us, again. I'm confused. What happened in the three days that we were apart?" I continue as I take my seat opposite her.

Lola takes her time placing the linen napkin on her lap before looking at me. I can see her hazel eyes are shiny from unshed tears. But she blinks them away and lifts her chin, a determined expression replacing the moment of sadness.

"Like I said in my text and on the phone, I let myself get swept up and need time to refocus on me. I'll be thirty in two weeks and I promised myself that I would not depend on a man—"

I cut her off to ask if this is about her being a sub to my Dom and her struggle with letting go. She admits that's part of the problem. I remind her it's her choice and that she's the one with the power in our D/s relationship. I also tell her we can step back from it if that would make her feel more comfortable about our relationship. I will do whatever it takes to make us work. We go back and forth some more, not bothering to eat the food that we ordered—it's all tasteless to me and she struggles to eat hers, too.

After too short a period, I sit back in my chair as I watch the woman of my dreams walk out of my life.

SEBASTIAN

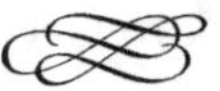

"Oh, so are we back to this again so soon, Steele?"

Whack!

"What the fuck is in your *bashka, kiska?*"

Bam bam!

"Do you need me to beat it out of your *zhopa*?"

Whack! Bam bam bam!

Thunders my personal trainer and former MMA champion Borya *The War Defender* Alexeyev as he knocks my distracted ass around the mat. We're sparring in the full gym on the first floor of my penthouse duplex.

Yeah, that pretty much sums it up. We're back to working out at five in the morning before I head to the office a few floors below. Eleven is over since I no longer have Lola to roll around in our bed each morning. Either to satisfy my morning wood in her always-wet-for-me sweet pussy or waking her up with a toe-curling climax from eating her honey like a starving bear. Hopefully sparring with the giant Russian will knock some sense into me after almost two weeks of moping around or snapping at everyone. My concentration has gone to shit.

I zap back to attention when one of Borya's massive fists connects with my right flank, sending me reeling in the opposite direction, nearly off of the mat. Fuck! That hurt. I give my head a firm shake as I rub my side with my wrapped hand; I turn back to face the giant.

"Fuck you, Alexeyev! Is that the best you have for me, *kiska*?" I challenge, then go at him with a series of well-placed punches followed by a quick roundhouse kick.

"*Da*, much better, Steele. Guess you aren't getting any more of that *sladkaya kiska*! What have I told you before? Be here or go jerk off. No room on this mat for *zhopas*! Meow. Meow."

That gets my head on straight. I see red pissed he's right about me not getting any more of Lola's sweet pussy and her dumping me fucking with my capacity to function for work and life. Like hell if I'll let her craziness distract me from my duties and responsibilities to STEELE's growth and derailing me from my CEO path. If Lola wants to stay apart and deny what we had was good, then fuck it. I have to move on, too. With that in mind, Borya and I finish the rest of the session like two bulls facing off during rutting season. Game on!

* * *

"Hey, man. What's been eating your ass these last couple of weeks?"

My youngest brother Harris asks me as we're sitting in my office with Haley going over a new security protocol that they want to implement across all the STEELE divisions.

"Oh, leave him alone, nosy! If he wanted to tell you, he would," Haley admonishes with a scowl as she pushes her glasses back onto the bridge of her nose.

The twins are the youngest of the Steele clan and a double surprise for our parents, who had not planned on having more children. Then a twofer to boot. Roger is three years older and had been the baby of the family until Harris and Haley popped up—Harris older by mere minutes.

Although fraternal, they share a similar love of technology with Haley being a hacker and Harris a coder. We tease them for being nerds, but they're wizzes at what they do, which led to the approval for them to create a new subsidiary STEELE Technology and Cyber Security. As co-heads, they're responsible for all of STEELE and external clients from around the globe, including Jackson Corporation. They're smart as fuck and we've grown to depend upon them, even if they're now the babies.

Haley is a shy beauty who I can remember used to follow Lachlan and me around like a little stray puppy until she was in her gawky teens. Her looks—like Harris'—match the rest of us with jet black hair. Hers hangs mid-back in a silky curtain. Our signature gray eyes in her are soulful, set in her heart-shaped face with cheeks that display dimples when she smiles or laughs. Unlike now, since she's frowning in consternation at her twin.

Harris who couldn't care less that Haley does not approve of his questioning behavior rises from the conference table to stretch his much taller frame. At six feet, one inch, he's got five inches on his twin. He runs his hand through his short hair, then strides to the mini refrigerator below the drinks cabinet on the opposite wall.

"Anyone wants a bottle of water or something stronger,

eh Baz?" He teases squatting down to pull one out for himself.

"Yeah, I'll only have a water, thank you very much," I respond.

I ignore the rib, grateful for the slight change in subject as I'm not eager to discuss my love life with my younger siblings.

The thought of calling the relationship that I had with Lola my love life gives me pause, and I wonder whether I love her. The more that I think about it, I'm certain that I care for her deeply and could see it growing into love easily. But… Oh well, she's squashed that with the heel of one of fuck-me sandals.

"Seriously, Baz, either you're looking like a lost puppy or you're biting everybody's heads off. I mean it, you're a mess." Harris continues ignoring Haley's loud sigh as he passes both of us a bottle.

I take my time to unscrew the cap, then swallow before I respond. We're a tight-knit family, so I'm not ashamed to admit what happened to him.

"Lola ended things almost two weeks ago out of the blue and it sent me for a loop," I confess.

Then take another sip of water and stare out of the floor-to-ceiling windows. The city stretches before me with unobstructed views of the Hudson River to the west, the East River opposite, and Manhattan to the south from Midtown to Battery Park. It's a sunny, cloudless day, so the vista is breathtaking from the forty-ninth floor of The STEELE Tower.

I get lost in thought for a moment until I hear Haley cough softly to get my attention. I return my gaze to the Dynamic Duo as we nicknamed them and smile brightly. I'm the eldest, so I want to project positivity and the ability to move past problems to my siblings. I feel responsible for them as their leader, both as big brother and as future CEO.

"So, after Borya knocked some sense into my wussy ass during our training session this morning, I'm back on track!" I tell them, slapping my palms on the table in front of me and leaning forward to look them directly in their eyes. "Now, tell me more about your latest brilliant scheme to save the corporate world from black hats."

* * *

LATER THAT NIGHT while I sit alone at the breakfast bar in my large, family style kitchen eating Indian food that I had delivered, I let my mind roam. Pre-Lola I went to LEVELS to satisfy my need to eat dinner at Level 4 Restaurant, fuck away the stress of the day, and to flex my Dom proclivities.

Now, I can acknowledge my relationship with Lola opened my eyes to me not wanting to return to my previous playboy ways of fuck 'em and leave 'em. As crude as that may appear, I was always respectful to the women, and the encounters were always consensual. I always made certain to fulfill their needs before my release—a part of my fetish.

Being in an exclusive—albeit short-lived—relationship made me realize that I'm at a point in my life where I can successfully dedicate my time to work and a woman. Neither has to suffer from lack of my attention. I'm reminded of the conversation that I had with my college roommate from Harvard right before his wedding.

"I get it Baz, and you can tease me for turning from a playboy to a soon-to-be married man. But I'll tell you now that when the right woman comes along, the one who's worth it, she'll change your mind like Lauren changed mine."

I laugh and finish putting my platinum cuff links on while I walk over to the valet for the jacket of my morning suit.

"Scott, man, you are nuts! Whatever you say, that won't be me anytime soon. I have an empire to grow and to lead—sort of what you're supposed to do with your family's business. Remember, hint, hint. No time for a relationship that will detract me from my goals."

Fast forward seven months and here I sit admitting that I want more and that Lola is the woman for me, just like Scott predicted. Sure, I'll give her some time. But I'm not giving up on us or our future together. I snagged her the first time with an offer that she couldn't refuse, and I'll reel her in again.

LOLA

"Lola, you have a delivery."

I look up from my computer monitor to see Blair standing in the doorway to my office on the third floor of Lola's Coterie New York. In the arms of the deliveryman is the largest bouquet of roses I've ever seen in my life. Not just your typical red roses, rather stunning lavender with silver highlights. The incredible scent of a sweet and citrusy fragrance wafts into the room.

Caught by surprise, I'm slow to ask him to place the laden vase on the conference table. So, of his own volition, he moves to it and places them in the center with a grateful sigh. Shaking his arms out as he walks to me, he withdraws a white envelope of fine linen stationary from his messenger bag. He puts the note in my hand as I sit awestruck in my chair.

"Thank you," I tell him and reach into my drawer for my wallet to give him a sizable tip.

"No, ma'am," he says shaking his head and walking backwards. "The sender already provided the tip. Enjoy your flowers!"

He turns on his heels and walks out of the door. Blair slowly leaves my office, gazing lovingly at the exceptional display of rare roses. I get up from my desk to stand beside their beauty as I open the envelope.

My Dearest Lola,

You enchant me. It was love at first sight where you enraptured me with feelings of love and adoration. I will give you time to yourself, only because you requested it. But know that you are mine and I am yours forever.

These fifty Sterling Silver Roses symbolize my love for you knows no bounds. I will never let you go. We belong together. I intend to make you face the truth and punish you soundly for your transgressions.

Your love forever,
Baz

I crumble to my knees and bow my head, overwhelmed by my former lover's declaration. It's unexpected and I have no defense against it. I love him, too. If he were here at this moment, I could not protect my heart from Baz—damn Lydie.

I love this man, so it seems as much as he loves me. As Leonie says it's a *coup de foudre*—a stroke of lightning love at first sight. I stand and bend over the gorgeous bouquet to take a whiff of the fragrant flowers. I grip the edge of the table to maintain my balance. My eyes close as I remember our intense love affair as if it were yesterday, and we never parted.

The sound of my mobile ringing pulls me from my memories. With a sad exhalation, I head to my desk to answer the call.

"Hey, what's going on with you? You have answered none of my calls and texts!"

Speak of Leonie and she appears. I take a seat back behind my desk and gaze longingly at the roses before I answer her questions.

"Sebastian just sent the most extraordinary bouquet of silvery lavender roses with a note of his love for me," I answer.

I finger the card with his bold monogram in gray displayed on it. Then, bring it to my nose when I detect a trace of his sexy cologne, Creed Aventus. The iconic name derived from ventus the wind. Illustrating the Aventus man as destined to live a driven life. Ever galloping with the wind at his back toward success. The scent of bergamot, patchouli, musk, and vanilla tantalizes my nostrils and makes my pussy contract. I miss my lover.

"Oh, la la! What a fancy one!" Leonie laughs. "Will you give him another chance?"

I detect the note of sadness in her voice. Undoubtedly, she's thinking about her ill-fated romance with Sebastian's younger brother Roger. They, too, were a *coup de foudre.* Or so Leonie thought until Roger's demanding ways made her break free of him before it entangled them for too long. At least theirs was a fast break. Yet just as painful as I sense from the tone of her voice.

"No, I need to make my way and cannot afford to let him distract me, again. Besides, he has Lydie to make him feel better," I finish as I toss the note into the bottom drawer of my desk. I shut it with a decisive bang and return my attention to my best friend.

"Tell me what you've been up to these days. What's going on with you and Giovanni?" I ask to distract her from my melancholy love life. I think she and Roger make a better couple. But judging from the state of my relationship, I'm not the best judge of romance.

"Bof," Leonie scoffs. "He's in Paris and I'm in Milan for the shows. After Las Vegas, he told me he had to get back to his gallery to handle some business. Only, I see him on social media, all over the Internet hugging another woman. Men!" She huffs and continues on a stream of why she will never date again.

I can relate to her sentiment, as I also vowed to avoid those complications. But, as my gaze wanders to the lavish crystal vase, I can't deny the flutter in my heart that still happens when I think of Baz and what we shared. It may have been brief, but it was soul changing. As Leonie continues, I let myself drift to what should have happened upon my return to New York City from Las Vegas.

WITHOUT TURNING THE LIGHTS ON, I strip and crawl onto the mattress to straddle Baz as he sleeps contentedly on my side of the big bed hugging my pillow close. His beautiful face is lit by the moonlight as I gaze lovingly at him.

Gently placing my palm on his face covered in stubble, he sighs and rubs his cheek against my hand, the murmur of my name falling from his parted lips. My heart skips a beat. He's gorgeous and all mine.

"Baz, baby, I missed you so much," I whisper huskily in his ear.

The tips of my peaked nipples brush against his bare chest and cause me to shiver in anticipation of this man deep inside of me, our bodies bonding into one. Beneath me, I feel his thick shaft come to life as it grows in response to the heat of my hot, wet core eager to encase him. With a groan, Baz reaches for me, his large hands grip my hips to hold me steady. He raises his pelvis to grind his burgeoning shaft against my dripping pussy lips. I cry out and press back against him, the thin cotton of his sleep shorts not much of a barrier for our combined heat.

"Lola," he groans, thrusting up and holding me tight.

"Baz," I respond in a passionate whimper, grinding against his lengthening ten-inch dick. "I missed you so much, baby. It's so good to be home with you."

Sebastian's gray eyes fly open as he realizes this encounter is not a dream, but the real deal. Without hesitation, he easily flips us, putting his muscular body on top of my curvy one, his hips already beginning to piston against my fiery core. His Dom coming to the forefront to take control of our lovemaking.

I open my thighs wider to give him better access and lock my ankles together against his tight ass, encouraging him to drive into me. One of his hands slides between our fevered bodies to tease my engorged clit. Baz uses the other to yank his shorts past his hips, then grips his massive cock in preparation to impale me with it.

With a satisfied mewl, I throw my head back and close my eyes when his tip breeches my pussy lips. He pumps unabashedly into me, skin-on-skin. Our cries of mutual satisfaction fill our bedroom as we chase our climaxes.

Fuck, I missed my man so much. He feels so good inside of me. His guttural growls of pleasure turn me into one of Pavlov's dogs as my body responds to his—

"ARE YOU EVEN LISTENING TO ME?" Leonie's roar breaks through my reverie.

Shit, I got so caught up that I missed most of her conversation. With a contrite tone, I apologize to her and ask that she repeats herself as I promise to pay careful attention.

For the next ten minutes, I listen to Leonie and her concerns with Giovanni and Roger. Of the two, I prefer Roger, not because he's Sebastian's brother, but because Giovanni is not dependable and reappears in Leonie's life when he's in between women. Although I'm shocked to hear that he asked her to be exclusive and wants to make a go at a genuine relationship with her. Her hesitancy is because of her attraction to Roger.

He's an ass because he taunted her in Monte Carlo at the Grand Prixe after party chatting up another well-known supermodel. I promised Leonie that I wouldn't talk to Sebastian about it. But that didn't keep me from giving Roger my death glare. What's up with the Steele men? Assholes.

Since Leonie is heading to Hong Kong next, we plan to catch up on her way back to Paris with a stopover in New York for a few days. I'm psyched to see my best friend and vow to make our time together fun and free of the Steele brothers. We'll go clubbing at the new spot Butterfly that caters to the glitterati. Giovani will think twice about his frolicking when he spies Leonie dancing the night away with hunky celebrities. We won't go to LEVELS New York like we did the last time we were together in the city. After we chat some more about fashion gossip, we end our call and I return to work.

* * *

IT'S BEEN a week and aside from the roses, I haven't seen nor heard from Sebastian. I guess he meant what he wrote in his note, that he would give me some time to myself. Just as well. Since at that moment, I was so weak I would have run right back to him and moved into his penthouse again. Not going to happen. Especially since I have a dinner meeting with Patrick Rockett. The Dom that I met at LEVELS the night Sebastian and I were hooking up for the second time and whose company Rockett Construction is the competitor to STEELE International.

Part of me accepted his offer because I knew that it would piss Sebastian off and partly because I swore to live my life. Pat is an attractive Alpha male, so it's no hardship to spend the evening with him. With that in mind, I freshen up my makeup and tidy my form-fitting, red Roland Mouret stretch-crepe dress that features a gold zipper along the entire back. It hugs my curves and with my stilettos make me feel sexy.

Blair gives me a wolf whistle as I pass her desk on my way to the elevator.

"Go home! We've reviewed the upcoming projects each night. Enough! Have some fun. I know I will," I add with a wink.

"Will do! I'll head out in a moment," Blair replies.

I wonder if she and Luc are still going strong. It's been a while since I spoke with my mentor. I make a mental note to call him tomorrow. Tactfully, I'll ask about his status with Blair. Luc is such a gentleman, that I doubt he'll reveal much of his personal life to me. Sebastian always argued that Luc wanted more from his relationship with me than just being my benefactor turned second father figure. Inwardly, I roll my eyes as I slip inside of the Bentley Bentayga.

I smile at Stan, my New York driver. Then, chuckle to myself as I think of the many nights he drove me to my trysts with Sebastian at LEVELS. Now, he's taking me to dinner with Pat at L'Atelier de Joël Robuchon, the two

Michelin star restaurant at the Four Seasons Hotel New York. Oh my.

The bar area is lively as I make my way to Pat, who doesn't see me yet. His distraction with his mobile gives me the chance to observe him. He's a handsome man with a ruddy complexion, short red hair, and green eyes around six feet, three inches tall. Most intriguing about him is his sexy Scottish accent. If I hadn't met Sebastian first, Pat's charms could easily sway me.

The women near him try to catch his eye, but I don't feel a sense of jealousy as I would if he were Sebastian with hawks circling. With a devious glint in my eyes, I walk up to him and place my tiny palm on his massive chest—a reminder of his university rugby days. Damn, but he is fit. I give his pecs a squeeze and laugh softly when he jumps to his feet in surprise.

"Hey—" He starts before realizing it's me.

Pat's startled look fuels my mischief as I rub his chest more before tilting my cheek up for his kiss. Promptly, he responds as he wraps his brawny arms around my waist, lifting me to my toes to pull me close.

"Good evening, Mr. Rockett. Nice to see you," I murmur in his ear.

The women, who were only moments before ogling him, glare at me with their nostrils flared. I snicker to myself and move away from his tempting embrace. Again, he's not Baz, but I had to make myself feel better and ward off the wannabes angling for the Scottish billionaire.

"Aren't you a pretty sight, lass," Pat drawls, his accent thickened with his desire for me, his gaze caressing my body from head to toe.

With a coy smile, I respond, "Thank you. Shall we go to our table?"

"Och aye, briagha" Pat answers. The roles are reversed as his Dom replaces the startled gent, his green eyes sparkle impishly.

My pussy clenches and I lower my gaze submissively. To which a rumble in his chest emerges as a low growl. I lick my lips and press my thighs together, aching for relief I haven't had in weeks.

Pat grips my elbow and guides me to the maître d' another female who gawks at him before collecting herself. Her plump lips curve into a flirtatious smile as she leads us to our table in the center of the dining room. With his impressive physique and commanding presence, eyes follow us. I hold my head up high and gracefully sit in the chair that Pat pulls out for me.

Once we're settled and placed our order, I ask what business he wants to discuss with me.

"Ah, *leannan,* I want to finish what we started twice already, at the Cellar and the charity gala. Each time Steele rudely interrupted our dalliance. Now that you're a free woman, it's my chance to woo ye, lass."

I take a sip of my wine as I hedge for time. My mind going wild as I wonder what makes him think Sebastian and I aren't together anymore. I have told no one but Starr and Leonie. Visions of Sebastian doing a scene with another woman at LEVELS, on a date with some man-eater, or worse yet with Lydie makes my stomach flip. Could Pat have witnessed Sebastian's assignations?

Before I retch all over the pristine linen tablecloth, I excuse myself for a trip to the bathroom. In its relative safety, I can use the breathing techniques that Starr taught me. I need all the self-control that I can muster.

. . .

"WHAT... THE... FUCK... LOLA!"

I turn quickly, startled by the voice. A red-faced Sebastian stands in the doorway to the ladies' room. His fists clenched at his sides and his gray eyes shooting lethal daggers at me.

"What is it with you and bathrooms, Sebastian!" I say through clenched teeth.

I reference his invasion of the bathroom at my celebratory dinner at Per Se after we signed the expansion deal. This time, I won't let him have me. I will stand strong and not give in to his dominance. As much as I want him, I'm determined to safeguard my happiness more.

"What are you doing in a hotel with Rockett!" Sebastian yells back at me.

Da fuck!

How dare he insinuate that I'm meeting Pat for sex This man towering over me thinks so little of me and has no respect for me! He's the one running around with different women every night or his supposed family friend. Blatantly flaunting the fact that we're no longer together. I snap.

"How dare you!" I hiss, unable to contain my fury at his audacity.

Sebastian moves closer into my personal space. He boxes me in and lowers his head to glare into my eyes. I refuse to move back. Instead I stand my ground lifting my chin to return his steely glare. I won't be the first to speak.

"One more time... What... are... you... doing... in... a... hotel... with... Rocket?" Sebastian grits through his teeth, his breath hot on my face.

For a moment, I'm hypnotized by his dominance. I close my eyes to gather my strength to ward off his magnetism. Although my body aches to lean into him, I straighten my spine. Opening my eyes to once again meet his gaze.

"Whatever I'm doing is of no concern of yours"—I raise my hand to stop him from interrupting me—"You and I are not exclusive. Hell, we're not even a couple. So excuse me. I have a date waiting for me."

I push a gobsmacked Sebastian out of my way, but pause at the door.

"I could very well ask you the same question, Mr. Steele," I scoff with my perfectly arched eyebrow lifted accusingly.

The parting shot ricochets off the walls as we glower at one another in a heated silence. The air is thick with tension—whether lustful or loathsome is hard to decipher. My body is afire with anger and need for this man. We're on the edge, but not pleasurably.

When Sebastian opens his mouth to respond, I remain firm. I dismissively toss my hair over my shoulder. Without a backward glance, I open the door and leave him standing with his mouth agape. I will not give him the opportunity for a comeback.

My inner cheerleader is remorseful while my Independent Woman salutes. Me… My world rocked. Sadly, not enjoyably.

LOLA

Sweat drips down my spine, sending a shiver across my body as my feet relentlessly pound the treadmill at the swank fitness club near my apartment rental. The front and back of my Sweaty Betty Ultra Run sports bra drenched from my exertion lives up to its name. Fortunately, the black leggings camouflage and wick away the perspiration.

Every few minutes I alternate the pace or incline to maintain the burn in my muscles. Ten more minutes left in my grueling workout—my alternative form of release.

It's not quite subspace, but the rhythmic pulsations lull my mind into an active meditation. The drift happens, just not as sexually satisfying. The runner's high definitely doesn't compare to orgasmic euphoria.

I realize it wasn't the pain from the actual spanking that had thrilled me. Rather Sebastian's display of dominance that formed my need for him to possess me sexually. His power and control over me made my blood race directly to my core, engorging my clit and activating the muscles of my inner walls. The freedom from thinking for myself that allowed him to take over relaxed me.

The nerd in me researched why spanking enthralls me. According to the *Kama Sutra*'s "Blows and Sighs" chapter, spanking activates the lower chakras where sexual energy rests. The sensation moves through the entire spine like the flash of a lightning bolt. It's a way to release or awaken one's kundalini—sexual energy or chi. A spank or smack sends that chi up the spine from the root chakra, eliciting the chain reaction for a full-body orgasm.

After binge-reading the complete book—in between moments of self-induced release—I no longer feel guilty about my need for punishment and embrace my submissive desires. Even my Independent Woman approves. I won't go so far as a full-time D/s relationship, only during sex. Exactly what Sebastian and I had established and enjoyed.

Despite my revelation, I cannot go back to Sebastian. His cheating with Lydie is a nonstarter. He ruined any chance of us reigniting our passionate love affair. Yes, it is love for me. From the way he tenderly held me or the smoldering look in his gray eyes caressing my body. I sense he was on the cusp of loving me, too.

The cool-down ding from the treadmill ends my musings. My head is clear, ready for the day ahead.

* * *

"Blair, hey, you just poured a ton of sugar in your tea!" Billie exclaims, snagging the crystal bowl from her.

Blair mutters a curse as she moves the cup aside and rests her fingertips against her forehead. Silently, she shakes her head with her eyes closed.

"What's going on with you? I noticed you haven't been

yourself since I arrived yesterday. Do you want to talk about it?" A concerned Billie asks softly.

We're at Norma's in the Parker Meridien Hotel on Fifty-seventh Street, one block west of the boutique. I figured a change of scenery for a breakfast meeting would be nice since Billie is in town. Really, I wanted to avoid bumping into Sebastian. Three times since his latest bathroom invasion is more than enough. I'm way too weak now that I've admitted my sexual preference. But smart enough to not put myself in that devil's path.

"Billie is right. You've been distracted for a few days now," I chime in.

Blair peeks at us through her fingertips before she lifts her head with a sigh.

"I'm so sorry, Lola, for letting my personal life interfere with my work—"

I raise my hand to stop Blair as I shake my head to assure her she has nothing to be sorry about. Everyone has their moments and my company is not strict where staff can't be human. Hell, my head has been in the clouds for a while. Hypercritical much?

"I'm not sure if I should discuss it with you… It's about Luc… and me," Blair pauses, raising a cautious gaze to me.

Not surprised in the least. The pair have spent a lot of time together outside of the office since we arrived in New York. Their outings to the ballet, dinners with Luc's New York associates confirmed my suspicions months ago. Luc is too much of a gentleman to discuss his private affairs, so I've only hinted at him and Blair as a couple. Each time, he changed the subject. Until now, Blair hadn't mentioned it other than to ask to leave the office early occasionally.

I place a reassuring hand on her forearm and squeeze.

"Luc is like a father to me. His well-being is of the

utmost importance. However, I am a woman and know what it's like to need to talk to a friend about my love life," I smile, pleased when her eyes shine in relief.

The three of us exchange stories as we enjoy fluffy omelets and scrumptious pancakes—at least I went for a run this morning.

Luc and Blair are not officially a couple, but they've made out a few times. He's hesitant since she's seventeen years younger than him. Plus, she's the daughter of his friend who asked Luc to help her find a job.

He recommended Blair as an assistant three years ago. She was interested in fashion and not her family's manufacturing business. I was trying to handle all aspects of my company despite Luc's advice to focus on the creative design side and let an assistant handle the day-to-day tasks. After a one-month trial period, Blair proved herself to be efficient, dependable, and clever when balancing the activities that didn't need my constant or immediate attention. Blair is a valued member of my team, so I advise her to give him time.

Billie laments being single and wants a man who's a powerful match to her feisty, independent self. Someone as she says who has cojones—she's a Southern belle, not a wilting flower. Her last boyfriend only wanted the petite, brown-skinned beauty as a trophy on his arm she shares. Her big green eyes darkens with disgust.

I'm tempted to tell Billie to come with me as my guest to LEVELS New York so she can experience a Dom. Despite the concrete nondisclosure agreements they signed, I'm not revealing that part of my private life to my employees. Instead, I assure her that the man of her dreams is out there waiting for her.

My mobile chirps with a text message from Leonie. She's

landed and headed to my apartment rental. I remind her the concierge has the spare key for her. As I hit send, a marvelous idea pops into my head: Girls' Night Out!

* * *

"THIS MUSIC IS PUMPING! I'm hitting the dance floor to shake my thing," a tipsy Billie announces after she applies gloss to her pouty lips.

She along with Leonie, Blair, and I sip Whiskey Sours and Manhattans gathered around our VIP booth at the opening night for the exclusive club Butterfly. I promised my girls a fun night to boot our not so titillating love lives squarely in the rear.

My gaze roams around the opulent club full of the glitterati. Celebrities, socialites, fashionistas, and billionaire tycoons wear their sexiest, most revealing outfits. Bottles of top-shelf liquor and magnums of champagne sit atop the tables in booths like ours.

Partiers pack the dance floor with their booty shaking as they grind and gyrate to the DJ's booming tunes. Those not fortunate to have a booth stand two deep at the three bars or perch on stools at high-top tables surrounding the dance floor.

"Hold on," I shout over the music to Billie. "I'm coming with you!"

We weave through the crowd as the heady scent of various perfumes and colognes mixed with sweat assails our nostrils the closer we get to the dancers. I love it! The sensuous, undulating sea of bodies calls me to revel with them.

Billie and I make quite the sight as we dance in the middle of the crowd. Billie in a glittering sea-green sequin tank dress that skims the tops of her thighs. Her ample bust nearly spilling over the top as she raises her arms overhead. She draws appreciative stares from the drop-dead gorgeous guys closing in on us as she seductively shimmies to the beat.

I match her moves with some of my own as I drop it low. The silver spangles of my fitted, strapless mini dress catch the LEDs like a spotlight. My shoulders shake as I rock back up to stand tall in my strappy sandals. Lost in the beat, I jump when brawny hands grip my hips to pull me against a massive chest. Trapped in the man's hands, I can only peer over my shoulder to see his face. Patrick Rockett. Damn.

"Aye, *leannan*, damn is correct," he rumbles in my ear. "You are a siren in your itty-bitty dress."

His warm breath sends goosebumps to the surface of my feverish skin. The sensation of his thick dick grinding into my ass as his grip tightens on my hips nearly causes me to swoon. Whether it's the cocktails or the heat, I have the sudden desire for the man in whose embrace I shiver to be —Sebastian. I shake my head at Patrick as I pull away from him. He's a Dom, but a well-bred man first. Patrick lets me go without argument.

"Hey, handsome! Who are you?" Billie's accent is as thick as Patrick's accent.

Her eyes sparkle in delight as her gaze slides over the burly billionaire. My surprised gaze lifts to Patrick, who towers over Billie and me. I notice his nostrils flare and his emerald eyes darken in lust for the petite vamp. Obviously, her siren's song is more appealing than mine, I laugh. Patrick slips his muscular arms around her tiny waist, lifting her from the floor as their hips slowly move despite the music's upbeat tempo. I won't need to invite Billie to

LEVELS. She's found her Dom with very enormous cojones. To that, I can attest.

Leonie and Blair drag me back to the dance floor just as I step off. Our shenanigans and laughter save me from asking Stan to drive me to Sebastian's penthouse pronto. Those thoughts fade away as more attractive albeit drooling guys pivot towards us. *The Lion* is on the loose and I will have fun!

LOLA

"I can't believe it's almost three months since I broke up with Roger," Leonie sighs as we stare at photos of him looking extraordinarily suave in a bespoke tuxedo.

Last night while we lived it up at Butterfly, he attended a charity gala with a stunning raven-haired heiress clinging to his biceps. His intense gray eyes captivate you, drawing you in even though it's only his two-dimensional image.

In another shot, despite her gaze of adoration as she presses her palm against his broad chest, Roger remains coolly aloof. His icy stare unchanged by her intimate touch.

I recall his stoic demeanor during my initial meeting with STEELE. His expression revealed no emotion, even when Leonie and the other models sashayed around the conference room in skimpy lingerie. His intense gaze redoubled.

However, that standoffish persona vanished proven when Sebastian and I witnessed Roger and Leonie at The STEELE Tower. The morning after dinner at Per Se, he carried her onto the family's residential elevator. Their long limbs tangled as their lips locked in an amorous kiss. Only Sebastian's discreet cough stopped Roger from hiking Leonie's leg around his hip as he thrust his pelvis into hers.

When he's with Leonie, the distant man changes into a fiery lover whose electricity sends shock waves through the enamored bombshell. A smoking hot couple whose flame burned out too quickly for either to come to terms. Which explains Leonie's sullen mood shift as she continues to scroll through the gossip website.

"She's the woman he wants," Leonie frowns disapprovingly as she mimics Roger's baritone voice. "A 'serious-minded partner' and not a 'wayward woman who cannot stay focused for over five minutes!'"

I hold my breath, not sure if the giggle I'm suppressing is inappropriate until Leonie bursts out in raucous guffaws. Gleeful tears trickle from the corners of her glowing amber eyes.

We cut our laughter short when the next photo pops up. Lydie stands beside the heiress; Sebastian and Roger flank them. The caption informs the viewer Sebastian and Roger are two of the world's eligible billionaires. Along with their brothers Malcolm and Harris, they're pronounced The STEELE Quaternity.

The amused tears turn tragic as Leonie and I wail over our former lovers. The fun lasted less than twelve hours.

"See I told you Sebastian lied to me the entire time we were together!" I screech in frustration. "Family friend, my ass! That bastard was fucking her for sure! That asshole jerk—"

I stalk around the living room, anger escalating. Last night I was so close to giving in to his charms. The "we belong together," his possessive Captain Caveman antics at the Four Seasons, memories of his enormous cock pounding into me had me ready to give in… again.

"No!" I slap my palm on the table so hard Leonie's iPad lifts and she jumps. "The STEELE Quaternity my ass! The Controlling Cads is more like it."

Leonie gives me a high five. "Giovanni the scoundrel, too. None of them are good enough for us, *Chérie. Tous les mecs sont des cons!*"

True, they're all assholes. We deserve better than what they offer.

The ring of my mobile interrupts our man-bashing tirade. I'm surprised to read Robin Sanchez-Waghorn's name on the display. I answer, curious what the realtor has to tell me so early on a Saturday morning. My curiosity turns to elation when she delivers monumental news. The Sutton Place penthouse is back on the market. The owner asked if I'm still interested, they re-accept my original offer plus an immediate close. Without hesitation I tell Robin to get the paperwork ready, I want to take ownership by end of day on Monday. We end the call with plans to meet at the penthouse to show Leonie this afternoon.

"Congratulations, *Chérie!*" Leonie exclaims as we jubilantly dance around the soon-to-be-empty rental.

"THE VIEW IS SPECTACULAR, Lola! You can sit on the terrace and sip tea as the sun rises or end the day with a glass of Chardonnay."

I agree with Leonie. The view of the East River sealed the deal since it reminds me of the one I had from my family's apartment further north of Fifty-seventh Street. The familiarity comforts me. It lessens the pain of the unexpected loss of my parents when they died two months shy of my eighteenth birthday. I envision myself just as Leonie described. The first night, I'll toast my parents and my return home.

The sunny, spacious penthouse in a magnificent, Rosario Candela designed building is by far my favorite of all the others Robin selected to meet my needs. It's exactly what I'm looking for in my new home. The proximity to the boutique is a bonus. A seven-block drive across Fifty-seventh Street from Sutton Place to Fifth Avenue and I'll be at the office. Sure, the crosstown traffic is daunting, but it's still a quick commute.

"You know, since you have your final project for your interior design degree, I want you to do my apartment!"

After more than sixteen years as a successful supermodel, Leonie is in her last semester at the Paris American Academy. The years of staying in remarkable homes and hotels sparked her interest in residential design. With her desire to look beyond the catwalk, Leonie chose a path that remains a part of the creative end of business. Her taste and style are perfect for her new career.

"Oh, Chérie! Merci beaucoup pour votre gentillesse..."

Overwhelmed, Leonie's eyes fill with tears. As we embrace, I join her knowing we cry not just for happiness. But in addition to the emotions roiling in our minds about the men we love.

* * *

FORGET CLOUD NINE. My excitement breaks through the stratosphere. Robin and I finished the closing on my penthouse an hour ago. The contract included an addendum for certain light fixtures to remain. Something about the co-op board and maintenance of the property's historical value.

The process ended quickly since the seller's broker handled the signing with a general power of attorney. A niggle in my mind made me wonder why the owner was absent unlike the last time and pointed to the name appeared differently from the previous paperwork. However, Robin assured me all was in order.

What I care about are the keys in my hand—the penthouse is mine. Robin gave them to me on a sterling silver Tiffany key chain with a star charm. I plan to spend the night. So, Blair arranged a cleaning crew and a bed with linens. I'll bring my favorite Dom Pérignon Rosé Vintage 2005 Champagne and pick up dinner from Mr. Chow. Until Leonie transforms it into my home, I'll stay at the rental. But tonight, I'll celebrate.

"Lola, Luc is on the line for you," Blair's voice rings out from the intercom on my desk.

Funny, Luc usually calls my mobile. He called through the office line as an excuse to get Blair on the phone. The distance she placed between him and herself has drawn him out of his reluctance. Soon he'll give in to admitting she means more to him than he's let on. Smart move by Blair.

"Bonjour, Renard Argenté. Comment allez-vous aujourd'hui?" I ask, a sly smile on my face.

"Bonjour, petite chérie. Je vais bien, merci," he responds distractedly.

Yup, Blair's put it on him, I giggle to myself. Go, girl!

Luc and I discuss business, including my upcoming trip to Paris and London. The past few months spent in New York and Las Vegas with only one visit to Paris and Luc handling in-person work is not enough. Meetings scheduled with suppliers and distributors among other activities require my presence. We arrange logistics and plan to meet in Paris in two weeks. With my base in New York settled,

I'm ready to split my time between the States and Europe regularly.

Now is an agreeable time for the trip since my attention will focus on the LA, Dubai, and Abu Dhabi boutique openings. The LA property is perfectly situated as an anchor store amongst other high-end retailers in STEELE's outdoor mall on Rodeo Drive. Tomorrow, I meet with the Retail Properties Division team. The agenda includes the final paperwork on the LA location and discussion on two spots in Dubai and three in Abu Dhabi.

No matter how Sebastian irks me, he is extremely organized with a knowledgeable staff. The ease of our business relationship is opposite of our combustible love affair.

Once I catch Luc up on my end, I poke the bear.

"Why didn't you call me on my mobile?" I innocently ask.

A brief silence followed by a throat-clearing cough shows my theory is correct. Luc used the call as an excuse to interact with Blair. Before he can answer my question, I continue.

"Did you need to speak with Blair about something? I mean, normally—"

"Lola..." He interrupts.

Two clues he's agitated are his use of my name as opposed to *petite chérie,* and his French accent is thicker. Good, gotcha on the ropes, Silver Fox! I sit forward, ready to spar. These men will learn today, I nod decisively.

"I do not always call you on your mobile. Particularly during business hours I avoid an interruption of your creative flow or perhaps a meeting. Why are you asking me such nonsense?"

Luc's flustered. His tone is never harsh with me. Still, I won't back down. Now for the TKO.

"Hhhmmm... I'm surprised Blair answered. I thought she'd already left for lunch with Antonio. Oh, silly me, it's not 12:30, yet."

This time, the silence is deafening. The jealousy is thick. Well... get 'em while he's down.

"Oh Luc, I need to catch her before she leaves. He's taking her to that cozy restaurant near—"

"Lola, I have another call. Adieu!"

Abruptly, Luc ends our call and I race to Blair to tell her what happened. As I reach her desk, her mobile rings and I snatch it from her hands.

"It's Luc! Let it go to voicemail!" I huff. Damn, isn't running supposed to condition me?

I relay the conversation with Blair. At first, she hides her annoyance. But by the third call in a row from Luc, she's slapping high fives with me. We listen to the messages and read several texts. We decide to not respond until tomorrow afternoon. He can roast for a little while. Maybe that will help him put on his big boy underwear.

Since neither of us has lunch dates, Blair and I order salads. We video conference Billie in from Las Vegas to give her the latest update on Luc. She gets a laugh out of it and tallies score one for Blair, zero for Luc.

Then, I get a shock when Billie tells us Patrick visited her only days after she left New York. Apparently, the bonnie Scotsman is more than entranced by Billie's siren song. He calls her each night and invited her to Hawaii for the weekend. The smart lass declined and hasn't done more than kiss Patrick. Her adage: why pay for the cow if you can get the milk for free? Billie's hard-to-get tactic works. I'll definitely keep it in mind for future use. Billie has a meeting, so we end the video call with promises of regular Girls' Chats with Leonie included in the next session.

The rest of the day goes smoothly, allowing us to leave shortly after four. At the top of the stairs on the second level of the boutique, I observe it's bustling with shoppers and attentive staff. They're not trained as salespeople, rather consultants who advise shoppers on their purchases of ready-to-wear pieces and bespoke designs. A thrill runs through me as I sense how proud my parents would be of me. With that thought in mind, I stride through the customers introducing myself and offering suggestions. So involved in helping my customers, I don't realize over an hour passed until Stan calls my mobile. I ask him to give me ten minutes to finish with a client.

My passion to give women an air of sultriness in sexy lingerie continues beyond my initial realization as a thirteen-year-old. I knew I'd found my destiny when I watched Elizabeth Taylor wearing a silk lace-trimmed slip in the classic movie *Butterfield 8.* The bombshell leaning against the wall in nothing but her slip and high-heel shoes sipping liquor from a crystal glass remains forever etched in my brain. Lola's Coterie was born.

As ALWAYS, Mr. Chow is delicious. With my hunger beyond satisfied, I make my way to the terrace where the stars glow. I envision my parents gazing down from Heaven and raise my champagne flute in salute: Thank you, Daddy and Mommy, for loving and believing in me. I'm home, again!

Sitting cross-legged on the terrace floor, I stare at the night sky and finish nearly all the bottle of Dom Pérignon. The bubbles tickle my nose. The carefree feel the delicious vintage fills me with loosens my inhibitions. I rise from the terrace floor to make my way to the bedroom where the temporary bed awaits me.

The white fluffy pillows, downy comforter encased in silk, and matching silk sheets encase me in a cocoon of sensuality. I feel like a bride on her wedding night. With thoughts of being ravaged, I rip the tank and joggers from my body, eager to lie naked in the middle of the bed to await the command of my lover. My fingertips trail fire over my fevered body as my thoughts drift to my Dom Sebastian Steele. My nipples pebble and my pussy weeps. I miss him and want him beyond all measure of sanity. Yes, he cheated on me. But his dominance, ability to elicit multiple pleasurable orgasms from my body, and most of all his love make me burn for him despite Lydie Fucking Jackson.

I close my eyes and fantasize about my lost Baz.

"On your knees, Little Pet," his mesmerizing voice makes me drop gracefully to the floor at his feet.

My pussy quivers and my nipples peak in response to his command. I lick my lips and eye the bulge straining against the crotch of his leather pants. My Dom has a ginormous dick. I shiver in anticipation.

"Eager tonight, are you, Little One?" He asks seductively as his thumb circles my full lips. "You enjoy sucking me off, do you not?"

The rough growl causes goosebumps to break out across my heated skin. My mouth moistens at the thought of his colossal dick driving savagely down my throat as he relentlessly fucks my face, chasing his climax. I close my eyes and sigh. I love the sensation of my Dom's pulsating dick deep down my throat, twitching before it spews forth a torrent of his seed. I silently vow to swallow every bit, not allowing a drop to spill from my swollen lips.

"Yes, Sir," I moan as I squeeze my thighs together to ease some pressure built from my desire for his cock to take me.

"Have at me, Little Pet. Show your Dom how much you love to please me."

Without hesitation, my fingers pull the leather cord on my Dom's pants to loosen the lacing that separates my mouth from his thick length. As I pull the pants past his narrow hips, his bare crotch appears. So, I'm not the only naughty one tonight. I lick my lips, eager to have him in my mouth. His clipped pubic hair surrounds the beauty of his massive cock—all ten inches of it in all of its glory engorged before my hooded gaze. The pants fall to the floor and I wrap my small hand around his massive length. With a tug, I pull his bulbous tip into my mouth. My tongue circles around his massive head and pokes the slit, lapping the pre-cum from the seam. Yum.

My other hand toys with his sac, shifting the weight of his balls in my palm. He's a virile male with loads of jizz to fulfill all of my desires. I take a deep breath to slide his thickness to the back of my throat. I moan as he throws his head back in bliss. The Dom is under my control.

I continue my ministrations easing his massive girth from my mouth then back to my throat deepening the reach on each stroke. His muscular thighs shake as he nears his peak. I slow the onslaught to make him beg me, turning the tables for only a moment. The sub becomes the Master.

"Fuuuck... Little Pet! You feel so good.... Aaaahhhhh!" He groans as his jizz gushes down my throat.

My fingers fly to my core to satisfy my pleasure. The eager digits dive between my wet, swollen folds, stroking my inner walls and G-spot in a frenzy. As I near the edge, I pinch my pleasure nub and scream my release around his turgid staff. Shock waves rip through my core. Our mutual climaxes convulse our bodies.

BAAAAAZZZZZZ!!

My sole scream reverberates around the empty bedroom—a reminder I am alone and not with my lover. I roll over onto my side to curl into a ball wrapped in frustration despite my intense release. My body continues to quake from the aftershocks of my illusion while my mind comes to terms with Sebastian choosing Lydie over me. Tears trickle from my tightly shut eyes that refuse to see the truth. Why can't Sebastian be mine and only mine? Sleep pulls me under and I give in to the peace it offers.

SEBASTIAN

Fuck… me. Lola still loves me and wants me as much as I love and want her.

My hand fists my thick, hungry cock in time with the rhythm set by her fingers as they pump in and out of her sweet pussy—my pussy. I want this woman more than I've wanted anything in my life. She's mine and I will not stop until she has my ring on her finger and my baby in her belly.

The view of Lola in bed masturbating while she fantasies about me is enough to make me race over there to prove how much I am hers and she is mine. Enough with the games, I will make her mine forever. Fuck Patrick Rockett and Lydie. I won't let anyone come between us again.

A zing shoots from the base of my spine to my heavy balls. My rock-hard dick expands in my hand in preparation to release the orgasm that has Lola's name on it. With one last tug, I throw my head back and roar like a feral beast just as my Petite Seductress screams my name. I nearly fall off the breakfast bar stool when I black out from the intensity of my release. Thick creamy jizz gushes onto my bare chest and abs, then coats my hand. It seeps through my sweatpants as it drips onto my lap. Once the shudders stop and I can see straight, I head to the shower to clean up the proof of my unceasing desire for Lola.

"SEBASTIAN! What the fuck are my cameras doing in Lola's apartment, you asshole?"

What the fuck? Is that Harris bellowing outside of my bedroom? What the fuck is he doing in my penthouse, I wonder as I wrap a towel around my hips.

The door to my bedroom slams against the wall as a livid Harris storms inside. His face is a mask of fury. His gray eyes shoot daggers when he spies me standing in the middle of the room.

"What… the… fuck… are… my… cameras… doing… in… Lola's… apartment… you… asshole?" Harris yells.

Fuck! What made me think giving my family access to my penthouse was a bright idea? He must have seen my laptop in the kitchen, still tuned into Lola's penthouse. Yeah, I didn't quite tell him why I needed the special cameras he designed. Rather, I alluded to needing them to monitor staff stealing supplies.

Lame, yes, but I couldn't exactly tell him it was to watch my ex in her new apartment. The same apartment that I originally bought under a shell corporation to prevent Lola from moving in to it instead of staying at my penthouse. I set up the ruse to prevent her from buying the Sutton Place penthouse when I realized I preferred her here in my bed. It wasn't the owners pulling the penthouse off the market; it was me.

When I realized Lola would not come back, I told Robin to let her know it was available again. I want to keep Lola near. I included the addendum in the contract so I could put Harris' surveillance cameras in the light fixtures to monitor her. I need to determine whether she's dating someone else like that fucker Rockett. Unscrupulous, sure, but I let nothing get between me and something that I want.

"I'm removing my cameras tomorrow, asshole! Don't even think you can stop me," Harris berates me.

His steely gaze rakes over me. His eyes narrow, and he cocks his head, lifting his eyebrow.

"Did you just rub one out while you watched her? Is that why you took a shower this late at night?"

I can only stand there silently as I have no defense; he makes his case.

"What a loser," Harris mutters as he shakes his head. "You're lucky I don't tell Mom. She'll have your balls, creep."

The thought of him blabbing to our mother jump-starts my brain. I draw on my Dom to gain control of the situation.

"Harris, you are right. I deceived you," I start inwardly relieved when he looks surprised that I didn't lie. "As I told you, Lola is everything to me. I pledged to her I would give her time since she requested it, but know that she is mine. It may be much to monitor her, but you are an Alpha male. Would you not use any means to monitor your woman?"

Fortunately, Harris agrees, but remains adamant about the immediate removal of his cameras. To avoid Lola's suspicions, he'll go under the guise of an inspector sent by the board to ensure the light fixtures remain intact. The task will go smoothly since Robin will assist him by relaying the message to Lola and getting her keys. The arrangements made, Harris leaves with the corkscrew he planned to borrow.

I'm not overly upset by this turn of events. He may have

remotely disabled the cameras, but the files autosave to an undetectable backup server. Beyond even his tech savvy self.

A quick conversation with my private investigator replaces the sophisticated technology with old-fashioned footwork and photography. Until Lola is back at my side, I'll prevent anyone else from claiming her.

* * *

"PARDON MY TARDINESS. An urgent overseas call delayed me," I say to those gathered in the conference room, but I lock my eyes on Lola.

Her hazel orbs dilate as she unconsciously licks her plump lower lip. I ache to nip and suck it into my mouth. The memory of her taste fades each day. If all goes as planned, her succulent tongue will dally with mine soon. My dick twitches at the thought of her skillful appendage.

I stride to the table and unbutton my suit jacket. Sliding my hand down the muscular plane of my torso, momentarily hovering over my crotch. I delight in Lola's eyes darkening as her gaze follows the path of my palm. I lick my own full lips as I take the seat opposite my beauty, whose eyes widen when she sees my burgeoning bulge. As our eyes meet, I pin her with my penetrating Dom stare. Lola's sharp intake of air makes me smirk—she's bitten the bait.

Until now, my Retail Properties Division team handled affairs directly with Lola. Out of respect for her time request, I stayed in the background. Although I kept a watchful eye on the goings-on. So, I'm very much aware of each new boutique's property location and timeline.

Relationship aside, it's still all about generating revenue and having the partnership with Lola's Coterie make up for the money lost in the Rockett Construction fiasco. My goal for CEO in just over six months is very much on track.

So far, her New York and Las Vegas boutiques are profitable with expectations of surpassing the initial projections. It's a sound business deal that I will not screw up. I'm living up to the promise I gave Lola when we made a go at a relationship. We even included an addendum to the contract to solidify the partnership. No matter what occurs between us personally, business will continue unscathed.

STEELE Galleria Rodeo Drive is the best spot for her Beverly Hills boutique since an anchor store recently moved into a freestanding space in one of our West Hollywood storefronts. I held the SGRD specifically for Lola not to curry favor. But for the potential increase in revenue for the site since hers will be the only luxury lingerie store in the vicinity. Our marketing division will work with her team to make a tremendous splash, ensuring a successful opening.

The United Arab Emirates locations in Abu Dhabi and Dubai require a trip to view the three and two spots in each city, respectively, before we make the ultimate decision. Their openings will coincide one week apart for logistical reasons. No need to travel to the other side of the globe unnecessarily.

They schedule the trip for three weeks from now if Lola's time is available. I'll clear my calendar for a chance to be with her on my Gulfstream G650 private jet for thirteen uninterrupted hours.

Lola furtively peeks at me over the course of the meeting. Each time she blushes when our gazes connect. I slowly rub my thumb back and forth over my lower lip, imagining it thrumming her clit.

A thrill runs through me as she sucks her lower lip between her teeth. When she slowly releases her swollen lip and keeps her mouth slightly open, I nearly cum in my trousers. I shift in my seat to adjust my cock discreetly. Zipper marks undoubtedly formed on my turgid length. A look of triumph lights Lola's eyes when she detects my discomfit. I tilt my head in affirmation and curl the corner of my lip in a half smile. She needs to know she affects me as much as I do her.

The meeting continues peppered with our secret foreplay. Lola hastens to gather her personal effects, but I have other plans for my Petite Seductress.

"Lola, a word," I command.

I suppress a laugh when she jumps like a frightened rabbit cornered by the wolf. She's not so far off. My gray eyes are predatory, latched on her. She will not dodge me today—or any day going forward.

"Mr. Steele, I have another meeting—"

"Oh, Lola, I can take it for you. No worries."

I could kiss her assistant, Blair, except that Lola would stab me with her stiletto. Instead, I nod my thanks as Blair hurries from the room. I return my gaze to a shocked Lola, who's staring after Blair's retreating figure as the door closes. No escape.

Instead of speaking immediately, I wait until Lola faces me. I want her full attention.

"Are you pleased with the situation?" I ask, knowing she'll assume I'm referring to our personal relationship.

Flustered, she lowers her head as she places her tablet inside of her attaché.

"Mr. Steele, as you said, 'don't mix business with pleasure.' So, excuse me," Lola snaps with flashing eyes.

Quickly, I round the corner of the table to block her path to the door. She halts inches from my chest. Another sharp intake of air forces a growl deep in my chest. Lola jerks her eyes to my face. The raw need she sees makes her involuntarily sway towards me. I seize the opportunity to grip the back of her neck to draw her body flush to mine while tilting her head back to swoop my lips onto hers.

The surprise move parts them. I brazenly slip my tongue into her mouth, sweeping around until I catch her tongue and suck it into my mouth. A moan falls from Lola's parted lips as she fists my suit jacket. Our tongues dally just as I planned. We relish the taste and feel of one another.

Reluctantly, I move away. I don't want to push Lola too far. I have to reel her in slowly or risk her slipping off the line.

I take a deep breath of her alluring perfume; hints of tuberose, ylang-ylang blossom, and pear make my mouth water. I close my eyes for a moment to let her scent infuse every cell of my body.

"Have dinner with me now," I tell her, my voice husky with desire.

Lola tries to move away, but I tighten my grip on her neck and tilt her head back up. She's gorgeous with kiss-swollen lips and hooded eyes. Her flushed cheeks mimic the heat on mine. I lean my forehead against hers. We exchange breaths and our souls reconnect.

"You asked for time... Two months, Lola. Have dinner with me," I start, then continue when she softens against me. "Only dinner. We can take it slowly. You can trust me not to take you beyond your limits."

I add the D/s reference to judge her reaction. Against my legs, Lola squeezes her thighs together. Yes, she hasn't let go of her sub needs. I groan and grip her hip with my free hand. Pressed against me, Lola senses the power she has over me. My dick pokes her belly, but she knows it's her choice.

"Let go and just feel," I remind her in a rough whisper as I brush my lips against the shell of her ear.

"Baaazzz..."

Lola's groan reminds me of her in the throes of passion last night. I nip and suck my way from her ear along her jaw and down her throat to travel back up the opposite direction to cover her mouth once again. We gasp when our lips touch. Lola slides her arms around my neck and pulls me down to her. I lift her from her feet and hold her tightly as our kiss deepens. We remained locked together, reacquainting our bodies.

"Say yes to dinner now or it's yes to me feasting on you spread before me on this conference room table," I growl into her neck.

Lola shivers and pants yes. I sense she means the latter, but it will be dinner. Again, a slow pace.

Gently, I lower Lola to the ground, letting her body slide against mine. I hold her firmly by the waist until she's sure on her feet. Once settled, she lowers her head as her cheeks deepen in color. I hold her chin between my thumb and index finger as I bend my knees to align our eyes.

"No need for embarrassment. I miss you, too. A lot," I reassure her with a soft kiss to the tip of her nose.

Her smile makes my heart skip a beat.

Lola finishes packing her attaché. Meanwhile, I send a text message to my assistants Melody Lawson and Tina Nickles to apprise them of my change in plans for the rest of the workday. I also ask them to have my driver bring the sedan out front. I'm sure they're surprised since I usually leave the office around seven in the evenings. My days are fourteen hours long—a testament to my unwavering dedication to STEELE's success. Since I'm heading out early, I tell them to wrap up whatever they're working on and call it a day.

The sense of being stared at causes me to lift my gaze from my mobile to find Lola peering at me. Her cheeks flush when I catch her hooded stare. A smirk lifts the corner of my mouth—gotcha securely on my line. Defiantly, she tosses her hair over her shoulder and quirks her eyebrow.

"Still cocky, I see," she says to deflect.

I stand from leaning my hip against the table to tower over her. I may have decided to go slow, but I will not allow my Little Pet to sass me. Quickly, I crowd Lola to back her up against the sideboard across from the table. She jumps and squeaks when her plump bottom bumps into the furniture. As I brace my hands against the top on either side of her waist, I lower my lips to press them against rim of her ear.

"Are you ready for punishment so soon, Little Pet? As always, your cocksure mouth needs me to fill it. You realize we do not have to go slow as I originally suggested," I gruffly respond, allowing my breath to tickle her skin.

Lola trembles with pleasure as her next inhalation catches in her throat. Purposefully, I maintain mere inches between our bodies. The heat building between us is scorching. It radiates between us in waves.

With a sharp nip to her lobe, I pivot on my heel to stride to the door. Sweeping my palm towards the opening, I tilt my head to the side, pinning Lola with my Dom stare.

"Shall we?"

I watch Lola's plump ass and curvy hips in the black-ribbed wool dress molded to her luscious body. The high-heel shoes lift her butt and lengthen her shapely legs. My palm itches to smack her ass to watch in fascination as it jiggles. My dick twitches at the memory of being deep inside of her bottom hole. Fuck, I need her. I shake my head to clear those thoughts and follow Lola like a homesick puppy. Strong Dom missing alert…

As we walk past the other executive suites, one of my younger brothers Malcolm calls out to us. We detour into his office. At only two years apart, he's my doppelgänger: same six feet, four inches in height; gray eyes; black hair; clean shaven or 5 o'clock shadow covers a firm jaw. As kids, he strove for his own identity, hating being in my shadow. Fortunately, we grew past the teenage angst to develop a close relationship.

Malcolm rises to greet us and pulls Lola into an embrace. He winks at me over the top of her head before giving her a squeeze. A growl falls from my lips and he laughs, releasing her from his tentacles.

"Good to see you again, Lola," he starts with a twinkle in his eyes. "I spoke with Adrienne Anthony, Starr Knight's studio manager. Apparently Starr is out of the country at an ashram in India and unreachable. So, we must connect when she returns."

Again… When the hell did they speak? What the hell is Malcolm talking about? Why didn't he tell me he communicated with Lola? Before I can demand answers, Lola responds.

"It's so good to see you again, too, Malcolm! Thank you for dinner. The—"

"Whaaat???" I yell, my eyes zipping between Lola and Malcolm.

The cool, in-control Dom now completely off the grid. My mind plays a scene of Lola and Malcolm dining by candlelight in a romantic restaurant. Her eyes shiny from the champagne they drink with dessert. He leans over the table to lick cream from the corner of her lips. Lola's laugh rings out. Other men turn to stare jealously at Malcolm. The lovestruck couple leave the restaurant to finish dessert at Malcolm's penthouse in The STEELE Tower. While I lay alone in the big bed Lola and I once shared two floors above…

I snap my head in Malcolm's direction when his words filter through my nightmare.

"—concept could fit well with our latest Jackson Hole venture. New amenities attract unique guests while the regular ones find more reasons to keep coming back to stay. Once I meet with Ms. Knight, I'll fill you in."

As the president of STEELE's Entertainment Properties Division, Malcolm oversees our casinos, hotels, and resorts. His latest project Jackson Hole at STEELE Resorts is in partnership with Lydie and her younger brother Lucien. The concept is members-only, high-end beach clubs for the jet set. It's his second foray with LEVELS New York, Paris, and London BDSM/dine/dance clubs in co-ownership with Lucien. Basically, Jackson Hole is LEVELS on the beach minus the BDSM.

Since a baffled expression lingers on my face when he finishes, Malcolm sighs dramatically realizing that I wasn't paying him the least bit of attention.

"Get your head out of your ass, Baz. Lola and I had dinner last week to discuss business. B-U-S-I-N-E-S-S. Got it?" He admonishes me. "Lola met Starr Knight, the owner of the Beverly Hills-based fitness studio and wellness center Starr Light Fitness & Wellness. She plans to expand into international fitness retreats at luxury resorts and to add a second center location in the Caribbean. Lola told me about Starr since she had an exceptional experience at her first retreat in Fiji on the private Laucala Island. Are we clear?"

I have to hold back an eye roll getting chastised by

another Dom, especially my younger brother. I risk a peek at Lola to find her hazel eyes glowing warmly with suppressed laughter. Malcolm drapes his arm around her shoulders as he joins in her glee. How low can an Alpha male sink?

"Crystal clear, brother. Now, back off my girl. We're going to dinner," I chide to regain control.

Lola's eyes widen. I frown at her, then realize I referred to her as my girl. Oh boy. Instead of addressing the term of endearment, I grasp her hand and pull her from the office.

"Have fun," Malcolm taunts.

I throw a glare over my shoulder at him as I usher Lola through the door. His booming laughter carries across the office suite. Fucker.

"Possessive much?" Lola asks as she tries to tug her hand from mine.

Not having it. I squeeze her hand and glance down at her. No way am I letting Lola go.

"Yes," I answer definitively.

LOLA

Sebastian is definitely trying to get in my good graces and off of my shit list. I acknowledge as I sit oh so comfortably in his Gulfstream G650 private jet on my way to Paris. With a base price of sixty-five million dollars, it's the epitome of luxury travel. During the four months that Sebastian and I dated, we used his jet for frequent trips domestically and abroad. Luc also has a custom model that frequently over the six years we've known each other I've flown in. Of course, he's had a few upgrades as recent ones hit the market. Private jets without a doubt surpass commercial and charters by miles —no pun.

This latest lure comes on the tail end of two weeks of romantic dates, phone calls late into the night, and dozens upon dozens of exquisite Sterling Silver Roses, each with a touching—sometimes lascivious—note. I blush just thinking about the hedonistic pleasures Sebastian promises: lave your glistening pink pussy until you beg me to stop; cuff you to my pommel horse and spank your engorged clit; lock your legs in my spreader bar and plunder your tight ass. My core clenches at the graphic visions. Damn, I miss my man.

Sadly, he still insists that we take it slow. So we haven't had a date at LEVELS New York, yet. How unfortunate, I sigh. Sebastian also refuses to touch me beyond kisses and hand holding. Snooze. I want those full lips suckling my peaked nipples. His enormous hands gripping my hips as he pistons deep inside of me from behind.

Sebastian's denials only make me crave him more. It's probably some Dom-mind trick designed to drive the sub insane with sensual need. Their unsatisfied arousal high, way beyond the pleasurable torture of edging.

Each night, I have to release the pressure built from our dalliances with the help of my new BOB—Battery Operated Boyfriend. Not quite Sebastian in size or sensation. But it gives me a bit of relief. When I teased Sebastian about needing to use it after one of our explicit phone calls, he called me back on FaceTime deliciously naked. His mouth-watering body leaning against the headboard of the bed we shared. That night, both of us eased the load.

The sight of Sebastian vigorously pumping his thick ten-inch girth with his muscular thighs spread wide, his heavy balls hanging between them was something to behold. Particularly when ropes of his creamy semen shot all over his bare chest, his pecs, and abs tight with tension. He threw his head back as he squeezed his eyes shut and yelled my name. My mouth waters just thinking about his taste and the feeling of his girth stretching my throat. Yum.

My Captain Caveman. My Dom. My Baz.

"Lola?" Billie asks. "Luc just called me because you're not answering your mobile."

Damn. I forgot to turn my mobile back on once we were in the air. So busy fantasizing about Sebastian. It's been two hours, so I wonder who else may have tried to reach me. Well... really, I only wonder if Sebastian called or sent a text message.

My mobile chirps with multiple voicemails, texts, and emails. It distracts me from wondering why Luc called Billie and not Blair. I thought they were back on track. I make a mental note to ask Blair after I handle these incoming communications.

Half an hour later, I'm through the backlog. But disappointed not to hear from Sebastian. It's about eleven thirty at night back in New York City. I expected at least a call.

Doubt surfaces at the edges of my mind. Now that I'm gone, is he at LEVELS to ease his Dom and sexual needs truly? Before me, Sebastian was the quintessential Alpha Billionaire playboy who only fucked a woman one time. Then on to the next one whenever the urge arose. He was highly sexual. When we were together, we fucked regularly. As many as four times a day.

I haven't had the guts to ask if he was active these past three months. Really, it's not my place since I broke up with him. Even though it was his fault. That damnable Lydie. Could he be with her now?

I also haven't told him I witnessed their post-sex cuddling in one of the penthouse's guest suites. Yes, I'm a wimp. I like a touch of pain with pleasure. But I'm not a masochist. The answers could only lead to more heartache. Something I have no interest in experiencing so soon. Particularly since Sebastian and I are seemingly working on our relationship.

Although I know trust is the foundation of any relationship and even more so a D/s one, as Sebastian emphasized repeatedly during our lessons, I still wonder. Now, I'm tense and it has nothing to do with sexual buildup.

To avoid going further down the path of madness, I call Luc. It's early morning in Paris, so I'm not sure what could be so urgent for him to call me now. I brace myself since the last time I received an urgent early morning call, the police were at my family's door to tell me a car crash killed my parents. I shudder at the thought and send a loving prayer to them. With trepidation, I tap Luc's number.

"Lola! I've been trying to reach you."

I hold my breath to wait for the dreadful news.

"Splendid news, *petite chérie*!"

His unexpected exuberance forces the air from my lungs. I nearly faint from the rush of blood to my head. Did he really just say "splendid news"? Thank you for that relief.

Luc says he wanted to be the first to tell me ANDAM the prestigious fashion awards nominated Lola's Coterie for the Best Breakthrough Collection. I squeal. In my haste to jump from my seat, I nearly drop my mobile. I barely hear another word out of Luc's mouth as I dance around the cabin.

I put Luc on speaker to share the news with Blair and Billie. They join in my dance, bumping hips and slapping high fives. Once I'm seated again, Luc fills me in on the details. Afterwards, we end the call with plans for a celebratory dinner at Arpège. The three Michelin star restaurant is my favorite in Paris. Luc and I make a habit of dining there for milestones and anniversaries.

My next call is to Sebastian. I'm excited to tell him. Plus, it's the perfect excuse to call. His mobile goes straight to voicemail. I try not to think the worse. It's hard since Sebastian only turns his mobile off when we were having sex or doing a scene at LEVELS.

"Drink up, *Ms. Best Breakthrough Collection Nominee*!"

Billie giggles as she hands a flute of Dom Pérignon Rosé Vintage 2005.

Sebastian rubbed it on thick by stocking my favorite champagne on board. Still, at this moment, he's remains on the cusp of my shit list. I'll give him the benefit of the doubt. For now.

With a sigh, I down the entire glass. Billie and Blair exchange glances. I shrug and lift my flute for some more. I might as well, take the edge off with a few glasses of the ambrosial bubbly.

* * *

IT'S refreshing to walk into Lola's Coterie Paris. The flagship location is in the former home of a courtesan to a French king. It was his gift to her after she bore him their first of four children. He wanted them to live royally in the opulent *maison.*

The decor sets the mood with the air of a boudoir: sparkling Baccarat crystal chandeliers; silk wallpaper; scenes of Parisian streets hand-drawn on accent walls; light hardwood floors; vamp and shell pink colors with platinum touches; beveled mirrors. The warm and creamy, sweet and clean, sensual and sophisticated, woodsy fragrance wafts through the hidden atomizers. Soft French background music by Josephine Baker and Edith Piaf delights the ears. Stylish, sexy shopgirls assist fashionable, gorgeous women and men. The boutique invites patrons to relax in an atmosphere of splendor and entices them to indulge their inner sexpot or to gift their lover with pieces.

Standing amongst a gathering of mesmerized fans—patrons and staff alike—stands Leonie. Ever the muse for Lola's Coterie, she wears one of the Las Vegas collection's beaded and silk camisoles, a pair of skinny jeans, and strappy sandals. Her hands move animatedly as she chats with her admirers, the tinkle of multiple bracelets punctuate each word. She offers advice on their selections and tips to look flawless in lingerie. As she shows body angles to highlight curves, Leonie sees me. Her liquid amber eyes and dazzling smile light up the room.

Yes, it's terrific being back in Paris.

"Lola, *Chérie*!" Leonie gushes, rapidly covering the distance between us as she stalks towards me like the feline she's named for.

"How long have you been here? I'm so glad to see you!"

She pulls me into an embrace as she whispers, "*Félicitations*! Luc told me about the ANDAM nomination."

"Merci beaucoup, mon amie!"

We do our little celebratory shimmy—dance in a circle, holding hands, and bouncing on the balls of our feet. Then turn our attention back to the others. They delight in our exuberant reunion.

The most rewarding part of my job is engaging with patrons. So, I take the time for fittings, explanation of materials and care, and gift suggestions. Their feedback whether positive or negative helps me to better my collections. It's all about the wearers. They agree an evening wear line that harkens to lingerie would be favorable. Something I had considered, now I'll make a priority.

Several ideas for fresh pieces pop into my head. I'm eager to put them in my sketchpad. It's as though I'm plugged back into my creative fuel.

After a while, Leonie and I bid them adieu. It's time to get to the business side of Lola's Coterie. We scheduled Luc to meet us in my office in thirty minutes. On the ride in the elevator to the top-floor atelier, Leonie peeks at me sheepishly.

"Gio is in Paris. We haven't seen each other in over a week. He asked me to dinner"—she rushes on when I open my mouth to complain—"But I told him I have plans."

"Good, because I haven't seen you in weeks..." I reply with a huff. "Besides, I thought you broke up since he was gallivanting with other women."

That Giovanni, such a handsome devil.

I send a silent prayer Leonie doesn't go back on her word about moving on from him. He's nowhere near being ready to settle down. The billion-dollar playboy, an Italian nobleman to boot, attracts women with no effort. They throw themselves at him.

Leonie is the exact opposite. She intrigues him because she doesn't take his shit and has her own millions, fame, and admirers. Giovanni may not settle down now. But when he's ready, I'm sure he would prefer Leonie. If she still wants him by that time.

The elevator doors open to the all-white atelier bathed in natural sunlight from the skylights and oversized windows. The whitewashed hardwood floors and matte-white walls act as the perfect backdrop for any fabric, color, or texture. The open space includes workstations for staff. Glass walls separate my office and a conference room from the primary area. I prefer to sit amidst the action, but have privacy when necessary.

Blair and Billie sit outside of my office at an antique partner's desk. Their mobiles glued to their ears while they type rapidly on their laptop keyboards. They arrived before I did since I detoured to my flat.

Leonie's mobile chirps. Her eyes widen at me and she pulls her lower lip between her teeth when she sees the name on her screen. I snatch it from her with a raised eyebrow. Giovanni, of course. She grabs it back and turns away to respond to his text message. Whatever, she's a grown woman. I'll be there for her either way. BFF and all.

"Lola, Luc's on his way up now," Billie informs me.

I glance at Blair to gauge her reaction since once again Luc contacted Billie instead. Blair refuses to meet my eyes. She pointedly keeps her attention on the monitor. I'll leave it for now since this is work time.

Damn, these girls will drive me nuts with their men issues. Hell, I have enough of my own. Especially since I still haven't heard from Sebastian. Shaking my head, I stroll into my office to sit at my drawing desk ready to put the thoughts of the evening wear collection to life.

The morning is a blur of activity. Once Luc arrives, we have several meetings with vendors and internal marketing and finance teams. Leonie stays for the marketing meeting as her input is invaluable. She takes her role as Lola's Coterie muse seriously. The success is due in part to her representation of the brand.

Before she leaves, Leonie pulls me aside to tell me we're going to a party tonight after dinner. Giovanni invited us and "we can't say no" she insists. I give in, needing to have a distraction. Sebastian is a no show all day despite my messages.

Time to get my groove on. No sitting in my empty flat dejectedly watching my mobile for me. No ma'am!

* * *

London is dreary with rain, just like my mood. Sadly, I'm not as wet too.

The past week in Paris may have had my creativity at a

peak. But those were the only juices flowing. Sebastian and I spoke briefly a few times. He claims to have had meetings that kept him busy. The time difference didn't help the situation. So no late-night FaceTime sex to stave my needs. And I left BOB in New York. How the hell does Sebastian satisfy his cravings?

I try not to dwell on thoughts of him with someone else —especially not Lydie. Leonie did her best to distract me. Giovanni's party was a blast, after all. He was extremely attentive of Leonie. His possessive eyes never left her as we danced in the crowd. Another upside is Sebastian called me the next day after he saw me on social media and the Internet surrounded by gorgeous men. Jealous much? Well, too bad.

The rain pelts unceasingly on the windows of my office. The leaden gray sky reminds me of Sebastian's eyes when he's aroused. The memory of him staring up at me as he used his skillful tongue to eat my pussy has me shifting in my seat. I close my own eyes to revel in the flashback that plays in my mind.

A chirp draws my attention out of the clouds and to my mobile. The text message from LEVELS London makes me clench my thighs. Tonight is Masquerade Night—how apropos.

Thankful that I upgraded my seven-day guest pass to the New York flagship to an All Access Global Membership, I reply YES to RSVP. With a mask on, I can at least select a black voyeur bracelet. I'll live vicariously through others' lustful encounters...

With more wanton excitement than I've had in a week, I head down to the boutique's couture collection floor to select tonight's attire.

SEBASTIAN

Lola's absence is equivalent to me missing a limb. I need it desperately. But it's not there, only its phantom presence tricks me.

For two weeks, she's been in Europe on business and it feels like two months. The only upside is the barrage of unexpected work I've had to deal with dominating my time. I haven't had an idle moment. Otherwise, my thoughts would continuously stray to Lola.

I've only had time for a few brief calls with her. Not enough to have phone sex and definitely not enough for FaceTime fucking.

The five-hour difference makes it inconvenient to connect. By the time my business day ends and I'm crashed on my sofa or bed, it's after two in the morning for Lola. She seemed distracted the last time we spoke, or perhaps irritated. I hope she's not having as difficult of a time with her business affairs as I am with mine.

Somehow an undetermined employee accessed one of our corporate servers to download confidential data on

STEELE's global VIP list. They compromised personal information such as names, addresses, and credit card details for high rollers who frequent our casinos and royalty and the über-wealthy who stay at our properties. It was a well-orchestrated job that could involve more than one person from within STEELE and externally.

Harris and Haley's cyber security team detected unusual activity from a non-STEELE IP address. It was their latest security protocol they just implemented across all the STEELE divisions that triggered the alert. The system immediately started the shutdown of the transmission and isolated the source. The process is complex and meticulous. So it will take time. Undoubtedly the Dynamic Duo will resolve the issue.

In the meantime, the handling of the communications with the VIPs lands in my wheelhouse. Our father delegated the task to me even though the division impacted falls in Malcolm's purview. The undertaking is the perfect opportunity to flex my future CEO finesse.

Forget an email or conference call, this demands face-to-face conversations to avoid legal and public relations nightmares. Fortunately, the compromised individuals are only in New York City and London—the total of twenty out of thousands. Thank fuck.

Since last week, I've met with everyone in the city. As expected, they were beyond pissed and threatened legal action. That the security protocol not only interrupted the download, but sent a zap to delete the receiving server's system eased the VIPs' concerns. That along with our legal team's preemptive contract that assures full financial compensation for any damages caused by the breech directly.

Tomorrow morning, I fly to London. The Brits are more

stiff upper lip than Americans, so I expect fewer threats of "taking you to the cleaners" and "ruin STEELE forever." Not that it'll be a cakewalk. Shit, I would end STEELE if it were me.

My mobile dings with a Google alert for Lola Lewis. I smirk as I think of Lola asking me if I'm possessive much. Yup. She'd add obsessed stalker if she knew I have an alert for any mention of her name on the Internet.

What… the… fuck!

I damn near crush my mobile.

Lola's shaking her ass dancing in a tight-as-fuck red mini dress. Her toned thighs on full display damn near to her crotch. She was at some party with Leonie a few hours ago—this after the last one of Mattei's. Guys circle around her, reaching out to touch her body in various places—her hand, her waist, her fucking hip. All the while, she's laughing with her arms overhead, twirling, bumping, grinding.

I may very well have a coronary.

I grit my teeth in irritation, pissed that I didn't fully reclaim her from the get-go. Take it slow, I said… Lure her in… Give her the time she needs… Don't rush her…

Fool.

That probably explains her reticence. Lola's mind is on other guys and far from me. Clearly, she fell off my hook.

Would this have happened if I were still a playboy, not spending more than two fucks with various hookups? Absolutely not.

Would I even care? Hell no! My only priority was to give them immense pleasure and to relieve my needs.

Lolas has me all fucked up.

Not giving a damn it's three in the morning, I call her. Furious, I use facial recognition to unlock my mobile. The current scowl that adorns my face renders the capability useless. With a herculean effort to rein in the myriad of emotions roiling in my mind, I set a neutral expression.

The telltale click precedes my finger jabbing at the phone icon. Favorites... Huh. For a moment I wonder if Lola even has me listed in her Favorites. If so, by what name? Baz... Sebastian... Sir... Idiot? Yeah. I continue to seethe while the call connects.

Damn if it doesn't go straight to voicemail. Un-fucking-believable.

At first, I thought it was Lola saying hello, so I started heatedly to demand what she's doing. But no. It's only her message. I end the call even more pissed off than before since she never turns her mobile off.

If she's fucking someone she picked up at that party. Or some schmuck wrapped himself around her hot little body after they fucked, limbs tangled, passed out from the exhaustion of going at it for hours...

Grrrrr!

I scroll through more photos, scandalized as I scan for likely suspects. Shit, it could very well be any of these losers. They're all sniffing around her, jockeying for her attention.

The captions magnify Lola's obvious delight in the men fawning all over her: Lola Lewis lingerie designer flocked by sexy admirers; partygoers can't get enough of the curvaceous Lola Lewis; revelers want more of the lingerie world's top creator, Lola Lewis; known for her sexy lingerie pieces, Lola Lewis looks luscious dancing long into the night. Each picture, not to mention the annoying blurbs, makes me see red.

Gone is the simpering pseudo-boyfriend. The Dom in me takes over. When I see her, I will mark her ass red with my palm prints. Lola will explain why she chose to defy me to mess around with other men. She knows she belongs to me and me only. I just told Lola how possessive I am of her. Yet, she purposefully sought gratification from others.

My mobile dings, again. This time it's a text message from LEVELS London.

Lola Lewis Masquerade Night RSVP YES

A wicked chuckle rumbles up from deep within my chest, bursting past my down-turned lips. Deviously, I narrow my eyes in glee—excellent.

Oh, my Petite Seductress, you will get punished sooner than I expected. You dare go to a LEVELS club without me as your paired Dom, leaving you open to the whims of another to slake your sub needs. Hhhmmm. You forget who's your Dom, Naughty Pet. These transgressions will not go unchecked.

My dick springs to life as it lengthens down my thigh inside my gray sweatpants. The anticipation of Lola naked —except for a mask—with her delectable body strapped to a red leather spanking bench on the main stage at the Cellar with her pink pussy dripping to a puddle beneath her as I spank that ass is enough to cause pre-cum to gather at my expanding tip. The bulbous head as red and angry as the one above my shoulders. Both heads are of the same mind: Lola will learn her lesson at Masquerade Night and be mine fully by the end.

I intend to spank her plump bottom until it's so inflamed, even a feather lightly brushing over its rounded curves will elicit a yelp from her pouty mouth. Then fuck her like a wild caveman claiming his mate until her womb fills with my seed. Every one of Lola's holes will leak with my jizz. My scent permanently fused to every inch of her skin. No doubt will remain to whom she belongs.

Me.

I have to wonder whether Lola is provoking me on purpose. The little vixen loves punishments. With my insistence that we take it slow with only FaceTime for self-induced climaxes, I'm not giving her the satisfaction that she craves. Lola's complained about the lack of intensity from the video calls. Plus taunted me enough with hew new BOB and the vivid details of her use of the fake dick. Her behavior over these past two weeks may be a subconscious cry for my attention—not for those suckers who are hanging around her. Well, I've got her message loud and clear.

Whatever Lola wants, Lola gets.

LOLA

The sweat on my palms makes it difficult to adjust the red enamel bracelet around my wrist. The clasp is too delicate for my clumsy fingers. The two ends circle my wrist, then slide off before I can attach one to the other. In consternation, I bite my lower lip to make my third attempt. Foiled again.

The last time I was at a LEVELS, I wore a wide, black leather collar with a silver ring for a delicate matching chain to dangle from the collar to Sebastian's hand. At first, my Independent Woman balked at being led around like a dog on a leash. But the sub in me appreciated the collar symbolized Sebastian as a Dom who claimed me as his sub. I was his alone, and he was mine. Not exactly a wedding band, but the meaning was just as powerful.

Now my choice of bracelet color shows my availability to others. I no longer have a Dom. To avoid unwanted interactions amongst club participants, the system requires partnered subs to wear collars given to them by their Dom;

partnered Doms wear gold bracelets; available subs wear red; available Doms wear white; voyeurs wear black.

This detail of consensual connections is one of the many reasons I feel safe being a member of LEVELS. They enforce strict protocols members, their guests, and applicants must follow. From nondisclosure agreements to no-names given unless provided by the person to super tight ongoing background checks and other security measures. In addition, no judgement!

As though she senses my nervousness, without a word of annoyance or appraisal, the LEVELS London greeter slips the jewelry from my hand and deftly closes the clasp. She returns my relieved smile with a perfectly brilliant one of her own.

Damn. Every staff member at each of the LEVELS locations looks as though they just strode off the catwalk, I giggle to myself.

With more confidence, I straighten my shoulders before I nod my head at her to signal my readiness to enter Peepshow on the BDSM side of the club.

It's fascinating how Malcolm and Lucien Jackson—I adore that incredibly hot *Sexy Chef*—selected locations for their uniqueness and double entendres. The New York flagship in one of the former warehouses of the Meatpacking District plays on the area's name. Put a club where men pack their meat into willing women and willing men allow women to pack them with their toys, or any combinations or groupings thereof.

For consistency and members' comfort, locations share the same layout:

> Main entry foyer has two sides with two greeter stations for access to Dine & Dance levels and BDSM levels, an All-

> Access member can choose from any of the seven levels: 7th Sky Lounge that offers a bar, restaurant by day dance club by night, coverable pool that's open for the summer, and a glass-retractable roof; 6th and 5th multilevel dance club with two bars and a lounge for food and drinks; 4th Level 4 Restaurant and bar open for breakfast, lunch, and dinner; 3rd has twelve private suites for members to continue their pleasure apart from the BDSM levels; 2nd Peepshow for BDSM with seating alcoves, main stage, performance rooms, and a bar that serves non-alcoholic mocktails; below ground the Cellar BDSM dungeon with mocktails bar. The Dine/Dance members only have access to the party levels—Sky Lounge, Dance Club, and Level 4 Restaurant.

London is the third after Paris of the exclusive, luxury, members-only clubs. Its site is a former bank set in the City of London, also known as The City and Financial District. They use the original vault for private parties. Locked behind its massive, thick steel door, who knows what all goes on inside. This LEVELS is an ode to the debauchery of money and the wealthy who wield it as power over others. How appropriate the Sky Lounge provides an unobstructed view of the Tower of London.

Now it's my turn to enter the beast's lair. Despite my bravado, my heart races uncontrollably as soon as the double doors open to Peepshow. My senses amplify as my mind adjusts to the carnality before me.

The space is dimly lit with spotlights on the main stage and several of the smaller platforms where demonstrations in bondage and Shibari are active. Shrouded in shadows, the seating alcoves cluster along the perimeter. Only glimpses of movement prove their inhabitants' presence. Desirable, sensuous men and women appear in various stages of dress or nudity while they partake in all forms of sexual activity.

The atmosphere is pure bacchanalia. Melodic thrumming of sultry music accompanies the moans and groans of the revelers. While the air is heavy with the mixture of expensive cologne, alluring perfume, and immeasurable arousal. The heady aroma alights on my tongue as I gasp from the thrill of the visions. Unconsciously, one of my hands glides along my hip while the other strokes my beaded nipples. Caught up in the rapture, I seek my gratification.

A third and fourth hand join mine to explore my body. I jump from the unexpected touch as a squeak slips from my mouth. Twisting to peer up and over my shoulder, my eyes meet a pair of ice blue ones framed by an ornate gold half-mask. The gold highlights the flecks in his eyes—gorgeous.

"Pardon my boldness, beauty," he rasps in my ear.

I shiver from his warm breath tickling my lobe and the deep carnal tone of his voice laced with an ultra-posh Queen's English accent.

His enormous hands slide beneath my much smaller ones as he continues, "But I could not allow you to pleasure yourself. Leave it to me to elevate your arousal."

To emphasize his intent, the captivating man lifts my jewelry-wrapped wrist to match his that bears a white enamel bracelet. He's an available Dom.

"Come, beauty. Tell me what your sexy fantasy entails. Perhaps I may help you bring it to life."

No longer stunned by his assertive appearance, my brain turns back on to release my immobile tongue.

"As much as I appreciate your offer, I only just arrived and haven't navigated the room in my pursuit of a partner," I start re-gaining confidence. "However, should I not engage with a suitable Dom, you and I can meet in an hour at the bar."

Gently, yet with enough force to make my point, I detach myself from his clutches. With a smile and a nod, I saunter away without further engagement. Way too much too soon.

The next hour I roam the floor at Peepshow as I hold off on immediately searching for an appealing partner. It's awkward without Sebastian. Instead, I take in the activities on display in the performance rooms: a male-male-male-female ménage with triple penetration; a Domme, her male sub, cock and ball bondage, and a St. Andrew's Cross; two female subs and their Dom use intense breath control; still others with two men and three women, so on and so on.

Yup, Masquerade Night allows members to sate their most explicit appetites uninhibitedly.

Just as I'm meandering to the bar to meet the bold Dom, I see two familiar forms huddled together near the shadows. I don't want to jump to conclusions, so I move closer, sure to keep others between us. The voices carry over the backdrop of Peepshow—a toe-curling baritone and an annoying lockjaw. Now I'm certain the pair are Sebastian and Lydie.

What. The. Fuck!

I stumble as I pivot on my five-inch mules. A man catches me. But I hurry away for fear the motion will draw Sebastian and Lydie's attention to me. I mumble a hasty thank you and rush to the ladies' room. Once inside, I lock myself in one stall. The blood pounds in my ears. Clutching my chest, I try to slow my breathing like Starr taught me at the Fiji retreat before I hyperventilate. Inhale one. Exhale one. Inhale two. Exhale two. Inhale thr—

That bastard!

No wonder Sebastian was so unavailable and couldn't

spare me time but a few minutes. Too busy hugged up with that wench Lydie. A-fucking-gain!

How stupid am I? I broke my vow to never go back to Sebastian. See where that got me… Screwed over, again!

The minutes tick by. I grouse some more, crying then stewing in the stall. The sounds of other members entering and leaving keep me from exiting my temporary refuge. As soon as it quiets down, I'll fix my face. Then get the hell out of LEVELS posthaste. A break in the comings and goings gets me moving.

My face is puffy and red from crying. Fortunately, the waterproof makeup didn't smear. I don't carry a handbag to LEVELS, so I make use of the plush cotton washcloths dampened with cool water. One more dab and I'm out.

The door opens to three women. The first to enter is none other than Lydie with her mask still in her hand. She halts when she sees me. But gets bumped further past the entry by the couple who are more engrossed in each other to notice the sudden tension in the bathroom. A loud moan follows the clicking of the lock on the largest stall at the end. Lydie and I never stop staring at one another.

I refuse to let her see how upset I am, so I stride to the door with my head held high, eyes straight ahead.

"Lola, wait," she says as she catches me by the arm. "We need to talk."

"Fuck you, Lydie"—there goes subtlety—"There isn't shit for us to talk about." I snarl as I yank my arm from her hand.

Instead of letting me go, Lydie tightens her grip, and I jerk to a stop. She is taller than me by a good four inches and surprisingly strong. Damn… I need to add strength training to my running.

I stare up to find her emerald eyes no longer lit with

arrogance and disdain as they were every time she and I crossed paths. A quick scan of her face reveals a humbleness that wasn't there previously. I nod my acquiescence as the door opens again to more women.

"Not here," Lydie states.

I follow her down a quiet separate hall to a door where she places her palm on the panel. The door opens with a soft click to a private room. Not trusting Lydie, I beckon her inside ahead of me. A small smile returns her usual self-possessed glint to her eyes. I cock my eyebrow and she raises her hands, palms forward in peace. The door shuts behind us.

"First, I must apologize for my poor behavior, Lola."

I stand still, shocked by her words. With a self-deprecating nod, she continues.

"Yes, I was totally wrong and should never have treated you as I did. Please allow me to explain," she pauses, and it's my turn to nod mutely.

"As you know, Sebastian and I grew up together. Although he is best friends with my younger brother Lachlan, Sebastian and I share the commonality of being the eldest sibling and future leader of our family's company. As we grew older and took over more responsibilities in our business roles, I leaned on him for support. He became my confidante."

Lydie pauses, closes her eyes, and takes a deep breath before she continues.

"My father does not believe a woman can run Jackson Corporation. He wants Lachlan to take over from me despite the successes I've achieved. Lachlan loves me and will do nothing to ruin our relationship. My father's consolation prize is to marry me off to a man from another powerful and wealthy family as a business merger."

My jaw drops and I shake my head in complete disgust. Damn, isn't this the twenty-first century and not the 1800s? Lydie exhales at my reaction.

"Yes, I see you agree with me how ludicrous is his idea. Sebastian became a ray of light for me in that I could marry him, please my father, and with Sebastian's support persuade my father to allow me to run Jackson."

Again, Lydie gauges my reaction. I press my lips together to not comment. She takes that as my permission for her to go on.

"You changed the plan that only I created—Sebastian was completely unaware. He loves you and cares for you unlike any prior woman. You may have changed my plan, but you also changed the flagrant playboy who never dated a woman or spent time with one more than once."

My mouth drops open, again. Whaaat??? But Lydie goes on.

"I'm working with a therapist to deal with my issues and part of the process is to right wrongs. It's selfish of me, but I hope you can forgive me."

The entire time Lydie spoke, my mind was reeling. Sebastian loves me? Then why did they have sex? I demand an answer from her for those very questions. She has the decency to appear sheepish.

"Oh, yes, well, I had a bit too much to drink and after midnight showed up at Sebastian's penthouse professing my love. To which he fed me espresso and crackers to sober my ass up so I could go to bed and leave in the morning. What you saw and heard was him supporting me in standing firm against my father's antiquated belief. And yes, he truly loves you. As a matter of fact, he's here looking for you. But these masks make it pretty difficult." She laughs as she twirls her mask by the string.

I search Lydie's face for the slightest sign on insincerity. But find none. Only relief shows as though a weight is off her shoulders.

Tonight is chock full of shocks. I may need a defibrillator before it's over.

"Okay, I see," I start. "You really pissed me off and caused a hell of a lot of heartache and anguish for Sebastian and me. I could go on, but I have to get to my man. I appreciate your honesty and forgive you." I raise my hand to stop her interruption to continue.

"The Steeles and Jacksons may not share the same blood in their veins. But you might as well, since your families are so intertwined. I plan to be in Sebastian's life, so you and I will have to be amicable. We may not be BFFs, but we will be respectful of one another. Deal?" I ask hurriedly as I hold out my hand, eager to leave.

Lydie's face breaks into the most beatific smile—fuck, she's as gorgeous as everyone else here—and shakes my hand.

"Deal, Lola," she grins. "Now, I am on my own quest to find myself a lover. Another suggestion made by my therapist." Lydie winks and opens the door to a fresh beginning for all of us.

SEBASTIAN

Oh, well, isn't this just rich…

Lydie is at LEVELS London tonight. Amongst the members, she's spotted me the one second I lifted my mask from my face to wipe my eye. Damn.

I sure as hell hope Lola doesn't happen upon us as Lydie goes on about an apology for her atrocious behavior towards Lola. Good for Lydie she has a therapist to help her overcome her Daddy-approval issues. Hopefully, she has marrying me out of her head, too. No more late-night booty calls by her to my penthouse. So, there's a major win at least. I cannot allow Lydie to fuck up my re-claiming Lola now.

"—understand. So, please forgive me, Sebastian. I never meant to cause you any angst. I was just too blinded by proving myself to my father and thought you would be the match he would approve."

Lydie stops to eye me warily. In response, I nod and incline my head to tell her I understand and forgive her. But I'm looking for Lola and don't need her seeing

Lydie with me. She agrees and excuses herself to the loo.

Finally.

Now I can continue my perusal of the crowd.

I spot a petite, dark-haired woman who has a red enamel bracelet on her slim wrist. If Lola is here seeking a Dom, I will lose it. She better have a black enamel bracelet as a voyeur to observe others' sexual escapades. Especially since Masquerade Night gets wild. Still a safe place with only consensual play amongst adults. But fewer inhibitions because of the anonymity the masks provide members.

As I approach the potential Lola, she turns. Even through the decorative mask that covers her entire face, I can see her eyes are a vivid blue. She peeks up at me and tilts her head in question. Before I can shake my head a definitive no, I glimpse Lydie striding towards me. Beside her struts another little woman with raven colored hair.

This one speeds past Lydie to rush over to me as she snatches her mask off her face.

Thank fuck! It's Lola. My excitement is short-lived as she scowls at me, then jabs her long-manicured finger in my chest. Ow, damn.

"Really, Sebastian! Lydie said you were here looking for me. But ohhh nooo… You're hooking up with someone else. Dam—"

Swiftly I grab her wrist—noting the red bracelet and the punishment it will incite. Then turn her back to my front as I reach my other arm across her torso to grip her opposite hip. Her slight frame pinned to my chest while my growing cock pokes her lower back.

Fuck yeah, it's on. My dick twitches in agreement.

"Hold on there, Naughty Pet," I growl in her ear. "So soon you forget who is the Dom and who is the su—"

"Fuck... You, Sebastian! Naughty my as—"

I swing her around and pepper her plump bottom with a volley of slaps. Lola dances on her toes, shifting her body to avoid the unforgiving blows. Now, that's the only dancing long into the night she will do, and only for me.

I ignore her curses and cries for me to stop. Instead, I lower my hand to spank the sensitive area where her butt meets her thighs. Lola yelps in response. Next, the backs of her thighs receive my unwavering attention. Lola remains unyielding, too stubborn to give in. Fine by me.

"Enough... Sebastiaaan! Ouch..."

"When are you going to learn, Naughty Pet?"

Despite her protests, Lola's body betrays her arousal. The scent of her sweet pussy floats to my nose. I inhale deeply. My mouth waters as the aroma triggers my memory of her delectable taste. I lick my lips, then press them to the delicate shell of her earlobe.

"Do you really want me to stop, Naughty Pet? Before you deny it, think long and hard. Your body tells me otherwise. Tell me, Pet, if I were to slide my finger within your folds, would I find you sopping wet?"

The vixen forgets I know how much she craves punishment. Her body needs it to release tension or to ease her nerves. A kink she discovered a little over a year ago when one of her two lovers who was a Dom spanked her before they had sex.

Her need started us doing an anonymous scene together at LEVELS New York. She was in search of a Dom to relieve her nervousness before her meeting to expand her lingerie company. Of all the available Doms there that night, I'm thankful it was me who saw her first. However, neither of us knew the very next morning we would face each other in a conference room to negotiate a multimillion-dollar business deal. Fate, I wonder.

Now, Lola growls in frustration, knowing I speak the truth. She cannot deny her responsiveness to my touch—be it a caress or a swat—nor the pleasure it gives.

Her little body tightens in embarrassment. But loosens when she feels my fingers slowly stroke down her inner thigh to the hem of her clingy negligee.

The lingerie she wears is enough to make me punish her. Glittery black jet beads form the shapes of flowers, leaves, and vines embroidered on sheer skin-tone mesh. Thin black boning accentuates her narrow waist and the flare of her curvy hips. Lola's blush pink nipples wink at me while her mound hides behind artfully placed beads that form the shape of a vase. Lola's lush body is an Eden I intend to plunder for eternity.

"Oh Baazzz."

My name slips past her parted lips on a long exhale as my fingertip brushes her swollen nether lips.

"Let go and just feel, Naughty Pet. Coat my finger with your succulent juices," I grunt, my girth trapped in my trousers painfully.

Lola spreads her thighs, raising the negligee higher to give me better access to her ambrosial core. With a slow rhythm, I slide my thick finger in and out before I add a second digit.

"So tight and wet for me, Pet. You do not disappoint your Dom."

Lola purrs in contentedness as she rubs her pussy against my palm. Music to my ears; pressure to my cock.

So infatuated by Lola, I didn't notice the members who turned to watch our impromptu demonstration until their murmurs of approval breach our bubble. The gathered crowd includes Lydie who stands stock-still fascinated by the performance. Her blush deepens to a bright red from her hairline to her bosom when our eyes meet. Slowly, Lydie retreats beyond the circle. This intimacy would never happen between us. I sense she still wants it despite what she says, but acknowledges it will never happen.

I return my gaze to Lola, who leans languidly against my body. Her eyes are half closed and a soft smile lingers on her angelic face. I kiss the top of her head before I wrap my arm around her waist to keep her steady as I lead us to the double doors. Our peepshow ends.

Lola's soft curves press into my side as we wait for the elevator to take us to Level 3 for my private suite. Since I live in New York and frequently visit London for business, I have suites set aside for my personal use only at those LEVELS locations. It's one of many privileges my investor status affords me.

With Lola in my life and having her flagship boutique in Paris, we'll need a personal suite at LEVELS Paris. I make a mental note to send a text message to Taylor Hunt, the head of membership to make the arrangements immediately. Perhaps Lola and I will take a side trip to select our preferred suite before we return to New York.

The ding signaling the elevator interrupts my thoughts. More members arrive to partake in the festivities. Some men turn their heads in Lola's direction. Her alluring body outlined in her revealing lingerie proves too enticing for them. From behind elaborate masks, their eyes scan her bountiful curves from head to toe.

My caveman instincts kick in. Possessively, I move Lola behind me to protect my mate from the challenge of other males. I stand to my full height of six feet, four inches, a projection of Alpha power and strength. I will fight any man who dares to come between me and my woman. Lola is mine.

Sensing their imminent demise, the men move on in search of easier to obtain playmates.

"Where are we going?" Lola asks as the doors close and the elevator starts its ascent.

I cup her face to tilt her lips to mine as I capture her mouth. She tastes divine. After a mind-blowing kiss, I respond to my Petite Seductress.

"We are going upstairs to my private suite to continue your punishment," I smirk.

Lola's eyes open wide, no longer lulled by the bliss of her orgasm. She raises a perfectly arched brow and cocks her head to the side.

"How presumptuous of you, Sebastian," she retorts.

I crowd her space, using my larger body to push her into the corner. Then bend my knees to level our eyes.

"Really, Naughty Pet? Now you question your Dom?"

"Who says you're *my Dom*? You were just chitchatting with your hookup for the night only moments before I walked over to you," Lola accuses, a flicker of sadness sweeps across her face.

"You are mistaken. I thought she was you with her black hair and petite, curvy frame," I reassure Lola while softly stroking her cheek.

Her ample chest expands on a deep inhale as she considers my words. More emotions from sadness to doubt to hope cross her lovely features.

"I came tonight because I knew you would be here—"

The doors open, cutting off my declaration. I gesture for Lola to go ahead of me. Then take her hand to lead her to my suite. The hallway is quiet because of the plush carpet and soundproof rooms. Low sensuous music is the only testament to what awaits you behind the doors.

At the end of the hall, I place my palm on the panel to unlock my suite. Lola enters ahead of me. I enjoy the sight of her ass as she sways her hips. Her fuck-me heels make her butt sit up proudly, just like my dick.

As though she senses my thoughts, Lola peers at me over her shoulder. Her waist-length hair hangs like a silky curtain. It begs for me to wrap it around my fist and pull on its glossy strands until she arches her back in surrender.

"Sebastian, we need to talk."

The most dreaded words fall from her mouth sufficiently ending my reverie. My heart skips a beat at the thought of her ending any chance we have at getting back together before we can even start.

I gesture for her to sit on the extra-large, hard-carved mahogany wood bed. The only appropriate piece of furniture. A pommel horse and chaise with brass rings wouldn't do for a serious conversation.

Lola perches on the foot of the bed and glances up at me. I incline my head for her to speak first.

"I want your commitment as an exclusive couple. What do you want, Sebastian?"

This is what I most adore about Lola. She is a smart, direct woman who doesn't give a shit about who I am or the size of my bank account. She's about me, not the glamour of being on a billionaire's arm.

With renewed hope, I settle beside her. Then pull her into my arms to hold Lola close to my heart that beats for her only.

"You. I want you, Lola. I want us. Period," I profess. "I promised you before, I'm yours, Lola. Only you."

Lola leans back to stare at my face. Her imploring hazel

eyes search for any deception. I open up to her to show my sincerity. Satisfied, she nods, then pulls my face to hers, locking our lips together. Our tongues probe and stroke one another in a passionate tango.

I shift us so she lies beneath me, my body pressing her firmly into the mattress. I want to possess her, mark her as mine.

"I want you, Lola. I crave you."

My whisper hoarse, barely audible as I brush my lips over the soft skin of her delicate throat.

Lola shivers, responsive as ever. I must have her now. I can no longer take it slow or wait another moment.

I stand and strip my clothes off. Lola lies back on the bed with hooded eyes now scanning me with heat. Each article of clothing I remove causes her eyes to spark with blatant desire. Unconsciously, she plays with her nipples, tugging on the taut tips through the material of her lingerie. She draws her lower lip between her teeth and widens her legs to me in welcome.

Fully naked, I stalk over to the armoire. There's a particular toy I need to use on Lola tonight.

Returning to the bed, I make haste removing the negligee that's taunted me with hints of the sinful body covered by it. Unable to resist, I lower my head to her puckered nipple. I latch on to suckle from her plump flesh. Lola bows her body, pushing her D-cups further in my face.

Fuck. I've missed the delicacy that is Lola.

My sensitized dick thumps her thigh, reminding me it's time to reclaim my Petite Seductress fully. I pick up the spreader bar and attach it to her ankles ensuring the fit is secure, but not overly tight. The width prevents her from closing her legs from my entry. But first, I have to be sure Lola is ready for me. If she hasn't been with anyone since me—as is my hope—I must prep her for the intensity of my thick ten inches.

I trail kisses from her full tits down her belly to her bare mound. I lift her legs over my head to put the spreader bar behind my back. As I settle between her thighs, I take a deep inhale to fill my nostrils with the savory aroma of Lola's arousal. A glance up her body shows she's already in the throes of passion with her head thrown back and her eyes closed. With a smirk, I take my first sample in months of Lola's sweet essence.

My tongue glides along the edges of her labia, teasing her to open for me. As if on cue, Lola whimpers when her juices flow from her core. I use the tip of my tongue to catch each drop, savoring her unique flavor.

Lola's mewl spurs me on to probe past her folds to the interior of her channel. The rough texture of her G-spot demands my attention. I pass my tongue over it again and again, sending Lola into a tizzy. She tries to clamp her legs around my head with her need for release. But the spreader bar restricts her movement.

I don't want to prolong her pleasure, only heighten it to get her loose and sufficiently wet for the pounding that I won't be able to control. It's been too long without her.

I add two fingers to her core as my tongue pulls on her engorged clit. The finger fucking combined with the sucking and laving of her clit shoots Lola into a jackknife. I growl and use my free hand to press onto her lower belly to hold her in place. With a strangled cry, Lola settles back into the pillows, barely able to keep her hips from shifting closer to my mouth.

I continue to eat her pussy like it's the first meal I've had in three months. Which is the case since I haven't had her in all of this time. I more than make up for it as I lick and nip until her juices gush into my eager mouth.

Once I've had my fill and she's ready for me, I slide on top of her pliant body. I disentangle her hands from my hair and hold them above her head in one hand while the other aligns my cock dripping with pre-cum to her channel. Without hesitating, I surge forward to impale Lola on my thick length. She wails in response.

"So tight, baby. Fuuuck... Are you still only mine, Lola?" I demand as I drive my girth deep within her core.

My eyes roll back as the overwhelming sensations of once again being one with my baby course through my body. I shudder and demand she answers me.

"Oh yeeesss... Baz... Only you.... Oh fuuuck... Only you, baby... Aaahhh," Lola moans, meeting each of my frantic thrusts with one of her own.

Our bodies need no further direction as we reclaim one another the way man and woman have known from the dawn of time.

Lola is mine, and I am hers. I satisfy my caveman.

* * *

Lola

I thought the goings-on at Peepshow amplified my senses, but nothing compares to Baz's ability to heighten my desires. This man brings out every emotion in me—joy, pain, pleasure, love...

Once again I let him win. I let him conquer me. For good.

LOLA

Awesome…

The only word that comes close enough to describe the past few weeks with Baz.

All during the night and into the morning of our reunion, he only let me sleep for an hour or less. Each time, I awoke to his lips suckling my nipple, his teeth nipping my clit, or his fat cock stroking my pussy walls. He made good on his promise to fill each of my holes, too. By the time we left LEVELS London, both sets of my lips were puffy, my muscles ached, and I staggered out the door bowlegged.

Baz meanwhile strutted like a peacock, proudly flaunting its feathers.

Instead of returning to the Royal Suite where I was staying at Claridge's for the week, Baz took us to his palatial estate in the ultraexclusive Kensington Palace Gardens. Just as his duplex penthouse in New York City is on Billionaires' Row, his West London home is on Billionaires' Boulevard. As I always say, there's the rich, and then there's the wealthy…

Baz made it his mission for us to christen each room over the three days we stayed. That was a hell of a lot of christening with at least forty rooms over five floors—including the attic. Let's just say he gave me the grand tour and then some.

A surprise trip to Paris took us to LEVELS in the 7th Arrondissement Palais-Bourbon Le Faubourg. Similar to Lola's Coterie Paris, the club inhabits the former Parisian home of a pampered courtesan to another French king—those randy royals.

The beautiful *maison* on a tree-lined street sits behind duplicates of the original double carriage doors and features a spacious interior courtyard. Baz explained they host grand soirees during the warm-weather months under the stars and strings of fairy lights.

He decided we needed to select one of the private suites for our exclusive use. Baz wants to be sure we have one specific to us since I have my flagship boutique in the city and split my time here. We chose a new decor and our favorite toys. I giggle to consider a room in a sex club a sweet gift, albeit an ultraposh one.

When we finally arrived back in New York, Baz insisted I move in with him. But I declined on the basis we need not rush into living together again. Plus, Billie's words of "why buy the cow when you can get the milk for free" floated into my head. A definite reminder that Baz and I moved in together too soon after meeting. Only a week had passed. I made myself too accessible to him. Even though I enjoyed spending almost every non-work hour with him. This time, it's best for us to have our own space. Breathe a little. My version of take it slow.

* * *

"Lola, what sense does it make for you to live all the way over on Sutton Place when your Lola's Coterie New York is right below our penthouse?" Baz complains, exasperated since we've been discussing me moving back in with him for the past ten minutes. "And to top it off, by yourself! When you can just move back in here."

Secretly, I'm glad he wants me to move in right away. It proves his commitment to us as a couple. But I have to stand firm.

"No, Baz. I want this to be right. We need to have our own space—"

"That's absurd! We had three months of 'our own space' and quite frankly, it sucked!" Baz erupts. His hands thrown up in irritation as he swipes a thick lock of ebony hair out of his eyes.

His hair already disheveled from plowing his long fingers through it makes him look even more rakish than usual. I'm concerned he may just pull it out by the roots.

At the image, a laugh bubbles past my lips despite my attempt to hold it back.

"What the hell is so funny?" Baz demands.

Baz's reaction makes my giggles worsen. Doubled over, I hold my sides and laugh so hard I snort. That only adds to my mirth. Baz's irritation increases as I continue to laugh harder.

"Oh... So the big bad Dom is a big wimpy baby!" I rib him, catching my breath. "Waa, waa, waa!"

And just like that, Baz turns the tables when he spins me around and spanks my ass.

"You think I am entertaining, Little Pet? Let me show you how hilarious I can be..." He chuckles sinfully at my shock.

* * *

Just the thought of the limitless pleasure Baz gives makes me squirm with need in my seat next to him as we fly to the

United Arab Emirates. Besides incredible, non-stop make-up sex daily—even if I go home to my penthouse or he goes to his—we accomplished business-related tasks.

Baz's first order of business was to move my New York office back to the executive floor of STEELE International. I gave in to that move since the suite of offices is larger than the two rooms above my boutique. Plus, the unobstructed views of Manhattan are fantastic from the floor-to-ceiling windows on the twenty-ninth floor.

On the opposite wing from Baz's offices gives him a sense of closeness not afforded him with me living in my penthouse "all the way over on Sutton Place." Not to mention the incredible scenes of secretary and demanding boss we play behind the darkened glass walls of the sound-proof offices. Definitely worth setting aside my independent streak for clandestine orgasms.

"Hey, babe, private jokes?" Baz asks, poking my ticklish side.

I pull his hand away from my flank to kiss his fingertips before nipping then sucking them between my full lips. A shudder runs through me when Baz's eyes widen in surprise. The normally flint gray orbs darken to lustful onyx.

"Oh, just thinking about you, Sir." I purr, slipping his thick fingers from my mouth. "And the pleasure you so kindly provide me."

A sharp intake of breath precedes Baz shifting in his seat. My gaze drops to his crotch where a bulge forms from his massive cock awakening at my seduction. Hhhmmm.

"Lola, excuse me. I hate to interrupt."

Disappointed I have to look away from a promising sight, I glance up. Baz reaches for his laptop to cover the burgeoning evidence of his unexpected arousal. Unaware of the sexual tension around her, Blair continues.

"The report you requested just came through and we set the con call to start in fifteen minutes. Would you like for me to set up at the table?"

Thwarted by work, I slip past Baz. Knowing he won't dare do anything in response, I purposefully let my butt glide past his face. Tease, temptation, and a raincheck rolled in one. In frustration, Baz growls low in his chest.

"Until later, Sir..." I whisper in his ear, sure to brush my ample breasts against his arm.

Another growl and I follow Blair to the front of the jet.

Billie stands by the table with her mobile at her ear and her laptop in her arm, ready to get started. I have the best assistants ever. And to think I wanted originally to do everything myself, from the design to the administrative tasks. Luckily, Luc disengaged that madness from my mind. Things are more efficient now. I can focus on the creative side of the business—doing what I love the most.

Before we leave Dubai, we must have another Girls' Night Out. I need to catch up with them on Luc and Patrick. Blair's been mum while Billie regularly gushes about the bonnie Scotsman. Funny how the men appeared interested in me at first. Well, at least Baz thinks both. I still doubt Luc thought of me beyond a mentee. All turns out as it should. A Starr tenet I've grown to appreciate.

"Splendid job! The production schedules for the Abu Dhabi and Dubai collections are on track for the openings," I say happy to have the cultural differences worked out.

"Yes. It's good we had a focus group to determine the female patrons' comfortability levels," Billie adds.

"Very true. Also, your pieces are pretty much worn beneath clothing, so less likelihood of issues," Blair nods.

"It's like unwrapping a present to find an exquisite surprise!"

Our laughter carries through the jet. The chirp of my mobile draws my attention. Luc is on the line. I glance at Blair, but she's busy chatting with Billie. I excuse myself to take the call on the sofa.

"Ciao, Luc, comment ça va?" I ask as to his well-being once settled and staring out the window at the expansive sky.

"Comme ci comme ça, petite chérie," Luc responds.

I perk up at his despondent tone and ask him what's on his mind, fluently conversing in French. He has an obligation that prevents him from meeting us in Abu Dhabi tomorrow. He's delayed a day or two and will meet us in Dubai.

"I know how important the location selections are for you, Lola," he states. "But I will make it in time for the Dubai sites. You can send a video of the ones in Abu Dhabi. However, I trust your judgment and I know Steele wants the best for you."

On the tail end of our call, Blair's mobile chirps a text message. Her expression changes from perky to disappointed. I slide into the seat opposite her at the table and look at her questioningly.

"Oh, nothing," she says airily as she flips her mobile face down on the table blocking the screen from view. "Nothing at all."

"So you say, but your body language busts you," I tell her with my eyebrow cocked in disbelief. "By any chance was that a text message from a certain French nobleman?"

Blair swings her gaze in my direction, shocked that I guessed correctly.

"Mmm hmmm... So I thought! You don't have to say anything"—I raise my hand to stop her from speaking—"For now at least. But you will spill when we have a Girls's Night Out before we leave Dubai!"

Billie giggles and prods Blair with her elbow.

"So busted!" Billie grins. "Blair refuses to tell me anything. Now, you must divulge all over cocktails at a club for visitors. We'll need some liquor to get us through this drama!"

The rest of the thirteen-hour flight we spend on more prep work, dinner, and sleeping. Despite the bedroom being soundproof, I just can't finish what I started with Baz while Blair, Billie, and the other STEELE staff members are on board. I blush at the thought.

We land shortly after seven in the morning. Several helicopters wait to fly us to the STEELE Abu Dhabi. The impressive complex comprises four towers that resemble modern sculptures. With varying heights of over 1,000 feet and 80 floors, SAD is nothing less than breathtaking elation as it dominates the skyline. The signature gray glass exterior gleams in the desert sunshine. Two towers offer sought-after residences; one tower features the luxury hotel and mall; the fourth tower provides optimal office space. On the ground level, benches under trees and other greenery with water misters make for a respite from the heat. Phenomenal.

Baz and I take the rapid elevator to one of the Rulers' Suites on the top floor. Blair, Billie, and Tina Nickles, who's one of Baz's assistants, and other staff go to a separate bank of elevators to access their suites a few floors below. We agree to meet in the lobby in ninety minutes.

"This is an incredible property, Baz!" I blurt as soon as we're alone on the elevator.

His eyes light up when he turns to me to respond.

"This project is one of my favorites. Since it covers each

of the STEELE divisions being residential, entertainment, and retail, my entire family worked together to make it a success. Not to mention the top-notch security installed to protect the elite clientele."

Baz's excitement radiates on his face. He truly loves his family. A bit of wistfulness strikes me when I think of my parents and how much I miss them. As though sensing my sudden mood change, Baz strokes my cheek before tilting my head back to kiss me senseless.

"They would be proud of you, babe," he whispers while his thumb strokes my cheek. "You're not alone. You have me, and my family is eager to have dinner when we get back."

I can only nod since tears of happiness clog my throat as I lean my forehead against his firm chest. The heady aroma of his cologne fills my nostrils. So I burrow deeper into Baz, gaining support from his strength. Moments later, the elevator doors ding open.

My breath escapes me once again. This time because of the jaw-dropping view. Spread before us is the dazzling water with glittering ripples that reach across to the other shoreline. The megayachts moored at the complex's private marina bobbing on the waves resemble toys from this lofty height. The sandy beach dotted with umbrellas calls to me. With a wistful sigh, my gaze moves to the interior.

The sheer opulence of the suite rivals the panorama. A cue from the family's name influences the decor that features platinum, white gold, and white marble with gray and black veins running through it. They cover the walls in white silk while the ceiling is white-gold leaf with crystal chandeliers and strategically placed recessed lighting. White and dove gray furniture made of silk and leather is throughout the seating areas. The primary space is vast with plenty of sunlight and a light airy feel. I can only imagine the decor for the four bedrooms, baths, dining room, and other spaces must be just as resplendent.

"Come on, Lola, we have little time," Sebastian says as he grabs my hand and pulls me away from the living area. "I have something even more captivating to show you."

ANOTHER NOTCH on the Christened Room Bedpost later, we meet the team in the lobby. Everyone changed into lighter clothing to account for the sultry desert heat. Women opting for loose-fitting cotton shift dresses with jackets and the men swapping their wool suits for linen cotton blends. Sunglasses, mobiles, and attachés abound.

A quick walk through one of the all-glass, air-conditioned corridors that connect the hotel to the other towers takes us to STEELE International, Inc. UAE. Similar to the New York City headquarters, the executive level is on the top floor and the view again is spectacular.

Seated in a conference room facing the enticing water, it's hard to concentrate on business. But concentrate we must.

Gathered around the table sit staff from Lola's Coterie Paris and STEELE New York and UAE. The opening of my boutique requires members from both companies to work together as one team. LCP marketing, sales, legal, and finance staff flew in yesterday afternoon. Less of a time change accounts for their perkier attitudes.

STEELE's staff in attendance include the same departments less sales. Additionally representatives from retail, design and construction, logistics, security, technology, and cultural affairs round out the group. The talent everyone brings to the table is impressive. I'm confident Lola's

Coterie Dubai's success will match that of New York and Las Vegas.

The combined marketing teams discuss their plan including the ad and branding campaigns, magazine and television interviews, opening party guest lists, and invitations to social events that I should attend. Another team covers logistics for travel and accommodations for out-of-town guests and staff along with activities since the event will cover two days in Abu Dhabi. After the lunch break, the STEELE retail team shares an in-depth presentation covering the three available spaces. The rest of the departments layout the agenda for tomorrow's sessions.

I thank everyone, and we end the workday at three due to the eight-hour time difference.

"I'M SO EXCITED! I can't wait to see the stores tomorrow!" I exclaim to Baz as we sit at one of the hotel's three Michelin star restaurants overlooking the marina.

Determined to beat jet lag, Baz and I took a nap when we returned to our Rulers' Suite to give us energy to stay up for dinner. Even Baz was too tired to do more than spoon me against him. A refreshing shower followed. Now rejuvenated, we dine on scrumptious seafood and vintage wine.

Billie, Tina, and Blair went out for dinner and to a club with some STEELE UAE staff. In the morning, everyone will meet in the lobby instead of at the office since it connects the mall to the hotel. The retail team will give us a tour of the recommended stores before we make the ultimate decision.

"I'm pleased with the presentation the retail team made. Those store options are A1 on the scale we use to categorize space," Baz responds. "The anchor location closest to the hotel entrance is my first choice, followed by the one near the street entrance. The one in the middle requires foot traffic directed to it as opposed to an entryway with organic passersby."

"I would love to walk through after we eat…" I offer Baz my most-winning smile.

"Since this is a business negotiation, Ms. Lewis, what would I get in exchange for granting you access to the mall after hours?" Baz asks with a cocked eyebrow.

"Oh, Sir, I will need your help to reach the top shelves in the stockroom. You see, my manager didn't leave a ladder for me to use. So, I will need to sit on your strong shoulders to—"

"Check, please," Baz calls to a server who passes our table.

SEBASTIAN

Dubai is one of my favorite cities in the world and holds a special place in my heart.

After I graduated Harvard Business School with my MBA, my father sent me here as part of the team that managed the opening of STEELE's first office in the UAE. I value the experience as I handled various aspects of the project from site selection to land negotiations to construction plans to the hiring of staff. Hell, even the carpet selection fell in the realm of my responsibilities.

My father wanted me to know all sides of our family's business and how to run it. It was a three-year process that helped to hone my skills as STEELE's next generational leader.

Since SD I's initial opening, two additional towers for a five-star hotel and luxury residences joined the office tower at the original site. SD II's expansion across the street includes a multi-level mall with an office tower above and a residential tower.

The boom for housing and commercial space has

exploded over the years. People and businesses from all across the globe have made Dubai their home or established an office. Work and big money requires distractions. Thus the need for high-end shops, top-rated eateries, movie theaters, and concert halls. STEELE provides it all.

I'm thrilled Lola agreed to open Lola's Coterie Dubai. The boutique is perfect to join the other luxury retailers in the SD II Mall. Despite what people may think, the women in the UAE enjoy wearing the latest fashions, including lingerie. I can vouch for their desire to appear and feel sexy.

The two spots set aside for Lola to choose from are the best in the entire mall. One opens directly onto the street with an entrance inside to the mall's interior. The other space is near the office entrance. The presentation the retail team shared with us emphasizes the benefits of both. But I prefer the street-front space since she can showcase her new evening collection in the windows. Modesty is still appropriate in the UAE. So Lola can take advantage of the windows to make passersby aware of the clothing side of Lola's Coterie. Either way, the decision is for her to make.

"Lola, this space offers you the most exposure, even if it's larger than you want."

Luc's voice cuts through my thoughts, bringing my attention back to where we stand in the store available at the front of the mall. I was glad when he didn't show up in Abu Dhabi. Thank fuck! I'm still working on my trust of his intentions with Lola. Since Lola and I are just back together, I keep my mouth shut. No need to make her jump back into the water just as I reeled her into my boat.

"I don't know, Luc. It's a lot larger than I expected. Bigger than any of my other boutiques, including Paris. Sebastian, what do you think?"

My heart warms. Lola asking my advice after her "mentor" told her his opinion. Big step forward. Perfect time for cool points.

"I agree with Luc," I start, casting my eyes in his direction. He looks shocked by my words. Yeah, grandpa. Take that.

"You can showcase your new evening collection in the windows. With modesty very appropriate in the UAE, you can take advantage of the windows to make passersby aware of Lola's Coterie clothing side. Draw them in with the dresses that resemble lingerie, then get them to buy the dresses and the real lingerie. A win-win situation.," I finish with a nod to Luc. Solidarity, my brother.

"Baz! That's a fantastic idea! So smart!" Lola gushes as she claps her hands. "Then, it's settled. This is the location for Lola's Coterie Dubai!"

A satisfied smile blooms on my face. Score!

* * *

"Do I look all right?" Lola asks as we head to a party thrown by some friends I met years ago.

I let my gaze travel over Lola's lush body. She looks like a goddess in a red silk chiffon sleeveless gown with a cape detail that sweeps from the shoulder straps to the floor behind her as she walks. Her full breasts accentuated by the vee front and wrapped waistband make my mouth water. Light through the bottom shows the faint outline of her legs lengthened by the sky-high strappy sandals she wears. Being in the UAE, she modestly covers her shoulders with a glittery, embroidered sheer wrap while we're outdoors. Her hair falls loose in lustrous waves down her back. The rare, red diamond earrings and matching bangles, two on each arm, that I gifted her for the opening of Lola's Coterie Las

Vegas shine. I note how they enhance her beauty as we sit in the back of the chauffeured Rolls-Royce Corniche that I keep in Dubai. Gorgeous Girl.

Damn. I can't wait to ravage my Petite Seductress when we get back to the hotel.

"More than all right. You look like a dream," I assure her.

The jewels sparkle as she reaches forward to kiss me softly on the lips.

"Thank you, baby," Lola whispers. "I want to make a good impression on your friends."

She peeks at me from under her thick lashes. I lean my forehead against hers and whisper words that have been on the tip of my tongue for months.

"I love you, Lola Lewis. You impress me and that's all that matters."

Lola's jaw drops and her eyes brighten with tears as she leans back to study my face. Shit, I didn't mean to upset her. Quickly, I pull her onto my lap to hold her close. I press my lips to the top of her head as I croon to her.

"Lola, baby. I've wanted to tell you for so long. You mean everything to me. I thank my lucky stars that you've accepted me back into your life. I was lost without you, my love. Never for a moment think you are less than. You are my everything."

Lola shudders in my arms. We remain as one until the car stops at the party venue. Lola slips off of my lap and straightens her gown before she dabs her eyes with the handkerchief I handed to her.

Just as the door opens, she puts her hand on my forearm to stop me from stepping out of the car.

"I love you, too, Baz. I've loved you from the start."

My heart melts and I sit back in the seat. But Lola shakes her head.

"Your friends haven't seen you in a while and threw this party for you. We have to go in. If only for a little while," she smiles. Her hazel eyes glow with her love for me.

For me, the Dom playboy who said he'd never fall in love and scoffed at a permanent relationship.

Well, that was before Ms. Lola Lewis... Petite Seductress... Little Pet... Soon-to-be Mrs. Sebastian Steele.

As EXPECTED, Lola charms all the guests. The women flock to her and the men leer with lust-filled eyes. She floats about the room with ease. No one is immune to Lola's wit and grace, I smile proudly to myself.

"Hi, Sebastian. It's been awhile."

The purr comes from Vanessa O'Sullivan the Irish ex-pat I fucked regularly when I lived in Dubai and often when I returned for business. She is not someone I want to deal with now that things are well with Lola. I learned from Vanessa not to dip more than once with a woman—too clingy. Shit.

I scan the room and see Lola speaking with a cluster of women. Perfect. Hopefully, I can get this conversation with Vanessa over with fast.

"Hello, Vanessa," I start only to stop when she slips her hand under my evening jacket to reach for my crotch.

I grab her wrist and pull her hand away. Another quick search around assuages my fear that someone saw her bold-as-fuck move. Deftly, I pull her out of the others' sight. This ends now. No Lydie miscommunication happening again. I will make it crystal clear for Vanessa.

"Vanessa, do not put your hands on—"

"Sebastian, sweetie, I only wanted to greet you properly," she purrs, pressing her body close to mine.

I jerk back, but stand firm. She is not the type to back down if she senses a weakness. The Dom in me takes over.

"Vanessa, you will never touch me again. Not in greeting or for any other reason. Good night."

I pivot and without a backwards glance return to the party, seeking Lola out. I catch her glancing about the room, looking for me. When our eyes meet, her smile lights the room.

Fuck, I'm a goner for this woman.

Once beside her, I bend down to kiss her on the lips not giving a damn what others may think. I need to taste her sweetness to banish the sour thought of Vanessa from out of my mind. Lola sighs softly as she melts against me.

"No need to act all possessive, Steele. We get it, you've got the best girl as usual. No offense to you, ladies."

I laugh as I take my lips from Lola's delectable mouth to bro hug Porter Huntington. As Vanessa was a tryst, Porter was a partner in crime while I was in Dubai. It's been almost a year since we last saw one another.

"Porter, let me introduce you to the love of my life, Lola Lewis. Lola, this is my wonderful friend Porter Huntington."

Huntington ever the Casanova takes Lola's hand in his as he bows and kisses her knuckles.

"A pleasure to meet the woman who has captured the heart of Sebastian *Never Fall in Love* Steele," he smirks at me over Lola's hand.

"*Enchanté,* Mr. Huntington," Lola starts. "The pleasure of Baz's heart is all mine."

With that, the group laughs. Once again, Lola is the one to capture everyone's heart.

. . .

"WHAT A LOVELY EVENING! Your friends are so welcoming," Lola smiles as we walk into our Rulers' Suite at SD II. "Well… Of course there was that dreadful woman who made a grab for your crotch…"

I nearly trip over Lola's cape, so taken aback by her comment. Damn. I didn't think she saw what happened with Vanessa. Sheepishly, I glance at Lola, who's turned to stare me directly in the eyes. My pulse quickens in anticipation of an argument. Blasted Vanessa O'Sullivan!

"For a moment, I thought I'd have to take off my earrings and sandals to handle her myself. Luckily, you moved her aside and corrected the situation pronto," Lola ends with a smirk.

I scan her face and realize she's not angry with me. Thank fuck! Without hesitating, I scoop her over my shoulder in a fireman's carry, swat her plump ass for giving me palpitations, and stride to the bedroom. Time to make love to my girl. Her laughter rings out and fills my heart with joy.

Yup, Lola Lewis Soon-to-be Mrs. Sebastian Steele has captured my heart forever.

SEBASTIAN

"You will suck me, Little Pet. Every... Little... Inch."

My hips thrust forward with each grunt as I tower above Lola lying supine on the most recent addition to our suite at LEVELS New York. The adjustable table resembles one found in a doctor's examination room. At the foot of the narrow leather-padded bench, the legs split with suede-lined cuffs at the foot. The midsection hinges to allow an upright position or one angled down to the floor. Arms in more cuffs attached to hinged slabs allow for a movement like angel wings.

Ah, and what an angel Lola appears. My favorite types of fruit cover her supple body. Delectable figs with the downy softness of their skin and their plump bottoms blush violet remind me of Lola's lusciousness after a satisfying spanking. Pears shaped like Lola decorate her thighs. Pomegranate seeds made famous for their temptation and sensuality by Greek literature lead a sticky trail from her neck to her mound. The sight of my massive cock burrowing deeper down her throat makes my balls ache. A zing shoots down my spine, straight to my sac. My dick weeps pre-cum in relief.

"Suck... Me."

My growl makes my Little Pet shudder and amp up her tantalizing ministrations. To reward her, I bend my body over hers to gorge on the abundant cherries, grapes, and strawberries that fill her pussy. It's sweeter than ever. I lap at the juices running down her quivering thighs. Then nibble her swollen lips and clit before I spear my tongue between her folds to withdraw a wet cherry. As I chew the tasty treat, I nearly choke on it when Lola nips my engorged tip.

"Fuuuck!" I bellow.

The hum of Lola's teasing laughter shoots vibrations along my shaft, prompting more seed to fill my heavy balls. To prevent an unwanted early release, I pull my dick from her mouth with a pop as I stand.

"Naughty Pet. I know you nipped me to earn a punishment," I chide with a raised brow as I stroke my length. "I am more than happy to oblige."

Despite the blindfold covering her eyes, I can tell by the bowing of her body that she's eager for a spanking. That pleasure I will not give to her as she has not earned it... yet. Instead, I pull nipple and clit clamps and an anal plug from a drawer in the large, double-door armoire. The treasure chest contains a plethora of our favorite toys—Wartenberg Wheels, cords, dildos, vibrators, and so much more.

My lips pluck a piece of a peach from her left nipple and pull them both into mouth. I suck her bud until it tightens. The pinch of the clamp changes Lola's soft mewls to a sharp yelp. Now that she knows my intentions behind the suckling, she tenses when my mouth engulfs her right nipple.

The licks and nips I make along her pomegranate trail cause Lola to writhe wantonly on the bench. The pain of the clamps forgotten.

The delicious combined aroma of her arousal and the fruit makes my mouth water in anticipation. I lap at her thighs and pussy soaked with the ambrosia until she nears her climax. Her body bows and she tries to push her core further into my mouth as her thighs tremble with intensity. The sudden bite of the clit clamp abruptly stops Lola's pending release. A wail follows a frustrated growl that slips from behind her clenched teeth as she flops down against the buttery soft leather of the bench.

Next I carefully insert the medium-size plug coated generously with lube in her puckered hole—a star twinkling at me. Slow, deliberate pressure applied to her back entrance gives Lola time to adjust to the object. Her protests soon turn to sighs once I fully seat the plug within her ass. The red crystal glitters in the ambient lighting.

Stunning.

My attention focuses on the cornucopian spread before me. I continue my feast. A bite of plum, a taste of raspberries, a morsel of nectarine burst with flavor in my mouth. When Lola's skin emerges with only traces of fruit juice, I return to her head.

Just the mushroom tip of my dick pressed against her mouth is enough to signal her to envelop my girth. A groan of pure bliss escapes my lips from the warmth wrapped around my length. I rise onto the balls of my feet to gain further access down Lola's open throat. My angel is definitely heaven sent.

. . .

"Feel better, babe?" I ask Lola, seated in the extra-large claw-foot tub as I slide a sudsy sponge over her bountiful breasts.

Her taut nipples floating on the surface dance in and out of the foam.

Since we returned from the UAE and I reminded Lola about my family coming over to my penthouse for dinner, she's been on edge. Her nerves peaked the closer the day arrived for my family to visit. Their first official meeting has my love anxious. She needed a scene at LEVELS New York to ease her anxiety.

"Ooh yes, baby. Much better, thank you," Lola murmurs contentedly.

She leans her back against my front and widens her legs to allow the sponge to stroke further along her body, dipping in and out of her curves. With her arms draped on the tub's rim, Lola lays herself bare to my sensuous cleaning. A soak in the tub and bathing one another after we play is one habit we established early in our relationship. We enjoy it as much as our lovemaking. The act of caring so intimately for each other brings us closer.

"I went shopping at Eataly NYC in the Flatiron District this afternoon. They have the best of everything and so fresh from Italy! I know you love when I make saltimbocca. We'll start with Mushroom and mozzarella arancini followed by saltimbocca, a tomato and burrata salad with basil oil. Ooh... And garlic sticks! For dessert—"

"You mean besides you?" I tease her as I nibble the sensitive area where her neck meets her shoulder. She's getting wound up again. Her nervousness making her ramble. So, I distract her.

"You and I will save that for the post-party!" She giggles, tilting her head to the side to give me more access. "A selection of sorbet and gelato to end the meal on a lighter note. After coffee we'll drink Limoncello Gin Collins."

Lola slips away to face me, the amber in her hazel eyes glow with her mounting excitement.

"If you don't mind, I'd like to set up a table on the large terrace off of the living room. We can decorate with strings of fairy lights, bright pillows on the furniture, soft music playing over the surround sound system... Recreate an Italian alfresco dining extravaganza!"

Lola's enthusiasm is irresistible. Hating the loss of her body against mine, I cross the tub and pull her back into my arms. With my face nuzzled in her hair, I can join her glee.

"Whatever you want, my love... Whatever you want."

I FOLLOW the sound of conversation into the kitchen, perplexed by a man's voice in my penthouse... A man's deep voice engaged with Lola's light laughter bouncing off the walls of my home.

What. The. Fuck.

"—so kind of you to offer... Ooh!"

Lola's startled exclamation spurs me to slam into the kitchen, ready to drop kick some motherfucker flat on his ass. The door bangs into the wall, the sound of plaster hitting the floor makes Lola and the man jump in surprise.

"What the fuck is going on?" I demand as I stride across the marble, eyes blazing. "Who the fuck are you?"

In my periphery, Lola's mouth is a perfect O shape. Her eyebrows reach her hairline as she stands in shock at my entrance and domineering manner.

The man stands his ground. If I'm not mistaken, he puffs up his chest. I narrow my eyes into slits. My fists clench. My body poised to spring at him. Shit, if I can take on Borya, I can take this guy. He's two inches shorter than me and about fifteen pounds lighter. I'll annihilate the asshole.

"Sebastian!"

Lola's cry pauses my forward motion. But my gaze remains steady on my opponent. Obviously untrained in the art of war, he glances at Lola.

"What the fuck are you looking at my woman for? Answer my questions... Now," I say, my voice deadly.

"Hey, man, I meant no harm. I just offered my help," he responds, palms up. "I thought she was the caterer."

"Yes, Sebastian. He's a part of the crew you hired to help set up the terrace for dinner tonight," Lola adds.

"Really? The terrace is about thirty feet beyond that door. So, again... What the fuck is going on?" I demand.

"Is everything all right?"

A woman in her fifties steps through the kitchen door and plants herself between the man and me. She surveys the situation, then turns to face me.

"Mr. Steele. Please allow me to introduce myself and my employee. I'm Mrs. Cartwright, the party planner your assistant Ms. Lawson hired for your dinner this evening."

She pauses and turns her gaze to the man. With a flare of her nostrils, she takes a deep breath and continues.

"This is Blake, a recent hire. I apologize for his behavior and assure you I will deal with him properly. Do you approve of the rest of my team completing the task?"

I rake my gaze over Blake from head to toe before I respond.

"Security will see him off the premises," I give him the once-over again. "Mrs. Cartwright, we would appreciate you finishing the job, thank you."

Lola picks up the penthouse phone to the concierge and

asks for security to come upstairs to the kitchen immediately. Her wide-eyed stare stays on my face. Wary of my next move. I don't blame her as I'm wound tight, about to blow.

Moments later, four members of the security staff stride into the room. Their eyes take in the scene. No doubt sensing the tension in the air.

"Mr. Steele, Ms. Lewis, how may we help you?" The leader asks, flicking his gaze to Mrs. Cartwright and Blake.

"Please remove this man from the premises following the protocol. Thank you," I respond.

"Yes, sir, Mr. Steele."

Blake throws a glare in my direction. But the guards hustle him out, avoiding any further confrontation.

"Mr. Steele, Ms. Lewis, I apologize greatly. We will finish expeditiously. Our services are in kind," Mrs. Cartwright tells us.

I will not allow some asshole's poor behavior to prevent payment. So, I thank her for her offer. But we will pay her as contracted. She thanks us graciously before returning to the terrace.

Now that Lola and I are alone, I brace myself for an argument. My gaze settles on her at last. Still clutched in her arms, a pot top nestled against her heaving bosom. She traps her lower lip between her teeth. Then glances over her shoulder in the direction Mrs. Cartwright left the kitchen. Lola swings her gaze back to me. Her eyes sweep up and down my body as her eyes darken and her breath quickens. I raise my eyebrow in question.

Lola dashes to me, grabs my arm, and pulls me into the walk-in pantry.

"Fuck... That was hot! I have to have you... Right... Now!"

And have me she does. When at last we exit the pantry and check on the party planners' progress, they're long gone. Mrs. Cartwright left a pleasant note on the terrace table thanking us and apologizing for Blake's unacceptable behavior, again. She promises the servers will be up to par.

Well, I thank Blake for the best *aperitivo* I've ever had in my life.

"LOLA, THIS WAS DELICIOUS!" My mother, Shelley beams. "I feel like I'm back on holiday in Positano at Villa Sogno! That's our home on the Italian Rivera. You must come the next time we're there."

At those words, my mother stares at me pointedly. I press my lips together to stifle a chuckle at her blatancy. Lola, however, claps her hands and bounces in her seat.

"Thank you so much! I was so very nervous to meet you all. But you've made me feel so welcome. Thank you."

She bows her head, then lifts it, smiling at everyone seated around her. The entire Steele clan is present. The elliptical table is the perfect shape to allow all eight of us to see each other. While we enjoy the view through the frameless tempered glass around the edge of the terrace. The many lights of the Manhattan skyline do not compare to the ray of light my Lola projects.

"I propose a toast," Morgan with his Limoncello Gin Collins in hand stands at the end opposite to my mother. "To the first and the last woman our eldest son Sebastian has ever introduced to his family. We welcome you, Lola!"

"Here here!"

"Bravo!"

"*Cent'Anni!*"

"Cheers!"

"*Salute*!"

With my glass raised, I look around the table at my father, mother, sister, and brothers. My heart is full of joy and a peace I never knew could exist ten months ago. My gaze lands on Lola. Her eyes meet mine and her smile brightens even more.

I know she's happy with me and how our relationship progressed these past two months. When my father stated the proposal, it almost made the words "will you marry me" slip out of my mouth.

However, as elated as Lola and I are right now, I never ask a question I may get a no answer. Lola's not ready to tell me yes… yet. So I won't ask her to marry me tonight. Even though the words fight to escape my mouth. I rein them in for a more suitable time.

A time that is without a doubt in the very near future. That is my mission.

LOLA

"We have so much to catch up on!"

Leonie's tinkling laughter floats over our FaceTime call. I've missed my BFF. With both of us super busy at work, we haven't had time for a lengthy conversation since Paris. It's so good to hear her voice.

"*Chérie, tu me manques tellement!*" Leonie exclaims. "It's been forever since we said more than hi and goodbye! Just business-related emails with sketches, colors, fabric swatches… Tell me everything I missed in your personal life."

I laugh at her snuggling back on the settee in her bedroom lifting a cup of tea, ready for the gossip. She wears a Lola's Coterie cream silk dressing gown over the matching tank top and sleep shorts. The color highlights her golden caramel-colored skin beautifully. Her glossy, mahogany hair swept up in a messy bun and her flawless face is bare of makeup. The supermodel lounges at home look at its finest!

"He told me he loves me!" I gush as I almost bounce off of my sofa.

"He who???" Leonie asks as she tilts her head, squinting her eye with a raised eyebrow.

"Baz, girl!! He told me he loves me when we were in Dubai on our way to a party his friends threw for him."

Leonie sputters as the sip of tea dribbles from her open mouth. Her amber eyes widen as she stares at me in shock.

"Ce qui!!! Etes-vous sérieusement en train de me dire que Sebastian Steele vous aime??"

I giggle and ecstatically nod like a human bobblehead. Yes, I am seriously telling her he loves me! Sebastian *Dom Playboy* Steele loves me and only me. A thrill rocks my body, shooting from the top of my head to the tips of my red-polished toes. Baz has been so attentive since he uttered those three words. I swoon at the memory.

"Oui! Il m'aime beaucoup!!" I whoop.

"C'était merveilleux, Chérie!" Leonie smiles with tears in her eyes.

She understands how much it hurt me when I saw Sebastian with Lydie. Damn, I forgot to tell her what really happened at his penthouse.

"Leonie! You won't believe what Lydie told me..."

After I fill Leonie in on the details, her mouth hangs open for a second time. She has to excuse herself to get a refill of tea. As she walks with her iPhone, she shakes her head and mutters to herself in French.

When she settles on her settee, we dissect the entire situation and surmise that Lydie isn't as bad as we thought. She had her reasons with her father's archaic thought process and expectations. Leonie agrees for the sake of my relationship with Sebastian, I should move forward and be cordial with Lydie. No need to prolong the issue. Especially since Baz was not in the wrong.

"And his family is so nice. I cooked an Italian extravaganza for dinner alfresco on the largest terrace at Baz's penthouse," I steer our chat to a more appealing topic.

Leonie's eyes light up as she leans forward expectantly. Her teacup clasped in both hands before her bosom.

"Give me the deets! How did his mother act towards you? What did his father say? Who was there..." She trails off.

We realize at the same time she's thinking about Roger. Her intense ex-lover flew in from Paris to join us. He was pleasant during dinner. But I sensed his thoughts were elsewhere. I really would like to speak with him about his contributions to their breakup. Leonie doesn't want me to speak to Baz either. She and Roger will have to figure out their deal without my interference. No matter how much I want to help.

"Baz's mother is wonderful! Her name is Michelle, but everyone calls her Shelley. She complimented me on the meal and invited me to their villa in Positano. When she extended the invite, she glared at Baz as if she dared him to say no!"

"Really? You must have made an excellent impression on her to extend an invitation after just meeting you!" Leonie nods sagely.

"I know, right!" I laugh, then add, "His father Morgan even toasted me as the first and hopefully last woman Baz ever introduced to his family!"

"*Merde!* That's fantastic, *Chérie*! I'm so happy for you!" Leonie beams.

"In fact, his sister Haley invited me to dinner tomorrow. La Goulue, one of your favorites," I add smiling back.

Leonie rubs her flat belly as she licks her lips, "Mmm mmm mmm! I'm so jealous. Get the *Moules sauce "Poulette!" Non, non, le Pavé de saumon aux lentils*!"

I laugh and shake my head in disagreement, "Sorry, sweetie! You know I'm rather partial to the House Specialty *Le soufflé au Fromage*. Yummy!"

"By the way, how did you like the designs I sent for your penthouse?" Leonie asks. "Do you like the library?"

We chat about each of the rooms, brainstorm ideas, and timelines. So far, I'm impressed with Leonie's plans. Just like her, the aesthetic is incomparable. We account for her modeling schedule, classes, and travel to showrooms like the D&D Building here. If all goes as expected, she'll finish in two months.

With promises for more FaceTime and a meetup in LA, we end our call.

* * *

"SEE, if you lived in our penthouse instead of just spending the night, you could always take our elevator to meet Haley. A total breeze."

I throw a wry glance over my shoulder at Baz as I finish tying the belt on my Diane von Furstenberg wrap dress. For a moment, he tempts me to jump back in bed with him. His sizable frame is all sprawled out on his back with his hands folded behind his head. My gaze travels from his tousled hair, over his gorgeous face with sexy stubble, down his sculpted chest and eight-pack abs. The silk sheet just reaches to the v-cuts of his Adonis belt and emphasizes the outline of his massive dick resting on his muscular thigh. Damn.

"Like what you see, my love?" He taunts while shifting his hips side to side, making his dick bounce.

Baz locks me in his Dom stare as he slides his fingertips

down his chest, along his happy trail, and under the sheet to stroke his hardening length. I lick my lips and swallow.

"Are you just using me for the pleasure I bestow upon you, Little Pet?" He croons, stretching languidly.

I flare my nostrils and purse my lips to keep from moaning out loud. No… No… No… I will dine with Haley. Period. Instead of a response, I bend at the waist to wrap the strings of my sandals around my ankles. An added shimmy of my hips precipitates the sound of rustling sheets.

A squeal pops from my mouth as Baz grips my hips and with knees bent thrusts his cock against my ass. His thick thighs bear my weight easily as he lifts me from the floor. Grunts and growls fill the air as he humps me. When his climax nears, Baz lowers me to my feet. I spin around on wobbly legs, eager to see what he'll do next.

His hooded gaze locks on mine. Staggering back, he tugs at his engorged dick as it pulses. Muscles taut in preparation. One last pull. Great ropes of creamy semen spurt from the reddened tip like a geyser. I'm enthralled, unable to take my eyes from the spectacular sight.

Spent, Baz falls back onto the bed with his feet on the floor, throwing his arm over his face, breathing rapidly.

"You'll be the death of me yet, Little Pet," he pants.

* * *

I'M LISTENING TO HALEY.

But I swear, my body is back in the bedroom with Baz. He's the walking personification of hedonistic sex. I can't decide if he's Bacchus, Hedylogus, Min, Freyr, Kuni, Priapus, Cupid, Xochipilli, Kurupi, or every god of love, sex, fertility, and sweet talk in the history of mankind. My womb throbs thinking about him. I'll worship at the altar of Temple Baz for the rest of my life!

I squirm in my seat, excited by his Captain Caveman words he imparted as I untied my dress to switch into a fresh one.

"No, you cannot change your dress. I marked you with my scent on purpose. As you walk past other men and sit in the restaurant amongst them, intuitively they will know you are taken. And it will remind you that you are mine."

"—his birthday? Since he never plans—"

"Wait, what?" I ask startled out of my reverie by the word birthday.

"Baz's birthday is later this month. What do you have planned? He does nothing for it himself. My mother and I usually throw a party for him. We don't want to conflict with what you have planned."

I stare mutely at Haley for a minute. Damn, all this time and it never occurred to me to ask Baz about the date of his birthday. What a sucky girlfriend…

"You'll probably think I'm the worse. But I didn't know Baz's birthday. We've been so all over the place, I never remembered to ask him," I respond sheepishly.

Haley pushes her glasses up onto the bridge of her nose. Her expressive face can't hide her surprise. Fortunately, she doesn't berate me or look at me with pity.

"I can understand. Don't worry about it. His birthday is on the 30th. We have a few weeks to plan something fun." She looks at me from beneath her lashes. "That is unless you want to have a private celebration."

No way will I isolate Baz's family. This is an important step in our relationship. We have plenty of birthdays ahead of us. I shake my head in response.

"What do Shelley and you have planned? I'd love to be a part of it."

Haley's mobile buzzes on the table. As if by kismet, it's their mother. A warm smile spreads across Haley's heart-shaped face. Her dimples pop out, adding to her sweet beauty.

"I have to take this call. It's my mom," she tells me.

Before Haley can say hello, I hear Shelley asking her if she's spoken to me about Baz's birthday, yet. Haley peeks over at me and laughs. I join her.

"Right on cue!"

After little to no arm twisting, Shelley agrees to join us for dinner to discuss ideas. Haley and I share things about ourselves as we await Shelley's arrival. Haley just turned twenty-nine, fluent in French, and is fiercely loyal to her family. We share a lot in common from food to movies, even favorite color. It'll be good to have a friend who's constantly in the city besides Blair. I can't be as free with her since she's my employee. I can see Haley and I forming a great friendship.

"Hi, girls!"

Shelley bends over to hug us before she sits in the chair the maître d' pulled out for her. She's a striking woman in her mid-fifties with shoulder-length, wavy black hair and expressive brown eyes. I smile at the Steele Matriarch who I can tell is the boss of the family. As her feisty New Yorker personality affirms.

"I'm so glad you'll let us throw Baz's birthday party with you! Let me tell you, I love my family fiercely and we love to be together for birthdays, holidays, just because. I'm not a smother mother. No! It's their choice. They just love their parents so..."

She tweaks Haley's cheek. A diamond ring mounted on a

platinum band catches the light. The stone is so ginormous it reminds me of the stunning engagement ring Elizabeth Taylor wore. Similar to her 29.4-carat emerald-cut diamond she referred to as "My ice skating rink." Shelley's diamond may not be almost 30 carats, but it's not far off. I absolutely adore it!

"Yes, Mom!" Haley turns to me as she laughs heartily. "Lola, don't think we're odd. But we are a close-knit family. We don't pry and we have lives. So no fear!"

"Oh, I don't mind at all. I'm an only child and with my parents gone, I miss having a family," I end wistfully.

Shelley stands and pulls me into a tight embrace. Her genuine warmth brings tears to my eyes and I can't stop a few from falling.

"Lola, darling," Shelley starts. "Baz told us about your parents and how strong you are. You've made an immense change for the better in my son. He's finally opened himself up to love a woman who's deserving of his love. So, when Morgan says we welcome you, we truly welcome you into our fold."

She pulls away slightly to wipe my face before she continues as she stares intently in my eyes.

"He also meant it and we all agree that you are the first and better be the last woman Baz introduces to us!"

Shelley gives me another hug, then bustles me into my seat.

"Now, I say we have it at Villa Sogno. We haven't been there all together in a while. The weather is perfect this time of year. Swim at the beach, go out on the boat, dine alfresco! Lola, have you been to Positano?"

A born and raised New Yorker, Shelley speaks faster than I do. I can only laugh. Happiness replaces my tears.

Haley joins in with chuckles of her own. While Shelley stares between the two of us.

"What? What did I say? Oh… Too much?" She laughs at herself.

The server places our meals in front of us. In a comfortable silence, we savor the delicious dishes. I paid homage to Leonie and ordered *le Pavé de saumon aux lentils*. As I eat, my mind processes Shelley's words. Baz spoke of me to his mom and more than likely Malcolm and Roger mentioned me, too. She and Morgan must have been suitably impressed. Good.

"Positano is a favorite spot. I did a photo shoot with Leonie *The Lion* Beaulieu for a collection four seasons ago. Should we make it a three-day trip or is that too long?"

"Darling, that's not long enough! What with the travel time and it being the season… How about five?" Shelley counters.

I can tell where Baz learned his negotiation tactics…

"Then it's a deal!"

"Ooh! What fun we'll have! I can't wait!" Haley claps.

"How was dinner?"

"It was so nice! Haley and I will be BFFs. You guys are lucky to have Shelley as your Mom."

Baz pulls me tighter as we sit on a chaise sipping drinks, a Jackson Scotch for Baz and a Whiskey Sour for me. The Manhattan skyline spread before us. I snuggle against his powerful chest with a contented sigh.

"Yeah. We lucked up with our parents. Don't get me wrong, we argue, have misunderstandings, and all the things any family goes through. But we are loyal, supportive, and love each other dearly. We wouldn't be where we are without each other."

He kisses the top of my head.

"Are you truly happy we're together Lola? Do you mind my parents saying what they did the other night? Be honest."

I stop for a moment to think on it. Then, shift around to peer into his gray eyes.

A vulnerability I never noticed before lies in their depths. It makes me think back on what Shelley said about Baz finally opening himself up to love. He's a confident and experienced son, businessman, and Dom. But he's never had an actual relationship with a woman beyond sex. As much as I'm scared of being hurt. I now realize Baz is afraid of me hurting him, too. We've had enough heartache and anguish.

"Yes, Baz. I am truly happy we're together. No, I don't mind what your parents said. It was wonderful. What about you?"

Baz's gaze intensifies.

"I love you, Lola. I love you more than I ever thought I could love someone outside of my family. So, yes, I'm truly happy we're together. No, I don't mind what my parents said. It was indeed wonderful."

The kiss he gives me makes stars float behind my closed eyes. Stars that rival the ones that sparkle above us.

SEBASTIAN

"I saw Rhys Rockett at the club the other day. He wasn't as smug as usual. I imagine word got to him about the deal you completed last week?"

When my father mentions club, for a second, my mind goes to LEVELS New York. A visual appears of my parents in a scene where my mother waits bound to a St. Andrew's Cross while my father brandishes a flogger. It fries my retinas. I shudder at the thought.

I dislodge it from my head with a shake that brings the Union Club to the forefront. The Steele men have been members of the one hundred-eighty plus year old, exclusive social club since its founding as the first of its kind in New York City. Despite being notorious for denying membership to sons, they have always accepted us. A Steele as a founding member helps.

"When he first entered the squash courts, he almost turned tail seeing me standing there with Benson," my father continues. "He tried to save face by greeting us. But the cocky grin disappeared."

Morgan despises Rhys more than I loathe his eldest son, Patrick. Morgan never divulged what took place years ago. But I have a sense it was because of a woman. Perhaps my mother, who's just as evasive about the disdain my father harbors.

"Good. The sly bastard. Excellent job, Baz," Malcolm nods his head and tips his glass of Scotch at me in salute. "I saw Alastair last night at LEVELS parading a sub around the Cellar. Since he's a member, I was cordial. But didn't strike up a conversation."

I snort into my rocks glass as I stretch my legs out. We're on board Morgan's G650 headed to Naples, where we'll board *Serendipity* the megayacht he gave to Shelley for their thirtieth wedding anniversary.

Gifts and anniversaries prompt me to glance back at Lola where she sits chatting animatedly with my mother and Haley. My heart soars at the happiness on her face. I knew she needed more women in her life who would give her the comfort of a supportive family. Every time I think of how strong Lola is in the face of losing her parents at barely eighteen, encourages me to make up for it.

I jump around when something hits my chest. Harris tossed his stress ball at me. Fucker.

"Good grief, Baz... You just can't stop peeping at her. She's still there, Lost Puppy."

He and Malcolm make goo-goo eyes and clutch their hearts. Loud guffaws fill the cabin. I cringe, but couldn't care less. That's my girl.

"Leave your brother alone. You two need to settle down," Morgan admonishes them. "I remember the first time I saw your mother where she worked as a shopgirl at one of our men's clothing stores. She was the most beautiful woman I'd ever seen. Immediately, I knew I had to make her mine. I stare at her every chance I get."

At the suggestion they settle down, Malcolm and Harris zip their lips. Malcolm preoccupies himself with refilling his drink. Harris checks his newfangled gadget.

Right.

"I'VE BEEN on some of the most renowned yachts in my life. But this... this is beyond exquisite!"

Lola and I stand on the sixth deck of *Serendipity* watching the sunrise over the Gulf of Naples. She was too excited to go inside of our suite. I can't blame her. *Serendipity* is a majestic boat. The largest megayacht in the world has a length of six-hundred feet, nine inches. That extra nine just to nudge past the next yacht down. At least for now, *Serendipity* holds the record since everyone competes for the prize of the biggest on the water. There are already rumors that a Russian oligarch contracted a prominent builder specifically to outsize *Serendipity*.

It's definitely a beauty to behold. The all-white, sleek design boasts seven decks. The top for the bridge; the sixth for four palatial suites where my parents, Malcolm, Haley, and I stay; the fifth deck for four suites where Roger and Harris and up to four close friends stay, plus our private library, office, family and dining rooms with galley; the remaining decks accommodate twenty-four guests in staterooms, quarters for eighty-eight crew, helicopter pad, submarine and water vehicles and toys garage, swimming pool, spa, gym, barbershop and salon, disco, living and dining areas, and an entertainment deck with a bowling alley, cinema, pool room, cards room, and game room. The open-air decks hold chaises, beds, tables, televisions, and dining spots. *Serendipity* is a floating haven for rest, relaxation, and partying.

When we arrived on board, everyone went to their suites to rest until we reach Positano. The vibrant colors of the rising sun playing on the Tyrrhenian Sea's crystal blue surface awed Lola. So, we detoured to my favorite spot on the fifth deck near my suite.

"My father bought her for my mother as a thirtieth wedding anniversary. They keep *Serendipity* here during the season. Then transport her to the Caribbean for the fall and winter months."

"Your dad really does it big! Your mom's engagement ring is as incredible as her boat!"

Lola's laugh tinkles in the air before ending on a yawn. I scoop her up and carry her to our suite.

"Time for bed."

Her giggles continue as I take her dress off, then tuck her in bed. She hums a striptease between yawns as I undress, making me wish we weren't so tired. Instead of ravaging her, I slip under the covers and pull Lola into my arms.

"Sweet dreams, princess," I whisper into her hair.

A FEW HOURS LATER, I wake before Lola and lie on my side watching her sleep. A slight frown furrows her brow as she murmurs. The gentle pressure of my kiss smooths her scowl. On an exhalation, Lola sighs my name. Still asleep, her lips curl up into a smile as she reaches for me. Denial is impossible. I slide my body closer to hers, resting her cheek on my chest. It's my turn to sigh.

While I embrace Lola, my fingertips trace along her naked back. Her warm skin is soft. I could lie here all day, but I know we should approach Positano any moment. We need to disembark for Villa Sogno. Based on Lola's excitement about the boat, I'm sure she'll want to see the spectacular sight of the colorful hillside town at our arrival.

"Babe, wake up," I briskly rub Lola's back while I kiss the top of her head. "We're not far and you'll want to see the landscape."

"Mmm… Mmm… Mmm."

Lola arches her back and stretches like a cat, lifting her arms overhead. Her more-than-a-mouthful boobs appear from beneath the sheet.

I can't stop myself from pulling her plump nipple into my mouth, suckling on her tit. Lola's coos stiffen my cock. A quick roll and I pull her under me, settling my hips between her warm thighs. My mouth still on her breasts alternating between the mounds, I cup her ample ass to angle her entrance to prepare for my dick.

"Ooh… Baz. You're so big, baby…. Damn… ahhh," Lola hisses as my girth expands her pussy.

My lips continue to ravage her breasts, knowing my ministrations will stimulate her core to release her juices. Lola's luscious body creates generous amounts of lube naturally. She is the most responsive woman I've ever been with, and I play her body like a fine instrument. Her high notes of pleasure music to my ears.

"Yaaasss! Right there. Right there! Yes… Yes… Yes…" She stutters with each powerful thrust.

Nothing is more important than Lola's climax. I continue to pound into her, circling my hips and changing my angle to spur her release. My dick pulses when her inner muscles grip it greedily.

"Cum on my cock, Lola. Cum for me now!"

Her body spasms as she comes undone, her mouth open in a silent cry.

One orgasm is never enough. My thrusts continue until I've wrung multiple climaxes from her core and she begs me to stop. Only then do I chase my release. I flip her onto all fours and slam into her from behind. The force shifts her towards the headboard. I grip her hip in one hand and her hair in the other, bowing her body to gain better access. Lola screeches and writhes, tilting her pelvis to open further for me. A few spanks to her butt cheeks make her explode. Her whimpers beg me to cum.

"Fuck, Lola! You… feel… so… fucking… good! No need to beg, baby. I'm right… with… you!" I roar my release.

Stars dance before my eyes and my thighs shake. Unable to squat any longer, I collapse onto her back, then roll us to the side. I spoon Lola while our breathing returns to normal. I give a silent thanks for the soundproof walls.

Freshly showered and dressed, we stand beside my parents at the front of the sixth deck. This spot offers the best vantage point to see the town as we pull into the coastal waters off the Positano shore. Everyone else headed to the third deck. The crew prepares the tenders to take us to the marina, where we'll drive up a hillside road to the villa.

"The early light's beauty drew me here for the photo-shoot. That campaign was one of the most popular we ever created. Leonie channeled Sofia Lauren. Everyone loved it," Lola shares.

"I adore it here. It brings such wonderful memories," my mother responds, as she gazes with affection at my father and squeezes his hand in hers. "When we came as part of our honeymoon, we knew this would be a regular spot for the two of us, then our family."

Morgan stares down at my mother with such love in his eyes. I want the same with Lola.

"Villa Sogno is a gem! You'll love it!" My mother

continues dragging her eyes from my father to the approaching shoreline.

Moments later, we disembark and climb into the Mercedes-Benz G-Wagens my parents keep at the villa. Roger arrived yesterday, so my parents and Malcolm ride in the SUV Roger drove down to meet us. Harris and Haley hop into the back of the one I drive with Lola in the passenger seat.

During the two-mile ride, Haley and Lola chat about their favorite places to eat while Harris and I chime in on our preferences. It's great everyone has claimed Lola as part of our clan. Being the first child to bring home a partner puts pressure on me for Lola to get along with my family. Both are important. So, I prefer we like each other, rather than to be at odds or merely polite.

All talk stops as we approach the gates to Villa Sogno. As Shelley said, it's a gem set atop the highest hill. An abundance of flowers covers the lower stone wall surrounding the base of the property at its perimeter. Their beauty welcomes you with vibrant colors and fragrant aroma. At once, your mind is at ease, ready for the dreamlike atmosphere.

We pass through the wrought-iron gates and climb further up the hill past terraces for gardens and lemon trees, seating and entertainment areas, and the swimming pool and cabana. The property covers several acres in a prime location, the real estate developer in me notes every time I arrive.

I pull into the motor court next to Roger to the side of the villa. Lola hops out first and claps her hands at the incredible cliffside views of Positano and the rugged Amalfi coastline this vintage retreat offers.

The sun sparkles on the azure waters of the Tyrrhenian

spread out into the distance. *Serendipity* appears but a miniature version as it floats amongst other boats below us. The marina, beaches, restaurants, and shops line the streets. Other villas, residences, and hotels pack the cliffs. The view is second only to the villa itself.

The staff greets us and unloads our belongings. I take Lola by the hand as I stride along the path lined with potted flowers and plants to the portico. A mosaic floor leads to the double wooden doors framed by terra-cotta urns with miniature lemon trees. Their citrusy scent reminds you of being in Italy.

Once inside, we walk the terra-cotta floors beneath colorful frescoes and dramatic Renaissance paintings. The spacious, airy main floor has the living room, family room, study, bathrooms, dining room, and kitchen among other rooms. Several outdoor areas including loggias and balconies are perfect for reading a book or watching the sea as the sun goes down. The second and third floors have twelve oversized bedrooms with en suite bathrooms and sitting areas. Villa Sogno has occupied this land for years, and my parents did a magnificent job of respecting its history while bringing it into the present. It has a modern Baroque style.

"This has got to be the most spectacular estate I have ever seen aside from Luc's ancestral chateau. The view… the fragrance… the peacefulness… the home… Words can't describe it," Lola exclaims.

"Darling, I told you you'd love it! You can stay as long as you want. Or come back anytime. Perhaps a part two of your photoshoot?" Shelley responds, pleased Lola is so taken by the villa.

"That would be delightful! Thank you!" Lola smiles

graciously, then beams at me with her hazel eyes shining. "Yes?"

I squeeze her hand back and nod.

Damn. My throat too clogged with emotion won't vocalize an answer. Maybe I am a wuss after all.

LOLA

"What do you think of this?"

Haley and I stand in a fine watches shop perusing at a selection of vintage Rolex, Patek Phillipe, Audemars Piguet, and Vacheron Constantin. I know they're more than likely overpriced, being sold in a jet-set spot. But I couldn't find anything that resonated with me in New York at the auction houses or dealers.

Baz collects vintage timepieces, so I want to be sure it's one he'll cherish since it's the first birthday gift I've given him. A smile lifts my frown as I think of the future we can now have together.

His family is amazing and accepts me as one of their own brood. Yesterday, Morgan and I had a lengthy conversation about some ideas he has for Lola's Coterie. He's a no-nonsense, straight shooter. His wealth of knowledge comes from his years of running the retail stores division for STEELE to prove his mettle for the CEO role, as Baz is doing now.

The Steele Patriarch is a handsome, distinguished older

man who's the mold for his sons. Their unmistakable similarities in height at six feet, four inches, black hair with Morgan's salt and pepper strands cut short, piercing gray eyes, and fit physique. Judging by his authoritative manner and Shelley's reactions to it, he passed his Alpha Dom gene to his sons, too. Funny how Baz's parents remind me of us. Except his father is more of a player being ten years older than Shelley!

I chuckle to myself just as Haley points to an Audemars Piguet that looks as powerful and dominant as Sebastian, and just as complex.

"That's it!" I proclaim triumphantly. "Thanks, Haley!"

"An extraordinary piece," starts the salesperson who presented us with the tray of watches. "This is the limited edition Titanium Grand Complication watch. Only three made. It features a 44 mm black clay bezel titanium circlet and croon posh pieces. The ceaseless almanac shows the durations in a fractional second chronograph, minute repeater, day, month, and year..."

He croons on and on about the watch. Magnificent, yes. But okay already. I pick it up with the soft, white gloves he provided to Haley and me before he allowed us to touch any of the fancy dancies. I use my discerning designer's eye to check for any imperfections. None found, I stop him.

"I'll take it. Please gift wrap it with the certification and original box, thank you."

"Of course, madame. Excellent choice! He will enjoy it immensely," he pauses to gaze at me. "It's $778,000 plus applicable taxes. How would you prefer to pay?"

As I said, this is my first gift to Baz. It has to be special. With all the lavish presents he's given to me, this ranks with them. Not a competition or you bought me, I owe you situation. Every occasion he glances at the time, I want him to think of me and his birthday celebration here. With that thought in mind, I happily hand the salesperson my Black AMEX Centurion Card.

"Sebastian will love it!" Haley claps gleefully before pulling me into a tight hug.

While they wrap the watch up, we stroll through the shop. So many beautiful pieces. We pause at the collection of diamond rings. They're all drool worthy.

"Your mother's ring is far superior to these trinkets," I tease. "I wonder why she's not wearing it now. I would wear it every day for the rest of my life if it were mine!"

Haley ducks her head, causing her hair to fall across her profile like a curtain. She refuses to glance my way. Then walks at a clipped pace to the other end of the store. Odd, I think. I hope I didn't sound nouveau riche. Elizabeth Taylor is an icon to me. Shelley's ring reminds me so much of Liz's many pieces. I follow Haley.

"Haley," I touch her arm as she stands in front of the cuff links' display case. "Please forgive my lack of tact—"

She cuts me off with a wave of her hand, "No, no. You did nothing wrong or distasteful—"

"Madame, your gift is ready."

The salesperson hands the discrete package to me with a flourish. I glance back at Haley, who has an expression of relief on her face. Despite what she said, I wonder if I didn't offend her.

We thank the salesperson and I link arms with Haley to walk a few streets over. We promised Shelley we would pick up Baz's cake from her favorite bakery in town. She stayed at Villa Sogno to manage the party decorators and caterers and the villa's staff for the influx of guests, some of whom will stay at the property.

As the head of STEELE International, Inc.'s STEELE

Foundation that builds and manages attractive, affordable housing for urban, lower-income families, Shelley grew accustomed to throwing elaborate galas and events. She's the family's go-to party planner. Haley convinced me it's best to leave Shelley to her task.

Haley doesn't broach the subject of Shelley's ring again. Instead, we chat about what we're wearing tonight for the party and who's coming.

I agreed with Shelley we should invite their cousins the Jacksons and some of Baz's closest friends. Lucie Jackson, their family's Matriarch, is best friends with Shelley. As Baz explained the women spent most of their adult lives together when Lucie moved to New York alone. After meeting, they formed a closer bond than they had with their families. It remained strong even after marriage when they went from a shopgirl and a bartender to socialite wives of multibillionaires.

Lucie and Connor drove over from their nearby villa. Lachlan flew in from Aberdeen, Scotland, where Jackson Corporation has their UK headquarters. Baz sent the helicopter for Lucien, who's at his villa in Monte Carlo. Laurent, the youngest of the siblings, sent Baz a vintage lacquer humidor filled with Jackson Cuban Cigars since he's unable to make it. I give a silent thanks Lydie declined because of a business conflict.

Baz's Harvard roommate Scott and his wife Lauren with whom we had dinner several months ago at Le Bernardin in New York arrive later today. Some of his friends from Dubai and London flew in this morning for a few days. They round out the list to twenty.

"I've not met the Jackson parents nor Lachlan. What are they like?" I ask Haley.

At the mention of Lachlan's name, Haley stumbles.

"Are you all right? Did you trip on something?" I ask, glancing over my shoulder at the ground.

Haley pushes her glasses back up the bridge of her nose. Her eyes dart away.

"My foot caught on a crack," she shrugs. "Anyway, here's the bakery."

Again, she avoids my eyes and waltzes ahead of me through the door.

* * *

"IT IS such an absolute pleasure to see you again so soon, Lola. You look ravishing, luv," Porter Huntington kisses my hand as he greets me on the terrace.

Baz's party begins on a terrace one level below the villa. The view at night just as spectacular with the lights of the villas and hotels along the cliffside, the waterfront restaurants and shops, and the boats moored at sea or docked at the marina. The breeze is warm with the ever-present fragrance of flowers and lemons wafting through the air.

Shelley did a fantastic job with the transformation of the terrace from a lush verdant space where you can unwind to a festive party spot. The decorations, musical quartet, and bar service keep the guest in lively spirits. One of Lucien's two Positano restaurants catered the dinner and provided the servers. The cocktail hour gives guests time to arrive, Porter being one of them.

"You are too kind, sir," I respond with a dramatic curtsy.

"Sir?"

A shiver runs down my spine at the sound of Baz's commanding voice spoken against the shell of my ear. His unexpected closeness sparks sensuous thoughts.

"Really, Little Pet?"

"Aah… Correction… Fine gentleman," I babble.

"Better… However, you will correct yourself on your hands and knees later," he finishes with a nip to the delicate shell.

I cover my yelp with my hand and blush, avoiding Porter's quizzical gaze.

"Well, here's the birthday boy!" Porter claps Baz on the back in a bro hug. "And this gorgeous creature hasn't abandoned you, yet! Well done, old chap!"

"No, if I have my way, Lola will never leave me," Baz responds.

"Hey, hey! Happy birthday, man!"

The three of us turn towards the deep voice. A striking male strides over. He resembles a movie star. His fit, six-foot-four-inch frame topped by a face so incredible it takes your breath away. Blazing green eyes lock in on you as your gaze takes in his thick, dark brown hair slicked back from his chiseled cheekbones and strong jawline. The cleft chin adds to his Cary Grant vibe. Wow.

"Thanks, Lach. Glad you could make it after all," Baz grabs his outstretched hand as he pulls him into a bro hug.

"Of course! It wouldn't be a party without me," he teases, green eyes dancing in delight.

"Babe, this is Lachlan Jackson. Lach, this is my girl Lola," Baz introduces us.

"So nice—"

"Finally, I get to meet—"

We laugh at the exchange. In my periphery, I notice Haley watching Lachlan's every move. Hhhmmm. Now I know why her "foot caught on a crack" when I mentioned his name earlier. She's attracted to him. This family and their love lives. I'll suss out this one later. With hope faster than I have Leonie and Roger… But right now, it's all about my love life.

The evening is a success. Delicious dishes with ingredients fresh from the Tyrrhenian Sea dazzled our palates. Flavorful wines and Prosecco from their cellar fill crystal glasses and flutes. The camaraderie enhanced by everyone's love for Sebastian. My heart is full as I hand his gift to him. I have the honor of presenting last.

"Thank you, my love," he smiles as he kisses my lips tenderly.

The ambient lighting from clusters of torches set about the terrace sparkle in the gray depths of his eyes when he shreds the wrapping paper from the wooden, hinged box. Then widen in surprise at the magnificent watch nestled in the soft leather lining.

"Lola," he breathes out.

My insides melt at his awed expression. The sound of the others' ohs and ahs fill in the silence. I can only smile, thrilled that he's so taken by his gift. Perfect.

"Put it on already, Sebastian! Don't just slobber all over it," ribs Scott.

Baz laughs and slips his platinum Rolex Day-Date watch off his wrist. That little number is a beauty, too, with its unique meteorite and diamond-set dial bezel on a President's bracelet. He swaps one handcrafted piece for another. Then holds it aloft for all to see.

"This is an exceptional timepiece, Lola. I know my watches and this is—"

I press my fingertips to his lips as I shake my head.

"You are priceless to me, Sebastian. Nothing in this world or beyond compares to you. Think of my love whenever you glance at the time," I respond.

Baz presses his lips together as his gray orbs moisten. He

clears his throat and closes his eyes for a moment to collect himself.

I press my lips to his as I murmur, "I love you."

Baz exhales and opens his eyes to stare into mine.

I smile slightly, shaken by the intensity of his gaze, and raise my eyebrows in question. The room is silent and feels tense suddenly. I bite my lower lip as my nerves tingle.

Baz inhales deeply, then exhales slowly. He reaches into his pocket and slips off his chair to drop to one knee in front of me. My heart stops as I see a small, black box in his hand. My wide eyes fly back to his as my mouth drops open. No way!

"Lola. Marry me. I want it all with you, my love. And I want it now."

Before I can answer, Baz opens the box, takes my hand in his, and places the ring on my finger. Then, he pulls my hand to his lips to kiss the ring.

The ring that's his mother's diamond engagement ring I lusted after from the moment I saw it on her finger at La Goulue. Tears form in my eyes as I peer up to search the group for Shelley. When I spot her wrapped in Morgan's arms, she smiles and wipes tears of joy from her eyes. With a nod, she kisses her fingertips and blows it to me.

I'm so choked up with emotions I can only nod wordlessly in response to Baz.

"Words, Little Pet. I will have your words," Baz rasps just as full of emotion as I.

My pussy clenches and my nipples pebble as my Dom-cum-fiancé commands me.

"Yes, Sir," I answer, my voice low and throaty with love and heightened desire.

I smile through my tears of joy as my ice skating rink glimmers in the light.

SEBASTIAN

"You are doing well, son. STEELE exceeding revenue projections for three consecutive quarters. Your impressive leadership of your division, the company, and of your younger siblings. Now, a lovely fiancée to settle you down—start on heirs to continue our legacy," my father looks at me pointedly with a cocked eyebrow. "You make your mother and me proud, Sebastian."

My gaze flicks to Lola, who's floating in the Tyrrhenian with Haley, Lauren, and Huntington's date. It's our last day in Positano. Our favorite spot to soak up the sun and to swim in the crystalline waters is at beautiful Fornillo Beach.

It's a little hidden secret in Positano on the Amalfi Coast. Unlike tourists, those in the know spend time here. The overcrowded hot spots hold less appeal. The small, pebble stone beach sits at the bottom of the plunging cliff face below the town with an unobstructed view of the sea. Two ancient stone watchtowers flank the ends of the beach. A bathhouse with lounge chairs and a restaurant provide amenities for beachgoers.

Shelley and Lucie shopped with their friends. While Malcolm and Lucien drove to a potential site for some new venture they plan. Roger, Harris, and Scott eat at the restaurant. My father, Connor, Lachlan, Porter, and I sit on lounge chairs near the shoreline.

"I had urged a more permanent alliance between the Jackson and Steele families. Sebastian and Lydie would have made an excellent strategic match," Connor harrumphs.

My Limoncello Gin Collins chokes me. Lachlan glances at me apologetically. My father releases a barely audible sigh.

"Our combined businesses would increase revenue and monopolize the markets," Connor continues blatantly unaware of our reactions and silence. "I told Lydie a marriage would be conducive to both company's bottom lines."

It's unbelievable he would voice such inane thoughts on the heels of my proposal to Lola. No wonder Lydie bowed out of attending my birthday party. She probably guessed Connor would say something ridiculous. More than likely, he berated her for not closing his deal.

"Father," Lachlan starts before my father or I can speak. "With all due respect, Lydie and Sebastian are not chess pieces. I say the best of luck to Lola for agreeing to stay with this guy for eternity!"

He raises his tumbler in a toast.

"Here's to a long life and a merry one. A quick death and an easy one. A pretty girl and an honest one. A cold beer—and another one! Cheers!" Chimes in Porter with his glass of Guinness stout.

"Agreed!" Morgan adds with his eyebrow cocked as he stares at Connor.

"What are we toasting to?"

Our heads pivot to see Lola and the girls approaching. Her curvy body makes the innocent pink seersucker bandeau bikini sinful. She stressed about wearing a swimsuit that wasn't too revealing since we were going to the beach with my father and Connor. But damn. There's not much she can do about her luscious body. Fuck. I'm thankful.

She slips onto my chaise and gives me a chaste kiss on the cheek. Then takes my drink for a sip.

"Aah… Refreshing! Cheers!" She laughs.

Everyone can't help but join her infectious happiness. Even Connor, who offers a small smile with a shake of his head. Undoubtedly wishing it were Lydie beside me.

"Oh, just wishing you and Baz the best. Really, you!" Lachlan roars heartily.

"Whatever, jerk," I throw my towel at his head.

Deftly catching it, he stands to offer it to Haley.

"Here, Haley. Your brother's aim is off. I'm sure he meant to give you a towel to dry yourself off…" He adds rolling his eyes at me over his shoulder.

Haley fidgets with her bikini top, then blushes as she peeks up at Lachlan. She stammers a thank you and something about going to the restroom. Then rushes off, wrapping the towel around her body.

"Maybe there's hope, yet," murmurs Connor.

I shift my gaze to Lachlan, whose sharp, green eyes follow Haley's retreating figure, oblivious to his father's remark. Lola didn't miss a thing. She nudges me and goes after Haley. Lachlan must sense my stare because he turns to me with a smirk.

"Race you to the pontoon, lovestruck!"

Interesting.

We climb onto the deck and settle on an empty spot

facing the beach. My muscles appreciate the hard swim since the only workouts I've done comprised wrestling Lola beneath me. I stretch my shoulders and turn to Lachlan.

"Spill," I demand.

Lachlan jerks his head in my direction, his eyes scan my face for my mood. I maintain a neutral expression. He knows he better tread lightly regarding my sister.

"What?" He rejoins.

"Do not fuck with me, Lachlan," I threaten.

Wasn't he just sitting there listening to my father speak of my leadership of my siblings? He knows me well enough after these years, I'm difficult on fuckers messing with my kid sister.

"Sebastian, fuck off."

"*Ciao, ragazzi.*"

Two leggy Monica Bellucci lookalikes stand over us. Their minuscule bikinis barely cover their abundant assets. One reaches for Lachlan's cheek and the other grins at me.

Lachlan and I glance at each other. A nod sets our squabble aside to avoid a bigger one if Lola sees a woman flirting with me. Without hesitation, we dive back into the azure waters.

Lola waits for me at the shoreline. I grab her by the waist and toss her into the surf, diving in after. I've got a Siren to conquer. Lachlan and his bullshit can wait. For now.

* * *

"I WAS WONDERING why Haley acted weird when I mentioned your mom's engagement ring the other day. I thought Haley reacted to my comment about the size of the diamond."

Lola tells me as she stares at her ring with a broad smile.

"I told them when we had our first dinner date it reminded me of Elizabeth Taylor's famous Ice Skating Rink Ring," she continues. "You realize I'm a huge fan of hers since she inspired me to create Lola's Coterie after seeing her in *Butterfield 8* as a young teen."

"Yes, babe, I noticed," I answer with a smirk. "You've told me about your fan worship of your idol only a million times…"

"Whatever, Baz," she retorts with an eye roll and smirk of her own.

I spank her ass, admiring the way her tanned flesh jiggles and reddens. Then pull her squealing onto my lap. We're alone aboard *Serendipity* on the fourth deck. The party is over, and everyone heads back to the actual world from Villa Sogno. But my dream rests comfortably in my arms.

"I'm glad you like it," I tell her as I lift her hand up to watch the diamond sparkle. "It's a family heirloom passed to the first son to his first son for generations. My mom recognized one day it would go to my wife. When I asked her for it, she told me she's glad it's you."

Lola spins around to face me with tears in her eyes. Her arms wrap around me as she buries her face in my neck. Her body trembles with each sob.

"Shhh, please don't cry, my love. Tell me, what's wrong?" I ask as I rub her back to soothe her.

Lola's cries continue unabated by my soft caresses. My heart breaks as my mind jumps to the loss of her parents. It must be hard to not have at least one parent for thirteen years. The death of both at the same time is unimaginable.

Now, it's her wedding. Lola won't have her mother to help her pick out a dress or her father to walk her down the aisle.

My parents understand her situation and told me they

would step in. I'm not sure how Lola will react. But I expect she'll be gracious.

"I miss my parents, Baz," she whispers.

"Ba—" My voice catches in my throat. "Babe, I know. I know."

I pull away to lift her face so her eyes meet mine.

"No one can replace your parents or their love for you," I gaze into the depths of her sad hazel eyes. "My mother told me to let you know she'd love to help you select your dress and plan our wedding. My father said he'd walk you down the aisle."

She speaks. But I kiss her lips softly to stop her.

"You don't have to decide now. Just realize they… Hell, we all love you and want our wedding day to be one of joy. Whatever you want. However you want it—"

I stop her again so she hears me correctly.

"But… We're getting married after your Dubai boutique opening."

A beat passes. Lola's emotions play across her face like an exaggerated cartoon character. Sadness; confusion; shock; indignant. The firecracker is lit. I hold my breath for the bomb to detonate.

"Hold on… Did I hear you correctly?"

I pull my lips over my teeth and raise both eyebrows with a nod. 10… 9… 8… 7

"Whaaaaat?" She screeches.

Lola momentarily forgets her tears as she jumps to her feet and glares down at me. Her hands on her hips and her feet in a fighting stance. Lola is ready to rumble.

"You cannot be serious, Sebastian! That's only eight weeks from now!"

She pauses to stare at me for verification. I nod again.

She throws her hands up and paces the deck, muttering. Every few steps, she turns to look at me and I nod.

"Lola. Did I not say 'and I want it now' when I proposed to you?" I remind her. "What did you think I meant?"

"Oh, no you won't! You will not turn this around on me, Sebastian Steele!" She growls.

It's difficult. But I hold back my laugh at the petite pistol starter. A neutral expression drops over my features. I have to win this negotiation. Funny how it always comes down to a deal with us.

First at LEVELS New York, I had to persuade her to allow me as her Dom that night. After the initial meeting for her expansion plans, she gave in to my offer of teaching her the fine points of a D/s relationship. Her move into my penthouse instead of a rental proved a very satisfying repartee on the kitchen banquette. I intend to win this bid, too.

"Lola, why forestall the inevitable? If it is the work, hire as many planners as you need. Unless you are not sure..."

She stomps her feet. Then shadow boxes while growls and curses fall from her lips. I can't contain my chuckles any longer. Lola has exploded.

My sides hurt from laughing so hard. Lola dives on top of me, knocking me back onto the sunbed. We wrestle and she ends astride me. Her fiery core grinds on my dick. Oh, I get it. My Petite Seductress thinks she can use her feminine wiles to change my mind.

Not going to happen.

"Baz, baby, you realize I love you and have absolutely no doubts about us. None... what... so... ever," she purrs, circling her hips with each word. "So what is another six months, hhhmmm?"

My dick protests. But I lift Lola off of me and sit up straight with her beside me.

“No. You had your way for three months. Unnecessarily I might add since I had done nothing wrong,” I cock my head at her as I drop the gauntlet.

A beat passes as she glares at me, and I raise my eyebrow at her. 10… 9… 8… 7… 6

“I cannot believe you’re only giving me two months to prepare for our wedding, Sebastian!” Lola wails as she flops back on the sunbed.

Success!

LOLA

Sebastian knows, and I do. He didn't persuade me to have our wedding so soon. I want it as much as he does. Well, he was eager to put a ring on it. And boy did he with this super stunner! I laugh to myself as I wave my left hand in the air à la Beyoncé.

"Okay giggly goo, we have work to do you know."

I glance across the immense table strewn with bridal magazines, legal pads, colorful stickies, fabric swatches, and other wedding prep items at Shelley. Haley was correct. Leave Shelley to her world of party planning. She's a firm taskmaster and the epitome of organization amid craziness. And this right here is insanity… eight weeks. No, seven weeks, three days to be exact. Good grief.

Not to mention my upcoming trip to LA for a few days; finalization of the Abu Dhabi and Dubai boutiques' collections and pre-opening party tasks; everyday responsibilities of running my company. Oh, and the redesign of my penthouse that Baz recommended I turn into a corporate apartment since I'm moving in with him to "our penthouse where you belong." He wasn't having it when I told him my plan to stay on Sutton Place so we could savor the moment I move in after the wedding. "Not happening, Lola!"

Which is exactly why I took him up on his suggestion to hire as many planners as I need. With Shelley spearheading the operation, Baz is right, it won't take long.

Haley, Leonie, two wedding planners, and I sit in Shelley's home office in her STEELE Tower duplex penthouse on the fifty-seventh and fifty-sixth floors floors. If one considers three generously sized rooms an office. An anteroom for two assistants' desks, a sitting area, and a bathroom, a conference room, and her inner sanctum with en suite bathroom comprise Shelley's version of a home office. She runs her private activities from here and her foundation work from that office on the executive floor of the corporate office.

She and Morgan live on the top two floors. Baz and I are below. So it's convenient. Some women may find living so close to their mother-in-law a nightmare. But Shelley is not the meddling type. Plus, I don't mind the company of an older woman in the absence of my mother. Not that Shelley is an old woman. She's a sexy vixen! And it's obvious Morgan can't get enough of her.

Blair has a conference call she can't reschedule and Billie joins us via video conference from Las Vegas.

"Right! Return to Earth, girl. Time is precious," Billie teases me in her Southern drawl.

"*Oui, Chérie.* Get it together. Tick Tock..."

Leonie chartered a private jet to New York as soon as I told her about my engagement. In her excitement, she dropped her iPhone and lost the FaceTime call. I tried calling her back, but didn't get an answer. My consternation ended when she called me from the tarmac at Le Bourget

Airport to tell me she'll see me in a few hours and to have bottles of Dom Pérignon Rosé Vintage 2005 Champagne on ice. That was last night. Now, it's time for work.

"Yes, yes, sorry," I smile apologetically for my wandering thoughts.

"I understand your distraction, which is why you have us to keep you focused," Shelley smiles warmly. "With all you have going on you need not get bogged down in the minutiae. We'll narrow the choices to a few based on what you prefer. Then you make the big decisions like your dress, bridesmaid dresses, colors, invitations, flowers, venue, food, cake. Sebastian will handle your honeymoon. Sounds good?"

This is a monumental relief. It's my wedding, so my involvement is paramount. But I acknowledge I can't do it all. With a light heart, I return Shelley's smile.

"Thank you so much! You do not understand how stressed I've been in just a few days," I respond. "Eight weeks to plan a wedding..."

Haley laughs.

"Girl, you must know by now when Baz wants something, nothing will stop him!"

"You speak the truth!" We crack up.

Tap. Tap. Tap.

Sergeant Shelley raps her Montblanc champagne gold rollerball pen on the surface of the table. Once all eyes fix on hers, she clears her throat.

"Ladies, shall we begin?"

"Yes, ma'am!" We salute.

The other night Baz and I discussed key decisions for the bridal party. We prefer an intimate number of our closest loved ones. Leonie as my maid of honor paired with Malcolm, Baz's best man. Haley as my bridesmaid paired with Lachlan, his best friend. Then Blair and Billie paired with Roger and Harris, respectively.

Leonie and I spoke of her concerns about being with Roger if he were a groomsman. But I assured her Baz understood and chose Malcolm as best man since he's the oldest brother of the three. She's still nervous to interact with Roger. So, I told her I was fine with Giovanni as her plus one. My BFF's happiness is just as important as mine.

Haley was just as pensive as Leonie when she agreed to being my bridesmaid. I want to include her since she's my future sister-in-law. Also, I genuinely adore her. We've grown close over the last five weeks. She confessed to me she's had a crush on Lachlan since she was a kid. But not ready to move beyond family friends. Particularly since he's Baz's best friend—her ultra-protective eldest brother. I promised her I won't mention anything to Baz. Not that I'm keeping secrets from him. Rather, I'm maintaining her privacy.

For their dresses, we let them choose gowns in the wedding colors and that complement their bodies. They vary in height, but all curvy. So, what flatters most.

"Ooh, Haley and Billie! A designer friend of mine just sent photos of his latest formal dresses to me!" Leonie exclaims. "Here. Scan through these. I saw a few that could be *parfait*! Billie I'll text message the link to you now."

She nods while Haley eagerly swipes through the photos on Leonie's iPhone. Their ebony and mahogany heads bob yes and no over the mobile.

"These two would look great on you," Leonie states.

"And this one... Ooh, no that one for you!" Haley adds.

She turns to me and says, "Leonie and I will go over the dresses with Billie and Blair. Then show you our selections by tomorrow."

"Excellent!" Shelley claps. "Now for you, Lola. What are you thinking for your gown?"

My gown is a whole other story. I know I want three—for the ceremony, dinner, and after party. I'm not the princess type. Instead, the mermaid or sheath styles suit me best. I like a little vavavavoom action. Baz will love to see my curves accentuated by the flattering fit.

"I have little time for a custom gown," I lament with a sigh. "I never dreamed of my wedding dress like most little girls. I always sketched the lingerie trousseau! But I want a special gown so I can see Baz's eyes light up when I stand at the top of the aisle."

Shelley nods, "Don't you fret, darling! One of the most important things I learned by being Morgan's wife is a billionaire's influence goes way beyond the norm! I'm sure Baz told you whatever you want, you will have, unquestioned."

She and the planners make notes to book appointments starting tomorrow with designers in New York City in person and virtually for Paris. She's as determined as me to find memorable dresses.

As for the colors, Baz and I are strong, bold individuals with a flair for the unexpected. Our palette has to represent us well. I'm partial to orange and fuchsia. Hues on the same side of the color wheel work well together. Their undertones will act as a seamless gradient rather than two contrasting shades. I opt for neutral supporting colors to ensure the vibrant shades pop wherever they're featured. A striking, winning combination of a dynamic couple and their wedding colors.

The guests are the next item to tackle on Shelley's master to-do list. My side comprises Luc, Leonie, Blair, Billie, Starr, and some friends I've gained in the industry—

about forty. Baz, thus the Steele clan, has a much larger list. It accounts for our wedding being the family's first. The need to invite family, friends, society members, business associates, and political figures increases their number significantly. I understand and leave it to Shelley to decide. Truly, the only person I need there is Baz.

As though we drew her in through telepathy, Shelley's assistant announces the invitation company rep's arrival. Shelley uses them for her most important events since their unparalleled designs are exceptional. We spend the next hour discussing my preferences and reviewing options. Then plan to provide her with the final number tomorrow.

Sergeant Shelley maintains her Double VIP list by guest category for such occasions as an unexpected party or event. So a day's notice poses no problem.

"The venue is up to you, Lola," Shelley starts. "STEELE has the best in the city, well honestly anywhere. But do you have a preference?"

I remember how STEELE42's beauty impressed me when I attended a charity gala there with Baz the first month we met. It's one of their award-winning entertainment venues that specializes in weddings, parties, and galas for society's best both in the United States and abroad.

It was a bank. When STEELE refurbished it, they strove to keep the integrity of the space with the original columns, teller windows on the sides, the vault, and more original details. I was most awed by the vaulted ceiling that twinkles in the dim lighting with a replication of the constellations. Since STEELE42 is one of Baz's favorite venues, I ask Shelley to plan for that space. She smiles delightedly and agrees it's perfect.

"Now, on to the most appetizing part!" I shimmy in my chair.

My girls laugh. But don't deny it. Women after my heart.

The food and drink tasted so divine at the gala I ask for Lucien to cater the wedding. For the cake Shelley insists we use her good friend Sylvia Weinstock. She's *The Queen of Cake* whose delicious confections cross the lips of high society, celebrities, or anyone who can afford her chefs d'oeuvre. Who am I to argue? I can't wait for the cake testing set in two days. Yum!

Flowers play a major part in our relationship. The endless vases Baz sent to my suite at STEELE Monte Carlo, the everyday bouquets he sends to me at the office and home, the exquisite Sterling Silver Roses he used to entice me back. They're small tokens that bring a lot of happiness. I want the venue decked out in them. Not one to waste, we'll donate the flowers to the nonprofit children's hospital for which Baz is a patron. Shelley's florist joins us virtually to discuss ideas. We schedule an in-person appointment before the cake tasting.

Shelley confirms what Baz mentioned to me the other night. The official press release announcing our engagement and upcoming wedding will be distributed in the morning. She needed the details we worked out today to complete the announcement. She warns me from her experience with Morgan to expect paparazzi, the nosy, and jealousy. Suddenly, it becomes oh so real. Despite what may come, I wouldn't have it any other way.

"Here's to an exceedingly productive day, Ladies!" Shelley toasts with more of my favorite Dom Pérignon.

"Cheers!" We chorus as we raise our Waterford Crystal flutes filled with the tasty champers.

I send a silent toast to my parents, who I know watch on with love.

* * *

"SHELLEY IS WONDERFUL! You're lucky to have such a nice mother-in-law, *Chérie*," Leonie clinks her flute to mine.

We parted from Shelley and Haley with hugs and kisses a few hours ago. Now, we're ensconced on a terrace at my STEELE Tower penthouse sipping more Dom P. Hell, we're more than sipping, we've finished two bottles.

I wanted her to stay here. But she declined, preferring to stay at my Sutton Place penthouse to "get a true feel for the space." I believe she wanted to avoid being in the same building as Roger. After I told her he's in Paris, she agreed to spend time here after the wedding prep session. Her expression went from guarded to relieved. Now, it's blissfully happy from the bubbly.

"How are you and Giovanni?" I ask since she hasn't mentioned her on-again-off-again lover after I extended her plus one to him.

She stares beyond the glass surround at the city view for a moment. Then shifts in her chaise to face me.

"Oh, *Chérie*, I just don't know if I want to—"

Abruptly, she sits up and swings her feet to the floor, staring with wide eyes over my shoulder. Surprised by her reaction, I turn to figure out the cause for her concern.

Roger!

Fuck!

He's striding over to us with that intense gray-eyed gaze of his pinned on Leonie. I hear her quick inhalation of breath and turn to face her. Her normally golden-caramel complexion is ashen. Her mouth opened in shock.

What. The. Fuck.

I jump to block his path to her. He will not hurt my best friend again. I don't give a damn what I promised her.

"Stop!"

I put my hands up and glare at Roger and at Sebastian, who I notice stands behind him.

"Leonie doesn't want to see you. So, please go," I tell him. Then forcefully I add, "Now, Roger!"

He blinks away from Leonie. His eyes cut to mine. I don't waiver before him. I meet his stare with my own hazel eyes blazing.

"Roger, bro, you need to slow down," Baz tells him, putting his hand on Roger's shoulder to pull him back. "You're freaking them out. Not cool, man."

The air is tense until I hear movement behind me. I peer over my shoulder to see Leonie putting her shoes back on and gathering her things. She's a bit wobbly from the champagne, but determined to leave.

"Lola, I have to go. I'll call you later," she whispers in French.

I know she's upset because she rarely calls me Lola.

"No!"

We jump around to stare at Roger who raised his hands palms forward in surrender. His stare less intense, but still focused on Leonie.

"Please, Leonie, I just want to speak with you. Just for a moment... Please," he beseeches in a voice rough with emotion.

Collectively, we hold our breath for Leonie's response. She sighs again, but nods her head in acceptance. I start to speak, but she shakes her head. I sense she's trying to control her emotions, so I give her the space she requests. The glare I give Roger would set him on fire. Sebastian turns to Leonie and asks if she's comfortable speaking with Roger. She nods, again. We leave them on the terrace and head to the living room.

"What the fuck, Sebastian?" I round on him once we're out of earshot. "I told you Leonie was here! Why did you let Roger come over without telling me? You said he was in Paris!"

"Whoa, babe," he responds with his hands up in supplication. "He told me he needed to make things right with her before our wedding. She wasn't answering his calls or text messages. He had no other choice."

I narrow my eyes at him, not assuaged by his answer.

"Fuck that! If Leonie wanted to speak with him, she would have answered. To put her on the spot is unacceptable," I retort.

"I'm sorry. I should have told you so you could have prepared Leonie. But he's sincere. Trust me. I know my brother. He won't hurt her. Besides, they're adults and capable of working out their love life. We did, right?"

I give it to him. Baz is so good. He easily flipped the conversation to make me focus on us.

"Okay, you're right. But she's my best friend. I will allow no one, and I mean no one to cause her pain. She's a kind, loving woman who deserves respect. I don't care if Roger is your brother. He better not fuck up, Sebastian."

He enfolds me in his muscular arms, pressed firmly to his chest, and kisses the top of my head.

"He won't, my love. He won't."

Roger better not, I think to myself as I allow Baz to lead me to the sofa.

I tuck my legs under me, angled to see through the glass wall onto the terrace. On the chaise I vacated, Roger sits forward with his elbows resting on his knees, his hands clasped together. Leonie returned to her chaise, perched on its edge with her hands folded in her lap. At first they stare at each other, apparently waiting for one to speak. Roger breaks the silence.

We can't hear what's being said. However, Leonie's response to Roger's lengthy utterance has her hands moving rapidly in agitation. Roger shakes his head, speaking again. They exchange words for some time before Leonie nods and stands, a sign she's ended their conversation.

I rise, too, but Baz grabs my arm to stop me from going onto the terrace.

"What?" I ask, throwing him a glare over my shoulder.

"Wait a minute, Lola. Give them a moment," he responds, then points his chin in the terrace's direction.

Roger rose to stand before Leonie much as I blocked him earlier. He cups her face in his hands, then tips her face up towards his. Leonie's body shudders in response when he slants his mouth over hers in a scorching kiss.

Well, damn.

The intensity of their passion makes me blush and turn away. Baz pulls me onto his lap, and I can't help but peek at them again. Leonie clutches the front of Roger's shirt in her hands as she swoons from his embrace. Roger's mouth moves to trail kisses along her jaw and throat as he murmurs words only she can hear. She trembles, then pulls away, shaking her head while her hands no longer hold him, rather they push him away. Startled by her abrupt reaction, Roger loses his grasp on her. Leonie spins around, scoops up her belongings, and rushes to the door, swiping her face. Coming upon Baz and me, her eyes widen and she covers her mouth on a sob.

"*Merde*," she whispers.

"Leonie!" Roger calls to her as he strides through the open door. He too pauses when he sees us and wipes a hand over his face with one hand and attempts to adjust his pants from the not so discreet enormous bulge at his crotch.

"Fuck," he mutters.

No one moves until Leonie tells me she's leaving as she hastens to the front foyer. I follow her this time, not letting Baz stop me.

"I'm coming with—"

"Non, non... Je vais bien, mer—"

I cut her off, not believing for a moment she's fine. I grab my handbag from where I left it on the entry table before I turn to tell Baz. He and Roger stand watching us. Baz nods in understanding. Roger shakes his head dejectedly. I purse my lips and take Leonie by the hand as the elevator doors open. She squeezes my hand in response as she smiles through her tears. I understand exactly how she feels: wanting him, but not wanting the pain.

"Time for something a little more potent than Dom P., *oui?*"

Leonie's snort of laughter starts us on a fit of giggles.

She'll be just fine.

LOLA

Instead of returning to Paris, Leonie continued on with me to Beverly Hills earlier than we planned for some much-needed girls' time before business meetings start.

The night she spoke with Roger on the terrace, we went to my Sutton Place penthouse. She admitted she still loves him, but is afraid of being hurt again. She assured me he had said nothing untoward. She was overwhelmed.

While we drank shots of tequila, Roger called and sent text messages she refused to answer. Until his last voicemail when he threatened to come over to see her in five minutes. She promptly called him back.

He apologized for upsetting her. His agreement not to pressure her and to give her space made Leonie feel better. For the sake of peace at the wedding and out of respect for Baz and me, they decided to hold off on any further conversations.

I wonder at his reaction when she arrives with Giovanni. Two Alpha Males, one lioness...

"Lola... Hey girl... Lola?"

Once again, Starr's gentle voice pulls my mind from rampant thoughts distracting me from my meditation session.

Focus, Lola! Like Baz said, Leonie and Roger can figure out their relationship without my interference. Well, at least I hope so.

I shake my head to clear my ruminations. Then open my eyes to see not only Starr's angelic face, but Leonie, Haley, Blair, and Billie peeping at me. My cheeks redden as I laugh in embarrassment.

"No judgement... But again, Lola!" Starr's dimples appear as she joins in.

The first stop to jumpstart our girls' time was to Starr Light Fitness & Wellness Beverly Hills for yoga and meditation classes. The concentration vinyasa requires prevented my mind from wandering. Instead, I tuned into my breath and the sequence of challenging asanas Starr used in the flow. The vigorous physical and mental workout was just what I needed as opposed to the slower pace of a Hatha class. Starr's dynamic teaching style made it fun.

After a few minutes in the steam room and a quick shower, we head to lunch at nearby Crustacean Beverly Hills. The modern Vietnamese fare specialties include delicious seafood that's the perfect light meal after yoga.

We settle on the gray suede seats at a banquette near the Walk on Water. The path runs from the front door through the restaurant between tables. Interspersed with wood and weight-bearing glass, the water below appears to offer a glimpse of the ocean's depths. Aside from the cuisine, the path is the eatery's highlight.

When the server arrives, we order An Sum—Crustacean's version of dim sum—to share and salads for our meals. I haven't spoken with Starr in a few months, not since her return from the ashram in India.

"Have you spoken to Malcolm Steele, yet?"

"No, we keep playing phone tag. Right now he's it!" She laughs. "I was unreachable in India, then traveled a few more weeks. He was away on business followed by holiday in Italy."

I forgot I hadn't told her about my engagement. That's where Malcolm was recently.

"Oh, well, you see..."

Exaggeratedly, I brush my left hand against my cheek. I removed my ring for the class and locked it in the safe at the center. Now, Starr's eyes bug out of her head as the light bouncing off of my rink nearly blinds her.

"Holy shit! Are you serious with me right now? That's humongous!"

Her quiet calm, namaste, om, center your mind blown clear out of the water. We giggle at her reaction. The server places our drinks on the table with a smile, enjoying our mirth.

"Here's to the woman who got her man!" Starr raises her sparking water in a toast.

I smile graciously at my friends as they raise their glasses to my happiness. Just as glad they like one another. My little circle expands nicely.

"*D'accord*, where do we go for our Girls' Not Out?" Leonie asks.

"The latest hot club to open is the Remy West Hollywood," Billie who knows all the West Coast happenings responds. "Their It thing is dancers bound by ropes Shibari style suspended from the ceiling. It has a BDSM vibe if you know what I mean."

She giggles and lifts her eyebrows up and down.

Leonie and I glance at each other, then snort. If only she knew we're All Access Global members of LEVELS. But then I remember Patrick Rockett is AAG, too. She's probably been there plenty of times with him. Holy shit we're all kinky! I laugh uncontrollably.

"What did I say?" Billie asks, confused.

"Oh, Billie, nothing! It's aah… How do you say… graphic!" Leonie giggles. "Let's meet at eleven in the lobby. *Oui?*"

Billie nods, accepting Leonie's save.

"What are you wearing?" Haley asks. "I have a black mini dress or a light blue sequin romper."

Fortunately, the conversation switches to a safer topic. Blair chimes in on how well the light blue would contrast with Haley's gray eyes and ebony hair. Meanwhile, Leonie's eyes still twinkle with glee.

* * *

"WHAT THE—"

I screech when enormous hands grab me from behind as I walk into my Penthouse Suite at the STEELE Rodeo Drive, an iconic property at Wilshire Boulevard. As a scream rises in my throat, a hand covers my mouth and the other wraps around my waist locking my back to a massive chest. Fuck me!

"Surprise, Little Pet."

My legs give out. But for Baz's arm banded about me, I would have crumpled to the floor. My pulse races as the adrenaline pumps through my veins. My armpits tingle and my palms are damp. I close my eyes.

Once Baz lowers his hand, I take a deep inhale. Which serves to push my breast into his hand that slipped inside of my dress. My breath catches when he pushes the lace of my bra to the side and tugs my nipple into a turgid nub. My pussy clenches.

My head lolls to the side as he plants open-mouthed kisses along my neck. A nip followed by a long suck forces a hiss from my lips. His new habit of marking me with "Baz Love Bites" starts my juices to collect in my core. The combination of the nipple tweaks and mouth assault drives me wild with lust. I rub my thighs together, hoping for some kind of relief.

"You cannot cum until I give you permission, Naughty Girl," Baz chastises me as he plunges two thick fingers past my G-string into my wet, aching pussy. My inner walls greedily suck the invading digits deeper into my channel.

Blatantly disobeying Baz, I rock my mound against his palm in sync with his thrusts as he finger fucks me.

WHAP… WHAP… WHAP WHAP

"Naughty… Naughty… Naughty Pet," Baz punishes my pussy with slaps that coat his hand with my juices. "You want me to put you over my lap to spank… this… round… ass."

He couples each word with a thrust of his groin against my bottom. I writhe and moan my response. My orgasm is so close, so close. I'm delirious with need.

"Aaaahhh, Sir… Please may I cum…" I beg pitifully.

Baz flips us around, braces my palms against the suite's door, and kicks my legs apart. The sound of his zipper opening makes my pussy quiver in anticipation. I don't have long to wait.

The force of his thrust as his enormous dick slams inside of my pussy lifts me to the balls of my feet. My calves strain to hold me in position.

His pistoning strokes intensifies as I feel him expand in size. His snarls and grunts trigger my release as I wail with relief. Baz effortlessly lifts me from the floor with one hand hooked under my thigh, opening my core to his brutal thrusts. My pelvis slams into the hard, wooden door. I fear the hinges will break from his power.

I love it! I slap my palm against the door as I throw my head back.

"Yaaaasssss!"

"You want my fat cock to fuck your tight, juicy pussy, Naughty Pet," Baz grunts in my ear. "Your pulsating heat around my dick. Take it! Take… every… fucking… inch!"

My pussy spasms with wave after wave of my third orgasm. I can't even think straight anymore. I can only respond with grunts of my own.

"Uh… Uh… Uh… Uh!"

My inner walls clamp down hard on Baz's dick. He roars and jackhammers my pussy. His thick length swells, stretching my channel to the point of pain. His tip hits my cervix and I cry out.

"Fuuuck!" I scream. "Oh… Fuuuck, Baaazzz!"

His cock unleashes ropes of creamy cum deep within my core. Bathing my pussy with his seed.

Another orgasm rocks me. I'm too spent to utter a sound. I lean heavily against the door and let Baz pump into me until every drop of his cum empties within my womb.

"Lolaaaa… Fuuuck!"

My body shivers at his primal call. My mate claims me again.

* * *

SEBASTIAN WAS NOT THRILLED I left him after hours of making love to go to a club. But, hey, he came two days early… literally.

My girls and I sit in the VIP area of the Remy West Hollywood. Billie was right. This is a hot spot. The Shibari tied dancers hover inches above the crowd. The colorful silken cords artfully swathe their long, toned limbs. They blindfolded some. While others stare boldly at the revelers. The dungeon-like atmosphere adds to the BDSM theme. It's a nice attempt at a sex club. But it doesn't compare to the LEVELS locations.

I chuckle as I lift my Manhattan to my lips, thinking of how discerning my sexual tastes are now. Eleven months later, and I'm no longer the novice ashamed of my sub inclinations. I proudly embrace my Independent Woman and submissive.

RAWR, Sir!

"Time to get our groove on one more time, Ladies!" Blair announces as she pulls Billie to her feet. "Let's go. No time to decorate the banquette!"

She's right. We've been dancing and drinking for the past three and a half hours. It's about that time. Besides, I have an even hotter fiancé in bed waiting for me. Girls' Night Out is fun. We enjoy each other's company and our drinks. But, hey… I finish the last of my cocktail and join my friends on the dance floor. One more shimmy and I'm out.

The DJ's music and callouts have everyone bouncing to the beat. I throw my hands up and shimmy in my gold backless, strapless mini dress. It's one of my latest designs for the evening wear collection. A band at the top connects to the front panel that circles around my rear, dipping dangerously low to the crack of my ass. The chain-mail material shimmers in the lights. Leonie already requested one for a movie premier she's attending in a few weeks.

I shy away from a guy who's dancing too close only to bump into another one who's behind me. I slide away. But he slips his hand around my waist. Turning to face him, I peer up into Baz's smirking face. The devil!

He bends to reach his lips to my ear as he whispers, "I will wrap you up in my silks, Little Pet. Then fuck you as you swing from the ceiling."

Damn!

Baz twirls me around and with bent knees, he grinds his pelvis into mine. The sensation of his hard dick against my soft mound breaks goosebumps across my skin. We move as one for a few songs, glued at our groins. Our foreheads pressed together. My arms draped around his neck with my fingers gripping his hair. His hands clutch my hips possessively. As the next tune begins, he whispers in my ear.

"I am not staying. Just reminding you what you are missing, Little Pet…"

With his mission complete, Baz strides away. He leaves me standing with my mouth hanging open, pussy wet and wanting. Torn between my man and my friends, I hesitate.

"Go! Be with your boo!" Billie laughs and shoos her hands at me.

Leonie, Haley, and Blair nod, giving me the thumbs up as they continue to dance.

I only hesitate a moment. Blow kisses to them. Then rush after Baz, pushing my way through the pulsating crowd. He's so tall I can spot him ahead of me. I slip my hand in his and he smiles down at me.

"Excellent choice, Little Pet," he whispers against my ear.

Excellent choice indeed, I smile.

LOLA

"We're a family and we support one another, Lola."

Morgan says to me with a fatherly smile that makes my heart soar.

Baz and I just arrived at Meridian Teterboro the deluxe FBO at the private jet airport. It surprised me to see the entire Steele clan other than Roger aboard. I guess he'll meet us in Abu Dhabi since he's in Paris.

Blair and Billie left two days ago to coordinate with the STEELE teams. Leonie and Luc flew in yesterday. Ever the supermodel, she wanted to acclimate to the environment before interviews and the red carpet.

An unexpected fitting for my wedding dress delayed my departure by two days. However, Blair and Billie assured me they would handle everything in my absence. I'm confident all will be well. They've proven themselves more than capable with the New York and Las Vegas boutique openings.

"Morgan, thank you so much! Everyone being there means so much to me," I smile warmly at him.

Shelley stands from where she sat with Morgan and takes my hand, "Lola, darling, come! Haley and I must brief you on the latest updates."

I cast a glance over my shoulder at Sebastian. He and Morgan chuckle as they salute Sergeant Shelley. I can't complain. My future mother-in-law has morphed into my fairy godmother. She meets all of my needs even before I voice them. When Baz and I return from our honeymoon—destination still unknown to me—I'm taking Shelley and Haley on an in-laws' getaway to thank them for all they've done. They more than deserve it.

Settled at the conference table, Haley's fingers fly across the keyboard of her laptop. Without moving her gaze away from the screen or slowing down, she nods in greeting.

"Right on time! You can view the latest program on these tablets. I'll make adjustments to the master file from my laptop. Take a moment to review it. Then we can go into details."

Haley is a genius. She created a cloud-based software program and coordinating app to compile each component of my wedding into one user-friendly, easily accessible and updated organizer with virtual assistant. Shelley insists Haley patents and sells licenses of it.

I agree. Brides, planners, vendors all will benefit. The Steele family knows how to generate more wealth!

"Haley, this is fantastic! You've done so much more since I last saw it," I exclaim, slapping high five with Shelley. The girl is good.

Shy Haley blushes as she pushes her glasses up the bridge of her nose. Well aware of her brainiac intelligence. But not one to boast, she gives a self-deprecating shrug.

We jump into wedding planning mode for the next few hours. We set the date for a week after Lola's Coterie Dubai opening. Baz gave into an extra week to give me time to address any unforeseeable issues. He refuses to let post-opening situations delay our wedding. He won't let me forget canceling the Cabo San Lucas getaway he surprised me with after the Las Vegas party. I more than made up for it by treating him to a spa day. I gave him the best happy ending ever!

Once the press release went out, my publicist moved into overdrive funneling appropriate interview requests and television appearances with local, national, and international media. The gossips' tongues can't stop wagging. They proclaimed I snagged the most eligible and lusted after bachelor in the world. Some implied my non-existent pregnancy spurred the quick nuptials. Others speculated I married him to benefit Lola's Coterie.

Social media accounts and bloggers devoted to us popped up overnight. The monikers *Couple of the Century* and *SeLo* trend on Twitter and Instagram. Major topics: What's Lola wearing today? *SeLo* Spotted! Lola's Baby Bump! *SeLo* Breakup Countdown! Whether the posts are true or false, the likes, reactions, shares, and comments are off the charts. Celebrities and the wealthy are uppermost in people's minds.

Baz doesn't have a social media presence other than the STEELE corporate handles. I have mine on Instagram to post behind-the-scenes photos and my activities and on Pinterest some boards for my favorite foods, recipes, and inspiration. Nothing particularly personal, just enough to keep people interested. My follower count rose from hundreds of thousands to millions. The comments now include snarky haters. Funny enough, my loyal fans defend me. I stopped reading them. Better for my wellbeing, Starr told me.

My marketing team had to add three people to handle the increase in demand for Lola's Coterie social media and public footprint. The vice president told me the number of Google Alerts increased over two hundred percent and the languages are no longer predominately English and French. The Asian and South American countries increased their coverage of Lola's Coterie, Baz, and me. Marketing monitors Baz from a business standpoint. But when I started dating him, I set up alerts to keep track of his name and what he was up to in the news. #NotAStalker

Shelley's warning was correct. And every day it increases. It's sheer madness!

"I'm sorry I missed your last wedding ceremony dress fitting, Lola."

Haley's voice brings me back to the planning. Another Shelley prediction rings true for my wedding dresses.

Each of the designers we met with were eager to create my dresses even with less than eight weeks to finish. I narrowed them down to Mr. Valentino, Reem Acra, Naeem Khan, and Amsale. After reviewing the sketches, I fell in love with the exquisite long-sleeve, lace mermaid gown with a cut-out in the back by Mr. Valentino. The elegance, drama, and sensuous lines made it the clear winner for my ceremony dress.

For contrast at the reception, I chose the Reem Acra sleeveless, deep-vee sheer mermaid gown overlaid with hand-stitched flower appliqués and a silk satin belt with a diamond brooch. It harkens to our theme of abundant flowers.

In the end, I opted to alter dresses from my evening wear collection for my rehearsal dinner and post-reception party dresses. Baz made the point with all the photos picked up by media. It would be an organic way to promote my new line.

Mr. Valentino and his team brought my gown to New York since I couldn't make it back to Paris for the last fitting. It's just as well since the dress needs to be there for my return from the UAE. No worries of it going missing. It's now safely ensconced with my other dresses in my new temperature-controlled walk-in closet in our STEELE Tower penthouse.

"No worries. I'd rather everyone see it when I walk down the aisle," I wink at Haley.

"I'm sure you look stunning," Haley smiles.

"Oh, indeed! She looks divine!" Adds Shelley, who I was happy to have there for her support. "All three gowns and her rehearsal dinner dress are sensational!"

"How do you feel about your bridesmaid dress?" I ask Haley.

Leonie already told me she's ecstatic about her Elie Saab custom creation. Since he has a studio in Paris and is her good friend, he made her gown specifically for her matching our color palette. It's a dreamy strapless column of silk organza layers in various shades of the orange and fuchsia hues.

Haley also chose one of his designs. Her halter-top column dress follows the same layers as Leonie's.

"I love it! So light and moves beautifully," she exclaims. "Very dreamy and romantic."

Blair's and Billie's dresses suit them perfectly and match the color theme. Blair chose an orange empire gown that accentuates her lithe figure. Billie opted for a fuchsia gown with a draped neckline and body skimming silhouette.

Baz and the groomsman will wear classic, bespoke tuxedos in black with boutonnieres.

Our updates move to the RSVP list. The final total of three hundred people may seem astonishing. But it's not out of the ordinary, Shelley assures me. She whittled it down from the original four hundred after Morgan and Baz added their lists. As long as everyone enjoys themselves and the delectable dishes Lucien crafts and the yummy cake Sylvia Weinstock makes, I'm happy.

Now, I'm sketching some exclusive designs for the Beverly Hills boutique. The anchor store location at STEELE Galleria Rodeo Drive is optimal. Spread across three levels in the open-air mall, two above ground facing the Drive and the interior courtyard and one below grade with a glass wall and double doors opening onto the courtyard. Passersby from all directions can access the entrances.

The windows will display the glitzy gowns and luxury lingerie perfectly. The opening is just in time for awards season. With Leonie's advertising campaign highlighting the evening wear, I'm positive celebrities and Hollywood's elite will order the custom creations.

Baz was smart to wait for my boutique to fill the retail space. Lola's Coterie Beverly Hills will be the only luxury lingerie store on Rodeo Drive. The lack of competition combined with my unique pieces and our joint marketing teams working to hype up the launch will ensure significant exposure and traffic. Thus impressive revenue gains. My man, the future CEO of STEELE International, Inc.

I lean across the armrests to buss his cheek. Startled, he jumps in his seat, his hands fumble with the tablet he held.

"Sorry, baby!" I giggle.

I can't resist his gorgeousness—I'm engaged to a stud. I pull his face to mine and kiss him silly. Once we come up for air, I rest my forehead against his with a sigh. I love him so much and cannot wait to be his wife, Mrs. Sebastian Steele. Independent Woman or sub, I'm old-fashioned. I intend to take his name, Lola Steele.

"I love you, too, babe," he murmurs, so attuned to my attitude he knows without me speaking a word my state of mind.

For the rest of the flight, I cuddle against his side in total bliss.

* * *

"Luc!" I cry as I rush over to hug him. "I've missed you so much! I have a lot to tell you."

We're having lunch at one of the hotel's restaurants at the STEELE Abu Dhabi complex. I left Baz in our Rulers' Suite so I could have some private time with Luc. I know they only tolerate each other for my sake. My wish is for them to be more friendly. They're both important to me.

Luc's been my support for over seven years, stepping in as a mentor and father figure after losing my parents. Fortunately, now that he's put a ring on it, Baz has relaxed his stance on Luc secretly crushing on me. My Captain Caveman may still growl, but at least he won't bite.

"Oh, *petite chérie*, it's so good to see you!" He responds holding me in a tight embrace. "I guess as much since I saw a certain article in the *Financial Times* about a pair dubbed the *Couple of the Century*. Or perhaps it was the *International Herald Tribune*? Oh no, it was *The Asahi Simbun*."

Laughing, we settle at the table, and I hold out my left hand to him. His smile is genuine as his eyes brighten with unshed tears.

"Félicitations pour vos fiançailles!" He says. "Steele is a man of honor after all. Are you truly happy, *petite chérie?"*

I nod enthusiastically, *"Bref, je crois que nous sommes, sans l'ombre d'un doute, amoureux!"*

No doubts whatsoever. Baz and I love one another, I smile happily. Luc nods, satisfied with my response.

Sitting up, I reach for his hands. Surprised, he lifts his gaze to mine.

"Luc, for over seven years you have been my rock. A staunch supporter of my business endeavors, financial guru, and father figure," an emotional hitch catches my words.

I clear my throat to start anew.

"Luc, it would lift my spirits if you would walk me down the aisle and sit in the front row beside the chairs reserved for my parents' memory. Then at the reception, thank guests for coming and give the toast in place of them. I would also love if you would dance with me."

The unshed tears well in his eyes, turning the stunning dark blue orbs black with unbridled emotion. Luc squeezes my smaller hands between his larger ones and nods, too emotional to voice his answer.

We sit quietly for a moment. Then he squeezes my hands again. His emotions back in check.

"Steele couldn't find a bigger ring to profess his love for you, *petite chérie*? Ah, the cheapskate!"

Luc's joke instantly shifts the somber mood to a light one. I snort loudly and cover my mouth with my hand. My ice skating rink dazzles Luc with its brilliant light.

SEBASTIAN

My woman stuns on the red carpet. The paparazzi flashbulbs shimmer against the metallic material of her mauve, one-shoulder, ankle-skimming gown. When she walks, her toned legs peek from behind a hip-high slit that meets the ruching on one side of her waist. The strappy sandals that match the color of her dress make her petite frame taller. Shimmery metallic eye makeup stresses the golden flecks in her hazel orbs. For added drama, her glam squad crimped her hair, flowing down to her waist in a raven arrow aimed at her luscious ass.

In celebration of this opening party, I gifted Lola a pair of pink diamond chandelier earrings to grace her swanlike neck. Never jaded, she whooped and smothered me with so many kisses she had to reapply her lipstick and I had to wash the dusty pink color off of my face. I can't wait to see my dick tinged pink when as she promised to "thank you properly later, Sir." My length twitched.

I step back to allow the cameras full access to her beauty.

Lola poses and smiles radiantly. My ring shows big and bold on her hand, placed sensuously on her hip. Turning her megawatt smile in my direction, she beckons me like the Petite Seductress I first nicknamed her at LEVELS New York that fateful night twelve months ago. Unable to resist her call then or now, I stride over to take my place by her side. A gentle kiss to her upturned pouty mouth seals the deal.

Yup. *Couple of the Century.*

"Lola!"

We pivot to see Leonie stalk the red carpet towards us. Another irresistible beauty. *The Lion* commands the crowds' attention without even glancing their way. Their shouts of her name only elicit a brief smile as she's determined to reach her best friend.

Leonie captivates in a burnt-orange sequined one-sleeve, fitted gown that reaches one knee then flares at the other like a mermaid's tail to angle down to the top of her foot. Her long legs make quick work of the red carpet in open-toe stilettos. Each sway of her hips reflects the light of the incessant flashbulbs. Her signature mane piled in a bedhead tousled style.

A flicker of irritation shoots through me when I see she's accompanied by Giovanni Mattei. For my younger brother's sake, I'd hoped Leonie would arrive alone. I glance around, but don't see Roger. Good, I'll warn him.

"Lola! *Chérie*! How marvelous you look!"

The BFFs hug and the paparazzi start their blitz again. Now that she's caught up to her friend, Leonie affords the press her full attention. She and Lola pose together and apart, ensuring their best angles. Meanwhile, Mattei and I stand to the side. I shoot a quick text message to Roger to let him know not to freak out and to maintain his cool. Mattei is no chump, so it could get ugly real fast. I await Roger's response when I see the three dots show he's answering right away. As expected, he's pissed, but promises not to start shit. Good.

Lola calls to me, and I join them for more photos. Fortunately, Mattei keeps his distance and doesn't join us in the shots. As I stand between the two of them, the crowd goes wild. In my periphery, I see Roger walking on the red carpet with Malcolm, Harris, and Haley. I call them over to get in the pictures. The rarity of all the Steele siblings in one frame will make for excellent social media posts and traditional media coverage.

I don't hesitate when I refer to all of us as Steeles, since I have a feeling Roger won't let Leonie wander much longer. After his drunken confession to me last month, it's only a matter to time.

As they approach, I feel Leonie stiffen and shift to move away. I won't let her. I tighten my hold on her waist. The professional in her won't cause a scene, so she relaxes at my insistence and beams for the cameras. Roger doesn't hesitate to stand beside Leonie and place his arm around her possessively. He didn't even acknowledge Mattei's existence. Now fully assembled, the flashes nearly blind us as the paps go crazy for the best shots.

"Luc!"

Lola calls to her mentor as she waives him over to us.

I've cut him some slack. Particularly since Lola is officially mine. He smiles at her with the affection of a proud father. So that helps. I'll do anything to make Lola happy. I clap him on the back and invite him to stand on Lola's other side. Luc nods in acknowledgment of my olive branch and we pose for more shots.

"Lola, Leonie, Sebastian, Luc, you have news crews to speak with," Billie says as she steps behind us.

"Thank you, Billie! You look gorgeous!" Lola says enthusiastically.

And she does. Lola has some attractive friends. But no one compares to my love. I slip her hand into mine and follow Billie to the awaiting crews. Lola winks at me. Her eyes twinkle brighter than the pink diamonds that adorn her ears.

Just inside the boutique, I spot my father deep in conversation with some prominent businessmen from the UAE. Their wives peruse pieces from the collections while engaged in conversation with my mother. They exemplify a power couple I hope to replicate with Lola.

We finish the interviews that interspersed questions on Lola's Coterie collections and rapid rise to success to details on our upcoming nuptials. Lola answered the business-related questions with gusto. But deftly avoided substantial responses on our personal lives. She kept it simple with we're in love and look forward to our future together.

The less fodder given to the media, the better. As with most old money families, the Steeles like media coverage to further our business gains, but prefer intimate aspects to remain private.

"Honey, how are you holding up?"

My mother materializes next to me. I smile down at her and wrap my arm around her shoulders. She's an inch taller than Lola and fits under my chin with her heels on.

"Good, thanks Mom. How are you? You've been so busy with our wedding plans. Thank you so much," I squeeze her close.

I love my mother dearly. She's grounded since she didn't grow up wealthy and made sure we were, too. She always has our best interests at heart and loves my father passionately. Shelley's the epitome of a dedicated wife and mother. I hope that Lola and I can have an amazing family, too.

"Now you know I don't mind at all. You're our first baby to marry. We have to be sure everything is perfect! Your father and I are very proud of you."

She pauses as her eyes mist with tears. She takes a deep breath and I squeeze her again. Her words make even the Dom in me blink back tears. I strive to make my parents proud of me. It's so good to hear it from both of them.

"We're very pleased with Lola, too. She'll make an excellent wife for you, smart, independent, loving. She's not after your name or wealth. She reminds me of myself," she laughs. Then adds, "Although I was a shopgirl, and she owns the shops!"

We crack up over her joke.

"Yes, well, each generation improves upon the prior one," she smiles as her gaze lands on Lola who's charming a group of guests, mainly men.

My mother must sense me bristle because she laughs and pushes me in Lola's direction.

"Go! You and your father are so alike! Possessive Alpha males," she shakes her head.

"—the truth! You have the figure for modeling your designs—"

"What did you just say?" I demand, moving between Lola and some git flirting with her.

He backs up, locking eyes with me. He's about my height and broad. Not that it matters. I'll still knock him on his ass.

"You... Come with me."

I hear Malcolm. But don't see him since I refuse to take my gaze from the fucker. Without waiting for his response, Malcolm takes him by the arm, and Roger flanks him. Quickly, they move him through the clusters of guests.

A small hand slides along my back. Instantly, I'm soothed by Lola's touch. I take a deep breath and pull her into my arms, nuzzling her hair. Her seductive perfume fills my nostrils. She's a balm for my agitated psyche.

"Thank you for protecting my honor, Captain Caveman," she murmurs, suppressing a giggle.

I chuckle against her hair. Then flip it because I can, and Lola loves it.

"Are you being a smartass, Naughty Pet?" I demand, pulling back to pin her with my no-nonsense Dom stare. "You know, I can always take you to the stockroom to administer a proper spanking for your sass, Little Shopgirl."

A shudder runs through my sub-cum-fiancée and her pupils dilate. The tip of her tongue darts out to moisten her lips as her eyes scan the guests, wondering if they overheard. When they alight on mine, I nod with a smirk. Right.

"Okay lovebirds, I need Lola."

Another man trying to monopolize my woman's time. With a sigh, I relinquish her to Luc, who laughs good-naturedly at my obvious annoyance.

"Don't worry, Steele, I won't keep her long. There are some business associates who want to meet her. You're welcome to join us."

I decline again, mending fences with Luc. I'll give him a chance to earn some of my trust. I leave them to it and network with other guests.

"Do not even think about it."

Haley jumps when I come up behind her and take the sheer negligee from her hands. Her face reddens and her glasses slip down her nose.

"Dammit, Sebastian! Stop being a jerk!" She retorts,

shoving her glasses back in place, glaring up at me. "You're not my father, you know!"

I have to hold back a laugh. She's been repeating those same words to her four older brothers all of her life. If I wasn't so protective, I would feel sorry for her. Oh, well. It is what it is. Which reminds me.

"What's going on with you and Lachlan?" I ask, narrowing my eyes at her.

Haley sputters, and her blush deepens. She's so flustered she can't speak.

"Sebastian! Are you pestering your sister?"

Again Shelley materializes out of thin air, this time to admonish me. For a moment, I'm transported back in time to when Lachlan and I were sneaking out of my room to go to a party. Unbeknownst to us, Haley who was forever tagging along followed. But tripped on the rug right outside of my parents' room. They woke from her cries and reprimanded Lachlan and me.

"No. She doesn't need a piece like this see-through negligee," I answer, then glance around and hold up a more modest piece. "This is better."

Haley snatches it and puts it back.

"Bugger off, Sebastian!"

My mother and I watch as she storms off. Then we glance at each other and laugh. As she dabs the corners of her eyes, my mother speaks first.

"Leave your sister alone, Sebastian. She's a grown woman, Big Brother."

"Yes, Sebastian, let her be."

Lola slips her arm around my waist as she stares up at me with a raised eyebrow. Outnumbered, I acquiesce... for now.

"Fine. Let's get back to the party. Shall we?"

I offer my mother and Lola my arms to escort them to where my father stands talking to some people Lola should meet. The light in Morgan's eyes when he sees my mother approach is like glancing into a mirror. I feel the same way about Lola.

She's the light of my life and I'll forever be happy to have her at my side.

SEBASTIAN

"*Spasibo* for the trip, Steele. Now let's see if I can knock you back to the Big Apple, *da*?"

I have more pent up energy than release options. Sparring sessions with Borya is just what I need.

It's been a week since the Abu Dhabi opening. Rather than returning to New York, we spent some days in Abu Dhabi. The usual post-opening work preoccupies Lola. More media coverage interviews, photoshoots with Leonie in the desert and around the city, in-boutique private parties for the city's wealthiest women. Lola's exhausted.

Leaving me to my own devices...

Borya flew in three days ago to Abu Dhabi, then traveled with us to Dubai. We train twice a day before my workday starts and in the evenings before dinner. I can't let my mind wander to my blue balls when I have the fist of a giant Russian coming towards my face. Lola thinks my slightly crooked nose that broke in a fight as a teen gives me a more edgy and less pretty boy appearance. Well, I don't need for it to happen again. Borya would smash the bones to bits. Forget crooked. He'd decimate my nose.

Roger flew back to Paris after Abu Dhabi to avoid drama with Leonie and Giovanni. Everyone else stayed and worked from the STEELE offices in Abu Dhabi and now Dubai. It's good for employee morale to see New York flagship executives in the branch offices. Morgan especially inspired them since he stays in New York or travels to London and Paris.

We've had meetings, lunches, and dinners with our respective teams and top-level leadership. It's good to hear their feedback and address their concerns in person. One of my goals as CEO is to spend three days in each office every month.

Tonight is the opening party for Lola's Coterie Dubai, so Borya and I hit the mat early. I'll have time to grab a protein shake, take a shower, and get dressed. Lola's booked until ninety minutes before we leave. My poor baby. She'll get to unwind soon.

"*Privet, mal'chik!*"

Whap Whap Whap!

An unrelenting succession of blows to my torso reminds me to refocus or risk permanent body damage. I pivot to the right and land a few punches to his flank. Quick to recover, Borya roundhouse kicks at my retreating form. I fake left and jab right. The action of our session is intense. We go at it for an hour before we stretch and cool down.

"Good job, Steele. You should join me in a double MMA match, *da*?" He claps me on my back when we head out.

"Nah. Gotta look pretty for my girl," I respond, reminding him of his taunts to me about my obsession with Lola.

A grimace appears on his face, the closest to a smile that

his lips can create. Followed by a deep, rumbling sound that's his version of a laugh booms around the boxing gym at STEELE Dubai I.

"*Veselaya*, Steele!"

We leave the gym floor and head over to the juice bar for our shakes before returning to the hotel.

"See you tonight. Maybe a girl will find you pretty too, Alexeyev," I smirk, patting his cheek.

"*Veselaya*, Steele!" His laugh follows me as I stride to the elevator bank for the Rulers' Suites.

As expected, our suite is empty. I checked my mobile on the elevator. Other than business communications and a voicemail from my mother, I didn't hear from Lola. I open my calendar app and filter today for her schedule. She's in a meeting with a textile vendor who specializes in fabrics by local artisans. Impressed by the samples he sent, she was eager to meet him. She considers the cloth incorporated into the UAE collections a friendly gesture of inclusivity and respect for the culture. The STEELE UAE cultural affairs team agreed.

I shoot a text message to tell her I'm back. Then strip out of my hoodie and shorts. I close my eyes, as I duck under the spray from the multiple shower heads and tilt my head back, bracing my hands on the marble wall. The warm water sluices down my rock-hard body. The ache in my muscles from the strenuous workout lessens. I drop my head and roll my neck, getting the kinks out.

Thoughts drift to Lola—my luscious beauty. I groan as my dick lengthens, and the girth thickens. What I would give to bury myself balls deep in her tight, wet heat. I groan again when I think about how we haven't made love in days. Days… Damn.

My hand slips from the steam slick wall and slides down

between my eight-pack abs, the well-defined ridges taut under my fingertips. The texture of the trail of hair leading from below my navel to my groin contrasts with my bare skin. I suck in a ragged breath at the vision of Lola naked on her knees before me with her eager mouth open wide to receive my ready rod. Her hooded eyes bore into mine, filled with lust.

They're her full lips that wrap around the base of my dick, not my hand, as she takes me down her throat. My ten inches fill her cavity. Her gag reflex spasms sending a zing to my heavy balls. I squeeze my eyes tight, not wanting to lose the vision before I can blow my load.

A cool breeze touches my warm back. A small hand covers mine. My eyes fly open, but the steam fills the glass enclosure, hampering my sight. But my sense of smell recognizes my mate—Lola. Here in the shower with me, not in my head.

"Please allow me, Sir."

Her soft, wet curves meld to my back as she slips her hand under mine. I drop my forehead to the slick wall and brace myself on my forearms for what promises to be a leg wobbling experience.

Lola does not disappoint.

As she trails nips followed by kisses along my back, one hand massages my sac and the other grips and tugs my turgid cock. The rhythm she sets alternates between gentle and painful, keeping a delicate balance that has me close in moments.

"Fuuuck… Lola… Shit, that feels so good," I grunt as my palms slap the wall.

A pinch to my tip sends me rocking onto the balls of my feet, driving my hips forward to pump against her hand.

Lola senses how close I am to release, so she speeds up her pace.

"Lolllaaa," I roar as my dick jumps in her hand and ropes of creamy cum splash onto the wall.

My hips move on their own since my mind left. Lola snakes her hand that was on my balls up my torso to pinch my nipple.

Dayummm!

My cock hardens again and I grab her wrists to pull her in front of me, facing the wall. I bend her ninety degrees and put her hands in place of mine on the marble. I grip my dick and line it up to her slit, then check in with her.

Lola flicks her long raven hair over her shoulder and lifts her heated gaze to mine. She licks her lips and nods. Without breaking eye contact, I slam into her tight pussy. Her inner walls greedily suck me in deep. Lola mewls and lifts to her toes, bowing her back to grant me better access.

I grip her curvy hips tightly and piston into her, chasing our climaxes. I ride Lola and she bucks against me, meeting each of my thrusts with her own. The sound of our wet skin slapping against each other reverberates in the shower.

I bend my knees and tilt her body back towards mine to change the angle. As I hit deep within her, Lola screams her release, her pussy clenching my dick like a vice. I roar and continue my onslaught. She writhes wantonly, demanding more. With unimaginable joy, I give her what she wants—whatever Lola wants, Lola gets.

Our bodies continue the feral dance of the ages until I wrench three more orgasms from her core and she's begging me to stop. Only then do I release my load with a roar of her name. Sated at last, we slide to the floor of the shower. I pull Lola between my still quivering thighs and wrap my arms around her, nuzzling her hair.

"Thank you, my love," I murmur.

Lola's contented sigh makes my heart swell more than her lush body makes my dick grow.

"I'm sorry I've been so busy, baby," she says as she shifts to peek at me. "I promise after this opening, I'll make it up to you at our honeymoon—destination still unknown to me… Okay?"

"I know, babe," I respond sincerely. "You know I respect your company and your work ethic. I want you to succeed and achieve your goals."

I lift her chin to kiss her lips softly, then continue, "How could I want less for you than I do for myself?"

"Thank you, my love," she whispers as she smothers me with heartfelt kisses.

"FUCK YOU, YOU SLIMY DICK!"

CRASH!

Roger? What the fuck is going on!

I spin around to see him and Mattei exchanging blows in the middle of the fucking party. The opening night party for my woman's boutique in a STEELE property. Not happening.

I beat security to the fray. Malcolm and Harris grab Mattei as Luc and I grab Roger. Roger struggles against our hold as does Mattei who tries to shrug my brothers off. Roger and Mattei are bulls in a lingerie shop that knocked over two mannequins.

Suddenly, they stand stock-still when my father storms over. He is pissed.

All eyes turn to Morgan, including that dickhead Mattei. He must have done some shit for Roger *The Responsible* Steele to lose control. And at a highly public event—never. That goes against every cell in his physiology.

"You will cease this outrageous, infantile behavior at once and apologize to Ms. Lewis and her guests. Then leave. Do... you... understand?" Morgan issues his edict.

His Dom stare knocks Roger and Mattei down several notches. In fact, they're below ground by the time he finishes his chastisement of them. Everyone else stands in silent awe of his power.

Roger gains control first and turns to seek Lola out in the crowd gathered around. I too scan for her, hoping she's not as upset as I imagine. I spot her standing between my mother and Leonie. Haley, Blair, and Billie stand near them. All have shocked expressions on their faces. Damn.

Mattei tries to walk to them. But Malcolm puts his hand on his chest to stop him since Roger headed their way already. Mattei has the sense to back down.

"Lola, I apologize for my poor behavior. Please forgive me," Roger beseeches.

With grace, she nods her head and accepts his outstretched hand. Her eyes meet mine and I offer her a consoling smile to which she nods.

"Mother, Leonie, I ask for your forgiveness, too," Roger says to both of them, but his eyes lock on Leonie whose amber gaze shies away.

I can see his shoulders rise and fall on a disappointed sigh in response to her reaction. Then, he turns to the guests and apologizes to them before he excuses himself from the event.

As he passes me, I squeeze his shoulder to offer my support. He nods without breaking his stride.

Next, Mattei apologizes. The Italian nobleman exudes charm as he bows to the women and to the crowd. His accent laid on thick as he issues his apology like a statesman at the Colosseum.

He takes Leonie's hand in his and kisses it with a flourish. She won't meet his eyes either. Then he speaks in her ear. But she shakes her head. Denied, he pivots and struts out the door without a backwards glance.

Good.

"Now, let us return to the celebration of Lola's Coterie Dubai. As a token of STEELE International, Inc.'s gratitude for welcoming our newest partner to the UAE, we gift each guest twelve hundred Emirati Dirhams for use at her Dubai or Abu Dhabi boutiques."

Morgan speaks into the ensuing silence while holding Lola's hand in unification.

The crowd cheers and raises their glasses in salute.

"Enjoy!" Lola exclaims as she beams at the guests then up at Morgan.

Crisis averted, I join them as my mother slips her arm around Lola and whispers in her ear. Lola nods and turns to me.

"Well, as they say, 'all publicity is good publicity.' Your name in people's mouths is what you want. So don't worry," I say.

"Oh, I know. I'm more concerned about Leonie."

She thanks Morgan, gives me a hug, then excuses herself to go talk to her best friend. Leonie looks shaken, but brightens when Lola reaches her. They speak briefly and head to a private corner.

"Talk to your brother, Sebastian. Or I will. He knows better than to act boorishly, particularly at one of our business functions."

I follow Morgan's directive and step away to call Roger. He answers on the first ring.

"Sorry. That was a shitshow Lola did not deserve. Does she really forgive me? Are you going to kick my ass?"

He sounds like a wreck, so I don't add to his ill ease.

"Yes, and no. Dad gave the guests gift cards. What the fuck happened?" I ask.

Roger clues me in on the details. I tell him I understand. But remind him to keep his shit together in the future. Then tease him about not being responsible. Roger grouses over the gibe. We hang up with a reminder about breakfast.

LOLA FELL ASLEEP QUICKLY after all of tonight's drama and the long week she's had with both boutique openings. I watch, mesmerized by the woman I love more than life. Thankfully, her sleep is peaceful.

I bend over my sleeping beauty and inhale her natural scent, a combination of her lavender body wash, shampoo, and luscious Lola.

"Sweet dreams, princess," I whisper into her hair.

Then leave the bedroom, closing the door softly before I exit the suite.

Until tomorrow, Mrs. Steele. Until tomorrow.

LOLA

Mmmhhhhmmm.

As I waken, last night replays behind my closed eyelids. Roger, his face flushed red and intense stare locked with unrestrained anger on Giovanni before he punches him in his face. Giovanni falling backwards into mannequins that crashed to the floor. Gio charging Roger. Then Sebastian, Luc, Malcolm, and Harris holding them apart. The guests shocked speechless. Hell, I froze, too.

Thank God for Morgan. He prevented a catastrophe. I felt sorry for Roger and Giovanni after he castigated them. Oh, well. The gift cards… Brilliant.

Poor Leonie was too distraught. I had to console her. We still don't know what caused the battle of the Alpha males. Ever the professional, she refused my offer to go back to the hotel. *The Lion*—brave woman—continued on until the end.

I agree with Baz about any publicity being good. Still, I shudder to read the event's report from my marketing team.

This bed is so comfy, I could stay in it all day. In fact, that's exactly—

My fingers brush over cold sheets and not the hot torso of my fiancé. Sitting up, I notice Baz's side of the bed remains untouched. Weird.

"Sebastian?"

I call as I sit up, holding the sheet to my bare breasts. A scan of the bedroom proves it empty, and the door shut. No sound comes from the bathroom or walk-in closets. What the fuck?

As I reach for my mobile on the nightstand, my gaze lands on a single Sterling Silver Rose next to a white linen envelope—Baz's personal stationery. Curious but hesitant, I open it and pull out a handwritten note.

My Dearest Lola,

I know how strongly you feel about tradition, so I cannot wake with you held tightly in my arms this morning. But every morning after this one, the sun will rise with you wrapped in my loving embrace.

Each hour until I see you walk down the aisle to me, you will receive one Sterling Silver Rose. As these twelve months have shown, my love for you knows no bounds. Tonight we become one, Mrs. Sebastian Steele.

Love your Husband & Dom forever,
Baz

MY VISION BLURS as tears fill my eyes. Several times I have to swipe them away as they fall before I can finish reading Sebastian's note. Is he serious? The aisle? Tonight? He can't possibly mean we're getting married in Dubai now and not next week in New York.

With trembling hands, I reach for my mobile and tap his number.

"Good morning, my love."

I can only sit on the line as my sobs increase just from hearing his deep voice so full of love for me. Lightheaded, I fall back onto the fluffy pillows, clutching the mobile to my breasts.

"Lola? Baby? Are you all right?"

I take a deep, cleansing breath. Then bring my iPhone back to my ear.

"Fuck… I think she's fainted."

"Whaaat?"

"Call Mom! She'll get her!"

"No way, bro! You scared her off."

"Shut the fuck up, Harris!"

A vision of the Steele brothers worried running around in circles reminds me of the Three Stooges and their antics. Except there's four of them. Hysterical laughter bubbles out of my mouth, followed by uncontrollable snorts.

"Fuck! Now she's laughing hysterically! Lola! You're freaking me out now, babe!"

More suggestions filter through the mobile. And my snorts turn to cries of joy. We're getting married tonight!

"LOLA, darling, you had Sebastian and the boys ready to run to the suite! Sebastian was beside himself! He told me, 'damn tradition!'"

Shelley laughs as we sit in the STEELE Dubai I Spa waiting for our manicures and pedicures to dry. After a full day of beauty treatments, they have pampered us into silky smooth, ultra-relaxed, glammed-up dolls. Just what I needed after the shocks of last night and this morning.

"Yes! Luc called me hyperventilating!" Chortles Blair. "I thought we'd have to ring for the medic to resuscitate them!"

I give her the eye since she's been quiet about their status. She giggles.

Leonie, Haley, and Billie join in on the laughter. We're loud as our voices echo around the nails room. But it doesn't matter since Baz reserved the entire spa just for us. He wanted me to unwind with my girls and his mom undisturbed.

In fact, he bought out the entire hotel for our three hundred guests. They were in Abu Dhabi for the last two days at the SAD hotel and arrived here this morning. He didn't want me to see anyone and become suspicious. So he kept them there, being entertained with an assortment of activities. So clever!

"Pardon me, Ms. Lewis."

One of the spa aestheticians stands at the door. A Sterling Silver Rose wrapped in white silk held in her outstretched hand.

As promised, Baz sends a single rose each hour. I smile happily and beckon her to bring it to me. It smells divine. I add it to the vase filled with four others I've collected since we arrived.

"How romantic," sighs Billie with a wistful look in her big green eyes. "I'm so happy for you!"

"Shelley, you raised a good man," Blair chimes in.

"Thank you, Blair," Shelley responds and lifts her glass of citrus-infused water in toast. "May you all marry your romantic, good man!"

She smiles and glances at each of us. But she winks at

Leonie, who blushes and averts her eyes. Which makes me wonder if Shelley knows about Roger and Leonie's *coup de foudre* relationship.

"Ladies, we hope you enjoyed your spa sessions! You seem sufficiently rejuvenated! The restaurant awaits you!" The manager announces.

"Excellent, right on schedule," Sergeant Shelley responds. "We'll have your bridesmaids' luncheon. Then you can rest for two hours before the glam squad arrives."

My heart leaps with joy.

"I cannot wait to become Mrs. Sebastian Steele. The countdown continues!"

Shelley smiles and the girls cheer.

The nail technicians return to help us remove the toe separators and to add moisturizing oil to our cuticles. We chat about my upcoming nuptials as they finish. Then head to our private changing rooms.

I STEP into the lobby first and spin in a circle, feeling carefree in my bohemian-style silk-crepon mini dress in a cornflower floral pattern. The plunging vee-neckline draws the eye to the flattering waist cutouts and flowy tiered skirt. I swept my hair up in a messy bun to showcase the lace-up open back. Paired with flat sandals and a straw top-handle bag, it's a breezy relaxed outfit. Perfect for my bridesmaids' luncheon.

"Don't you look so cute!" Billie declares as she joins me.

"Thanks! As do you, lovely!" I respond admiring her silk halter-back maxi dress. The yellow color makes her green eyes pop.

Once everyone appears, we head to the restaurant. As we walk through the lobby, I recognize some of our guests.

They stop to offer their congratulations and express their gratitude for an exciting trip. I thank them for joining us in our celebration and tell them we'll see them soon.

Shelley introduces me to some guests unknown to me. Everyone from prominent politicians to business tycoons, to celebrities eagerly extend their best wishes and delight at being a part of our nuptials.

The five-star treatment continues when we arrive at the restaurant and sit at the best table overlooking the dazzling water. More guests stop by to introduce themselves to me. The buzz is palpable. Shelley was correct again—our wedding is the most talked about of the decade.

"I want to thank all of you for all that you've done to help me with my wedding and for being such a supportive mother-in-law and friends," I tell everyone after we place our order. "I have special gifts for you. But I didn't know this was happening now. So they're in New York. I promise to give them to you as soon as I return."

Just as I finish, an attendant appears at the table with a basket filled with the gifts. How in the world? I swing my gaze to Shelley, who claps her hands and smiles in excitement.

"Oh, darling! We knew your wedding would be here all along. So we planned for everything to be in Dubai. Plus, your bridesmaids' gifts!"

My eyes tear and I wave my hand in front of my face to stop the flow. Damn! I'm so emotional recently.

"Thank you! Thank you!"

I rise and hug Shelley. Then hand out each of the gifts. The girls oh and ah over the diamond drop earrings that they'll wear to complement their dresses.

"These are absolutely exquisite! Thank you!" Blair exclaims hugging me fiercely.

"OMG! They're the most gorgeous things I own!" Billie adds as she circles her arms around both of us.

A teary Leonie holds her pair up to sparkle in the light. They're bigger than the others since she's my BFF and maid of honor. Instead of one drop, hers has three.

"*Merci, Chérie,*" she whispers as she hugs me close.

The last gift is for Shelley. Baz had to help me with hers since it's hard to shop for a woman who has so much. Her grounded personality and intense love of her family dictated her present.

"Lola… This is so thoughtful… Thank you, darling," she says, holding back her tears. "This will sit in the center of the living room table amongst our photos."

I crouch beside her chair and hug her tightly. So happy that she likes the handmade Buccellati Rose sterling silver framed photo of Sebastian and me, a photographer friend of mine captured in honor of our engagement. Baz knew she'd love it and place it with the rest of their family snapshots—her way of welcoming me into the Steele clan.

"Shelley! Lola!"

I glance up to see Lucie and Lydie Jackson approaching us. Lucie beams and Lydie smiles softly.

"Congratulations, Lola," Lucie hugs me. "We're so pleased for you."

The Jackson Matriarch like Shelley is in her mid-fifties and a dynamo. Her black, wavy bob highlights her angular cheekbones and hazel eyes. The silk wrap dress fits her curves and the strappy sandals show off her long legs. At five feet, eleven inches in her heels, she's six inches taller than me in my flats. We became acquainted in Positano. She's fun-loving and feisty. The perfect mate to bristly Alpha Connor.

Lydie pulls me into a hug, too.

"Yes, congratulations to you!"

"Thank you! So good to see you again," I tell them. "You should join us. They can make room for two more!"

Today, my happiness knows no bounds. They decline. But magnanimously, I insist. If Baz can extend an olive branch to Luc, I can do the same with Lydie. Shelley smiles at me knowingly.

The servers add place settings for them and they give their orders. We hold ours until theirs are ready, instead nibbling on appetizers. I have a form-fitting wedding gown to don in a few hours. So my meal comprises grilled chicken breasts... no carbs... no bloat. Leonie nodded sagely when I told the server my selection. She's in complete agreement and chose the same.

"Where are you going for your honeymoon?" Lucie asks as she sips her champagne.

I throw my hands up and shrug. Baz still hasn't told me our destination or for how long. Every time I mention it, he just smiles and tells me not to worry. When I told him I need to know what to pack, he smirked "nothing." I've given up asking.

"I have no clue and Sebastian is mum. I don't even know what to pack," I lament. "Do you know, Shelley?"

She's the taskmaster. So if anyone knows, she does.

She smiles mysteriously and swipes her fingers over her lips to zip them closed.

No such luck.

"Well, honey, don't worry. Sebastian has excellent taste. He won't disappoint you," Lucie pats my hand and glances at Shelley.

She keeps smiling. But shakes her head.

"I promised Sebastian I wouldn't tell. Sorry, Lola, darling," Shelley responds.

"I trust him. So it's all good," I admit.

The luncheon moves to us swapping stories about relationships we've had and Lucie and Shelley's words of advice for a successful marriage. I take note since they're married for over thirty years. Particularly their counsel on handling possessive Alpha males, and I'm certain in both of their cases Doms.

"Always listen more than you talk so you can understand how to respond if you have a disagreement," offers Lucie.

Shelley nods and adds, "Don't lose yourself in their lives. Maintain your friendships, work, activities."

"Yes, and your personality. If you were feisty and independent when you met, don't change. That's what attracted them to you. Don't simper like women who clamor for their attention," Lucie says.

"Oh and most important, be a proper lady in public, but a sex kitten in the bedroom! Pleasure them in the way they love the most regularly without fail!"

Shelley and Lucie burst out laughing as they high five each other. Shelley dabs the corners of her eyes. She's laughing so hard she cries. Lucie covers her mouth with her hand and giggles some more. Clearly, they have private jokes.

"Mom!"

Haley and Lydie call out in unison. Haley's face reddens in embarrassment. While Lydie covers her ears, shaking her head.

"What?" Shelley asks, hitching her shoulder.

"You're grown women. You know what we mean!" Lucie declares.

The rest of us join in their glee, and our laughter fills the restaurant.

Yup, I knew it. Shelley and Lucie are Independent Women-cum-subs like me.

We continue to enjoy ourselves through the rest of the luncheon. More guests drop by with Shelley providing introductions when necessary. Attendants bring two Sterling Silver Roses in mini vases for my collection. We decline dessert and end with tea.

"Lola, time to rest before getting you ready," Shelley announces with a raised eyebrow, tapping the bezel of her Chopard L.U.C. XP Esprit by Fleurier Peony watch.

"YOU LOOK SO BEAUTIFUL, LOLA!" Leonie gushes as she touches a handkerchief under her teary eyes. "*Tu es magnifique, Chérie*!"

"Oh, how absolutely stunning and sexy!" Haley exclaims.

"Simply divine," sighs Blair.

"Sebastian will snatch you away before the ceremony even starts!" Laughs Billie.

I feel all that they say and more as I stand before the full-length mirror in the dressing suite beside the ballroom. Mr. Valentino outdid himself. Before joining the other guests, he came by to ensure my gown fits perfectly. It does.

The sensuous lines hug my curves and dramatically flare into an elegant, cathedral-length mermaid train. I peer over my shoulder at the cut-out in the back that makes it as much of an exit dress as the deep-vee in the front makes a statement. The fitted long sleeves add a touch of the demure to the provocative gown. The impeccable detail of the lace exemplifies the craftsmanship of his atelier. It's a masterpiece.

The traditions continue. My mother's diamond earrings adorn my ears as something old and to have her close to me.

My gown represents the new. Shelley lent Sebastian's grandmother's cathedral-length silk tulle veil to me as the borrowed. My face will remain symbolically covered for his eyes only until Baz lifts my veil at the altar. I custom designed a lace G-string for the blue—perfect for fidelity.

So we don't see each other before we exchange our vows, we set our photo session for after the ceremony while guests enjoy the cocktail hour. We even signed the marriage license separately. I'm not risking a single thing.

"Lola?"

The photographer and videographer call for me to pose alone and with my bridesmaids, then with Shelley. They followed us discreetly throughout the day, capturing candid shots. Baz has a set following him, too. We want to see all that happened while we were apart.

One of the wedding planners enters the suite to tell us it's time.

My heart jumps. I hold back the tinge of panic with deep breaths. Starr came by earlier and we mediated before I put my gown on. Opening my eyes, I ask for a moment of privacy. I need to speak to my parents. Everyone nods and Shelley lingers to check on me. But I shake my head. I walk to the glass wall of windows and look to the heavens, feeling the warmth of the sun on my face. I close my eyes and whisper a prayer of love and thanks. Then a moment of silence as I feel their love wrap around me.

One more deep cleansing breath and I walk to the suite door. Luc waits just outside. He scans my face with concern. I smile and air kiss his cheeks to let him know I'm all right. When I pull back, his eyes shine with tears. He takes a moment to collect himself. Then extends his arm for me to hold.

Leonie hands my bouquet to me and gives me air kisses,

too. She adjusts my train behind me and fluffs my veil into place. Luc and Leonie, my support for over seven years by my side once again.

I love them dearly.

We line up behind the rest of the bridal party at the side of the open doors to the ballroom where the ceremony will take place. The second ballroom will host the reception. The harpist plays the processional music. The sound pure and light. The groomsmen and bridesmaids pass through the doors and make their way down the aisle. Leonie glances over her shoulder at me with a smile before she too glides down today's catwalk. The doors shut for my grand entrance.

"Are you ready, *petite chérie*?"

I smile up at Luc, full of confidence, "Yes."

He nods and we walk forward. The wedding planner smiles and wishes me luck. Then opens the doors.

There are three hundred guests. But my eyes only see Sebastian at the end of the aisle, waiting for me before the altar. He stands tall like the powerful man he embodies, be it Dom or future CEO. The expression of love on his face fills my heart with bliss.

Yes, without a doubt I am ready to become Mrs. Sebastian Steele at last.

SEBASTIAN

"*No way, bro! You scared her off.*"

Harris' lame ass joke hit me harder than I admitted to my brothers. Even though I know it's not true, his words have been on repeat in my mind all fucking day. Beyond satisfying a woman sexually for a night or two, I've never been in a relationship. I never had to worry about her leaving me.

Lola left me twice.

The first time after an argument—true, I was a dick. The second time over a misunderstanding I wasn't even aware happened. Lola just left… Poof… For three months. Despite the promise we made to talk things through before doing something we'd regret.

We're stronger now. But it wouldn't surprise me if she pulled a Julia Roberts and turned into a runaway bride. That would be a tough scenario to recover from.

After an early morning sparring session with Borya and a run on the treadmill, we met my brothers, Scott, Porter, Lachlan, Lucien, and Laurent for breakfast. Bro Bonding, as

Laurent calls it. The youngest Jackson is their company's director of cigars and a rebellious playboy who loves to party. He's game for any opportunity to drink and have fun.

While at the table, Lola calls me. She went from silent, to sobs, to hysterical laughter. She freaked me the fuck out. I wasn't sure if she was angry I surprised her with our wedding here in Dubai or if she changed her mind. Even the Dom in me lost control and couldn't demand her words.

Finally, Lola spoke. Relief flooded my body. The adrenaline slowly drained from my veins. Hell, I was about to race back to our suite to get her to answer me. Damn not seeing her before over vows.

Once again level-headed, Roger *The Responsible* suggested I call our mother. She stepped in and met Lola at our suite to take her for the spa day I arranged. Text messages from her assured me Lola wasn't doing a runner. Thank fuck!

"I know you're not still thinking Lola's ditching you. Are you?"

Fucking Harris. At it again.

"No, you ass. And she's not ditching me," I respond, glaring at him as we sit in my office.

I had to keep my mind busy and couldn't take another grueling session with Borya. Tina scheduled meetings for me with some wedding guests who have been waiting to get on my calendar. So, it works out well. Except for Harris.

When we finished breakfast, everyone continued their own way. Borya had friends to catch up with. Malcolm and Lucien took an appointment for a potential restaurant/club. Roger met with planners for a new residential tower complex. Lachlan settled into one of the guest offices with his laptop. Scott and Porter returned to their wife and date, respectively. We left Laurent flirting with two wedding guests.

Harris… He's in his little brother mood and bugging me to death. Stretched out on the sofa, typing on his laptop.

"Well, you've been reading the same paragraph for the past five minutes," he answers with his eyebrow raised.

"How the fuck do you know what I'm doing on my laptop?" I demand. "You better not have some high-tech gadgetry hooked into my system."

His guffaws fill the air. Then he wipes his eyes. Everyone is hysterical today…

"Bro, you are so lame! You *are* still thinking about Lola! You might as well admit it," he chuckles.

"You did not answer my question, Harris. How the fuck do you know what I am doing on my laptop?" I repeat, giving him my Dom stare.

He only laughs some more, grating on my sensitive nerves.

"Oh, don't pull that Dom shit with me, Little Puppy."

I sit back in my chair and tent my fingertips as I continue to stare at him.

"Okay, okay already," he throws up his hands. "I don't have any 'high-tech gadgetry hooked into' your system."

He stares back at me, "It was a guess… an intelligent guess I might add. Your eyes were spaced out. Obviously not seeing what was on your screen. Rather, what's playing in your head."

Harris sits back triumphantly and folds his arms over his broad chest with a smirk. His eyebrow cocked in challenge.

Damn. Busted.

With a sigh, I close my laptop and pace the floor.

"See that's why I came to hang out with you. You're too

uptight. Relax, Baz. She loves you. We all can see it. Don't let the blips of the past fog your bright future."

I stop, shocked. When did my kid brother grow up? He's dropping advice like he's our father. Impressed, I turn to him.

"Thank you, Harris. That means a lot to me," I smile, feeling better now than I have all day.

Recharged, I return to work and Harris clicks away on his laptop. He even stays during the meetings. Periodically, I'll glance his way to see him studying me to be sure I'm all right. It's different since I'm usually the one watching out for my siblings. I smile, nodding my head, grateful for his support.

When the last meeting goes longer than intended, Harris stands up.

"Excuse me. The groom needs to return to the hotel. Tina can schedule a follow-up appointment. I'm sure you understand."

I hide my chuckle with a cough and rise from my seat at the conference table. To confirm the meeting ended, I shake his hand.

"Congratulations again, Sebastian. My wife and I offer our best wishes to you and your beautiful bride."

"Thank you and we'll see you at the reception," I respond, clasping both his hands in mine.

As soon as he leaves, Harris circles his fingers in the air, signaling I need to wrap it up.

A flare of nerves hit. But I think of how peacefully Lola slept as I watched her this morning. I take a deep breath—Lola taught me to channel my inner calm.

We're good, we're good. I exhale the mantra that replaces Harris' earlier words. We're good, we're good.

. . .

THE AIR RUSHES from my lungs when the doors to the ballroom open and my bride stands at the top of the aisle. Lola is an absolute vision of elegant beauty. Her enchanting smile teases me from behind a blusher that reaches her hand holding her bouquet. The long, sheer veil modestly covers her curvaceous body clothed in an extraordinary lace gown.

The fit accentuates Lola's greatest assets. The curves of her generous breasts peeks from the plunging neckline. Her narrow waist tapers to her rounded hips. I'm confident the back of the gown cups her full bottom.

The seductiveness of her body balanced by the delicate floral-patterned lace, long sleeves, and flare of the gown's shape below her hip bones. Her regal carriage enhances the graceful style. Lola is the embodiment of a sensuous, classic beauty.

As she nears, I can't help but match her smile that sparkles more brilliantly than the diamonds in her ears. She's stunning. Shelley told me Lola's gown didn't call for jewelry other than her mother's earrings. So I didn't gift her a suite of diamonds as I intended. Her wedding ring and hand harness will make up for it.

They're walking so slowly, I'm tempted to snatch her before she makes it to me. Malcolm must sense my urge. Discretely, he places a restraining hand on the back of my arm. I nod and practice another deep breath. Relax!

Luc smiles at me and agrees to give away the bride. Lola beams at him. Then turns her loving gaze to me.

My heart skips a beat.

I clasp her small hands in my larger ones as soon as she gives Leonie her bouquet. Everyone laughs at my eagerness. I shrug. I don't give a damn.

As we face each other listening to the officiant, the room

fades away. We're lost in our own world, filled with love and joy. No one can touch us.

A soft cough brings us back to the room. The officiant awaits the exchanging of our vows.

I clear my throat, and with a loud confident voice I declare my eternal love for Lola. Tears glisten in her eyes. But her voice is clear and carries through the ballroom.

Malcolm opens the jewelry case. The lights hit the enormous diamonds of Lola's custom hand harness and her band. She gasps, as do the bridesmaids. Her wide eyes fly to mine and I smirk. Yeah, no one will miss you being mine, Little Pet.

She lifts her hand to admire the harness. A chain of diamonds connects to her eternity band on her middle finger to a pear-shaped diamond that rests atop her hand connected to a diamond double bracelet. Her engagement ring sits on her ring finger. The harness is removable. So she can wear her band and ring together.

The guests murmur, suitably impressed. Point made and duly noted.

Grinning, Lola places my classic platinum band on my finger. She holds my gaze as she flicks the tip of her tongue across her plump bottom lip. Then brings my hand to her mouth to kiss my ring.

My dick twitches. Fuck me.

The officiant pronounces us husband and wife.

With a smirk, I lift her veil and kiss Mrs. Sebastian Steele silly.

The guests stand, clap, and whoop.

I end the kiss with little nips to her swollen lips; she mewls. Damn. We may not make it to the reception.

Leonie places Lola's bouquet in her hand and fluffs her

veil and gown as we turn to our guests. Their cheers follow us as we saunter hand in hand down the aisle.

As soon as we clear the double doors, I pull Lola to the side and kiss her again, cradling her lush ass. My hard length grinds into her soft mound. We groan, full of desire heightened by our newly forged bond. Like a caveman, I want to claim my mate.

She pants, pressing the full length of her body against mine. Lola is as desperate as I am eager to consummate our marriage.

"Oh, Baz, baby," she groans against my lips.

"Ahem."

Malcolm and the rest of the bridal party stand at the doors, blocking guests from witnessing our PDA.

Lola giggles and wipes her lipstick from my mouth.

"Later," she purrs.

My parents and Luc appear. One glance and my mother knows what we were doing. She smiles and shakes her head.

"Photo time!" She says gaily.

Everyone laughs and heads to the atrium. Fortunately, it doesn't take long since we had photo shoots solo and with our parties separately. With the family and group shots complete, we go to the second ballroom for the reception. The wedding planner tells us the guests finished the cocktail hour and sit at their tables awaiting our entrance.

The hair and makeup teams touch up Lola and the other women. Once they're primped, we head en masse to the reception.

I notice the awkwardness of Haley and Lachlan. Once more I wonder what's going on with them, if anything. I haven't broached the topic with Haley since the Abu Dhabi opening and Lachlan since Positano. It's on the top of my list now we finished the wedding.

Lola assured me Giovanni wasn't coming. I was adamant. No one fucks with my family. I don't give a damn if Leonie wants him here. No. The way she glances sideways at Roger and he stares at her adds them to my list.

Now that I've opened my eyes, blinded by jealousy, I observe Luc's interest in Blair. Based on their brief exchanges, it's clear they've had something going on for a while. Good.

My mega concern lies with Billie and Rockett. When Lola asked if I would accept Rockett as Billie's plus one, my head almost split. I asked her when the hell that happened and she told me a few months ago.

They met at some club when Lola went partying with her girls. She claims it was accidental and Rockett didn't know Billie worked for her until later. I told Lola he's full of shit and using Billie to get information on Lola's Coterie and subsequently STEEELE. She agreed she thought the same thing, but Billie signed an airtight nondisclosure and non-compete agreement. Plus Lola asked Billie outright, and she swore her loyalty to both of us. Funny enough, Malcolm says he's seen Rockett at LEVELS New York with the petite beauty. Lola just laughed when I told her.

He's here at our wedding. But I said one wrong move, and he's out. Period. Billie who came to me after Lola spoke with her agreed.

"Ready, Mr. Steele?"

Lola's sweet voice pulls me back from my musings. I kiss her lips softly and murmur yes. She nods to the wedding planner, who opens the double doors.

The emcee announces, "Ladies and gentlemen, presenting Mr. and Mrs. Sebastian Steele!"

Lola gazes up at me with such love my breath catches. She tips her chin up for another kiss to seal our final deal.

Happily, I oblige my wife. The guests stand to applaud as we enter the ballroom.

We make our way to the dance floor for our first dance. Another surprise for Lola is our song. It symbolizes all that I feel for her and want to give her. As the strains of Adele's "Make You Feel My Love" begin, Lola's eyes tear.

When the live voice of the songstress carries over the sound system, Lola's eyes zoom to the stage then back to me. She trembles in my arms, the emotion too much. I pull her as close as two can be without further intimacy. I rock her as I whisper the words in her ear. Her tears make my eyes prick with moisture. I press my face against the top of her head. Cocooned in our love, we let our bodies speak to each other.

As Adele's mesmerizing voice sings the last word, I kiss Lola, and she melts against me. I hold Lola in my arms as I smile my thanks at Adele. She nods and continues with another of her soul-stirring ballads as Lola and I take our seats to prepare for Luc's message and toast.

I wrap my arm around Lola's shoulders and hold her close. Her emotions have been high and Luc stepping in for her parents is difficult for her. She nuzzles her head against my neck and links her fingers with both of my hands.

Luc's speech is passionate. He too gets caught in emotions. Unashamed to let his voice thicken with the tears that stand in his eyes, he does well by Lola. She rises and they embrace. Her little body quivers and I ache to hold her to my chest. But I know she needs her time with Luc. He whispers in her ear and she nods. Then they smile at me, and I stand to welcome my wife back into my arms.

"I love you, baby," I murmur as I hold her close.

"I love you, too," she whispers.

While the meal begins, Lola excuses herself and goes

with Leonie to freshen her makeup. When she returns, she stuns me again. Her latest gown shows more of her voluptuous figure. Still a mermaid fit with a deep-vee front, but sleeveless. Delicate flowers cover the sheer material. A belt cinches in her waist while a diamond brooch glitters in the middle. It reminds me of a garden of pure pleasure.

"You like Mr. Steele?" She asks as I take her hand and twirl her around.

"Absolutely, Mrs. Steele," I tell her, bobbing my eyebrows as I gaze at her mouthwatering breasts.

One false move and she'll spill out. Then Borya and I will have that double MMA match he asked me about to fight every man off of her.

"Abso-fuckable-lutely," I purr in her ear.

Lola giggles, "Come on, Captain Caveman. Time to mingle with our guests."

She takes my hand, and like a Little Puppy I follow her, tongue hanging out.

We spend some time circulating amongst the guests as they eat their seated meals. Lola enchants every one of them. Her elation is palpable. She always touches me on my hand, my cheek, my back. Each time, a thrill runs through me. Soon, I'm pulling her into a closet somewhere.

The wedding planner steps over to let us know it's time for more toasts. We settle at our table and prepare for words from our family and friends.

Leonie stands before us like the Queen of the Savannah. She exudes feline grace. Her toast is touching with a story of how she and Lola first met and now are sisters for life. Lola dabs her eyes and blows kisses to her BFF.

Malcolm steps beside Leonie and pulls her into an embrace as her emotions overwhelm her. I chance a peek in Roger's direction. As I guessed, his face resembles stone and his intense stare riveted on Malcolm. Who's now rubbing Leonie's back and whispering in her ear. Oh shit.

Fortunately, Leonie collects herself and disentangles from Malcolm's arms. She returns to the table. Roger's gaze tracks her every move. When she's close, he stands and helps her into her chair. She touches his chest and briefly leans against him. The relief on his face is clear. Perhaps I can check them off my list.

Malcolm's voice cuts through the murmuring as he regales us with a fairy tale story of my miscreant behavior until the Lovely Lola saved me from imminent doom. The guests roar with laughter. I roll my eyes at the charmer. He laughs, and the meal continues.

Right before the parent dances start, Morgan stands to face us.

"Lola, we welcomed you into our family once. But now we embrace you as our daughter-in-law and daughter of our heart. Your love for our son is true as his love for you is infinite. You will forever be a Steele."

Lola sobs softly in my embrace, and I kiss her temple as I rub her arm.

"Sebastian."

I raise my gaze to my father.

"As we tell you often, you make your mother and me proud. The eldest child who cares for and supports your siblings, they admire and respect you. As a dynamic leader in our family's company, our employees and business associates accept and appreciate your guidance and skills."

He flickers his gaze between Lola and me.

"Sebastian, now that you settled down with a woman who matches and complements you personally and professionally, I officially hand over the reins of CEO and Chairman of the Board of STEELE International, Inc. to you. You will lead our family's business into the next generation and your children after you. You earned it on your own, son. Here's to your success."

The room explodes in thunderous applause. My siblings whoop and holler the loudest. My mother claps with tears in her eyes. Lola hugs me close and whispers how much I deserve it. I'm stunned—months earlier than expected.

My father beams at me and nods.

I stride over to him and we embrace. As he pats me on the back, he tells me he's so very proud of me and he expects great things from me and Lola. A power couple like him and my mother, he adds.

At his words, I choke up. That's exactly what I hoped to replicate with Lola. My father sees it in us. I'm beyond words, and can only nod. Now I understand how Lola feels when she's too caught up to verbalize a response. The thought makes me chuckle and clears my head.

"Thank you, Dad. I will make you proud."

"I know you will, son. I know you will."

The band starts the music, and he pats me with affection on the back.

The partner dances begin with Lola and Luc, then my mother and me, followed by the rest of the wedding party. I'm happy to have Lola back in my arms. She sings along happily as we dance amongst the guests.

After a while, she tosses a bouquet—she's saving her original—that Billie catches. I toss her garter—no revealing of my baby's leg, so it's at her knee. Porter swats it away from him, so it falls into Lachlan's hand, who also looks dubious. They don't know what they're missing; I chuckle.

Not one to behave like a child, I feed the forkful of cake into Lola's open mouth. Her seductive hum vibrates through the fork straight to my dick. My hooded eyes lock on her lips and I lick the frosting stuck at the corner. Yum.

She feeds my bite to me and licks her little pink tongue across her full bottom lip with a smirk. She is so not getting away with teasing me all night, I whisper in her ear. She shivers and her hazel orbs darken with lust.

Leonie comes over and whisks Lola away before I can make good on my promise. They return just in time for her favorite artist Beyoncé's first song. All the single ladies jump up. Lola struts her stuff in a shimmery metallic purple fitted slip dress with black lace bra cups from her evening wear collection. Sky-high strappy sandals lengthen her toned legs. She's shaking her ass like a matador with a red cape before a bull.

I give her three songs, and I snatch her from the floor.

"Time for the first consummation of the night, Mrs. Steele," I say huskily in her ear.

She purrs in response, the vixen.

LOLA

This morning I awake wrapped in Baz's arms just as he promised me. And I'm Mrs. Sebastian Steele...

"Ooohhh..."

Baz's dark head rests between my quivering, spread thighs. His muscular arms wrap around them with his firm hands holding me in place.

I'm locked in position, unable to shift my body. Only accept the onslaught of his lips sucking on my engorged clit, still sensitive from his ministrations into the early light of dawn.

"Fuuck... Baby... So good—ah, ah, oooh..."

As my hundredth climax rips through my pussy, it wracks my body with uncontrollable spasms. Baz continues to lave my seam, causing a second orgasm to follow the first.

It's too much.

My fingers tangled in his thick strands attempt to push his voracious mouth away from me to no avail. He's a tyrant, demanding more as a third wave crashes over me.

My eyes roll back as I thrash my head from side to side. Unsure if I want more or if I want the extreme sensations to cease, I push and pull at his head. He chuckles knowingly against my lower lips.

"Baz... Please no more..."

My pleas fall on his deaf ears covered by my thighs pressed against his head.

His slate-gray eyes watch my pitiful struggle as his tongue flicks lazily over my distended nubbin.

Unable to look away from his intense stare, I watch helplessly as Baz settles deeper between my legs. His wide shoulders push my sore thighs further apart.

Another round... Fuck...

His fingertips slide over my pussy lips to part them. Warm air blows across the sensitive flesh.

I shiver in response as a smaller orgasm massages my inner walls. My mind floats on a cloud.

Gentle licks stroke my core, bringing me back to Earth. Kisses trail from my inner thighs to my calves to caress the arches of my feet lightly.

At last, Baz sits back on his haunches. My juices cover his nose, mouth, and chin. My core clenches at the sight.

He lowers his head to form another path of kisses up my legs, over my belly, to suckle my pebbled nipples.

My body bows off the bed in ecstasy.

Wet, open-mouth kisses climb up my slick chest to my neck where powerful sucking marks my heated skin. Satisfied with his claim, Baz brings his swollen lips to mine and I taste myself on his insistent tongue.

"Mmmmmm..."

"Good morning, Mrs. Sebastian Steele. I love you, baby."

I wrap him in my arms, pulling his massive torso to cover mine, enjoying the pleasure of being beneath his muscular body. His biceps bulge as he lowers from his hands to his forearms, holding my face between his hands reverently.

My pelvis cradles his as I double wrap him with my thighs. His enormous cock nestled between our steamy bodies.

"Good morning, Mr. Steele, Sir," I purr, my lips pressed to the shell of his ear.

His deep chuckle reverberates through us. A quick shift of his hips and he grips his thick length before sliding it between my swollen pussy lips.

"Aaahhhh... So big... Oh yes... Ssir!"

The bed rocks with the force of Baz's thrusts. I can only hold on tight while he chases his release. Always determined for me to find my pleasure before him. Now it's his turn.

If this is what he meant by me waking every morning in his arms forever, an abso-fucking-lutely good morning they will prove to be.

Moments pass before either of us can move. Limp from the exertion, we rest, allowing our bodies and minds time to come down.

With a contented sigh, Baz rolls onto his back, carrying me with him. He smoothes my tousled hair from my cheek and kisses the top of my head as it rests on his chest. His fingers make patterns across my back, continuing to calm me.

I nuzzle into his caress as I rest my hand on his pecs. A glint catches my eye.

"Baz! When did you put this on me?" I ask, sitting up to stare at my right wrist.

He presses his lips to my side, and I shiver.

"While you dreamed of me, my Sleeping Beauty," he murmurs against my skin.

The Cartier Love bracelet diamond-paved in platinum is yet another gift from my husband. The timeless elegance of the piece is stunning. Its symbolism of a chastity belt that locks the loved one from any but the lover who has the key is powerful.

With a smirk, I reach into the nightstand to withdraw my red jewelry box.

"Your turn," I purr as place the box on his chest and brush my lips against his in thanks.

He returns my smirk and sits up. His Love bracelet is also platinum. But no diamonds as his is a quiet elegance.

I remove the screws and place the bracelet on his left wrist, right below his wedding band. So even if he removes his ring to spar with Borya or for some such reason, the bracelet remains as a symbol of me holding the key to his love. I kiss his palm and he cups my face for a kiss.

"I'm yours forever, baby, as you are mine. Thank you."

"You're so welcome, my lo—"

His mobile vibrates with a call on his nightstand.

Damn... Back to reality already. Our post-wedding brunch must start soon, and that's Sergeant Shelley to remind us. When Baz nods his head in confirmation, I laugh and climb out of bed to head to the shower.

Gotta love my mother-in-law. Impeccable timing!

SEBASTIAN

"You appear well rested, Baz."

Harris' smirk taunts me.

But I laugh. My kid brother proved his level of maturity yesterday. He was correct in his assessment then and now. I clap him on the back as we end our bro hug.

"Marriage does a man good. You should try it soon," I tease him and he stutters, his face flushing red.

I know full well he's only twenty-nine and nowhere near ready for a wife. Hell, it took me until I was thirty-five for a relationship and thirty-six for marriage.

"Don't worry, bro," I assuage his fears. "You'll know when you're ready. In fact, she'll let you know like Lola did with me. One glance and one touch and I was hooked for life!"

I wave my left hand, showing him my wedding band.

He mumbles and scampers off in the opposite direction. My booming laughter follows him.

"You've scarred him for life, Sebastian."

I turn my gaze to Lydie, who I hadn't realized came to

stand next to me. Her green eyes twinkle with mirth. I search her face for any signs of jealousy or trouble. I find none and release the breath I held, apprehensive she'd act up since Lola and I married. Thank fuck.

"Probably," I smile down at her. "At least until he 'meets The One' like Scott told me."

I put it out there to gauge her reaction. Not a flicker of emotion aside from her glee passes across her face. Good.

"How are you doing?" I ask, concerned genuinely.

We hadn't spoken except briefly regarding business since LEVELS London. Relief filled me since she hadn't gone postal and meant what she told Lola and me about seeing a therapist to work out her Daddy issues. Based on the normal conversations we had, I know her sessions have a positive impact on her. She seems more like her old self—confident, at ease, in control. I'm pleased for her. She'll find someone who deserves her love. Not someone her father wants to form alliances with for his gain.

"Great. I'm actually taking some time off. A much-deserved extended holiday, in fact," she beams.

"I'm happy for you, Lydie. I truly am," I respond.

"Hey lovebird! Where's your mate?"

Porter strides over to us. The debonair gent greets Lydie with a bow, then shakes my hand. I notice Lydie doesn't flinch at his reference to Lola. Progress, for sure.

We talk some more before we part to sit. I go in search of Lola, who I find chatting with Starr Knight. The ebullient beauty smiles at me as I approach. Her brown eyes glow with an inner warmth. Another new friend I'm thankful Lola has added to her circle.

"Good morning, Sebastian!" She stands as she hugs me. "Your aura is at peace, good!"

Not for a minute do I think she's quirky. Lola and I have

taken some private virtual yoga and mediation sessions with her, and it works. I grin back at her.

"Good morning, Starr. I am at peace. Namaste," I clasp my palms together in front of my heart and bow to the light in her.

"Namaste," she bows in return.

As I straighten, I catch sight of Malcolm eyeing Starr from a distance. His stare is so focused he doesn't notice me observing him. He makes his way over. But a redheaded wedding guest waylaid him. A look of annoyance crosses his face when she steps before him.

Meanwhile, Starr excuses herself to head to the airport. She's off for another trip to an Indian ashram. Lola tells her we'll reschedule our sessions for after her return or ours. Then cocks an eyebrow at me, still piqued I haven't told her our honeymoon plans. Oh well. She'll learn soon enough.

"Where did she go?"

Lola and I turn to see an agitated Malcolm peering over our shoulders in the direction Starr walked away. We glance at each other and laugh. Not another one! My list grows.

* * *

ALONE WITH LOLA AT LAST.

After brunch, Lola had some post-opening work to handle for a few hours with Luc. So I went to the office to meet with my father and siblings to discuss my transition to CEO and Chairman of the Board. I spoke privately with each of them to confirm their agreement with the change. As the eldest doesn't guarantee they really want me as their leader. I did not need for concern based on their enthusiastic responses. My father's speech last night proved his belief in me.

We decided the transition will start the week I return from my honeymoon and last for two months. He will make himself available as needed. But determined to have me fully on board within that timeframe. I assured him I'm up to his charge. Pleased, he clapped me on the back and left us to return to our mother with whom he had plans to take shopping. If people knew she had the Mighty Morgan wrapped around her finger, they'd laugh.

Just like Shelley and Morgan, Lola has me whipped. My goal is to keep her happy and surprised by what's coming at all times. She deserves nothing but joy for the rest of her life after being without a family since her parents passed away. Sure Leonie and Luc make up a part of her support system, but as my wife, we're bonded forever. Plus, my parents and siblings already love Lola. Soon we'll have our own family. Her happiness fuels mine.

Starting with our honeymoon. I wanted to make it an experience she'd never forget. Not the typical week at an all-inclusive Hawaiian beach resort or a big city trip to LA or New York or a Caribbean Sea cruise. No. Only something as unique and bold as Lola and me will do for our special time, starting our lives together as husband and wife.

I had Blair and Billie clear her schedule for two months. She'll be mine undisturbed and not distracted, fully focused on us. The best way to disconnect from the rest of the world and to remain in our universe is to go off the grid. No laptops, tablets, mobiles—aside from two emergency satellite phones. Lola, me, and the bits of clothing I'll sometimes let her wear. I can stare at her heavenly body all day and night.

We'll navigate the globe making stops in the Seychelles, Mauritius, the Maldives, Bali, Fiji, Bora Bora, and Tahiti.

Private islands and beachfront bungalows await us. No neighbors, no guests, only the properties' staff. Bliss.

Lola was beyond excited when I surprised her with our itinerary. She jumped into my arms and covered my face with kisses. I had to put her down or we would miss our caravan.

I planned for the first night of our honeymoon to be just as remarkable as the island hopping. But opposite to the beach. Only an abundant amount of sand is similar.

Now she bounces next to me on the seat of the Range Rover as we traverse the Arabia Deserta to kick off our honeymoon. Our destination is a tent next to an oasis outside of Dubai. Not just any tent. We're glamping in a luxury, temperature-controlled one. The floor covered in Persian rugs and oversized silk pillows; the walls lined with handwoven tapestries; a large, round bed strewn with sumptuous silk bedding takes up most of the interior space; a modern bathroom in a separate tent adjoins the main one.

As we hop out of the SUV, Lola's mouth drops at the romantic sight. Under a canopy sits two chairs, and a table covered with savory local dishes, wine, flowers, and flickering candles. The tent stands just behind the canopy with its flaps tied back to show the interior and netting covering the entry. A butler waits to assist us.

She squeals and throws her arms around my neck lifting onto her toes to kiss me passionately murmuring words of love. I return her kiss just as zealously.

After we eat dinner and each other, sated we lie on our backs stargazing through the night. The top of the tent is clear so the stars shine brightly above us.

I take Lola's left hand adorned with my rings and harness in mine and kiss her open palm. She turns her beautiful face towards me. Her hazel eyes shine as she smiles with a palpable intensity, mirroring my love for her.

Our future holds as many infinite possibilities as the uncountable stars above. They're so close, we can grab them and soar to heights unknown.

* * *

Sebastian & Lola's Story Continues: *Deepen My Desires*

STEELE INTERNATIONAL, INC.
A BILLIONAIRES ROMANCE SERIES

Deepen my DESIRES

SEBASTIAN & LOLA PART III

Charmaine Louise Shelton

Deepen My Desires Sebastian & Lola Part III
Copyright © 2021 by Charmaine Louise Shelton

All rights reserved. No part of this book may be reproduced or transmitted in any form or by any means, electronic or mechanical, including but not limited to photocopying, recording, or by any information storage and retrieval system without written permission from the author.

ISBN: 978-1-7363429-2-3 (Paperback)
ISBN: 978-1-7363429-1-6 (eBook)
Published by CharmaineLouise New York, Inc.
Sexy Fantasies Fulfill Your Desires Publications

Deepen My Desires Sebastian & Lola Part III is a work of fiction. Names, characters, businesses, places, events, and incidents are either the product of the author's imagination or used in a fictitious manner. Any resemblance to actual persons, living or dead, or actual events is purely coincidental.

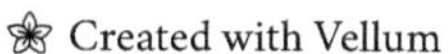
Created with Vellum

I dedicate this novel to those whose bond to their loved one proves stronger than steel.

Fulfill Your Desires.

xoxo
Charmaine Louise

ABOUT DEEPEN MY DESIRES SEBASTIAN & LOLA PART III

The white-hot love affair of Sebastian and Lola—who can't get enough of his controlling ways—concludes with a final fight for their happily ever after in their soul mates romance story.

The sparks fly once again when a lover from Lola's past threatens to upend her lovefest with her new hubby when Simon demands more than her luxury lingerie company's partnership... He wants Lola.

What's a girl to do when her hormones rage and the man she loves questions her loyalty?

Join their Sexy Fantasy as Sebastian and Lola face their biggest hurdle as this love triangle takes them around the globe!

Sebastian and Lola's love story is a standalone trilogy in the series. Get a glimpse of their dynamism in other books.

Anthem: "Deeper and Deeper" Madonna
https://www.youtube.com/watch?v=sJV29ZQIUhs

Playlist:
https://www.youtube.com/playlist?list=
PLXwYvn0e218Chf-HjF7o7_s0BxYm-WNL9

Visit CharmaineLouiseBooks.com

LOLA

"I want to have a baby with you, Lola."

Sebastian Steele—the former multibillionaire playboy now my husband of eighteen months—murmurs to me as he traces shapes with his fingertips on my bare, flat belly.

Shocked to hear his words, I stiffen. An ice bucket of water douses the fiery heat swirling around our post-climax bodies.

We just made passionate love, and my core still buzzes from Baz's skillful touch—mouth, lips, tongue, fingers, ten-inches…

I roll over to face him in bed at my best friend turned sister-in-law Leonie Steele, formerly Beaulieu, and Baz's second younger brother Roger's new, multimillion-dollar chalet in Verbier, Switzerland. I need to know how serious Baz is about a baby.

As I stare into his dove gray eyes that shine in the moonlight from the wall of windows in our suite, I search his handsome face for any sign of a joke. No guile, only earnestness, and dare I think hopefulness show.

Damn.

Why now?

I thought we addressed this issue months ago.

First Baz only hinted at a baby all nonchalant like. A reference to the need for the next head of STEELE International, Inc., his family's multigenerational, multibillionaire dollar luxury real estate development and management corporation based in New York City.

Baz, previously president of the Retail Properties Division, earned the CEO role when his father Morgan announced his retirement and named Baz his successor at our wedding, as Morgan's father named him. Each of his siblings works at STEELE: Malcolm, second oldest, president of the Entertainment Properties Division; Roger, president of the Residential Properties Division; Harris and Haley, youngest and fraternal twins, co-founders of the subsidiary STEELE Technology and Cyber Security.

Who needs "the next head of STEELE" only eighteen months after being appointed and Baz is only thirty-seven years old now, nowhere near retirement age? Really? Cue the biggest eye roll of the millennia…

I didn't open my mouth.

Then a couple of months passed, and he mentioned having a baby outright.

I told him we should spend our first few years as a couple, no need to rush into a family. We'd rushed enough—meeting one week; living tougher the next week; a couple for four months before our disastrous breakup…

Plus, we have our career goals that dominate our focus. The growth of Lola's Coterie my luxury lingerie and now evening wear collection boutiques and Baz as CEO and

Chairman of the Board. We're both driven and acknowledge the importance of our businesses. Particularly since my growth ties in with STEELE as their retail spaces serve as my boutique locations around the globe.

Baz agreed. That is, until he brought it up again just now...

I blame Leonie and Roger for running around proud parents of identical twin boys, Rodolphe Beaulieu Steele and Gaspard Beaulieu Steele. They just turned three-months old and nothing is more adorable than The Twins. To see my bestie so ecstatic with her husband of four days, Roger, and her *beaux fils*—beautiful sons as the Parisian and Tunisian beauty in her own right calls them—makes my heart swell with love.

Since Leonie and Roger prove a young couple can successfully balance a family while they excel in their careers—Leonie as a megamodel turned interior designer with her newly created division at STEELE—influenced Sebastian clearly. Not to mention how they cannot keep their hands off each other. Who said babies end a steamy sex life?

Can I see Baz and me like Leonie and Roger living their best lives? Hell yes! But...

I can't get over the loss of my parents in a tragic car accident when I was seventeen years old and left all alone in the world.

The thought of having children only to leave them makes me violently ill. Sweat breaks out on my skin and dry heaves rack my body, dizziness overtakes me. Realistically I know there's no way to see the future, and no one has kids expecting their own deaths, but it's hard for me, even fifteen years later.

The upside came from my friendships with Luc

Montaigne and Leonie, who he introduced to me eight years ago. Luc became my mentor, Vice Chair of Lola's Coterie, and a father figure. That is after I literally bumped into him one evening in Paris where I was an apprentice at a lace atelier after graduating from the Fashion Institute of Technology in my native New York City.

Le Renard Argenté, fifty-two and the multibillionaire CEO and Chairman of the Board of his family's multigenerational banking empire Banque Montaigne headquartered in Paris with branches worldwide, took me under his wing. The Silver Fox lives up to his name as a sexy and fit older man who is the last *duc* of his family's noble line.

When he introduced me to Leonie, she agreed to become the spokesmodel for Lola's Coterie. It was one move that skyrocketed my company to the stratosphere. To have *The Lion*—the world renown face of fashion houses and cosmetics companies—represent my lingerie brand made Lola's Coterie a household name.

Luc and Leonie became my surrogate family along with Leonie's parents, *Papa* Guy and *Maman* Joséphine. Sadly, Luc lost his wife and son in childbirth one year before he met me. We helped each other to survive our shared grief of losing loved ones unexpectedly.

So while I'm super happy for Leonie and Roger, I'm still hesitant to move forward with a child. I've put off thinking about it. But they influenced me, too. Especially since we arrived in Verbier yesterday to celebrate not only their marriage, but Christmas and New Year's. Spending time at the Christmas market and at dinner makes me want what they have for Baz and me.

"Babe, don't look so stricken. Just think more about it. For me, for us. Okay?"

Baz's softly spoken request pulls me from my musings. His eyes now fill with concern and a touch of sadness.

My throat clogs, and my chest constricts. I can only nod in response.

"Words, Little Pet. I will have your words," Baz corrects me in his commanding Alpha Dom voice.

I shiver and bite my lower lip as a thrill rushes through me.

To think just over three years ago I was first introduced to a D/s relationship by my onetime lover Simon Blanchett. The hot AF Alpha Dom spanked me before giving me the most intense orgasms and sense of release I'd ever experienced. He awakened the need in me.

Until Baz... The only man I submit to now after my Independent Woman realizes I can still roar in the boardroom, but purr in the bedroom. I give Sebastian control with our fucking willingly, but with enough sass I'll forever need a spanking. Indeed, a total win-win situation. Give it to me, baby!

"Yes, Sir," I answer firmly.

"Good. Now go to sleep, you earned your rest, Little Pet," Baz says with a smirk.

He kisses my lips, but ends with a nip for a touch of pain with the pleasure before he rolls me back over to spoon again.

I lie wrapped in his warm, loving embrace as my mind continues to work over the issue.

Once his breathing evens out, and his hold lessens, I slip from our bed.

I pad to the bathroom to clean up, then put on one of Lola's Coterie cashmere lounge suits and matching slippers. A quick peek at Sebastian assures me he's still fast asleep. For a moment, I stare at his gorgeous face, so peaceful. I love this man with all of my heart and soul and want both of us happy.

With a sad smile, I turn for the suite's main door.

The massive chalet sits quietly. How's the Christmas tale go? Not even a mouse stirs. Dim lighting from wall sconces and ceiling pots make my way visible. It's a comfy and chic custom-built chalet with all the top amenities and accoutrements expected by a posh family.

Roger gifted it to his new bride as one of his wedding presents. Leonie whose favorite holiday is Christmas named it *Chalet de le Joie* since it's the time of year most filled with joy.

Verbs, as the in-the-know jet-set call Verbier, is a town in the Swiss Alps. A part of the Valais canton in the southwest of Switzerland, France borders Verbier to the west with Italy to the south. It's the most exclusive ski destination in the world.

It's the winter version of Monaco, with the difference being people who go to Monaco want to watch or be watched. Whereas Verbier has an understated style where wealth is glamorous, stylish and tasteful. People are here for the reasons one goes to a ski resort—the superb skiing. Not to mention the phenomenal bars and restaurants; the après-ski is perfect for party lovers. Verbier is a glamorous winter playground.

Leonie and Roger's luxury chalet occupy the area south of the Médran lift. They're slightly away from town along Rue de Médran, where the extra space means they are rarely overlooked and have a private, exclusive vibe. The residential compound is opposite to the STEELE Verbier Hotel & Resort that's closer to the heart of the village square. The concept is for the STEELE Verbier Chalets to access the resort for its five-star amenities. The most important include the luxury thermal bath spa and the three Jackson Corporation restaurants headed by the Steele siblings' cousin Lucien *The Sexy Chef* as he's known by his millions of followers.

The STEELE Verbier had its grand opening during last year's ski season. They planned the Residential Properties Division's completion of the by-application-only compound of ten state-of-the-art chalets and private clubhouse to take occupancy for this year's season. As always, both top-notch properties deserve the STEELE stamp.

I make my way down the back set of stairs that open out on a windowed walkway. It connects the huge chef's kitchen and butler's pantry with a cluster of rooms.

Not that Leonie cooks! Over the years, *Maman* Josy taught their Tunisian family's traditional recipes to me since cooking is one of my favorite pastimes.

A giggle bubbles up as I think about the time Leonie burned water… Yeah, she boiled it right out of the pot and burnt the whole kit and caboodle! *Maman* Josy banned her from *Le Beaulieu Manoir's* kitchen for a week. It's surprising Leonie didn't burn down her family's ancestral mansion on the westernmost part of the outskirts of Paris in Neuilly-Auteuil-Passy. The majestic property features manicured park-like grounds, stables, tennis court, swimming pool and cabana, and a palatial French Rococo mansion. A part of the 16th arrondissement, it's in the wealthiest neighborhood.

They built the hamlet between the thirteenth and seventeenth centuries. Later, during the reign of Louis XV, it became a fashionable country retreat for French elites. The Beaulieu's twenty acres of land border Bois de Boulogne with parts of the acreage awarded to their ancestors by the monarch.

So growing up überwealthy, Leonie really does not need

to cook at *Le Manoir* or here. Not that I did either with a mother who was a high-powered medical attorney and my father was one of the world's top cardiologists. They were multimillionaires. I just love to cook and enjoy the fruits of my labor, and Baz loves my curves.

The fully stocked pantry offers tons of options for a warm cuppa; I opt for chamomile tea. Once it's ready, I return to the walkway and curl up on a settee. Then bundle an oversized cashmere throw around me; it engulfs my petite body.

Listlessly, I gaze out the windows as the early morning light sparks beyond the Swiss Alps. So lost in thought, I don't hear anyone approach.

"Hey. What are you doing up so early?"

I glance over my shoulder to find Leonie.

The sad expression on my face makes her pause.

"What's wrong?!" She asks urgently as she sits beside me hurriedly. "Why are you out here and not upstairs with Sebastian? Did something happen?"

Her feline amber eyes narrow as she searches my face for the cause of my distress. We've become one another's defenders over the years. To take on boyfriends and touchy-feely fans in a heartbeat.

I sigh and wipe a hand over my heart-shaped face. With a smile, I shake my head. The glossy raven tresses sway with the movement. "Sebastian and I—"

"I'll kick his ass! I don't care if he's Roger's brother! What did he do to you?!" Leonie demands, her French accent thickening with her emotions as her eyes glow fiercely.

Another giggle surfaces through the pain, and I hold up my hands to stop her.

"No. It's not what you guess," I say. "He wants to have a

baby for a while now. At first he only hinted at it, later he mentioned it outright. Now, being around The Twins and seeing how happy you and Roger are and how you're making the family thing work, Baz brought it up again earlier this morning. I couldn't fall sleep. I stayed up thinking long after he fell asleep. So I came down here for some chamomile tea."

I twirl a strand of hair around my fingers. My gaze goes back out the floor-to-ceiling windows and to the beauty of the snow-covered Swiss Alps beyond. Puffs of snow fall from a leaden sky.

It's Christmas morning and a picturesque wintry day. My best friend knows I should enjoy a cuddle with my hubby instead of sitting down here all alone. She waits for me to continue.

Moments later, I shift on the settee to face Leonie.

"I do want children, and I know we can make it work, too," I start. Again, I look away. "But I'm scared about them losing one of us like I lost my parents at seventeen. It's really so hard..."

My voice cracks and tears fill my hazel eyes as my lower lip trembles.

Leonie scoots closer and pulls me into an embrace. Her maternal instincts make her rock me and hum softly as she rubs my back soothingly.

I'm sure she's thinking about how I felt that night when the police came to my family's apartment on Manhattan's Upper East Side. Only a few hours before, I'd wished my parents a good time at dinner with their out-of-town friends.

I give Leonie a squeeze before I sit up, drying my eyes with the backs of my hands. I take a deep cleansing breath like Starr Knight—our close friend and yogi, who helped me get through the rough patch after I left Baz early on—taught us. On the exhale, I nod, the decision made.

Again, Leonie waits for me to speak, knowing her BFF so well and how I like to think things through uninterrupted.

"I can't not live because of a what may happen. I want what you and Roger have just as much as Sebastian. Hell, probably even more"—I chuckle and clasp her hands in mine—"What do you think? Am I being silly?"

Leonie squeezes my hands and shakes her head. Her long mahogany waves settle around her like a lion's mane.

"Absolutely not! You had a traumatic experience that's not so easily overcome. Luc and I helped you and being around my parents did, too. But it still had to be hard"—she squeezes my hands again and continues—"But now, you have a man who loves you madly and an even bigger family with the entire Steele clan. You have the support of many loved ones. 'Live. Live. Live' as Auntie Mame says!"

I giggle again at her reference to one of her favorite movies about the eccentric, carefree socialite who let nothing or anyone make her change course—much like Leonie.

"There you are!"

"We've been looking all over for the two of you!"

Sebastian and Roger stride down the hallway, their long legs make quick work of the distance between us. Baz cocks his head to the side and narrows his eyes when he notices my tear-stained face.

"What's wrong, baby? What happened? Are you sick?" He asks rapidly as he rushes to kneel before me.

Leonie pats his shoulder and squeezes it. He glances at her, puzzled.

"Take her upstairs. Despite how nice it is for us to have

some BFF alone time, I'm positive Lola would rather be with you than in this walkway with me," she says grinning.

Baz nods and scoops me in a bride-like hold. I wrap my arms around his neck as I nuzzle against him, breathing in his sexy cologne that's imprinted on my brain as love and safety. Creed Aventus. The iconic name derived from ventus —the wind—illustrating the Aventus man as destined to live a driven life, ever galloping with the wind at his back toward success. How apropos.

Roger claps him on the back as we pass.

Sebastian acknowledges him barely as he murmurs soothing words in my ear.

In what seems like no time, we're back in our suite. Baz stands me by the bed and strips the lounge suit from my body, then tucks me under the covers. He takes off his long-sleeved t-shirt and sweatpants.

My body instantly responds to his muscular six-foot-four-inch frame and massive cock, even flaccid it's major.

He catches sight of my hungry gaze—knowing how my other favorite pastime is to suck him off—and smirks.

"First, tell me why you left our bed and ended up in the walkway in tears, babe," Baz says as he scoots under the bedding beside me.

We promised one another honesty above all, a lesson we learned after our breakup.

"I'm scared to have children only for them to lose me or you like I lost my parents," the words tumble from my mouth in a rush.

Baz nods and cups my face to pin me with his intense gaze.

"My love, I cannot imagine your pain. I can only try to ease it with my love for you"— he says then kisses me deeply—"But we have to live our lives and not let the past, no matter how tragic, stop us. Yes?"

I take another cleansing breath as I say a silent prayer to my parents for their strength.

"Yes, Baz. Let's have a baby, my love."

The most beatific smile crosses Sebastian's face, lighting his gray eyes to the color of molten platinum.

"Second, let's get started right. Now."

LOLA

"Hey! Starting without me, I see!"

The tinkling laughter of my buddy Starr makes me laugh in my crystal tumbler filled with a Manhattan cocktail over ice.

I flew out to the West Coast for business at my Lola's Coterie Beverly Hills and Las Vegas boutiques. My marketing team and I plan to review campaign locations for my new collections along with vendor meetings I'll handle in person.

My personal assistants Blair Thomas and Billie Chandler accompany me. Blair came from New York City with me on Baz's Gulfstream 650, and Billie joined us from Las Vegas. It's funny how all these years later, after denying to Luc I needed an assistant and insisting I could take care of all aspects of my company, I have two.

It's been five years since Luc made the referral for Blair. As the daughter of an English manufacturing magnate, she comes from a wealthy family and really doesn't have to work. But she set her heart on being in the fashion industry.

So Luc did his friend a favor and introduced his daughter to me.

At first I was hesitant until Blair flashed a determined expression with her cerulean blue eyes. Her gusto and attention to detail won me over quickly.

Like Blair, Billie chose not to follow in her family's footsteps to pursue her love of fashion. Her family comprises affluent Southern politicians. Billie—who reminds everyone of a petite Tyra Banks with her wavy, medium-blonde balayage hair, pecan-colored skin, and green eyes—was tired of being arm candy for her ex-boyfriend. She moved to Vegas. Shortly after I began construction on my boutique at STEELE Las Vegas, Malcolm introduced me to her. Here we are three years later.

Although I wonder how much longer either will remain as my PA since they paired off with Luc and Patrick Rockett, respectively. When Billie started dating Patrick, Sebastian nearly had a coronary as Rockett Construction is STEELE's top competitor, not to mention how Pat was interested in being my Dom initially... Fortunately, the brawny multibillionaire Scotsman became enthralled by Billie's siren song.

Along with Leonie and Haley, Blair, Billie, and Starr have become my girls over the years. We can't wait to get tougher for a Girls' Night Out or a Girls' Getaway—especially if it's one of Starr's international luxury fitness retreats. Tonight is no different, minus Leonie, since the Hot Mama is still on her honeymoon.

"Hey yourself! You're late and the party starts once I arrive!" Billie jokes as she stands to hug Starr.

Blair rises, too, and quips, "Yeah, and you know I cannot resist my Whiskey Sour for too long! My Scottish blood from my mother's side demands it as soon as I enter a bar!"

I wave my hand and add, "*Voilà!* Your drink mademoiselle, nice and fresh just how you prefer it!"

The server appears to place Starr's favorite mojito cocktail in front of her. She grins and raises it for a toast.

"Here's to good friends and excellent drinks. May they forever be as one!" She winks, then adds, "And here's to our girl Leonie who's definitely having a hotter time than us right now!!"

We burst out into giggles while the other patrons at the restaurant in STEELE Rodeo Drive glance our way. The vibe is elegant, but relaxed, so they smile at our joviality. The restaurant run by Lucien through Jackson's partnership with STEELE is a popular Michelin-starred eatery like his other establishments.

When Sebastian and I travel, we stay at a STEELE property—being they own so many worldwide, we never run out of options. Hence, with my frequent trips to the West Coast, the Penthouse Suite here has become my home away from home.

While in town, my peace of mind and workouts happen at my yogi buddy's Starr Light Fitness & Wellness Beverly Hills. For my thirtieth birthday twenty months ago, I attended her first international retreat at the private Laucala Island in Fiji. I was like Humpty Dumpty since Starr had to put me back together again after my breakup with Sebastian.

"Okay, ladies, time to dish about your fabulous holidays in chichi Verbs!" Billie says as she claps her hands once the server completes our order. "Then Blair, you must admit to some details about your time with *Duc* Luc, give us some tiny morsel for a change. After I'll tell you all about my Highland adventures!"

Starr and I share some highlights from our fabulous Winter Wonderland Christmas and New Year's.

Happily, I note how her sorrel brown eyes sparkle whenever she mentions Malcolm. As Baz's doppelgänger—same six feet, four inches in height; gray eyes; black hair; clean shaven or 5 o'clock shadow covers a firm jaw—I can understand her pleasure. Only two years apart, some confuse the brothers for twins.

I smile to myself and wonder when the next of the STEELE Quaternity will be off the market. The media dubbed Baz, Malcolm, Roger, and Harris as the STEELE Quaternity—the most sought-after of the world's eligible billionaires. Since my marriage and now Leonie's, the number has diminished by half. I expect Malcolm in a matter of time…

"Er, Lola? Who's—"

Blair's words get cut off by a sexy French accent in a baritone that once made my pussy juices flow. Shocked, I turn and look up six feet, three inches of a well-formed male into the ice-blue eyes of drop-dead gorgeous Simon Blanchett. They bore into my hazel orbs. I'm spellbound.

"Lola?"

Caught gaping at him, I flush from my hairline to my chest. Damn! Even after all these years, Simon's dominant masculine presence still takes my breath away. What the hell is wrong with me??

"I thought that was you, *belle*," he continues in French with a smirk.

My attraction obvious as he bends over to double kiss my cheeks. He's like a great white shark in open water that scents one drop of blood.

Baz is the only man for me. My body just had a visceral reaction to my original one-night Dom who helped me to discover my desires for BDSM. I shake my head to dispel the fog. *Get it together, Mrs. Steele!* I chide myself.

"Simon… Bonsoir," I respond as my fluency in French takes over. "How nice to see you. Allow me to introduce my friends."

I use the introductions to get my head together and regain control of the situation.

We chat for a moment and learn we're in town on business for the next week. His eyes light up.

"How fortuitous! I have a business proposition to discuss with you. Rather than interrupt your evening, have dinner with me tomorrow night. We can meet in the lobby if you prefer, then go to Spago. I remember how you enjoy large cuts of meat," Simon says.

Damn.

He has a way of making innuendos so effortlessly.

But I am intrigued since I've been considering ramping up Lola's Coterie online presence. Who better to partner with than Blanchett Retail Enterprises, SAS, the largest online luxury retailer in the world?

I first met the commanding self-made multibillionaire at a retailers' event in London three and a half ago. He was persistent then, just as he issued his directive to me now.

With that mastery and confidence, it's no wonder Simon could build his online shopping platform with a few thousand dollars and no formal college education. Three years before we met, he was already generating millions of dollars in revenue. Soon, his company will surpass Amazon—a feat.

I like to tell myself his brilliant business acumen drew me to him—I thought I could learn a lot from his success and apply it to Lola's Coterie. But I fooled myself. I desired his controlling ways.

Even though that's in the past, if he has an idea for me, I

won't pass it up. Of course I'll tell Baz. After I find out the details...

"Sounds intriguing, Simon. Seven works for me. I'll meet you by the concierge desk. Good night," I respond confidently as my Independent Woman charges to the forefront.

"Bien, jusque-là, belle," he responds. His glacial eyes pin me to my seat. Then he turns and bids the girls a good evening.

I watch—like other women in the room—as he strides to a table with well-dressed men in bespoke business suits. My designer's eye can pick up on the high-quality tailoring and fabrics. When my gaze returns to our table, the girls stare at me with wide eyes. It's pretty comical.

"Oookay, then..." Starr says, fluttering her eyelashes dramatically.

Blair and Billie mimic her movements, and they laugh.

I wave my friends off and assure them nothing is amiss. I don't mention my brief relationship with Simon. Although I know Malcolm and Patrick are Alpha Doms, and I'm positive Starr and Billie partake in their sexual pursuits, we've never spoken about it.

Dinner continues with delicious dishes, fine wine, and pleasant conversation.

But Simon has my mind on overdrive, more than likely on purpose. I push the distracting thoughts aside and refocus on my friends. Tomorrow will take care of itself. *Be present,* a Starrism I've adopted.

* * *

"YOU LOOK WONDERFUL, Lola. The photos do not come close to your radiance. Married life has given you a special glow."

Interesting. Simon must follow me in the media. Why else would he mention photos?

Not that I was by any means attempting to impress him, but I put a bit more razzle-dazzle into my outfit.

A white wool-crepe midi dress with an off-the-shoulder neckline artfully folded to frame my collarbones. The nipped-in waist and darts at my hips highlight my curvy figure. Plus the color stresses my sun-kissed skin from the week Baz and I spent aboard *Serendipity,* his parents' megayacht cruising the Mediterranean Sea after we left Verbier.

I kept my hair and makeup simple with an upswept style and a natural palette, matte red lipstick for the zinger. To add height to my petite frame sky-high, glittery Swarovski crystal strappy sandals adorn my feet.

Most importantly, I wore my elaborate diamond hand harness attached to my eternity band and my Ice Rink engagement ring. My Captain Caveman wanted to ensure no one would mistake me for a single lady. And I want to drive that point home to Simon tonight.

I am here for business only.

"Yes," I respond, then lean forward to pin him with my hazel stare. "Tell me about your business proposition."

A smile plays at the corners of Simon's full mouth as he runs his fingers through his wavy flaxen hair. A lock falls over his eye and it reminds me of how I slipped it behind his ear that night in his Parisian penthouse.

I glance away.

"Of course," Simon replies. His eyes scan my face before he continues, "Lola's Coterie could benefit from being a part of the new luxury e-commerce portal my company plans to launch in the next six months. The brands represent the absolute best in their categories and offer exclusive and unique items sought after by the highest echelons of the überwealthy. We handpick the brands and the clients must apply to the portal, then pay a significant annual access fee."

Simon pauses to gauge my reaction. Then adds, "Ordinarily you would sign an ironclad or rather a steel-clad nondisclosure agreement being your husband's company includes a retail division."

He stops again and pins me with his mind-blanking stare, the blue of his eyes turns dark sapphire at the edges.

"But you and I have a history built on trust. I can still trust you, *non, belle*?" Simon asks.

I swear my body temperature rises instantly and my underarms prickle. The heat on my face lets me know my cheeks flushed from his reference to that night.

Damn! Simon took control again.

I lift my glass of Marcassin Estate Chardonnay to my lips. The movement catches his eye. Good. Before the rim touches my alluring, red-stained mouth, I stare directly into his hooded eyes, then respond.

"Yes, Simon."

This time I speak those words, I know the sub always has the true power in the D/s relationship. I set the limits and can choose to stop at any time. I'm in control.

The smile stretches from one corner of Simon's lips to the other and his eyes sparkle in delight. With a nod, he lifts his wineglass in salute. Touché.

We spend the rest of dinner discussing the venture's details. He answers the questions I think off the cuff knowledgeably. This dinner was no ruse to get in my panties again.

It appears a sound opportunity that would increase Lola's Coterie's exposure on the Internet and add another stream of revenue—the potential remarkable. I let him know the need to speak with my team and Sebastian about it.

Simon agrees. Then tells me he'll be in New York City next month so we can schedule a meeting at his US offices. At that point, we'll sign NDAs prior to the presentation. Our assistants will organize the best date for all parties.

When we return to STEELE Rodeo Drive, Simon walks with me to the elevator bank for the VIP suites. As it so happens, he's in the other Penthouse Suite that's accessed by the rear door of the elevator I use to access my suite.

"I won't ask you to tell me your reason for ignoring my calls, text messages, and visits to your flagship offices after our magnificent night together. I respect you, Lola, and your decision not to be my sub. No matter how much I wanted to continue our relationship," he says as we part through the separate elevator doors on the top floor. "But I will tell you Steele is a very lucky man who better treat you right."

I stare at the man who had I met later when I was in a different mindset could have been the one. With a nod, I hold out my hand.

"*Bonne nuit*, Simon."

"*Bonne nuit fais de beaux rêves*," he replies as he clasps my hand between his much larger ones.

I can only hope Baz's dreams are sweet after I call him to say I had dinner with Simon, albeit it for business.

SEBASTIAN

Fuck. Me.

Simon Blanchett is the man who introduced my wife to spanking. The man who owns the largest fashion e-commerce platform in the world on which many of STEELE's brick-and-mortar clients host their online presence.

Not a direct competitor to our Retail Properties Division per se, but on a personal degree, he's my archrival...

Almost three years ago the woman who fell into my arms at LEVELS New York—the flagship location for the global, luxury, members-only BDSM/dance clubs created by Malcolm and Lucien—took my breath away. My body jolted from her touch and my cock sprang to life from her sinful little body—my Petite Seductress.

Before our scene Lola told me her last lover was a Dom who spanked her for the first time and she enjoyed it. A feral growl ripped from between my clenched teeth. I wanted to rip his fucking head off. Mine!

Now I'm going to rip the head on his shoulders and the one in his pants off.

To have the absolute audacity to approach my wife—business opportunity or not—goes beyond the code. No Dom addresses another's sub without explicit permission. As an experienced Dom, without a doubt he's aware of that respectful conduct.

It took every ounce of my control not to call my second flight crew to file a plan for an immediate trip out to LAX. But for the fact Lola asked me to trust her—the basis of our relationship, marriage and D/s—I would have been at Blanchett's suite door in a matter of hours. He's lucky I didn't have his ass kicked out of my hotel.

Instead, I called my personal trainer and former MMA champion Borya *The War Defender* Alexeyev to our session an hour early. The big Russian grumbled to meet at 4:15 in the morning, but complied since I pay him a sizable salary to be on call.

Our sparring gave me a chance to release the tension—and need for reckoning—before my workday began.

That was a month ago.

Lola, Luc, Blair, and I sit across from Blanchett, our respective teams beside us. Not in his offices as he planned originally. Rather in the conference room of STEELE's twenty-ninth floor executive floor where Lola has her suite of offices down the corridor from mine. This meeting occurs on my territory, no power exchange with Blanchett ever.

My forebears chose this Billionaires' Row location at the corner of Fifty-Seventh Street and Fifth Avenue to build the modern, gray-tinted glass fifty-seven story mixed-use skyscraper. It's function to impress clients and to intimidate competitors.

Through its floor-to-ceiling windows, the city stretches out with unobstructed views. Central Park to the north, the Hudson River to the west, the East River opposite, and the rest of Manhattan to the south from Midtown to Battery Park. On a sunny, cloudless day like this morning, the panoramas are riveting.

The decor—as sleek as the exterior—features platinum silk wall treatments, ebony wood floors, dove gray and white leather furniture, crystal light fixtures, Lucite tables, steel accents, and original artwork. The reception area has a spacious desk. Three attractive receptionists with headsets in their ears and custom-tailored light gray dress suits and skin-tone heels that serve as uniforms sit behind it.

The majesty of our power awes all who enter SI's headquarters.

It's the exact chord I want to strike with Blanchett. Despite his nonchalance, I sense his vulnerability at being in my presence.

When Lola told me who he was to her, I had my guy do an extensive background check on Blanchett. Nothing unseemly stuck out: thirty-nine; street smart; tech savvy; philanthropic; respected by his employees and peers; in between subs he usually keeps for a few months.

But his Achille's heel lies in his feeling less than since his formal education ended at eighteen. Whenever he's interviewed, Blanchett scoffs at those with higher levels of education and throws shade on them. He prides himself on being self-made through his grit and "not a fancy degree that hangs on a wall collecting dust and not money."

A dominant man such as myself who comes from a wealthy family and attended Harvard University, both undergrad and Business School—as my family's legacy—

irks Blanchett. Not to mention Lola denying him as her Dom, yet she's with me.

My guy also found Blanchett holds a Global All Access membership to the LEVELS clubs—New York, Paris, London. Lola told me he wanted to take her to the Paris location, but she freaked out after their encounter and never returned his calls. Good!

Blanchett's behavior during this meeting will be the deciding factor in his interest of Lola's company or of the woman herself.

Game fucking on.

"Mr. Steele, the nondisclosure agreement is acceptable."

STEELE's General Counsel for New York brings me back to the conference room.

I thank her, and her administrative assistant passes a copy to each of us. Once they're signed, my gaze goes to Blanchett.

"You may proceed," I tell him.

Only a slight change around his eyes hints at his irritation with my undisguised command. His expression shutters as he recovers quickly. Blanchett signals to his team lead, and their presentation begins.

During the course of the ninety minutes, I observe Blanchett. He keeps to a professional demeanor and addresses Lola appropriately. It appears his interests lie in the new portal and a partnership with Lola's Coterie.

Luc and I ask questions along with members of Lola's team and STEELE's marketing team. Blanchett allows his people to answer, but adds to their responses as necessary. His display of leadership and grace combined with the solid opportunity prove a partnership with his company has the potential to be worthwhile.

The CEO of STEELE International, Inc. in me sets

personal issues aside. I acknowledge the deal could benefit Lola's Coterie significantly. The potential for other STEELE retailers not already associated with Blanchett Retail Enterprises could increase their revenue, too.

As it always concerns me: does the deal have a high profit margin and will it add to STEELE International's bottom line? Yes, well, it's a go. No, then no go.

Lola expresses her likelihood of participating and tells Blanchett we will discuss it amongst ourselves, then get back to him next week.

After we married, Lola was appointed to STEELE's board of directors as I was to Lola's Coterie. I've taken on an advisory role to her similar in capacity to Luc. Final decisions lie with her ultimately.

Blanchett nods his acceptance, and the meeting ends.

"Luc, do you plan to attend the Hearts of Love Foundation Gala?" Blanchett asks in French as he strides around the table to where we stand. "I sit on the board and see Banque Montaigne listed as a sponsor this year."

Luc pauses in his conversation with Lola to face Blanchett. Then assesses him coolly as only aristocrats can without coming across as rude.

I have to laugh to myself when I realize two men from Lola's past stand before me.

Luc, who I swore wanted to fuck her despite being her "mentor." Fortunately, I've let go of my jealousy of her relationship with Luc. For one since she wears my rings and two since he and Blair appear to be an item.

Blanchett, well…

"Yes. Where I invest my money, I invest my time," Luc responds.

Being fluent in French—Italian and Russian—I understand what's spoken and Blanchett's subtle attempt to isolate me from the conversation, not realizing my language abilities.

Rule Number One: never underestimate an opponent.

Rule Number Two: know your opponent's allies.

Luc responds in French, but shifts his stance to encompass Lola, Blair, and me. He knows my fluency and undoubtedly what Blanchett sought to accomplish.

I reconsider my thought of this being strictly business. It's obvious Blanchett still has some degree of interest in Lola, or he's just pissed I got what he wanted.

As a dominant Alpha male, I don't blame him. But oh the fuck well. Lola is mine.

However, I would never hamper my wife's business goals. So I won't speak on Blanchett's behavior with her further. Rather, I smile and join in on the conversation; Blanchett attempts to hide his surprise.

Rule Number Three: keep them on edge.

Rule Number Four: remain vigilant at all times.

One wrong move and both heads will roll.

THE SENSUOUS PULSATING rhythm of the music combined with the moans of those being pleasured or punished strum through my body. Lola and I enter the BDSM dungeon known as the Cellar at LEVELS New York for a night of hedonistic passion.

The flagship is situated inside a multilevel brick warehouse in the historic Manhattan neighborhood of the Meatpacking District as a play on the area's name. Put a club where men pack their meat into willing women, and willing men allow women to pack them with their toys.

The historic reference continues with the decor. The lobby is minimal and industrial. The fixtures and furniture that appear well worn are high-end, modern replicas used to add authenticity without the grime of old pieces. The two sides have coordinating greeter stations that allow access to the separate Dine & Dance levels and the BDSM levels.

All Access members can choose from any of the seven levels. While the Dine/Dance members only have access to the party levels—Sky Lounge, Dance Club, and Level 4 Restaurant. For consistency and members' comfort, locations share the same layout with varying views:

> Seven levels: 7th Sky Lounge that offers for the Meatpacking location a stunning, 360-degree view of Manhattan and across the Hudson River to New Jersey's shoreline, a bar, restaurant by day dance club by night, a coverable pool that's open during the warmer months, and a glass-retractable roof; 6th and 5th multilevel dance club with two bars and a lounge for food and drinks; 4th Level 4 Restaurant and bar open for breakfast, lunch, and dinner; 3rd has twelve private suites for members to continue their pleasure apart from the BDSM levels; 2nd Peepshow for BDSM with seating alcoves, primary stage, mini-stages, performance rooms, and a bar that serves non-alcoholic mocktails; below ground the Cellar a BDSM dungeon with mocktails bar.

Since the club caters to the crème de la crème of society, male and female. Members include the likes of US Attorney Generals, international politicians, royalty, and high-powered industry titans. Entry is rigorous and participation consensual. The most wealthy and influential prefer their sexual proclivities remain private.

LEVELS offers a judgment-free safe haven with the relative protection one can expect from the signed ironclad nondisclosure agreement required from every member and their guests. Patrons relax and indulge their every whim or socialize at the dance clubs or restaurants.

Tonight Lola and I plan to indulge.

Recently I've loosened up and agreed to join the public spaces sans masks. Lola complained I was being overly Captain Caveman since we only ventured out during Masquerade Night.

True, after we married, I didn't want another man seeing what is mine. But she pointed out the fact we didn't wear masks before and she was mine. Thus our faces remain uncovered and it's a regular night.

Even though her tantalizing curvy body is on full blast in her Lola's Coterie playsuit. If you can call a black satin belt with continuous holes that winds around her body from her neck to the outsides of her lush tits, doubled below them to wrap around her slim waist and ample hips then to cup her crotch for a naughty bondage look a suit of any kind. Her nipples and areoles covered by diamond pasties and her bare pussy by a sheer flesh-tone crotchless thong. Her shapely legs lengthened by matching fuck-me mules.

She wore her raven hair out in lustrous waves that skim her ass as her hips sway. Her mouth a pouty red I can't wait to see stain my cock.

Above the belt, my diamond collar adorns her neck. The pavéd center loop connects to a thin platinum chain I hold in my hand as we walk. The Cellar's lighting makes my collar sparkle, leaving no doubt Lola is my sub.

When we come out to play, she wears a platinum band that matches mine instead of her wedding jewelry to avoid any damage to the pieces.

As Lola removed her wool cape at the Cellar's double doors, my lower jaw hit the floor and my dick hardened down my leather covered thigh. I had to adjust its length in my pants because of the uncomfortable confines. I understood then why she wouldn't let me see her before we left our duplex penthouse.

Naughty Pet.

My cock twitches at the thought of spanking that luscious ass and watching the flesh jiggle as it blooms from blush pink to crimson red. Oh, she'll wear my marks tonight.

I also know Lola did it on purpose to incite a punishment. My woman loves the release I help her reach.

Naughty, Naughty Pet.

My smirk falls off my face when I spot Blanchett in the center of the dungeon. He's standing on a demonstration stage with a vamp red leather spanking bench and a petite raven-haired woman who stares up at him adoringly. From this distance I can't discern his words to the members gathered, but the hairs on the back of my neck rise all the same.

This motherfucker.

He has a sub who bears an extremely close resemblance to my wife!

What. The. Fuck?!

"Sir, what's wrong?"

Lola's pillowy tits press into my back, the heat of her body seeps through the thin cotton of my lace-up, long-sleeved shirt. She rises on her toes to whisper in my ear since I halted abruptly, and she bumped into my back.

I narrow my eyes at Blanchett while I reach a hand behind me to hold Lola in place. Damned if I'll let him see her half-assed naked! He may have had sex with her years ago, but this is now. And I'm not having it.

Mine!

Lola being busy as usual slips around my other side. She

peers up at my face, then her gaze follows mine. When she sees Blanchett strapping the sub to the bench, Lola's eyes widen in shock.

Quickly, she glances at me to gauge my reaction. Her mouth set in a perfect O, and the wrong cheeks redden as she flushes with embarrassment. Lola also picked up on the startling resemblance between her and Blanchett's sub.

Since Blanchett's background check noted he's in between partners, he must have requested of the LEVELS concierge an introduction to a woman fitting Lola's description, or he happened upon this one. Either way, this clears shit up for real.

He's not over Lola at all.

SEBASTIAN

"J*oyeux Anniversaire!*"

"Happy Birthday!"

My parents, the Beaulieus, and Luc celebrate The Twins' six-month birthday the day after Roger and Leonie return from their two-month-long honeymoon in Verbier.

Lola and I flew into Paris last night for the party, to update Roger on another bullshit legal claim, and for a meeting with Blanchett to complete the deal with Lola's Coterie.

Yeah, like I said, I don't let personal impede a sound business deal. So, Lola's moved forward with the partnership.

However, I made it clear to her should Blanchett so much as smile at her in a way I find inappropriate, I will finish him. Then I'll buy his fucking company and enfold it within STEELE International.

Fuck with a Steele and see what happens.

However, I refuse to let my mind dwell on any negativity right now. I'm here to celebrate my adorable nephews.

We're in Roger and Leonie's triplex penthouse in The STEELE Tower Paris gathered around the dining room table with Rodolphe and Gaspard sitting in their high chairs. They're bedazzled by the flickering candles on the identical cakes before them.

As everyone sings, The Twins bounce and wave their arms in amusement. Each has one little tooth that gleams in the light. All the drooling and tears led to their first tooth. Each time I see them, they surprise me with their growth.

I still can't believe it's been half a year already and three months since Lola promised we'd start a family of our own.

As Roger and Leonie bend over to blow out the candles, a pang hits my chest when they lean in to kiss The Twins' chubby cheeks and Gaspard says, "Dada, dada!"

Roger looks stunned.

"Dada, dada."

Everyone looks over to Rodolphe, and he waves his arms, repeating the words.

Roger has tears in his eyes as he lifts first Gaspard, then Rodolphe into his arms. He kisses their cheeks and holds them close.

Leonie wraps her arms around the three of them. Roger buries his face in her hair. It's an unexpected, momentous occasion that overwhelms the first-time parents.

The room is silent save The Twins and their baby sounds.

"Well, Dada, don't get all sappy on us!"

We glance at Harris, who laughs.

"I'm ready for some cake, bro!"

Everyone laughs at the jokester.

While Roger continues to hold The Twins and turns to

me, Lola helps Leonie cut the cakes made by the Twins' *grand-mère* Josy.

"How's married life treating you, bro?" I ask as I reach for Rodolphe, then nuzzle his cheek, inhaling his baby scent.

"Incredible, man! Now I know why you went all loopy after you married Lola!" Roger chuckles and his eyes dance. Then turns serious. "I never would have thought I could be so happy. Having my wife and my sons makes me complete. I won't allow anyone to harm them or to come between us, ever. They're mine, all mine."

Then he glances towards our wives and back at me.

"So, how's progress on fatherhood for you?" He asks, his famous intense stare locking on me. "You guys seemed pretty eager before you left Verbier."

I take a moment to consider our progress. Lola had just taken her three-month birth control injection before we left for Roger and Leonie's wedding. Since we agreed to have a baby, Lola told me the other day she didn't renew it this month when I asked her about it.

So I'd say we're making excellent progress. I can't wait to have a sweet-smelling bundle of my own.

As if agreeing with me, Rodolphe raises the same gray eyes as mine to gaze at me so like his father. Then the mini Steele laughs, drool slipping down his chin.

I laugh and wipe his mouth as I tell Roger he won't be the only dada for long!

We spend the next half an hour opening presents. With The Twins' development in mind, the gifts include stacking toys with different-sized rings and multi-colored cubes; cars, trains, and balls that roll, light up, and make music to encourage crawling; roly-poly toys; sturdy toys that encourage pulling up to standing; to keep them entertained, colorful board books.

The Dynamic Duo give them some gadgets claiming one is never too young for technology.

Luc bought them their first stock portfolios. The men were more impressed and had a lengthy discussion about the growth potential.

Afterwards, we go to the cinema room with aperitifs.

Haley surprises Roger and Leonie with a compilation movie of our first family Christmas and New Year's. No one even realized she was taking footage while we were together. Some scenes from us skiing, the angle straight on as though we were still on the piste; making s'mores at the outside firepit; The Twins first snowfall; the New Year's Eve fireworks in the village.

She has it set to some of Leonie's favorite Christmas songs, including "Christmas Canon" and Andrea Bocelli and Céline Dion's "The Prayer."

She gives Haley an enormous hug as tears well in her amber eyes.

Haley impresses everyone, and we request copies. Always prepared, she hands out artfully packaged copies to each of us.

Then everyone departs since we have a busy workday tomorrow.

My parents and Lola and I take the family's private elevator to our respective penthouses on the two floors below Roger and Leonie. Our residences occupy the top floors, twenty-eight through thirty-two.

The Tower is in the Front de Seine district of Beaugrenelle in the *quinzième*. Like its New York City counterpart, it's mixed-use with commercial and residential space plus the largest mall in Paris. The views of the Seine and of the Eiffel Tower are incredible, especially at night when the spectacular light display flits across the monumental iron structure.

Malcolm, Harris, and Haley return to their suites at the STEELE Place Vendôme. Guy and Josy leave for their family's ancestral home, *Le Beaulieu Manoir*. Their driver will take Luc to his mansion first as both live in the posh *seizième* arrondissement.

"Good night, sweethearts. I can't wait for our next grandchild!" My mother Shelley exclaims as she hugs Lola and me before we step off the elevator.

"Now, do not pressure them, Shelley," my father admonishes.

She lowers her eyes, but winks at us.

I'll never get over how my father and mother share a D/s relationship, too. In the bedroom, since my mother is as independent as Lola. I guess our kids will wonder the same about us I chuckle to myself.

I give my mother a squeeze and whisper in her ear, "Me, too."

Lola's smiles, but remains silent.

I clasp her hand and lead her off the elevator. Once inside, we go to our bedroom.

"I can't believe how much Rodolphe and Gaspard grew since we saw them. What do you think Roger and Leonie feed them?" I stop when I realize breast milk. No need for the visual of my brother's wife.

Lola makes a noncommittal sound as she walks into the bathroom. She tosses her dress onto a chair. Her round ass beckons to me as I watch the thong disappear between her ample cheeks.

The water turns on from the shower.

I follow her, my cock hardening at the thought of her luscious body slick with water and soapsuds, steam playing peekaboo with her curves. As I stroke my bulge through my boxer briefs, I slip behind Lola where she stands at the sink wiping her makeup off.

"How about we make a baby and give The Twins a cousin, hell, maybe two?" I murmur against Lola's neck as my lips trail open-mouthed kisses to her bare shoulder.

My hands cup her natural D-cup tits. They're more than a handful, even for my sizable hands. I heft their weight and tweak the plump nipples that sit high on the pillowy mounds until they harden to points, pulling on them persistently.

"Mmmmmm… Baz," Lola mewls, grinding her hips against my tented boxer briefs. "Please fuck me, Sir."

With a low growl, I nip the sensitive skin where her neck meets her shoulder. Lola cries out, and I smile satisfied against her skin before I lap at it to soothe the bite of pain.

"So tender, so sweet, Little Pet," I croon seductively.

Lola squirms, and I spank her ass in quick succession, one cheek after the other. She rises on her toes and braces herself against the vanity top. Her hips roll with each slap.

"Aaaahhh… Yeeesss, Sir," she moans.

My hand snakes around her hip to cup her mons through the silk thong, stroking my thick, long middle finger along the damp crotch. The tip of my nail scrapes her swollen clit beneath its hood.

Lola yelps as her body jerks in response.

I continue to play with her nipples as I grind against her, driving Lola's hips into the edge of the counter. My body folds over hers as I force her to bend at the waist, her torso parallel to the vanity top and her lower half pinned by my muscular legs.

A swift kick to widen her stance allows me to move between her legs, humping my groin against her ass.

Fuck, she feels so good. I growl in her ear to let her know just how pleased I am with her delectable body. It's my playground.

When I sense Lola's on the cusp of an orgasm, I stand abruptly and rip her thong off, then toss her over my shoulder. A smack to her ass settles her in place as I stride to the steamy glass-enclosed shower.

Once inside, I place Lola on her feet and angle the showerheads to rain water on her. Then lather the lusciousness of Lola in the enticing bodywash she uses. Its sultry bergamot, lemon, ylang-ylang, peach, and green notes drive me wild.

My fingers slip over her slick skin as she writhes with pleasure, eyes closed and head tilted back. Her soft sighs make my cock throb. But her pleasure first, as always.

I dip my fingers between her folds, now even more wet from the shower. Lola mewls and tightens her grip on my shoulders as she rises to her toes to wrap one leg around my hips.

A swat to her ass stills her pussy undulating against my palm as she attempts to ride my fingers.

"I will give you your pleasure, Naughty Pet."

The rumble sends a shudder through Lola. She presses her torso against mine as she wraps her arms around my neck. Anchored to me, her needy whimpers thrum in my ears.

My gentle thrusts in her pussy increase in pace and pressure. When a third finger joins the other two, Lola's inner walls tighten and flutter with her impending orgasm.

I coat the thumb from my left hand with some of her pussy juices, then press the tip against her bottom hole. The tight ring of muscles gives way to my invasion of her most private hole as I alternate thrusts to her pussy with those to her ass. The erotic, tight fit proves too much for Lola.

"Cum for me hard all over my fingers, Little Pet," I command. "Cum. Right. Now!"

I punctuate each word with deep thrusts.

Lola throws her head back and keens as wave after wave of her climax racks her body. She quakes in my arms. Her greedy pussy and ass muscles clench on my fingers over and over.

All the while, I continue to move within her holes rhythmically and murmur provocative words to inflame her passion.

"Splendid girl, Little Pet," I praise Lola.

"Thank you, Sir," she whispers as her heated forehead rests on my chest.

I kiss the top of her silky head and steady her as I rinse the suds off. A slap of my palm against the panel turns the water off, and I help her from the shower. Wrapped in a warm bath sheet, I dry Lola off and sit her on the oversized terrycloth ottoman. Then I strip out of my boxer briefs and towel off.

Lola's lust-filled hooded stare watches my every move. She never fails to tell me how much my sculpted frame turns her on just as much as my ten inches.

I stroke my length and smirk when the gold in her hazel eyes spark with renewed carnal interest.

"Oh, my Little Pet, you will have my cock deep inside of you. It's time my seed fills your womb and takes root," I say advancing on Lola.

For a brief moment, the spark dims in her eyes. I dismiss it in my heightened state and pick her up to carry her from the bathroom. Lola tenses when I place her on our bed, but relaxes when I kiss her silly.

Lola falls back against the pillows when I crawl up her lush body, trailing kisses in my wake. Her knees fall apart as the head of my cock nudges her swollen seam.

We groan in unison when I breech her tight pussy with my wide girth. I set a pace of long and even strokes, sure to touch every surface of Lola's warm, wet sheath. The sensation sends ripples of ecstasy along my spine.

Lola cries out as her pussy spasms with another orgasm. It squeezes my dick like a vice.

I want to make it last, so I dip my head to pull her turgid nipple into my mouth. As I suckle deeply, just the way Lola likes it, she bows her back and digs her nails into my scalp to lock me to her breast.

"Ooohhh… Baaazzz. So good, baby, so good," Lola moans as she meets each of my thrusts with one of her own.

I reach beneath her and cup her round ass in my hands to keep her in place. Unable to hold back any longer, I drill her into the mattress repeatedly. The frisson of my climax starts at my toes and works its way up the backs of my legs. It increases the force of my pistoning strokes into Lola's sopping wet pussy.

Her pussy grips my cock and hungrily draws me further inside until I hit her cervix.

It's the trigger to my release.

My speed increases as I growl through each spurt of my release, "Take it. Take every last drop of it, and give me a son, Lola!"

The copious amounts of my seed shoot deep in her womb, bathing it thoroughly. The caveman in me throws his head back and roars.

"Mine, Lola! You are mine and only mine!"

Images of Blanchett with Lola run through my head.

Followed by thoughts of him fucking a sub who resembles my woman drive me over the brink.

Yeah, I want a baby with Lola. But I also want to make her belly swell with my seed as a sign she is mine completely.

Like Roger said, *"Having my wife and my sons makes me complete. I won't allow anyone to harm them or come between us, ever. They're mine, all mine."*

That just about sums it up.

LOLA

"Lola!!! What. The Fuck?! Are you serious with me right now?!"

I jump ten feet when Sebastian's angry bellow startles me. I damn near stab myself in the eye as I apply mascara at my vanity in my dressing room of our New York City duplex penthouse in The STEELE Tower.

Simon and I signed the contracts last month during our meeting in Paris. Today, we have our first gathering with our combined marketing and sales teams.

Obviously I need both eyes…

Sebastian storms in. Through the reflection I notice his face is an angry shade of red and his dove gray eyes flash daggers in my direction.

Oh fuck…

"What—"

"NO! Just stop! You fucking lied to me for weeks now! All the millions of times we were 'making a baby,' you laid beneath me and lied!! How could you, Lola?! Do you think this is some sort of a game? All you had to say was *I need more time*!! We've been married for damn near two years. What would another six months matter?! We promised we would always tell each other the truth. And. You. Fucking. Lied. To. Me. Lola!!!"

I can only sit in astonishment. Never has Sebastian spoken to me in this manner or been this furious. My mind runs through reasons and comes up blank. What the hell did I lie… Oh no. There's no way he could know…

"Yeah you know, don't you?! I can see it in your face, Lola!"

He folds his arms across his massive heaving chest and stands with his feet planted wide, staring down at me. The look of pure disgust on his handsome face makes me flinch.

We stare at each other, knowing who speaks first loses leverage. Our relationship started with a deal, and we always fall back on the rules of engagement.

But I'm at fault, so I give in. I won't lie further and can only pray he'll forgive me.

"Baz, I just need more time, especially with the new e-commerce portal partnership. To get pregnant now wouldn't let me get the work done. I—"

"Are you serious with me right now?! You lied to me about stopping your birth control injection so you can WORK?! No fucking way, Lola! That's a poor-ass excuse!!!" Sebastian shouts as he throws his hands in the air.

The veins in his neck bulge and the corners of his lips turn into a sneer. He looks me up and down, shakes his head, and strides from the room.

"Baz!! Wait!!!" I scream as I leap from the tufted stool. It crashes backwards to the hardwood floor. "Sebastian, I'm SORRY!!!"

His long legs carry him from our bedroom to the outer sitting room swiftly. I rush to reach him. He slams the door shut behind him, and the wooden frame shakes with the force. It stops me in my tracks.

Damn!

I take but a moment to fling the door open and race out the door. I glance towards the stairs as I hasten in that direction, only to hear the ding of our private elevator down the hall.

He's leaving our home!

With a burst of speed, I run to catch Sebastian. Our eyes meet through the two inches before the doors close as I skid to a halt in front of them. When I see tears in his eyes, I cry out in agony and slap my palms against the wood.

Oh, no… What the fuck have I done???

A sob tears from between my lips as I crumble to the floor. Pain like I've never known pierces my heart. It's as though a piece of my soul ripped from the deepest part of my body, leaving me with an irreparable void.

I have no idea how long I sit there with tears streaming down my cheeks. Minutes? Hours?

When the house phone rings, I drag myself to my feet and go into the closest room to answer. It's Blair. She had the concierge call since I didn't answer my mobile. I left it in my dressing room.

The meeting starts in fifteen minutes.

Damn.

I reason with myself Sebastian won't speak to me at this moment, so I ask Blair to buy me time. Twenty minutes, and I'll be ready. Back at my vanity after washing my face, I check my mobile and only see missed calls and text messages from Blair—nothing from Sebastian.

Again, I tell myself it's best to let him calm down before I contact him. In reality, I don't want to miss my meeting. Besides, Sebastian of all people understands the importance of being professional and accomplishing one's business goals.

Hell, I should be upset he's upset. I wouldn't stop him or expect him to get pregnant with an important deal to finish.

The idea of Baz pregnant makes me giggle.

We'll be all right.

"WHY DON'T we continue these discussions over dinner? We can order some food in and knock this out."

Blair's suggestion would make sense if Sebastian and I hadn't argued this morning.

I pause to consider my options. I haven't heard from him all day. When I dropped by his office, Melody Lawson—one of his two personal assistants—told me he was out at appointments for the rest of the day followed by a business dinner.

Either I could go home and wait for him or get this done and get home around the same time as him. We can talk then.

I ignore the niggle in my chest and shoot Sebastian a text message to let him know I'm working through dinner and will see him after his business engagement.

"Excellent recommendation, Blair! Lola, you agree, *non?*" Simon says. His ice-blue eyes regard me intently.

I shrug off any hesitation and smile brightly, "Of course! Let's get this done!"

Simon beams, and Blair pulls up the menu for our favorite Thai restaurant.

The time flies as we work and eat and work some more. Before I realize it, four hours pass. Shocked, I check my mobile for any communication from Sebastian. Seeing none, I turn my attention back to the others and finish the last bit on the plan.

Thirty minutes later, Simon and I stand at the private elevator that connects the STEELE offices to the family's residences. I smile up at him.

"That was incredibly productive!" I say.

"*Oui*, we accomplished much," Simon begins, staring at me. "But you seemed distracted at times. Are you all right? Nothing wrong at home I hope."

Surprised he caught my lack of focus and would ask about my personal life, I glance away and shake my head.

"I have quite a few projects going on. But all run smoothly. I appreciate your concern," I tell him, purposefully ignoring the "at home" comment. Like I need another reason for the Wrath of Captain Caveman...

"Simon, I'll walk you to the main elevators."

Blair's voice interrupts Simon's next words.

He closes his mouth and nods. Then he bows to me before he strides in the direction Blair indicates. With his back to her, Blair raises an elegant eyebrow at me in question.

I ignore her, too, and place my palm on the elevator call panel as I bid them good night.

When I step off on the fifty-fifth floor for the second level of our duplex, a sense of sadness overtakes me. I haven't heard from Sebastian. He didn't respond to my text message. I murmur a prayer he'll forgive me as I walk through our darkened sitting room. Just as I reach the bedroom door, a lamp flicks on.

"Where have you been, Lola?"

Once again, Sebastian startles me. I glance over my shoulder to find him dressed as earlier, seated on a chair by the fireplace. He has a crystal snifter of amber liquid in his hand—undoubtedly his favorite Jackson Special Blend Scotch.

I swallow as I take in the closed expression on his face and the aloof body language. He's not letting me in. My mouth sours as a wave of nausea hits me.

"In my offices. We worked through dinner. I sent a text message to you. Melody said you were out at appointments, then had a business dinner. So I figured we would catch up later." The words tumble from my lips in a rush.

Sebastian lifts the glass to his mouth and sips as he peers at me over the rim. His unchanged gaze locks on me.

"With Blanchett?" He asks, watching me closely.

"Yes," I reply. But when a flash gleams in his eyes, I add, "Of course, with both of our teams present the entire time!"

Sebastian merely stares at me; no response or reaction to my statement.

I swallow and press on.

"How—" I have to clear my suddenly dry throat. "How do you feel now?"

He continues to gaze at me as he swirls the liquid, then puts the snifter on the knee of his leg crossed over the other. Pointedly, he pushes the sleeve of his suit jacket back to glance at his Audemars Piguet watch. The birthday gift I gave to him and said, *"You are priceless to me, Sebastian. Nothing in this world or beyond compares to you. Think of my love whenever you glance at the time."* Moments after, he proposed to me in front of our family and friends in Positano.

Fuck…

"Well, considering it is after ten at night and my wife just returns home after we had our first major argument this morning because she lied to me, I could be better," he replies in a bland tone.

I cross the room in a hurry and drop to my knees in front of him. I clasp his free hand between mine and stare up at him beseechingly.

"Baz, my love, please forgive me. I did not intend to hurt you… hurt us. I was selfish and should have been honest with you. Will you please forgive me?" I plead.

Sebastian stares back at me, then takes a sip of his Scotch before he places it on the side table.

"I forgive you, Lola. I know how important your company is to you," he stands and looks down at me as I continue to kneel before him. He scans my face, then he continues.

"You let me know when you are ready to have a baby, Lola. You already know I am. I will not ask again," Baz says.

I watch as he walks to our bedroom without a backwards glance. Then cover my face with my hands and cry, knowing the irreparable void just widened.

SEBASTIAN

I cannot believe how easily Lola lied to me. Looked me dead in my face every single fucking day for weeks and lied with no remorse whatsoever. Not a tell to observe. Her nonchalance shocks me.

Had the receptionist at her gynecologist's office not called the duplex's landline and I answered, I never would have known. Ever.

Fortunately for me, my sneaky wife left her umbrella at their office yesterday. Bad luck for her.

All I could see was red. A swirling cyclone of anger centered on the vortex of how Lola would lie to me after all we've been through. So. Fucked. Up.

But the reality hit me, and it hurt so badly I had to get away before the pain of anguish took over from the blinding fury.

We've known each other for nearly three years and married for twenty-two months. I told Lola from the start a D/s relationship requires trust and open, honest communication. If having a baby now is a hard limit, then I would respect her wishes.

Those same principles apply to our marriage. Without them, it dooms the situation for failure and pain of another sort. Heartrending doubt in us.

I'm no wuss and can't remember the last time I cried. But the idea Lola cares so little for us and what we're trying to achieve as a couple cut me to the quick.

Prior to Lola, I never had a relationship beyond satisfying my Dom needs and physical release with a woman one night, maybe two. Lola changed my playboy ways, and I don't regret it. Her love gave me reason to settle down.

But her actions make me wonder if I should have kept to the course I set for myself: remain business focused. I adjusted my ways for her—for us—and she could care the fuck less. Her work is still more important to her than our marriage.

And that's what's so messed up. I give in to change so our relationship can work, and she stays the same for selfish reasons.

Obviously we're in this marriage for better or for worse. But I needed time this morning, and I need it now. The scheduled ten days of business travel couldn't have come at a more opportune time.

So I stalk into my dressing room and continue to pack my luggage as I started an hour ago.

"Wh… What are you doing? Where are you going, Sebastian??"

Caught up in my thoughts, I didn't hear Lola enter the room. I turn to find her clutching her hand to her chest and her eyes wide, glistening with tears. Her gaze bounces between my open garment bag and wheelie.

I don't answer right away. Let her wonder, get a sense of my pain.

Again, she's so self-absorbed she forgot I leave for visits to several STEELE properties in South American cities tomorrow morning. She begged off accompanying me because of the meetings with Blanchett—how fucking convenient.

A vicious growl rumbles from my mouth at the thought.

Lola gasps, assuming I directed the feral sound at her.

I have to stop myself from rolling my eyes in annoyance. Instead, I respond snarkily, "South America for business. Remember? Oh no, that's right, you're too focused on your more important work with Blanchett. Nothing compares, right, babe?"

A subtle jab at her claiming nothing in this world or beyond compares to me

As I stride into my bathroom for my toiletries kit, I throw a scowl at her over my shoulder. At this point, I don't give a damn how immature I behave.

"Baz," Lola cries as she hurries behind me. "That's not fair! You're more important to me and nothing compares to you!"

When she reaches for me, I jerk away and snatch my kit off the shelf.

"Lola, listen, I get it. Don't worry yourself. Why don't you go get ready for bed?" I face her and add, "The jet departs early, so I'm sleeping in one of the guest suites. Wouldn't want to disturb your rest for another long workday. Good night, sweetheart."

* * *

THE SORROW in Lola's eyes as she stood at our elevator watching me leave for Teterboro at 4 a.m. still stings twelve days later. Some issues arose that kept me longer than expected. With the time changes and how Melody packed my schedule to avoid a lengthy time away, Lola and I communicated little.

On the flight back, I vowed to settle this and to move forward. I let emotion cloud my judgement and didn't give her a chance to explain fully. Not that I won't be pissed, but we can talk it out like adults.

I last told her I'd arrive tomorrow morning. But the meeting moved up, allowing me to arrive earlier than expected. I picked up some dinner from Mr. Chow's Lola's favorite high Chinese cuisine restaurant before my driver Edgar Gonzalez took me home. The delicious food has my mouth watering, along with the thought of Lola doing her happy dance, shimmying her grip-worthy hips.

Now, my driver pulls up to the residence side of The STEELE Tower. As we near the curb, I notice a tall, blond man in conversation with a petite raven-haired woman. Something he says makes her throw her head back and laugh; his eyes fill with mirth.

I blink to make sure I'm not hallucinating since I didn't even know he was still in New York City. No. Fuck me if it's not Blanchett and Lola standing in front of the entrance to our home.

A string of expletives falls from my mouth. I can't catch a break with bullshit, can I?

Rather than asking Edgar to continue on past the building, I have him pull right up next to the gleeful couple. As my mother says, never air your dirty laundry in public. I'll put on an Oscar-caliber performance: husband returns home from a business trip and sweeps wife off her feet in front of her former lover, leaving him with his dick in his hand.

I don't wait for Edgar to get the door; he can give my luggage to the bellman who will leave it at the penthouse's service entrance. Jumping out, I grab the bag of food and saunter over to Lola and Blanchett a broad grin on my face.

"Lola, sweetheart!" I call as I near them.

Her head swivels in my direction. Wide eyes full of surprise blink at me—she must not believe her eyes either—and her mouth forms a perfect O.

I don't allow my gaze to shift to Blanchett until I wrap my arm around Lola, place my hand on her ass, and kiss her possessively. With my lips still on hers, I glance over at him. Then I stand to my full height, an inch taller than him.

"Blanchett, how good of you to walk my wife home from the office. The progress of the portal pleases me. What are the latest updates?" I ask.

Rule Number Three: keep them on edge.

They stare at me, unsure how to respond.

Blanchett recovers first. His eyes slide to Lola and back to me before he answers.

"Steele, what a surprise. Lola did not mention your return," he says.

I grin wider and ask, "You don't believe Lola tells you details of our private lives, now do you?"

"Of course I don't!" Lola exclaims as she peeks up at me, eyes searching mine for a clue to my true mood.

To dispel her anxiety, I chuckle and bend down to kiss the top of her head. I eye Blanchett. "Well then, we'll bid you a good night!"

I nod at him, and without awaiting his response, I hustle Lola along with me as I stride past the doorman into the building.

She keeps up on her sky-high stilettos and doesn't utter a word until we're on our elevator.

"Sebastian! You're home early! Why didn't you tell me? I would have fixed dinner for you," Lola says hurriedly, staring up at me, then tilts her head down. "Oh, is that Mr. Chow?"

She squeezes my side where her hand rests to get my attention.

I glance down at her and search her face.

And the winner for best performance in a love triangle drama goes to Sebastian Steele…

Lola fell for my act.

"The better question, how much time has Blanchett spent at our home while I was away on an extended business trip?" I ask her.

She stumbles backwards as though the words knocked the breath from her lungs. Her mouth opens on a gasp and closes as her eyes scan my face.

Lola sputters, "Wh... What do you mean? How can you think I'd allow any man to spend time at our home, Sebastian?"

I cock an eyebrow.

"Sebastian," she says, exasperated. "We need to talk."

The elevator doors open to the first level of our duplex, and I gesture for her to go ahead of me.

"That was my plan and why I picked up food from one of your favorite restaurants. How the hell would I know you and Blanchett had other plans?" I say as I follow her to the entry double doors.

Lola spins and glares at me. The gold flecks in her hazel eyes blaze.

"We didn't have 'plans,' Sebastian! Simon just walked me around the corner from my boutique! How the hell can you call that 'plans'?" She demands, glaring at me, face flushed scarlet with anger.

Oh, so she's upset? How rich!

I ignore her and slap my palm on the entry pad to unlock the double doors. Then without looking at Lola, gesture for her to go ahead of me into our duplex. As she passes, I swear I hear her growl. To keep from chuckling, I bite the inside of my cheek and shake my head.

She drops her handbag on the side table and drapes her coat on the chair beside it before she bends over to remove her over-the-knee boots. The roundness of her ass and the curve of her hips in the black leather pencil skirt call me to push her against the wall and fuck her raw.

It's been too long since we last had sex, and my cock weeps in dismay. But I'll be damned if I give in to the temptation of Lola's lush little body. I'm still pissed with her, and we need to resolve this situation before we can move forward.

So I drag my hungry gaze away. Once again I shake my head, then discreetly adjust my throbbing length.

"Listen, Lola. I'm calling it as I saw it," I respond as I stride past her to the kitchen. "Let's eat before we get into it."

"Fine," she huffs as she follows me in her stockinged feet.

We wash our hands and fix our plates in silence. Not the comfortable silence of a happily married couple, rather the tense silence of an ill-at-ease pair.

Lola heads to the kitchen banquette with our plates.

My eyes rove over her voluptuous figure as her hips sway. My dick tents the front of my tracksuit pants.

Down, boy! Not now.

"White or red?" I ask as I clear my throat.

She glances over her shoulder and bites her plump lower lip in consideration of her wine choice.

I can think of another pair of lips I'd like to bite. And suck. And lave… My facial expression must give away my carnal thoughts based on the sudden heat in Lola's hazel orbs.

Her scorching gaze takes me in from top to toe, hesitating on my enormous bulge. She licks her lips and flares her nostrils. More than likely her thoughts run to her love of sucking me off.

My dick twitches, and she smirks.

"Red, please," Lola murmurs seductively.

Ah, the color of passion. How apropos.

I take another moment to watch her sashay to sit down, then turn to the Sub-Zero wine storage. Along with the bottle, I grab two glasses and pocket the opener. When I place the bottle and glasses on the table, Lola inclines her head towards me with another smirk.

"Happy to see me?" She asks. "Or is that a corkscrew in your pocket?"

I cock my head and grace her with my smirk as I quip, "Wouldn't you love to know?"

Quick as a flash, Lola snakes her hands inside my pants and grips my junk. Her small, soft hand glides along my hard length and squeezes my ample girth. When she rubs her finger across my weeping tip, I grunt and my hips jerk of their own accord.

Lola shifts on the bench and uses her free hand to tug my pants and boxer briefs to drop at my feet. On a satisfied sigh, she leans forward and engulfs my cock with her warm, wet mouth as her hand grips my thick base. Her tongue swirls around the shaft, lowering until my bulbous tip hits the back of her throat. Her gag reflex kicks in, but she doesn't stop.

Instead, Lola lifts her hooded gaze to mine and hums.

The vibrations rock me to my core. My hands dive into her hair to hold her head in place as my hips piston forward. In fast, out slow, in fast, out slow. Long and even strokes. I maintain the controlled pace, barely giving Lola time to catch her breath.

Her splutters and strips of saliva clinging from her lips to my cock fuel my drive. As the first tingles of my orgasm begin at the base of my spine, I increase my pace and rise onto the balls of my feet.

Lola's hands wrap around the backs of my thighs, pressing into the taut muscles. Her whimpers around my dick zing along my nerve endings. Her blown pupils stare up at me.

Fuck!

My hips buck and I plunder her mouth, losing all control. My only thought centered on the orgasm charging through my body, from down my spine and up from my toes to join at the base of my hard-as-steel cock and heavy balls.

"Take it… Take every inch of me… Fuuuckkk!" I bellow as I throw my head back and roar my release, my body shuddering from the force.

My vision blackens and my hearing dulls as I collapse forward, slapping my palms on the wooden table and on the suede bench back.

Slowly, I return to myself to feel Lola licking my spent dick and massaging my empty balls leisurely.

"Mmmmmm… Better than Mr. Chow's any day, Sir," she moans in a low and throaty voice, well-fed by me filling her belly with my seed.

I can only grunt in response as I pull away with a pop.

Her hazel eyes dance in delight as she wipes the corners of her mouth with her pinky finger.

For the third time, I shake my head. Damn, what this woman does to me. As I've always told Lola, she has the power in our relationship. She just took control and brought me to my knees.

"Yes, well, eat up. We still need to talk," I say as I tuck my now happy cock back in my pants.

Out of my periphery, I notice Lola's shoulders sag before she rearranges herself on the bench. Ordinarily, I would never leave her unfulfilled. But where we are is not normal. We need to clear things up so we can get back to that happy couple. Pronto.

I take my seat opposite her and pour the wine in our glasses. My heart tugs when I see Lola glance at me wistfully.

"Sebas—"

"Lola—"

We speak at the same time.

I tilt my head towards her and sit back.

Lola clears her throat and starts again, "I am so very, very sorry, Sebastian. Never should I have lied to you. Ever. Nor do I blame you for being angry with me."

She takes a sip of wine for fortification and continues, "I do want to have a baby, babies, with you. With no doubt."

Lola pauses to lean forward and reaches for my left hand. As she stares at it, she rubs her thumb over my platinum wedding band. Then her tear-filled eyes lift to me.

"I love you, Baz. Only you, forever you. Not Simon or anyone else can ever compare to you or what we share," Lola whispers, her voice warbles with emotion.

She entwines our fingers and brings our joined hands to

her lips to kiss them. With an imploring look, Lola stares into my eyes.

"Please, Baz, I want to finish this project first. It launches in five months. Can we please wait until then?" She asks as she squeezes my hand.

I contemplate her request and her actions that led us to where we are now. It is not my wish to interfere with her business, and I understand her commitment. The kicker is, I'm more committed to us than Lola. However, I won't belabor the issue. But I will get my point across.

"One would think after all this time, their loved one would be honest," I respond. "All I ask of you is your honesty, Lola. Had you discussed your decision with me, we would have avoided the argument."

The tears spill from her eyes and my heart clenches. I wipe her face with my other hand and nod.

"As I said before I left, we can wait until you're ready. However, going forward, let's decide together, Lola, as a couple, not as individuals. Do you agree?" I finish as I cup her cheek in my hand.

She turns her face to kiss my palm, then nuzzles against it with her eyes closed on a sigh. Lola rises from her seat to embrace me.

I stand and pull her into my arms. With our bodies fully pressed together, Lola wraps her arms around my neck and nods with her forehead against my chest. Her tears wet my long-sleeved t-shirt.

Petting her back, I say, "Words, Lola. I will have your words."

She pulls back and rises onto her toes to look me square in the eye.

"Yes, Sebastian, my love. Absolutely, yes."

SEBASTIAN

"Sebastian, we've known each other for a very long time. There is absolutely no way you can hide your feelings from me. So don't even try it. Spill it, buddy."

I'm at Quality Meats for lunch with Lydie Jackson—the eldest of the Jackson siblings and my childhood friend for whom I've become a confidante since we're in the same position. She's working to take over the helm at Jackson Corporation from her father, just as I did with STEELE from mine. Both of us consider ourselves the leaders of our siblings and responsible for their wellbeing.

Over the years, she's turned to me for advice, especially since she craves approval from her father, Connor. Lydie will do anything to prove she's as good as a son to lead. The son in question is Lachlan, my best friend and the second oldest of the Jackson clan. He's one year younger than Lydie and their father's preferred heir. But Lachlan is a reluctant heir apparent because he loves his older sister more than he wants to please Uncle Connor. He refuses to hurt her, knowing how much she wants to run their company.

For now, Uncle Connor is holding out on making his final decision since he's not retiring for a few months—it's been up in the air the last couple of years. He continues to hope Lydie will marry and turn to her family life and Lachlan can step up to CEO.

Despite being a stunningly gorgeous woman—only six inches shorter than me in high heels, waist-length dark brown hair, and intelligent green eyes known as the signature Jackson family trait—I've never felt a sexual attraction to Lydie.

Lola however thought differently and broke up with me because she mistook my conversation with Lydie as an affair—albeit from Lola's perspective, the visual was rather damning. From the moment they met, Lola perceived Lydie wanted more and only held back because I hadn't made a move and was a serial playboy who fucked different women without commitments.

Little did I know Lola was correct, and Lydie confessed. She thought I solved her problem since her father would accept me as her behind-the-scenes co-head of Jackson Corporation—the perfect merger of STEELE and Jackson.

Uh, not.

I told her under no circumstances we would ever be more than friends, and Lola was the only woman for me. In the end, Lydie realized her errors and apologized to Lola and me. After which, Lola and I renewed our relationship and married months later.

Understandably I'm more than hesitant to disclose the baby drama Lola and I are dealing with to Lydie. Not to mention the fact Lola would have my balls and thus would end any chance of me carrying on the Steele line. So instead I feign work-related stress.

"You're right. I have a new deal in the works that's

proving to be more of a headache than I expected. We have delayed the conclusion for the foreseeable future because of outside forces. So don't mind me," I respond, partially true since the new deal is having a baby obstructed by Blanchett.

Lydie arches her elegant eyebrow and narrows her emerald eyes as she scans my face for any fakery. A full minute later, she nods and lifts her glass of 2007 Sassicaia to her full, ruby lips.

"Okay, let's go with that then," she says with a wry smile. "So tell me, what else is going on with you?"

We fall back into an easy conversation no different from the ones we used to have prior to Lola and I dating. Every month Lydie and I would meet for lunch or dinner and talk on the phone between face time. With Lydie spending more time on the West Coast and focused on her new boyfriend plus me with Lola, our schedules don't allow our get-togethers.

The conversation goes from catching up on our lives since we last saw each other at Roger and Leonie's wedding seven months ago to a business proposal for another STEELE-Jackson partnership. It's light and enjoyable.

Time passes quickly as we chat and eat. I walk Lydie to her car where her driver holds the door open. She turns to me before she gets in.

"It was so good to see you, Sebastian. Perhaps the next time Chase is in town, the four of us can go to dinner," Lydie says with a bright smile.

"That would be nice. And I can give him The Talk, even though I'm sure Lachlan did it already," I smirk.

Her laughter floats around us as I kiss her cheek. "You know he did! Even Laurent had his say in the matter. It's a wonder Chase didn't run away!" Lydie shakes her head as her lustrous hair sways with the movement.

"Excellent," I chuckle. "I'll let Lola know about dinner."

I step back and watch Lydie's Duo-tone cognac and black Bentley Mulsanne glide into traffic. Then stride down Sixth Avenue to head back to my office.

Yeah, it was good to see Lydie. And even better to see her happily involved with another man.

"So, how was your lunch with Lydie?"

I glance at Lola, fork midway to my mouth, as we sit on the terrace off the living room eating the dinner she made and set up like a picnic.

Over the past month she's been extra attentive: sending text messages to me during the day to check in; coming home by six each evening; cooking dinner a few times a week; vamping up her Petite Seductress. I in turn have moved forward and not mentioned a baby or my concerns about Blanchett. So it's been nice and we're back on track.

"It was good. She asked about you and suggested we have dinner with her and her new boyfriend Chase the next time he's in town," I respond, then hold back my chuckle when Lola's eyes widen, and she sputters her wine.

"Yup, Lydie has a new beau who appears serious. Serious enough, her brothers gave him The Talk, and I told her I would, too," I add.

Lola's head bobs, and she claps her hands in glee.

"That's the best news ever! Now she won't have time to moon over you… Sebbie," Lola gibes in reference to Lydie's childhood nickname for me that Lola despises.

I shake my head as I roll my eyes. Women.

"Tell me about your day. How's the progress on the portal?" I say, changing the subject deftly.

Lola smirks in acknowledgment of my tactic, but goes

on to answer in lengthy detail. Then mentions a business trip to Paris for meetings with Blanchett's operations and tech teams next month.

"I want you to come with me. Tina checked your calendar and said your schedule could permit the trip," Lola finishes expectantly having spoken with my second personal assistant.

My teeth grind at the thought of her going to Paris to be with Blanchett. Paris, where they fucked. You can bet your ass I'll be there.

Besides, it's our two-year anniversary. I wonder if Lola even remembers since she didn't mention it…

"Of course, babe, I'll confirm with Tina in the morning and ask her to arrange the G650," I answer in an even tone.

"Thanks, baby, you're so good to me!" Lola squeals and climbs onto my lap. "Now it's time for dessert… Sir."

Her seductive purr coupled with her round ass grinding on my groin makes my cock spring to life. From alfresco dining to alfresco fucking. Our penthouse duplex on the fifty-fourth floor with no other buildings around has its perks.

I stand and carry Lola to one of the double-size chaise lounges to spread my tempting treat before me.

I set Lola on her feet. My hands glide along her flanks, hips, and legs to pull the hem of her silk maxi dress up and off. One tug and the tiny scrap of pink lace covering her pussy falls to the floor. Lola in all her luscious naked beauty takes my breath away.

I bow my head to her full D-cup tits to draw a plump nipple into my mouth, puckering in the cool night air. A few lusty sucks followed by sharp nibbles of first one then the other tasty morsel have Lola shifting from one foot to the other as she gasps. I growl and stretch her out on the chaise lounge.

Time to partake.

Her raven hair fans out to frame her gorgeous face flush rosy from her arousal. She bows her back on a throaty moan as she looks down her body at me on my knees between her legs, open wide in full invitation.

"Look at my pretty, little, pink pussy glistening so wet for me, Pet"—I lean forward and brush my nose along her slippery seam and inhale deeply—"Mmmmmm. And it smells delectable. Let us see just how delicious it is, Pet."

Lola writhes and mewls as I lave from her puckered hole along her slit to her clit in one long swipe of my flattened tongue. The tip teases her bundle of nerves until it's engorged, and her thighs clamp around my ears to lock me against her honeypot.

With a wicked chuckle, I nip her inner thighs, place my palms on them, and brush my fingertips against her puffy pussy lips as I press her legs apart again. I watch as her pussy quivers.

"Ooohhh… Sir… Please…" Lola moans, her hips lifting from the chaise lounge to seek my mouth.

"Ah, ah, ah, Naughty Pet," I chastise, then smack her throbbing pussy three times in quick succession.

The squelching and her breathless cries make my cock ache.

But her needs come first—literally. I lift her legs to rest the backs of her thighs on my shoulders as I reposition myself to continue my ministrations with gusto. My determination to bring Lola to orgasm three more times becomes my sole purpose. Groans fall from my mouth in pleasure as her musky and sweet taste cross my palate.

"Ohhhh my Go—"

Her strangled cries cut off as her body shudders from the strength of her climax. Heels knock against the back of my neck as she bucks against my mouth.

I don't let up.

"Aaaahhh… Sssirrr… No more, please!" Lola wails after one orgasm follows another.

She tosses her head from side to side and digs her nails into the cushion. Her inner thigh muscles strain to clench around my head.

Instead, I hold her legs apart while I lap up her juices as she rides out the waves of her climaxes.

"So sweet, just like fresh honey. Tell me your pussy is my personal honeypot, Pet," I growl, my eyes traveling up her body to her reddened, dewy face. "Open your eyes and tell me. All mine!"

Lola's eyes flutter open. Her unfocused expression lets me know she's past a coherent state. But she attempts to follow my command.

"Yes, Sir," she whimpers. "All yours, Sir."

With a satisfied nod, I rise to my feet above her, sprawled out on the chaise to strip out of my clothes. I make quick work of the linen sweater and trousers as I kick off the slides. My clothes land on top of Lola's dress as I discard them without a care.

Single focus: bury my turgid length balls deep in Lola's sopping wet pussy.

I take a moment to stroke my cock. The bulbous tip a vivid red and dripping pre-cum. As my gaze travels over Lola's lush body, so ready for penetration, my dick swells and hardens further.

She must sense my need and lifts her arms in welcome.

On a primal growl, I pounce. Lola squeals.

One hand fists my thick base while the other grips her

hip in preparation. I glance at her face and pause. Lola's nod unleashes my pent-up passion.

"Hands above your head, Pet, against the back of the chaise. Do not move them, no matter what happens," I command in my stern Alpha Dom voice.

"Yes, Sir," Lola pants, fully aroused and ready for more.

One brutal thrust, and I make my mark—tip against her cervix and balls slap against her ass.

"Fuuuckkk… Feel so good," I bark, buried deep within Lola's tight core.

"Fuck, yesss!" She screams once I bottom out. "Oohhhhhh…"

My hips take on a mind of their own as they pull back, then slam forward over and over again. I plunder Lola's pussy as she braces herself against the chaise lounge. The grip on her hip increases painfully, sure to leave a bruise.

My other hand lowers to above her shoulder to prevent Lola from sliding back and forth as I piston inside her throbbing pussy.

Looking down at her, I snarl, "You are mine, Lola. You know that, do you not?"

So caught up in our carnal pleasure, she's unable to respond verbally. Her head bobs as her mouth hangs slack, issuing soft mewls and moans.

Enthralled by her big tits bouncing with each thrust, I lower my head to latch onto one pebbled nipple. My tongue flicks, then wraps around the pert tip to suck hard.

The action triggers Lola to buck her hips as her pussy walls flutter then clamp down on my cock. She orgasms again with a carnal scream.

My dick swells unbelievably in response.

Her nipple drops from my mouth with a pop as I throw my head back and let off a feral roar. No longer even strokes, my movements become unhinged with the need to reach my release. Caveman grunts and growls fill the air around us as my peak draws near.

"Cum for me, Pet. Cum with me now!" I snarl ferociously.

Lola keens and stiffens as her entire body jolts with one last orgasm.

"Good, girl," I praise her as I bury my face in her sweaty neck, overtaken by my toe-curling climax.

She shudders beneath me.

Fuck Blanchett. Lola is mine, all MINE!

SEBASTIAN

"The inventory systems for the portal will connect seamlessly with your Paris, London, New York, Las Vegas, and Beverly Hills warehouses' tracking systems to ensure delivery of packages to clients within the specified distances. The New York and Paris warehouses will coordinate the shipping for international deliveries. This program proves most effective and efficient for other partners with similar locations to yours. Just as important, we put extensive cyber security measures in place to prevent information breaches. Any questions?"

Harris and Haley flew over to Paris with us to take part in the technology portion of Blanchett's meetings. As the Dynamic Duo—tech and hacker wizzes, respectively—the twins were best suited to handle this presentation.

They question Blanchett's team while Lola, Luc, Blair, and I listen on.

As it turns out, the timing for this trip coincided perfectly with a legal update for Roger and STEELE Paris. Yesterday morning, we met with Blanchett. Later that afternoon, our father, Malcolm, our Paris and New York legal teams, and Leonie gathered in Roger's offices. Afterwards we had dinner with our mother, Lola, Guy, and Josy joining the rest of us.

Blanchett Day Two ends with this meeting.

Fortunately, he's been professional and allowed his teams to run the meetings. Occasionally he's glanced in Lola's direction for longer than necessary. But averted his eyes when I glared at him across the conference room table.

Fucker.

I'm keeping it civil for business sake.

Lola appears oblivious. Her attention focused on the presentations and discussions. Her rapt concentration and well-thought comments and suggestions prove her business acumen.

Luc and I exchange looks of pride.

"If this satisfies Haley and Harris, then I give my approval to move forward. However, I require coordination with STEELE Technology and Cyber Security on all matters. Their team will keep me abreast."

Lola's command of the conference room would make anyone doubt she's a sub in the bedroom, I chuckle to myself. Her Independent Woman is at the forefront to handle her business.

The contradiction makes my cock pulse.

"Although my team comprises the best in the field, I will agree to your request," Simon responds.

I note he said request as opposed to Lola's requirement. A glance at her proves she didn't miss his word choice either.

"While I am sure your team is excellent, my business reputation is of the utmost importance. I trust Haley and Harris to handle my technology affairs implicitly," Lola states with her hazel eyes locked on Blanchett unwaveringly.

He has the grace to nod and break the standoff.

Blanchett better had or I would have stepped in. Or Luc from the way he leaned forward zoning in on Blanchett.

"Of course. Whatever Lola wants," Blanchett quips with a wide smile.

I have to contain my need to punch him in the mouth for using my phrase for my wife. Instead, I turn to Lola.

"Are you satisfied with the progression or do you have any other concerns before the meeting ends?" I ask, wanting to get the fuck out of here before I lose my hold on civility.

Lola glances at me and smiles.

"Yes, you and Luc?" She asks.

Out of my periphery, I catch a glimpse of Blanchett tightening his jaw in a struggle to hold back a comment. I play it up to spite him.

"I agree with you regarding the tech responsibilities and find the launch well in hand. Luc?" I respond.

Luc shares his feedback and adds some suggestions that everyone agrees would benefit the portal overall. Blair adds some thoughtful insights, and her marketing acumen shines through. Luc smiles at her in adoration.

I grin to myself knowing that look firsthand and cast one at Lola who smiles back.

Then she turns to Blanchett.

"This has been a productive two days, Simon. We appreciate your teams' efforts and their work towards a successful launch," Lola starts as she glances around the room at each face. "Unless you have additional information, we can adjourn our meeting."

Blanchett shutters his emotions when he senses my assessment of him, then smiles brightly.

"Lola, as always you hold the power, and we are at you will—"

"What exactly do you mean, Blanchett?" I demand as I rise from my seat and lean towards him with my palms on the table. I'm poised to leap across and knock the shit out of him.

This motherfucker has just shredded the last thread on my civility.

Our eyes lock. A momentary flare of anger sparks his icy eyes before he holds his hands up in capitulation.

"I mean no disrespect, Monsieur Steele. I merely mean our partner's wishes take priority," he says. Then adds, "Nothing more, I assure you."

A small hand on my arm and a discrete cough from Harris ease me down several notches. But not completely.

"Be sure to respect my wife, Blanchett. I give zero fucks whether you respect me," I respond as I stand and take Lola's hand.

I turn to his team and add, "Thank you for your time and work."

Lola, Luc, Blair, Harris, and Haley rise and gather their things. They thank Blanchett's teams before he and his managers walk us to the elevator.

"We'll provide the weekly updates as scheduled. Safe travels home," Blanchett says as he shakes our hands.

I give him an extra-firm squeeze as a reminder. Then usher Lola through the elevator doors.

"Well, that was entertaining," Harris quips when the elevator descends.

Lola snorts, and everyone laughs heartily.

* * *

So Lola didn't forget our second wedding anniversary after all I smile to myself as I stretch out on the oversized beach towel after thanking her sufficiently.

I glance over at my wife, still buzzing from making love under the warm sun of the Maldives as the Indian Ocean waves caress our toes.

Lola surprised me with a trip to a private island for the next ten days.

"I want us to leave everything and everyone behind as we celebrate our anniversary, my love."

My eyes close as I revel in the aftereffects of our lovemaking. Nothing beats Lola on my lap, wrapped in my arms, held with her back to my chest while our bodies connected, taking in the incredible sight of the expansive turquoise, aquamarine water. Not a soul for miles as we rocked in rhythm with the water lapping around us.

The ultimate in peace and tranquility.

"Mmmmmmm, Baz… Can we stay forever?"

I chuckle as I roll over and plank above Lola. Her hooded hazel eyes meet mine, darkened yet again with erotic lust.

She slips her arms around my neck and pulls herself up to slant her mouth over my lips. Our tongues tangle as we explore one another. The taste of the tropical fruit juice still lingers. I lap at it with a hum.

"Mmmmm… Yes, babe. Forever and ever," I respond, desperate to show Lola just how happy she makes me.

I lose myself in her body once again. Slowly I sink my cock within her core, still soaked from our combined essence. Her greedy pussy grips me as I slide deep.

Both of us groan when I bottom out.

Intent on making it last, I hold still to allow us to feel our intimate connection. Right now, it's not about fucking until we're breathless and spent. We need to reaffirm our vows. Take time to just let go and feel.

I told Lola that from the moment she asked me to teach her the ways of a D/s relationship. In almost three years we've been to together, I remind her regularly. Today makes it extra special since we became husband and wife two years ago. Bound forever as one.

Soft sobs bring me back from my musings.

I lift my head from Lola's neck to find tears falling from the corners of her eyes down the sides of her face. My heart constricts.

"What's wrong, baby?" I ask, concerned by her abrupt change in mood.

Lola shakes her head. But I urge her to speak with murmurs of love and reassurance. She raises her gaze to me.

"I love you so much, Sebastian. I hate we argued. I never want us to part at odds again"—she takes a deep breath and continues—"Promise me, please."

An overwhelming desire to engulf Lola with my everlasting love overtakes me. I groan and start to move within her, hoping my actions speak better than any words I can offer, as choked up as I am by raw emotion.

With my face buried in her neck, I slip my arms under her shoulders to cradle the back of her head. Steady strokes of my cock as I pull out to the tip, then slide back in at a slow pace cause Lola to bow her back. Her contented sighs replace the soft sobs.

I shift the angle of my penetration to nudge her most sensitive spot with each inward stroke. Lola feels so fucking good I can't help the nonsensical words and sounds emanating from my mouth. She's right there with me as she coos against my damp hair.

We reach our climax as one on strangled cries of ecstasy.

My cock jerks and shoots my seed deep within her womb as Lola's pussy flutters along my length, milking every drop.

On a groan, I collapse on top of her, my breath blowing her hair from her cheek. My lips find the delicate area where her neck and shoulder meet. I trail open-mouthed kisses up her throat, tasting the salty flavor of her sweat-covered skin, until I reach the shell of her ear.

"I love you so much, too, Lola. I promise to never part from you at odds ever again," I thrum against her lobe in a voice deepened by desire.

* * *

Lola

The sound of Baz's laughter as he cracks up at my corny joke makes my heart swell with love. His gray eyes shine brighter than the sun as it sparkles on the infinite expanse of azure blue waters in front of us.

We have one more day in Paradise, and truly I never want it to end. I wasn't joking when I asked him if we could stay forever. I mean it even more now than I did that first day.

It's been a peaceful time for us to reconnect and to lose ourselves in each other. No distractions and no interference, just like our honeymoon two years ago. Beyond perfect.

I know Simon still bothers Baz, and he's making every effort to not let his Captain Caveman loose. When Simon referenced "Whatever Lola Wants" followed up with his "power" comment, I could feel the heat radiate off of Baz. The temperature in the room increased tenfold in seconds, then plummeted when Baz stood to face off with Simon.

Without a doubt, Baz would have throttled him right

then and there had I not placed my hand on Baz's arm to pull him back from the battle. He was ready to strike. With his MMA training and his possessiveness of me, Baz would have decimated Simon. Then again, Simon is a worthy opponent with his knowledge of Krav Maga. Alpha males…

Thankfully, nothing worse happened.

I meant it when I said I love Baz so much. It's so true, and it's made me feel horrible about the baby situation. Once Lola's Coterie completes the portal, things will be better. Baz and I will be better, that I vow.

"Babe, you're too much!"

Sebastian's words draw me from my musings, as do his continued chuckles.

"Come on, Ms. Jokes. Let's go for a swim," he says, standing to his feet and pulling me up to mine. "I want to check out the reef one more time."

He hands my snorkel tube and mask to me. Then he places his set on his face and carries our fins to the water's edge. We make quick work of donning our gear, before we dive into the crystal-clear, warm water of the Indian Ocean.

Baz's playful mood extends to its depths. He makes faces around his snorkel while his gray eyes dance behind the mask. As we near the reef, he swims after the colorful fish as they scatter from our intrusion of their watery home.

I can't help but to join in his friskiness. The sunlight filters to the bottom, and we swim around in the brilliant rays. I flip my legs as I channel my inner Ariel mermaid to race past Baz to the coral reef ahead of us.

After we investigate the nooks and length of the reef, we resurface to float on our backs lazily. The tranquility of the water lapping around our buoyant bodies lulls us in the heat of the sun.

Suddenly, the water erupts with loud splashes and whistles. Startled, Baz grabs me and pulls me to his chest as he treads water. I screech and cling to him with my face buried in his neck.

My God, what the hell is—

Baz's laughter cuts my thoughts off. He loosens his grip and turns me around.

"Spinner dolphins! It's a pod of dolphins! Damn... I didn't know what the fuck was happening!" He exclaims pointing at the offensive creatures excitedly.

I let go of the breath I was holding and throw my head back, laughing. All I could think of was Jaws and how no one would ever find us.

"Holy crap! I almost keeled over from fright!" I yell. "Damn if they didn't sneak up on us!"

The dolphins swim and leap in the surrounding air, but are careful not to do any harm. The majestic mammals take my breath away. I've never been this close to them before.

Baz reaches over and skims his hand along the back of one as it passes by. I mimic his movement and touch the slick side of one near me. Their whistles and clicks increase as they continue to romp around. Then, as unexpectedly as they appeared, the pod dives below the surface.

We put our masks back on and watch as the dolphins swim away. Once they're out of sight, we resurface, and Baz kisses me silly.

"I love you, Mrs. Steele," he murmurs against my swollen lips.

"I love you more, Mr. Steele," I whisper as I stare into his hooded gray eyes.

It's a magical end to our enchanted anniversary getaway.

LOLA

"*Chérie!* It's so good to see you!"

I glance over from the white board covered in ideas for the latest pre- and postnatal collections to see Leonie padding towards me. We're in the conference area of my atelier above Lola's Coterie New York, and Leonie just arrived for the first of several meetings planned while she and Roger are here. Next month the entire Steele clan, Josy, Guy, Luc, Blair, Billie, and Patrick will go to Steele Southampton Village for their annual Labor Day fundraiser.

Even though it's only been a month since we last saw each other, it feels like forever. Since I moved to New York, then married Baz, Leonie and I have gone from practically spending every day together in Paris to a few days a month or so. Now she's married to Roger and has The Twins leaving even less time.

I miss her and jump up to pull her into a tight hug.

"Hey! You're early! When did you get in?" I ask.

Leonie tosses her mahogany mane of waves over her

shoulder and smiles brightly. Her amber eyes glow with mischief as she rubs her hands together.

"I told Roger not to tell Sebastian so I could surprise you! We arrived last night and made sure the coast was clear before we entered the family's private elevator," she exclaims gleefully. "Surprise!"

We laugh and hug again.

"Well, well, well… The gang's almost all here! Only Haley is missing."

Leonie and I part to find Billie and Blair heading towards us, beaming.

"You weren't due in until later this afternoon!"

They embrace and catch up a bit before we settle at the table with my design team. We proceed with the meeting for the new pieces, including the ones Leonie sketched. After we separate the yeas from the nays, we impress everyone with the final selection.

"I love the new collections, *Chérie*. Well done!" Leonie says as she does our happy shimmy dance. "When will you have the samples ready? I can't wait to see the outcome."

I nod in agreement. The collections are fantastic and go along with the concept of sexy mamas with a need for functional lingerie before and after childbirth.

"Yes, this turned out well! We should have the samples to the—"

"Pardon me, Lola. I didn't realize you'd be in a meeting."

I shift in my seat. Another surprise—it's Simon. I rack my brain for a memory of an appointment scheduled with him and come up empty. I turn to Blair and Billie, but they shake their heads and stare at me in wide-eyed shock.

Quickly, I recover and stand to greet him.

Simon pulls me in close and kisses my cheeks, close to the corners of my mouth. When he steps back slightly, I notice Leonie's raised eyebrow and questioning look. I blink and return my gaze to Simon.

"Hi, how are you? Did we have a meeting scheduled? I don't recall one in my calendar," I stammer.

Simon smiles and his ice-blue eyes glitter.

"*Non, belle*. I have business in New York and thought I'd stop by to see you. Ask you to lunch so I can update you on the portal," he says with his hands still holding my arms. "But if you are busy, let's have dinner, *non*?"

I blink again, unable to formulate a sentence.

"*Excusez moi, monsieur*. I'm Leonie Steele, Lola's sister-in-law. We are in the middle of a meeting now and we have plans with our husbands later. Too bad you came all of this way for nothing, *non*?" Leonie smoothly intercedes as we often do for one another when faced with unwanted attention.

I smile at her and nod. She gave me time to get my word together.

"Yes, Leonie is correct, Simon. Now is not a good time, and I jam-packed my schedule. If the update is urgent, Blair may be available to discuss it with you as she handles the portal," I respond.

Silently Simon stares into my eyes, piercing my soul with his now arctic blues. Then he inclines his head and releases my arms before he steps back further.

"I see," he starts. "I apologize for my intrusion. I will have my assistant touch base with yours regarding the update. Next time, I will make certain to get on your calendar, Lola. I'd hate to disturb your work or family plans."

He turns to nod at Leonie, who stands beside me, after to Blair.

"I bid you all adieu," Simon says before he pivots and strides to the elevator.

Once the doors close behind him, I stalk to my office with Leonie on my heels. I close the door behind us and sag onto the sofa, throwing my head back and screaming silently.

Damn, that man gets to me every single time!

When I raise my head, Leonie sits across from me on a chair, assessing me with feline eyes. She cocks her head to the side.

"Spill it, *Chérie*," she demands.

I tell her how things are going with Baz, me, the baby, and Simon in a non-stop stream of confessions. It's been forever since we last spoke about our lives and I need to off load in the worse way.

Thankfully, Leonie lives up to her BFF status and sits in silence nonjudgmental while I let it all out. Once I'm done, she takes a moment to absorb it all before she speaks.

"I understand, *Chérie*. But I must agree with Sebastian. Simon wants you back and being an Alpha male, he won't let up. Be firm with him and make it very clear you are no longer interested in him beyond your professional partnership," Leonie says.

She arches her elegant brow when I don't respond right away.

"Yes, yes, of course! Baz is the only man for me, Leonie," I say as I rise to my feet to pace the floor. "I just don't want to mess up this deal. It's important and I want nothing to go wrong. I'll speak with Simon."

I stop to face Leonie, and she eyes me for a moment again. Then she nods and rises, too.

"*Bien!* Now, let's review the photo shoot details. I miss being in front of the camera, you know!" She says with a wink as she sashays out of my office.

Visions of Sebastian's head exploding if he saw Simon

holding me flit across my sight. I shake my head to rid it of the terrible thoughts before I follow Leonie through the door.

God forbid…

* * *

"LOLA!!! WHAT THE FUCK?!"

"What are you yelling about?! I'm the one who should be pissed since you had me fucking followed, Sebastian Steele!!"

Sebastian and I snarl at one another as he throws photo after photo after photo of Simon and me: Simon touching my lower back; me laughing at whatever the fuck he said; Simon staring at me with my back turned; me leaning over his shoulder at something he's holding.

Un-fucking-believable!

My husband had me tailed by his guy for weeks. Weeks!! Capturing damning photos of Simon and me in scenarios that were innocent!

"How could you, Sebastian?!" I shout as I pick up a photo and rip it to shreds angrily shaking my head. "This proves nothing! Do you hear me, N-O-T-H-I-N-G!!"

"Yeah?! Then you explain to me why the fuck Blanchett has his hands all over you? Huh? Why, Lola?!" Sebastian shouts back, waving one of the four-color pieces of "evidence."

I glare at him as my nostrils flare.

"Yeah. Thought so. No answer," Sebastian says as he throws the photo on the table between us.

I watch it flutter to land on top of the others. My eyes fill with tears, but I'm determined not to let them fall like the photo.

A deep inhale and exhale does little to calm me down. I turn my back to Sebastian and swipe at my eyes.

"You said you were meeting him for work, for business, for the fucking portal. I trusted you to tell me the truth, Lola," Sebastian ends his tirade in a lower tone of voice.

I spin around to face him, angered once again. Damn my tears!

"That is the truth, Sebastian! I never lied to you. It was for work," I say. Then add, "No different from you and Lydie."

Sebastian's face turns the brightest shade of crimson imaginable. Smoke tendrils seep from his ears. For a second I fear he'll combust.

"Are you seriously comparing my longtime family and business relationships with Lydie to you and Blanchett?!?!" Sebastian shouts.

When I nod, his eyes widen, then narrow to slits. His lip curls into a feral snarl.

Uh oh. I brace myself. But nothing could prepare me for the words that drip from his mouth scathingly.

"I… Never… Fucked… Lydie."

My knees buckle, and I have to grab ahold of the table's edge to prevent myself from collapsing to the floor in a broken heap.

"But you fucked Simon. Did you not, Lola?" Sebastian pauses to look me up and down. "So no. You cannot compare my situation with Lydie to yours with Blanchett."

The tears that threatened to spill now fall unceasing from my eyes. I drop my chin to my chest and sob.

I cannot believe this has gone so far. How could I have known Sebastian would react in this manner. He won't listen to anything I say. It's beyond the simple point of "let's move on."

His anguish is deep-seated. His assigning someone to follow me shows how far Sebastian's trust of me has fallen. Then to throw my one night with Simon in my face. Too low of a blow.

I can sense Sebastian watching me, waiting for a response, any answer. But I can't give it to him right now. I need some space.

Without a glance in his direction, I straighten my spine and stride from the room. When I reach the entry foyer to our duplex, I grab my handbag from the console. My hand stops inches from the front door's knob.

"So, that's it? You're going to leave as usual. Not even stick around to clear this shit up?" Sebastian asks from behind me.

When I don't answer, he sighs and continues.

"Well then go, Lola. If Blanchett is in town, go cry on his shoulder. No doubt he will welcome you with open arms," Sebastian says, then walks away.

My heart clenches. But I leave despite the pain in my chest that chokes words from my mouth that could end the pain for both of us.

Time. I just need some more time.

LOLA

Weeks later, I sit at a conference room table in Paris. I have the final run-through of the e-commerce portal. Luc and Blair sit with me at Blanchett Enterprises, SAS, while Haley and Harris join via video conference. Sebastian has business engagements he couldn't break.

After I left our duplex, I checked in at the St. Regis Hotel New York for a few days. I needed the time to get my head together and for Sebastian to calm down. So I sent a text message to him to let him know I was in the Presidential Suite. Prior to my deal with STEELE, the suite served as my home in New York whenever I came in for business.

Sebastian acknowledged my text with a brusque, *fine*.

Over the weeks, I went to work and threw myself into the photo shoots, collections finalizations, and the contentious portal. I just wanted it done already. I kept the end goal in mind each night I laid my exhausted head on the pillow when I came home late from the office.

Often Sebastian was already in bed or soon returned

home from his late hours at STEELE. He never mentioned that night to me or asked about my work activities. It wasn't as though Sebastian was rude, he just refrained from speaking too in-depth about anything. He stuck to the basics. And we made love rarely.

Occasionally, I would catch Baz staring at me with a raw expression of hurt. But he would turn away or leave the room before I could address it.

A mirthless snicker escapes my lips as I recall the somber times we've had recently.

The incessant drone of voices around me stops. The sudden silence pulls me from my thoughts, and I glance around the room at the concerned faces staring at me.

Damn.

"Lola, are you all right?" Simon asks from across the table. "Does the presentation displease you?"

I straighten in my leather chair, then clear my throat as I touch my fingertips to it.

"Ah, yes. I mean no. I'm fine and so is the presentation. I had a tickle in my throat. Excuse me," I respond with a slight cough.

I can sense Luc and Blair eyeing me, but I don't turn to them.

"Kindly continue, thank you," I add, then smile.

Simon stares at me for a second longer than necessary. His ice-blue eyes scan my face before he inclines his head and motions for the marketing vice president to continue her slideshow.

Periodically, he glances in my direction. But I avoid his questioning gaze.

When the veep finishes, Blair asks questions regarding the promotional campaigns. An in-depth discussion ensues.

The suggestions she makes are on point. As always, Blair impresses me with her acumen.

The financial presentation occurs next. Numbers are my kryptonite, so I leave them to Luc to handle. He points out improvements, and the team makes the adjustments. When he's satisfied, Luc turns to me, and I agree. He proclaims the structure sound, and Simon concurs.

Haley and Harris make last-minute tweaks to the tech aspects that Simon's team missed. He teases how he must become a client of the Dynamic Duo's subsidiary. Everyone laughs, and once again Simon's eyes land on me.

I avert my gaze and squirm under his intense stare.

Luckily, the last presentation begins, and I focus on the operations team. Billie takes over for Lola's Coterie since that area falls in her wheelhouse. She too makes amendments to the Blanchett team's process. Billie's knowledge proves as impressive as Blair's.

After hours of review, the meeting ends. Haley and Harris sign off from New York. The rest of us stand and stretch from sitting for so long. Luc, Blair, and Billie chat about their evening plans. Luc and Blair intend to hang out at Luc's mansion while Billie goes to dinner with Patrick, who flew in with her from Las Vegas.

"What are your plans, Lola? Do you want to join us?" Billie asks.

"Actually, I reserved a table at Arpège for dinner to celebrate the portal's completion," Simon interjects. "I know it's your favorite restaurant, Lola."

Luc makes his patronizing Gallic "*Bof!*" He narrows his eyes at Simon and opens his mouth.

I cut him off, "Sounds good. What time shall we meet?"

Simon smiles broadly and tells me he'll pick me up from The STEELE Tower Paris at eight o'clock. Then we part.

I ignore the looks from Luc, Blair, and Billie. I know what I'm doing.

"YOU LOOK LOVELY, *BELLE*."

I glance down at the black figure-hugging crepe dress that's ruched to highlight my waist before it falls to an asymmetric split hem. I paired it with black stretch satin above the knee stiletto boots. I left my hair to cascade down my back in waves and my face with natural hues of makeup.

"Thank you, Simon," I respond as I fall in step beside him. I choose to ignore his proffered arm.

We leave the lobby of The Tower residence and slip into his chauffeur-driven Rolls-Royce Phantom. We keep the conversation easygoing as we make our way through the Parisian streets. The traffic is light, so we arrive at the restaurant in no time.

Once seated, we order, and I select one of my favorite dishes, Coquilles Saint-Jacques à la Bretonne. Simon opts for the grilled abalone with garlic buckwheat. The sommelier returns and pours the wine.

As I sip my Chardonnay, I observe Simon over the rim. He chats amicably with the sommelier while they discuss the merits of the wine selection. Simon's hearty laugh fills the surrounding air.

Women flick their gazes in his direction like moths to a flame. Some even eye me as competition.

Simon will never lack a woman's attention.

I smile against the rim and take another sip.

The sommelier leaves, and Simon turns his attention to me.

"Tell me, *belle*. Are you happy?" He asks softly, his eyes boring into mine.

I cock my head to the side and stare back at him. I hazard a guess he's not asking about the portal, but I feign ignorance.

"Simon, the portal is brilliant. It further proves how astute you are as an entrepreneur. Thank you for thinking about Lola's Coterie. It's the perfect opportunity for a conducive partnership," I respond and lift my wineglass in salute.

He raises his and smiles. Then shakes his head after he takes a sip.

"*Belle,* I am happy the outcome pleases you. You are never far from my mind. However, my reference was not to the business, rather to you and your personal life"—he takes a sip of his wine before he continues—"Are you happy in your marriage, *belle*?"

The sip of wine sputters as I gasp at his inappropriate question. I never thought Simon would come right out and ask such a thing. But then, he is a dominant and never hesitates to go after what he wants. Apparently, he still wants me as Sebastian guessed.

Damn.

I dab my lips with the linen napkin, then meet his heated gaze.

"Simon, that is not an appropriate question for you to ask—"

"You did not answer my question, *belle*. Are you happy in your marriage?" He queries again. "If not, leave Steele. I will take care of you like the treasure you are to me."

I push back from the table and rise.

Simon hastens to stand and catches my wrist as I turn to walk away.

"Lola, wait. I do not mean to upset you. Please sit down," he beseeches me. "You appeared sad at the meeting, and I know the only thing to hurt you and cause you to disregard your business is your husband."

I glance at Simon over my shoulder and lock blazing hazel eyes with him.

"I am extremely happy in my marriage, Simon. I am not at all happy you would ask such a personal question of me," I state emphatically.

He has the decency to lower his gaze, then he glances back up at me.

"I apologize, *bell—*"

"Also, do not call me *'belle'* anymore, Simon," I correct him sharply.

He nods, then says, "Come. Finish dinner, and I will keep my comments to myself. We have much to celebrate. *D'accord?*"

I appraise him for a moment, then nod when I note sincerity in the depths of his blue eyes.

"D'accord, Simon."

He helps me back into my chair and sits across from me. Simon continues as the perfect gentleman for the rest of dinner. The conversation is stilted at first. But after more wine, we relax into a friendly banter. We finish with delicious millefeuille croustillant and soufflé au citron Meyer desserts.

Once we stop in front of The Tower residence, Simon shifts in his seat to face me. His eyes shine in the dim interior lighting.

"Lola, it pains me I missed my opportunity to be with you"—he holds up his hand to stop me from interrupting him—"I will forever wonder what our lives would have been like had we been in a relationship. I respect you and will not make another advance towards you. But do know, I stand by my words. Should Steele muck things up, I will always be there for you, Lola."

Simon smiles sadly and steps from the car. He helps me out and walks me through the lobby to the private elevator.

I turn to him and smile softly.

"Thank you, Simon. Know that had you and I met later than we did, things may have been different. I love Sebastian, and he is my heart, my soul mate. You will find a woman who has that same love for you. *Bonne nuit*," I respond.

Simon bows, and I step into the elevator.

The doors closing signal the end of that chapter in my life. It's time to get home to my love.

"AAAH... LOLA... BABE..."

I slide my tongue along the slit of Baz's cock, swirling and tasting him as he lies in our bed asleep. The weight of his dick growing as it goes from flaccid to hard in my mouth.

After I returned to our Paris penthouse, I called for the jet. One minute I was in Paris, the next I was racing through the door of our New York bedroom. Relief flooded through me when I saw Baz asleep in bed, in all his naked glory on his back with one arm thrown over his face, the other resting on my pillow. Gorgeous.

A smile lifts the corners of my lips when my name falls from his mouth. Even in sleep, he wants me only. My husband. My lover. My Dom.

I purr around his thick girth, and he pumps his hips as his fingers clasp the back of my head. I relax my jaw muscles and allow him to use me for his pleasure.

Still asleep partially, Baz groans and guides my movements to match his pace.

His taste of musk and of his bodywash makes my mouth water. I slip a finger in and out of my slippery wet folds in time with his thrusts. Our moans and groans ring out in the room.

"Fuuuck, babe! You feel so fucking good… Mmmmmm," Baz grunts as he begins to piston and hit the back of my throat.

Offering no resistance, his shaft slides down my throat on each reentry. The sounds of his pleasure bring me to climax. My shuddering body triggers his release with the thickening of his massive dick in my mouth.

"Yeeessss… Aaaahhhh!!!" Baz roars as he holds my head still and his seed shoots down to my belly.

When his grip lessens, he pulls me on top of his heaving chest. Our bodies line up, and he nuzzles my neck.

"I missed you, Lola," he murmurs in a voice rough from sleep and his cries of passion.

"I missed you, too, Baz," I respond, content to be in his arms again.

Then I straddle him and lean over to place my hands on either side of his head. I brush my nose against his and grind my pussy against his still hard cock.

"Next time, I want your big dick inside of my greedy pussy so your seed can fill my womb. I want my belly full of your baby, not just your cum, Mr. Steele" I whisper.

Baz stiffens beneath me, then bolts upright, wrapping his arms around my waist. He leans back to stare into my eyes.

I smile at the shock in his gray depths, and I nod.

"Yes, Mr. Steele. Give me your baby, your heir."

On a whoop, Baz flips us over and aligns his pelvis with

mine. Notched together, he slams into me on a guttural, feral growl.

My Captain Caveman makes good on my request and fills me with an abundance of his seed all night into the early morning.

When my body can take no more, Baz rolls to his back and tucks me into his side. As we drift off, I tell him I won't get my birth control injection next month.

It's time we make our family and deepen our love at last.

LOLA

"I love the different shades of ocean blues around the Hamptons. Mixed with the warm tones of caramel and orange and a base of eggshell white, it's the perfect palette for a beachfront home."

Roger smirks, "Really? Well, you told me you're not interested in redecorating our home at the compound. So, what's with 'the perfect palette'?"

Leonie nudges his side with her elbow and rolls her eyes.

"Just a comment, smarty pants," Leonie responds. "Is that all right with you?"

"*Just* saying..." He quips. "You declined the opportunity, babe."

Baz and I along with Blair, The Twins, Nanny Grace, Roger, and Leonie are on board the STEELE Sikorsky helicopter heading to the Southampton Village Heliport. Billie will fly in with Patrick on his helicopter later this afternoon and stay at his beachfront property.

Already at the beachfront compound are Morgan, Shelley, Malcolm, Starr, and Harris. Haley and her "we're just friends" Callum also left early. They're prepping for tonight's sunset dinner on the beach—a traditional New England Clambake. And I cannot wait, yum!

Leonie's parents and Luc should have landed by now at the private airport for the Hamptons. They flew in on Luc's new Gulfstream G700. He heard how much we enjoyed our flights for Verbier in the STEELE jet, so he ordered one even though he has a plush G650. This trip his excuse to try his new toy. Leonie and I teased he's a spoiled *duc*!

"Bro, it's been eight months. You haven't learned, yet?" Baz chuckles. "Sometimes you have to not say a word!"

"Yeah. Happy wife, happy life and all that," I say, glancing up from her laptop.

Then I turn to The Twins in their car seats and add, "Learn that lesson now, Little Pumpkins, and you'll be all right."

Rodolphe waves his car in the air while Gaspard claps and says, "Dada, Dada!"

"Yeah, Dada," Leonie laughs and points to Roger as she claps.

Everyone joins in, and The Twins' laughter is the sweetest of all.

Malcolm, Harris, and Haley meet us at the heliport with two Black Badge Rolls-Royce Cullinans and a Suburban. The guys load up the Suburban with our luggage while Blair and I hop into the back of Malcolm's SUV.

Nanny Grace and Leonie secure The Twins in the middle row of the SUV Haley drove. Then Nanny Grace slips onto the third row, and Leonie sits between The Twins.

When Roger opens the driver's door, Haley crosses her

arms over her chest and cocks her head to the side, peering up at him.

"Oh, so you think you're just going to bogart my ride, Big Brother?" She asks.

Roger pinches her cheeks and grins.

"You're so cute when you're annoyed, Baby Sister," he says wiggling her face. "I love you with all my heart. But I will drive any vehicle with my wife and sons in it."

Reluctantly, Haley relinquishing the SUV to her brother. But not without giving him the stink eye as she walks around to climb into the passenger seat.

"Don't feel bad, *Chérie*," Leonie tells her. "Roger does the same thing to me. He refuses to let me drive The Twins anywhere. Either he drives or Eric. *C'est la vie*."

Haley nods, then says, "Only because of my nephews did I give in to you, Roger..."

He winks at her and starts the engine.

We pull up to the compound's private road. A security guard in a gatehouse triggers the oversized wooden gates set between stone pillars with wrought iron lanterns to swing open. A long driveway of pressed oil and natural stone rolls out before us like the yellow brick road.

We're not in Kansas! This is Southampton luxury living at its finest.

Once past the impressive gates, it's another world. The property rests on ten acres all beachfront. Its incredible surroundings include native trees, grassy areas, and closer to the ocean sandy dunes. The briny scent of the ocean through the open windows fills my lungs. The calls of seagulls ring out.

On either side of the primary driveway, secondary ones appear as we drive along. Malcolm pulls off to one on the right. Roger turns onto one of them to our left and Harris follows.

A shorter driveway ends in a circle before a classic Hamptons-style three-story mansion. Sea green shutters lean against gray weathered shingles. Beneath the windowsills flower boxes filled with yellow and red blossoms add to the beauty of the home.

"Here we are," Baz says as Malcolm pulls to a stop at the front door.

We hop out, and I wrap my arm around Sebastian's waist as I gaze at the house. Atop the widow's walk, an antique weathervane idly switches direction with the breeze. The top half of the dark green Dutch door stands open. It's absolutely picturesque.

I glance up at Baz to find him staring at me with a soft smile. His aviator sunglasses reflect mine. He drops his head to kiss me sweetly.

"All right, see you guys at the main house," Malcolm says before he continues along the circular driveway with Blair.

"See you later!" She exclaims as she waves.

We stride through the front door where the interior doesn't disappoint. It's a center hall with a double staircase rising along the walls. The cream, pale green, and dusty yellow hues complement the stone floors. Canvas covered furniture with the accent colors fill the great room. It's comfy and elegant.

But as always, the view of the ocean out of the wall of windows takes my breath away.

Drawn to the endless expanse of the Atlantic Ocean, I walk over to step onto the deck. Out on the private beach, caterers prepare for the clambake. They dug the pit and lined it with large stones and wood. The fragrant scent fills the air. I love being in Southampton Village!

"Come, let's get settled, then meet up with everyone at the main house," Baz says.

I nod and follow him back inside.

We spend the next hour getting situated. I ordered some new bikinis with matching pareos and workout clothing. The staff put everything away before we arrived.

The day turns into evening, and we go to the beach for a seafood feast with the backdrop of a spectacular sunset. The perfectly steamed clams, lobsters, potatoes, and corn on the cob topped with melted butter and paired with local beer and white wine make for a scrumptious meal. Dessert options include warm blueberry and apple pies with vanilla ice cream. Afterwards, we sit around the bonfire chatting.

I smile over at Rodolphe and Gaspard asleep in their mesh beach cots, Blair found online. They enjoyed their first taste of seafood. The greedy little monsters wanted more! So with full bellies, they doze during the rest of our beach time.

"Time to make our baby, Mrs. Steele," Baz murmurs against my windblown hair as I sit between his legs and lean my back against his broad chest.

Wrapped in the warm cocoon of Baz and an oversized blanket, I don't want to move. But nod, and we gather our things and bid everyone a goodnight.

"Don't forget beach yoga at seven tomorrow morning!" Starr calls out to me, as she sits huddled up with Malcolm.

I give her the thumbs up and loop my arm through Baz's as he we walk along the sandy path to our golf cart. I lean my head against his shoulder as we take the short ride.

When we get home, we take a steamy shower to rid our bodies of the sand before we climb into our bed. We make love with the full moon's light bathing us in its glow. Then we collapse with Baz's body spooning mine.

We whisper I love you and fall into a restful slumber.

* * *

"WHAT A GORGEOUS START to the day! I'm so glad the summer weather continued into September."

"It could stay summer year-round as far as I'm concerned."

The girls and I spread our yoga mats out on the sand at the beach in front of the Shelley and Morgan's house. Originally, Starr wanted us to gather for a sunrise meditation at six-thirty, but after the long night we convinced her to start later—if only by half an hour.

I fold into Child's Pose to release tension and to prepare my mind and body for our session.

After the mediation, Starr undoubtedly has a vigorous flow planned with a dharma talk during Savasana. My consistent Skype sessions with Starr over the last two years increased my endurance and ability to handle more advanced asanas. I look forward to today's practice.

"Let us begin. Come to a comfortable sitting position with your palms face up on your knees, fingers in Gyan Mudra. Center your mind…"

Starr takes us from a reflective guided meditation through a sequence of asanas that build up to the challenging peak pose of Scorpion Handstand.

In practicing asanas, the point isn't to twist oneself into a pretzel and the more you can bend, the better. Rather, the focus on the breath and releasing the mind to move the body.

Starr loves to push our ability to focus, and Scorpion Handstand requires lots of it.

I'm beyond grateful for Savasana as we settle onto our

backs. With our eyes closed and our minds open, Starr speaks to us about surrender. Despite the purpose of her dharma talk, I can't help but wonder if she surrenders to Malcolm's Alpha Dom as his sub!

Just as we stand to take a dip in the ocean, here they come...

"Rats, did we miss the yoga?" Patrick jokes in his Scottish accent.

It turns out he and Callum know each other, and it surprised them to find the other with us.

Last night at the clambake, Billie teased how she and Haley are into bangers and mash. The visual of the double entendre made her blush and Callum sputter his ale.

"Of course it's over since I left you snoring almost two hours ago!" Billie replies, her Granny Smith apple green eyes sparkling in the bright sunlight.

With her wavy, medium-blonde balayage hair and pecan-colored skin, everyone says she's Tyra's doppelgänger. Billie is curvy like the megamodel, but a petite version at five feet, four inches. Patrick towers over her by eleven inches.

He scoops Billie into his arms and carries her off to the water as she giggles.

"I saw you with your pussy in the air holding the position for me to come over, grab your thighs, and fuck you until you saw stars in the daytime."

A gasp slips past my lips as my pussy clenches and my nipples pebble beneath my white bandeau bikini. I sway in Baz's sudden embrace as he presses his front into my back with his hands on my lower belly.

He makes his arousal known with his lengthening dick sandwiched between us.

"Can you back up your claim, Monsieur Steele?" I purr.

Baz chuckles, his warm breath tickles my neck. "Absolutely, Naughty Pet. Come back to our house, and I will show you."

"Bye, guys! See you later!" I tell the others.

* * *

THE NEXT FEW days are so relaxing. We do more yoga, lounge around the pool, swim in the ocean, or hang out on the entertainment level of the primary house to bowl, play in the arcade, or watch movies.

It's good to unwind with everyone since it's the first time we've all been together in a few weeks.

Baz's laughter comes easily, and he jokes with his siblings. They along with Patrick and Callum played a rowdy game of touch football on the beach.

Between drooling over the gleaming muscles, the girls and I cheered them on. My parents-in-law, Leonie's parents, Luc, and The Twins watched from the sidelines.

Patrick and Callum told them American football sucks and isn't even football since the ball stays in the players' hands more often than not. They insisted on a round of rugby—"the real man's sport."

We couldn't care less as long as the guys remained sweaty.

I giggle about it as I slip into my side-cut-out my white silk maxi dress. The soft caress of the material swirls around my body as it falls to the tips of my crystal-embellished ankle strap sandals.

"You look stunning, Mrs. Steele."

A glance over my shoulder reveals Baz in the doorway of my dressing room.

He's delectable in an untucked white linen button-down

shirt with the sleeves rolled midway up his muscular forearms and white linen pants with a pair of white leather slides. The Audemars Piguet watch I gave to him for his birthday on his wrist and his wedding band puts a smile on my face.

His sun-kissed skin makes his gray eyes even more translucent. Two-day stubble covers his cheeks and chin. With his hair combed back, his bone structure stands out. Baz is a sight to behold.

And all mine!

The corners of my mouth lift in a grin, and I twirl for him. As I stop, my hair swings over my shoulder to cascade past my hip in glossy waves. My eyes shine with love for my man.

"I love you," Baz says. "But you're missing something."

He holds up his hand and the light catches the diamonds glittering in his palm.

My diamond and platinum choker—at least that's what those unfamiliar with BDSM would think. Tonight Baz wants me to wear one of the collars he gave to me as his sub.

Okay… So he needs to prove I'm his, huh?

I blush under the intensity of his stare and bow my head. He makes my heart race uncontrollably.

"Come. Put this on and let's get to the party," Baz continues. "Later we'll make our own fireworks."

Now, my pussy throbs. We have hours before the party ends.

Damn.

Baz smirks at me knowingly and puts my collar around my neck before he takes my hand to lead me to the golf cart out front.

A quick ride along a path separate from the driveway—

that's lined with cars waiting to reach the party's valets—and we arrive at Morgan and Shelley's house.

The giant side lawn, aglow by thousands of fairy lights and lanterns, has two sumptuous pavilions, one for dinner and the other for dessert and dancing. Beyond it, on the beach, several bonfires burn. Waitstaff mill about with trays of champagne and wines or hors d'oeuvres. To one side a band plays lively music piped through speakers, also out on the sand.

Guests mingle, sipping drinks in the different areas, all dressed in the theme of the annual STEELE White Party.

It's already bustling since it's the party of the season and everyone wants a ticket for a chance to see and be seen amongst the world's elite. Not to mention raising funds for STEELE Foundation.

As soon as we're spotted, people approach to get a word with Baz or to take a photo of us for the society pages.

Automatically, I smile for the cameras and snicker inside. Oh boy…

Baz slips his arm around my side right below my braless boob so his fingers brush underneath it and hugs me close. Did anyone say, "Captain Caveman?"

Finally, we spot people we know and make our way to Billie and Patrick.

"Hey! I love your dress!" I gush to her.

She has on a strapless white-on-white dress that falls to the floor. Her apple green eyes stand out against her tanned skin and twinkle when she smiles.

"Thanks, you look fantastic, too!" Billie responds.

Patrick smiles at her. His hand on the back of her neck slides down as he strokes her possessively.

"Hi! You're finally here!"

I turn to see Leonie and Roger striding over. A giggle

escapes when Leonie when she notices my collar. I smirk, and she winks.

We chat for a few minutes, then return to mingle before the waitstaff serves dinner.

I catch sight of Haley and Lachlan talking off to the side. It appears serious, so I don't interrupt them with a greeting.

The Jacksons, who also have a compound nearby, came over for the party. Laurent, the playboy, flirts shamelessly with three female guests. Lydie who seems to be with her new boyfriend Baz mentioned laughs with some industry titans—she's a killer in the boardroom. Lucien, whose Southampton restaurant caters the event, holds court in the dining pavilion for last-minute preparations.

A quick scan of the crowd reveals Leonie's parents in conversation with Connor and Lucie while Morgan and Shelley stand next to them chatting with other guests. The couples make a powerful trio and became fast friends over the past two years.

Baz and I visit a third tent for the silent auction.

Luc offered two weeks at his family's ancestral seat. In his case, it's a magnificent chateau on one hundred acres of park-like grounds and forests once used as royal hunting grounds. Excursions for cooking and wine lessons and tours of the countryside round out the visit.

STEELE went further with a six-week-long trip around the South Pacific. Two-week stays at three five-star hotels and resorts in Fiji, Tahiti, and Hawaii make for a memorable holiday. Plus, use of a STEELE private jet and helicopter to transport the lucky couple. The imagery for the display is so vibrant and romantic, I want to put a bid on it!

The gong rings to announce dinner.

We follow the guests to the dining pavilion and take our seats. The Steele clan disperses across the room, sitting at tables with guests to make everyone feel welcome and included.

Shelley makes her speech, and the emcee keeps the party going through dinner and on to the dessert and dancing. A DJ famous for his skills on the turntables spins popular music that gets the guests on their feet.

The fireworks display from a barge offshore lights up the inky night sky with vivid sparklers, crowns, glitter, and crosettes. We cheer with each round, delighted by the glitziness.

"I have an explosive pistil with your name on it, Little Pet. Shall we?"

For the rest of the night and well into the early morning, Baz makes me oh and ah in erotic, toe-curling delight. At the rate we're going, I'll be pregnant soon!

* * *

"I CAN'T BELIEVE *Mr. Responsible* let you take The Twins and drive into the village without him."

Leonie bites her lip and raises her eyebrows at my comment.

We're heading back to our Cullinan after a couple of hours shopping on Main Street. Baz and the guys went to play golf.

When Leonie hesitates in her answer, I turn to face her.

"Wait a minute. Do you mean to tell me you did not let Roger know?" I ask incredulously, stopping in the middle of the sidewalk.

She shrugs and presses the key fob to unlock the doors.

"Leonie! He's going to be so pissed off with you!" I say as I buckle Rodolphe in his car seat. "And do not give me that *Bof* shrug!"

Leonie laughs and responds, "Don't worry! We'll return before them. So stop yammering and get in the car already. I took advantage of his absence to prove I can handle driving us around—alone."

I shake my head and step up to the passenger seat.

Along the way, we chat about our final dinner tonight before we leave in the morning. We spent an extra week after Labor Day because it was just so nice to hang out.

"It's amazing how time flies! I cannot believe The Twins will be one year old in a couple of weeks—"

WHAM!

The SUV veers off the road and crashes head-on into a tree. Leonie and I jerk forward as the front end smashes, then bounce back when the airbags deploy. The Twins' cries fill the car along with my pained moans.

My ears ring as my head pounds from my forehead being slammed by the airbag. I try to turn to see Leonie, but can't see, blinded partially by the airbag dust and blood dripping in my eyes.

Relief sweeps through me when the back doors open. Thank God, someone helps us.

"Is everyone okay?" I ask. Still unable to move with my legs trapped by the front of the SUV, I shift my gaze sideways.

The chilling tendrils of horror close in when two masked faces stare at me and without a sound take Rodolphe and Gaspard from their car seats.

"Nooooooon," Leonie yells, now frantic and forcing her body to move. *"Ne prends pas mes bébés!!!"*

Unable to think in English, she screams at them to not take her babies.

I hear a cry and scuffling.

In her haste and limited eyesight, Leonie misgauges the

height and falls out of the SUV. I hear her leap to her feet to run after the kidnappers. Screaming, she pounds after them, fueled by the cries of The Twins.

As if in a dream, the kidnappers peel away. Their tires kick up gravel from the side of the road.

I hear Leonie screaming in sheer heart-wrenching agony. Tears stream down my cheeks and my screams join hers.

SEBASTIAN

"What the fuck's going on?"

I demand down the mobile line when I see Roger drop his club and race after Harris. He's already running to their golf cart. Luc and Callum close in on them, the sound going in and out as I run, too.

Behind me, Malcolm and Patrick shout questions.

"Harris! What the fuck is going on?!" Roger yells as he jumps into their cart.

Without taking his eyes from the path, he shakes his head and says, "Your Cullinan crashed."

The world tilts.

Lola!

Frantically, Roger ends my call, and I dial her mobile. No answer. I dial my father.

"Where are Lola, Leonie, and The Twins?" I yell.

He sucks in a shocked breath, then responds, "Dammit! They went into the village. What's happened?"

I fill him in, then my other line rings. It's Luc.

I start yelling over the line, demanding to know where the app places them.

"Where?" I hear Roger ask Harris.

He tells him it's the road from Main Street toward our compound. His app alerted him to the crash along with the STEELE Cyber Security emergency team. First responders are en route to the scene.

"The scene." My nightmare. Bile rises in my throat as my stomach clenches. I pray they're not injured. Especially since Lola's parents died in a car accident. I nearly puke on the spot. I have to pull on my control to keep ahold of my emotions to allow my brain to function like a leader.

When we get to the country club's parking lot, we abandon the cart and race to the Suburban just as Roger, Luc, and Callum jump from their cart. All of them are on their mobiles.

I go for the driver's door, but Malcolm stops me.

"You're too keyed up, bro," he starts, then continues when I interrupt. "I got this, get in."

By the time we get to the car crash, the police cordoned off the area. Fire engines and ambulances line the road. Cars backed up prevent us from getting any closer.

We leave the SUV and rush to the yellow caution tape.

An officer stops us, but Roger and I yell it involves our wives and Roger's sons. When he reaches for his radio and doesn't lift the tape to give us access, I duck under and run to the first ambulance.

My stomach clenches again when I catch sight of the Cullinan's crushed hood. The force of the impact decimated it.

FUCK!

We step up on the back of the ambulance and see Lola on a stretcher.

Her eyes widen when she sees me. Mine widen when I see the bloody gash on her forehead.

"Leonie? The Twins?" Roger asks.

Lola bursts into tears, and Roger's knees buckle.

I pull him out of the way and climb on board. I don't have time to help him. I have to see to my wife first.

"Lola, baby, what happened?" I ask urgently as I kneel beside her.

"Sir, please give me room. I have to attend to her wound now," a paramedic says as he nudges me.

I swivel my head and give him a death stare.

He doesn't back down and points to Lola's head.

"She can have a concussion, spinal injury, and we don't need the wound to get infected. Kindly step aside," he states.

Lola touches my arm, and I glance back at her. She shakes her head, then winces. The collar around her neck, unlike mine, is there to limit damage to her spine.

I move to allow the paramedic to work.

"The Twins… they kidnapped them!" Lola wails as fresh tears fall from her red eyes.

My heart stops.

The world falls off its axis.

Adrenaline pumps through me, and I race out of the ambulance, screaming Harris' name. He has the app on his phone and can tell us where The Twins are right now.

"Where are they?" I ask when he runs towards me.

He shows me, then we race to Roger where an officer has him on the side of the ambulance.

"We know where they are!!" Harris and I yell simultaneously.

Officers come running, and Harris shows them another of his apps.

Two dots blink green on a map with heat signatures of

four other individuals in various locations. The coordinates place The Twins near to where we stand. The street view shows a secluded house on a private lane.

Just then Roger's mobile rings with a call from our father.

"A person contacted me with a ransom demand of $10 million," he says without preamble. "Each."

"We've got The Twins via their trackers, and—"

"Quelle? Veux-tu dire??"

Leonie stands behind the officers with Lola. They clutch each other. At that moment, I notice the bruising on Leonie's face, too.

Roger strides over to her and pulls her into my arms as I embrace Lola.

Leonie peers up at him and asks again, what does he mean.

Tightly holding her, he explains, so only we can hear that every member of our family has a tracker in case we get lost or kidnapped. She questions why he didn't tell her about The Twins having them, and he tells her it slipped my mind.

Then Leonie and Lola frown and ask if they have one, too. We nod and tell them we'll explain after we get them home. Leonie whispers it's all her fault.

Roger tells her not to think such nonsense. Then kisses her head and nods to the paramedic to take her back inside the ambulance.

I kiss Lola and tell her to stay with Leonie and the officers. She clings to me, and I hug her once more before I move to my brothers.

Meanwhile, the officers plan an extraction and send a unit to the compound to monitor the communications from the kidnappers.

Roger, Harris, and I insist upon accompanying the extraction team.

The officers see we won't let them deny us, so they give in on the condition we remain in the patrol car. No one knows whether the kidnappers have weapons.

We agree.

Luc promises to take care of Leonie and Lola. Since he's known them longer than Roger and I combined, we trust he won't allow any harm to come to them.

Malcolm drives them and Callum back to the compound.

"More people arrived at the house!" Harris exclaims as he monitors his app's feed. "What the fuck?! Haley is there now!!"

Roger and I swing our gazes to the front seat where Harris sits beside the sheriff.

"Whaaat?!?!" We yell at the same time.

Then we tell the sheriff to drive faster.

Shortly thereafter, we arrive at the house. According to the app, The Twins still blink green in the same room with a heat signature next to them. However, ten heat signatures surround three others in another room while four appear in a third one beside The Twins.

The STEELE's security team lead for our compound flags us down.

"Mr. Steele," he says to Roger. "We have the situation under control. Ms. Steele alerted us to the kidnapping, and we used the tracking app to locate your sons. They're with the team medic. The kidnappers are being held by other members of the team. Come with me, sirs."

Just as he said, we see our team with three men who sit handcuffed in the middle of the floor. One is jabbering on about not being a part of the kidnapping. His voice gives me pause. It's Antonio Velasquez, the guy from Leonie's school.

What. The. Fuck!

If Delia Shaw, the woman who fucked with Roger is behind this, I'm going to finish the psycho bitch once and for all!

Raised voices draw my attention from the asshole Antonio.

Roger, our security lead, and I rush into the next room. Two of our team members stand aside, but at the ready. Delia runs screaming like a banshee with her arms outstretched and long nails ready to claw at Haley.

Surprisingly, Haley stands her ground in a defensive posture. No one is prepared for what happens next.

"You BITCH!"

WHAM!

"You fucked with my brother."

WHAM! WHAM!

"You tried to steal my nephews!"

WHAM! WHAM! WHAM!

"Stay. The. Fuck. Away. From. My. FAMILY!!!"

Haley whales on Delia.

"I've got your number, bitch, and it's all legit. You're going away for the rest of your miserable fucking life," Haley ends in a deadly tone made more terrifying after her shouts and thrashing.

Delia—whose face already shows signs of swelling—stares with one open eye up at Haley. Delia's busted lip trembles as she mumbles how sorry she is for all she's done.

Haley refuses to give in and tells her it's too fucking late.

The officers rush in, and we explain what happened. They proceed to arrest Delia, who starts crying assault.

When they ignore her and read the Miranda warning, she doesn't have the sense to shut the fuck up.

Instead, she slings more baseless claims against me and curses while they take her away.

Bye, bitch!

"Mr. Steele, your sons are safe and sound."

Roger turns to face the door and sees the security medic as noted by the word on the front of his uniform's bulletproof vest. He and another team member hold Rodolphe and Gaspard, who wear black adult-size t-shirts.

When they see him, they call out Dada and reach their arms out.

Tears fill my eyes, and my breath escapes me at the sight of their reddened faces puffy from crying. Two strides and they're in his arms. He squeezes them so tightly to his chest they squirm and cry some more.

Never in my life have I been so terrified. All sorts of crazy thoughts ran through my head. Nightmarish and ghastly things are done to children, and I would end anyone who would harm what's mine.

I know for a fact I would be beside myself if something happened to a child of mine.

Harris, Haley, and I enfold our arms around Roger and hug The Twins and him. We're a tight-knit clan, and I feel the love flowing from us to them. Even The Twins calm, hiccups replace their sorrowful sobs.

We take a moment to absorb the intensity of the situation.

Then I squeeze them and look at each of their faces. Mine, like theirs, streaked with tears. But the steely glint in my eyes shows I'm back to business. As the eldest sibling, I always take on the responsibility of my brothers and sister —no matter their ages.

"Let us go. Haley, call Leonie. Harris, you get Dad on the line. He needs to prep for our arrival"—I turn to the security lead—"I want a full briefing with the team, the police, and the FBI. We will meet in my father's office in an hour."

Big brother, CEO, Alpha Dom, all in one take charge.

When we reach the compound's perimeter fence, armed security members stand spaced in intervals along its full length. At the front gates, two of their armored Suburbans block the entry and dozens more armed members stand around them. We are on full lockdown.

"ROGEEERRR!!!"

Leonie roars as she runs out of the house.

She throws her arms wide, pulling The Twins and him into her embrace. She trembles as sobs rack her body. He murmurs words of love and lets her know they're fine to soothe her anguish.

Josy and Guy join them, and they hug in a unit as he did with his siblings. The pile on continues when they make room for our mother and father.

He notices the others hovering, not wanting to interrupt. So he gives them a nod and suggests we move inside.

We settle in the living room where Leonie and Roger hold The Twins on our laps. She checks them over one at a time, rubbing her hands over their bodies and holding their faces to look into their eyes. He tells her they're fine since the medic did an examination, and he assessed them on the ride over.

But *Maman Lionne* ignores him.

The silence broken by Malcolm.

"That bitch is going to pay," *The Enforcer* declares. "No way will she get away with this shit. I want answers now!"

Everyone shares his sentiment, and we decide to have the briefing here instead of in the office for more space.

Before they arrive, Leonie and Roger take The Twins upstairs to bathe and redress them. The forensics team took their clothes for evidence, thus the t-shirts.

Lola's who's been sitting on my lap quietly turns to me and whispers, "I can't believe this happened. I was so scared, Baz... What would happen if we had a baby and I… I…"

Her words cut off on a choked sob. Lola buries her face in my neck as her body trembles with emotion.

I can only imagine her fright. Instantly I remember her concerns about having a baby and one of us dying to leave the child alone, as happened with her and her parents. My heart breaks.

"Lola… Babe, look at me," I say when her sobs worsen. "Oh baby, listen to me. It's all right now. The Twins, Leonie, you are all safe and sound. Come, let's go home."

I stand with Lola wrapped around me like a monkey clinging to a tree. As I rub her back, I glance at my father and he nods, understanding without uttering a word. My mother also nods and smiles encouragingly.

"We'll let you know if something comes up, son. Go take care of your wife. You've been through a hell of a time," Morgan says gruffly, the Alpha Dom Steele Patriarch as always.

Lola whimpers, and I squeeze her in my comforting embrace. I have more than enough strength for both of us. I vow to watch over her and our children with my life.

* * *

"BAZ, I NEED YOU… PLEASE."

I wake up two days later to Lola stroking my cock, and her desire whispered in my ear.

Her full D-cup tits press against my back, the points of

her peaked nipples jutting into me. Sleep falls away, followed by memories that come back in a flash.

Lola's soft cries as she relived the nightmare of the crash coupled with the pain from the loss of her parents filled the last two nights. During the day, she stayed huddled under a throw sitting on the deck staring out into the distance of the Atlantic Ocean, lost in thought.

Starr came by each morning to do breathwork and meditation with Lola. It helped her to clear her mind, but she remained quiet. Starr assured me Lola just needed some time and not to worry.

I smiled, thinking how lucky Malcolm is to have a woman like Starr in his life. It's time he settled down, too. I chuckled as Starr left the house with Malcolm, and he helped her into the golf cart before they returned to his house.

And she was right, judging by Lola's persistent caresses of my now fully engorged cock.

"Baz, wake up," Lola says louder as my cock jerks in her hand.

On a groan, I roll and plank over her body as I stare into her hooded hazel eyes. They widen with urgency when I hesitate.

Lola reaches up and slips her hands into my hair to tug me down on top of her. She widens her thighs to give me more space to settle against her mound. Lifting her hips, she slides her wet pussy lips along the length of my dick and moans.

"Now… Baz…" she demands.

"Little Pet, who is in control?" I growl in her ear as I lift away from her pussy. "You or me?"

Lola moans incoherently and bows her back.

"Words, Little Pet. I will have your words," I growl, staring down at her.

She licks her lips then pulls a corner into her mouth with her teeth before she nods, "You, Sir. Only you, Sir."

I reward her with a brutal thrust as I lift her thigh onto my forearm and grip the base of my cock. The angle and depth make Lola throw her head back and keen. Her nails dig into shoulders as she clings to me.

Lola needs it rough to take away the pain, just as spankings relieve the tension in her body.

Without hesitation, I give my baby exactly what she needs and more. My hips snap forward and backward as I drive deep within her tight core, not easing up on the demanding rhythm. I rock in and out of her body, entranced by her gasps and the squelching of her abundant juices.

Her pussy muscles clamp on my cock, and it twitches inside of her core. She can feel every ridge, every vein, and every one of my ten inches as I drill her into the mattress repeatedly.

Lola cries out from her climax, but urges me on by throwing her other leg over my shoulder and tilting her pelvis up to meet each of my pistoning strokes.

"More, Sir, please!" She begs through clenched teeth.

I ramp up my pace and latch onto her pebbled nipple with my teeth, then suckle strongly.

Lola squeals and thrashes beneath me. Her eyes roll to the back of her head and close in pleasure.

"Open your eyes and look at me fucking you, Little Pet," I command as a watch her gaze drop to the space between our sweaty bodies.

My thick dick plunges in and out from my tip to my root

as her greedy pussy grips it. The sight spurs both of us on and we buck as Lola cums again with a throaty moan.

"Oh... Oh... Oh... Oh..." she pants with each well-placed thrust of my throbbing cock.

"This pussy is mine, Little Pet. Mine to fill with my seed. Mine to put my baby inside of you. Do you want that? Do you want me to put my baby inside of your womb, Little Pet," I growl like the feral beast I've become as I fuck my mate raw.

Lola squeezes my dick so hard I howl.

"Yeeessss... Sir!" She screams from my dominant possession as another orgasm rips through her pulsating pussy.

"Then take it. Take... every... fucking... drop!" I roar as my cock jerks and my seed coats her womb.

Lola writhes beneath me as I wring one last orgasm from her wrecked pussy.

I collapse on top of her, spent from my mind-blowing release, and she wraps her arms and legs around my shuddering body.

"Thank you, Baz. I needed your passionate dominance, my love," Lola says in a voice filled with sated desire.

On a groan, I roll us over and bury my face in her damp hair. My lips brush her ear, and she trembles.

"Feel better?" I ask.

"Mmm mmm good," she purrs and squeezes my cock still buried within her folds.

It thumps, and I grind up into her as I circle my hips.

"Excellent because we are just getting started, Little Pet," I growl.

SEBASTIAN

"*Sebastian, I need you to come to my doctor's office. Now. The address is—"*

As I race up the steps of the elegant townhouse off Fifth Avenue on Sixty-fourth Street, I can't hold back my panic.

Over the last few weeks Lola's suffered from nausea, extra tender tits and nipples, food repulsion, and tiredness. She refused to admit she may be pregnant and wouldn't take an at-home test despite the six packs of two I brought home. She blamed her symptoms on coming off of the birth control injections.

When I asked her about her period not coming, she claimed it was never regular before the injections. I tried to cajole her into at least seeing the doctor in case she had a stomach virus or the flu. But no…

Now she's at the doctor and asking me to come. I don't even know what type of doctor he is, general practician or gynecologist.

God forbid it's bad news. I'll lose my damn mind.

Edgar weaves my Mercedes-Maybach S 650 Sedan

through the congestion of New York City midday traffic like a pro. The doctor's office is only seven blocks north of The STEELE Tower, but it takes longer to drive than if I had just jogged over.

Visions of Lola's belly round with my baby, then of her holding my child appear before my eyes. As much sex as we've had since she woke me with a blow job on her return from Paris, she should be pregnant with a brood!

I chuckle to myself at the thought.

The other morning I caught Lola in front of the full-length mirror in her dressing room, staring at her profile with her hand on her belly. I started to enter, but hesitated when she sighed and rubbed her eyes. From the distance, I could see her hazel orbs glistened with unshed tears.

Not wanting to intrude on her private moment, I backed away.

I guess part of her hesitancy in finding out the truth is her fear. I do know Lola wants a baby as much as I do. She's been pretty damn gung ho with our efforts, often starting the sex and not stopping until we're both too sore to move.

It dawns on me to Google the doctor to find out his specialty. Just as the results populate, Edgar opens my door. So absorbed in my thoughts, I didn't notice we arrived at the address Lola gave to me.

Since I'm a second from seeing with my own eyes, I put my mobile away and hop out. In my haste, I take the steps three at a time and burst through the front door. A second door leads to the foyer where a receptionist sits behind an ornate wooden desk.

"Hello, may I help you?" She asks as her gaze travels from my face down my body back up to my eyes.

I shake my head at the reaction women have when they see me—or my brothers for that matter, The STEELE

Quaternity of multibillion-dollar bachelors, now only two single ones.

I ignore her lust-filled expression and reply, "Yes, my wife Mrs. Sebastian Steele is with Dr. Rice. Kindly take me to her."

The receptionist's shoulders droop at the mention of my wife, but she rises and gestures for me to follow her.

I don't bother to shake my head; I just ignore the exaggerated sway of her curvy hips as she sashays ahead of me. I avert my eyes and notice the walls display multiple photos of newborn babies.

Well, that answers my question: Dr. Rice is an OB-GYN and Lola is here. Ding, ding, ding! We have a winner, folks!

YES!

I feel like Lola and want to break out in a happy shimmy dance, except the receptionist might think I'm a nutcase. So I do a discreet victorious fist pump behind her back.

"Right this way, Mr. Steele," she says as she points to a closed door and steps aside.

"Thank you," I nod and knock on the door, then walk in after the doctor calls out to enter.

Immediately, my eyes seek Lola. She's sitting on the examination table in a gown. The shocked expression on her face makes my heart flutter with hope of a positive outcome. I hasten to her side and take her hand.

"Are you all right?" I ask, brushing my thumb over her knuckles. Her hand is icy, so I rub both of them between mine to give her some warmth.

My eyes dart to the doctor for answers.

"Mrs. Steele is perfectly fine, Mr. Steele. Or shall I call you Papa?" Dr. Rice smiles, the corners of his brown eyes crinkling.

Despite having an inkling of the situation, my mind blanks, and I freeze.

Lola squeezes my hands when I fail to respond.

"Baz?" She asks hesitantly. "Did you hear Dr. Rice? Are you okay?"

Slowly the cogs churn again, and I come back online.

"WHOOHOO!!!!!" I shout as I fist pump both hands in the air above my head and gyrate my hips in my version of a happy shimmy dance. "Call me Big Poppa, baby!!!"

Lola and the doctor laugh uproariously as I strut around the room handing out imaginary cigars to imaginary people.

Once I make my way back to my glowing wife, I swoop her off the table and swing her high. Then hold her close against the length of my body as I kiss her until her toes curl.

We don't realize Dr. Rice rose from his stool until we hear a soft click of the door.

"How do you feel, Sexy Mama?" I ask Lola as I sit on the visitor's chair with her snuggled in my lap. "How is my baby?"

I rub her belly and kiss her hair. My heart soars.

"We're good, Big Poppa," Lola laughs. "I was so nervous, though. I really didn't want to know, but I didn't want to do anything to harm our baby just in case I was pregnant. Holy cow, can you believe it? I didn't expect it to happen so—"

I cut off Lola's nervous rambling with another breathtaking kiss.

Her fingers dive into my hair and tug on my scalp as we devour one another. Soft moans slip from her mouth into mine. Lola's round ass squirms against my cock, and it begins to lengthen and thicken in response to her gyrations.

"Fuck, Naughty Pet, if you do not stop, I will take you

right here, right now," I chastise her with a smack to the top curve of her ass.

Lola hums in delight and attempts to move again.

"Not now, I want to talk to Dr. Rice," I tell her and carry Lola to the examination table. "I'll get him now. Behave!"

I chuckle when Lola pouts. Roger told me how horny Leonie was all throughout their pregnancy. I should have known Lola was preggie from her increased carnal appetite.

Dr. Rice was waiting outside of the room and returns to show us our baby on the ultrasound.

"You see, from the imaging, all looks good. Based on the timing of Lola's last birth control injection, lack of her monthly menses, and her levels, I place Lola at twelve weeks," he says. "At eighteen weeks, we'll perform another scan to detect your baby's gender, if you wish to know in advance."

"Absolutely!"

"Yes!"

Lola and I exclaim at the same time, then laugh.

Dr. Rice smiles and tells us to meet him in his office to discuss care, plans for birth, and a pediatrician. Before we leave, we'll schedule each of Lola's appointments for follow-up visits.

"Lola, you're so beautiful. The glow you have is even more resplendent now that Dr. Rice confirmed your pregnancy. I love you, sweetheart," I say as I watch her dress.

She bows her head, and I hear her sniffle.

Right away, I rush over to her and pull Lola close as I bend my knees to press my forehead to hers. The golden flecks in her hazel eyes shine as her tears spill down her rosy cheeks.

I kiss each one and murmur words of love.

We hold one another for a few moments, then I step

back and put her stilettos on her feet. My fingers caress her calves, the backs of her legs, her hips, and across her lower belly as I rise to tower over her. Lola moans softly and wraps her arms around my neck.

"When we get home, I will show you just how much I thank you for giving me the gift of a child, Mrs. Steele," I say huskily.

Lola's eyes flare with lust, and she rises to her toes for one more sultry kiss.

Lola

"Congratulations! You're pregnant, Mrs. Steele."

Dr. Oscar Rice has been my gynecologist since I moved to New York permanently. I chose him based on friends' recommendations and since he's an obstetrician, too. I knew eventually Baz and I would have children, so I didn't want to have to change doctors.

It scared me to death something was wrong when I was sick every morning and had a major headache. Instead of addressing the issues, I put my head in the sand… The possibility of me being pregnant wasn't my first thought. I figured I experienced side effects from having the birth control injections for so many years.

In a roundabout way, I asked Leonie questions about the early stages of her pregnancy with The Twins. Being the BFF she's always been to me, Leonie didn't make any judgments or ask me any specifics. She did urge me to see the doctor to rule out any sickness.

So this morning, I gave in and scheduled an appointment. Luckily, Dr. Rice had an opening. When he told me those words, I became dizzy and had to lie down on the exam table to let the wave pass.

He assured me all was well, and dizziness was another symptom.

I knew I had to call Baz and have him come right away. I didn't want to face it alone. And he'd want to be here.

My heart swelled with happiness when he reacted the way he did. Even though my heart stopped when he didn't respond at first. Whew!

Baz is so cute. He put each of my appointments in his calendar before we left the doctor's office. He insisted I get the same date and time as the first patient of the day. *"Bright and early, so Dr. Rice is sharp."*

The administrative assistants and receptionist were in awe of him, so whatever he wanted he got…

It didn't bother me in the least. Baz is mine and now that I'm carrying his baby, it sealed our deal!

I giggle remembering how our relationship started with a deal, his proposal was a deal, and now our first baby is the consummation of our deal.

"What's so funny, babe?" Baz asks as he kisses my knuckles.

We're on our way home, and I cannot wait to jump his bones. I squeeze my thighs together to ease some ache. Damn, pregnancy makes me horny AF.

"Oh, I see, Naughty Pet has an ache that her Dom needs to take care of for her. Is that correct, Naughty Pet?" He asks with his gray eyes shining like molten platinum.

I whimper in response and peek at him from beneath my eyelashes. Ever the sexual submissive.

"Yes, Sir," I reply.

Baz chuckles darkly, and his eyes spark with carnal lust.

I glance out the window and smile when I see The STEELE Tower across Fifty-seventh Street.

YES!

Baz and I nearly race through the lobby, so eager to get butt naked and fuck as Ice-T raps. Once in the hallway of our duplex's second floor, we strip the clothes off of each other.

I barely have him free of his jacket before Baz slams me against the wall and thrusts his ginormous dick in my throbbing slick pussy. Guttural groans fall from our mouths upon penetration.

Thankfully Baz takes Dr. Rice's assurance we can have as much sex-wild and gentle-as we want, barring any discomfort on my part.

None whatsoever, I think as Baz jackhammers deep inside my welcoming pussy. His tip hits my G-spot, then his length strokes it as he pistons inside of me. His girth stretches me to the point of pleasurable pain.

"Uh… Uh… Uh… Nnh…" I gasp with each feral plunge.

Baz growls and grunts indecipherable words as he takes us higher and higher to the pinnacle of erotic ecstasy.

I squeeze my eyes shut and dig my heels into his firm ass when a powerful orgasm takes hold of me. I feel it from my lower belly to my pulsating pussy to my sensitive clit, all the way to my curled toes. A bolt of lightning zings through every cell of my body to set me ablaze.

"Oooooooo!" I cry out as I explode.

My body convulses from the waves of pleasure.

"MINE! MINE! MINE!" Baz roars as he rises on the balls of his feet and lifts my leg to his shoulder, driving deeper inside of my spasming pussy.

Even as his dick unleashes a torrent of cum inside of me, Baz continues to pummel my pussy. He grinds his pelvis into mine, leaving not a millimeter of space between us. His body quakes from his release. Then his knees buckle, and we slide down the wall to settle on the floor, where he pulls me into his lap as his big dick pops out of my well-fucked core.

"Did I thank you sufficiently, Little Pet?" Baz pants.

"Yes, Sir, more than I could ever desire," I sigh as I nuzzle against his heaving damp chest contentedly.

He chuckles and kisses the top of my head. His warm breath tickles my scalp as he trails his lips along my hair.

"Excellent," he murmurs.

"When should we tell everyone?"

After we returned to our right minds, Baz carried me to our bathroom and filled the massive marble tub with warm water and fragrant oils for us to soak our sore muscles.

Leaning my back against his chest, I consider his question. We're meeting everyone in Capri for Thanksgiving in a couple of weeks, then Verbier for Christmas. I'm torn between the two occasions. I'd rather wait and give us more time to make sure everything is fine with the baby.

I voice my concerns to Baz, and he agrees with his usual "Whatever Lola Wants" response. He's beyond happy and will give me the world if I ask for it.

We decide to tell everyone at Christmas and make the announcement one of our presents. Shelley and Morgan will be so excited. I remember the many times she hinted or outright asked when Baz and I will have a baby like Roger and Leonie.

I can't blame her. She had five children and loves to have kids around. Even after over two years of being married to Baz, the size of his family and extended family with the Jacksons and close friends awes me coming from a family of only three.

But I love it and can now contribute to the Steele ranks with a baby of our own!

I turn around to face Baz and place my palms on his cheeks.

"Thank you, my love, for giving me a loving family and now a baby of our own," I say.

Tears sparkle in his gray eyes, and he kisses me silly once again.

LOLA

"Lola honey, are you all right? You look a bit peaked."

Baz and I ride in the Sikorsky with Morgan, Shelley, Malcolm, Starr, Harris, and Haley en route to Roger and Leonie's Villa dei Fiori in Capri for Thanksgiving.

We flew to Naples on the Gulfstream G650 an hour ago. The move from one aircraft to the other doesn't sit well with my queasy stomach. I drank ginger tea with lemon on the private jet to settle my nausea, but didn't have time for a cuppa on the helicopter.

Ugh…

I smile wanly at Shelley, but can't risk opening my mouth to vocalize an answer. Fortunately, Baz chimes in.

"Yes, Lola had a touch of food poisoning last night from the Thai takeout we ate for dinner"—he rubs my hand and continues—"She'll settle down once we get situated at the villa."

Shelley eyes me for a moment, and Haley and Starr watch on in silent observation.

I smile and use Baz's tactic: don't avoid, admit a partial truth.

"Yes, ignore me," I say with a grimace dramatically.

They nod, and I turn to glance out of the window. How the hell much longer until we land??

Moments later, the Sikorsky touches down on the helipad at the rear of the villa. Leonie and Roger stand holding The Twins, waving at us.

Morgan and Shelley alight from the back of the helicopter first, followed by Baz and me. Malcolm and Starr, then Harris and Haley disembark next. We wave and troop over.

"Hey, Little Pumpkins! Did you miss your favorite auntie?" I ask as Baz scoops Gaspard out of Roger's arms.

"And your very favorite uncle?" He adds giving Malcolm and Harris the side eye with a grin.

We make our way around to the terrace where Guy and Josy sit. They flew in this morning. Everyone exchanges greetings before Leonie and Roger show us to our sumptuous bedroom suites.

Villa dei Fiori has fast become one of their most cherished homes. It's where they had their babymoon when Leonie was nineteen weeks pregnant and they'd been back together for nine months. She fell in love with Lucien's former home the moment she set eyes on it. So, of course, Roger bought it for her.

The salmon-colored stucco exterior with white trim around the windows, columns, and roof lines blend beautifully with the lush greenery and stunning sea views from all sides. The sea-edge gardens, bountiful with camellias, magnolias, and palm trees prove as captivating as the impressive views of Mount Vesuvius, the Peninsula of Sorrento, the entire Gulf of Naples, and Anacapri. Its private swimming pool set in the side garden's grass and its exclusive sea access with a second plunge pool below makes it a unique property.

Baz and I, the siblings, and Guy and Josy take advantage and stay on different occasions. Since Morgan and Shelley have Villa Sogno across the Tyrrhenian Sea in Positano, this is their first visit.

"Oh! This is a stunning villa! I love the gardens with all the fragrant flowers," Shelley gushes as we walk to their suite first. "I'm surprised Lucien gave it up."

Roger chuckles and responds, "He drove a hard bargain. But it was worth it to see the smile on Leonie's face when I gave it to her."

Morgan nods, then adds, "I know the feeling, son. Nothing is better than your wife's happiness. Remember my words well."

As we pass through the villa, Roger points out the rooms for a mini tour. The antique furnishings, Murano glass fixtures, and unobstructed views charm everyone.

However, Morgan and Shelley are even more pleased with their enormous corner suite and balcony overlooking the sea. The cobalt blue, champagne, and gold color scheme with crystal chandeliers and wall sconces, silk fabrics, plus a bathroom in floor-to-ceiling travertine slabs make for a lavish set of rooms.

"Very nice indeed," Morgan says as he takes in the suite.

Baz and I head to our plush suite. I can't take another moment without giving in to the need to throw up. Yuck!

We make it just in time. Baz kneels beside me to hold my hair out of my face and rubs circles on my back to soothe me. I groan and sit beside the toilet.

He goes to the sink and brings back a glass of cool water.

I take some sips and close my eyes as I rest it against the

marble wall. My stomach rumbles, but doesn't explode again. I open one eye to peer at Baz.

His expression is one of concern and guilt.

"Help a preggie lady up, would you?" I smile, not wanting him to feel bad. It's not his fault. Blasted hormones!

Baz lifts me to my feet and helps me to the sink where I brush my teeth. He leans his sexy butt on the edge of the vanity with his muscular arms folded over his broad chest and watches over me.

"Do you want to join the others for lunch or stay here and rest? Either way, I'm with you," he says.

I shake my head and respond, "No, no. Let's go down. Some toast and tea will do me wonders."

On our way back outside for an alfresco lunch in the seaside garden, Harris catches up with us.

"How're you feeling, Sis?" He asks, concern etched on his handsome face.

"I'll feel much better once I get something in my stomach. Thanks for asking," I respond with a smile as I loop my arm through his.

We find Leonie, Roger, The Twins, Malcolm, Starr, and Haley seated on blankets in the grass near the lunch table. As we reach them, Leonie bursts out laughing, then starts to snort uncontrollably.

"What's so funny?"

They glance up to find us behind them.

"Oh, just the rigors and demands of travel," Starr deadpans.

Malcolm sits back on his hands, all smug with a cocky grin on his face. The Alpha Dom took his carnal tastes to the skies for fifteen hours.

Sebastian snickers and I snort.

"No comment…" Haley says, rolling her eyes, disgusted

as usual with hearing about her brothers' sex lives, even as innuendos.

She glances down at her mobile and smiles. Then types a response at lightning speed. When she raises her head, her cheeks flush and her eyes shine. No longer wearing her glasses makes the dove gray orbs more expressive. Happy Haley, hmmm interesting.

"What's up, Baby Girl?" Roger asks, knowing the nick-name drives her crazy.

Still in la-la land, Haley startles, then responds rushed, "Oh, uh... Callum's over in Sorrento."

When she doesn't continue, Roger prods her. He wants to take Haley to dinner. So Roger tells her he can come here if they want. He's more than welcome. They agree, and Roger arranges for the helicopter to pick him up in an hour.

As it turns out, her brothers think Callum could be an excellent match for their little sister. He proved himself during Labor Day weekend as a guy who's worthy of Haley, has his own fortune, and blends well with the Steele clan. The girls and I love he's a Scottish duke, but the guys couldn't care less. Baz hired his guy to conduct an extensive background check on Callum as soon as they met him while we were in Verbier for Christmas last year. Nothing in it caused concern.

Haley being with Callum and not with Lachlan sits better with Sebastian and with the rest of the guys. Baz can't get past his best friend with his younger sister. Baz had been suspicious since we were at Villa Sogno when he proposed to me. Then at our Labor Day party, he argued with Lach after he saw him in an intense conversation with Haley. It has strained things with the friends since.

Leonie's parents and my in-laws appear. We gather around the table for a delicious lunch of flavorful local dishes prepared by the chef and served by the staff with wines from the villa's prized cellar.

The chef prepared a simple meal for me with toast, meats, and ginger tea with lemon. My stomach calms, and Baz rubs my thigh under the table.

Fortunately, no one comments on my requests. Leonie just peeps at me, then smiles to herself.

Shortly after we finish eating, Callum touches down. Haley goes to greet him, and some time later they join us for Limoncello Gin Collins on the lawn furniture. Her lips appear swollen, and his eyes gleam.

Mmhmmm.

"How are things with you, Callum?" Morgan asks as he sips his digestif. "I read in the *Financial Times* renewable energy is on the rise for another year in a row for Scotland."

They get into a discussion on Callum's family's business, Graham Energy, Oil & Gas Company, based in Aberdeen, Scotland. His father still leads the company as CEO, but he's in the process of grooming Callum for the role in five years. His younger brother and sister hold positions, too.

The conversation flows easily with everyone's participation.

The siblings grew up discussing business to prepare for joining their family's legacy while I worked hard from a teenager to grow Lola's Coterie. All of us volunteer in some way to help others, so we're a well-rounded group. All of our perspectives add to the conversation.

As we continue to chat, Baz reaches over and pulls me onto his lap. Content to relax in his arms, I snuggle against him and drift off, exhausted from the travel.

* * *

"LET'S BEGIN WITH SOME BREATHWORK."

Each morning Starr starts our day with yoga in the sunroom facing the sea. Aside from the girls, the guys join us. Starr's influence runs deep.

I admitted my pregnancy to her so I did nothing to harm my baby. Since Starr taught Leonie during her pregnancy via Skype and served as her doula, I asked her to do the same for me.

After Starr suggested we meet for morning yoga on our first night here, I pulled her aside to let her know. She was so excited for me, but kept it hush-hush.

I haven't even told my BFF yet. So I don't want anyone else to find out before Leonie.

Baz thought it was a good idea to let Starr know, especially since she's been my yoga teacher all these years and would know prenatal modifications. He agreed she'd be perfect as my doula, too.

So far, I've avoided showing my baby bump. Instead of a bikini, I opted for cut-out maillots and flowy dresses. Even when we do our yoga sessions, I wear a tank top with loose-fitting pants. My petite frame carries my pregnancy well.

Baz of course noticed—and relishes—my bigger boobs.

Even though we welcomed the guys to yoga, we're kicking them out so we can have some much needed Girls' Time. We have a lot to catch up on and only two days left before we go our separate ways until Christmas.

After a peaceful Savasana and light sharing namaste, we kick Baz, Roger, Malcolm, Harris, and Callum out of the sunroom.

"So, spill with Callum and Lachlan, Haley," Starr says as soon as she shuts the door behind them.

Haley turns scarlet and reaches to push her glasses up the bridge of her nose. It's her nervous tell she can't stop even after wearing contact lenses for the last couple of years.

"What do you mean?" She asks, not realizing we know she's bluffing.

We giggle at her gaffe.

"Oh, don't play the innocent, Ms. Kiss Me Until My Lips Swell Steele!" Leonie laughs.

On a breathy sigh, Haley fills us in on the last couple of months since she saw Lachlan at the Labor Day fundraiser. The drama of her love triangle with one man who's her brother's best friend and one man who's had his eye on her since Harvard Business School proves more intriguing than any telenovela I've seen!

"Well then, what about you, Ms. Comfy on Malcolm's Jet Knight?" I add to avoid the teasing coming around to me and my hormone-induced nausea.

Now it's Starr's turn to blush. Her chestnut-colored skin adds a crimson hue to her cheeks.

Haley smirks.

"Fine! He's a monster!" Starr laughs as she holds her hands two feet apart in front of her.

We fall onto our mats, snorting as Haley sings at the top of her lungs with her fingers in her ears.

Once we catch our breath, Starr fills us in on how Malcolm fills her and not just with his "monster" dick. It's obvious they're really into each other. I'm happy for my good buddy and brother-in-law.

By the time Starr finishes her tales, Shelley and Josy come in the sunroom to invite us on a shopping trip to Capri town between the Piazzetta and Via Camerelle. It's one of the most fashionable centers in the world, with high-end boutiques and jewelry stores.

Grateful for the distraction, I'm the first one to agree.

Less than an hour later, we're strolling along the streets, popping in and out of the boutiques filled with designer pieces and handcrafted items by local artisans.

Most of the people in the shops and on the streets recognize Leonie. She takes it in stride when they ask for her autograph or a selfie. Our security detail keeps any overzealous fans at bay—precautions Baz and Roger implemented after the Labor Day situation.

My shopping spree is complete when I order two pairs of bespoke Canfora Sandals, my favorite, purchase some hand-painted silk scarves, including three ties for Baz, and perfume that reminds me of the island's natural scent.

"Lola, honey, the sun did you some good. You're glowing."

I glance up into Shelley's smiling face as she loops her arm through mine. Her expression of genuine joy makes me wonder if she can tell I'm pregnant. I feel horrible not admitting it yet, but it's only a few more weeks before Christmas.

"Yes, the fresh sea air and warm sun make a tremendous difference," I grin using Baz's tactic once again. "Plus, your son makes sure I eat properly and rest."

Shelley throws her head back and laughs. Her brown eyes shine with mirth.

"I'm sure he does! My boys better treat their women well. Right, Starr and Leonie?" Shelley adds with a wink at the girls.

They giggle and nod their agreement.

Maman Josy cups Leonie's face and says, "And you treat those boys well, *non?*"

"Oui, Maman, absolument!" Leonie smiles lovingly at her mom.

I sigh and swallow back my tears as I unconsciously

place my hand on my belly. I wish my mother were here with me.

How in the world am I going to raise my baby without my mother's guidance? Who's going to give me tips for teething pains? Or just listen as I share my thoughts on motherhood?

I bite my lip to hold back a cry and glance away from Leonie and *Maman* Josy. It hurts too much, and my hormones are making me overly sensitive and emotional.

"You know Josy and I are here for you, Lola, honey. We may never replace your mother. But know we love you dearly and will help you in any way."

Shelley's kind words break the dam, and I sob.

She pulls me into her arms and rocks me gently as she hums a soothing tune.

"*Chérie*! What's the matter?!" Leonie cries as she rubs my back.

Shelley answers for me, just as her son did before. "She's fine, just a bit overwhelmed. Let's head back to your villa, shall we?"

Leonie agrees and takes my arm while Shelley holds the other. Josy, Haley, and Starr gather around us, and we make our way back to the Mercedes-Benz G-Wagens. The security detail follows, then drives us to the villa.

Determined not to upset anyone, I put a smile on my face and tell them I'm fine. Since we had lunch in town, I go to my suite and curl in the bed for a nap. Baz and the boys went boating with friends. So I have time to get myself together before Thanksgiving dinner tonight.

"THIS IS FANTASTIC! I agree we should have an opulent Edwardian-themed-*Gigi* party!"

Leonie and Roger finished giving everyone a tour of the vintage steam yacht he bought for her. She named it *Gigi* after her favorite film.

I can't wait to plan the soiree.

Leonie and I do our happy shimmy dance, then continue on to the bow where we'll have cocktails before Thanksgiving dinner begins.

The last few days have been full of swimming at our private beach or in the pool and excursions to the Blue Grotto, Monte Solaro, and Villa di Tiberio. The Blue Grotto thrilled The Twins when their laughter echoed inside of the water-filled cavern.

Leonie wanted to save *Gigi* for last as the highlight and setting for our Thanksgiving dinner as we cruise around Capri for three hours. They time it for cocktails at sunset and dinner by torchlight—electric since they don't want to risk damage to the boat.

We dress in semi-formal attire with the guys in suits and the women in dresses. The Twins wear shirt and shorts one-piece sets with socks that mimic shoes and outdo us all.

Once we're gathered at the bow with drinks in hand, Morgan leads us in expressing his thanks over the past year. Each of us takes a turn ending with Roger. It's obvious he's already emotional after Leonie's heartfelt words of gratitude for their lives together and most of all for the safety of their sons.

Coming on the end of her touching speech and tears, he holds her close in his arms and address us.

"Thanks can never express the depth of my feelings for all of you and others who are not present. Your love and support from the start of that fiasco to the joy of our wedding with the addition of my in-laws and the wonderful holidays we shared to the return of our sons mean more than you can imagine. Mom, Dad, all of our lives you raised us to be a close-knit clan. This past year proves you succeeded. I love you all beyond measure."

Roger lifts his glass and proclaims, "Now let us enjoy this Thanksgiving dinner and here's to many, many more!"

"Hear, hear!!"

"Bravo, Roger! We love you, too!!"

"Happy Thanksgiving, everyone!!"

Baz nuzzles my neck and whispers, "Happy Thanksgiving to my babies. I love you with all my heart."

SEBASTIAN

I glue my eyes to the monitor where the screen shows an alien-looking world of red clouds and swirls, much like Mars. In the center floats my baby, my son.

He's the size of a cucumber, but looks like a mini human —no martian features. His facial expression appears peaceful with closed eyes. Tiny fingers of one hand wrap around the umbilical cord while he sucks the thumb of the other.

Dr. Rice tells us our baby boy can hear our voices in utero with studies proving he can recognize us once he's born.

Yeah, I made a super baby!

"A boy for you, Mr. Steele," Lola says as she squeezes my hand and smiles at me. "Are you pleased?"

I cup her beautiful face between my palms and brush my lips over hers before I kiss her softly. With my forehead pressed to hers, I whisper words of love.

This woman carries my child, the next generation of the

Steele clan, the son of the eldest son. Lola probably doesn't comprehend the magnitude of her pregnancy.

Each first son before me laid the groundwork for the following generations to grow STEELE International, Inc. into a multibillion-dollar corporation. The subsequent generation added to our family business' success. As the head of this generation, it is my duty to continue that upward trajectory set by those before me and will be the responsibility of my son. My heir.

I take a deep calming breath to re-center myself, then kiss the tip of Lola's nose before my gaze returns to the monitor.

"I'll print some images for you," Dr. Rice offers.

"Oh, wonderful! We can show everyone when we arrive in Verbier next week," Lola says full of excitement.

My face nearly splits as I grin and respond, "Yes, the perfect present!"

* * *

"HEY, hey, hey! The gang's all here!! Merry Christmas Eve!"

Roger and Leonie laugh as Harris makes his way through the front door after Lola and me, arms laden with gifts. They tease he looks like a young Santa Claus.

He rejoins with, "A sexy AF one, no doubt! And no last-minute presents for me, Roger dear! Let's see if you get coal in your stocking this year…"

Malcolm and Starr enter behind him, and the girls hug while Malcolm and Roger bro hug.

"Good to see you, man!" Roger tells him.

"Still looking goofy, bro!" Malcolm teases.

Haley walks in looking glum, and Roger pulls her into a bear hug, lifting her off her feet.

As per Lola's intel, Haley was going through some relationship issues, so he tries to cheer his baby sister up posthaste. *Duke* Callum will rue the day if he hurts our little sister. I'll *duke* his ass.

"You better have brought your, A game or I'm going to leave you in the powder tomorrow morning for our Christmas Day run!" Roger teases Haley. "Don't blame me when your googles get covered in snow!"

She rolls her eyes and retorts, "Even on my worse day, I can outrace you, Roger!"

Guy and Josy enter carrying The Twins. They cared for Rodolphe and Gaspard while Roger and Leonie enjoyed their first wedding anniversary.

They scoop The Twins up and hold them close. These past few days are the longest they've been apart from them. They laugh at their parents' overzealous kisses and pat their faces with their chubby hands.

I smile to myself at the thought of my parents taking care of our baby while Lola and I spend quality time together. I cannot wait for our baby to be born!

Speaking of my parents, they're last to enter, and they greet Roger and Leonie warmly.

"This tree is even bigger than last year's," my mother says, smiling as she takes a glass of hot mulled wine. "I love the new decorations!"

Everyone makes their way to their suites while Leonie and Roger tend to The Twins.

"I can't wait to tell them!" Lola exclaims as she rubs her belly. "This sweater is warm even if it hides my baby bump."

I walk back out of the bathroom to slip my arms around Lola from behind. My sizable hands cradle her belly that reminds me of a basketball, though I would never tell Lola. She's still getting used to her body changes.

"Then you should take the sweater off, babe. You don't want to overheat," I tell her.

She switches out of the turtleneck into a silk camisole, not wanting to give away her baby bump before we make the announcement after dinner.

Lola and I head back downstairs to the dining room where Josy chats with the chef she favored last Christmas about tonight's dinner. It's like the holiday before, in honor of the French tradition of l*e Réveillon de Noël* for the Christmas meal.

We relish in each other's company as we dine on fine dishes and excellent wines. The conversation flows easily.

Once we're gathered in the great room and exchanged our first gifts as our tradition for Christmas Eve, Roger stands and pulls Leonie to her feet with him. The two female Bichon Frise puppies Roger gifted Leonie and The Twins scamper around their feet, playing with a toy.

"Well everyone, Leonie and I have some news to share with you," Roger gazes from one smiling face to the other before his eyes turn to his wife's gorgeous face.

"We're twenty weeks pregnant with a baby girl!!" Leonie announces, grinning like the Cheshire Cat.

Everyone whoops and hollers.

"Congratulations!!"

"*Oh, Mon Dieu*!"

"Awesome news, Roger and Leonie!!"

"*Fantastique, Mon Trésor!*"

When the well-wishing ends, I clear my throat and stand, too.

"Roger and Leonie, Lola and I are so thrilled for you! Once again you'll make us an aunt and an uncle—the most favorites, of course," I pause to pull Lola into my side. "And we will make you an aunt and uncle, too. The most favorite is up to the others."

At first everyone smiles and nods. Then the room erupts when they realize what I mean about us expecting a baby, too.

"We're twenty weeks, too!" Lola gushes as she rubs her belly covered by an oversized sweater. "Can you believe it, BFF?!"

"Oh, Lola, Sebastian! We're so happy for you, too!!" Leonie exclaims as she hugs a beaming Lola and they start to cry, overcome with hormonal emotions.

Undoubtedly Leonie remembers Lola being upset this time last year as she sat in the windowed walkway in the early morning debating having children with me then or later.

Now here we are a year later, and we're both expecting. This Christmas is going to be even more special than the last!

The doorbell chimes, and Shelley waves Roger off as she heads to the entryway to answer. Everyone is present, so we're not sure who it could be.

Roger glances down at Leonie, and she shrugs her shoulders.

Everyone turns to the entry, wondering who has arrived at this late hour.

Shelley returns to the great room with Lachlan behind her. She glances at Haley questioningly, then at me worriedly.

Lachlan strides right in and stops in front of Haley, clasping her hands in his. Without his emerald green eyes leaving her dove gray ones, he addresses Morgan and Baz.

"No disrespect, Uncle Morgan. We're like brothers,

Sebastian. But Haley is mine, and I won't go another day without her for anyone."

Silence descends on the great room. Talk about the other shoe drops, rather the third…

"What the fuck, Lachlan?!" I growl as I advance on my best friend. "What do you mean Haley is yours?"

Lola puts both of her hands on my arm to hold me back. She knows I won't pull away and risk hurting her and our son.

"Baz, babe, let them be. It's Haley's decision, not yours," Lola says calmly.

"*Oui*, give them some privacy," Leonie adds, then turns to Haley and Lachlan. "Haley, go to the library. No one will disturb you, *Chérie*."

"Leonie—" Roger pins her with his intense stare.

"*Non*! Enough of the big brother meddling! Let Haley live her life," Leonie demands, her fierce feline gaze sparking golden amber.

Haley nods, and she leaves the great room with Lachlan in tow.

Malcolm, Roger, Harris, and I glare after them. I swear I hear Harris growl. He's the most easygoing of us, but he's extremely protective of his twin.

"Now, Sebastian, Lola, boy or girl?" Josy asks, clapping her hands to diffuse the situation. "We must know how to prepare, *non*?"

Lola jumps right in and tugs me to the sofa.

"We're having a… baby… BOY!!" She shouts as she shimmies in her seat beside me.

Her exuberance melts the arctic chill from the air in the room. No one can resist her joy, especially me.

I wrap my arm around her shoulders and lean over to kiss her temple. Then I face our family.

"Yes, a son! A healthy baby boy! See for yourselves," I say as I stand to pass out color copies of the ultrasound images I had in an envelope.

"Fantastic! You're right, Josy, we have so much to prepare!" My mother gushes. "June will be here before you know it."

"A girl and a boy at the same time! Busy, busy, busy!" Starr laughs.

I notice how Malcolm watches her with what appears to express longing. Could he have the baby bug, too? Starr doesn't catch his look since she's chatting with Lola and Leonie.

Malcolm must sense my stare and shifts his gaze to me. He purses his lips and crosses his arms over his chest when I raise an eyebrow questioningly.

I chuckle. Yeah, right. He's smitten.

LOLA

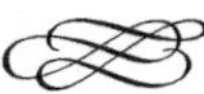

"I know you'll be busy with your pregnancy, your work with Lola's Coterie and STEELE, and your volunteering with the girls. But… I'd love if you'd design my nurseries… Please, bestie?"

Leonie, Haley, Blair, Billie, Starr, and I sit in my chill room on the first floor of my New York City penthouse while The Twins play with their Bichon Frise puppies and toys on a blanket. The boys including Morgan, Luc, Patrick, and Lachlan went to the STEELE box at Madison Square Garden for the Knicks versus the Los Angeles Lakers basketball game.

The girls and I take advantage of some time alone. It's been a month since we left Verbs and the first time we've all been together.

As the Head of STEELE Children and Young Adults Division and since she did a fantastic job with my Sutton Place penthouse, Leonie would be perfect to help me. The last few weeks I tried with Shelley's assistance, but Leonie just has that special touch.

The Twins' nurseries—nine in total, no less—are spectacular and suit each of Leonie and Roger's and their grandparents' residences. We need eight: our and Morgan and Shelley's New York City penthouses; our and their Southampton Village beach houses; our and their Paris penthouses; Josy and Guy's Paris mansion; our London mansion.

It's a Herculean task. I give Leonie my puppy dog eyes.

"Of course, *Chérie*! I was hoping you'd ask!" She says clapping her hands as her amber eyes twinkle in delight.

Leonie has always had an eye for design. The combination of being the world-renowned megamodel *The Lion* for almost nineteen years and as the daughter of an old, wealthy Parisian merchant family that travels seeking antiques, antiquities, and fabrics instilled in her a love for the aesthetics. Transitioning into interior design was her dream for years.

"Merci! Merci beaucoup, mon amie!" I thank her with a huge sideways hug to avoid bumping our bellies. "We must start with the nurseries here and in Southampton Village. The ones in Paris and London can wait since we won't travel abroad until after the summer season."

Since Baby Boy is due in June, Baz and I decided to stay out in The Hamptons after they're born. Time away from the city during the sultry New York summer proves just the solution. Who wouldn't prefer to be on the beach?

Shelley already told us she and Morgan will stay out there and not go to Positano for the summer. So Baz and I will have plenty of support.

"Do you want to remain true to your interiors or go with unique designs? Have you decided which rooms you want to convert? Oh, and Shelley showed me some incredible heirloom pieces from their family we can incorporate like we did for The Twins. Not to mention antiques from mine and pieces from the collections of Beaulieu Enterprises. I know just the ones…"

We jump right in on ideas. Leonie sketches on a pad I pull from my secretary desk as her creative juices flow from her head to her fingers. In no time at all she has several options from themed to traditional, down to the layouts and the color palettes.

I love them!

"Do you think Nanny Grace would make a blanket for Baby Boy? Rodolphe and Gaspard's are beautiful," Haley says. "They'll treasure them forever."

Nanny Grace hand-crocheted two navy blue cashmere blankets. Everyone admired the fine stitchwork of the intricate design. The center panels have entwined B and S for Beaulieu and Steele, surrounded by a twelve-inch border of swirls and whorls. She made matching beanies and booties to complete the sets.

I clap my hands together and lace my fingers as I bounce on the sofa.

"Ooooh! That would be phenomenal! Will you ask her for me, Leonie?" I say. "I'd love to combine Baby Boy's initials."

"Have you chosen a name, yet?" Starr asks.

Baz and I thought of some options and narrowed it down to two. We want to wait until the day he's born to pick based on which feels best once we set eyes on Baby Boy.

I share our decision with the girls, and they understand.

"Being that you and Lola are due at the same time, I spoke with Anita since she's a doula now. She can help you, Leonie, while I help Lola. It's better for you both with me in the States and Anita in Paris. We can give you the attention you need without concern for distance," Starr says.

I smile at her for such a brilliant suggestion.

After Baz and I made the official announcement, I told Leonie about admitting my pregnancy to Starr first since the yoga sessions concerned me in my prenatal state. And how I asked her to be my doula. I did not know when I asked Leonie was expecting too and would want to have Starr help her again.

Of course, my easygoing BFF took it in stride. Leonie rarely allows situations to become problems. It reminded me of her favorite saying: *"Only solutions, Lola!"* She figured she'd make do with a referral from Dr. Berger, her OB-GYN.

Now Starr offers the perfect solution!

Anita Green is the wife of Norman Green, Roger's boxing coach and personal trainer and the former world heavyweight champion nine years straight—eight by knockout. At Roger's suggestion, Norman opened eponymous chains of branded gyms through STEELE's Entertainment Properties Division when he retired. One for underprivileged youth and another as exclusive elite training facilities for the über-wealthy and star athletes.

In her own right, Anita is a star yoga instructor with a flourishing global practice and with her degree from the culinary school at Le Cordon Bleu started a meal plan delivery service. Norman added her customized plans to the paid offerings of the elite facilities and complimentary healthy snacks to the youth. She also took over the food services in both chains. They're a dynamic couple who raise the bar in the fitness industry.

Anita became Leonie's yoga instructor once she was further along in her pregnancy, and Starr wanted her to have hands-on attention not possible through their Skype sessions. Over the years, Anita and Leonie, then with the other girls, became close. She's now a part of our clique.

"Wonderful, *Chérie*! I remember when Anita completed her doula training. She'll be perfect, *merci*!" Leonie gushes. "I'll send a text message to her now."

"While we're on the topic of baby plans… Leonie, Sebastian and I want to meet with Nanny Grace's agency for selecting a nanny and a nurse," I say, remembering the conversation we had a few nights ago. "Baz and I figure you can speak with the owners since they're based in Paris before we meet with their New York City office."

Grace Hart is one of their stellar nannies who's also a trained nurse. The überwealthy and celebrities use her agency to hire their nannies, nurses, and governesses. Their training is top-notch in everything from changing a diaper to language lessons to disarming a would-be kidnapper. Even though Baz has a security detail for me, it's good for the nanny to have training.

"*Absolument!* Nanny Grace is the best! Roger and I will call them tomorrow morning Paris time. Perhaps we can video conference into the call the head of this office," Leonie responds.

The house intercom rings, and I answer it to Shelley on the line. The spa day with her best friend and the Jackson Matriarch Lucie ended early. Shelley asks what we're up to, and I tell her to come down since we're talking baby plans.

When she arrives, we fill her in on the latest. She's just as excited as we are about the developments.

"More grandchildren to spoil," she laughs, clapping her hands. "I cannot wait!"

My heart fills with joy. I may not have my mother here, but Shelley and Josy have lived up to their word and helped me in every way. I know my mother would be happy for me. And I send a silent prayer to her.

"EXCUSE ME, everyone. May I have your attention? I have an announcement to make."

We're in the private East Room of Per Se, my favorite restaurant in New York City. It's also where we celebrated the deal between Lola's Coterie and STEELE over three years ago.

I smiled to myself as we walked in, and my gaze went to the stunning views of the Manhattan skyline and Central Park clear across Columbus Circle to Fifth Avenue. The other side of the East Room is a glass panel that overlooks the restaurant's main dining room. But prior to our arrival, the staff closed the silk drapes for privacy.

Then my thoughts shift to the feral way Baz fucked me in the ladies' room against the vanity after he spanked my ass until it was on fire. He pounded into me from behind like a man possessed until he came with an explosive roar. The shock on Baz's face when he realized he lost control and took me bareback was priceless.

Even though I was pissed with him, I returned to his penthouse right after we straightened our clothing. His declaration to take my last hole proved more tempting than my anger. My pussy and ass clench with the memory.

Now my gaze travels around the circular table to Luc, who smiles encouragingly. He and Baz agreed with my newest business decision. It's a long time coming.

With a nod, I stand and smile at Blair.

"Years ago I thought I was Wonder Woman and could do every aspect of Lola's Coterie by myself. From the design to the marketing to the management of the Paris flagship and the London boutique. My wise mentor told me to focus on the creative design side and let an assistant handle the day-to-day tasks. In came Blair and she blew me away with her efficiency, dependability, and cleverness when balancing the activities that didn't need my constant or immediate attention."

Then I turn to Billie seated beside Patrick and smile.

"I learned from my experience with Blair to find someone I can rely on to handle my business affairs long distance for Lola's Coterie Las Vegas. Thanks to Baz's director of STEELE's West Coast retail properties, I met Billie. I needed someone who could handle the contractors, staff, and clients who like me could charm the best of them, but can turn into a spitfire when necessary."

Everyone laughs when I waggle my eyebrows.

"Over the years, you've proven yourselves to be incredible in your jobs, but also wonderful friends. With Baby Boy on the way, I realize once again, I cannot do it all"—I raise my glass of iced lemon ginger tea—"So this decision was a no-brainer. Blair I would like to offer you the position of my chief marketing officer and Billie my chief operating officer!"

Blair and Billie gasp while the others stand and clap, then raise their glasses in a toast.

"So deserved, *Chéries*!"

"Whoohoo! Congratulations!"

"*Félicitations!*"

"Cheers!"

After a few moments, I quiet everyone down and turn back to Blair and Billie.

"Do you accept?" I ask, hoping they answer in the affirmative. "I mean, just don't leave a preggie lady hanging, no pressure!"

Billie jumps up and gives me a hug, and Blair does the same. They agree wholeheartedly. And the servers appear with chilled bottles of Dom Pérignon Rosé Vintage 2005 and a variety of desserts.

"We'll drink for you, Leonie and Lola!" Malcolm teases.

Lachlan adds, "We know it's your favorite bubbly, Lola!"

"Awww… Don't tease my sisters. Although I must say you are missing out, ladies!" Harris chuckles.

Leonie laughs, and Roger pops Harris on the back of his head good-naturedly.

We spend the rest of the time chatting and enjoying one another. The boys rehash the basketball game, including the "incredible last second three-pointer by LeBron *King* James." Billie jokes about her date with another basketball superstar. But Patrick whispers in her ear, and her eyes widen as she turns bright pink. He sits back and smirks.

I giggle knowing Patrick being an Alpha Dom must have told her just how he feels about her date with another man. Baz squeezes my thigh under the table, and I can't help but snort.

Starr who sits next to me covers her mouth with her linen napkin to hide her laughter. Then Malcolm silences her with words said in her ear.

It cracks me up further to realize how each of my friends —who despite being Independent Women—find themselves attracted to Alpha males, Doms or not. Sometimes when you're in control of your business, career, life… it's a relief to turn over control to your lover. No need to think, just feel as Baz tells me.

"What is going on in that busy mind of yours, Little Pet?"

Baz's warm breath tickles my neck as he leans over to murmur in my ear. His lips trail along the side of my neck, making my nipples pucker against the silk of my blouse and my pussy clench with need. My mind was already on lascivious thoughts. He just drove me closer to the edge.

"Well, Sir, since you asked… A vision of my wrists bound by red silks to the corners of our bed with my ankles in the spreader bar. My legs thrown over your shoulders as you kneel above me, pounding your ginormous dick into my dripping, tight pussy. The bed creaks from your powerful thrusts as though the frame may crack at any moment. I scream your name—hoarse from my previous carnal cries—as you wring a fourth orgasm from my wrecked pussy. Sweat drips from your chin to land between my bouncing breasts. You bow your head to lap it up, then suckle my peaked nipples voraciously until I cum again. Head thrown back, eyes shut, a roar rips from your throat as you blow your load deep inside my pussy. It squeezes every drop from your cock."

I lift my lowered gaze to his and smile in triumph when I see his pupils blown and his mouth slack.

Baz flares his nostrils and smirks, "Well my Petite Seductress, let us return home to make your vision our reality."

My grin widens, "Yes, Sir. Thank you, Sir."

SEBASTIAN

"Where are we going? The water has the most beautiful shades of blue and green! Look! Are those dolphins over there?"

Lola's excitement as she peers out the window in her seat beside me on our Gulfstream 650 makes me chuckle.

At twenty-six weeks pregnant, she's two-thirds of the way through our pregnancy. It's month six with only three months left to go. I'll be a father in no time. Holy shit!

Roger reminded me I need to take Lola on our babymoon before she's twenty-eight weeks. Leonie had the great idea of taking Lola to the Caribbean since it's less than three hours from New York City or an hour from Miami by plane just in case we need a doctor.

That was a few weeks ago, and it gave me time to decide to stay at a STEELE beach resort or to rent a private villa. In the end, I chose to invest for our family—the three of us and the rest of the Steele clan.

What can I say? It's the big brother in me to care for my siblings.

I researched private islands instead of giving money away to an owner for a villa rental and not doing our usual of a STEELE property stay.

The private island realtor suggested by a business associate helped me to narrow down the location to the Exumas. More specifically to an island within the chain of the Exuma Cays known as the yachting, sailing, and fishing paradise of the Bahamas. The location offers an ideal spot for relaxation and fun activities.

The forty-million-dollar investment of Bougainvillea Cay lies in one of the most beautiful parts of the Bahamas. It features over five hundred acres of lush, tropical land with a network of paths and walkways. Surrounded by crystal clear turquoise waters, it boasts many white sandy beaches, three inner lakes, and different elevations for stunning views. An airstrip for us to fly in and out with ease makes it perfect for quick getaways. Another plus is its proximity to STEELE Exumas should we wish to use the recreational, spa, or dining facilities.

Two properties round out the island. A palatial two-story, ten-bedroom beachfront villa with saltwater pool, four guest cabanas, and a caretaker's house and an actual castle built by an Englishman in the 1930s. We can rebuild it into a spot for the kids to take over, especially as they grow into teenagers and want their space apart from the adults. I'll leave it to Leonie to design through her STEELE division.

My parents and siblings can build their villas along the coastline that features natural coves for privacy. With his STEELE division, Roger can create a clubhouse on the largest beach for our family to gather. We'll add docks with lifts for sailboats, Jetskis, and other water toys.

Bougainvillea Cay will be the Steele Caribbean retreat. A

spectacular place for our family to gather for the winters, as we do at Steele Southampton in the summers and *Chalet de la Joie* for the holidays.

I reach over and place my palm on Lola's round belly. Now it's bigger than basketball, but smaller than a beach ball. My fingers caress her baby bump and tweak her newly outie belly button.

Lola giggles and slaps my hand away.

"Tell me! Why and where have you kidnapped me?" She demands. "At least you didn't blindfold and gag me. Well… Not that I would have minded!"

"Naughty Pet. You will soon find out," I respond as I sweep her much longer hair aside to nuzzle the side of her elegant neck. "Patience, Pet. Patience."

Lola gasps when I nip her soft skin between my teeth and suck hard. Once satisfied a mark will appear, I lick and kiss the area to soothe her.

My Petite Seductress drives me crazy with need. Her pregnancy body is a whole new world for me to explore and to delight in. From her sensitive oversized nipples to her Double-D tits to her ample ass and grip-worthy hips.

Mine!

Our pilot announces we'll land in fifteen minutes.

I grin at Lola when she looks from me to the window and back again. I'm sure she can see the cays and from our flight time guess we're in the Bahamas.

She just smiles and takes my left hand in hers to kiss my platinum wedding band. Then she lifts her hazel gaze to my dove gray one.

"Wherever we may be and why, you captured me the moment I first saw you at LEVELS New York. My vision locked on your magnetic gray eyes and a thrill rushed through me as if a jolt of electricity shocked my very soul. I love and trust you, Mr. Steele," Lola says with a twinkle in her eyes.

My heart beats wildly. This woman is the best thing to happen to me in my life, ever. Never afraid to show my true self to her, my eyes glisten with tears.

"Thank you, my love," I murmur as I slant my mouth over hers for a soul-shocking kiss.

Before we landed, I pointed out the window for Lola to take in the majesty of our private island. I didn't tell her it was ours. I wanted to wait until we were at the villa.

When I finished giving her a tour of the primary residence, we changed into bathing suits and headed to the beach for lunch at a table set on the warm white sand. Staff stand at the ready to serve us.

I help Lola into her chair after I place a bougainvillea flower behind her ear, then sit across from her. Once they place our appetizers before us and pour our beverages, they depart. They'll return for our entrees.

"How do you like Bougainvillea Cay?" I ask as Lola takes in the turquoise water, clear blue sky, and endless sand.

She turns her gaze to me and grins, "I love it! I've never seen such a picturesque private island. The flowers intoxicate me. Thank you, baby!"

My chest swells with pride.

"Do you like it enough to make it our new Caribbean retreat?" I ask nonchalantly as I pop a delectable grilled shrimp in my mouth.

No sound comes from across the table. So I glance up to see Lola's eyes wide, and her mouth hanging open in shock.

I laugh so hard I nearly choke on my morsel of conch fritters.

"Welcome to Paradise, baby," I grin.

Lola rushes over to me, and I pull her onto my lap as she flings her arms around my neck and kisses me until we're breathless. She pulls back and rubs her nose against mine.

"Thank you, so much," she whispers. "It's perfect, my love."

I tighten my arms around her and brush my lips on hers.

"I would take all the credit if I could. But Roger reminded me to take you on a babymoon so we could spend time as a couple before Baby Boy comes. Then Leonie suggested the Bahamas. So here we are," I respond.

Lola beams and kisses me again. Then laughs, "So you bought an island?"

I chuckle, embarrassed by my enthusiasm. But when I explain its use as a family getaway like Southampton and Verbier, Lola agrees wholeheartedly.

We discuss plans for making the island our own as we enjoy a delicious meal of fresh fish prepared with local flavors and tasty sides, including pigeon peas and rice. Virgin Bahamas Mama Punch and cool water keep us refreshed in the warm sun. A delicious guava duff dessert completes our meal.

The staff leaves us after they clear the table. They return to the caretaker's house until we request their service.

Total privacy on our private island.

I take Lola's hand and lead her to the sunbed with a double umbrella, the only other item on the expanse of powdery white sand. We stretch out and lean back to gaze at the Bahama Blue water of the Atlantic Ocean.

Lola shifts on the sunbed to face me.

My eyes travel from her messy bun to her luscious tits in the triangle bikini top to her round belly, past her bikini-bottom-clad mound, down her toned legs to her red-painted toenails.

Sexy Mama Alert.

"You know bougainvillea is symbolic of abundance, prosperity, and passion. But most of all of fertility. How apropos, Mr. Steele?" Lola says as she touches her fingers to the vibrant pink flower in her raven hair.

A feral grin forms on my face. It pleases my caveman to provide for my mate, give her pleasure, and fill her belly with my baby. A growl rumbles from low in my chest.

Lola purrs in response and drags a fingertip from her ear down her throat to circle a beaded nipple. Her lust-filled eyes never leave mine. Instead, they spark with a carnal inner fire that threatens to consume me.

"Spread your thighs for me and present your pretty pink pussy, Little Pet," I command in my deep Alpha Dom baritone.

I smirk when Lola shivers visibly, and a soft cry falls from her mouth. She loves it when I control her sexually.

Being the vixen as always, Lola pulls the strings on her white bikini bottom slowly. Her heated gaze warms me more than the Bahamas sun. Just as unrushed, she slips the bottoms from her bare mound. She takes my request a step further and places two fingers on either side of her pussy seam to pull her juicy lips apart.

My cock jumps and my mouth waters at the sight of her glistening, pink folds.

"Are you satisfied with the view, Sir?" Lola asks seductively as she stares at my growing bulge pressing against my sky-blue trunks.

The clear outline of my mushroom head leaves no question of my arousal.

I mimic her moves and lift my hips to peel my trunks down my muscular legs unhurriedly. My ten inches spring free and slap my eight-pack abs. It aligns with my happy trail of dark hair as it reaches my belly button.

Lola licks her lips, dragging her little pink tongue from one corner of her mouth to the other. Her hooded eyes rake over my hard pecs, abs, and rod as I stroke my chest down to grip the base of my cock.

"Are you satisfied with the view, Little Pet?" I ask, repeating her question.

Lola smirks and raises her hands behind her neck.

When she pulls the string loose of her bikini top and it falls down to reveal her delectable tits, I nearly blow my load. I have to pinch the tip of my dick to distract myself.

"Tit for tat, Naughty Pet?" I rumble, and she quakes. "Hands and knees. I want to mount you from behind."

Lola hastens into position. She tosses her hair over her right shoulder to peer back at me over her left one. She bites her plump lower lip when her gaze lands on my fisted cock as I advance on her.

I lean forward and bury my face between her thighs.

Her cries of ecstasy drive me to increase the intensity of my licking inside her pussy and sucking her engorged clit. Lola squeals and drops to her forearms when I smack her dripping folds.

I slip one finger inside of her pussy, then flex and curl it to stretch her walls and stroke the rough textured nugget on top. She needs to be soaked and ready for my invasion.

"Cum for me, Little Pet," I command, adding a second thick digit and increasing the rhythm. "Cum now!"

Lola bows her back in a deep arc, throwing her head back as she keens. Her body shakes from her climax.

Just as her greedy pussy grasps my fingers, I pull out and jam my throbbing cock inside. I grunt and Lola yowls.

Her pussy still flutters from her orgasm around my dick as I pound into her. Barbaric growls and grunts fill the air in opposition to the calm lapping of the ocean waves on the sand. The scent of our fucking mingles with the salty air. Sweat drips down my spine and a sheen forms on Lola's back. Erotic energy surrounds us.

I grip her hips harder as she writhes on my dick, pushing back to meet each of my thrusts with vigor. She clenches her pussy walls, and I groan.

"So fucking good, Little Pet… So tight… So wet…" I grunt, then spank her jiggling ass cheeks one after the other.

"More, Sir! Harder!" Lola cries out in wild abandon as she slaps the sunbed.

I give her what she wants; what she needs. The sound of flesh on flesh—groin to ass, balls to clit, palm to ass—fills our ears.

"Right there! Oh… My… Go—" Lola screams as her body shudders from another carnal climax "Yeeessssss!!"

Caught in her sexual thrall, I lose my mind as I bury myself in her wet heat. Lola's last orgasm makes my rhythm falter as she clamps down on my cock.

I have to shut my eyes from the sight of her writhing beneath me to regain control. My left hand reaches under Lola to wrap around her throat and pull her upright, her back flush with my front.

She mewls still in the midst of her orgasm.

It's time for my release. My hips grind in circles to allow my dick to hit every inch of her pussy. Shallow thrusts followed by deep strokes until the tingle of my orgasm turns into a mind-blowing tsunami.

I throw my head back and howl to the heavens.

We collapse in a state of sheer euphoria.

"Happy Valentine's Day, Mr. Steele." Lola whispers throatily when I spoon her in front of me.

I rasp, "Happy Valentine's Day, Mrs. Steele."

LOLA

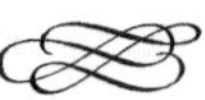

"*Mon amie,* I have to thank you for two weeks of sheer bliss in Paradise! If Baz didn't have to go to Australia for business in Sydney and Melbourne, we would have stayed for a month instead of only two weeks!"

I tell Leonie as we sit on sofas wrapped in oversized cashmere throws in her living room in Paris.

Baz and I left the Exumas a few hours ago. He took the larger G700 private jet to Australia and I flew to Paris on the G650. Baz wasn't pleased I wasn't returning to New York City while he was away for ten days. He worries about me being further along in my pregnancy.

I'm sure the idea of me being in Paris without him—the same city as Simon—weighed on Baz's mind, too. He does not need to fear at all. That page turned months ago!

But I explained I won't be able to fly much longer and want to see Leonie before neither of us can travel. Since she has The Twins, it's easier for me to go to her.

He relented after he spoke with Roger. He assured Baz

he wouldn't let me out of his sight. Even the security detail isn't enough for them. The Cavemen are super protective of Leonie and me with us being pregnant.

I could only smile at their possessiveness. Once I agreed to limit my activities to Lola's Coterie Paris, The STEELE Tower Paris, *Le Beaulieu Manoir,* and shopping, Baz relaxed.

Roger even said he'd accompany Leonie and me when venture out to buy baby items. He's going to stay true to his word, traipsing around stores with two preggies and all. Good luck with that, brother!

While I'm here, I'll work out of my flagship and take care of some baby prep needs. I arrived on a Saturday, so today we'll hang out in order for me to get some rest, then tomorrow go over the nurseries' status. We're enjoying some tea and cookies while Rodolphe and Gaspard nap in their rooms. The puppies chase each other, gamboling with a chew toy.

"No need to thank me, *Chérie*! I'm sure you would do the same for me. I don't blame you for wanting to stay. When you sent the photos, Roger teased we'd crash your baby-moon and move into a guest cabana!" Leonie's laughter fills the room.

Then she claps her hands in glee as her amber eyes sparkle.

"I cannot wait to get started on the castle! It's gigantic. *Les petits enfants* will love pretending they're storming the castle or are princes and a princess. Baz is right, the castle will make the perfect spot just for them, especially as they get older and want time away from us," Leonie adds.

I nod, "It definitely will let their imaginations run wild. Baz and I role-played an erotic *Sleeping Beauty...*"

Leonie bursts out in a fit of giggles, then clutches her belly and grimaces.

"Daphne didn't appreciate being shaken. She just jabbed me!" Leonie says wide-eyed as she rubs the painful area. "*C'est la vie*. At least it's just one foot or hand and not two like with The Twins!"

I agree and rub my belly, remembering the boxing match Baby Boy had on the jet. His pokes were so intense I had to lie down in the bedroom for the last part of the flight. The thought of two babies at once makes me shudder. How the heck did Leonie do it? I muse as I shake my head in awe.

"You thrilled Roger with the idea of a family retreat in the Bahamas. The Beaulieus have a private island in Greece, but my father leased it in perpetuity to a luxury resort. We would stay, but it's not the same with other guests around. I can't wait to go to Bougainvillea Cay!" Leonie says smiling again.

We talk some more about the changes we want to make and the type of villa she and Roger prefer for their home. First on the list are the clubhouse and the docks, since there's room in the primary residence and the guest cabanas for everyone until they complete their villas.

Roger promised to share some of his ideas after dinner. He wanted to give Leonie and me time to catch up.

"And Malcolm is excited about selecting the boats. You know Mr. Fast Cars and Motorcycles! He's investigating sailboats and other water toys," I giggle mimicking him riding his Harley-Davidson at top speed. "Starr teases him all the time about a boy and his toys!"

"Well, she'll go gaga over the endless stretches of beach for yoga and the trails throughout the island for hikes. Not to mention swimming in the interior lakes," I say envisioning the exercise sessions Starr would come up with while we're on island.

My mobile rings, and Starr's name appears on the

screen. I laugh and tell Leonie guess who as I answer on speaker audio.

"Hi, honey! How was your flight? Do you and Baby Boy fell all right?" Starr asks.

I tell her all is good, and I didn't return home. Instead I went to Paris to visit Leonie and to take care of some European business before I'm too far along.

Of course Starr already knows. As it so happens, Baz told Malcolm, who in turn told her. She and Malcolm want to make sure I made it in safely, and Baby Boy is fine.

In the background, I hear Malcolm ask if I'm okay, and Starr relays our conversation.

"Okay, well, other Hot Mama, Malcolm says you better take care, too! We'll leave you guys to it. Have some Girls' Time fun for me!" She says. "Oh, and don't forget to do your Kegel exercises and breathwork."

Leonie and I promise to follow Starr's prenatal instructions and tell her to thank Malcolm for his concern, too. We end the call with plans to meet up when I fly to the West Coast to visit my Las Vegas and Beverly Hills boutiques before my travel time draws to a close.

My goal is to attend to as much work at each boutique as possible before I give birth in June. Despite witnessing Leonie's bounce back after The Twins, I can't be sure how my body will react and don't want to risk not being able to attend to Lola's Coterie. My original baby!

I say a silent thank you for Blair and Billie already rocking it out in their new roles. They'll be my saving grace in the coming months. Even more so than they were before. My mind is at ease.

Leonie and I get back to talking. But my mobile rings again, this time with a FaceTime call from Baz. She laughs and goes to the kitchen with the puppies on her heels.

"Tell my brother hi for me, *Chérie*. And not to worry!" She says over her shoulder.

I answer the video call with an enormous smile on my face. This man is the definition of an overprotective first-time father.

"Hi, my love. Baby Boy and I arrived safely, and we feel great! No need to worry. How's your flight going?" I ask in an attempt to answer his questions and to redirect his thoughts.

Knowing me so well, Baz raises his eyebrow and purses his lips.

With a shake of his head, he responds, "Oh, don't even try it, babe. Deflection won't work. Your flight attendant told me you retired to the bedroom with a pained expression..."

I roll my eyes. Damn. Spies everywhere.

We talk some more, and I vow to take it easy for the next two days. Otherwise, Baz informed me he'll be here in no time and will cart me to Dr. Berger's office stat—Leonie's OB-GYN. Not wanting to go that route, I reaffirm my pledge.

Satisfied, Baz ends the video call with kisses for me and his son.

My heart flutters, and Baby Boy pokes my belly as though responding to his father.

Baz gets as big a kick out of it as I, although mine was physical...

When Leonie returns, Roger enters with her and gives me the once over with his intense dove-gray stare. With a nod, he leaves us and pulls his mobile from his jeans pocket. Undoubtedly he's calling his brother to make a report on his assessment of me.

Leonie and I watch him leave, then turn to each other.

We bust out laughing and hold our bellies to keep our babies from rocking too hard. Tears pop out of the corners of our eyes when we try to come up for air.

It feels so good to spend quality alone time with my best friend. And even better to share our pregnancies with each other. It's a blessing I'm so grateful to experience.

* * *

"OH, *chérie*! You look so good and happy!"

Maman Josy pulls me into her warm embrace once Leonie, Roger, The Twins, and I stand in the magnificent entry foyer of *Le Beaulieu Manoir*. Their ancestral home never ceases to amaze me.

Leonie is right. I'll definitely find some jewels for Baby Boy's Parisian nursery amongst her family's collections. I love the idea he'll have true antiques to fit in with the history of the city.

I squeeze *Maman* Josy to infuse an extra burst of love and thanks.

"Come, let's have brunch, then we'll get into the goodies," she says as she takes Gaspard and Rodolphe's hands with the puppies in tow.

Roger offers Leonie and me his arms and we loop ours through his as he follows *Maman* Josy.

We walk past beautifully appointed salons to an all-glass solarium that overlooks the rear rose garden. They set a table for our Sunday brunch, a tradition *Maman* Josy enjoys preparing as proved by the sideboard arranged for a buffet-style service with an abundance of platters. The delicious aroma of savory and sweet dishes fills the air. Spices, meats, and baked goods blend to make my mouth water and my stomach to growl.

We just settle in our seats when *Papa* Guy's voice booms in the solarium.

"*Bonjour, mes filles et mon fils!* Rodolphe, Gaspard come to your Grand-père!"

We turn to find him striding into the room, ever the man of the estate. He's impeccably dressed in bespoke blazer, shirt, and trousers with Gucci loafers. After he scoops up The Twins, he hugs us and gives us double kisses. Then plants a soft kiss on *Maman* Josy's upturned lips.

His obsidian eyes scan Leonie and me as he takes us in from our heads to our rounded bellies. With a satisfied nod, he takes his seat.

"Come, let us eat," *Papa* Guy commands.

And eat we do!

Maman Josy is an incredible cook. Her skill of combining traditional Tunisian delicacies with Parisian cuisine makes for delectable dishes. Add in her baking specialties, including double-chocolate soufflés, and one can't ask for anything more.

Yum-my!

Throughout brunch, we chat and enjoy one another's company. Bougainvillea Cay thrills *Maman* Josy when I show them photos. *Papa* Guy regales us with his deep-sea fishing tales from his trips to the best fishing waters around the world. He's looking forward to those of the Exumas. It's been a while, he says.

Roger tells them he and Leonie will design a villa with living quarters for them. They beam when I assure them they're welcome to come and go as they wish, whether Baz and I are on island.

"*Merci, mes enfants*!" *Papa* Guy says in his deep baritone.

"Now, let's go upstairs. I had the servants move some pieces I think will be perfect for Leonie and you to select from for your nurseries," *Maman* Josy says as she rises from the table.

Papa Guy helps her, and they smile at each other as she touches her hand to his cheek. Their love is palpable.

The relationship they and my in-laws have are couple goals for Sebastian and me. Love at first sight and happily married for over thirty years is what I want for us. I know Leonie agrees; I think as I watch her grinning at her parents.

"Oui, *Maman*! I can't wait to see what goodies we have. There are some pieces I remember from before I'd like to use for Daphne," Leonie says as she rubs her baby bump. "They were too girly for The Twins. Now… Yippee!"

We laugh.

Guy assures Roger their staff will help us so the two of them can watch the Real Madrid and Manchester United football match.

After Leonie and I swear to not move or lift a single thing, not even a sheet, Roger concedes. As we part at the elevator, he gives us another warning, including calling Sebastian if I don't listen.

Maman Josy shoos them away with a bubbly laugh that makes her amber eyes glow when the door opens.

"*Chéries*, you'll learn to let your husbands talk and worry, then let them have their way. But on your terms," she says with a wink as she nods her stylish curly ebony bob.

Her words remind me of the advice Shelley and Lucie gave to us at my bridesmaids' luncheon in Dubai. Particularly their counsel on handling possessive Alpha males, and I'm certain in both of their cases Doms.

"Always listen more than you talk so you can understand how to respond if you have a disagreement," offered Lucie.

Shelley nodded and added, "Don't lose yourself in their lives. Maintain your friendships, work, activities."

"Yes, and your personality. If you were feisty and independent when you met, don't change. That's what attracted them to you. Don't simper like women who clamor for their attention," Lucie said.

"Oh and most important, be a proper lady in public, but a sex kitten in the bedroom! Pleasure them in the way they love the most regularly without fail!"

Shelley and Lucie burst out laughing as they high fived each other. Shelley dabbed the corners of her eyes. She laughed so hard she cried. Lucie covered her mouth with her hand and giggled some more.

Clearly, they had private jokes.

But now, after being married to Baz for thirty-two months, I get them, too!

Maman Josy, Leonie, and I step off the elevator into the Beaulieu family collections.

They dedicated the entire fourth floor of the massive mansion to their family's archives of antiquities, antiques, paintings, furniture, and clothing in temperature-controlled and damage-proof rooms. Generations of goodies cataloged in books with photos and details on each room door for easy access.

I can guarantee no other home in the world has such an elaborate setup for their family's archives.

"*Ooohhh, fantastique, Maman*!" Leonie claps in glee when she spies a beautiful hand-painted wooden cradle Josy set aside. "This is just the one I was thinking about! It's from before the Revolution, *non*?"

She's unfazed completely by the wealth and history of her family.

I smile and walk amongst the selections in admiration. The pieces *Maman* Josy displays are more than fantastic. Now, I wonder whether it's appropriate for me to have any of them, removing them from the family. They're Beaulieu heirlooms.

Maman Josy must sense my hesitancy. She's as in tuned to me as her daughter. *Maman* Josy wraps her arm around my shoulder and places her other hand on my belly.

"*Ma fills,* Guy and I want you to have any pieces your heart desires. We are blessed Leonie brought you into our family. You are a true daughter to us," she says with a smile, her eyes full of sincerity. "Come, I thought of Baby Boy when I saw this cradle."

I place my hand over hers on my baby bump and return her smile with tears shining in my eyes—damn hormones. My throat too thick with emotion, so I can only nod.

Once again I say a silent prayer for the loving family I have with me in my life and for my parents who continue to watch over me and now their grandson.

"YOU DIDN'T OVEREXERT YOURSELF, did you, babe?"

I'm back at our penthouse in bed doing a FaceTime video call with Baz. His worried platinum eyes search my face for any sign of fatigue.

"No, my love, brunch as usual, was delicious. Then the staff helped us with the selections. Leonie and I never lifted one pinky finger. Scout's Honor," I respond with a smile and three upright fingers.

Baz nods, and I tell him all about the pieces for the nursery. He's just as excited as I am for the beautiful items.

When I yawn, he tells me to go to sleep and to stay in bed later tomorrow morning. Work can wait.

It's nine in the morning Baz's time in Melbourne. So he's up and already at the STEELE offices, ready to start his day, while I'm just in bed at eleven at night.

"Okay, I will," I promise as I burrow under the bedding and sigh. "We love you."

Baz smiles, "I love you both very much. I miss you. Sweet dreams, babe."

Before he ends the call, my eyes close.

Baz knows me so well, I think as I drift into a peaceful slumber.

SEBASTIAN

Beautiful.

My hungry gaze rakes over my Naughty Pet. Her glossy raven tresses cascade to the floor. The line of my Naughty Pet's slim back leads to her lush ass. She's bound by red silk ties around her wrists and ankles to the vamp red spanking bench padded with suede leather. Her belly full with my son, my heir, cradled in the soft suede and silk pouch beneath the bench.

Her comfort is of the utmost importance at this stage of her pregnancy—thirty-three weeks and counting.

But my Pet craves punishment.

I growl my pleasure at the sight of my mate presented to me for her punishment. A punishment she so rightly deserves for disobeying my command.

"Yes, yes, Sebastian, I promise already!" Lola says, her voice tinged with irritation.

I don't give a damn she's annoyed I want her to take it easy. She's been traveling nonstop the last three weeks since we returned from Bougainvillea Cay: Paris, London, a brief stop in New York

City, Las Vegas, Beverly Hills, back to New York City after a go-see in Dallas.

Now she wants to visit a STEELE row of retail stores on Main Street in Southampton Village for a Lola's Coterie pop-up shop this summer.

"Oh Baz, the helicopter ride is brief," Lola continues as she slams her Hermès attaché closed with a huff. "I'll be back this afternoon."

"Why can't you let Billie take care of the walk-through? Isn't that why you promoted her, so she can handle the 'operations' of Lola's Coterie?!" I retort.

She throws the stink eye at me over her shoulder as she bustles to our private elevator.

"I will see you later, Sebastian. Have a good day at work. I love you," she calls as she steps through the open doors.

I roll my eyes to the heavens for strength, then settle on her face—lit from within, from her mommy's glow.

"Make sure you go easy today. I'll call you to check in"—when Lola winks at me like a sassy vixen, my mood softens—"I love you, too."

Lola grins in victory, knowing she has me wrapped around her little pinky.

"Take care with my son!" I shout as the doors close.

She blows kisses at me and disappears from sight.

"SEBASTIAN! IT'S LOLA! SHE FAINT—"

When I saw Billie's name appear on the screen of my mobile, I knew it was bad news. I race out of the conference room on the Executive Floor of STEELE in the middle of a budget meeting with my Retail Divisions Team. All heads turn towards me as I run to the private elevator, yelling with my mobile to my ear.

"WHERE IS SHE?!?!"

"Mr. Steele! I called for Edgar to bring your car around to meet you in the building's front now."

I glance over my shoulder as I reach for the elevator call button. Then thank Tina with a quick nod. My PA is always on point and in tune with my needs after all of these years.

"She's resting in the back of the car. But she slipped to her knees before we could catch—"

"WHAAAAT?!?!?!?!" I scream, the word reverberating around the enclosed space.

Billie's voice chokes, startled by my ire.

"I'm so sorry, Sebastian!!" Billie cries. "Lola says she didn't hurt herself. But she should still see Dr. Rice. Blair called him, and he's meeting us at the hospital. We're landing on the roof, so you can meet us there—"

"Tell him not to worry... I'm fine... Please."

Lola's strained voice in the background makes my chest tighten as my heart clenches.

I don't want to stress her further, knowing it can cause her blood pressure to rise and harm our baby. We don't need any problems with him added to what's happened with Lola. So I tamp down on my anger with her for not heeding my request to rest.

FUCK. ME.

When I lay eyes on Lola as Dr. Rice and the nurses rush her from the Sikorsky to the hospital roof's door, I lose my control nearly. I have to bite down on my molars to keep from blowing my top.

Her eyes are closed in her pallid face—no longer glowing as it was this morning—covered partially by an oxygen mask. The lids flutter when the nurse calls me by my name to step out of the way.

Stormy gray orbs meet dull hazel ones.

Lola blinks, then grimaces.

"Is she all right?! How's our baby?!" I demand as the medical team hurries her past me into the hospital with me on their heels.

"She's stable. But we'll know more when we monitor her and the baby," Dr. Rice responds in between commands to the others.

I follow the team as far as they allow to the doors of an operating room on the obstetrics floor. A nurse turns to block my path and points towards a waiting room down the hall. Reluctantly, I head to it once again with my mobile to my ear to alert my parents.

That happened over a week ago. Fortunately, neither Lola nor Baby Boy suffered any repercussions from her fall. Not one test or observation revealed any harm to either of them. I said a prayer of thanks then and repeat one now.

Even as my erect cock twitches in my gray sweatpants, appreciative of the beauty spread before me.

Lola's round ass reddened by the spanking I gave her moments ago. The imprints of my palms and fingers leave my marks on her soft skin.

I trace my fingertips along the edges, then palm the heated flesh and squeeze.

Hard.

Lola hisses past the ball gag. Her body tenses, and she bows her back, seeking the pleasure from the pain.

"How do you feel, Naughty Pet?" I ask, not wanting her to sense any discomfort from the binds or the position. The spanking, well…

Lola glances over her shoulder in my direction and nods twice. A red silk mask on her face—a playtime one over her eyes and not one for oxygen atop her mouth. Instead, a cherry red ball gag parts her full lips.

"Excellent. Do you understand why you are being punished, Naughty Pet?" I ask as I pick up the next implement and run it through my fingers.

Time to step it up, I chuckle low in my throat darkly.

The fringes of the suede flogger glide along the soles of

her feet, up the backs of her calves and thighs, then along her dripping pussy seam to between the crack of her rosy ass.

Lola whimpers around the gag and nods twice. She shivers from the erotic touch of the toy. The scent of her arousal—a carnal perfume—fills my nostrils.

I inhale deeply and close my eyes.

Mmmmmm.

"Ten. One for each city you insisted upon traveling to, despite me asking you to take it easy. Plus two as encouragement to listen to your husband," I say as the flogger arcs through the air and lands on Lola's left ass cheek with a THWACK. Then I follow it with another strike on her right ass cheek. THWACK!

"AAARGH!!!" Lola yowls past the gag as she pulls against the restraints.

I tsk and walk around standing before her.

Lola turns her head to track the feel of the flogger as I drag the fringes along her flank, over her shoulder, and place the butt beneath her chin. She shivers, and not from the cold.

"You forgot to count, Naughty Pet," I smirk. "Oh, well, we must start from one."

A mewl escapes her mouth, and she drops her head. The thick waves conceal her gorgeous face.

I lift the butt to raise her head on a level with my face as I squat before her.

"Naughty Pet, how do you feel?" I ask.

Without hesitation, Lola bobs her head and stretches her neck to reach closer to me. I stroke her cheek and purr in her ear.

She trembles.

Abruptly, I step away and reposition myself behind Lola.

The flogger makes contact with her round rump again and again as she mumbles the count. The last strike has her keening, a combination of pain and pleasure.

My dick throbs and drips pre-cum from the mushroom tip.

Quickly, I release the silk ties and lift Lola's limp body into my arms. Lost in subspace, Lola's head lolls against my broad chest. Her breathing is strong, and her face flushed.

I stride over to the swing and strap Lola in the harness. With care, I remove the ball gag from her swollen lips and slant my mouth over hers.

The passionate kiss wakes my Sleeping Beauty. She returns it with a voracious one of her own, sighing in satisfaction.

Once we part, I lift the mask from her eyes.

Lola blinks to regain the sense I deprived her of from the moment we entered our new playroom. The original Valentine's Day gift I created for us. Lola thought I was Captain Caveman before, but now…

I refuse to allow others at LEVELS New York to see my mate's voluptuous body further enhanced by her pregnancy. No fucking way.

Not willing to give up our BDSM lifestyle, I hired a renowned designer to create a custom playroom on the second floor of our penthouse. Every toy, apparatus, and accessory Lola and I incorporate into our erotic delights dwell here.

The sex swing is the latest goody I insisted upon adding to our repertoire. It offers the perfect solution to fuck Lola inclined on her back while she's seven months pregnant and more. I love her baby belly, but it lessens our frontal connection.

Lola smiles when she realizes she's in the swing. It's fast

become her favorite apparatus, even over the spanking bench, her top choice.

She reaches for the cords elongating her torso. Her newly grown double D-cups lift, pointing her beaded nipples towards me. Lola smirks when she notices me lick my lips.

Well…

I latch onto her nipple and suckle it until she writhes in the harness. My hot wet mouth moves from one tit to the other, planting open-mouthed kisses in the hollow between her mounds.

When Lola cries out, I grip her spread thighs, swing her back, then impale her on my engorged cock in one deep thrust.

Both of us groan upon entry.

I swing Lola back and forth, driving into her soaked pussy. In and out. In and out. In and out. The squelching sounds and the smell of sex fill the playroom.

"Oh fuuuck… Sir… Yes… Yes.. Yeeesss!" Lola screams in ecstasy, her head thrown back and her eyes squeezed shut.

"Open your eyes, Naughty Pet! Watch me fuck my pussy!" I growl.

She obeys, eyes widening at the erotic sight of my thick dick plunging into her swollen pussy and my balls slapping her ass. As another massive orgasm overtakes her sensibilities, her mouth goes slack. Her greedy pussy walls clamp on my thick invasion.

My pulse pounds in my ears. With a carnal roar, I release a torrent of cum, enough to impregnate my mate again.

"LOLAAA!!!" I growl barbarically, throwing my head back to roar for the heavens.

. . .

"You were right, my love. I overextended myself… and put our baby at risk…"

Lola shakes her head sadly as she rests her back against my chest during our evening ritual of a bath. It's our time to reconnect after a day apart at work or with family or friends. Now, we recover from our scene.

I burrow my face into her silky hair as my fingertips cover her mouth. No. I will not allow Lola to dwell on what happened. Time to move on.

"Babe, don't. You're good. Baby Boy is good"—I shift her to face me, then cup her cheeks—"And I believe you learned your lesson. Correct, Naughty Pet?"

Lola peeks at me from beneath her eyelashes submissively. Then smirks, "Yes, Sir."

I laugh a deep belly laugh.

My Independent Woman-cum-sub will never learn.

SEBASTIAN

"Go Baz! Go! Don't lose them, bro! No one wants to listen to them gloat!"

Harris shouts over the crashing waves of the Atlantic Ocean as he trims the jib sheet of the new sailboat we're racing against Roger's team.

We're on a Guys' Getaway before Roger and I become dads for the second and first times in just over a month. Along with Roger, Lachlan, Lucien, Laurent, Borya, and my close friends Scott and Porter join us for the four-day getaway. The destination of choice is Bougainvillea Cay. The guys wanted to have time to try out the new toys Malcolm ordered for the island retreat.

The racing yachts are on top of the list. So now it's the United States against The Others. Malcolm, Harris, Scott, Borya, and I make up the US. Roger, Lachlan, Lucien, Laurent, and Porter—based in Paris, Aberdeen, and Dubai—comprise our opponents.

"Scott, adjust the mainsheet! Let's go, let's go!" I shout as I man the helm.

Exhilaration runs through me as we take to the open water at the top speed of fifteen knots. The balmy weather —clear of any rain—provides the best backdrop for being on the ocean. Salty spray flies back and lands on my face. I laugh as I lick it from my lips, not daring to move my hands from the wheel.

"Yeah, baby!! We're gaining on them!!" Malcolm whoops. "Let's get it, boys!"

Lucien chances a quick glance as we come abreast with their sailboat. Lachlan shouts orders for Porter and Lucien. They rush to adjust their sheets for optimum performance.

Aside from being Alpha males, we're a super competitive group. Not one of us likes to lose. So it's balls to the walls on both yachts.

We round the regatta buoy for the return stretch with The Others ahead. But we're on their asses! Damn near our bow to their stern.

As we overtake them, Porter gives us the finger and Borya yells back curses in Russian. Both crews hustle to reach the finish line. The winner's buoy beckons to us.

With a burst of wind in our sails, we pass the marker less than a minute ahead of Roger's sailboat. The US crew hollers in victory as we head for shore.

"Yeah, yeah, yeah. Whoop it up all you want. Congratulations already…" Lachlan says as he claps me on the back when he steps onto the dock.

"Tomorrow it's the JetSki relay, so let's see who's bragging then!" Laurent adds as he grabs Harris in a headlock.

At thirty-one, they're the two youngest boys of the Steele and Jackson clans. Laurent's bottle-green eyes sparkle with mirth as he noogies Harris in the back of his head. Evenly matched in muscle although Laurent at six feet, three inches has two inches on Harris, they wrestle as they've always done—two wolf cubs angling for dominance.

They're close, like Lachlan and me. Although I'm still not that keen on him and Haley, I've let it go to avoid a distance between my baby sister and me. Not to mention sparking Lola's ire. Not worth it.

However, should Lachlan misstep, I'll beat his ass senseless. And he knows it.

"Fuck off, Laurent! Sore loser," Harris retorts as he flips him off the dock and into the water.

Everyone laughs. Then Borya hauls Laurent from the water.

"*Davay rybka,*" Borya rumbles as he pulls the little fish back onto the dock. "We'll do a training tomorrow so you can learn to defend yourself!"

Again, we crack up. While Laurent rolls his eyes and shakes his head, slinging water over us.

"Time for celebratory drinks, boys!" I chuckle as I stride back to the villa. "The winners will even pay!"

"Aw hell, dude! Pay what? We're at your place!" Porter responds.

I chuckle and nod, "True!"

WE SHOWER and change into swim trunks. Then lounge on the beach drinking local favorite Kalik beers. In the outdoor kitchen, the chef grills vegetables, fresh fish, lobster, and steaks to go along with the pigeon peas and rice.

The sun dances on the waves as they lap onto the beach before us. Other yachts dot the horizon, taking advantage of the glorious weather. The Exumas live up to their name as one of the best yachting areas in the world.

"Okay, Pops, how do you feel?" Lucien asks as he lifts his bottle to his mouth.

I can't help the grin that spreads across my face at the thought of my son making his debut in five weeks. To hold him in my arms close to my heart is the first thing I'll do after I thank his mother for my ultimate gift.

"Oh brother, man. He's grinning like the Cheshire Cat. Sebastian the Alpha Dom playboy turned faithful married man, soon-to-be father will complete his transition to domesticated chap," laughs Porter. "I can't bloody believe it!"

"Well, my friend, believe it. And I'm thankful for it!" I respond as I tip my bottle in his direction. "I pray you'll find a woman who will make an honest man out of you. Although I don't know how lucky she'll be. Bless the poor lass!"

Porter throws his head back and guffaws.

"What about you, Daddy of Three? What're your thoughts on fatherhood?" Laurent asks.

Roger grins wider than I did. His usually intense stare softens whenever he thinks of Leonie, The Twins, and now Baby Daphne.

"Enjoy every day with your children. Cherish each moment. They grow up in the blink of an eye," he answers, leaning forward with his elbows on his knees as he glances at each of us. "Don't waste a second of your time with them. And just as important with the woman who gave them to you."

"Amen, brother," I say as I stride over to him and tap my bottle to his beer. "And I will add, take the advice of those who have gone through it. Roger has been an invaluable resource for me. Thanks, bro."

Roger grins and inclines his head.

"You're more than welcome, brother. Based on the way you've cared for all of us from childhood to now, you'll be an incredible father," he says sincerely.

Malcolm and Harris along with Lachlan, Lucien, and Laurent nod in agreement.

Now it's my turn to bow my head. Roger's words strike a chord within me. I know being the eldest, I've always taken the lead to care for my siblings. Sometimes unwanted as with Haley and Lachlan and some requested like a bully harassing Roger.

To hear him praise me for taking care of them so well it prepped me for fatherhood makes my heart swell with love and pride. Then for the Jackson brothers to agree, chokes me up.

I take a swig of Kalik to give myself some time to control my emotions before I respond.

They sense it and give me a moment. A brief, but comfortable, silence descends on our group. The sizzle of the food on the grill amplifies. The aroma tantalizing.

With a nod, I rise.

"Thank you, my brother. Now, let us eat. Team The Others will need their strength for tomorrow's challenge!" I quip.

Boisterous claps, whistles, and denials fill the air.

* * *

"THE PERFECT WAY TO end our retreat: pumping music, fine liquor, and most of all hot babes! Here's to Harris for the fantastic idea!"

Laurent says with a flourish as he raises his crystal snifter of Jackson Reserve Scotch in salute.

"Hear, hear."

"Za nashu druzjbu!"

"Yes, Borya, to our friendship!"

After two more days of testosterone-filled macho challenges, we had a tiebreaker this afternoon for the best water jetpack acrobatics. Malcolm, the biggest daredevil of us all, won. So the US beat The Others with flying colors, literally.

To celebrate and to cap off our Guys' Getaway, we came to STEELE Exumas Hotel and Resort for dinner at the restaurant run by Lucien. Afterwards, the singles—Harris, Lucien, Laurent, Porter, Borya—wanted to party at the resort's nightclub.

Everyone agrees to go.

Harris makes out with a leggy brunette in a micro dress damn near showing her ass cheeks. Borya sandwiched between two fashion models bumps and grinds on the center platform of the dance floor. Lucien has Miss Bahamas in a corner on his lap with his hand between her legs devouring her mouth.

While they flirt with the more than interested female guests, those of us in relationships hang out in our VIP section partaking in a rum tasting. Lachlan gained cool points when he declined an offer to dance from a Bahamian beauty with long curly hair and doe-shaped eyes in her sepia-colored face. Instead, he stayed seated at one booth in our area.

"You should have seen Scott's face when—"

"Excuse me, aren't you Sebastian Steele?"

Inwardly, I roll my eyes at the interruption. But in case it's someone who's business-related, I school my features and face the woman.

"Why do you ask?" I respond.

A stunning ash blonde woman stares at me with large

turquoise blue eyes. She scans me from my head to my lap, her gaze lingering on my groin.

I have to hold back a scowl from her blatant scrutiny of my crotch.

"My friends don't believe me"—she points out a booth in another section of the VIP with three other attractive women staring in our direction—"And I hate to be wrong, especially when it involves a fine man. So... Yes?"

This time I don't hold back my annoyance.

"Lady, whoever I may be, the one thing I am not is interested in you," I respond, waggling my left hand to show my wedding band. The platinum glints in the light.

She narrows her eyes and launches into an angry rejoinder as she points her red-talon finger at me.

Who do I think I am? I don't have to be a major asshole. All I had to do was answer the question. Just because my name is on the resort doesn't give me the right to act like a dick. Blah, blah, blah.

I glance over at the security guard and nod. I don't have time for this dramatic shit. I have the woman of my dreams at home, pregnant with my son. I left the days of fucking for release and to sate my need to dominate with a random woman behind once I met Lola. So I give zero fucks this blonde hates to be wrong or I pissed her off with my dismissive attitude.

He strides to our section and asks the woman to return to her table. She takes the hint and throws a nasty glare at me before she leaves with no further comments.

"Good grief. That was the worse pickup line ever," Scott laughs.

"And equally ridiculous reaction," Lachlan adds with an eye roll as he sips his rum.

Malcolm and Roger agree and return to our tasting.

My mind drifts to Lola. I cannot wait to get home to her, my soul mate love.

* * *

THE FLOOR-TO-CEILING WINDOWS not covered by the blackout curtains allow the moonlight to fall across Lola's sleeping form as she lies in our bed at the duplex penthouse.

Like a man obsessed, I stand beside her, staring down. She's stunning. Her raven hair fans out on her pillow. The glossy tresses shine from the moon's glow. Her belly so close to her due date reminds me of a beach ball beneath the sheet. My son growing inside of her womb. Almost ready to make his debut.

Lola sighs in her sleep and reaches her small hand for my pillow. She draws it near her face and sighs contentedly.

Eager to hold her in my arms, I strip out of my tracksuit and boxer briefs. Then slip under the sheets and curve my body around Lola's. I nuzzle her neck to inhale her sweet scent and palm her swollen belly with my sizable hand.

"Baz?" Lola asks in a voice husky from sleep.

"Yes, babe, it's me. And better not be anyone else, either," I respond, as possessive of my mate as ever.

Lola snorts, "Chill, Captain Caveman."

She glances over her shoulder as she brings her left hand up to tangle in my hair. Her Skating Rink Ring along with her eternity band sparkle in the moonlight. A tug to my hair and I growl. A quick nip to the sensitive area where her neck meets her shoulder elicits a squeal from her.

"I am not teasing, Little Pet," I growl.

Lola snorts again and scoots back against my body. Her lush ass wiggles against my cock that's happy to feel her soft warmness through the silk of her negligee.

"Missed me?" She purrs. Then mewls when I lift her leg and slide my cock into her tight pussy that's always wet for me.

"What do you think, Mrs. Steele?" I smirk, rolling my hips to deepen my thrusts.

Until the sunrises, I show Lola just how much I missed her.

LOLA

"These onesies are just too cute! Look at the little giraffes doing cartwheels!"

Starr giggles as she holds the tiny outfit up.

"I love it!" Shelley exclaims. "And get a load of this one with teddy bears!"

We're in nursery one at the duplex penthouse. Baz and I decided to keep one close to our bedroom, so it's two doors down. After the summer, Baby Boy will move into his suite of rooms that includes nursery two, a bathroom, sitting room, playroom, and a room for Nanny Janice Smart when she's at the penthouse. We moved her into an apartment on the thirtieth floor so she can be near at all times.

She's the ideal choice for us since she's trained appropriately as a nurse and has a master's degree in early childhood education. She can dress a scrape, teach early academics and social, motor, and adaptive skills, and disarm assailants. She's a total Wonder Woman!

Nanny Janice never married and is a mature woman in

her late forties. Equally as important, she has zero interest in Sebastian.

Also checked off my list is the completion of the nurseries here, Southampton Village, and Paris in our and Morgan and Shelley's and Guy and Josy's residences. Surprisingly, the London nursery only needs the furniture delivered. Leonie worked her magic and finished ahead of schedule.

Each nursery reflects our homes: the color palettes, and whether traditional, Parisian elegance, or beach chic interior design style. My favorite is the Southampton Village with its calming greens, blues, and tans. The bleached wood and hand-painted tiles keep with the nautical theme. I can't wait to stay at our home there.

The girls surprised Leonie and me with a dual virtual baby shower a week ago. It was so much fun to play the games and to open the many presents while we interacted on the giant screens in our respective media rooms.

Blair, Billie, Starr and Shelley decorated mine while Josy, Haley, Anita and Hettie Bailey—a friend of Leonie's from Paris married to Roger's good friend Joel—did Leonie's room. They decorated hers in shades of pink and cream and mine in blues and grays.

Lucien had our favorite dishes from his restaurants in both cities for our lunches. The only downside for me was not having *Maman* Josy's delectable desserts! Instead, Sylvia Weinstock the Cake Queen who made my wedding confectionery delight crafted a gorgeous and delicious cake in the shape of a cradle. It was an edible piece of art.

Instead of the baby showers being limited to women, they included the guys. Anita and Norman's daughter Antonia and Joel and Hettie's toddler son came, too.

Rodolphe and Gaspard, almost two years old, helped to hand presents to Leonie.

The whole affair turned into a fun fete we enjoyed for hours.

Since that time, I've had the urge to nest. Hence reorganizing the gifts we received from the shower along with others delivered in the last few days from friends, fashion colleagues, and business associates. I've even reordered Baby Boy's supplies in his bathroom!

Dr. Rice says it's natural instinct to use the burst of energy I've gotten to prepare for the baby's arrival. It's no different from mama birds, cats, and other humans—male included.

I drive Baz nuts with moving his things into an order I think works best. The other morning while I was in the library reorganizing the books to make room for the first editions of *The Bobbsey Twins* and *Winnie The Pooh,* he came in asking where I put his ties.

He didn't quite understand why I moved them from their drawers to racks behind his suits. I figured he picked a suit, then would move down the row to pick a tie.

Well, no. So I spent an hour putting them all back.

I roll my eyes at the memory. Then straighten up to glance at the onsies Starr and Shelley hold.

"Oh, those came from Anna Wintour. A baby boutique in Londo—"

A sharp pain in my lower belly and lower back makes me double over with a cry. The pain radiates down my legs, making my knees buckle. I whimper and clutch my belly when I realize I'm falling.

But instead of hitting the floor, two sets of hands hold me up.

"We have you, Lola, sweetheart!" Shelley exclaims.

"Deep breaths, Lola," Starr tells me in a calm manner. "Focus on your breath."

They maneuver me to the glider, and I sit gingerly. The bracelet on my wrist beeps. A second later, my mobile rings.

Baz.

Harris—the tech wiz—created a monitor to track vitals, particularly for erratic or elevated heart rates that deviate from the norm. Plus, it has a fall detection and a GPS tracker for location of the wearer. He gave one to Leonie and one to me. The app connects to the monitor, then alerts Baz, Roger, Harris, Starr, Anita, and our doctors.

Shelley answers my mobile while Starr checks my vitals.

"Lola! What's happening?!" Baz asks over the speakerphone.

I start to speak, but another cramp hits me and knocks the breath from my lungs. Instead, a pitiful moan spills from my lips as I grimace.

All morning my back bothered me, but I just assumed it was gas from the French onion soup I ate last night. I craved the crouton and broth. It was yummy then, but it repeated on me... So I ignored the pangs.

Wrong.

"I'm on my way up!!" Baz shouts and disconnects the call.

Starr asks me questions while Shelley answers a call from Dr. Rice's nurse. They relay my answers to her, and she advises we come to the hospital even though my water hasn't broken since my due date is tomorrow. Dr. Rice will meet us there.

Just as they stand me on my feet, Baz and Malcolm rush in the nursery room's door. Baz takes one glimpse at me and barks for his mother to call Eddie to bring the car around.

He and Malcolm carry me between them. Starr grabs my hospital bag.

"Hold on, babe, we got you!" Baz says as we hurry down the hallway to our elevator. "Just breath like Starr taught you."

"Yeah, Little Sis. Don't worry, just focus!" Malcolm adds with a nod. "You and Baby Boy are all good!"

I smile at his words, so similar to Starr's. She's definitely rubbed off on him. The grin gets wiped off my face a moment later when I feel a popping sensation, along with a slow trickle of fluid between my thighs.

OMG!!! Did I just pee on myself???

Embarrassed, I peek at Malcolm, then Baz. Neither one seems to notice. Shelley talks to Harris, who called because of the alert on his mobile. However, Starr picks up on my discomfort.

She raises her eyebrows and cocks her head to the side. Her silent question hangs between us.

I glance down at my lap, then at Starr with wide eyes as we descend in the elevator. I'm wearing a white off the shoulder loose tunic and black leggings. At least the dark color will hide the evidence of my oopsie. Although I'm certain it ruined my silk thong.

She nods in understanding and turns to Malcolm.

"Honey, before you put Lola on the car's seat, let me place a towel down," she says as she rubs his back.

Malcolm nods, and Baz's gaze shifts from me to Starr to Malcolm.

"Did your water break?" He asks softly.

I flush bright red and nod.

"It's okay, babe. That's good! Baby Boy is on his way!" Baz says with a smile so full of love my heart flutters with joy.

. . .

"FUCK!!!!!! WHAT THE HELL DID YOU DO TO ME, SEBASTIAAAANNN STEEEEELE?!?!?!"

I scream at the top of my lungs as I glare at him. Daggers don't even come close to the dangerous weapons of mass destruction I'm throwing in Sebastian's direction.

He stares back at me wide-eyed with his mouth agape. My Alpha Dom, Captain Caveman is no longer in control. He's in shock.

I've been in active labor for almost seven hours. Seven. Fucking. Contraction-Filled. Hours...

"HOW MUCH LONGER DAMMIT?!?!?!?!" I screech.

The contractions come faster and last longer now. I want to bear down. I feel a lot of pressure in my lower back, worse than before and now in my rectum. I want to push, but the labor nurse says not yet.

When I first arrived at the hospital, the nurses settled me in my suite at New York's best hospital renowned for its OB-GYN department, of which Dr. Rice is the head. Moments later, he arrived with his team. An anesthesiologist, a pediatrician, labor and delivery nurses, an OB tech, and a nursery nurse followed him into my suite.

They went to work in prepping me for the first stage of pregnancy, pre-labor. Dr. Rice explained in first-time pregnancies, it can take six to eight hours for my body to be ready for the actual delivery. Once my cervix dilates to ten centimeters, he expected the second stage to be as short as 20 minutes or as long as a few hours.

Hell to the no, no, no! Not another minute, let alone a few fucking hours!

"Let's have the labor nurse check your cervix. Since the contractions are coming closer together and occur for ninety seconds, you may be ready," Starr suggests as she massages my calves.

Shelley agrees, and Starr steps out. Malcolm and Morgan wait in the anteroom of my suite. I hear them ask how I'm doing as the door shuts.

Since Leonie and I are due around the same day, the family split between New York City and Paris. Haley and Harris flew to Leonie as support for her and Roger three days ago. I haven't had a chance to speak with my bestie today, so I don't know if she's in labor, too.

Right now, I can't think past this pain honestly.

FUCK!!!

"Let's have a peek, Mrs. Steele."

I raise my gaze to see the labor nurse and Starr walk through the door. She helps me to lean back against the pillows while the nurse peeks under the sheet.

"Well, well, well, Mrs. Steele, your cervix dilated to ten centimeters. I'll get Dr. Rice now," she says with a warm smile and a gentle pat to my knee.

"Oh, thank you, Lord!!!" I cry.

Baz takes my hand in his and smiles as he says, "Babe, you're doing so well. Soon it'll be over, and we'll have our Baby Bo—"

He yowls as I grip his hand with all my strength when an excruciating contraction rocks me to my core.

"FUUUCK!!!!!" I bellow, followed by a string of curses. I call Sebastian every name I can think of and then find some more.

The labor nurse chuckles as she leaves for Dr. Rice and the rest of the obstetrics team.

"Mr. Steele, would you like me to have a look at your hand?" She asks over her shoulder.

"No, thank you. That's all right," he grunts as he rubs his hand.

Shelley rises from the sofa and reaches for Baz's hand.

"Sweetheart, it's not the best idea to hold a woman's hand when she's in labor," she laughs as she massages his hand with her fingertips. "Ask your father and brother. I'm sure I broke one or two of your father's fingers over the years!"

Baz groans, "Lesson learned, Mom, thanks."

Dr. Rice enters, and I say a silent prayer.

"Sounds as though you're ready for me, Mrs. Steele!" He booms. "Let's have a look."

Baz growls softly when Dr. Rice takes a seat on the stool at my feet and lifts the sheet. He lowers his head and peers between my legs. My Captain Caveman is not pleased. I'm surprised he's lasted this long with the many exams Dr. Rice gave me over the months—at the end weekly.

"All right, Mrs. Steele, we're in the second stage of labor. The time to push is now," he says with a fatherly smile.

"Thank the good Lord!!!" I cry as another contraction hits me.

"He's crowning. Get ready to push, Mrs. Steele," Dr. Rice raises his eyes to mine and nods. "All right, now! Push!"

At once, I curse myself for not accepting the epidural when I had the chance. I feel as though I have a hundred of Baz's massive hard dicks battering my pussy for hours with no end.

"AAARRGGGHHH!!!" I growl as I bear down.

"Breathe with it, Lola. Breathe," Starr says as she stands to my right just in my line of sight. "Focus on your breath."

I take a deep inhale in preparation to increase the pressure within my belly and contract my abs. Holding my breath before I let it go as I push Baby Boy out.

"That's it, my love. You're doing well," Baz murmurs as he strokes my hair that Starr put into one long braid down my back.

My mind knows it's not his fault. Well, not entirely. But I just can't think straight at a time such as now.

"SHUT UP STEEEELE!!!" I growl as I slap his hand away from me with a kyber crystal-powered super laser stare from the Death Star. It's strong enough to destroy an entire planet. Or a Steele.

Baz opens his mouth, then thinks better of it speaking and closes it. He glances at Starr and she shakes her head, suppressing a giggle.

It's rare one sees my powerful husband at a loss and not in charge of a situation.

More contractions, more choice words, more killer looks, more pushing, and our Baby Boy makes his debut.

SEBASTIAN

Our Baby Boy is born!

Holy shit! I'm a father, a Dad, a Daddy.

"Mr. Steele, you may cut the umbilical cord now."

Dr. Rice's words pull me from my pleasant musings, and I glance at him. He hands a pair of sterile scissors to me with a broad smile and a nod of encouragement.

I shift my gaze to Lola, my sub, my love, my wife, the mother of my child. Her hazel eyes—softened by the miracle she achieved—stare back at me from a face flushed red and damp from the exertion of nine hours of labor.

My heart swells and my eyes well with tears. I lean over to kiss her on her lips, then press my forehead to hers as I close my eyes on a silent prayer of thanks.

"I love you, Mama Steele. Thank you," I murmur huskily as tears slip down my cheeks.

Lola reaches a small hand up to wipe the moisture away. She brings her wet fingertips to her lips, then places them on mine.

"I love you, Papa Steele. Thank you, my love," she whispers in a hoarse voice. "Cut the umbilical cord so we can hold our son."

She pats my cheek and sighs, exhausted from the delivery.

With a nod, I turn to Dr. Rice and do the honor. The pediatrician, Dr. Samantha Woods, takes our son off to the side in order to care for him. I split my gaze between her actions and Lola, who's being comforted by Starr. I confirm she's fine, then turn my full attention to our son.

"How is he?" I ask as I watch possessively over the doctor's shoulder while she tends to him.

She smiles at me and responds, "He's in excellent health! All ten fingers and toes! He weighs 7.8 pounds. An acceptable size for a male newborn. Congratulations, Mr. Steele!"

Relief washes over me. Then anxiety sweeps in when she places our freshly cleaned son in my arms. When I look at her in a panic, Dr. Woods smiles encouragingly.

I glance down at his mottled face. He may be tiny, but the weight of responsibility hits me in that moment. My son, my heir, and next generation of Steeles; the fruit of my loins. I am his father. His safekeeping ranks as my utmost priority along with his mother.

"Baz? What's taking so long? Is he okay?"

Lola's soft voice filled with concern calls me back to the suite.

"He's perfect, my love. See for yourself," I respond as I stride over to her and place our son on her chest.

Lola's face lights up with such love and joy when she stares at our son. Tears stream down her cheeks. Her fingers tentatively touch his soft jet-black hair, and his eyes open slowly.

Gray eyes and black hair. The Steele family traits continue.

Lola peers up at me and smiles angelically.

"Your son, my love," she whispers. "He looks like you, like a true Steele. Are you pleased, Baz?"

I nod, overwhelmed, and I bury my face in her damp hair.

AN HOUR LATER, a freshly washed Lola holds our son to her breast as she feeds him for the first time. They're skin-to-skin to help him stay warm as he gets used to being outside of her womb. Dr. Rice explained it's a great way for parents and baby to get to know each other right away. Our baby welcomes our gentle touches, and this closeness can help us to bond with him.

I rub his back beneath the blanket, wanting him to recognize his father, too. My hand is so much larger than his narrow back. I smile and pull my mobile from my pocket to take a video and some photos.

Lola giggles, and pats the bed beside her.

"Come, sit, Daddy," she says with a twinkle in her hazel eyes.

I smirk when for a moment my mind drifts to the fetish. But that's not our thing. Although we'll try anything once...

"Stop it! Sir..." Lola laughs. "Sit with us before the family comes in."

Family.

Now I have my family of Lola, Baby Boy, and me. Our family unit that fits inside of the Steele clan. Now I know how Roger feels. To have my own is the most incredible sense of responsibility. Mine to care for, mine to protect, mine to love forever.

MINE!!!

"Tell me, did Leonie go into labor? We're due on the

same day, remember?" Lola asks. Her eyes pop in concern for her best friend, even on the heels of her delivery.

I smile before I put my mobile in front of her to hold it as Baby Boy suckles at her breast. With a few swipes, I load the video Roger sent earlier.

"Here, see for yourself, babe," I say as the screen fills with a grinning Roger angling his mobile to capture Leonie, their baby, and himself.

"Ciao, Chérie and Sebastian! Guess who made her debut right on time? Your niece Daphne Beaulieu Steele! She looks exactly like her father—gray eyes and ebony hair," Leonie trills.

Roger moves his mobile closer to Daphne's heart-shaped face. Her little rosebud mouth purses and she opens her eyes to reveal the Steele traits.

"My sweet baby girl. Can you believe it, big bro?" Roger says in awe.

Leonie gazes at him with such love. Then faces the mobile again, and her amber eyes shine.

"Now it's your turn to send a video message. Nous t'aimons!" She laughs.

"Yes! We love you! Ciao!" Roger adds as he waves before the video ends.

Their intimacy tugs at my heart. This is what Lola and I have now. I'm beyond pleased!

As I put my mobile down, it vibrates with a call. A glance at the screen shows my mother's name. Lola and I have been so focused on enjoying these first few moments with Baby Boy we hadn't communicated with my parents, Malcolm, and Starr.

"Hi, Mom! We're all good. Give us a minute before you come in to meet your newest grandson!" I exclaim.

Lola laughs as she puts Baby Boy on her shoulder.

I rub his back to help him burp. The greedy bugger.

While Lola fixes her nightgown and robe, I cradle our son to my chest through the opening of my button-down shirt. He's warm from Lola and smells like a baby, just as I remember Harris and Haley.

"'I'm all set, Baz," Lola says on a yawn.

"You need to rest, babe," I respond and continue when she starts to object. "We'll announce his name, make the video, and take some more photos. Afterwards, everyone leaves. It's important you take care of yourself, Mommy."

She grins and nods in agreement.

I place Baby Boy back in her arms, and she nuzzles his hair, inhaling his unique scent. Before I let the others in, I take a moment to stare at my little family.

All mine!

As soon as my parents walk in, my mother makes a beeline for Lola and Baby Boy. She coos softly as she strokes his little leg.

"How are you, Lola, sweetie?" My mother asks. "You look so happy. But you need to rest. We won't stay for long."

My father agrees, "No, we won't keep you, dear. Only a quick peek. You need your rest."

I chuckle to myself, thinking how alike my father and I behave. My goal has always been to have a loving relationship like my parents and now to be the best parent possible as they were with us.

"Congratulations, Little Sis, bro! You did it," Malcolm says as he fist bumps with me. "Now, what do we call Baby Boy officially?"

My face splits in two nearly as I wrap my arm around Lola's shoulders while I pat my son's back. Lola turns him around to rest against her big boobs so he can face everyone. I hand my mobile to Malcolm for him to take the video.

"Dad, Mom, Malcolm, Starr, Roger, Leonie, Harris, Haley, meet Slade Steele!" I announce, beaming.

"Slade! I love his name!" Exclaims Starr as she claps her hands. "It means valley."

"It sounds badass!" Malcolm grins, his eyes twinkle with mischief.

My father grips my shoulder and smiles. "Well done, son, daughter! A strong name for the next generation of Steeles. Your brother- and sister-in-law had Daphne, a beautiful baby girl. Today is a great day for our family!"

LOLA

"*Chérie*! Slade looks more and more like Sebastian every day! I don't see a drop of my bestie in your son!"

Leonie's laughter comes across the screen as we FaceTime streamed to the television in the pergola on the ocean-facing deck of Baz and my Steele Southampton Village beach house. She's holding adorable Daphne dressed in a pink leopard-print onesie on her lap while we have our daily Girls' Chat.

Shortly after she gave birth, they flew to their hillside villa in Monte Carlo for the summer. Guy and Josy along with Nanny Grace made the seasonal move with them down to the "glitterati" capital of Europe, as Leonie calls the Mediterranean gem. Her parents bought a villa in the same STEELE luxury gated community to be near their grandchildren when The Twins were born.

As a mother of three and my best friend, Leonie has a wealth of knowledge she imparts on me. I relate more to her since she's only a year older than me at thirty-three. Her recent experiences from what to do about swollen ankles to having a doula for support before and during childbirth to the best oils for breast massages help me tremendously.

"I know right! Baz struts around like a proud peacock!" I giggle as I nuzzle against Slade's soft ebony curls.

It's been three weeks since he was born. Without a doubt, Baz is his father. As my mother used to say, "You have no nickel in that dime!" Slade is a miniature Baz.

Billie gave a set of beautiful leather-bound journals to me as one of her baby shower gifts. The first one has my notes, sketches, and my musings on nearly every page. Each day I update Slade's growth and development: when he first lifted his head; his sleep patterns; feeding schedule. I even doodle little drawings of him sleeping or with Baz.

I love to go back to the first page and read through. Baz teases me, but I don't care. Especially since he's become a professional photographer!

He's kitted out with the top-of-the-line digital camera, various lenses, flashes, you name it. During my pregnancy, he used his mobile to snap my monthly baby bump profile pic. Before Slade was born, Baz had a fashion photographer friend of mine advise him on "nothing but the best equipment." Now Baz takes so many shots of us, I feel as though we're at one of Lola's Coterie's photoshoots!

Not only still shots, but video, too. "It's important to mark milestones and to record our family like my parents did with my siblings and me, babe!"

I have to admit I love his enthusiasm and the time we spend going through his many libraries categorized by theme. If I didn't have my family photos and videos, I wouldn't have any means to show Slade his maternal grandparents.

That's another reason I never miss my calls with Leonie.

She, Luc, *Maman* Josy, and *Papa* Guy are my second family; the ones who helped me through the loss of my parents. Time spent with them is even more vital for me. And I'm beyond thankful for them.

Shelley and Morgan have been fantastic. Even before Slade was born, Shelley lived up to the promise she made to me in Capri. She and Morgan may not be my parents, but they certainly make every effort to care for me and to love me like one of their own.

From the moment we announced our pregnancy at Christmas to Slade's birth, my in-laws helped to ease the sadness that would creep up, compounded by my raging hormones. On the very rare occasion Baz couldn't make an appointment, Shelley would come with me. She and *Maman* Josy gave as much input in Slade's nurseries as Leonie did with her designs.

Morgan made sure I had the best suite at the hospital since he's the top donor. "You never know when you may need a quality hospital, Lola dear. Best to support one as much as financially possible," he told me with a chuckle and a wink.

Now we're all out at the beach compound for the summer. Normally they would go to the Mediterranean either to their Villa Sogno in Positano or aboard their megayacht *Serendipity*. Just like Leonie's parents, Shelley and Morgan want to be near their newest grandson.

They come by to check on Baz, Slade, and me regularly. But Shelley insists we spend this time to bond as a family. She says it's important for Slade to recognize his parents, and for us to acclimate to a newborn.

Which brings me to Baz.

Besides being a proud peacock photographer, he's an amazing father. He's taking a paternity leave from

STEELE International through September. Just as Baz did for Roger when he had The Twins, Malcolm has stepped in to cover for both brothers. Harris and Haley will chip in since two divisions along with the CEO responsibilities will require all Steeles on deck. Morgan will assist as necessary.

My thoughts drift back to our first morning here.

The sunlight streaming through the windows glows like orange fire behind my closed eyelids, still heavy from sleep. For a moment, I lie there and listen to the squawks of the seagulls as they soar above the Atlantic Ocean in search of their breakfast. The breaking waves splash onto the private beach in a soothing rhythm that lulls me to sleep briefly.

I'm exhausted.

My attention returns to our bedroom as I listen for interior sounds. The first things I notice are the loss of Baz's warm body wrapped around mine and the lack of breathing from his side of the bed. I crack one eye open to glance towards his pillow. An indentation serves as proof he slept beside me. I reach my hand out to touch the rumpled bedding. Cold.

The sound of his gentle baritone over the latest version of the fancy-schmancy baby monitor Harris created for Leonie originally is the third thing I notice. I lift it off of the night table and place it on my breasts heavy with milk as I lean against the headboard with a contented sigh.

My man is with his son.

"—understand your situation... Absolutely... But your Mommy needs her rest, Slade... You kept us awake all of last night. But that's okay. You realize why?... Because we love you so very, very much, my son. You are a gift."

The rustle of material and the coos of Slade float over the monitor. He's in Slade's nursery.

I imagine Baz changing his son's diaper or getting him dressed for the day. He's better at coaxing his son into his diaper than I by a long shot!

"Now, you have to feel better, Stinky Binky..."

I giggle at the nickname Baz gave to Slade. When Baz changed our son's first diaper, he gagged and ran out of the room holding his hand over his mouth. I laugh harder and snort at the memory.

Not one to back done from a challenge, Baz now aces the diaper and dressing routine. The night prior, he selects the outfits for the next day and lays them out on Slade's dressing table. His attire varies based on the activity: walking on the beach or visiting his grandparents or resting at home.

Again, I crack up at my silly husband.

"I appreciate you're hungry, Slade... Yes, okay... We'll sit on the window seat this morning and watch the seagulls eat their breakfast while you eat yours. Deal?... Good..."

Over the last three weeks, we found schedules and routines that work well—and some that were abysmal. The one I recognize Baz treasures the most is his morning time with Slade. A time father and son can bond alone.

And a time for Mommy to sleep in bed longer. I roll over to my side and place the monitor beside Baz's pillow. The hushed cadence of his voice lulls me back to slumber again. My eyes drift shut, and I rest just as my husband knows I need.

"—Daphne loves the carousel mobile Luc bought for her with the princesses and princes riding on the horses! It mesmerizes her. Are you even listening to me, *Chérie*?"

Leonie's question pulls me from my daydream.

"So sorry! I was thinking about Baz and his morning routine with Slade. They're just so cute!" I respond, giggling. "How's Roger with all three babies?"

Leonie's amber eyes glow with love for her man and children. The stories she tells me about their escapades make Baz and his shenanigans seem professional. Roger *The*

Responsible lives up to his name truly and cannot wait to organize his little family. Leonie balances his intensity with her easygoing attitude. What I love the most is how well they make it all work.

"Hey Leonie! How's my sister doing? And of course, how're my nephews and baby niece? They do realize they'll see their most favorite uncle in a few weeks?"

I glance up to see Baz standing beside me, waving at Leonie and making faces at Daphne. We laugh at his antics and Daphne coos waving her chubby arms in the air.

"Bonjour, big brother!! We're doing well, *merci*. Roger made the arrangements for us, my parents, and Luc to fly over together. You know your brother!" Leonie snorts.

"Oh, we know!" Baz and I respond simultaneously, then join her in boisterous laughter.

Our family will gather here as tradition for Labor Day festivities and the fundraiser. It'll be even better this year since we'll have our newest additions, Slade and Daphne. Even though Leonie and I video chat every day, I can't wait to see her in person!

The three of us talk, then Roger joins us. He had taken Rodolphe and Gaspard to the clubhouse for a playdate with other kids in the villa community. He sits beside Leonie and puts Daphne on his lap while The Twins climb into Leonie's lap.

"Hey, guys!" Roger says. "You look fantastic, Lola! How's my little nephew? Tell Slade his favorite uncle says hi!"

We spend the next hour talking. Baz and Roger trade war stories as Leonie and I giggle. It's such a peaceful time. Our little families growing together.

I still can't believe how fortunate Leonie and I are to have married brothers. We can see one another regularly and not lose our best-friend connection like so many women do when men come into their lives. The bonus of our children bonding as we did makes me so elated. Not to mention being blood relatives.

Grateful doesn't describe how I feel for my life.

After my adamant refusal to have a baby—I can finally admit I dodged the baby situation—I'm beyond thrilled at the joys of motherhood!

I find the connection between Slade and me is unconditional. The endless hugs, kisses, and loving gestures from my son remind me every day of the love I shared before he was born—as he grew in my body. I learned being a mother changes my life completely. Yet I love every single part of it from the body aches and labor pain to staring in his eyes as he feeds to his unique scent tickling my nose.

Prior to Slade, Lola's Coterie was my baby, my be-all and end-all in life.

I made it my sole focus not only for success, but as a dedication to my parents. I envision each success as a kiss and a hug from them; each setback I hear my father whispering his favorite saying in my ear, "Lola, are you a wolf or super wolf? Because there are no sheep in this family."

As I harness the super wolf that they raised me to be, it pushes me to work harder to turn each setback around. At their funeral, I promised them I would never forget how much they loved and believed in me and that I would make them proud.

In my heart, I know that they're pleased with all that I've accomplished in such a scant time—graduated FIT at twenty; completed an apprenticeship here in Paris at twenty-four; opened my first boutique on the Champs-Élysées at twenty-five; the second location on London's Bond Street at twenty-eight; expansion to New York City,

Las Vegas, Abu Dhabi, Dubai, Beverly Hills at thirty; future locations in Dallas, Tokyo, and Milan.

As I watch my BFF and her husband, I understand just as Leonie I can have it all—the success of my company, the love of my husband, and the blessing of my son—without the loss of myself and my goals.

My gaze shifts to the man beside me. I watch Sebastian and smile as I recall our chance encounter at LEVELS New York and the serendipity of him being the president of the company I planned to meet with for Lola's Coterie. He brought out my sexual sub and taught me I can still be an Independent Woman—my body shudders with desire for my Alpha Dom. We've come so far and have so much more ahead of us. My soul mate.

Baz glances over at me and smiles. His strikingly handsome face makes my panties wet no matter the circumstances. He must glimpse my want because his gray eyes twinkle and he bites his full lower lip as his nostrils flare.

It's been too long since he had me beneath his powerful body. I cannot wait until July 27. I have the time marked on my calendar: BAZ AND I FUCK ALL WEEKEND LONG!!!

Shelley and Morgan offered to babysit Slade for the weekend at their residence in the compound. Shelley smirked knowingly when I asked her to take care of Slade the other day. Not that she needs an excuse to keep her grandson.

"So what's the plan for the rest of your day? A stroll on the beach, or are you going into town to that cafe we like?" Leonie asks as she bounces a laughing Rodolphe on her knees.

He speaks to her in French, then turns to the screen and asks in English when he'll see us.

Leonie and Roger want them to speak as many

languages as they—French, English, Italian, German, and Spanish. It makes sense living in Europe with so many countries around them.

Baz and I plan the same for Slade since we speak English, French, Italian, and Russian. We want him fluent in multiple languages as a future leader at STEELE and to appreciate other cultures. Our children will be worldly and have broad educational backgrounds like us.

"Well, Ms. France, it's July 4. So we're having a clambake and watch the fireworks on the beach in front of Shelley and Morgan's house tonight," I tease.

Leonie laughs and nods her head.

"Oh, yes, of course. I forgot! Have fun for us!" She says.

Daphne wails, and Roger cuddles her on his lap as he turns to Leonie.

"Feeding time, *Maman*," he says with a wicked grin.

Leonie's face flushes bright red as she glances away from the screen. She shakes her head and giggles while she gathers The Twins.

"Talk to you tomorrow, *Chérie*!" She sings with a wave.

When the screen goes black, Baz turns to me.

"I'm with Roger… Feeding time, Mama!" He smirks as he licks his lips.

LOLA

"Good afternoon, Mrs. Steele. Welcome to Spa Bliss Southampton Village!"

The receptionist greets me cheerfully as I walk past other clients to her desk.

Shelley suggested their spa for my day of pampering. It's her favorite of all places available in the village. Their facility provides individual suites per client for the utmost in privacy and attention since all treatments occur within the suite, no need to move from one area to the other. Plus, they have decadent products and tasty spa meals.

Baz gifted me with the day. He told me to take some time for myself. Unwind and tune into me. He would take care of Slade so I could relax. It's a Mommy Day Off.

Although we both know he's gearing me up for our weekend of debauchery! YES!!!

I notice two of the female clients lift their gazes from magazines at the mention of my name. Their sharp eyes take me in from head to toe. Who knows whether they're former lovers or wannabes—Baz was a notorious playboy before we tied the knot.

Even after three years of marriage, women still have no shame in expressing their desire for my husband. They take his denial as a challenge and disregard me completely. As if I give a good goddamn…

"Good afternoon, thank you," I respond to the receptionist. Then wave my left hand glittering with my gigantic Ice Rink Ring and eternity band at the vultures, "Ladies."

They blanched at the sight of the massive diamonds. A few defeated nods and mumbles greet me in response.

Right! I thought so.

"Kindly follow me to your suite, Mrs. Steele. Your aesthetician awaits," the receptionist says pleasantly.

I'm so excited about my spa day! All of my preferred treatments: hot stone massage, steam facial, salt glow with body wrap, deep conditioning hair mask, manicure, pedicure, aromatherapy. Not to mention a full-body wax, so my skin is buttery soft for Baz to slide all over me this weekend!

We pass through a curtained archway to enter the foyer that leads to my suite. Soft instrumental music plays in the dimly lit hallway while lulling essential oils of bergamot, lavender, and ylang ylang waft around us. Immediately, I'm transported to a land of tranquility. I take a deep restorative inhale and exhale all stress and negativity as I prepare for a day solely focused on Lola.

WHEN BAZ CHASED me down to Luc's beachfront villa in St. Barth's after I broke up with Baz the first time, we soaked in the outdoor sunken tub. The air fragrant from the fresh, tropical flowers in the surrounding garden.

It was in that moment I wanted to verbalize my love for

him, but held back for fear of exposing myself to more pain. Instead, I told him with my body when I melded us together. I connected with him in the only way that a woman and a man can. I covered his body with mine and put him inside of me like a key in a lock.

My blood pulses in my veins as my body heats from the memory of our lovemaking. Baz is such a talented lover and Dom. An ache grows in my pussy, and I squeeze my thighs together for a bit of relief. I cannot wait until he gets back from taking Slade to his grandparents…

Meanwhile, I luxuriate in the tub here in our home. We recreated our St. Barth's experience on the deck near the side garden overlooking the Atlantic Ocean. The flowers may not be tropical, but their fragrant aroma wafts around me as the wind blows off the water.

I close my eyes and sink deeper into the warm sudsy water scented with sandalwood, neroli, and jasmine essential oils. The seductive blend heightens my desire for my man. With a sigh, I trail one hand from the side of my neck along my collarbone over the top of my heavy breast past my peaked nipple across my flat belly to the apex of my thighs. My long middle finger brushes against my puffy pussy lips to breach my seam—

"What are you doing, Naughty Pet?"

I gasp and jump from the unexpected sound of Baz's voice, thick with lust and displeasure. Water splashes out of the tub onto the stones. My hair tumbles from the messy bun and whips into my eyes as I swing around in his direction wildly.

The breath catches in my throat when I take in the sight of Baz.

He stands naked, towering over me at his full height of six feet, four inches of pure muscle. His olive skin darkened by the sun's rays. Flinty gray eyes scan my body, alighting on my mounds as they skim the surface of the water, the nipples sharp points despite the heat.

A low growl makes my hooded eyes move from the v-cuts of his Adonis belt where his engorged veiny dick with its bulbous angry red tip shiny from pre-cum juts towards me.

Like a hungry animal, my mouth salivates, and I lick my lips. I follow his happy trail up his eight-pack abs to his pecs. His Adam's apple bobs as he swallows thickly, just as taken by the sight of my wet flesh glistening in the sunlight as I am of his masculine beauty.

When our eyes meet, a frisson of eroticism shoots through my core. It throbs and floods in anticipation of the pounding Baz will give to me. We're both too wound up for slow lovemaking.

I. Want. Him. To. Fuck. Me. Raw.

Baz raises his eyebrow and cocks his head to the side. Too engrossed with ogling his body to answer his question, I drool. He waits patiently. The marble sculpture of David in the flesh.

"Nothing, Sir," I respond demurely as I lower my eyes in submission.

Another growl—louder this time—forces my eyes up to his again.

My core clenches.

"What I witnessed is far from the definition of nothing, Naughty Pet," Baz rumbles. "Hands and knees. Now."

My mouth drops open, then my eyes widen at Baz striding towards me. The thick muscles of his long legs flex with each step. Even his calves bunch as he prowls towards me. His eyes narrow on me as I sit dumfounded.

Oh my.

I scramble to get into position with a carnal cry. More water sloshes out of the tub in my haste. But even more liquid floods my greedy pussy.

My palms land on the wet stones and my knees anchor to the porcelain basin, my toes curl to gain purchase. I arch my back to present my ass for punishment to my Dom.

The water ripples like waves in the ocean before me when Baz steps down into the tub. Concentric circles break as they reach my hips. Closer and closer he comes.

I shudder.

"Widen your knees, Naughty Pet," Baz commands.

The waves of desire emanate from his body to hit me more forcefully than the roused water. He bends over my back to press his lips to the shell of my ear. His warm breath tickles the sensitive skin as he breathes.

"Naughty Pet, you were told to wait for me in the tub. You were not told to play with yourself. Your body is my playground alone," Baz says gruffly. "Lean forward. I want your ass on the surface. Those round globes floating, ready for your punishment."

Once again, I hurry to obey.

No sooner than I raise up, the heavy palm of Baz's hand strikes my left ass cheek with a sharp crack intensified by the coating of water.

"Count, Naughty Pet. Miss one and we start anew," he threatens.

I yelp and shift forward as I cry out, "One, Sir!"

Baz grips my left hip to hold me where he wants exactly and proceeds to fall into a steady rhythm.

Left, right, left, crease of my ass and thigh, right, left.

"You do not touch yourself unless I give you permission, Naughty Pet. And be still! Control your body," he rumbles.

As the spanking continues, they get harder and the

intensity mounts. I can barely concentrate to count and beg Baz to forgive me. My body strung so tightly from the effort to not cum until he gives me permission, thrums.

"Your ass is a beautiful rose. But I want to see the petals of your pussy, Naughty Pet. On your chest, spread your thighs wider, and hold your butt cheeks apart for me," Baz demands in my ear. "Do you understand?"

"Yes, Sir," I pant.

A dark chuckle slips from Baz's lips. The tip of his thick finger touches my swollen clit.

I whine and undulate my hips, aching to feel his touch inside my pussy. A smack to my pussy lips has me slipping on the wet stone as my hands slide forward and my knees slip on the basin. Before I can fall, Baz slips his arm around my waist and lifts me back into position.

"Oh no you will not, Naughty Pet," he growls. "Keep still, or I will add ten more."

My pussy flutters, and I mewl. A part of me wants to slip for more of a punishment. The other part wants to cum on his massive dick that's pressed against the crack of my ass, wedged between my back hole and my clit.

The dick wins when the tip brushes my rosebud.

More smacks to my pussy lips, and I count every single one like a good girl. Albeit a breathless, quivering mess of one.

Finally, after what seems like a century, I hear those sweet words.

"I'm going to fuck you until you cannot walk, Naughty Pet. Then we will start again," Baz promises with another dark chuckle as he strokes my ass covetously.

Before I can reply, the wide mushroom head of his cock sinks inside of my flooded channel followed by his turgid length in one brutal thrust.

We grunt in unison.

As Baz pummels me relentlessly, I feel every ridge, every vein, and every one of the ten inches of his massive dick.

"Fuuuck… Pet… I missed your tight, wet heat pulsating around my cock!" Baz growls, his hips buck and jerk with each word.

"Ooooh! I missed you, too, Siiirrr…" I moan as my pussy muscles clamp on his thick invasion.

Baz grunts and leans back. His palm connects with my ass, smacking one cheek, then the other in rapid succession even as his thrusts continue to rock into me.

He pulls his hips back and his still swollen cock slips from my core with a pop. Bereft from the loss, I keen with need.

"Do not fret, Little Pet. Your pussy is not the only hole to service me," Baz says with one more slap to my ass for emphasis.

I whimper and drop my head. My heavy breasts sway below me. Full with milk, awaiting relief from Baz, they ache with need.

The next sound from my mouth is a grunt when his tip breaches the rings of muscles in my puckered hole. His thick dick coated with the natural lubricant juices from my pussy plows into me—two inches in, one inch out—until Baz seats himself fully within my ass. His balls brush my sensitive clit.

"Fuuuuuuck. Me." He roars with feral dominance and desire. "Yessss!!!"

With that cry, Baz grips my hip with one hand and my throat with the other to hold me in place as he uses my bottom hole for his carnal pleasure.

Each thrust and each groan brings me closer to the edge.

I whimper and wiggle my hips to make his heavy balls slap against my clit. I need to cum. Now.

Baz must sense my need. He reaches his hand around my hip to tap, then to tug on my swollen nub. His groin slams into me over and over.

"Cum for me, Little Pet. Cum on my giant cock in your tiny ass!" He shouts ferociously.

When he pinches my engorged clit, I spiral out of control. A long, low keen rips from my mouth as my pussy spasms on air and my ass squeezes his dick. My vision blackens and my hearing fades.

The bliss of subspace overtakes me at last.

* * *

"HAVE YOU HAD ENOUGH, or do you want more?"

It's been a weekend of pure carnal bliss. Baz bathes me as we take one last soak in the outdoor tub before we meet Shelley and Morgan for dinner at their residence.

Just as Baz promised, he's fucked me until I can't walk. My wrecked pussy filled again and again with his seed.

I feel wonderful… and deliciously raw.

"Sir, I can never ever get enough of you," I purr. "But our Daddy and Mommy duties call."

I shift position to straddle his thighs and hold his handsome face in my hands. Leaning forward, I rest my forehead against his and breathe his breath.

Baz sighs and cups my ass in his sizable hands. His lips meet mine. A toe-curling kiss ensues. He squeezes my butt cheeks and lifts me from his thighs to stand.

"I love you, Mrs. Steele, and will never ever get enough of your body or of your love," he murmurs huskily. "Now, let's get our son."

Thirty minutes later, we're seated at the outdoor table on the deck, lit with torches. The chef grills steaks, lobsters, shrimp, and corn on the cob in the husk with seasoned melted butter. A fresh green salad with balsamic vinaigrette and raspberry sorbet round out our dinner.

Slade sleeps comfortably in a cot at the head of the table between Baz and Morgan. The men peek at him throughout our meal, even though Slade isn't awake and hasn't made a peep. He's our Sweet Babboo.

"Slade is a pleasure to care for, no problem at all," Morgan says fondly. "Shelley and I are more than happy to babysit him whenever you'd like some time off."

"Indeed! He's a joy!" Shelley adds as she rubs Morgan's forearm. "It's important for the two of you to stay connected. Remember what I told you at your bridesmaids' luncheon, Lola."

I giggle at her sage advice and nod.

"Absolutely, Shelley! So insightful and wise," I respond with a smile.

Baz and Morgan stare between us expectantly.

But what's shared during Girls' Talk stays between the girls. Shelley winks at me, and we slap our upraised hands before we burst into peals of raucous laughter.

The boys shake their heads and take swigs of their beers.

I have the coolest in-laws imaginable, I think with a grin.

SEBASTIAN

"Hey, guys. I hate to bother you during your baby leaves. If we could have avoided it, we would have done so. But Dad said it's best to run the situation by you."

Malcolm says over the video conference in my beach house office. He's at STEELE International's Asian headquarters in Tokyo to oversee our latest division combined project.

The plan requires Retail, Entertainment, Residential, and Children and Young Adults. Even Lola's input matters since her lingerie boutique will serve as an anchor for the mall—her largest location to date because of the popularity of her lingerie in Japan. Harris and Haley join for their take on technology and cyber security. So the gang's all here, as Harris loves to say.

"Fine, tell us the net net of the situation," I respond as I sit back in my chair at the conference table. The shift from beach bum to multibillion-dollar global company billionaire seamless.

Lola sits across from me with her tablet at the ready. She has a determined expression on her face. Her shift was as seamless as mine.

Despite being on a business call, my cock twitches as I watch her Independent Woman come to the forefront. I've told Lola before how much it turns me on to watch her take charge in the boardroom.

The bedroom however is mine all mine.

The last two weeks we've been fucking like rabbits, wild animals, whatever gets their jollies off to make up for the time we couldn't make love. And it's not one-sided. Lola's more demanding than me! Not that I mind, not one bit.

I thought her body was bodacious before. Now, my Petite Seductress could tempt a saint. Fuller hips, narrow waist, double D-cups full of creamy milk. Yum-my… She attributes it to her yoga and Pilates sessions with Starr and her conditioning and weight training with Borya. He's the only man I trust with my woman, barely. However, I thank them both. Job well done!

Not that her pregnancy body wasn't attractive to me. It abso-fucking-lutely enthralled me, as in mouthwatering. In fact, I can't wait to fill her belly with my baby again. Perhaps she's already pregnant, considering the gallons of jizz I put in her fertile womb.

A man can hope.

Lola must sense my erotic musings. Her hazel eyes survey me from across the table for a moment while Roger makes a comment. She arches an elegant eyebrow in question.

But I shake my head slightly and return my attention to the conversation at hand. Not the ideal impression for the CEO to have carnal thoughts of banging his wife in the middle of an important meeting. Particularly when said CEO's cock hardened to titanium.

"—We can also incorporate the children's clubhouse within the adults' and require a form of recognition to enter the section. The added security would ease my worries for The Twins and Daphne. Don't you agree, *Chérie*?" Leonie suggests as she turns to Lola.

She nods and leans forward, "I most certainly do agree, Leonie. Now, with the mind of a mother, I understand their concerns. The security wouldn't have to be imposing and scare the children. But obvious enough for those who shouldn't be there and warn them off."

Roger and I glance at each other over the screen and grin. Our wives—the mothers of our children—have become not only an integral part of our personal lives, but of STEELE. They prove their worthiness of heading a division, as with Leonie, and holding seats on the board, as with both of them.

Malcolm beams and sits back in his chair. He claps his hands and chuckles.

"Well, ladies, your points provide another perspective and solutions we can use to solve that part of the problem. Do you agree, Haley and Harris?" Malcolm asks.

The Dynamic Duo nod and go into tech lingo that's above my pay grade! Their knowledge of their industry astounds all of us each time we listen to them. They expound upon Lola and Leonie's recommendations.

After another hour, we call it a wrap.

Malcolm will finish his business in Tokyo, then make stops in Singapore, Hong Kong, Beijing, and Kuala Lumpur. He plans to make the most of the Tokyo trip with visits to cities in the area before he returns to the United States. He'll stop by Beverly Hills for business and pleasure. Starr will return with him to Southampton Village for Labor Day.

Harris leaves for site visits in South America. Several of our retail and hotel properties require a review of their infrastructure. He and his team will meet with the leadership and the staff for concerns and feedback before Harris makes changes. Afterwards, he'll fly here.

Haley is over the Pond in the United Kingdom. She's working on a project out of our London headquarters. Some new idea she has for cyber security. Although I believe Lachlan the bigger factor for the choice of her location. Haley can work anywhere in the world with her gadgets. However, London is closer to Aberdeen, Scotland than her base in New York City. How convenient? As though she can fool her big brother…

Roger and Leonie won't leave Monte Carlo until it's time for them, along with Guy, Josy, and Luc to fly here. Roger doesn't want Daphne to fly such a long distance now. She and Slade will celebrate their three-month birthdays when everyone arrives.

Lola uses the video connection for her Girls' Chat. She and Leonie start to catch up on what I do not know since they speak every single day. What might change in less than twenty-four hours, I have no clue.

So, I bid everyone safe travels and kiss Lola on her forehead. Then I head to the nursery for my daily father-son bonding. Nothing compares to being a father. Not my roles at STEELE or my volunteer and philanthropy work. Only my love for Lola ranks as high on my list.

Who'd have thought Alpha Dom playboy solely focused on proving my worthiness as leader of STEELE would fall madly in love with a petite spitfire, marry her, and beg for a baby?

Hell nah!

But here we are, and here I go, striding with a purpose to my son's nursery. I can't help but to chuckle at the irony. I'm ready for family life, but women still flock to me. No ring and no baby keep them away.

Only the other day on Main Street, a woman who's a part of our social circle and knows damn well I'm married, propositioned me. While I was on the line at the Maison Kayser bakery where I was buying Lola a few of her favorite *pain au chocolat*. Unwanted and unbelievable.

As I near the nursery door, I hear Nanny Janice talking to Slade. She's a godsend. The best choice for our needs. Especially since she's not at all interested in me. Thank fuck!

"Hi Nanny Janice," I say as I walk through the door. "How is my son?"

She faces me and smiles as I lift him from her arms.

"Hi, Mr. Steele. Slade just finished a bottle, and I changed his diaper. So he's all ready for you," she responds.

I thank her and give her the rest of the day off. Lola and I prefer to care for Slade ourselves as much as possible. We're hands-on parents. Just as our parents were with us—and mine still! None of that abandoned by the parents for the staff to raise bullshit for our children. The poor little rich kid. No.

A chuckle falls from my mouth as once again I refer to more babies. Hell, Slade just turned eight weeks. Surely Lola isn't ready. But then again, motherhood has changed her.

I've noticed her shift in focus from Lola's Coterie to our son over the last few months, even before she gave birth. Roger says the same happened with Leonie, who unlike Lola wanted a baby. But had to find the balance of being a wife, mother, and her successful careers in modeling and interior design.

Yeah, Roger and I have our Guys' Chats about fatherhood. He's been a great resource—just as my Dad—for me. We don't necessarily speak every day as Lola and Leonie do. But our chats are regular. And we value them.

Slade wiggles in my arms and draws me back to our bonding time. Today I want to take him for a walk on the beach, then sit and watch the waves roll in. He revels in the tranquility just as much as me. The sounds of the waves breaching the sand and the seagulls as they soar above soothe us both.

We walk downstairs and out across the deck to the beach. I strapped Slade in his harness, facing out so he can watch where we go. He's ah-gooing and laughing as we stroll along. His chubby arms wave as his legs kick when a seagull swoops around us, hoping for a bite of food.

Slade's growth and development amaze me. At Nanny Janice's suggestion, we've bought toys and a mobile to stimulate his senses. He's at the stage of learning faster. So Lola and I want to encourage it.

Since the beach is private, we don't encounter other people. I stop at our favorite spot and open the blanket before we settle on the sand. Slade sits on my lap facing the Atlantic Ocean. In the distance sailboats glide by, and a cruise ship makes its way along the East coast.

I take the time to meditate like Starr taught me years ago. Her yoga sessions continue to be a part of my fitness routine for the mind-body benefits. Hell, even Borya MMA champion meets with Starr!

A shift in the breeze brings the scent of Lola's Joy Jean Patou Parfum. It's intense and luscious with an alluring floral composition. Like Pavlov's dogs, my dick jumps to life in my cargo shorts—my go-to bottoms since they have plenty of pockets for Slade's accoutrements.

"Hi, guys," Lola's says. The sound of her voice washes over me like the waves on the shore.

"Hi, babe," I respond as she sits behind me, wrapping her thighs around mine and pressing her front to my back.

Cocooned within her soft, warm body, Slade and I lean back. Her pillowy tits super comfy.

We don't need to speak; just allow ourselves to connect in silence as we watch the waves. Slade falls asleep, and I put a cover over him as he lies on his belly atop the beach blanket. Then I pull Lola around to my lap.

She giggles and kisses me silly.

"How was your father-son bonding today, my love?" Lola asks softly.

She knows the importance of the time for me. Just as her time in the evenings is for her. Lola loves bath time with Slade.

I love how wet her clothes get, then cling to her lush tits. The pebbled nipples ready for me to suckle. Bath time has fast become my favorite evening routine, too. Followed by tucking Mommy in bed beneath Daddy all night long time. Thanks, Slade, for being splashy!

"It was good. He had an encounter with a hungry seagull," I respond and laugh when her jaw drops. "No contact made. It flew around us, hoping for food. Slade thought it amusing."

We stay on the beach for another thirty minutes before we go to my parents' home for a snack on their deck. They too look forward to my walks on the beach with Slade since we include a stop by their place before we return home.

"Malcolm gave me his take on the Tokyo situation

update. Tell me your thoughts?" My father asks as we settle at the table with coffee and cookies.

The four of us discuss the strategy, and my father agrees with our decisions. He's retired, but his input is still invaluable. Besides, he'll never fully give up STEELE. He's always willing to step in as necessary.

The maid brings out a few boxes and places them on the table. My mother thanks her, then turns to Lola and me with a grin.

"Nanny Janice and I spoke the other day about the developmental stage Slade is in now. So I ordered a few things. I sent some to Roger and Leonie for Daphne, too," my mother says as she bites her lower lip and raises her eyebrows above twinkling brown eyes.

She's about to burst with excitement.

Lola, my Dad, and I bust out laughing. My mother just can't help herself when it comes to her grandchildren.

"Well, if I'm fully honest, Nanny Janice, Nanny Grace, and I spoke about The Twins' stage, too. So they have a special delivery," my mother continues with a giggle as she claps her hands.

We spend the rest of our time discussing the merits of brightly hued toys that captivate babies because of the high-contrast patterns and bright colors, infant play gyms, mobiles, and anything else two-month-old babies can swipe at. Along with the benefits of pretend play for twenty-three-month-old toddlers' learning and development.

Afterwards, Lola, Slade, and I leave for home. We walk along the beach hand-in-hand. Slade sleeps in his harness peacefully. On the return trip we don't encounter greedy seagulls, just the gentle lapping of the waves on the shore.

All is right in the Sebastian Steele World.

LOLA

"My, my, my, Mrs. Steele, don't you look lovely this evening."

Baz says with a wolfish glint to his gray eyes as I walk down the stairs of our beach house.

We're headed to the village for Date Night with Leonie, Roger, Starr, Malcolm, Anita, and Norman. They arrived earlier for Labor Day next week.

It's the first time we've been together since Leonie and I gave birth almost three months ago. She and I wanted to take Anita and Starr out to thank them for being our doulas. However, Baz overheard our conversation and invited himself and the boys saying they're just as grateful.

Anita and Norman will stay through the Labor Day festivities and fundraiser. They're offering great silent auction items with custom VIP fitness training sessions with them for a year. The way they whipped Leonie into shape postnatal every person at the event will want to win the bid!

I'm just as happy with my mommy makeover regimen

from Borya and Starr. The intense kickboxing, strength training, and conditioning workouts with Borya trimmed the extra pounds and tightened my muscles. The vigorous yoga and Pilates sessions with Starr increased my mind-body connection, flexibility, and core strengthening. Not to mention the much sought-after yoga butt!

So I do a spin for Baz in my white broderie anglaise cotton romper with puffed sleeves and a utility-inspired belt to cinch my waist. The sweetheart neckline outlined in delicate crochet trim enhances my full breasts. Paired with platform ankle-tied espadrilles and my hair in a topknot, I'm ready for our night on the town.

"Thank you, Mr. Steele. You're pretty hot yourself, sexy," I purr, raking my eyes over him.

Baz dressed in all black linen—loose-fitting v-neck sweater and pants—loafers with his five o'clock shadow and tousled hair longer than usual oozes sex appeal. He's leaning against the banister with his hands in his pockets, staring up at me. The predatory gleam in his eyes makes my pussy clench.

Mine, all mine. Hot damn!

He smirks and holds his hand out to help me down the last few steps as I reach him. When my feet touch the floor, Baz sweeps me into his arms and nuzzles my neck.

"Thank you, Mrs. Steele," he murmurs. "I thank you for gifting me with my son truly."

I smile up at him, then my jaw drops when I see a necklace dangling from his fingertips. The extraordinary blue gemstone heart pendant sparkles in the entry chandelier light. My gaze follows the necklace as it moves towards me.

"This is a blue diamond heart. It represents our son Slade, your gift to me"—Baz places the platinum chain around my neck and closes the clasp—"Each child will have a pendant for you to collect on this necklace. I pray we will fill it as many times as you allow, my love."

Tears well in my eyes, and I sob.

Baz hugs me to his chest and strokes my back as he soothes me.

"Let's see how many times we can fill it, my love," I blubber as I cup his handsome face in my palms.

I rise to my toes and slant my mouth over his. We kiss until the front doorbell chimes. Baz grumbles and smacks my ass before he takes my hand.

Shelley and Morgan have all four grandchildren for the night, along with Nanny Janice and Nanny Grace as extra support.

Roger stands at the front door with his Mercedes-Benz G-Wagen behind him. Leonie waves from the passenger window.

"Hey! Ready to go?" Roger asks as he pulls me into a hug, then claps Baz on his back. "Malcolm and Starr are in his SUV on the driveway."

"Yeah, bro! Let's go," Baz replies.

We climb in, and I hug Leonie from behind.

"Of course the boys had to gate-crash our Girls' Night Out!" She laughs. "But I don't mind!"

"Me neither," I respond. "It'll make for a fun time for sure!"

During the drive to the village, we ask about their trip and how Daphne fared with her first overseas travel. The Twins are used to longer flights now.

Roger teases Daphne is a pro since she slept most of the flight. Leonie attributes it to a full belly, empty diaper, and plenty of sleep.

When we arrive at the restaurant, Anita and Norman wait for us at the bar. They're staying at STEELE's version of a bed-and-breakfast just outside of town. It's a luxury property with excellent amenities similar to the offerings found at their large resorts.

We move to banquets at the bar for cocktails while we catch up before we move to our table in the dining room. The Champ tells us about some of his encounters with celebrity clients—without divulging names—that crack us up. Then Leonie adds her handsy times with some of the fashion industries most prominent designers and CEOS of conglomerates. Roger however will hear none of it and growls his dissatisfaction.

Laughter ensues, and we decide it's time to move to our table. As we make our way through the bar and dining room, other patrons follow our progress. Some greet us and others—particularly the women— glower. Their jealousy transparent.

Ha! Again, oh well, ladies. The STEELE Quaternity drops to one, Harris.

Leonie looks fantastic in her fuchsia cotton eyelet off-the-shoulder mini dress. The slim-fitting bodice defined by an adjustable belt around the sheer waist panel and falls to a flouncy tiered hem shows off her toned, postnatal body. Although she's naturally fit, Leonie works hard for her camera-ready body. One would never know she's a mother of three children under the age of two and a newborn to boot!

It's obvious people recognize *The Lion* when their eyes light up as she passes them by. Never one to care about the attention she receives, Leonie struts to the table completely oblivious.

Starr and Anita also look marvelous in a fitted tube mini dress and a maxi dress with boob side cleavage, respectively. Their dedication to health and wellness apparent in their fit bodies any woman would envy, including me, and men drool over, including the men in the restaurant.

However, if I were a man, I wouldn't want to mess with either woman and risk the wrath of The Enforcer or The Champ.

Once we're settled at the table, we order our dinner and wine.

I turn to Leonie and nod. We raise our glasses to Starr and Anita.

"Starr and Anita, thank you for helping me through our pregnancies, from the breathing exercises to the Kegels to the last push. Without your support and friendship, our pregnancies would have been a lot more complicated," I say.

"Oh, so what we're chopped liver?" Baz asks as he nods at Roger.

Leonie laughs and responds, "Of course you and Roger are invaluable, Sebastian! *Merci beaucoup, mon frère!*"

Everyone laughs.

"Well, you're more than welcome," Anita says. "You have a beautiful, loving family, and I'm glad to have had a part in it."

"Absolutely!" Starr replies. "Bringing a baby into this world is a blessing and a joy. Here's to your health!"

We raise our glasses in a toast.

"Hear, hear!"

"Thank you so much!"

"Well said!"

"Here's to family and friends who are as close as our blood relatives!"

The rest of dinner we relish each other's company and delicious dishes. We end the evening with promises to meet in the morning for beach yoga and breakfast. The guys plan for golf and lunch. Then we'll meet for dinner at Shelley and Morgan's residence.

As we leave the restaurant, Leonie loops her arm through mine.

"Your pendant is *magnifique*! For Slade, *non*?" She asks.

"Yes! Baz just gave it to me before we left the house as my push present," I respond as my fingertips brush the diamond's surface.

Leonie lifts her wrist. A rose gold charm bracelet dangles from it with a lightning bolt, home, heart, and two boy and one girl figures. Some charms sparkle with diamonds and others in solid gold. It's a beautiful piece.

"Roger gave this to me before we left Monte Carlo. I thanked him with a blo—"

I cut her off before she gives me too much information. Leonie giggles and turns to hug Anita good night.

We say our farewells until the morning and hop into our SUVs. Anita and Norman decide to stroll back to the bed-and-breakfast to work off some crème brûlée dessert.

Once we arrive back at the compound, Roger drops Baz and me off while Malcolm and Starr continue to his beach-front home.

"Sweet dreams!" Leonie calls out as she and Roger drive away.

Baz and I wave until their red taillights disappear in the night.

"I know something sweeter than dreams, Mrs. Steele," he murmurs in my ear. "And I'm going to eat it up all night long."

SEBASTIAN

"Do you know how important today is for you, Slade? Say again... No, not just our beach time... Really?... I'll give you a hint. Candles, singing... Yup! It's your three-month birthday, son! You and your cousin Daphne will have your party together.... I know exciting isn't it! Your grandparents, aunts, and uncles are here to celebrate with the two of you. Remember how I told you blood in the veins isn't the only requirement for family. Love, loyalty, and respect make family. So *Grand-père* Guy, *Grand-mère* Josy, *Oncle* Luc, Auntie Blair, Uncle Patrick, Auntie Billie, Uncle Norman, Auntie Anita, Uncle Connor, and Aunt Lucie, Auntie Lydie, Uncle Lachlan, Uncle Lucien, Uncle Laurent, and Uncle Borya are here. I suspect Auntie Starr will be more pretty soon..."

Lola and I gave Nanny Janice the day off, so I'm getting Slade ready for his special day.

Their party will kick off our Labor Day festivities with the family beach bonfire and seafood feast tomorrow night and the STEELE fundraiser the next evening. We'll stay out here through the rest of September, then return to New York City.

I have a feeling Lola may want to stay here until we fly to Verbier for Christmas and New Year's. She'd prefer to work out of her office at our beach house and fly in as necessary to the city or whatever business destination requires her presence. Plus, Blair and Billie handle a lot of the day-to-day responsibilities for her. Lola can create her designs anywhere in the world.

As much as I'd like to do the same, I have business at STEELE's overseas offices to check in on matters since I've been away on paternity leave. Prior to Lola and Slade, I would have booked the trips back-to-back. However, I spaced them out with seven days each over the next three months. In the new year, I'll have Melody schedule the rest.

Hell, I don't mind. I'm living my dream: wife, son, family, STEELE. Perfect!

My parents plan to stay here until the end of the month, then go to the Med for time aboard *Serendipity* for a week. They deserve a break after helping us for months with Slade. But they can't stay away from their grandchildren for long. After their respite, they're going to Paris for time with The Twins and Daphne. Then they'll all fly to Verbier.

Which reminds me… I have to come up with some pretty awesome gifts for all the kids. No way will I let Harris beat me in the coolest presents like he did last year. In fact, I know two puppies are definite. The Bichon Frises Roger bought The Twins are too damn cute. For Slade, I'm leaning towards a pair of Siberian Huskies. Silver gray with blue eyes for STEELE. I have a breeder on the lookout for them now.

Slade wiggles in my arms, so I hurry to finish dressing him. Almost time for breakfast. And I do not want my son hollering at me. I'm the Alpha male who makes demands in this family, I chuckle to myself.

"Hey there, Daddy. Do you need some help?"

I glance up to find Lola standing in the archway that connects Slade's nursery to our suite of rooms. She's a sexy as fuck MILF. Her hair mussed from my hands gripping her long tresses. Lips swollen from my endless kisses. Toned legs bare beneath my sweater, she ripped off of me last night. Most of all, her heavy tits with nipples poking through like beacons.

I groan with desire at the sight of my gorgeous, curvy wife.

Lola giggles when she hears my need for her. Then she glances down at my burgeoning manhood. Hazel eyes twinkle with mirth as she stalks towards me. Hands behind her back make her bountiful breasts jut out.

I glue my eyes to them, and my mouth salivates.

"The help I need, Little Pet, cannot occur in front of our son," I smirk.

Lola giggles and leans into me, pressing her tits into my back as she reaches up to kiss my lips.

I capture her mouth and nip the full bottom lip between my teeth. Then lave it when she moans.

"Be a good girl and let me finish with our son," I say as I turn back to Slade and put his sandals on.

"I can feed him if you hold this for me," Lola says as I move to the window seat.

As much as I take pleasure in my morning time with Slade, I can't deny him fresh breastmilk. I gesture for Lola to sit, then settle beside her as I hold him out to her.

She smiles lovingly at me with sparkly wide eyes as she bites the corner of her lip. One arm reaches out to cradle Slade to her breast while the other holds her hand out to me. In it is a gift-wrapped box.

I frown and raise my gaze to hers.

She shrugs and holds the box out further.

Assuming it's an early present for Slade, I take it in hand.

"Open it," Lola whispers as she watches me intently.

It's my time to shrug. But I untie the white ribbon and rip off the platinum paper, anyway. When I lift the lid and move the tissue paper, my jaw drops, and my eyes widen in surprise.

Okay, so Lola beat Harris and me in the coolest, most awesome gifts way early…

Nestled on the bottom of the box rest two pairs of dove gray knit booties.

Speechless, I glance up at Lola.

She's sitting still, as though holding her breath. Her eyes scan my face, and she chews on her bottom lip voraciously.

"Booties?" I ask quietly.

Lola nods, unsure of my reaction.

I close my eyes and say a prayer of thanks. When I open them, tears glisten in my love's hazel orbs. With a whoop, I jump from the window seat and pick Lola and Slade up in my arms. I hold my little family close to my chest, lifting Lola from her feet and swinging them in the air.

Tears of joy fill my eyes as Lola hugs me with one arm and our son with the other while our Twins grow in her belly.

The endless hours of making love paid off doubly!

Lola's necklace will have two more diamond heart pendants. I hope at least one is pink.

* * *

Sebastian & Lola's Story Concludes for Now...

Turn the page for the Steele Family, Author's Note, and a Preview of Roger & Leonie's Trilogy

THE STEELE FAMILY

STEELE INTERNATIONAL, INC

Multigenerational, multibillion-dollar business luxury real estate development and management corporation

Headquarters & Family's Primary Residences:

The STEELE Tower, New York City

A modern, gray-tinted glass fifty-seven story mixed-use skyscraper on southwest corner of Fifty-Seventh Street and Fifth Avenue within Billionaires' Row

Global Offices:

- The United States of America (New York City, New Jersey, Chicago, California, Miami, Las

Vegas)

- The Caribbean (St. Maarten, St. Barth's, St. Lucia)
- The French & Italian Rivieras (Nice, Cannes, Positano, Capri)
- Monaco (Monte Carlo)
- The United Arab Emirates (Abu Dhabi, Dubai)

STEELE FOUNDATION: A STRONG AND SUPPORTIVE HOUSE

Builds and manages attractive, affordable housing for urban, lower-income families

Available for download at **bit.ly/STEELEFamily**

Author's Note

Thank you for reading Parts I-III of Sebastian and Lola's sexy, sizzling romance! I hope that you enjoyed the Happy For Now conclusion of their white-hot love affair. If so, I'd love to hear your thoughts, please share a review at **bit.ly/CLBooksSI126Review** and tell your friends.

Yeah baby! Sebastian and Lola's story gave lots of hints at what's next for the Steele clan in the Desires Series!

Click below for the answers to one steamy story featuring Power Couple Alpha Male Roger and easygoing Supermodel Leonie as their electrifying trilogy begins:

A Trilogy of Desires Roger & Leonie Parts I-III

It's never too late to start the Desires Series at the beginning. So catch up on the family's scorching, toe-curling trysts.

At **CharmaineLouise.com** take the ***Four types of lovers. Which are you?*** **Quiz** to match your Sexy Fantasy: sub, Voyeur, Dominatrix, or Dominatrix sub Switch.

Follow me on social media including my CLBooks Coterie Fan Club below or on your favorite channels below and subscribe to my newsletter at **bit.ly/CLBooksNewsletter** for a **Free Book**.

Fulfill Your Desires.

xoxo

Charmaine Louise

BB bookbub.com/authors/charmaine-louise-shelton
f facebook.com/CharmaineLouiseBooks
instagram.com/charmainelouisebooks
g goodreads.com/charmainelouisebooks

COMING NEXT: A TRILOGY OF DESIRES ROGER & LEONIE PARTS I-III

PRESENT DAY— DUBAI, UNITED ARAB EMIRATES

ROGER

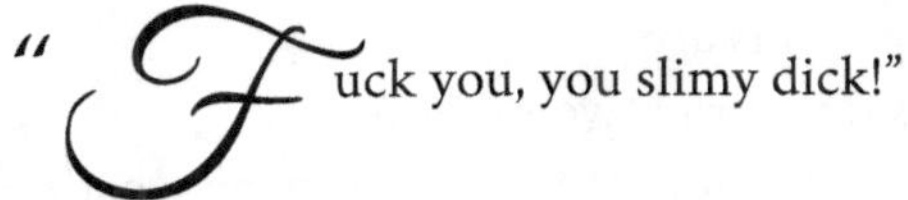

"Fuck you, you slimy dick!"

CRASH!

All I saw was red as that bastard Giovanni Mattei slid his hand up the dress of the blonde who'd been eyeing him for the past hour. We're at my future sister-in-law's opening night party for her luxury lingerie company, Lola's Coterie Dubai. The entire Steele clan is present to support her latest endeavor in her global expansion goal. Lola opened the flagship in Paris five years ago, followed by a location in London three years later.

Her initial goal to open boutiques in the United States started with New York and Las Vegas. But since meeting with STEELE Intentional, Inc. and my eldest brother Sebastian, the President of the Retail Properties Division, Lola's expansion now includes Abu Dhabi, Dubai, and Beverly Hills. Lola's Coterie Abu Dhabi opened last week, tonight is Dubai, and in a month another boutique will open in STEELE Galleria Rodeo Drive.

That fateful meeting a year ago between the two companies started a chain reaction. Sebastian and Lola dated within the week. Even moving in together. He surprised everyone since he was a notorious playboy.

Then, the spark hit me to fall for Leonie *The Lion* Beaulieu, the stunning supermodel, muse for Lola's Coterie, and Lola's best friend. Or as she calls it, *un coupe de foudre* —stroke of lightning, love at first sight. So we thought…

All I want to do right now is strike Mattei.

For the past year I've had to look at his smug face as he paraded around Monte Carlo, Las Vegas, Paris, the fucking globe with my woman on his arm.

Or at least she was for a brief two months.

The wildest two months of my life. I never knew what to expect with Leonie. One minute passionately wrapped in each other's arms, her long legs around my neck, my dick buried deep in her tight core. The next arguing about her not finishing reading assignments for her interior design degree from the Paris American Academy. The next, her feline amber eyes gazing lovingly at me to only narrow in anger when I reprimanded her lack of focus. My head aches as much as my dick just from thinking about Leonie.

What a fucking rollercoaster. We held on as long as we could before an argument went further than normal. Yeah, we had smaller disagreements. Bu nothing too major. The last one, though. No cuddles and coos of apology or incredible makeup sex could bridge the chasm we created. Words said, struck a chord and there was no going back. At least not at the time.

I let her get away from me once—well, I contributed hugely to her dumping me—and I won't let it happen again. First, I have to deal with the asshole she keeps going back to, fucking Mattei. He's always waiting in the wings to capture her with his charm. Only now she's distracted with the opening, as it's a work event for her representing Lola's Coterie. Mattei takes advantage of her lack of attention to *God's Gift* and shoves his hand up another woman's dress. Asshole.

Blondie wasn't the only one who couldn't keep her eyes or hands off the Italian playboy. Add the billionaire and nobleman status and he's irresistible to certain women. And any woman is irresistible to him... Without fail he flirted right back—a wink, a sly pinch on their rump, an unnecessary brush of his groin against their ass as he passed by them. Ridiculous.

Now observing Mattei and his shenanigans pisses me off. The self-proclaimed *God Has Shown Favor* shows only disrespect for Leonie. I would hate for his stupidity to upset her on such an important night. She deserves so much more. So I can't stop myself from telling him just that.

"You could at least have enough respect for the woman you're here with, then to feel up another woman within eyesight of her."

The sleaze turns his gaze towards me. His eyes take me in from head to toe as if assessing my seriousness.

Yeah, ass, I'm serious as fuck. If she's with him, he needs

to act like a man and not a randy teenager who can't control himself. It's the middle child in me that demands balance and loyalty. I want Leonie for myself, but until she's fully mine again, he will respect her.

"What I do is of no concern of yours, Steele."

I'm surprised he knows who I am since we've never spoken. He must recognize my shock as his smirk widens.

"Oh, I know who you are, Steele," he starts. "You're the loser who can't keep Leonie satisfied. So she keeps coming back to me. You see..."

He leans closer for dramatically to pseudo-whisper. But loud enough so the blonde can hear his words.

"I know how to make her cum so hard on my big dick screaming my name, she forgets all about your sorry ass."

Fuck Roger *The Responsible* who knows better than to act crazy in public. This asshole just sent me over the edge with a vision of him pounding into my woman. No... Fucking... Way.

"Fuck you, you slimy dick!"

CRASH!

In a blind rage, my fist connects with Mattei's jaw and he falls back into mannequins. As they topple to the floor, he recovers and clips me with a punch to the chest. Damn, I didn't expect the pretty boy to know how to fight. We're even at six feet, three inches. I have ten pounds of muscle on him, though. Plus, I spar regularly. I use both size and skill to my advantage.

We exchange only a few blows before my brothers Malcolm and Harris grab Mattei. Luc Montaigne, Lola's mentor, and Sebastian grab me. Security stands by, ready to step in to take over.

Still pissed, I struggle against their hold as does Mattei, who tries to shrug my brothers off. Unmatched by their combined strength, Mattei and I can only glare at each other. Itching to square off again. I give two fucks as the crowd stares on in silence. I want to finish this shit once and for all.

Until the figure of my father Morgan, the Steele Patriarch and Alpha Dom, storms over with such a wrathful look that Mattei and I stand stock-still.

Fuck. My father is pissed.

"You will cease this outrageous, infantile behavior at once and apologize to Ms. Lewis and her guests. Then leave. Do… you… understand?" Morgan issues his edict.

All eyes turn to him, including that dickhead Mattei. Morgan's Dom stare knocks us down several notches. In fact, we're below ground by the time he finishes his chastisement of us. Everyone else stands in silent awe of his power.

Morgan's words reset my out-of-control brain. I shake my head to dispel the angry red haze. Sure, Mattei was disrespectful to Leonie and said some stupid ass shit. But I never should have allowed it to get to me. It sent me on a downward spiral of jealousy, driven by an intense need to flatten him for having what is mine.

No matter the circumstances, I should have maintained command of the situation. Particularly at a highly public event held by STEELE. Before Leonie, this would never have happened. It goes against every cell in my physiology.

I gain control before Mattei and turn to seek Lola out in the crowd gathered around. I hope she's not as upset as I imagine. I spot her standing between my mother and Leonie. My younger sister Haley and Lola's assistants Blair and Billie stand near them. All have shocked expressions on their faces. Damn.

I notice Mattei tries to walk to them. But Malcolm puts

his hand on his chest to stop him since he recognizes that I headed their way already. Mattei has the sense to back down.

"Lola, I apologize for my poor behavior. Please forgive me," I beseech her.

With grace, she nods her head and accepts my outstretched hand. Her eyes meet mine before she searches for Sebastian, to whom she nods, too.

I turn my attention to the other women who stare at me, surprised by my unusual outburst.

"Mother, Leonie, I ask for your forgiveness, too," I say to both of them, but my eyes lock on Leonie whose amber gaze shies away.

My shoulders rise and fall on a disappointed sigh in response to her reaction. Not wishing to prolong the situation and knowing now is not the time to address Leonie's dismissal, I turn to the guests and apologize to them. Then excuse myself from the event.

As I pass Sebastian, he squeezes my shoulder to offer me support. I nod without breaking my stride. I don't even wait to hear Mattei's apology. I have to get out of here. Try to save some face from my lack of decorum.

Minutes after I exit the boutique, I feel my mobile vibrate in my trousers' pocket. I know who it is without even checking the name on the display. I answer on the first ring.

"Sorry. That was a shitshow Lola did not deserve. Does she really forgive me? Are you going to kick my ass?"

Of course it's Sebastian. I'm sure our father told him to call me or he would. I'd rather deal with my eldest brother than the elder Steele…

I must sound like a wreck since Sebastian doesn't go in on me, as would be his right. It's his woman's event for our family's company. He's the heir apparent to CEO and Chairman of the Board. So besides being the oldest who leads his siblings, he's the future leader of our multibillion-dollar business at which each of us leads divisions. I'm thankful when Sebastian doesn't add to my ill ease.

"Yes, and no. Dad gave the guests gift cards. What the fuck happened?" He asks.

I clue him in on the details. He tells me he understands. Baz is an Alpha male like me, although he's a Dom, too. So he understands protecting my woman's honor and my irrational possessive behavior. But he reminds me to keep my shit together in the future. Then teases me about not being responsible.

I grouse over the gibe. Then we hang up with a reminder about breakfast.

FUCK!

In my rage, I punch the wall. The plaster clatters to the floor, leaving a hole and splatters of blood. Too pissed to feel the pain, I stalk around the living room of my Rulers' Suite at STEELE Dubai I.

This shit is crazy. How can I allow myself to get so out of control that I make an ass of myself at a STEELE business function? So out of character for me—Roger *The Responsible*.

I roll my eyes in disgust at myself for letting Leonie upend my structured world. But I can't help myself. I call her mobile.

Leonie doesn't answer. What else is new…

I have no other choice than to leave a voicemail. How many will this one be? After twelve months, I've lost count. I just hope she'll listen to it and respond to me this time.

"How did we get here? Baby, I miss you. I'm so sorry. Tell me what to do. Please tell me, baby. Please…"

***

Click the Link Below or Visit books2read.com/u/bw1Lea For Your Copy

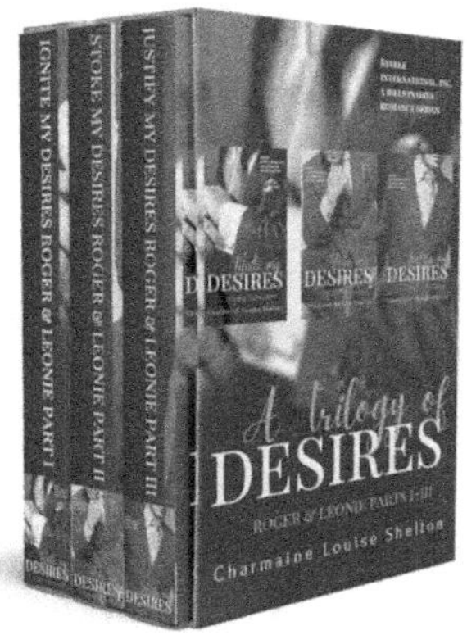

A Trilogy of Desires Roger & Leonie Parts I-III

STEELE International, Inc.
A Billionaires Romance Series Book 3

Ignite My Desires Roger & Leonie Part I

Click on the link below or visit books2read.com/u/md6EZR to get your copy.
Keep reading for a sneak peek!

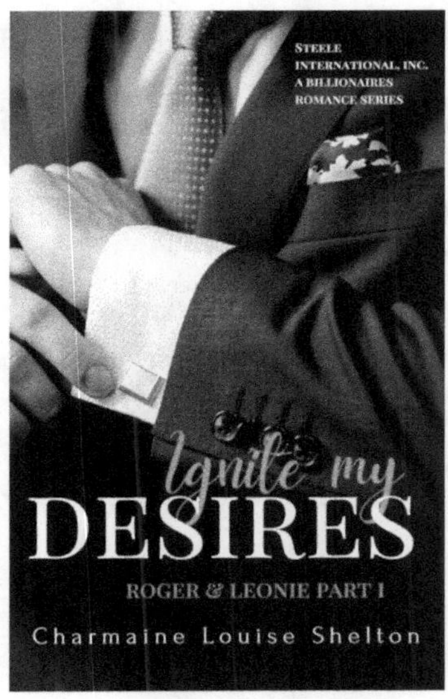

Ignite My Desires Roger & Leonie Part I

Books in the Series:

Discover My Desires Sebastian & Lola Prequel
(Available Exclusively to Subscribers)

Fulfill My Desires Sebastian & Lola Part I

Heighten My Desires Sebastian & Lola Part II

Ignite My Desires Roger & Leonie Part I

Stoke My Desires Roger & Leonie Part II

Justify My Desires Roger & Leonie Part III

Deepen My Desires Sebastian & Lola Part III

Capture My Desires Malcolm & Starr Part I

Embrace My Desires Malcolm & Starr Part II

Cherish My Desires Malcolm & Starr Part III

A Trilogy of Desires Sebastian & Lola Parts I-III

A Trilogy of Desires Roger & Leonie Parts I-III

A Trilogy of Desires Malcolm & Starr Parts I-III

Series Extras

Series Playlist

WELCOME TO CHARMAINELOUISE — THE SENSUAL LIFESTYLE

GLITZY. GLAMOROUS. STEAMY.

CharmaineLouise New York, Inc. invites you to indulge in *The Sensual Lifestyle* through **CharmaineLouise Books** and **CharmaineLouise Intimates**. CLBrands immerse you in ***Sexy Fantasies*** with CLBooks contemporary romance novels and give you ***Sexy Under Things & Loungewear*** with CLIntimates.

Charmaine Louise Shelton the Founder, CEO & Author of CLNY loves all things classic, elegant, feminine, and of course with an erotic edge! Favorite outfit of choice is a cashmere cardigan, leather pencil skirt, and seamed silk stockings with stiletto heels. Sexy Fantasy Type: sub with a dash of Voyeur. When not writing and designing, Charmaine Louise travels and spends time with her Maltese buddies, ZIGGY and Jynger.

CharmaineLouise — *The Sensual Lifestyle*

~ Visit online at **CharmaineLouise.com**

~ Subscribe to **CharmaineLouise Newsletter**

~ Find us on Facebook **@CharmaineLouiseNewYork**

~ Instagram @**CharLouNY**

CharmaineLouise Books *Sexy Fantasies* launched summer 2020. Sizzling, contemporary romance with your soon-to-be favorite Alpha Doms, Powerful Billionaires, and the women they lust after and love for second chances, insta-love, enemies-to-lovers, and more.

Want to chat it up and share your thoughts with other CLBooks Lovers? Read our blog, join our CharmaineLouise Books Coterie Fan Club and follow us on my author pages and social media to be in the know about the book release dates, exclusive content, giveaways, contests, and more!

~ **Purchase your eBook and paperback novels from my Author Page by clicking here!**

~ Read and subscribe to our blog ***The World of Sex***

~ Connect on **Amazon Author Page**

~ **Goodreads Author Profile**

~ **BookBub Author Profile**

CharmaineLouise Intimates *Sexy Under Things & Loungewear* debuted in 2003. Inspired by the sensuous sirens and sylph swans of the past and present, the hand crochet cashmere and silk collections are for the sexy: hence, the line names Ginger — Bombshell; Diana — Showstopper; Jackie — Timeless; Lena — Classic. Also known as The Movie-Star from Gilligan's Island; Ms. Ross The Boss; Mrs. Kennedy Onassis; Ms. Horne.

Do you thrive on seduction and being sexy lounging at home? Read our blog and follow us on social media to receive the tips, the latest additions to the collections, private sales, and more!

~ Read and subscribe to our blog ***The Art of Seduction***

~ Find us on Facebook **@CharmaineLousieIntimates**

~ Instagram **@CharmaineLouiseIntimates**

Fulfill Your Desires.

www.ingramcontent.com/pod-product-compliance
Lightning Source LLC
Chambersburg PA
CBHW060605100726
47907CB00006B/1506

* 9 7 8 1 7 3 6 3 4 2 9 6 1 *